THE WORLD OF TIERS

Volume 2 ===============================

THE WORLD
OF TIERS

Volume 2 ════════════

A PRIVATE COSMOS
BEHIND THE WALLS
OF TERRA
THE LAVALITE WORLD

Philip José Farmer

Doubleday Book & Music Clubs, Inc.
Garden City, New York

Published by arrangement with Ace Books
A Division of Charter Communications, Inc.
A Grosset & Dunlap Company
360 Park Avenue South
New York, New York 10010

ISBN: 1-56865-072-8

Printed in the United States of America

Contents

A PRIVATE COSMOS

INTRODUCTION

IT ALL GOES BACK TO MY CHILDHOOD OF ABOUT A YEAR AGO, WHEN I READ
The Maker of Universes. I recall it to have been a sunny Saturday in
Baltimore and its morning, when I picked up Philip José Farmer's book
with the green Gaughan sky and the gray Gaughan harpy (Podarge) on
the front, to read a page or two before beginning work on a story of my
own. I didn't do any writing that day.

I finished reading the book and immediately dashed off to my local
purveyor of paperbacks, to locate the sequel which I knew existed, *The
Gates of Creation*. When I'd finished reading it, the sunny morning in
Saturday and its Baltimore had gone away and night filled the day all
the way up to the top of the sky. The next thing that I wrote was not
my story, but a fan letter to Philip José Farmer.

My intention was not to tell the man who had written *The Lovers*
and *Fire and the Night* and *A Woman A Day* that I thought these two
new ones were the best things he had ever done. If he'd done a painting,
composed a piece of music, I couldn't compare them to his stories or
even to each other. The two books I had just then finished reading were
of the adventure-romance sort, and I felt they were exceedingly good
examples of the type. They are different from his other stories, styles,
themes, different even from each other, and hence, as always, incompa-
rable. I had hoped there would be a third one, and I was very pleased
to learn that he was working on it.

In other words, I looked forward for over a year to the book you are
presently holding in your hands.

In considering my own feelings, to determine precisely what it was
that caused me to be so taken by the first two books, I found that there
are several reasons for the appeal they hold for me:

1) I am fascinated by the concept of physical immortality and the ills and benefits attendant thereto. This theme runs through the books like a highly polished strand of copper wire. 2) The concept of pocket universes—a thing quite distinct, as I see it, from various parallel worlds notions—the idea of such universes, specifically created to serve the ends of powerful and intelligent beings, is a neat one. Here it allows for, among other things, the fascinating structure of the World of Tiers.

To go along with these concepts, Philip Farmer assembled a cast of characters of the sort I enjoy. Kickaha is a roguish fellow; heroic, tricky and very engaging. Also, he almost steals the first book from Wolff. The second book is packed with miserable, scheming, wretched, base, low-down, mean and nasty individuals who would cut one another's throats for the fun of it, but unfortunately have their lots cast together for a time. Being devilish fond of the Elizabethan theater, I was very happy to learn early in the story that they were all of them close relatives.

> A sacred being may be attractive or repulsive—a swan or an octopus—beautiful or ugly—a toothless hag or a fair young child—good or evil—a Beatrice or a Belle Dame Sans Merci—historical fact or fiction—a person met on the road or an image encountered in a story or a dream—it may be noble or something unmentionable in a drawing room, it may be anything it likes on condition, but this condition is absolute, that it arouse awe.
>
> —*Making, Knowing and Understanding*
> W. H. Auden

Philip José Farmer lives West of the Sun at the other end of the world from me in a place called California. We have never met, save in the pages of his stories. I admire his sense of humor and his facility for selecting the perfect final sentence for everything he writes. He can be stark, dark, smoky, bright, and any color of the emotional spectrum. He has a fascinating sense of the Sacred and the Profane. Put quite simply, he arouses awe. He has the talent and the skill to handle the sacred objects every writer must touch in order to convert the reader, in that timeless, spaceless place called Imagination.

Since I've invoked Auden, I must go on to agree with his observation that a writer cannot read another author's things without comparing them to his own. I do this constantly. I almost always come out feeling weak as well as awed whenever I read the works of three people who write science fiction: Sturgeon, Farmer and Bradbury. They know what's sacred, in that very special transsubjective way where personal specifics suddenly give way and become universals and light up the human condition like a neon-lined Christmas tree. And Philip José Farmer is special in a very unusual way . . .

Everything he says is something *I* would like to say, but for some reason or other, cannot. He exercises that thing Henry James called an "angle of vision" which, while different from my own a.v., invariably jibes with the way I feel about things. But I can't do it his way. This means that somebody can do what I love most better than I can, which makes me chew my beard and think of George London as Mephistopheles, back at the old Metropolitan Opera, in Gounod's *Faust,* when Marguerita ascended to heaven: he reached out and an iron gate descended before him; he grasped a bar, looked On High for a moment, averted his face, sank slowly to his knees, his hand sliding down the bar: curtain then: that's how I feel. *I* can't do it, but *it* can be done.

Beyond this, what can I say about a particular Philip José Farmer story?

Shakespeare said it better, in *Antony and Cleopatra:*

Lepidus. What manner o' thing is your crocodile?
Antony. It is shaped, sir, like itself; and it is as broad as it hath breadth. It is just so high as it is, and moves with its own organs. It lives by that which nourisheth it; and the elements once out of it, it transmigrates.
Lepidus. What color is it of?
Antony. Of its own color, too.
Lepidus. 'Tis a strange serpent.
Antony. 'Tis so. And the tears of it are wet.

(Act II, Scene VII)

Indeed, Sir, they are. It is the skill that goes with the talent that makes them so. Each of its products is different, complete, unique, and this one is no exception. I rejoice that such a man as Philip José Farmer walks among us, writes there, too. There aren't many like him. None, I'd say.

But read his story and see what I mean.

Now it is a cold, gray day in February and it's Baltimore. But it doesn't matter. Philip José Farmer, out there somewhere West of the Sun, if by your writing you ever intended to give joy to another human being, know by this that you have succeeded and brightened many a cold, gray day in the seasons of my world, as well as having enhanced the lighter ones with something I'll just call splendor and let go at that.

The colors of this one are its own and the tears of it are wet. Philip José Farmer wrote it. There is nothing more to say.

ROGER ZELAZNY

Baltimore, Md.

UNDER A GREEN SKY AND A YELLOW SUN, ON A BLACK STALLION WITH a crimson-dyed mane and blue-dyed tail, Kickaha rode for his life.

One hundred days ago, a thousand miles ago, he had left the village of the Hrowakas, the Bear People. Weary of hunting and of the simple life, Kickaha suddenly longed for a taste—more than a taste—of civilization. Moreover, his intellectual knife needed sharpening, and there was much about the Tishquetmoac, the only civilized people on this level, that he did not know.

So he put saddles and equipment on two horses, said goodbye to the chiefs and warriors, and kissed his two wives farewell. He gave them permission to take new husbands if he didn't return in six months. They said they would wait forever, at which Kickaha smiled, because they had said the same thing to their former husbands before these rode out on the warpath and never came back.

Some of the warriors wanted to escort him through the mountains to the Great Plains. He said no and rode out alone. He took five days to get out of the mountains. One day was lost because two young warriors of the Wakangishush tribe stalked him. They may have been waiting for months in the Black Weasel Pass, knowing that some day Kickaha would ride through it. Of all the greatly desired scalps of the hundred great warriors of the fifty Nations of the Great Plains and bordering mountain ranges, the scalp of Kickaha was the most valued. At least two hundred braves had made individual efforts to waylay him, and none had returned alive. Many war parties had come up into the mountains to attack the Hrowakas' stockaded fort on the high hill, hoping to catch the Bear People unawares and lift Kickaha's scalp—or head—during the fighting. Of these, only the great raid of the Oshangstawa tribe of the Half-Horses had come near to succeeding. The story of the raid and of the destruction of the terrible Half-Horses spread through the 129 Plains tribes and was sung in their council halls and chiefs' tepees during the Blood Festivals.

The two Wakangishush kept a respectable distance behind their quarry. They were waiting for Kickaha to camp when night came. They may have succeeded where so many others had failed, so careful and quiet were they, but a red raven, eagle-sized, flew down over Kickaha at dusk and cawed loudly twice.

Then it flew above one hidden brave, circled twice, flew above the tree behind which the other crouched, and circled twice. Kickaha, glad that he had taken the trouble to train the intelligent bird, smiled while he watched it. That night, he put an arrow into the first to approach his camp and a knife into the other three minutes later.

He was tempted to go fifty miles out of his way to hurl a spear, to which the braves' scalps would be attached, into the middle of the Wakangishush encampment. Feats such as this had given him the name of Kickaha, that is, Trickster, and he liked to keep up his reputation. This time, however, it did not seem worthwhile. The image of Talanac, The City That Is A Mountain, glowed in his mind like a jewel above a fire.

And so Kickaha contented himself with hanging the two scalpless corpses upside down from a branch. He turned his stallion's head eastward and thereby saved some Wakangishush lives and, possibly, his own. Kickaha bragged a lot about his cunning and speed and strength, but he admitted to himself that he was not invincible or immortal.

Kickaha had been born Paul Janus Finnegan in Terre Haute, Indiana, U. S. A., Earth, in a universe next door to this one. (All universes were next door to each other.) He was a muscular broad-shouldered youth six feet one inch tall and weighing 190 pounds. His skin was deeply tanned with slightly copper spots, freckles, here and there, and more than three dozen scars, varying from light to deep, on parts of his body and face. His reddish-bronze hair was thick, wavy, and shoulder-length, braided into two pigtails at this time. His face was usually merry with its bright green eyes, snub nose, long upper lip, and cleft chin.

The lionskin band around his head was edged with bear teeth pointing upward, and a long black-and-red feather from the tail of a hawk stuck up from the right side of the headband. He was unclothed from the waist up; around his neck was a string of bear teeth. A belt of turquoise-beaded bearskin supported dappled fawnskin trousers, and his moccasins were lionskin. The belt held a sheath on each side. One held a large steel knife; the other, a smaller knife perfectly balanced for throwing.

The saddle was the light type which the Plains tribes had recently adopted in place of blankets. Kickaha held a spear in one hand and the reins in the other, and his feet were in stirrups. Quivers and sheaths of leather hanging from the saddle held various weapons. A small round shield on which was painted a snarling bear's head was suspended from a wooden hook attached to the saddle. Behind the saddle was a bearskin robe rolled to contain some light cooking equipment. A bottle of water in a clay wicker basket hung from another saddle hook.

The second horse, which trotted along behind, carried a saddle, some weapons, and light equipment.

Kickaha took his time getting down out of the mountains. Though he softly whistled tunes of this world, and of his native Earth, he was not carefree. His eyes scanned everything before him, and he frequently looked backward.

Overhead, the yellow sun arced slowly in the cloudless light green sky. The air was sweet with the odors of white flowers blooming, with pine needles, and an occasional whiff of a purpleberry bush. A hawk screamed once, and twice he heard bears grunting in the woods.

The horses pricked up their ears at this but they did not become nervous. They had grown up with the tame bears that the Hrowakas kept within the village walls.

And so, alertly but pleasantly, Kickaha came down off the mountains onto the Great Plains. At this point, he could see far over the country because this was the zenith of a 160 mile gentle curve of a section. His way would be so subtly downhill for eighty miles that he would be almost unaware of it. Then there would be a river or lake to cross, and he would go almost imperceptibly up. To his left, seeming only fifty miles away, but actually a thousand, was the monolith of Abharhploonta. It towered a hundred thousand feet upward, and on its top was another land and another monolith. Up there was Dracheland, where Kickaha was known as Baron Horst von Horstmann. He had not been there for two years, and if he were to return, he would be a baron without a castle. His wife on that level had decided not to put up with his long absences and so had divorced him and married his best friend there, the Baron Siegfried von Listbat. Kickaha had given his castle to the two and had left for the Amerind level, which, of all levels, he loved the most.

His horses pulling the ground along at a canter, Kickaha watched for signs of enemies. He also watched the animal life, comprised of those still known on Earth, of those that had died off there, and of animals from other universes. All of these had been brought into this universe by the Lord, Wolff, when he was known as Jadawin. A few had been created in the biolabs of the palace on top of the highest monolith.

There were vast herds of buffalo, the small kind still known in North America, and the giants that had perished some ten thousand years ago on the American plains. The great gray bulks of curving-tusked mammoths and mastodons bulked in the distance. Some gigantic creatures, their big heads weighted down with many knobby horns and down-curving teeth projecting from horny lips, browsed on the grass. Dire wolves, tall as Kickaha's chest, trotted along the edge of a buffalo herd and waited for a calf to stray away from its mother. Further on, Kickaha saw a tan-and-black striped body slinking along behind a clump of tall grass and knew that Felis Atrox, the great maneless nine hundred pound lion that had once roamed the grassy plains of Arizona, was hoping to catch a mammoth calf away from its mother. Or perhaps it had some faint hopes of killing one of the multitude of antelope that was grazing nearby.

Above, hawks and buzzards circled. Once, a faint V of ducks passed overhead and a honking floated down. They were on their way to the rice swamps up in the mountains.

A herd of gawky long-necked creatures, looking like distant cousins of the camel, which they were, lurched by him. There were several skinny-legged foals with them, and these were what a pack of dire wolves hoped to pull down if the elders became careless.

Life and the promise of death was everywhere. The air was sweet; not a human being was in sight. A herd of wild horses galloped off in the distance, led by a magnificent roan stallion. Everywhere were the beasts of the plains. Kickaha loved it. It was dangerous, but it was exciting, and he thought of it as his world—his despite the fact that it had been created and was still owned by Wolff, the Lord, and he, Kickaha, had been an intruder. But this world was, in a sense, more his than Wolff's, since he certainly took more advantage of it than Wolff, who usually kept to the palace on top of the highest monolith.

The fiftieth day, Kickaha came to the Tishquetmoac Great Trade Path. There was no trail in the customary sense, since the grass was no less dense than the surrounding grass. But every mile of it was marked by two wooden posts the upper part of which had been carved in the likeness of Ishquettlammu, the Tishquetmoac god of commerce and of boundaries. The trail ran for a thousand miles from the border of the empire of Tishquetmoac, curving over the Great Plains to touch various semipermanent trading places of the Plains and mountain tribes. Over the trail went huge wagons of Tishquetmoac goods to exchange for furs, skins, herbs, ivory, bones, captured animals, and human captives. The trail was treaty-immune from attack; anyone on it was safe in theory, at least, but if he went outside the narrow path marked off by the carved poles, he was fair prey for anybody.

Kickaha rode on the trail for several days because he wanted to find a trade-caravan and get news of Talanac. He did not come across any and so left the trail because it was taking him away from the direct route to Talanac. A hundred days after he had left the Hrowakas' village, he encountered the trail again. Since it led straight to Talanac, he decided to stay on it.

An hour after dawn, the Half-Horses appeared.

Kickaha did not know what they were doing so close to the Tishquetmoac border. Perhaps they had been making a raid, because, although they did not attack anybody on the Great Trade Path, they did attack Tishquetmoac outside it.

Whatever the reason for their presence, they did not have to give Kickaha an excuse. And they would certainly do their best to catch him, since he was their greatest enemy.

Kickaha urged his two horses into a gallop. The Half-Horses, a mile away to his left, broke into a gallop the moment they saw him racing. They could run faster than a horse burdened with a man, but he had a good lead on them. Kickaha knew that an outpost was four miles ahead and that if he could get within its walls, he would be safe.

The first two miles he ran the stallion beneath him as swiftly as it would go. It gave its rider everything it had; foam blew from its mouth and wet his chest. Kickaha felt bad about this, but he certainly wasn't going to spare the animal if foundering it meant saving his own life. Besides, the Half-Horses would kill the stallion for food.

At the end of the two miles, the Half-Horses were close enough for him to determine their tribe. They were Shoyshatel, and their usual roving grounds were three hundred miles away, near the Trees of Many Shadows. They looked like the centaurs of Earth myth, except that they were larger and their faces and trappings certainly were not Grecian. Their heads were huge, twice as large as a human being's, and the faces were dark, high-cheekboned, and broad, the faces of Plains Indians. They wore feathered bonnets on their heads or bands with feathers; their hair was long and black and plaited into one or two pigtails.

The upright human body of the centaur contained a large bellows-like organ to pump air into the pneumatic system of the horse part. This swelled and shrank below the human breastbone and added to their weird and sinister appearance.

Originally, the Half-Horses were the creations of Jadawin, Lord of this universe. He had fashioned and grown the centaur bodies in his biolabs. The first centaurs had been provided with human brains from Scythian and Sarmatian nomads of Earth and from some Achaean and Pelasgian tribesmen. So it was that some Half-Horses still spoke these tongues, though most had long ago adopted the language of some Amerindian tribe of the Plains.

Now the Shoyshatel galloped hard after him, almost confident that they had their archenemy in their power. *Almost* because experience had disillusioned many of the Plains people of the belief that Kickaha could be easily caught. Or, if caught, kept.

The Shoyshatel, although they lusted to capture him alive so they could torture him, probably intended to kill him as soon as possible. Trying to take him alive would require restraint and delicacy on their part, and if they restrained themselves, they might find that he was gone.

Kickaha transferred to the other horse, a black mare with silver mane and tail, and urged it to its top speed. The stallion dropped off, its chest white with foam, shaking and blowing, and then fell when a Half-Horse speared it.

Arrows shot past him; spears fell behind him. Kickaha did not bother returning the fire. He crouched over the neck of his mare and shouted encouragement. Presently, as the Half-Horses drew closer, and the arrows and spears came nearer, Kickaha saw the outpost on top of a low hill. It was square and built of sharpened logs set upright in the ground, and had overhanging blockhouses on each side. The Tishquet-moac flag, green with a scarlet eagle swallowing a black snake, flew from a pole in the middle of the post.

Kickaha saw a sentry stare at them for a few seconds and then lift the end of a long slim bugle to his lips. Kickaha could not hear the alarm because the wind was against him and also because the pound of hooves was too loud.

Foam was pouring from the mare's mouth, but she raced on. Even so, the Half-Horses were drawing closer, and the arrows and spears were flying dangerously near. A bola, its three stones forming a triangle of death, almost struck him. And then, just as the gates to the fort opened and the Tishquetmoac cavalry rode out, the mare stumbled. She tried to recover and succeeded. Kickaha knew that the mishap was not caused by fatigue but by an arrow, which had plunged slantingly into her rump, piercing at such a shallow angle that the head of the arrow was out in the air again. She could not go much longer.

Another arrow plunged into the flesh just behind the saddle. She fell, and Kickaha threw himself out and away as she went down and then over. He tried to land running but could not because of the speed and rolled over and over. The shadow of the rolling horse passed over him; she crashed and lay still. Kickaha was up and running toward the Tishquetmoac.

Behind him, a Half-Horse shouted in triumph, and Kickaha turned his head to see a feather-bonneted chief, a spear held high, thundering in toward him. Kickaha snatched his throwing knife out, whirled, took a stance, and, as the centaur began the cast of spear at him, threw his knife. He jumped to one side immediately after the blade had left his hand. The spear passed over his shoulder, near his neck. The Half-Horse, the knife sticking out of the bellows organ below his chest, cartwheeled past Kickaha, bones of equine legs and backbone of the human upright part cracking with the impact. Then spears flew over Kickaha into the Half-Horses. One intercepted a brave who thought that he had succeeded where the chief had failed. His spear was in his hand; he was trusting to no skill in casting but meant to drive it through Kickaha with the weight of his five hundred pound body.

The brave went down. Kickaha picked up the spear and hurled it into the horse-breast of the nearest centaur. Then the cavalry, which outnumbered the Half-Horses, was past him, and there was a melee. The Half-Horses were driven off at great cost to the human beings. Kickaha got onto a horse which had lost its master to a Half-Horse tomahawk and galloped with the cavalry back to the post.

The commander of the outpost said to Kickaha, "You always bring much trouble with you. Always."

Kickaha grinned and said, "Confess now. You were glad for the excitement. You've been bored to death, right?"

The captain grinned back.

That evening, a Half-Horse, carrying a shaft of wood with a long white heron's feather at its tip, approached the fort. Honoring the symbol of the herald, the captain gave orders to withhold fire. The Half-Horse stopped outside the gates and shouted at Kickaha, "You have escaped us once again, Trickster! But you will never be able to leave Tishquetmoac, because we will be waiting for you! Don't think you can use the Great Trade Path to be safe from us! We will honor the Path; everyone on it will be untouched by the Half-Horses! Everyone except you, Kickaha! We will kill you! We have sworn not to return to our lodges, our women and children, until we have killed you!"

Kickaha shouted down to him, "Your women will have taken other husbands and your children will grow up without remembering you! You will never catch or kill me, you half-heehaws!"

The next day a relief party rode up, and the Tishquetmoac cavalry on leave rode out with Kickaha to the city of Talanac. The Half-Horses did not appear, and after Kickaha had been in the city for a while, he forgot about the threats of the Shoyshatel. But he was to remember.

THE WATCETCOL RIVER ORIGINATES IN A RIVER WHICH BRANCHES OFF from the Guzirit in Khamshemland, or Dracheland, on the monolith Abharhploonta. It flows through dense jungle to the edge of the monolith and then plunges through a channel which the river has cut out of hard rock. The river falls for a long distance as solid sheets of water, then, before reaching the bottom of the hundred thousand foot monolith, it becomes spray. Clouds roll out halfway down the monolith and hide the spray and foam from the eyes of men. The bottom is also hidden; those who have tried to walk into the fog have reported that it is like blackest night and, after a while, the wetness becomes solid.

A mile or two from the base the fog extends, and somewhere in there the fog becomes water again and then a river. The stream flows through a narrow channel in limestone and then broadens out later. It zigzags for about five hundred miles, straightens out for twenty miles and then splits to flow around a solid rock mountain. The river reunites on the other side of the mountain, turns sharply, and flows westward for sixty miles. There it disappears into a vast cavern, and it may be presumed that it drops through a network of caverns inside the monolith on top of which is the Amerindian level. Where it comes out, only the eagles of Podarge, Wolff, and Kickaha know.

The mountain which the river had islanded was a solid block of jade.

When Jadawin formed this universe, he poured out a three thousand foot high, roughly pyramid-shaped piece of mingled jadeite and nephrite, striated in apple-green, emerald-green, brown, mauve, yellow, blue, gray, red, and black and various shades thereof. Jadawin deposited it to cool on the edge of the Great Plains and later directed the river to flow around its base.

For thousands of years, the jade mountain was untouched except by birds that landed on it and fish that flicked against the cool greasy roots. When the Amerindians were gated through to his world, they came across the jade mountain. Some tribes made it their god, but the nomadic peoples did not settle down near it.

Then a group of civilized people from ancient Mexico were taken into this world near the jade mountain. This happened, as nearly as Jadawin (who later became Wolff) could recall, about 1,500 Earth-years ago. The involuntary immigrants may have been of that civilization which the later Mexicans called Olmec. They called themselves Tishquetmoac. They built wooden houses and wooden walls on the bank to the west and east of the mountain, and they called the mountain Talanac. Talanac was their name for the Jaguar God.

The *kotchulti* (literally, god-house) or temple of Toshkouni, deity of writing, mathematics, and music, is halfway up the stepped-pyramid city of Talanac. It faces the Street of Mixed Blessings, and, from the outside, does not look impressively large. The front of the temple is a slight bulging of the mountainside, a representation of the bird-jaguar face of Toshkouni. Like the rest of the interior of this mountain, all hollowing out, all cleaving away, all bas- and alto-relief, have been done by rubbing or drilling. Jade cannot be chipped or flaked; it can be drilled, but most of the labor in making beauty out of the stone comes from rubbing. Friction begets loveliness and utility.

Thus, the white-and-black striated jade in this area had been worn away by a generation of slaves using crushed corundum for abrasives and steel and wooden tools. The slaves had performed the crude basic labor; then the artisans and artists had taken over. The Tishquetmoac claim that form is buried in the stone and that it is revealed seems to be true—in the case of Talanac.

"The gods hide; men discover," the Tishquetmoac say.

When a visitor to the temple enters through the doorway, which seems to press down on him with Toshkouni's cat-teeth, he steps into a great cavern. It is illuminated by sunlight pouring through holes in the ceiling and by a hundred smokeless torches. A choir of black-robed monks with shaven, scarlet-painted heads stands behind a waist-high white-and-red jade screen. The choir chants praises to the Lord of The World, Ollimaml, and to Toshkouni.

At each of the six corners of the chamber stands an altar in the shape of a beast or bird or a young woman on all fours. Cartographs bulge from the surfaces of each, and little animals and abstract symbols, all the result of years of dedicated labor and long-enduring passion. An emerald, as large as a big man's head, lies on one altar, and there is a story about this which also concerns Kickaha. Indeed, the emerald was one of the reasons Kickaha was so welcome in Talanac. The jewel had once been stolen and Kickaha had recovered it from the Khamshem thieves of the next level and returned it—though not gratis. But that is another story.

Kickaha was in the library of the temple. This was a vast room deep in the mountain, reached only by going through the public altar room and a long wide corridor. It, too, was lit by sunlight shooting through shafts in the ceiling and by torches and oil lamps. The walls had been rubbed until thousands of shallow niches were made, each of which now held a Tishquetmoac book. The books were rolls of lambskin sewn together, with the roll secured at each end to an ebony-wood cylinder. The cylinder at the beginning of the book was hung on a tall jade frame, and the roll was slowly unwound by the reader, who stood before it.

Kickaha was in one well-lit corner, just below a hole in the ceiling. A black-robed priest, Takoacol, was explaining to Kickaha the meaning of some cartographs. During his last visit, Kickaha had studied the writing, but he had memorized only five hundred of the picture-symbols, and fluency required knowing at least two thousand.

Takoacol was indicating with a long-nailed yellow-painted finger the location of the palace of the emperor, the *miklosiml*.

"Just as the palace of the Lord of this world stands on top of the highest level of the world, so the palace of the *miklosiml* stands on the uppermost level of Talanac, the greatest city in the world."

Kickaha did not contradict him. At one time, the capital city of Atlantis, the country occupying the inner part of the next-to-highest level, had been four times as large and populous as Talanac. But it had been destroyed by the Lord then in power, and now the ruins housed only bats, birds, and lizards, great and small.

"But," the priest said, "where the world has five levels, Talanac has thrice three times three levels, or streets."

The priest put the tips of the excessively long fingernails of his hands together, and, half-closing his slightly slanted eyes, intoned a sermon on the magical and theological properties of the numbers three, seven, nine, and twelve. Kickaha did not interrupt him, even though he did not understand some of the technical terms.

He had heard, just once, a strange clinking in the next room. Just once was enough for him, who had survived because he did not have to be warned twice. Moreover, the price he paid for still living was a certain uncomfortable amount of anxiety. Always, he maintained a minimum amount of tension even in moments of recreation and lovemaking. Thus, he never entered a place, not even in the supposedly safe palace of the Lord, without first finding the possible hiding places for ambushers, avenues of escape, and hiding places for himself.

He had no reason to think that there was any danger for him in this city and especially in the sacrosanct temple-library. But there had been many times when he had had no reason to fear danger and yet the danger was there.

The clinking was weakly repeated. Kickaha, without an "Excuse me!" ran to the archway through which the unidentified, hence sinister, noise had come. Many of the black-robed priests looked up from their slant-topped desks where they were painting cartographs on skin or looked aside from the books hanging before them. Kickaha was dressed like a well-to-do Tishquetmoac, since his custom was to look as much like a native as possible wherever he was, but his skin was two shades paler than the lightest of theirs. Besides, he wore two knives, and that alone marked him off. He was the first, aside from the emperor, to enter this room armed.

Takoacol called out to him, asking if anything was wrong. Kickaha turned and put a finger to his lips, but the priest continued to call. Kickaha shrugged. The chances were that he would end up by seeming foolish or overly apprehensive to the onlookers, as had happened many times in other places. He did not care.

As he neared the archway, he heard more clinkings and then some slight creakings. These sounded to him as if men in armor were slowly—perhaps cautiously—coming down the hallway. The men could not be Tishquetmoac because their soldiers wore quilted-cloth armor. They had steel weapons, but these would not make the sounds he had heard.

Kickaha thought of retreating across the library and disappearing into one of the exits he had chosen; in the shadows of an archway, he could observe the newcomers as they entered the library.

But he could not resist the desire to know immediately who the intruders were. He risked one fast peek around the corner.

Twenty feet away walked a man in a complete suit of steel armor. Close behind him, by twos, came four knights, then at least thirty soldiers, swordsmen and archers. There might be more because the line continued on around the curve of the hall. Kickaha had been surprised, startled, and shocked many times before. This time, he reacted more slowly than ever in his life. For several seconds, he stood motionless while the ice-armor of shock thawed.

The knight in the lead, a tall man whose face was visible because of the opened visor of his helmet, was the king of Eggesheim, Erich von Turbat.

He and his men had no business being on this level! They were Drachelanders of the level above this, all natives of the inland plateau on top of the monolith which soared up from this level. Kickaha, who was known as Baron Horst von Horstmann in Dracheland, had visited the king, von Turbat, several times and once had knocked him off a horse in a joust.

To see him and his men on this level was startling enough, since they would have had to climb down a hundred thousand feet of monolith cliff to get to it. But their presence within the city was incomprehensible. Nobody had ever penetrated the peculiar defences of the city, except for Kickaha on one occasion, and he had been alone.

Unfreezing, Kickaha turned and ran. He was thinking that the Teutoniacs must have used one of the "gates" which permitted instantaneous transportation from one place to another. However, the Tishquetmoac did not know where the three "gates" were or even guessed that they existed. Only Wolff, who was the Lord of this universe, his mate Chryseis, and Kickaha had ever used them; or, theoretically, they were the only ones who knew how to use them.

Despite this, the Teutoniacs were here. How they had found the gates and why they had come through them to this palace were questions to be answered later—if ever.

Kickaha felt a surge of panic which he rammed back down. This could only mean that an alien Lord had successfully invaded this universe. That he could send men after Kickaha meant that Wolff and Chryseis were unable to prevent him. And that might mean they were dead. It did mean that, if they were alive, they were powerless and therefore needed his help. Ha! His help! He was running for his life again!

There were three hidden gates. Two were in the Temple of Ollimaml on top of the city, next to the emperor's palace. One gate was a large one and must have been used by von Turbat's men if they had entered in any force. And they must have great force, otherwise they would never have been able to overcome the large and fanatical bodyguard of the emperor and the garrison.

Unless, Kickaha thought, unless the invaders had somehow been able to capture the emperor immediately. The Tishquetmoac would obey the commands of their ruler, even if they knew they originated from his captors. This would last for a time, anyway. The people of Talanac were, after all, human beings, not ants, and they would eventually revolt. They regarded their emperor as a god incarnate, second only to the all-powerful creator Ollimaml, but they loved their jade city, too, and they had a history of twice committing deicide.

In the meantime . . . in the meantime, Kickaha was running toward the archway opposite the one through which the invaders must be stepping just now. A shout spurred him on, then many were yelling. Some of the priests were crying out, but several of the cries were in the debased Middle High German of the Drachelanders. A clash of armors and of swords formed a base beneath the vocal uproar.

Kickaha hoped that the hallway was the only one the Drachelanders were using. If they had been able to get to all the entrances to this room —no, they couldn't. The arch ahead led to a hall which only went deeper into the mountain, as far as he knew. It could be entered by other halls, but none of these had openings to the outside. That is, he had been told so. Perhaps his informants were lying for some reason, or perhaps they hadn't understood his imperfect Tishquetmoac speech.

Lied to or not, he had to take this avenue. The only trouble with it, even if it were free of invaders, was that it would end up in the mountain.

III

THE LIBRARY WAS AN IMMENSE ROOM. IT HAD TAKEN FIVE HUNDRED slaves, rubbing and drilling twenty-four hours a day, twenty years to complete the basic work. The distance from the archway he had just left to the one he desired was about 180 yards. Some of the invaders had time to enter the library and take one shot at him.

Knowing this, Kickaha began to zigzag. When he neared the arch, he threw himself down and rolled through the exit. Arrows slissed above him and kukked into the stone wall or bunged off the floor near him. Kickaha uncoiled to his feet and raced on down the hallway; he came to the inevitable curve, and then stopped. Two priests trotted past him. They looked at him but said nothing. They forgot about him when shrill cries stung their ears, and they ran toward the source of noise. He thought they would be acting more intelligently if they ran the other way, since it sounded as if the Drachelanders might be massacring the priests in the library.

However, the two would now run into the pursuers, and might delay them for a few seconds. Too bad about the priests, but it wasn't his fault if they were killed. Well, perhaps it was. But he did not intend to warn them if silence would help him keep ahead of the hunters.

He ran on. Just before he came to another forty-five degree bend, he heard screams behind him. He stopped and removed a burning torch from its fixture on the wall. Holding it high, he looked upward. Twenty feet from the top of his head was a round hole in the ceiling. It was dark, so Kickaha supposed that the shaft bent somewhere before it joined another.

The entire mountain was pierced with thousands of these shafts. All were at least three feet in diameter, since the slaves who had made the shafts and tunnels could not work in an area less than this.

Kickaha considered this shaft but gave up on it. There was nothing available to help him get up to it.

Hearing the scrape of metal against stone, he ran around the curve and then stopped. The first archer received a blazing torch in his face, screamed, staggered back, and knocked down the archer behind him. The conical steel helmets of both fell off and clanged on the floor.

Stooping, Kickaha ran forward, using the archer with the burned face, who had sat up, as a shield. He pulled the archer's long sword from his sheath. The man was holding his face with both hands and screaming that he was blind. The soldier he had knocked down stood up, thus preventing the bowmen who did see Kickaha from shooting at him. Kickaha rose and brought the sword down on the unprotected head of the soldier. Then he whirled and ran, stooping again.

Too late, some of the bowmen fired. The arrows struck the walls. He entered a large storage room. There were many artifacts here, but those catching his attention were long extendible ladders for use in the library. He set one upright, its end propped against the lip of a shaft in the ceiling. He placed the sword at the foot of the ladder, then picked up another ladder and ran with it down the hall, went through a doorway into a branching hall, and stopped below another shaft.

Here he propped the ladder against the edge of the hole in the ceiling and climbed up. By bracing his back against one side of the shaft and his feet against the other, he could thrust-slide his body up the hollow.

He hoped that the first ladder and the sword by it would fool his pursuers, so they would waste time shooting arrows up its dark hole. When they realized he was not to be brought down like a bear in a hollow tree, they would think that he had managed to get to a branching shaft in time. Then some of them would go up the shaft after him. If they were smart, they would delay long enough to take off their heavy chainmail shirts, skirts, leggings, and steel helmets.

If they were smart enough, though, they would also realize that he might be playing a trick. They would explore the halls deeper in. And they might soon be under this shaft and send an arrow through his body.

Inspired by this thought, he climbed more swiftly. He would back upward several inches, feet planted firmly, legs straining. Then he'd slide the feet up, then the back up, then the feet up—at least the walls were smooth and greasy-feeling jade, not rough steel, stone, or wood. After he had gone perhaps twenty feet upward—which meant a drop of forty feet to the floor—he came to a shaft which ran at right angles to his.

He had to twist around then so that he faced downward. He could see that the ladder still lay propped against the bright end of the shaft. There was no sound coming up the well. He pulled himself up and onto the horizontal floor.

At that moment, he heard a faint voice. The soldiers must have fallen for his ruse. They were either coming up that first tube after him or had already done so and were, possibly, in the same horizontal shaft in which he was.

Kickaha decided to discourage them. If he did find a way out, he might also find that they were right behind him—or worse, just below him. They could have passed bows and arrows from one to another up the shaft; if they had, they could shoot him down without danger to themselves.

Trying to figure out the direction of the shaft where he had left the first ladder, he came to a junction where three horizontal tunnels met above a vertical one. There the twilight of the place became a little brighter. He leaped across the hole in the floor and approached the brightening. On coming around a bend, he saw a Teutoniac bending over with his back to him. He was holding a torch, which a man in the vertical shaft had just handed to him. The man in the hole was muttering that the torch had scorched him. The man above was whispering fiercely that they should all be quiet.

The climbers had shed their armor and all arms except the daggers in the sheaths on their belts. However, a bow and a quiver of arrows was passed up to the soldier in the tunnel. The men in the vertical shaft were forming a chain to transport weapons. Kickaha noted that they would have been wiser to place six or seven in the tunnel first to prevent attack by their quarry.

Kickaha had thought of jumping the lone soldier at once, but he decided to wait until they had transported all the weapons they intended to use. And so bow after bow, quiver after quiver, swords, and finally even the armor was passed up and given to the man in the tunnel, who piled them neatly to one side. Kickaha was disgusted: didn't they understand that armor would only weigh them down and give their quarry an advantage? Moreover, the heavy thick mail and the heavy clothing underneath it would make them hot and sweaty. The only reason he could think of for this move was the rigidity of the military mind. If the regulations prescribed armor in every combat situation, then the armor would be worn, appropriate or not.

The soldier handling the material and those braced in the shafts bitched, though not loudly, about the heat and the strain. Kickaha could hear them plainly, but he supposed that the officers below could not.

At last, there were thirty-five bows, thirty-five quivers, and thirty-five swords, helmets, and chain-mail suits piled on the floor. There were more soldiers than that in the hall when Kickaha had first seen the invaders, so it seemed that a number were going to stay below. Among them would be all the officers, who did not want to take the time and trouble to remove their steel plates and chain. From the shouted conversation between the man in the tunnel above and an officer below—which could have been done quietly if the men in the shaft had relayed the messages—the man in the tunnel was a noncom, a *shlikrum,* an aboriginal word borrowed by the medieval German conquerors from Earth to indicate a master sergeant.

Kickaha listened carefully, hoping to find out if any men were climbing up other shafts—he did not want to be trapped or jumped on from the rear. Nothing was said about other climbers, but this did not mean that there were none. Kickaha kept looking behind him, like a bird watching for cats, but he saw and heard nothing. The *shlikrum* should have been as nervously vigilant as he, but apparently he felt that he was safe.

That feeling evaporated like a glass of water in a vacuum. The *shlikrum* had bent over to help the top man out of the shaft when Kickaha plunged his knife several inches into the man's right buttock. The man screamed and then went headfirst into the hole, propelled by Kickaha's foot. He fell on the man he was trying to hoist out; the two fell on the man below; and so on until ten men, shrieking, dropped out of the hole in the ceiling. They spludded on top of each other, the sounds of impact weakening as the layer of bodies increased. The *shlikrum,* who had fallen further than the others, landed sprawling on the uppermost body. Although he was hurt, he was not knocked out. He leaped up, lost his footing, and fell down the pile of bodies onto the floor. There he lay moaning.

An officer in a full suit of armor strode clanking to him and bent over a little to speak to him. Kickaha could not hear the words because of the uproar in the hallway, so he aimed an arrow at the officer. The angle was awkward, but he had trained himself to shoot from many angles, and he sent the arrow true. It penetrated the juncture of shoulder and neck plates and drove deep into the flesh. The knight fell forward and on the noncom. Kickaha was curious about the silvery casket strapped to the knight's back, because he had never seen anything like it before. Now was not the time to indulge his curiosity, however.

The soldiers who had been unpiling the bodies dropped their work and ran out of Kickaha's sight. There was a babble of voices and then silence after an officer roared for it. Kickaha recognized von Turbat's voice. It was only then that he began to realize the implications of this invasion and savage hunt for him.

Von Turbat was the king of the independent nation of Eggesheim, a mountainous country with perhaps sixty thousand citizens. At one time, as Baron Horst von Horstmann, Kickaha had had fairly amicable relations with him. After he had been defeated by Kickaha in a lancing joust and had then caught Kickaha making love to his daughter, von Turbat had been hostile. Not actively so, although he had made it plain that he would not be responsible for avenging Horstmann's death, if someone should kill Horstmann while he was under von Turbat's roof. Kickaha had taken off immediately after hearing this, and later, playing his role of robber baron, he had plundered a trade caravan on its way to Eggesheim. But circumstances had forced Kickaha to abandon his castle and identity and run for his life to this level. That had been a few years ago.

There was no reason why von Turbat should take such a terrible risk now to get revenge on Kickaha. In the first place, how had the king ever found out that Kickaha was here? How could he even know that Kickaha was von Horstmann? Why, if he had actually discovered the gates and their use, would he invade the dangerous city of Talanac? There were too many questions.

Meanwhile, from the low voices and following sounds of leather boots running, and the sight of the end of a ladder being swung out and moved away, it was evident that the Teutoniacs would be coming up other shafts. Kickaha doubted that many of them would be armored or heavily armed, since he now had the armor and weapons of the majority. Of course, they would be sending off for reinforcements. He had better get moving.

Then one of the men in the pile crawled out, and Kickaha sent an arrow through him. He quickly shot five more bodies on the theory that if any of them were able to revive, he was eliminating a potential killer. He was busy for about five minutes, running up and down and across and back and forth through the various tunnels. Three times he was able to catch the soldiers coming up shafts and to shoot the top man. Twice he fired down through shafts at men walking in the hallway.

But he could not hope to run swiftly enough to cover all the shafts.

And apparently the king was not counting casualties. The shafts originally entered were reentered, and lights and noises indicated that others were being climbed. Kickaha had to abandon all the weapons except for his knives in order to climb another vertical shaft. He intended to find a route to the openings of the shafts on the outside. There, high on the face of the mountain, above the Street of Mixed Blessings, he might be able to escape.

Von Turbat must surely know this, however; he would have archers on the streets above and below.

If he could only keep away from the soldiers in the networks of tunnels here until dark, he might be able to slip out across the jade cliffside. That is, he would if there were ornamental projections for him to use.

He became very thirsty. He had had no water all morning because he had been seized with the thirst for learning. Now the shock, the fighting and the running had dried him out. The roof of his mouth dripped a thick stalactitish saliva; his throat felt as if filled with desert pebbles dislodged from the hoof of a camel.

He might be able to go the rest of the day and the night without water if he had to, but he would be weakened. Therefore, he would get water. And since there was only one way to get it, he took that way.

He crept back toward the shaft up which he had just climbed but stopped a few feet from it. He smiled. What was the matter with him? He had been too shocked, his usual wiliness and unconventional thinking had been squeezed out of him for a while. He had passed up a chance to escape. It was a mad route to take, but its very insanity recommended it to him and, in fact, made it likely that he could succeed. If only he were not too late . . . !

The descent was easy. He came to the pile of armor. The soldiers had not yet approached this hole; they must still be coming up through shafts distant from this one. Kickaha removed his Tishquetmoac clothes and stuffed them in a mail shirt on the bottom of the pile. Hastily he put on a suit or armor, though he had to search to find a shirt and helmet big enough for him. Then he leaned over the hole and called down. He was a perfect mimic and, though it had been some years since he had heard the Eggesheimer dialect of German, he evoked it without difficulty.

The soldiers stationed below suspected a trick. They were not so dumb after all. They did not, however, imagine what had actually happened. They thought that Kickaha might be trying to lure them into range of his bow.

"*Ikh'n d'untershlikrum Hayns Gimbat,*" he said. "I am the corporal Henry Gimbat."

Hayns was a common first name throughout Dracheland. Gimbat was an aboriginal name, as were most of the names ending in -*bat*. Gimbat was especially common in that area of Dracheland and among the lower classes, who were a mixture of aborigine and German. There were bound to be several men of that name among the invaders.

A sergeant strode out and then stopped to peer up the shaft.

"*Vo iss de trickmensh?*"

"*E n'iss hir, nettrlikh. Ikh hap durss.*" Or, "He isn't here, of course. I'm thirsty."

"*Frakk zu fyer de vass?*" the sergeant bellowed. "You ask for water? At a time like this! *Shaysskopp!*"

The request was genuine, but it was also just the thing to take suspicion away from Kickaha. While the sergeant was raving, torches from both sides of the tunnel heralded the approach of soldiers who had climbed up. Kickaha left the shaft opening to speak to the officer of the newcomers. This knight had taken off his armor, after all, apparently because von Turbat thought that an officer should be in charge of the hunt.

Kickaha recognized him; he was Baron von Diebrs, ruler of a small principality on the border of Eggesheim. He had been at court briefly while Kickaha was visiting.

Kickaha kept his head bent so the helmet would put part of his face in shadow, and he made his voice less deep. Von Diebrs listened to him but paid no attention to his features. To the baron, Kickaha was just another faceless low-class soldier. Kickaha reported that the Trickster was gone without a trace. He also hastened to say that he had asked for water, but that the sergeant seemed to think it was an unreasonable request.

The baron, licking his lips, did not think it was unreasonable. And so bottles of water were lifted on the ends of poles by men standing on the ladders, and Kickaha got to drink. He then tried to drop back out of sight, so that he could get down to the hallway and, hopefully, out of the temple. Von Diebrs frustrated him by ordering him to lead the way up the shaft to the next horizontal level. Von Diebrs also swore at him for putting the armor on, and Kickaha had to remove the mail. He was ready to strike or to run at the first sign of recognition from the baron, but von Diebrs was only interested in searching for the barbarian killer.

Kickaha wanted to ask questions. He could not, however, without making the others suspicious, so he kept quiet. He crawled up the shaft and then took the bows and quivers and long swords passed up. After that, the party split into two. One was to go one way; the other, down the opposite direction. When the party of which Kickaha was a member met another search party, they were to go upward again.

The levels they had just left became bright and noisy. More men were coming in, reinforcements to press the hunt. Von Turbat, or whoever was in charge of the entire invasion, must have affairs under excellent control, to spare so many soldiers.

Kickaha kept with the original group, since none of them knew him. And when they encountered other groups, Kickaha said nothing. He still wore the helmet, since he had not been ordered to take it off. A few others also had helmets.

The walking became more difficult, because the shafts were now so narrow that a man had to duckwalk to get through and a party must travel single file. The soldiers had thought they were in top condition, but this type of progress made their legs ache and quiver and their lower backs hurt. Although he was not suffering, Kickaha complained too, so that he did not appear different.

After what seemed like many hours but was probably no more than eighty minutes, the party of six crawled from a shaft into a little round chamber. The wall opposite had large round openings to the outside. The men leaned over the edge and looked down, where they could see troops on foot and mounted knights in the Street of Mixed Blessings. Though they were small figures, their markings were distinguishable. Kickaha recognized not only the flags and pennants and uniforms of Eggesheim but those of at least a dozen kingdoms and a few baronies.

There were bodies and blood was spilled here and there. The fighting between the Teutoniacs and the Talanac garrisons must have taken place elsewhere, probably on top of the city.

Far below the streets was the river. The two bridges that Kickaha could see were jammed with refugees, all going outward and into the old city.

Presently, a Tishquetmoac rode down the long curving ramp from the street above and halted before von Turbat, who had just come out of the temple. The king got onto a horse before he would allow the Tishquetmoac to speak to him. This man was splendid in a headdress of long white curly feathers and a scarlet robe and green leggings. Probably, he was some functionary of the emperor. He was reporting to von Turbat, which must mean that the emperor had been captured.

There would be few hiding places for Kickaha even if he could get away. The people left in the city would obey their ruler's command, and if this was to report Kickaha's presence as soon as he was discovered, this they would do.

One of the soldiers with Kickaha spoke then of the reward offered for the capture of Kickaha or for information leading to the capture. Ten thousand *drachener* and the title, castle, lands, and citizens of the barony of Horstmann. If a commoner earned the reward, he and his family would automatically become nobles. The money was more than the king of Eggesheim got in taxes in two years.

Kickaha wanted to ask what had happened to Lisa von Horstmann, his wife, and von Listbat, his good friend who ran the barony in his absence. He dared not, but he sickened at the thought of what must have been their fate.

He leaned out of the window again to get fresh air, and he saw something that he had forgotten. Earlier, he had seen a knight just behind von Turbat, carrying a sword in one hand and a large steel casket under one arm. Now, this same knight accompanied von Turbat on the street, and when the king went back into the temple, he was followed closely by the knight with the casket.

Very strange, Kickaha thought. But this whole affair was very strange. He could explain nothing. One thing was certain, however: Wolff couldn't be operating effectively as Lord of this world, otherwise this would not be happening. Either Wolff was dead or captive in his own palace, or he was hiding in this world or in another.

The corporal presently ordered the party to go back down. Again, all the shafts in their sector were explored. When they reached the hallway, they were tired, hot, hungry, and cross. Their ill-feelings were made worse by the verbal assaults from their officers. The knights could not believe that Kickaha had escaped them. Neither could von Turbat. He talked with his officers, made more detailed plans, and then ordered the search renewed. There was a delay while bottles of water, hard biscuits, and dried sticks of meat were passed around to the men. Kickaha hunched down against the wall with the others and spoke only when spoken to. The others of his group had served together but did not ask him what his platoon was—they were too tired and disgruntled to talk much of anything.

It was an hour after dusk before the search was called off. An officer commented that the Trickster would not get away. For one thing, the flow of refugees at all the bridges had been cut off. Every bridge was heavily guarded, and the banks of the river opposite the city were being patrolled. Moreover, a house-to-house search was being started even now.

This meant that the search parties would not get the sleep they longed for. They would stay up all night looking for Kickaha. They would stay up all the next day, and the following night, if Kickaha was not found.

The soldiers did not protest; they did not want a whipping, ended by castration and then hanging. But among themselves, they muttered, and Kickaha paid attention to them to pick up information. They were tough, hardy men who griped but who would obey any order within reason and most senseless orders.

They marched along smartly enough though their thighs cried silently with pain. Kickaha had managed to get in the rear row of the platoon, and when they turned down onto a street with no natives and no other invaders, he disappeared into a doorway.

IV

THE DOOR HE STOOD BY COULD NOT BE OPENED FROM THE OUTSIDE, OF course. It was barred on the inside with the big bolt that all Talanac citizens used to protect themselves from the criminals that prowled at night.

Where there is civilization, there are thieves. Kickaha was, at this moment, grateful for that fact. During the previous extended visit to Talanac, he had deliberately become intimate with some of the criminal class. These people knew many hidden routes in and out of the city, and Kickaha wanted knowledge of these in case he needed them. Moreover, he found the criminals he knew, mainly smugglers, to be interesting. One of them, Clatatol, was more than interesting. She was beautiful. She had long, straight, glossy black hair, big brown eyes, very long and thick eyelashes, a smooth bronzish skin, and a full figure, although, like most of the Tishquetmoac women, she was just a little too wide in the hips and a little too thick-calved. Kickaha seldom required perfection in others; he agreed that a little asymmetry was the foundation of genuine beauty.

So he had become Clatatol's lover at the same time he was courting the emperor's daughter. This double life had eventually tripped him up, and he was asked politely to leave Talanac by the emperor's brother and the chief of police. He could return whenever the emperor's daughter got married and so would be shut up in purdah, as was the custom among the nobility. Kickaha had left without even saying goodbye to Clatatol. He had visited one of the little dependent kingdoms to the east, a nation of civilized peoples called the Quatsl-slet. These had been conquered long ago and now paid tribute to Talanac but still spoke their own language and adhered to their own somewhat peculiar customs.

While with them, Kickaha heard that the emperor's daughter had married her uncle, as was the custom. He could return, but instead he had gone back to the Hrowakas, the Bear People, in the mountains by the Great Plains.

So he would now get to Clatatol's house and find out if she could smuggle him out of the city . . . if she would have him, he thought. She had tried to kill him the last time he had seen her. And if she had forgiven him since, she would be angry again because he had returned to Talanac and had not tried to see her.

"Ah, Kickaha!" he murmured to himself. "You think you're so smart, and you're always fouling up! Fortunately, I'm the only one who knows that. And, big-mouthed as I am, I'll never tell!"

The moon rose. It was not silver, like Earth's moon, but as green as the cheese which the humorist-folklorists had said constituted lunar material. It was two and a half times as large as Earth's moon. It swelled across the starless black sky and cast a silver-green light on the white-and-brown streaked jade avenue.

Slowly, the giant orb moved across the heavens, and its light, like a team of mice pulling it along, strained ahead and presently was swarming over the lintel of the doorway in which Kickaha stood.

Kickaha looked up at the moon and wished that he were on it. He had been on its surface many times, and, if he could get to one of the small hidden gates in Talanac, he could be on it again. However, the chances were that von Turbat knew of their location, since he knew of the large gates. Even so, it would be worth finding out for sure, but one of the small gates was in the fane of a temple three streets above the lowest and the other was in the temple. The invaders were closing off all avenues out, and they had begun the house-to-house search on the lowest level. They would work upward on the theory that, if Kickaha were hiding, he would be driven upward until he would run into the soldiers stationed in the two levels just below the palace. Meanwhile, the other streets between would be patrolled, but infrequently, and by small bodies of soldiers: Von Turbat did not have enough men to spare.

Kickaha left the doorway and drifted out across the street and over the rampart and climbed down on the gods, beasts, men, abstract symbols, and cartographs which projected from the mountain face between the two streets. He went slowly because the hand and footholds were not always secure on the smooth stone and because there were troops stationed at the foot of the ramp leading from the street above to that below. They were holding torches, and several were on horseback.

Halfway down, he clung to the wall, motionless as a fly that detects a vast shadowy hand, threatening, somewhere in the distance. A patrol of four soldiers on horseback clattered along below. They stopped to speak briefly to the guards stationed on the ramp, then moved on. Kickaha moved also, came to the street, and slid along the wall, along the fronts of houses and into and out of shadowy doorways. He still carried his bow and quiver, although he could move more smoothly and quietly while climbing without them. But he might need them desperately, and he chanced their rattling and their clumsy weight.

It took him until the moon was ready to sail around the monolith in the northwest before he reached Clatatol's street. This was the area of the poor, of slaves who had recently purchased their freedom, of lodgings and taverns for the sailors and smugglers of the riverboat trading-fleets and for the hired guards and drivers of the wagon trading-caravans of the Great Plains. There were also many thieves and murderers on whom the police had nothing tangible, and other thieves and murderers who were hiding from justice.

Normally, the Street of Suspicious Odors would have been crowded and noisy even at this late hour. But the curfew imposed by the invaders was effective. Not a person was to be seen except for several patrols, and every window and door was barred.

This level was like many of the lowest streets, rubbed into existence when the Tishquetmoac had begun their labor of making a mountain into a metropolis. There were houses and shops on the street itself. There was a secondary street on top of these houses, with other houses on that street, and a tertiary street on top of those houses, and still another street on top of these. In other words, the stepped-pyramid existed on a smaller scale within the larger.

These housetop streets were reached by narrow stairways which had been rubbed out of the jade between every fifth and sixth house on the main street. Small animals such as pigs and sheep could be driven up the steps, but a horse would go up at peril of slipping on the stone.

Kickaha scuttled across the Street of Green Birds, which was immediately above the fourth level of houses of the Street of Suspicious Odors. Clatatol's house—if she still lived there—fronted the third level. He intended to let himself over the fence, hang by his hands, and then drop to the rooftops of the fourth level and similarly to the third level street. There were no projections on which to climb down.

But as he went across the Street of Green Birds, he heard the *kulup-kulik* of iron horseshoes. Out of the darkness cast by a temple-front porch, came three men on black horses. One was a knight in full armor; two were men-at-arms. The horses cracked into a gallop; the horsemen bent low over the necks of their mounts; behind them their black capes billowed, sinister smoke from fire of evil intents.

They were far enough away so that Kickaha could have escaped them by going over the fence and dropping. But they probably had bows and arrows, though he could see none, and if they got down off the horses quickly enough, they might be able to shoot him. The light from the moon was about twice as powerful as that from Earth's full moon. Moreover, even if their shafts missed him, they would call in others and start a house-to-house probing.

Well, he thought, the search would start now whatever happened, but . . . no, if he could kill them before the others heard . . . perhaps . . . it was worth trying. . . .

Under other circumstances, Kickaha would have tried for the riders. He loved horses. But when it came to saving his life, sentimentality evaporated. All creatures had to die, but Kickaha intended that his death should come as late as possible.

He aimed for the horses and in rapid succession brought two down. They both fell heavily on their right sides, and neither rider got up. The third, the knight, came unswervingly on, his lance aimed for Kickaha's belly or chest. The arrow went through the horse's neck; the animal fell front quarters first and went hooves over tail. The rider flew up and out; he held his lance most of the flight but dropped it and pulled up his legs and struck in a fetal position. His conical helmet, torn off, hit the stone, bounced, and went freewheeling down the street. The man slid on his side, his cloak ripping off and lying behind him as if his shadow had become dislodged.

Then, despite his armor, the knight was up and pulling his sword from its sheath. He opened his mouth to shout for whoever would hear and come running to his aid. An arrow drove past the teeth and through the spinal cord and he fell backward, sword *keluntking* on the jade.

A silver casket was tied to the saddle of the dead horse of the dead knight. Kickaha tried to open the casket but the key must have been on the knight someplace. He did not have time to look for it.

There were three dead horses, one dead man, possibly two other dead men. And no shouts in the distance to indicate that somebody had heard the uproar.

Carcass and corpse would not long remain unnoticed, however. Kickaha dropped his bow and quiver below and followed them. In less than sixty seconds, he was on the third level street and knocking on the thick wooden shutter over Clatatol's window. He rapped three times, counted to five, rapped twice, counted to four, and rapped once. He held a knife in his other hand.

There was no response which he could detect. He waited for sixty counts, per the code as he remembered it, and then rapped as prescribed again. Immediately thereafter, the sound of horseshoes came down to him and then an uproar. There were shouts and a bugle call. Lights began to gather on the street above and the main street below. Drums beat.

Suddenly, the shutter swung open. Kickaha had to dodge to avoid being hit in the face by it. The room within was dark, but the phantom of a woman's face and naked torso shone palely. An odor of garlic, fish, pork, and the rotten worm-infested cheese the Tishquetmoac loved puffed out past the woman. Kickaha associated the beauty of worked jade with these smells. His first visit had ruined him; he could not help it that he was a man of associations, not always desirable.

At this moment, the odor meant Clatatol, who was as beautiful as her cheese was dreadful. Or as beautiful as her language was foul and her temper hot as an Icelandic geyser.

"Shh!" Kickaha said. "The neighbors!"

Clatatol vomited another scatological and blasphemous spurt.

Kickaha clamped a hand over her mouth, twisted her head to remind her that he could easily break her neck, pushed her back so she went staggering, and climbed in through the window. He closed and locked the shutters and then turned to Clatatol. She had gotten up and found an oil lamp and lit it. By its flickering light, she advanced, swaying, to Kickaha and then embraced him and kissed him on his face, neck and chest while tears ran over these and she sobbed endearments.

Kickaha ignored her breath, thick with the resin-like wine and rotted cheese and garlic and sleep-clots, and he kissed her back. Then he said, "Are you alone?"

"Didn't I swear I would remain faithful to you?" she said.

"Yes, but I didn't ask for that. It was your idea. Besides," he said, "you couldn't be without a man for more than a week, as we both well know."

They laughed, and she took him into the back room, which was square except for the upper parts, which curved to form a dome. This was her bedroom and also her workroom since she planned smuggling operations here and dispensed various goods. Only the furniture was in evidence. This consisted mainly of the bed, a low broad wooden frame with leather straps stretched across it and mountain-lion furs and deer-hides piled on the straps. Kickaha lay down on this. Clatatol exclaimed that he looked tired and hungry. She left him for the kitchen, and he called out after her to bring him only water, bread, and sticks of dried beef or some fresh fruit if she had it. Hungry as he was, he couldn't stand the cheese.

After he had eaten, he asked her what she knew of the invasion. Clatatol sat by him on the bed and handed him his food. She seemed ready to pick up their lovemaking where they had left off several years ago, but Kickaha discouraged her. The situation was too enwombed with fatality to think of love now.

Clatatol, who was practical, whatever other faults she had, agreed. She got up and put on a skirt of green, black, and white feathers and a rose-colored cotton cloak. She washed out her mouth with wine diluted with ten parts of water and dropped a bead of powerful perfume on her tongue. Then she sat down by him again and began to talk.

Even though plugged into the underworld grapevine, she could not tell him everything he wanted to know. The invaders had appeared as if out of nowhere from a back room in the great temple of Ollimaml. They had swept out and into the palace and seized the emperor and his entire family after overwhelming the bodyguard and then the garrison.

The taking of Talanac had been well planned and almost perfectly executed. While the co-leader, von Swindebarn, held the palace and began to reorganize the Talanac police and the military to aid him, von Turbat had led the ever-increasing numbers of invaders from the palace into the city itself.

"Everybody was paralyzed," Clatatol said. "It was so absolutely unexpected. These white people in armor, pouring out of the temple of Ollimaml . . . it was as if Ollimaml Himself had sent them, and this increased the paralysis."

The civilians and police who got in the way were cut down. The rest of the population either fled into buildings or, when word reached the lowest levels, tried to get out across the river bridges. But these had been sealed off.

"The strange thing is," Clatatol said, hesitating, then continuing strongly, "the strange thing is that all this does not seem to be because of a desire to conquer Talanac. No, the seizure of our city is a, what do you call it, a byproduct? The invaders seem to be determined to take the city only because they regard it as a pond which holds a very desirable fish."

"Meaning me," Kickaha said.

Clatatol nodded. "I do not know why these people should want you so greatly. Do you?"

Kickaha said, "No. I could guess. But I won't. My speculations would only confuse you and take much time. The first thing for me is to get out and away. And that, my love, is where you come in."

"Now you love me," she said.

"If there were time . . ." he replied.

"I can hide you where we will have all the time we need," she said.

"Of course, there are the others . . ."

Kickaha had been wondering if she was holding back. He wasn't in a position to get rough with her, but he did. He gripped her wrist and squeezed. She grimaced and tried to pull away.

"What others?"

"Quit hurting me, and I'll tell. Maybe. Give me a kiss, and I'll tell for sure."

It was worthwhile to spend a few seconds, so he kissed her. The perfume from her mouth filled his nostrils and seemingly filtered down to the ends of his toes. He felt heady and began wondering if perhaps she didn't deserve a reward after all this time.

He laughed then and gently released himself. "You are indeed the most beautiful and desirable woman I have ever seen and I have seen a thousand times a thousand," he said. "But death walks the streets, and he is looking for me."

"When you see this other woman . . ." she said.

She became coy again, and then he had to impress upon her that coyness automatically meant pain for her. She did not resent this, liked it, in fact, since, to her, erotic love meant a certain amount of roughness and pain.

U

IT SEEMED THAT THREE STRANGERS HAD FLED FROM THE INMOST PARTS of the temple of Ollimaml a few minutes ahead of von Turbat. They were white-skinned, also. One was the black haired woman whom Clatatol, a very jealous and deprecating woman, nevertheless said was the most beautiful she had ever seen. Her companions were a huge, very fat man and a short skinny man. All three were dressed strangely and none spoke Tishquetmoac. They did speak Wishpawaml, the liturgical language of the priests. Unfortunately, the thieves who had hidden the three knew only a few words of Wishpawaml; these were from the responses of the laity during services.

Kickaha knew then that the three were Lords. The liturgical language everywhere on this world was theirs.

Their flight from von Turbat indicated that they had been dispossessed of their own universes and had taken refuge in this. But what was the minor king, von Turbat, doing in an affair that involved Lords?

Kickaha said, "Is there a reward for these three?"

"Yes. Ten thousand *kwatluml*. Apiece! For you, thirty thousand, and a high official post in the palace of the emperor. Perhaps, though this is only hinted at, marriage into the royal family."

Kickaha was silent. Clatatol's stomach rumbled, as if ruminating the reward offers. Voices fluttered weakly through the air shafts in the ceiling. The room, which had been cool, was hot. Sweat seeped from his armpits; the woman's dark-brass skin hatched brass tadpoles. From the middle chamber, the kitchen-washroom-toilet, came gurgles of running water and little watery voices.

"You must have fainted at the thought of all that money," Kickaha said finally. "What's keeping you and your gang from collecting?"

"We are thieves and smugglers, killers even, but we are not traitors! The pinkfaces offered these. . ."

She stopped when she saw Kickaha grinning. She grinned back. "What I said is true. However, the sums *are* enormous! What made us hesitate, if you must know, you wise coyote, was what would happen after the pinkfaces left. Or if there is a revolt. We don't want to be torn to pieces by a mob or tortured because some people might think we were traitors."

"Also . . . ?"

She smiled and said, "Also, the three refugees have offered to pay us many times over what the pinkfaces offer if we get them out of the city."

"And how will they do that?" Kickaha said. "They haven't got a universe to their name."

"What?"

"Can they offer you anything tangible—right now?"

"All *were* wearing jewels worth more than the rewards," she said. "Some—I've never seen anything like them. They're out of this world!"

Kickaha did not tell her that the cliché was literally true.

He was going to ask her if they had weapons but realized that she would not have recognized them as such if the three did have them. Certainly, the three wouldn't offer the information to their captors.

"And what of me?" he said, not asking her what the three had offered beyond their jewels.

"You, Kickaha, are beloved of the Lord, or so it is said. Besides, everybody says that you know where the treasures of the earth are hidden. Would a man who is poor have brought back the great emerald of Oshquatsmu?"

Kickaha said, "The pinkfaces will be banging on your doors soon enough. This whole area is going to be unraveled. Where do we go from here?"

Clatatol insisted that he let her blindfold him and then cover him with a hood. In no position to argue, he agreed. She made sure he could not see and then turned him swiftly around a dozen times. After that, he got down on all fours at her order.

There was a creaking sound, stone turning on stone, and she guided him through a passageway so narrow he scraped against both sides. Then he stood and, his hand in hers, stumbled up 150 steps, walked 280 paces down a slight decline, went down a ramp three hundred paces, and walked forty more on a straightaway. Clatatol stopped him and removed the hood and blindfold.

He blinked. He was in a round green-and-black striated chamber with a forty foot diameter and a three foot wide air shaft above. Flames writhed at the ends of torches in wall fixtures. There were chairs of jade and wood, some chests, piles of cloth bolts and furs, barrels of spices, a barrel of water, a table with dishes, biscuits, meat, stinking cheese, and some sanitation furniture.

Six Tishquetmoac men squatted against the wall. Their glossy black bangs fell over their eyes. Some smoked little cigars. They were armed with daggers, swords, and hatchets.

Three fair-skinned people sat in chairs. One was short, gritty-skinned, large-nosed, and shark-mouthed. The second was a manatee of a man, spilling over the chair in cataracts of fat.

On seeing the third, Kickaha gasped. He said, "Podarge!"

The woman was the most beautiful he had ever seen. But he had seen her before. That is, the face was in his past. But the body did not belong to that face.

"Podarge!" he said again, speaking the debased Mycenaean she and her eagles used. "I didn't know that Wolff had taken you from your Harpy's body and put you—your brain—in a woman's body. I . . ."

He stopped. She was looking at him with an unreadable expression. Perhaps she did not want him to let the others know what had happened. And he, usually silent when the situation asked for it, had been so overcome that . . .

But Podarge had discovered that Wolff was in reality the Jadawin who had originally kidnapped her from the Peloponnese of 3200 years ago and put her brain into the body of a Harpy created in his biolab. She had refused to let him rectify the wrong; she hated him so much that she had stayed in her winged bird-legged body and had sworn to get revenge upon him.

What had made her change her mind?

Her voice, however, was not Podarge's. That, of course, would be the result of the soma transfer.

"What are you gibbering about, *leblabbiy?*" she said in the speech of the Lords.

Kickaha felt like hitting her in the face. *Leblabbiy* was the Lords' perjorative for the human beings who inhabited their universes and over whom they godded it. *Leblabbiy* had been a small pet animal of the universe in which the Lords had originated. It ate the delicacies which its master offered, but it would also eat excrement at the first chance. And it often went mad.

"All right, Podarge, pretend you don't understand Mycenaean," he said. "But watch your tongue. I have no love for you."

She seemed surprised. She said, "Ah, you are a priest?"

Wolff, he had to admit, had certainly done a perfect job on her. Her body was magnificent; the skin as white and flawless as he remembered it; the hair as long, black, straight, and shining. The features, of course, were not perfectly regular; there was a slight asymmetry which resulted in a beauty that under other circumstances would have made him ache.

She was dressed in silky-looking light green robes and sandals, almost as if she had been getting ready for bed when interrupted. How in hell had Podarge come to be mixed up with these Lords? And then the answer tapped his mind's shoulder. Of course, she was in Wolff's palace when it was invaded. But what had happened then?

He said, "Where is Wolff?"

"Who, *leblabbiy?*" she said.

"Jadawin, he used to be called," he said.

She shrugged and said, "He wasn't there. Or if he was, he was killed by the Black Bellers."

Kickaha was more confused. "Black Bellers?"

Wolff had spoken of them at one time. But briefly, because their conversation had been interrupted by a subject introduced by Chryseis. Later, after Kickaha had helped Wolff recover his palace from Vannax, Kickaha had intended to ask him about the Black Bellers. He had never done so.

One of the Tishquetmoac spoke harshly to Clatatol. Kickaha understood him; she was to tell Kickaha that he must talk to these people. The Tishquetmoac could not understand the speech.

The fair-skinned woman, replying to his questions, said, "I am Anana, Jadawin's sister. This thin one is Nimstowl, called the Nooser by the Lords. This other is Fat Judubra."

Kickaha understood now. Anana, called the Bright, was one of Wolff's sisters. And he had used her face as a model when he created Podarge's face in the biolab. Rather, his memory had supplied the features, since Wolff had not then seen his sister Anana for over a thousand years. Which meant that, as of now, he had not seen her for over four thousand.

Kickaha remembered now that Wolff had said that the Black Bellers were to have been used, partly, as receptacles for memory. The Lords, knowing that even the complex human brain could not hold thousands of years of knowledge, had experimented with the transfer of memory.

This could, theoretically, be transferred back to the human brain when needed or otherwise displayed exteriorly.

A rapping sounded. A round door in the wall at the other end swung out, and another smuggler entered. He beckoned to the others, and they gathered around him to whisper. Finally, Clatatol left the group to speak to Kickaha.

"The rewards have been tripled," she whispered. "Moreover, this pinkface king, von Turbat, has proclaimed that, once you're caught, he'll withdraw from Talanac. Everything will be as it was before."

"If you'd planned on turning us in, you wouldn't be telling me this," he said. But it was possible that she was being overly subtle, trying to make him at ease, before they struck. Eight against one. He did not know what the Lords could do, so he would not count on them. He still had his two knives, but in this small room . . . ah, well, when the time came, he would see.

Clatatol added, "Von Turbat has also said that if you are not delivered to him within twenty-four hours, he will kill the emperor and his family and then he will kill every human being in this city. He said this in private to his officers, but a slave overheard him. Now the entire city knows."

"If von Turbat was talking German, how could a Tishquetmoac understand him?" Kickaha said.

"Von Turbat was talking to von Swindebarn and several others in the holy speech of the Lords," she said. "The slave had served in the temple and knew the holy speech."

The Black Bellers must be the as-yet unhooded lantern to illumine the mystery. He knew the two Teutoniac kings could follow the priest in the services, but they did not know the sacred language well enough to speak it. Thus, the two were not what they seemed.

He was given no time to ask questions. Clatatol said, "The pinkfaces have found the chamber behind the wall of my bedroom, and they will soon be breaking through it. We can't stay here."

Two men left the room but quickly returned with telescoping ladders. These were extended full-length up the air shaft. On seeing this, Kickaha felt less apprehensive. He said, "Now your patriotism demands that you hand us over to von Turbat. So . . . ?"

Two men had climbed up the ladder. The others were urging the Lords and Kickaha to go next. Clatatol said, "We have heard that the emperor is possessed by a demon. His soul had been driven out into the cold past the moon; a demon resides in his body, though not comfortably as yet. The priests have secretly transmitted this story throughout the city. They say for us to fight this most evil of evils. And we are not to surrender you, Kickaha, who is the beloved of the Lord, Ollimaml, nor should we give up the others."

Kickaha said, "Possessed? How do you know?"

Clatatol did not answer until after they had climbed the length of the shaft and were in a horizontal tunnel. One of the smugglers lit a dark lantern, and the ladder was pulled up, joint by joint, bent, folded, and carried along.

Clatatol said, "Suddenly, the emperor spoke only in the holy speech, so it was evident he did not understand Tishquetmoac. And the priests reported that von Turbat and von Swindebarn speak Wishpawaml only, and they have their priests to translate orders for them."

Kickaha did not see why a demon was thought to possess Quotshaml, the emperor. The liturgical language was supposed to scorch the lips of demons when they tried to speak it. But he was not going to point out the illogic when it favored him.

The party hurried down a tunnel with Fat Judubra wheezing loudly and complaining. He had had to be pulled through the shaft; his robes had torn and his skin had been scraped.

Kickaha asked Clatatol if the temple of Ollimaml was well guarded. He was hoping that the smaller secret gate had not been discovered. She replied that she did not know. Kickaha asked her how they were going to get out of the city. She answered that it would be better if he did not know; if he was captured, then he could not betray the others. Kickaha did not argue with her. Although he had no idea of how they would leave the city, he could imagine what would happen after that. During his last visit, he had found out just how she and her friends got the contraband past the customs. She did not suspect that he knew.

He spoke to Anana, who was a glimmer of neck, arms, and legs ahead. "The woman Clatatol says that her emperor, and at least two of the invaders, are possessed. She means that they suddenly seem unable, or unwilling, to talk anything but the language of the Lords."

"The Black Bellers," Anana said after a pause.

At that moment, shouts cannoned down the tunnel. The party stopped; the lantern was put out. Lights appeared at both ends of the tunnel; voices flew down from the rigid mouths of shafts above and ballooned from mouths below.

Kickaha spoke to the Lords. "If you have weapons, get ready to use them."

They did not answer. The party formed into a single file, linked by holding hands, and a man led them into a cross-tunnel. They duckwalked for perhaps fifty yards, with the voices of the hunters getting louder, before they heard a distant roar of water. The lamp was lit again. Soon they were in a small chamber, exitless except for the four-foot-wide hole in the floor against the opposite wall. The roar, a wetness, and a stink funneled up from it.

"The shaft angles steeply, and the sewage tunnel to which it connects is fifty feet down. The slide, however, won't hurt," Clatatol said. "We use this way only if all others around here fail. If you went all the way down this shaft, you'd fall into the tunnel, which is full of sewage and drops almost vertically down into the river at an underwater point. If you lived to come up in the river, you would be caught by the pinkface patrol boats stationed there."

Clatatol told them what they must do. They sat down and coasted down the tube with their hands and feet braking. Two-thirds of the way down, or so it seemed, they stopped. Here they were pulled into a hole and a shaft unknown to the authorities, rubbed into existence by several generations of criminals. This led back up to a network above the level from which they had just fled.

Clatatol explained that it was necessary to get to a place where they could enter another great sewage pipe. This one, however, was dry, because it had been blocked off with great labor and some loss of life thirty years before by a large gang of criminals. The flow from above was diverted to two other sewage tunnels. The dry tunnel led directly downward to below the water level. Near its mouth was a shaft which went horizontally to an underwater port distant from the outlets being watched by the pinkfaces. It was near the wharf where the river-trade boats were. To reach the boats, they would have to swim across the mile wide river.

Three streets up, within the face of the mountain, the party came to the horizontal shaft which opened to their avenue of escape, the dry tunnel slanting at fifty-five degrees to the horizontal.

Kickaha never found out what went amiss. He did not think that the Teutoniacs could have known where they were. There must have been some search parties sent at random to various areas. And this one was in the right place and saw their quarry before the quarry saw them.

Suddenly there were lights, yells, screams, and something thudding into bodies. Several Tishquetmoac men fell, and then Clatatol was sprawled out before him. In the dim light of the lantern lying on its side before him, Kickaha saw the skin, bluish-black in the light, the hanging jaw, eyes skewered on eternity, and the crossbow bolt sticking out of her skull an inch above the right ear. Blood gushed over the blue-black hair, the ear, the neck.

He crawled over the body, his flesh numb with the shock of the attack and with the shock of the bolt to come. He scuttled down the tunnel and into one that seemed to be free of the enemy. Behind him, in the dark, was heavy breathing; Anana identified herself. She did not know what had happened to the others.

They crawled and duckwalked until their legs and backs felt pain in the center of their bones, or so it seemed. They took left and right turns as they pleased, no pattern, and twice went up vertical shafts. The time came when they were in total darkness and quiet except for the blood punching little bags in their ears. They seemed to have outrun the hounds.

Thereafter, they went upward. It was vital to wait until night could veil their movements outside. This proved difficult to do. Though they were tired and tried to sleep, they kept awakening as if springing off the trampoline of unconsciousness into the upper air of open eyes. Their legs kicked, their hands twitched; they were aware of this but could not fully sleep to forget it nor be fully awake except when they soared out of nightmares.

Night appeared at the porthole of the shaft-end in the face of the mountain. They climbed out and up, seeing patrols below and hearing them above. After waiting until things were quiet above, they climbed over the ramparts and up the next wall and so to the next level of street. When they could not travel outside, they crawled into an air shaft.

The lower parts of the city were ablaze with torches. The soldiers and police were thoroughly probing the bottom levels. Then, as they went upward, the ring of men tightened because the area lessened. And there were spot-check search parties everywhere.

"If you're supposed to be taken alive, why did they shoot at us?" Anana said. "They couldn't see well enough to distinguish their targets."

"They got excited," Kickaha said. He was tired, hungry, thirsty, and feeling rage at the killers of Clatatol. Sorrow would come later. There would be no guilt. He never suffered guilt unless he had a realistic reason. Kickaha had some neurotic failings, and neurotic virtues—no way to escape those, being human—but inappropriate guilt was not among them. He was not responsible in any way for her death. She had entered this business of her own will and knowing that she might die.

There was even a little gladness reaped from her death. He could have been killed instead of her.

Kickaha went down a series of shafts after food and drink. Anana did not want to be left behind, since she feared that he might not be able to find her again. She went with him as far as the tube which led into the ceiling of a home, where the family snored loudly and smelled loudly of wine and beer. He came back with a rope, bread, cheese, fruit, beef, and two bottles of water.

They waited again until night sailed around the monolith and grappled the city. Then they went on up again, outside when they could, inside when they could. Anana asked him why they were going up; he replied that they had to, since the city below was swarming inside and outside.

UI

IN THE MIDDLE OF THE NIGHT, THEY CAME OUT OF ANOTHER HOUSE, having entered by the air shaft, and stepped past the sleepers. This house was on the street just below the emperor's palace. From here on, there would be no internal shaft connections. Since all stairways and causeways were guarded, they could reach their goal only by climbing up on the outside for some distance. This would not be easy. For forty feet, the mountain face was purposely left smooth.

And then, while they were skulking in the shadows at the base of the wall, they came across two booted feet sticking out of a dark alcove. The feet belonged to a dead sentry; another man lay dead by him. One had been stabbed in the throat; the other, strangled with wire.

"Nimstowl has been here!" Anana whispered. "He is called the Nooser, you know."

The torches of an approaching patrol flared three hundred yards down the street. Kickaha cursed Nimstowl because he had left the bodies there. Actually, however, it would make little difference to the patrols if the sentries were dead or missing from their posts. There would be alarms.

The small gate set in the wall was unlocked. It could be locked from the outside only; Kickaha and Anana, after taking the sentries' weapons, went through it, and ran up the steep stairway between towering smooth walls. They were wheezing and sobbing when they reached the top.

From below, shouts rose. Torches appeared in the tiny gateway, and soldiers began to climb the steps. Drums thoomed; a bugle bararared.

The two ran, not toward the palace to their right but toward a steep flight of steps to their left. At the top of the steps, silver roofs and gray iron bars gleamed, and the odor of animals, straw, old meat and fresh dung reached them.

"The royal zoo," Kickaha said. "I've been here."

At the far end of a long flagstone walk, something gleamed like a thread in the hem of night. It shot across the moonlight and was in shadows, out again, in again. Then it faded into the huge doorway of a colossal white building.

"Nimstowl!" Anana said. She started after him, but Kickaha pulled her back roughly. Face twisted, white as silver poured out by the moon in a hideous mold, eyes wide as an enraged owl's, she snapped herself away from him.

"You dare to touch me, *leblabbiy?*"

"Any time," he said harshly. "For one thing, don't call me *leblabbiy* again. I won't just hit you. I'll kill you. I don't have to take that arrogance, that contempt. It's totally based on empty, poisonous, sick egotism. Call me that again, and I'll kill you. You aren't superior to me in any way, you know. You *are* dependent on me."

"I? Dependent? On you?"

"Sure," he said. "Do you have a plan for escape? One that might work, even if it is wild?"

Her effort to control herself made her shudder. Then she forced a smile. And if he had not known the concealed fury, he would have thought it the most beautiful, charming, seductive, etc., smile he had seen in two universes.

"No! I have no plan. You are right. I am dependent on you."

"You're realistic, anyway," he said. "Most Lords, I've heard, are so arrogant, they'd rather die than confess dependency or weakness of any kind."

This flexibility made her more dangerous, however. He must not forget that she was Wolff's sister. Wolff had told him that his sisters Vala and Anana were probably the two most dangerous human females alive. Even allowing for pardonable family pride, and a certain exaggeration, they probably were exceedingly dangerous.

"Stay here!" he said, and he went silently and swiftly after Nimstowl. He could not understand how the two Lords had managed to go straight here. How had they learned of the small secret gate in the temple? There could be only one way: during their brief stay in Wolff's palace, they had seen the map with its location. Anana had not been with them when that had happened, or if she had, she was keeping quiet for some reason of her own.

But if the two Lords could find out about it, why hadn't the Black

Bellers also located it, since they would have had more time? Within a minute, he had his answer. The Bellers had known of the gate and had stationed two guards outside it. But these two were dead, one knifed, one strangled, and the corner of the building was swung open and light streamed out from it. Kickaha cautiously slipped through the narrow opening and into the small chamber. There were four silver crescents set into the stone of the floor; the four that had been hanging on the wall-pegs were gone. The two Lords had used a gate to escape and had taken the other crescents with them to make sure that no one used the others.

Furious, Kickaha returned to Anana and told her the bad news.

"That way is out, but we're not licked yet," he said.

Kickaha walked on a curving path of diorite stones set at the edges with small jewels. He stopped before a huge cage. The two birds within stood side by side and glared at Kickaha. They were ten feet high. Their heads were pale red; their beaks, pale yellow; their wings and bodies were green as the noon sky; their legs were yellow. And their eyes were scarlet shields with black bosses.

One spoke in a giant parrot's voice. "Kickaha! What do you do here, vile trickster?"

Inside that great head was the brain of a woman abducted by Jadawin 3,200 years ago from the shores of the Aegean. That brain had been transplanted for Jadawin's amusement and used in the body created in his biolab. This eagle was one of the few human-brained left. The great green eagles, all females, reproduced parthenogenetically. Perhaps forty of the original five thousand still survived; the others, the millions now living, were their descendants.

Kickaha answered in Mycenaean Greek. "Dewiwanira! And what are you doing in this cage? I thought you were Podarge's pet, not the emperor's."

Dewiwanira screamed and bit at the bars. Kickaha, who was standing too close, jumped back, but he laughed.

"That's right, you dumb bird! Bring them running so they can keep you from escaping!"

The other eagle said, "Escape?"

Kickaha answered quickly. "Yes. Escape. Agree to help us get out of Talanac, and we will get you out of the cage. But say yea or nay now! We have little time!"

"Podarge ordered us to kill you and Jadawin-Wolff!" Dewiwanira said.

"You can try later," he said. "But if you don't give me your word to help us, you'll die in the cage. Do you want to fly again, to see your friends again?"

Torches were on the steps to the palace and the zoological gardens. Kickaha said, "Yes? No?"

"Yes!" Dewiwanira said. "By the breasts of Podarge, yes!"

Anana stepped out from the shadows to assist him. Not until then did the eagles see her face clearly. They jumped and flapped their wings and croaked, "Podarge!"

Kickaha did not tell them that she was Jadawin-Wolff's sister. He said, "Podarge's face had a model."

He ran to the storehouse, thankful that he had taken the trouble to inspect it during his tour with the emperor, and he returned with several lengths of rope. He then jumped into a pit set in stone and leaned heavily upon an iron level. Steel skreaked and the door to the cage swung open.

Anana stood guard with bow and arrow ready. Dewiwanira hunched through the door first and stood still while Kickaha tied each end of a rope to a leg. Antiope, the other eagle, left the cage and submitted to a rope being tied to her legs.

Kickaha told the others what he hoped they could do. Then, as soldiers ran into the gardens, the two huge birds hopped to the edge of the low rampart which enclosed the zoo. This was not their normal method of progress when on the ground; usually they strode. Now, only by spreading their wings to make their descent easier, could they avoid injury to their legs.

Kickaha got in between the legs of Dewiwanira, sat down with the rope under his buttocks, gripped each leg above the huge talons, and shouted, "Ready, Anana? All right, Dewiwanira! Fly!"

Both eagles bounded into the air several feet, even though weighted by the humans. Their wings beat ponderously. Kickaha felt the rope dig into his flesh. He was jerked up and forward; the rampart dropped from under him. The green-silver-spattered, torchflame-sparked, angling walls and streets of the city of Talanac were below him but rushing up frighteningly.

Far below, at least three thousand feet, the river at the foot of the mountain ran with black and tossed silver.

Then the mountain was sliding by perilously close. The eagles could support a relatively large weight, since their muscles were far stronger than those of an eagle of Earth, but they could not flap their wings swiftly enough to lift a human adult. The best they could do was to slow the rate of descent.

And so they paralleled the walls, pounding their wings frantically when they came to an outthrust of street, moved agonizingly slowly outward, or so it seemed to Kickaha, shot over the street and seemed to hurtle down again, the white or brown or red or gray or black or striped jade face of the mountain too too close, then they were rowing furiously to go outward once more.

The two humans had to draw their legs up during most of the whistling, booming, full-of-heart-stopping-crashes-just-ahead ride.

Twice they were scratched, raked, and beaten by the branches of trees as they were hauled through the upper parts. Once the eagles had to bank sharply to avoid slamming into a high framework of wood, built on top of a house for some reason. Then the eagles lost some distance between them and the mountain wall, and the two were bumped with loss of skin and some blood along brown and black jade which, fortunately, was smooth. Ornamental projections would have broken their bones or gashed them deeply.

Then the lowest level, the Street of Rejected Sacrifices, so named for some reason Kickaha had never found out, was behind them. They missed the jade fence on the outer edge of the street by a little more than an inch. Kickaha was so sure that he would be caught and torn on the points that he actually felt the pain.

They dropped toward the river at a steep angle.

The river was a mile wide at this place. On the shore opposite were docks and ships, and outside them, other ships at anchor. Most of these were long two-decked galleys with high poop decks and one or two square-rigged masts.

Kickaha saw this in two flashes, and then, as the eagles sank toward the gray and black dappled surface, he did that which he had arranged with Anana. Confident that the eagles would try to kill them as soon as they were out of danger of being caught inside the city, he had told Anana to release her hold and drop into the river at the first chance.

The river was still fifty feet below when Dewiwanira made her first attempt with her beak. Fortunately for her intended prey, she couldn't bend enough to seize or tear him. The huge yellow beak slashed eight inches above his head.

"Let go!" she screamed then. "You'll pull me into the water! I'll drown!"

Kickaha was tempted to do just that. He was afraid, however, that the obvious would occur to her. If she could sustain altitude enough while Antiope dropped so that her head was even with Kickaha, Antiope could then use her beak on him. And then the two birds could reverse position and get to Anana.

He threw himself backward, turned over, twice straightened out, and entered the water cleanly, head-down. He came up just in time to see the end of Anana's dive. They were about 250 yards from the nearest of five anchored galleys. A mile and a half down the river, torches moved toward them; beneath them, helmets threw off splinters of fire and oars rose and dipped.

The eagles were across the river now and climbing, black against the moonlight.

Kickaha called to Anana, and they swam toward the nearest boat. His clothes and the knives pulled at him, so he shed the clothes and dropped the larger knife into the depths. Anana did the same. Kickaha did not like losing the garments or the knife, but the experiences of the last forty-eight hours and the shortage of food had drained his energy.

They reached the boat finally and clung to the anchor chain while they sucked in air, unable to control the loud sobbing. No one appeared to investigate on the decks of the ship. If there was a watchman, he was sleeping.

The patrol boat was coming swiftly in their direction. Kickaha did not think, however, that he and Anana could be seen yet. He told her what they must do. Having caught up with his breathing, he dived down and under the hull. He turned when he thought he was halfway across and swam along the longitudinal axis toward the rear. Every few strokes, he felt upward. He came up under the overhanging poop with no success. Anana, who had explored the bottom of the front half, met him at the anchor chain. She reported failure, too.

He panted as he talked. "There's a good chance none of these five boats have secret chambers for the smugglers. In fact, we could go through a hundred and perhaps find nothing. Meanwhile, that patrol is getting closer."

"Perhaps we should try the land route," she said.

"Only if we can't find the hidden chambers," he said. "On land, we haven't much chance."

He swam around the boat to the next one and there repeated his search along the keel. This boat and a third proved to have solid bottoms. By then, though he could not see it, Kickaha knew that the patrol boat was getting close.

Suddenly, from the other side of the boat, something like an elephant gun seemed to explode. There was a second boom, and then the screams of eagles and men.

Though he could see nothing, he knew what had happened: the green eagles had returned to kill Kickaha. Not seeing him, they had decided to take revenge on the nearest humans for their long captivity. So they had plunged out of the night sky onto the men in the boat. The booms had been their wings suddenly opening to check their fall. Now, they must be in the boat and tearing with beak and talon.

There were splashes. More screams. Then silence.

A sound of triumph, like an elephant's bugling, then a flapping of giant wings. Kickaha and Anana dived under the fourth boat, and they combined hiding from the eagles with their search.

Kickaha, coming up under the poop, heard the wings but could not see the birds. He waited in the shadow of the poop until he saw them rising out and away from the next boat. They could be giving up their hunt for him or they could be intending to plunge down out of the skies again. Anana was not in sight. She was gone so long that Kickaha knew she had either found what they were looking for or had drowned. Or had taken off by herself.

He swam along under the forepart of the boat, and presently his hand went past the lip of a well cut from the keel. He rose, opening his eyes, and saw a glimmer of darkest gray above. Then he was through the surface and in a square chamber lit by a small lamp. He blinked and saw Anana on all fours, knife in hand, staring down at him from a shelf. The shelf was two feet above the water and ran entirely around the chamber.

Beside her knife hand was the black hair of a man. Kickaha came up onto the shelf. The man was a Tishquetmoac, and he was sleeping soundly.

Anana smiled and said, "He was sleeping when I came out of the water. A good thing, too, because he could have speared me before I knew what was going on. So I hit him in the neck to make sure he continued sleeping."

The shelf went in about four feet and was bare except for some furs, blankets, a barrel with the cartograph for gin on it, and some wooden metal-bound caskets that contained food—he hoped. The bareness meant that the smuggled goods had been removed, so there wouldn't be any influx of swimmers to take the contraband.

The smoke from the lamp rose toward a number of small holes in the ceiling and upper wall. Kickaha, placing his cheek near some of them, felt a slight movement of air. He was sure that the light could not be seen, by anyone on the deck immediately above, but he would have to make sure.

He said to Anana, "There are any number of boats equipped with these chambers. Sometimes the captains know about them; sometimes they don't."

He pointed at the man. "We'll question him later." He tied the man's ankles and turned him over to bind his hands behind him. Then, though he wanted to lie down and sleep, he went back into the water. He came up near the anchor chain, which he climbed. His prowlings on the galley revealed no watchmen, and he got a good idea of the construction of the ship. Moreover, he found some sticks of dried meat and biscuits wrapped in waterproof intestines. There were no eagles in sight, and the patrol boat had drifted so far away that he could not see bodies—if there were any—in it.

When he returned to the chamber, he found the man conscious.

Petotoc said that he was hiding there because he was wanted by the police—he would not say what the charge was. He did not know about the invasion. It was evident that he did not believe Kickaha's story.

Kickaha spoke to the woman. "We must have been seen by enough people so that the search for us in the city will be off. They'll be looking for us in the old city, the farms, the countryside, and they'll be searching every boat, too. Then, when they can't find us, they may let normal life resume. And this boat may set out for wherever it's going."

Kickaha asked Petotoc where he could get enough food to last the three of them for a month. Anana's eyes opened, and she said, "Live a month in this damp, stinking hole?"

"If you want to live at all," Kickaha said. "I sincerely hope we won't be here that long, but I like to have reserves for an emergency."

"I'll go mad," she said.

"How old are you?" he said. "About ten thousand, at least, right? And you haven't learned the proper mental attitudes to get through situations like this in all that time?"

"I never expected to be in such a situation," she snarled.

Kickaha smiled. "Something new after ten millennia, huh? You should be happy to be free of boredom."

Unexpectedly, she laughed. She said, "I am tired and edgy. But you are right. It is better to be scared to death than to be bored to death. And what has happened . . ."

She spread her palms out to indicate speechlessness.

Kickaha, acting on Petotoc's information, went topside again. He lowered a small boat, rowed ashore, and broke into a small warehouse. He filled the boat with food and rowed back to the ship. Here he tied the rowboat to the anchor and then swam under to get Anana. The many dives and swims, hampered by carrying food in nets, wore them out even more. By the end of their labors, they were so tired they could barely pull themselves up onto the shelf in the chamber. Kickaha let the rowboat loose so it could drift away, and then he made his final dive.

Shaking with cold and exhaustion, he wanted desperately to sleep, but he did not dare leave the smuggler unguarded. Anana suggested that they solve that problem by killing Petotoc. The prisoner was listening, but he did not understand, since they were talking in the speech of the Lords. He did see her draw her finger across her throat though, and then he knew what they were discussing. He turned pale under his dark pigment.

"I won't do that unless it's necessary," Kickaha said. "Besides, even if he's dead, we still have to keep a guard. What if other smugglers come in? We can't be caught sleeping. Clatatol and her bunch were able to resist the temptation of the reward—although I'm not sure they could have held out much longer—but others may not be so noble."

He took first watch and only kept awake by dipping water and throwing it in his face, by talking to Petotoc, by pacing savagely back and forth on the shelf. When he thought two hours had passed, he roused her with slaps and water. After getting her promise that she would not succumb to sleep, he closed his eyes. This happened twice more, and then he was awakened the third time. But now he was not to stand guard.

She had placed her hand over his mouth and was whispering into his ear. "Be quiet! You were snoring! There are men aboard."

He lay for a long while listening to the thumps of feet, the shouts and talking, the banging and knocking as cargo was moved about and bulkheads and decks were knocked on to check for hollow compartments.

After 1,200 seconds, each of which Kickaha had silently counted off, the search party moved on. Again, he and Anana tried to overtake their lost sleep in turns.

VII

WHEN THE TIME CAME THAT THEY BOTH FELT REFRESHED ENOUGH TO stay awake at the same time, he asked her how she had gotten into this situation.

"The Black Bellers," she said. She held up her right hand. A ring with a deep black metal band and a large dark-green jewel was on the middle finger.

"I gave the smugglers all my jewels except this," she said. "I refused to part with that; I said I'd have to be killed first. For a moment, I thought they *would* kill me for it.

"Let me see, how to begin? The Black Bellers were originally an artificial form of life created by the Lord scientists about ten thousand years ago. The scientists created the Bellers during their quest for a true immortality.

"A Beller is bell-shaped, black, of indestructible material. Even if one were attached to a hydrogen bomb, the Beller would survive the fission. Or a Beller could be shot into the heart of a star, and it would go unscathed for a billion years.

"Now, the scientists had originally constructed the Beller so that it was purely automatic. It had no mind of its own; it was a device only. When placed on a man's head, it detected the man's skin potential and automatically extruded two extremely thin but rigid needles. These bored through the skull and into the brain.

"Through the needles, the Beller could discharge the contents of a man's mind, that is, it could uncoil the chains of giant protein molecules composing memory. And it could dissociate the complex neural patterns of the conscious and unconscious mind."

"What could be the purpose of that?" Kickaha said. "Why would a

Lord want his brain unscrambled, that is, discharged? Wouldn't he be a blank, a *tabula rasa,* then?"

"Yes, but you don't understand. The discharged and uncoiled mind belonged to a human subject of the Lords. A slave."

Kickaha wasn't easily shocked, but he was startled and sickened now. "What? But . . ."

Anana said earnestly, "This was necessary. The slave would die someday anyway, so what's the difference? But a Lord could live even if his body was mortally hurt."

She did not explain that the scientific techniques of the Lords enabled them to live for millennia, perhaps millions of years, if no accidents, homicide, or suicide occurred. Kickaha, of course, knew this. The agelessness was, to a slighter degree, prevalent for human beings throughout this, Wolff's universe. The waters of this world contained substances provided by Wolff which kept human beings from aging for approximately a thousand years. It also cut down on fertility, so that there was no increase in the birth rate.

"The Bellers were to provide a means whereby the mental contents of a Lord could be transferred to the brain of a host. Thus, the Lord could live on in a new body while the old one died of its wounds.

"The Beller was constructed so that the mental contents of the Lord could be stored for a very long time indeed if an emergency demanded this. The Beller contained a power-pack for operation of the stored mind if this was desired. Moreover, the Beller automatically drew on the neural energy of the host to charge the power-pack. The uncoiling and dematricising were actually the Beller's methods of scanning the mind and then recording it within the bell structure. Duplicating the mind, as it were. The duplication resulted in stripping the original brain, in leaving it blank.

"I'm repeating," she said, "but only to make sure you understand me."

"I follow you," he said. "But this stripping, dematricising, scanning, and duplication doesn't seem to me to be a true immortality. It's not like pouring the mental contents of one head into another. It's not a genuine brain transference. It consists, in reality, of recording cerebral complexes, forebrain and, I suppose, hindbrain, too, to get the entire mind—or don't Bellers have unconsciousnesses?—while destroying them. And then running off the records—tapes, if you will—to build an identical brain in a different container.

"The brain of the second party, however, is not the brain of the first party. In reality, the first party is dead. And though the second party thinks that it is the first party, because it has the brain complex of the first party, it is only a duplication."

"A baby speaks the wisdom of the ages," she said. "That would be true if there were no such thing as the psyche, or the soul, as you humans call it. But the Lords had indubitable proof that an extra-spatial, extra-temporal entity, coeval with every sentient being, exists. Even you humans have them. These duplicate the mental content of the body or soma. Rather, they reflect the psyche-soma, or perhaps it's vice versa.

"Anyway, the psyche is the other half of the 'real' person. And when the duplicate soma-brain is built up in the Beller, the psyche, or soul, transfers to the Beller. And when the Beller retransfers the mental contents to the new host, the psyche then goes to the new host."

Kickaha said, "You have proof of this psyche? Photographs? Sensual indications? And so on?"

"I've never seen any," she said. "Or known anyone who had seen the proofs. But we have been assured that the proofs existed at one time."

"Fine," he said with a sarcasm that she may or may not have detected. "So then?"

"The experiment took over fifty years, I believe, before the Bellers were one hundred percent safe and perfectly operational. Most of the research was done on human slaves, who often died or became idiots."

"In the name of science!"

"In the name of the Lords," she said. "In the name of immortality for the Lords. But the human subjects, and later the Lords who became subjects, reported an almost unendurable feeling of detachment from reality, an agony of separation, while their brains were housed in the Bellers. You see, the brains did have some perception of the world outside if the needle-antennae were extruded. But this perception was very limited.

"To overcome the isolation and panic, the perceptive powers of the antennae were improved. Sound, odor, and a limited sense of vision were made available through the antennae."

Kickaha said, "These Black Bellers are former Lords?"

"No! The scientists accidentally discovered that an unused bell had the potentialities for developing into an entity. That is, an unused bell was a baby Beller. And if it were talked to, played with, taught to speak, to identify, to develop its embryonic personality—well, it became, not a thing, a mechanical device, but a person. A rather alien, peculiar person, but still a person."

"In other words," he said, "The framework for housing a human brain could become a brain in its own right?"

"Yes. The scientists became fascinated. They made a separate project out of raising Bellers. They found that a Beller could become as complex and as intelligent as an adult Lord. Meanwhile, the original project was abandoned, although undeveloped Bellers were to be used as receptacles for storing excess memories of Lords."

Kickaha said, "I think I know what happened."

She continued, "No one knows what really happened. There were ten thousand fully adult Bellers in the project and a number of baby Bellers. Somehow, a Beller managed to get its needle-antennae into the skull of a Lord. It uncoiled and dematricised the Lord's brain and then transferred itself into the host's brain. Thereafter, one by one, the other Lords in the project were taken over."

Kickaha had guessed correctly. The Lords had created their own Frankensteins.

"At that time, my ancestors were creating their private custom-made universes," she said. "They were indeed Lords—gods if there ever were any. The home universe, of course, continued to be the base for the stock population.

"Many of the Bellers in the hosts' bodies managed to get out of the home universe and into the private universes. By the time that the truth was discovered, it was impossible to know who had or had not been taken over, there had been so many transfers. Almost ten thousand Lords had been, as it was termed, 'belled.'

"The War of the Black Bellers lasted two hundred years. I was born during this time. By then, most of the Lord scientists and technicians had been killed. Over half the laymen population was also dead. The home universe was ravaged. This was the beginning of the end of science and progress and the beginning of the solipsism of the Lords. The survivors had much power and the devices and machines in their control. But the understanding of the principles behind the power and the machines was lost.

"Of the ten thousand Bellers, all but fifty were accounted for. The 9,950 were placed inside a universe specially created for them. This was triple-walled so that nobody could ever get in or out."

"And the missing fifty?"

"Never found. From then on, the Lords lived in suspicion, on the verge of panic. Yet, there was no evidence that any Lords were belled. In time, though the panic faded, the missing fifty were not forgotten."

She held up her right hand. "See this ring? It can detect the bell-housing of a Black Beller when it comes within twenty feet. It can't detect a Beller who's housed in a host-body, of course. But the Bellers don't like to be too far from the bells. If anything should happen to the host-body, a Beller wants to be able to transfer his mind back into the bell before the body dies.

"The ring, detecting the bell, triggers an alarm device implanted in the brain of the Lord. This alarm stimulates certain areas of the neural system so that the Lord hears the tolling of a bell. Now, to my knowledge, the tolling of the alarm bell has not sounded for a little less than ten thousand years. But it sounded for three of us not two weeks ago. And we knew that the ancient horror was loose."

"The fifty are now accounted for?" he said.

"Not all fifty. At least, I've seen only a few," she replied. "I think what happened is that all fifty must have been cached together in some universe. They lay in suspended animation for ten millennia. Then some human, some *leb*—" She stopped on seeing his expression and then continued, "Some human stumbled across the cache. He was curious and put one of the bell shapes on his head. And the Beller automatically extruded the needle-antennae. At the same time, the Beller awoke from his ten thousand year sleep. It anesthetized the human through his skin so that he wouldn't struggle, bored into the skull and brain, discharged the human neural configuration and memories, and then transferred itself into the brain. After that, the human-Beller found hosts for the remaining forty-nine. Then the fifty set out on their swift and silent campaign."

There was no telling how many universes the Bellers had taken nor how many Lords they had slain or possessed. They had been unlucky with three: Nimstowl, Judubra, and Anana. She and Nimstowl had managed to inform Judubra of the situation, and he had permitted them to take refuge in his universe. Only the Black Bellers could have made a Lord forget his perpetual war against every other Lord. Judubra was resetting his defenses when the enemy burst through. All three Lords had been forced to gate through to Wolff's palace in this universe.

They had chosen his palace because they had heard that he was now soft and weak; he would not try to kill them if they were friendly. But the palace seemed to be vacant except for the taloses, the half-metal, half-protein machines that were servants and guards for Wolff and Chryseis.

"Wolff gone?" Kickaha said. "Chryseis, too? Where?"

"I do not know," Anana said. "We had little time to investigate. We were forced to gate out of the control room without knowing where we were going. We came out in the Temple of Ollimaml, from which we fled into the city of Talanac. We were fortunate to run into Clatatol and her gang. Not four days later, the Drachelanders invaded Talanac. I don't know how the Black Bellers managed to possess von Turbat, von Swindebarn, and the others."

"They gated through to Dracheland," he said, "and they took over the two kings without the kings' subjects knowing it, of course. They probably didn't know that I was in Talanac, but they must have known about me, I suppose, from films and recordings in the palace. They came here after you Lords, but heard that I was here also and so came after me."

"Why would they want you?"

"Because I know a lot about the secret gates and traps in the palace. For one thing, they won't be able to get into the armory unless they know the pattern of code-breaking. That's why they wanted me alive. For the information I had."

She asked, "Are there any aircraft in the palace?"

"Wolff never had any."

"I think the Bellers will be bringing in some from my world. But they'll have to dismantle them to get them through the narrow gates in the palace. Then they'll have to put them together again. But when the humans see the aircraft, the Bellers will have to do some explaining."

"They can tell the people they're magical vessels," Kickaha said.

Kickaha wished he had the Horn of Shambarimen, or of Ilmarwolkin, as it was sometimes called. When the proper sequence of notes was blown from it at a resonant point in any universe, that point became a gate between two universes. The Horn could also be used to gate between various points on this planet. All that business of matching crescents of gates could be bypassed. But she had not seen the Horn. Probably Wolff had taken it with him, wherever he had gone.

The days and nights that followed were uncomfortable. They paced back and forth to exercise and also let Petotoc stretch his muscles while Kickaha held a rope tied around Petotoc's neck. They slept jerkily. Though they had agreed not to burn the lamp much, because they wanted to save fuel, they kept it lit a good part of the time.

The third day, many men came aboard. The anchor was hauled and the boat was, apparently, rowed into dock. Sounds of cargo being loaded filtered through the wooden bulkheads and decks. These lasted for forty-eight hours without ceasing. Then the boat left the dock, and the oarsmen went to work. The hammer of the pacer, the creak of locks, the dip and whish of oars went on for a long time.

VIII

THE JOURNEY TOOK ABOUT SIX DAYS. THEN THE BOAT STOPPED, THE anchor was run out, and sounds of unloading beat at the walls of the chamber. Kickaha was sure that they had traveled westward to the edge of the Great Plains.

When all seemed quiet, he swam out. Coming up on the landward side, he saw docks, other boats, a fire in front of a large log building, and a low, heavily wooded hill to the east.

It was the terminus frontier town for the river boats. Here the trade goods were transferred to the giant wagons, which would then set out in caravans toward the Great Trade Path.

Kickaha had no intention of letting Petotoc go, but he asked him if he wished to stay with them or would he rather take his chance on joining the Tishquetmoac. Petotoc replied that he was wanted for the murder of a policeman—he would take his chances with them.

They sneaked onto a farm near the edge of town and stole clothes, three horses, and weapons. To do this, it was necessary to knock out the farmer, his wife, and the two sons while they slept. Then the three rode out past the stockaded town and the fort. They came to the edge of the Great Plains an hour before dawn. They decided to follow the trade path for a while. Kickaha's goal was the village of the Hrowakas in the mountains a thousand miles away. There they could plan a campaign which involved some secret gates on this level.

Kickaha had tried to keep up Anana's morale during their imprisonment in the hidden chamber in the boat, joking and laughing, though softly so that he would not be heard by the sailors. But now he seemed to explode, he talked and laughed so much. Anana commented on this, saying that he was now the happiest man she had ever seen; he shone with joy.

"Why not?" he said, waving his hand to indicate the Great Plains. "The air is drunk with sun and green and life. There are vast rolling prairies before us, much like the plains of North America before the white man came. But far more exotic or romantic or colorful, or whatever adjective you choose. There are buffalo by the millions, wild horses, deer, antelope, and the great beasts of prey, the striped Plains lion or Felis Atrox, the running lion, which is a cheetah-like evolution of the puma, the dire wolf and the Plains wolf, the coyote, the prairie dog! The Plains teem with life! Not only pre-Columbian animals but many which Wolff gated through from Earth and which have become extinct there. Such as the mastodon, the mammoth, the uintathere, the Plains camel, and many others.

"And there are the nomadic tribes of Amerinds; a fusion of American Indian and Scythian and Sarmatian white nomads of ancient Russia and Siberia. And the Half-Horses, the centaurs created by Jadawin, whose speech and customs are those of the Plains tribes.

"Oh, there is much to talk about here! And much which I do not know yet but will some day! Do you realize that this level has a land area larger than that of the North and South Americas of my native Earth combined?

"This fabulous world! My world! I believe that I was born for it and that it was more than a coincidence that I happened to find the means to get to it! It's a dangerous world, but then what world, including Earth, isn't? I have been the luckiest of men to be able to come here, and I would not go back to Earth for any price. This is my world!"

Anana smiled slightly and said, "You can be enthusiastic because you are young. Wait until you are ten thousand years old. Then you will find little to enjoy."

"I'll wait," he said. "I am fifty years old, I think, but I look and feel a vibrant twenty-five, if you will pardon the slick-prose adjective."

Anana did not know what slick-prose meant, and so Kickaha explained as best he could. He found out that Anana knew something about Earth, since she had been there several times, the latest visit being in the Earth year 1888 A.D. She had gone there on "vacation" as she put it.

They came to a woods, and Kickaha said they should camp here for the night. He went hunting and came back with a pygmy deer. He butchered it and then cooked it over a small fire. Afterwards, all three chopped branches and made a platform in the fork of two large branches of a tree. They agreed to take one-hour watches. Anana was doubtful about sleeping while Petotoc remained awake, but Kickaha said that they did not have to worry. The fellow was too frightened at the idea of being alone in this wild area to think of killing them or trying to escape on his own. It was then that Anana confessed that she was glad Kickaha was with her.

He was surprised, but agreeably. He said, "You're human after all. Maybe there's some hope for you."

She became angry and turned her back on him and pretended to go to sleep. He grinned and took his watch. The moon bulged greenly in the sky. There were many sounds but all faraway, an occasional trumpet from a mammoth or mastodon, the thunder of a lion, once the whicker of a wild horse, and once the whistle of a giant weasel. This made him freeze, and it caused his horses to whinny. The beast he feared most on the Plains, aside from man and Half-Horse, was the giant weasel. But an hour passed without sound or sight of one, and the horses seemed to relax. He told Petotoc about the animal, warned him to strain all shadows for the great long slippery bulk of the weasel, and not to hesitate to shoot with his bow if he thought he saw one. He wanted to make sure that Petotoc would not fall asleep on guard-duty.

Kickaha was on watch at dawn. He saw the flash of light on something white in the sky. Then he could see nothing, but a minute later the sun gleamed on an object in the sky again. It was far away but it was dropping down swiftly, and it was long and needle-shaped. When it came closer, he could see a bulge on its back, something like an enclosed cockpit; briefly, he saw silhouettes of four men.

Then the craft was dwindling across the prairie.

Kickaha woke Anana and told her what he'd seen. She said, "The Bellers must have brought in aircraft from my palace. That is bad. Not only can the craft cover a lot of territory swiftly, it is armed with two long-range beamers. And the Bellers must have hand-beamers, too."

"We could travel at night," Kickaha said. "But even so, we'd sometimes have to sleep in the open during the day. There are plenty of small wooded areas on the Great Plains, but they are not always available on our route."

"They could have more than one craft," she said. "And one could be out at night. They have means for seeing at night and also for detecting bodies at some distance by radiated heat."

There was nothing to do but ride on out into the open and hope that chance would not bring the Bellers near them. The following day, as Kickaha topped the crest of a slight hill, he saw men on horseback far off. These were not Plains nomads as he would have expected, nor Tishquetmoac. Their armory gleamed in the sun: helmets and cuirasses. He turned to warn the others.

"They must be Teutoniacs from Dracheland," he said. "I don't know how they got out here so fast . . . wait a minute! Yes! They must have come through a gate about ten miles from here. Its crescents are embedded in the tops of two buried boulders near a waterhole. I was thinking about swinging over that way to investigate, though there wasn't much sense in that. It's a one-way gate."

The Teutoniacs must have been sent to search for and cut off Kickaha if he were trying for the mountains of the Hrowakas.

"They'd need a million men to look for me on the Great Plains, and even then I could give them the slip," Kickaha said. "But that aircraft. That's something else."

Three days passed without incident except once, when they came upon a family of Felis Atrox in a little hollow. The adult male and female sprang up and rumbled warnings. The male weighed at least nine hundred pounds and had pale stripes on a tawny body. He had a very small mane; the hairs were thick but not more than an inch long. The female was smaller, weighing probably only seven hundred pounds. The two cubs were about the size of half-grown ocelots.

Kickaha softly told the others to rein in behind him and then he turned his trembling stallion away from the lions, slowly, slowly, and made him walk away. The lions surged forward a few steps but stopped to glare and to roar. They made no move to attack, however; behind them the half-eaten body of a wild striped ass told why they were not so eager to jump the intruders.

The fourth day, they saw the wagon caravan of Tishquetmoac traders. Kickaha rode to within a half mile of it. He could not be recognized at that distance, and he wanted to learn as much as he could about the caravan. He could not answer Anana's questions about the exact goal of his curiosity—he just liked to know things so he would not be ignorant if the situation should change. That was all.

Anana was afraid that Petotoc would take advantage of this to run for the caravan. But Kickaha had his bow ready, and Petotoc had seen enough of his ability to handle the bow to respect it.

There were forty great wagons in the caravan. They were the double-decked, ten wheeled type favored by the Tishquetmoac for heavy-duty Plains transportation. A team of forty mules, larger than Percherons, drew each wagon. There were also a number of smaller wagons which furnished sleeping quarters and food for the cavalry protecting the caravan. The guards numbered about fifty. And there were strings of extra horses for the cavalry and mules for the wagons. There were about three hundred and fifty men, women, and children.

Kickaha rode along to one side and studied the caravan. Finally, Anana said, "What are you thinking?"

He grinned and said, "That caravan will go within two hundred miles of the mountains of the Hrowakas. It'll take a hell of a long time to get there, so what I have to mind wouldn't be very practical. It's too daring. Besides, Petotoc has to be considered."

After he had listened to her plead for some time, he told her what he'd been thinking. She thought he was crazy. Yet, after some consideration, she admitted that the very unconventionality and riskiness of it, its unexpectedness, might actually make it work . . . if they were lucky. But, as he had said, there was Petotoc to consider.

For some time, whenever the Tishquetmoac had not been close enough to hear, she had been urging that they kill him. She argued that he would stab them in the back if he felt he would be safe afterward. Kickaha agreed with her, but he could not kill him without more justification. He thought of abandoning him on the prairie, but he was afraid that Petotoc would be picked up by the searchers.

They swung away from the caravan but rode parallel with it for several days at a distance of a few miles. At night, they retreated even further, since Kickaha did not want to be surprised by them. The third day he was thinking about leaving the caravan entirely and traveling in a southerly direction. Then he saw the flash of white on an object in the sky, and he rode toward a group of widely separated trees, which provided some cover. After tying the horses to bushes, the three crawled up a hill through the tall grass and spied on the caravan.

They were far enough so that they could just distinguish the figures of men. The craft dropped down ahead of the lead wagon and hovered about a foot off the ground. The caravan stopped.

For a long time, a group of men stood by the craft. Even at this distance, Kickaha could see the violent arm-wavings. The traders were protesting, but after a while, they turned and walked back to the lead wagon. And there a process began which took all day, even though the Tishquetmoac worked furiously. Every wagon was unloaded, and the wagons were then searched.

Kickaha said to Anana, "It's a good thing we didn't put my plan into action. We'd have been found for sure! Those guys"—meaning the Bellers—"are thorough!"

That night, the three went deeper into the woods and built no fire. In the morning, Kickaha, after sneaking close, saw that the aircraft was gone. The Tishquetmoac, who must have gotten up very early, were almost finished reloading. He went back to the camping place and spoke to Anana.

"Now that the Bellers have inspected that caravan, they're not very likely to do so again. Now we could do what I proposed—if it weren't for Petotoc."

He did, however, revise his original plan to cut to the south. Instead, he decided to keep close to the caravan. It seemed to him that the Bellers would not be coming back this way again for some time.

The fifth day, he went out hunting alone. He returned with a small deer over his saddle. He had left Anana and Petotoc beneath two trees on the south slope of a hill. They were still there, but Petotoc was sprawled on his back, mouth open, eyes rigid. A knife was stuck in his solar plexus.

"He tried to attack me, the *leblabbiy!*" Anana said. "He wanted me to lie down for him! I refused, and he tried to force me!"

It was true that Petotoc had often stared with obvious lust at Anana, but this was something any man would do. He had never tried to put his hand on her or made any suggestive remarks. This did not mean that he hadn't been planning to do so at the first chance, but Kickaha did not believe that Petotoc would dare make an advance to her. He was, in fact, in awe of Anana, and much too scared of being left alone.

On the other hand, Kickaha could not prove any accusation of murder or of lying. The deed was done, and it could not be undone, so he merely said, "Pull your knife out and clean it. I've wondered what you'd do if I said I wanted to lie with you. Now I know."

She surprised him by saying, "You aren't that one. But you'll never know unless you try, will you?"

"No," he said harshly. He looked at her curiously. The Lords were, according to Wolff, thoroughly amoral. That is, most of them were. Anana was an exceedingly beautiful woman who might or might not be frigid. But ten thousand years seemed like a long time for a woman to remain frigid. Surely techniques or devices existed in the great science of the Lords to overcome frigidity. On the other hand, would a thoroughly passionate woman be able to remain passionate after ten thousand years?

But Wolff had said that even the long-lived Lords lived from day to day. Like mortals, they were caught in the stream of time. And their memories were far from perfect, fortunately for them. So that, though they were subject to much greater boredom and ennui than the so-called mortals, they still weren't overwhelmed. Their rate of suicide was, actually, lower than a comparable group of humans, but this could be attributed to the fact that those with suicidal tendencies had long ago done away with themselves.

Whatever her feelings, she was not revealing them to him. If she was suffering from sexual frustration, as he was at this time, she was not showing any signs. Perhaps the idea of lying with him, a lowly, even repulsive, mortal, was unthinkable to her. Yet he had heard stories of the sexual interest Lords took in their more attractive human subjects. Wolff himself had said that, when he was Jadawin, he had rioted among the lovely females of this world, had used his irresistible powers to get what he wanted.

Kickaha shrugged. There were more important matters to think about at this moment. Survival outweighed everything.

IX

FOR THE NEXT TWO DAYS THEY HAD TO RIDE FAR AWAY FROM THE caravan because the hunting parties from it foraged wide in their quest for buffalo, deer, and antelope meat. And then, while dodging the Tishquetmoac, the two almost ran into a small band of Satwikilap hunters. These Amerinds, painted in white and black stripes from head to foot, their long black hair coiled on top of their heads, bones stuck through their septums, strings of lion teeth around their necks, wearing lionskin pantaloons and deer moccasins, rode within a hundred yards of Anana and Kickaha. But they were intent on shooting the buffalo in the rear of a running herd and did not see them.

Moreover, the Tishquetmoac hunters were after the same bison, but they were on the other side of the herd, separated from the Satwikilap by a mile of almost solid flesh.

Kickaha suddenly made up his mind. He told Anana that tonight was the time. She hesitated, then said they might as well try. Certainly, anything that would take them out of the sight of the Bellers should be tried.

They waited until the eating of roast meat and the drinking of gin and vodka was finished and the caravaneers had staggered off to bed. There were non-drinking sentries posted at intervals along the sides of the wagon train, but the caravan was within the borders of the Great Trade Path marked by the carved wooden images of the god of trade and business so the Tishquetmoac did not really worry about attack from men or Half-Horses. Some animal might blunder into the camp or a giant weasel or lion try for a horse or even for a Tishquetmoac, but this wasn't likely, so the atmosphere was relaxed.

Kickaha removed all harness from the horses and slapped them on the rumps so they would take off. He felt a little sorry for them, since they were domesticated beasts and not likely to flourish on the wild Great Plains. But they would have to take their chances, as he was taking his.

Then he and Anana, a pack of bottled water and dried meat and vegetables tied to their backs, knives in their teeth, crawled in the moon-spattered darkness toward the caravan. They got by two guards, stationed forty yards apart, without being seen. They headed for a huge ten-wheeler wagon that was twentieth in line. They crept past small wagons holding snoring men, women, and children. Fortunately, there were no dogs with the caravan and for a good reason. The cheetah-like puma and the weasel were especially fond of dogs, so much so that the Tishquetmoac had long ago given up taking these pets along on the Plains voyage.

Arranging living quarters inside the tightly packed cargo in the lower deck of a wagon was not easy. They had to pull out a number of wooden boxes and bolts of cloth and rugs and then remass them over the hole in which they would spend their daylight hours. The dislodged cargo was jammed in with some effort wherever it would go. Kickaha hoped that nobody would notice that the arrangements were not what they were when the wagon left the terminus.

They had two empty bottles for sanitary purposes; blankets provided a fairly comfortable bed for them—until the wagon started rolling in the morning. The wagon had no springs; and though the prairie seemed smooth enough to a man walking, the roughnesses became exaggerated in the wagon.

Anana complained that she had felt shut-in in the boat chamber, but now she felt as if she were buried in a landslide. The temperature outside seldom got above seventy-five degrees Fahrenheit at noon, but the lack of ventilation and the closeness of their bodies threatened to stifle them. They had to sit up and stick their noses into the openings to get enough oxygen.

Kickaha widened the openings. He hated to do so because it made discovery by the caravaneers more likely; while the wagon was traveling however, no one was going to peep into the lower deck.

They got little sleep the first day. At night, while the Tishquetmoac slept, they crept out and crawled past the sentries into the open. Here they bathed in a waterhole, refilled their bottles, and discharged natural functions which had been impossible, or highly inconvenient, inside the wagon. They exercised to take the stiffness out of muscles caused by cramped conditions and the jostling and bouncing. Kickaha wondered if he was so clever after all. It had seemed the most impudent thing in the world, hiding out literally under the noses, not to mention the buttocks, of the Tishquetmoac. Alone, he might have been more comfortable, more at ease. But though Anana did not really complain much, her not-quite-suppressed groans and moans and invectives irked him. It was impossible in those closely walled quarters not to touch each other frequently, but she reacted overviolently every time. She told him to stay to his own half of the "coffin," not to make his body so evident, and so on.

Kickaha began to think seriously about telling her to take off on her own. Or, if she refused, knocking her out and dragging her away some place and leaving her behind. Or, at times, he fantasized about slitting her throat or tying her to a tree so the lions or wolves could get her.

It was, he told himself, a hell of a way for a love affair to start.

And then he caught himself. Yes, he had said that: *love affair*. Now, how could he be in love with such a vicious, arrogant, murderous bitch?

He was. Much as he hated, loathed, and despised her, he was beginning to love her.

Love was nothing new to Kickaha in this or that other world . . . but never under these circumstances.

Undoubtedly, except for Podarge, who looked just like Anana as far as the face was concerned, and the strange, really unearthly Chryseis, Anana was the most beautiful woman he had ever seen.

To Kickaha, this would not automatically bring love. He appreciated beauty in a woman, of course, but he was more liable to fall in love with a woman with an agreeable personality and a quick brain and humor than with a disagreeable and/or dumb woman. If the woman was only reasonably attractive or perhaps even plain, he could fall in love with her if he found certain affinities in her.

And Anana was certainly disagreeable.

So why this feeling of love side by side with the hostility he felt toward her?

Who knows? Kickaha thought. *Evidently, I don't. And that in itself is pleasing, since I would not like to become bored and predictable about myself.*

The bad thing about this affair was that it would probably be one-sided. She might take a sensual interest in him, but it would be ephemeral and there would be contempt accompanying it. Certainly, she could never love a *leblabbiy*. For that matter, he doubted that she could love anyone. The Lords were beyond love. Or at least that was what Wolff had told him.

The second day passed more quickly than the first; both were able to sleep more. That night, they were treed by a pride of lions that had come down to drink at a stream shortly after the two humans arrived. Finally, as the hours had gone by and the lions showed no desire to wander on, Kickaha became desperate. Dawn would soon lighten this area. It would be impossible to sneak back into the wagon. He told Anana that they would have to climb down and try to bluff the big cats.

Kickaha, as usual, had another motive than the obvious. He hoped that, if she had any weapons concealed or implanted in her body, she would reveal them now. But either she had none or she did not think the situation desperate enough to use them. She said that he could attempt to scare the monsters, if he wished, but she intended to stay in the tree until they went away.

"Under ordinary circumstances, I'd agree with you," he said. "But we have to get back inside the wagon within the next half hour."

"I don't have to," she said. "Besides, you didn't kill anything for us to eat before we went back. I don't want to spend another hungry day inside that coffin."

"You had plenty of dried meat and vegetables to eat," he said.

"I was hungry all day," she replied.

Kickaha started to climb down. Most of the lions seemed to be paying no attention to him. But a male sprang into the air and a long-clawed paw came within six inches of his foot. He went back up the tree.

"They don't seem to be in a mood to be bluffed," he said. "Some days they are. Today, well . . ."

From his height in the tree he could see part of the wagon train, even in the moonlight. Presently the moon went around the monolith and the sun followed it from the east. The caravaneers began to wake. Campfires were built, and the bustle of getting ready for breakfast and then breaking camp began. Presently, a number of soldiers, colorful in long-feathered wooden casques, scarlet quilt-cuirasses, green feathered kilts, and yellow-dyed leggings, mounted their horses. They formed a crescent within which men and women, carrying pots, kettles, jugs, and other utensils, marched. They headed toward the waterhole.

Kickaha groaned. Occasionally he outfoxed himself, and this could be one of the occasions.

There was not the slightest doubt about his choice. It would be far better to face the lions than to be captured by the Tishquetmoac. While he might be able to talk them out of turning him over to the Teutoniacs, he doubted it very much. Anyway, he could not afford to risk their mercy.

He said, "Anana, I'm going north, and I'm going fast. Coming along?"

She looked down at the big male lion, crouched at the foot of the tree and staring up with huge green eyes. His mouth also stared. Four canines, two up, two down, seemed as long as daggers.

"You must be crazy," she said.

"You stay here if you want to. So long, if ever!"

He began to climb down but on the other side of the tree, away from the lion. The great beast arose and roared, and then the others were on their feet and pointing toward the approaching humans. The wind had brought their scent.

For a moment, the cats did not seem to know what to do. Then the male under the tree roared and slunk off and the others followed him. Kickaha dropped the rest of the way and ran in the same direction as the lions. He did not look back, but he hoped that Anana would have enough presence of mind to follow him. If the soldiers caught her, or even saw her, they would search the area on the premise that other fugitives might be nearby.

He heard her feet thudding on the earth, and then she was close behind him. He looked back then, not at her but for signs of the cavalry. He saw the head of one soldier appear over a slight rise, and he grabbed Anana and pulled her down into the high grass.

There was a shout—the rider had seen them. It was to be expected. And now . . . ?

Kickaha stood up and looked. The first rider was in full view. He was standing up in the stirrups and pointing in their direction. Others were coming up behind him. Then the lead man was riding toward them, his lance couched.

Kickaha looked behind him. Plains and tall grass and a few trees here and there. Far off, a gray many-humped mass that was a herd of mammoths. The lions were somewhere in the grass.

The big cats would have to be his joker. If he could spring them at the right time, and not get caught himself, then he might get away.

He said, "Follow me!" and began to run as swiftly as he had ever run in his life. Behind him, the soldiers yelled and the horses' hooves krok-krok-krokked.

The lions failed him. They scattered away, bounding easily, not panicked but just not wanting to turn to fight at this moment. They did not give him the opportunity he sought to flee while horse and rider were being clawed down by lions at bay.

Some of the cavalry passed him and then they had turned and were facing him, their lances forming a crescent. Behind him, other lances made a half ring. He and Anana were between the crescents with no place to go unless they hurled themselves on the lance-points.

"This is what I get for being too smart," he said to Anana.

She did not laugh. He did not feel much like laughing himself.

He felt even less like it when they were brought back, bound and helpless, to the caravan. The chief, Clishquat, informed them that the rewards had been tripled. And though he had heard of Kickaha, and of course admired and respected him as the beloved of the Lord, well, things had changed, hadn't they?

Kickaha had to admit that they had. He asked Clishquat if the emperor was still alive. Clishquat was surprised at the question. Of course the *miklosiml* was alive. He was the one offering the rewards. He was the one who had proclaimed the alliance with the pinkface sorcerers who flew in a wheelless wagon. And so on.

Kickaha's intention to talk the caravaneers out of keeping him captive by telling them the true situation in Talanac did not work. The empire-wide system of signal drums and of pony express had acquainted the frontier towns with conditions in the capital city. It was true that some of the news was false, but Clishquat would not believe Kickaha concerning it. Kickaha could not blame him.

The two captives were given a full meal; and women bathed them, oiled their bodies and hair, combed their hair and put fresh clothes on them. During this, the chiefs, the underchiefs, and the soldiers who had captured the two, argued. The chief thought that the soldiers should split the reward with him. The underchiefs believed they should get in on the money. And then some representatives of the rest of the caravaneers marched up. They demanded that the reward be split evenly throughout the caravan.

At this, the chiefs and the soldiers began screaming at the newcomers. Finally, the chief quieted them down. He said that there was only one way to settle the matter. That would be to submit the case to the emperor. In effect, this meant the high court of judges of Talanac.

The soldiers objected. The case would limp along for years before being settled. By then, the legal fees would have devoured much of the reward money.

Clishquat, having scared everybody with this threat, then offered a compromise which he hoped would be satisfactory. One-third should go to the soldiers; one-third to the civilian leaders of the caravan, the chief and chieflings; one-third to be divided equally among the remaining men.

There was a dispute that lasted through lunch and supper. The train did not move during this.

Then, when everybody had agreed, more or less amicably, on the splitting of the reward, a new argument started. Should the caravan move on, taking the prisoners with them, in the hope that the magic airboat would come by again, as the pinkface sorcerers had promised? The prisoners could then be turned over to the sorcerers. Or should a number of soldiers take the prisoners back to Talanac while the caravan moved on to its business?

Some objectors said that the sorcerers might not return. Even if they did, they would not have room in the boat for the fugitives.

Others said that those picked to escort the prisoners home might claim the entire reward for themselves. By the time the caravan returned to civilization, it might find that the escort had spent the money. And suit in court would be useless.

And so on and so on.

Kickaha asked a woman how the pinkfaces had communicated with the caravan chief.

"There were four pinkfaces and each had a seat in the magic car," she replied. "But a priest talked for them. He sat by the feet of the one who was in a chair in front and to the right. The pinkfaces talked in the language of the Lords—I know it at least when I hear it, though I do not speak it as the priests do—and the priest listened and then spoke to the chief in our language."

Late at night, when the moon was halfway across the bridge of sky, the argument was still going on. Kickaha and Anana went to sleep in their beds of furs and blankets in the upper deck of a wagon. They awoke in the morning to find camp being broken. It had been decided to take the prisoners along with the hope that the magic flying car would return as its occupants had promised.

The two captives were permitted to walk behind the wagon during the day. Six soldiers kept guard throughout the day, and another six stood watch over the wagon at night.

X

THE THIRD NIGHT, EVENTS DEVELOPED AS KICKAHA HAD BEEN HOPING they would. The six guards had been very critical of the decision to split the reward throughout the caravan. They spent a good part of the night muttering among themselves, and Kickaha, awake part of the time, testing his bonds, overheard much of what they said.

He had warned Anana to make no outcry or struggle if she should be awakened by the sentries. The two were rousted out with warnings to keep silent or die with slit throats. They were marched off between two unconscious sentries and into a small group of trees. Here were horses, saddled, packed, ready to be mounted by the six soldiers and two prisoners, and extra pack horses. The party rode out slowly for several miles, then began to canter. Their flight lasted the night and half the next day. They did not stop to make camp until they were sure that they were not pursued. Since they had left the trade trail and swung far north, they did not expect to be followed.

The next day, they continued parallel with the trade trail. On the third day, they began to angle back toward it. Being so long outside the safety of the trade path made them nervous.

Kickaha and Anana rode in the center of the party. Their hands were tied with ropes but loosely, so they could handle the reins. They stopped at noon. They were just finishing their cooked rabbit and greens boiled in little pots, when a lookout on a hill nearby called out. He came galloping toward them, and, when he was closer, he could be heard.

"Half-Horses!"

The pots were emptied on top of the fire, and dirt was kicked over the wet ashes. In a panic, the soldiers packed away most of their utensils. The two captives were made to remount, and the party started off southward, toward the trade trail, many miles away.

It was then that the soldiers saw the wave of buffalo moving across the plains. It was a tremendous herd several miles across and of a seemingly interminable length. The right flank was three miles from them, but the earth quivered under the impact of perhaps a quarter of a million hooves.

For some reason known only to the buffalo, they were in flight. They were stampeding westward, and they were going so swiftly that the Tishquetmoac party might not be able to get across to the trade path in time. They had a chance, but they would not know how good it was until they got much closer to the herd.

The Half-Horses had seen the humans, and they had bent into full gallop. There were about thirty of them: a chief with a full-feathered and long-tailed bonnet, a number of blooded warriors with feathered headbands, and three or four unblooded juveniles.

Kickaha groaned; it seemed to him that they were of the Shoyshatel tribe. They were so far away that the markings were not quite distinct. But he thought that the bearing of the chief was that of the Half-Horse who had shouted threats at him when Kickaha had taken refuge at the Tishquetmoac fort.

Then he laughed, because it did not matter which tribe it was. All Half-Horse tribes hated Kickaha and all would treat him as cruelly as possible if they caught him.

He yelled at the leader of the soldiers, Takwoc, "Cut the ropes from our wrists! They're handicapping us! We can't get away from you, don't worry!"

Takwoc looked for a moment as if he might actually cut the ropes. The danger involved in riding so close to Kickaha, the danger of the horses knocking each other down or Kickaha knocking him off the saddle, probably made him change his mind. He shook his head.

Kickaha cursed and then crouched over the neck of the stallion and tried to evoke from him every muscle-stretching-contracting quota of energy in his magnificent body. The stallion did not respond because he was already running as swiftly as he could.

Kickaha's horse, though fleet, was half a body-length behind the stallion which Anana rode. Perhaps they were about equal in running ability, but Anana's lighter weight made the difference. The others were not too far behind and were spread out in a rough crescent, with horns curving away from him, three on each side. The Half-Horses were just coming over the rise; they slowed down a moment, probably in amazement at the sight of the tremendous herd. Then they waved their weapons and charged on down the hill.

The herd was rumbling westward. The Tishquetmoac and prisoners were coming on the buffalos' right at an angle of forty-five degrees. The Half-Horses had swung a little to the west before coming over the hill and their greater speed had enabled them to squeeze the distance down between them and their intended victims.

Kickaha, watching the corner formed by the flank of the great column of beasts and the front part—almost square—saw that the party could get across in front of the herd. From then on, speed and luck meant safety on the other side or being overwhelmed by the racing buffalo. The party could not directly cut across the advance; it would have to run ahead of the beasts and at an angle at the same time.

Whether or not the horses could keep up their present thrust of speed, whether or not a horse or all horses might slip, that would be known in a very short time.

He shouted encouragement at Anana as she looked briefly behind, but the rumble of the hooves, shaking the earth and sounding like a volcano ready to blow its crust, tore his voice to shreds.

The roar, the odor of the beasts, the dust, frightened Kickaha. At the same time, he was exhilarated. This wasn't the first time that he had been raised by his fright out of fright and into near-ecstasy. Events seemed to be on such a grand scale all of a sudden, and the race was such a fine one, with the prize sudden safety or sudden death, that he felt as if he were kin to the gods, if not a god. That moment when mortality was so near, and so probable, was the moment he felt immortal.

It was quickly gone, but while it lasted he knew that he was experiencing a mystical state.

Then he was seemingly heading for a collision with the angle formed by the flank and front of the herd.

Now he could see the towering shaggy brown sides of the giant buffalo, the humps heaving up and down like the bodies of porpoises soaring from wave to wave, the dark brown foreheads, massive and lowering, the dripping black snouts, the red eyes, the black eyes, the red-shot white eyes, the legs working so swiftly they were almost a blur, foam curving from the open foam-toothed mouths onto thick shaggy chests and the upper parts of the legs.

He could hear nothing at first but that rumbling as of the earth splitting open, so powerful that he expected, for a second, to see the plain open beneath the hooves and fire and smoke spurt out.

He could smell a million buffalo, beasts extinct for ten thousand years on Earth, monsters with horns ten feet across, sweating with panic and the heart-shredding labor of their flight, excrement of fear befouling them and their companions, and something that smelled to him like a mixture of foam from mouth and blood from lungs, but that, of course, was his imagination.

There was also the stink of his horse, sweat of panic and labor of flight and of foam from its mouth.

"Haiyeeee!" Kickaha shouted, turning to scream at the Half-Horses, wishing his hands were not tied and he had a weapon to shake at them. He could not hear his own defiance, but he hoped that the Half-Horses would see his open mouth and his grin and know that he was mocking them.

By now, the centaurs were within a hundred and fifty yards of their quarry. They were frenzied in their efforts to catch up; their great dark broad-cheekboned faces were twisted in agony.

They could not close swiftly enough, and they knew it. By the time their quarry had shot across the right shoulder of the herd at an angle, they would still be fifty or so yards behind. And by the time they reached the front of the herd, their quarry would be too far ahead. And after that, they would slowly lose ground before the buffalo, and before they could get to the other side, they would go down under the shelving brows and curving horns and cutting hooves.

Despite this, the Half-Horses galloped on. An unblooded, a juvenile whose headband was innocent of scalp or feather, had managed to get ahead of the others. He left the others behind at such a rate that Kickaha's eyes widened. He had never seen so swift a Half-Horse before, and he had seen many. The unblooded came on and on, his face twisted with an effort so intense that Kickaha would not have been surprised to see the muscles of the face tear loose.

The Half-Horse's arm came back, and then forward, and the lance flew ahead of him, arcing down, and suddenly Kickaha saw that what he had thought would be impossible was happening.

The lance was going to strike the hind quarters or the legs of his stallion. It was coming down in a curve that would fly over the Tishquetmoac riders behind him and would plunge into some part of his horse.

He pulled the reins to direct the stallion to the left, but the stallion pulled its head to one side and slowed down just a trifle. Then he felt a slight shock, and he knew that the lance had sunk into its flesh.

Then the horse was going over, its front legs crumpling, the back still driving and sending the rump into the air. The neck shot away from before him, and he was soaring through the air.

Kickaha did not know how he did it. Something took over in him as
it had done before, and he did not fall or slide into the ground. He
landed running on his feet with the black-and-brown wall of the herd to
his left. Behind him, so close that he could hear it even above the rum-
ble-roar of the herd, was the thunk of horses' hooves. Then the sound
was all around him, and he could no longer stay upright because of his
momentum, and he went into the grass on his face and slid.

A shadow swooped over him; it was that of a horse and rider as the
horse jumped him. Then all seven were past him; he saw Anana looking
back over her shoulder just before the advancing herd cut her—cut all
the Tishquetmoac, too—from his sight.

There was nothing they could do for him. To delay even a second
meant death for them under the hooves of the buffalo or the spears of
the Half-Horses. He would have done the same if he had been on his
horse and she had fallen off hers.

Surely the Half-Horses must have been yelling in triumph now. The
stallion of Kickaha was dead, a lance projecting from its rump and its
neck broken. Their greatest enemy, the trickster who had so often given
them the slip when they knew they had him, even he could not now escape. Not unless he were to throw himself under the hooves of the
titans thundering not ten feet away!

This thought may have struck them, because they swept toward him
with the unblooded who had thrown the lance trying to cut him off. The
others had thrown their lances and tomahawks and clubs and knives
away and were charging with bare hands. They wanted to take him alive.

Kickaha did not hesitate. He had gotten up as soon as he was able
and now he ran toward the herd. The flanks of the beasts swelled before
him; they were six feet high at the shoulder and running as if time itself
were behind them and threatening to make them extinct like their
brothers on Earth.

Kickaha ran toward them, seeing out of the corner of his eyes the
young unblooded galloping in. Kickaha gave a savage yell and leaped
upward, his hands held before him. His foot struck a massive shoulder
and he grabbed a shag of fur. He kicked upward and slipped and fell
forward and was on his stomach on the back of a bull!

He was looking down the steep valley formed by the right and left
sides of two buffalo. He was going up and down swiftly, was getting
sick, and also was slowly sliding backward.

After loosing his hold on the tuft of hair, he grabbed another one to
his right and managed to work himself around so that his legs straddled

the back of the beast. The hump was in front of him; he was hanging onto the hair of it.

If Kickaha believed only a little in what had happened, the Half-Horse youth who had thought he had Kickaha in his hands believed it not at all.

He raced alongside the bull on which Kickaha was seated, and his eyes were wide and his mouth worked. His arms were extended in front of him as if he still thought he would scoop Kickaha up in them.

Kickaha did not want to let loose of his hold, insecure though it was, but he knew that the Half-Horse would recover in a moment. Then he would pull a knife or tomahawk from the belt around the lower part of his human torso, and he would throw it at Kickaha. If he missed, he had weapons in reserve.

Kickaha brought his legs up so that he was squatting on top of the spine of the great bull, his feet together, one hand clenching buffalo hair. He turned slowly, managing to balance himself despite the up-and-down jarring movement. Then he launched himself outward and onto the back of the next buffalo, which was running shoulder to shoulder with the animal he had just left.

Something dark rotated over his right shoulder. It struck the hump of a buffalo nearby and bounced up and fell between two animals. It was a tomahawk.

Kickaha pulled himself up again, this time more swiftly, and he got his feet under him and jumped. One foot slipped as he left the back, but he was so close to the other that he grabbed fur with both hands. He hung there while his toes just touched the ground whenever the beast came down in its galloping motion. Then he let himself slide down a little, pushed against the ground, and swung himself upward. He got one leg over the back and came up and was astride it.

The young Half-Horse was still keeping pace with him. The others had dropped back a little; perhaps they thought he had fallen down between the buffalo and so was ground into shreds. If so, they must have been shocked to see him rise from the supposed dead, the Trickster, slippery, cunning, many-turning, the enemy who mocked them from within death's mouth.

The unblooded must have been driven a little crazy when he saw Kickaha. Suddenly, his great body, four hooves flying, soared up and he was momentarily standing on the back of a buffalo at the edge of the herd. He sprang forward to the next one, onto its hump, like a mountain goat skipping on moving mountains.

Now it was Kickaha's turn to be amazed and dismayed. The Half-

Horse held a knife in his hand, and he grinned at Kickaha as if to say, "At last, you are going to die, Kickaha! And I, I will be sung of throughout the halls and tepees of the Nations of the prairies and the mountains, by men and Half-Horses everywhere!"

Some such thoughts must have been in that huge head. And he would have become the most famous of all dwellers on and about the Plains, if he had succeeded. Trickster-killer he would have been named.

He Who Skipped Over Mad Buffalo To Cut Kickaha's Throat.

But on the third hump, a hoof slipped and he plunged on over the hump and fell down between two buffalo, his back legs flying and tail straight up. And that was the end of him, though Kickaha could not see what the buffalo hooves were doing.

Still, the attempt had been magnificent and had almost succeeded, and Kickaha honored him even if he was a Half-Horse. Then he began to think again about surviving.

XI

SOME OF THE CENTAURS HAD DRAWN UP EVEN WITH HIM AND BEGAN loosing arrows at Kickaha.

Before the first shaft was released, he had slipped over to one side of the buffalo on which he was mounted, hanging on with both hands to fur, one leg bent as a hook over the back. His position was insecure, because the rough gallop loosened his grip a little with every jolt, and the beast next to him was so close that he was in danger of being smashed.

Shafts passed over him; something touched the foot sticking up in the air. A tomahawk bounced off the top of the buffalo's head. Suddenly, the bull began coughing, and Kickaha wondered if his lungs had been penetrated by an arrow. The bull began to slow down, stumbled a little, recovered, and went on again.

Kickaha reached out for the next beast, grabbed a fistful of fur, released the other hand, clutched more fur, let loose with the right leg, and his body swung down. Like a trick horse rider, he struck the ground with both feet; his legs and body swung up, and he hooked his left leg over the back just behind the hump.

Behind him, the buffalo he had just left fell, slid, stopped, on its side, kicking, two arrows sticking from it. Then the beasts behind it jumped, but the third one tripped, and there was a pile-up of at least ten mammoth bodies kicking, struggling, goring, and then dying as even more crashed into them and over them and on them.

Something was happening ahead. He could not see what it was because he was hanging on the side of the buffalo, his view blocked by tails, rumps, and legs. But the beasts were slowing down and were also turning to the left.

The buffalo on the right bellowed as if mortally hurt. And so it was.

It staggered off, fortunately away from Kickaha, otherwise it would have smashed him if it had fallen against him. It collapsed, blood running from a large hole in its hump.

Kickaha became aware of two things: one, the thunder of the stampede had lessened so much that he could hear individual animals nearby as they cried out or bellowed; two, in addition to the other odors, there was now that of burned flesh and hair.

The beast on the other side fell away, and then that carrying Kickaha was alone. It charged on, passing the carcasses of just-killed buffalo. It bounded over a cow with its great head half cut off. And when it came down, the shock tore Kickaha's grip loose. He fell off and rolled over and over and came up on his feet, ready for he knew not what.

The world seesawed about him, then straightened out. He was gasping for breath, shaking, sweaty, bloody, filthy with buffalo dung and foam and dirt. But he was ready to jump this way or that, depending upon the situation.

There were dead buffalo everywhere. There were also dead Half-Horses here and there. The living in the herd were racing off to the left now; the torrent of millions of tons of flesh and hooves roared by and away.

A crash sounded, so unexpectedly and loudly that he jumped. It was as if a thousand large ships had simultaneously smashed into a reef. Something had killed all of the beasts in a line a mile across, killed them one after the other within six or seven seconds. And those behind the line stumbled over these, and those behind rammed them and went hoof-over-hoof.

Abruptly, the stampede had stopped. Those animals fortunate enough to stop in time stood stupidly about, wheezing for air. Those buried in the huge mounds of carcasses, but still living, bellowed; they were the only ones with enough motive to voice any emotion. The others were laboring to run their breaths down.

Kickaha saw the cause of the dead and of the halted stampede. To his left, a quarter of a mile away and about twenty feet up, was an aircraft. It was needle-shaped, wingless; its lower part was white with black arabesques, its upper part was transparent coaming. Five silhouettes were within the covering.

It was chasing after a Tishquetmoac who was trying to escape on his horse. Chasing was the wrong word. The craft moved swiftly enough but leisurely and made no effort to get immediately behind the horse. A bright white beam shot out from the cylinder mounted on the nose of the craft. Its end touched the rump of the horse, which fell. The Tishquetmoac man threw himself out and, though he rolled heavily, he came up and onto his feet.

Kickaha looked around on all sides. Anana was a quarter of a mile away in the other direction. Several Tishquetmoac stood near her. A couple lay on the ground as if dead; one was caught beneath his horse. All the horses were dead, apparently rayed down by the craft.

Also dead were all the Half-Horses.

The Bellers had killed the horses to keep the party from escaping. They might not even know that the man and woman they were looking for were in this group. They might have spotted the chase and swung over for a look and decided to save the chased because they might have some information. On the other hand, both Anana and Kickaha were lighter skinned than the Tishquetmoac in the party. The Tishquetmoac did, however, vary somewhat in darkness; a small minority were not so heavily pigmented. So the Bellers would have decided to check them out. Or . . . there were many possibilities. None mattered now. The important thing was that he and Anana were, seemingly, helpless. They could not get away. And the weapons of the Bellers were overwhelming.

Kickaha did not just give up, although he was so tired that he almost felt like it. He thought, and while he was thinking, he heard a pound of hooves and a harsh rasping breathing. He launched himself forward and at an angle on the theory that he might evade whatever was attacking him—if he were being attacked.

A lance shot by him and then slid along the ground. A bellow sounded behind him; he whirled to see a Half-Horse advancing on him. The centaur was badly wounded; his hindquarters were burned, his tail was half charred off, and his back legs could scarcely move. But he was determined to get Kickaha before he died. He held a long heavy knife in his left hand.

Kickaha ran to the lance, picked it up, and threw it. The Half-Horse yelled with frustration and despair and tried to evade the spear. Handicapped by his crippled legs, he did not move fast enough. He took the lance in his human chest—Kickaha had aimed for the protruding bellows organ below the chest—and fell down. Up he came, struggling to his front legs while the rear refused to move again. He tore the lance out with his right hand, turned it, and, ignoring the spurt of blood from the wound, again cast it. This surprised Kickaha, who was running to push in on the lance and so finish him off.

The arm of the dying centaur was weak. The lance left his hand to fly a few feet and then plunged into the earth before Kickaha's feet. The

Half-Horse gave a cry of deep desolation—perhaps he had hoped for glory in song here and a high place in the councils of the dead. But now he knew that if a Half-Horse ever slew Kickaha, he would not be the one.

He fell on his side, dropping the knife as he went down. His front legs kicked several times, his huge fierce face became slack, and the black eyes stared at his enemy.

Kickaha glanced quickly around him, saw that the aircraft was flying a foot above the ground about a quarter of a mile away. Apparently it was corraling several Tishquetmoac who were fleeing on foot. Anana was down. He did not know what had happened to her. Perhaps she was playing possum, which was what he intended to do.

He rubbed some of the centaur's blood over him, lay down in front of him, placed the knife so it was partly hidden under his hip, and then placed the lance point between his chest and arm. Its shaft rose straight up, looking from a distance as if the lance were in his chest, he hoped.

It was a trick born out of desperation and not likely to succeed. But it was the only one he had now, and there was the chance that the Bellers, being nonhuman, might not be on to certain human ruses. In any event, he would try it, and if it didn't work, well, he didn't really expect to live forever.

Which was a lie, he told himself, because he, in common with most men, did expect to live forever. And he had managed to survive so far because he had fought more energetically and cunningly than most.

For what seemed a long time afterward, nothing happened. The wind blew coolly on the blood and sweat. The sweat dried off and the blood dried up. The sun was sinking in the last quarter of the green sky. Kickaha wished that it were dusk, which would increase his chances, but if wishes were horses, he would ride out of here.

A shadow flitted over his eyes. He tensed, thinking it might be that of the aircraft. A harsh cry told him that it was a crow or raven, coming to feed. Soon the carrion eaters would be flying in thicker than pepper on a pot roast: crows, ravens, buzzards, giant vultures, even larger condors, hawks, and eagles, some of which would be the mammoth green eagles, Podarge's pets.

And the coyote, the Plains fox, the common wolf, and the dire wolf would be following their noses and running in to the toothsome feast.

And the greater predators, not too proud to eat meat which they had not brought down, would pad in from the tall grass and then roar to frighten away the lesser beasts. The nine hundred pound palely striped Plains lions would attend with much roaring and snarling and scrapping among themselves and slashes and dashes at the smaller beasts and birds.

Kickaha thought of this and began to sweat again. He shooed a crow away by hissing and cursing out of the corner of his mouth. Far away, a wolf howled. A condor sailed overhead and banked slowly as it glided in for a landing, probably on some fallen buffalo.

Then another shadow passed. Through his half-closed eyelids, he saw the aircraft slide silently over him. It dipped its nose and began to sink, but he could not follow it without turning his head. It had been about fifty feet up, which he hoped would be far enough away so that they might still believe the lance had gone into his chest or armpit.

Somebody shouted in the language of the Lords. The voice was downwind, so he could not distinguish many words.

After a silence, several voices came to him, this time from upwind. If the Bellers were still in the craft, then it had moved between him and Anana. He hoped that a Beller would get out and walk over to examine him; he hoped that the craft would not first fly to a point just above him, where the occupants could lean out and look at him. He knew that the Bellers probably had hand-beamers and that these would be in readiness. In addition, the Bellers left in the craft would be using the larger projectors to cover those outside.

He did not hear the footsteps of the approaching Beller. The fellow had undoubtedly had his beamer on Kickaha, ready to shoot if he thought Kickaha was pretending to be dead or unconscious. Kickaha would not have had a chance.

But luck was with him again. This time it was a bull buffalo. It rose behind the Beller and, bellowing, tried to charge him. The Beller whirled. Kickaha rolled over, using the dead Half-Horse as a shield, and looked over it. The buffalo was badly hurt and fell on its side again before it had taken three steps. The Beller did not even use his beamer. But his back was momentarily turned to Kickaha, and the attention of those in the craft seemed to be on the other Beller on the ground. He was walking toward Anana's pile of buffalo.

At the bellow, one of the men in the craft turned. He swung the projector on its pivot. The Beller on the ground waved reassuringly at him and pointed to the carcass. The fellow in the craft resumed watching the other Beller. Kickaha rose and rushed the man, knife in hand. The Beller turned slowly and he was completely taken by surprise. He swung his beamer up, and Kickaha hurled the knife even if it was unfamiliar and probably unsuited for such work.

He had spent literally thousands of hours in practicing knife-throwing. He had cast knives of many kinds at many distances from many angles, even while standing on his head. He had forced himself to engage in severe discipline; he had thrown knives until he began to think he was breathing knives and the sight of one made him lose his appetite.

The unending hours, the sweat, frustration, and discipline paid off. The knife went into the Beller's throat, and the Beller fell over backward. The beamer lay on the ground.

Kickaha threw himself at the weapon, picked it up, saw that, though not of a familiar make, it was operated like the others. A little catch on the side of the butt had to be depressed to activate the weapon. The trigger could then be pulled; this was a slightly protruding plate on the inner side of the butt.

The Beller in the rear of the craft was swinging the big projector around toward Kickaha. Its ray sprang out whitely and dug a smoking swath in the ground; it struck a mound of buffalo, which burst into flames. The projector was not yet on full-power.

Kickaha did not have to shoot the Beller. A ray struck the Beller from the side, and he slumped over. Then the ray rose and fell, and the craft was cut in half. The others in the cockpit had already been struck down.

Kickaha rose cautiously and shouted, "Anana! It's me! Kickaha! Don't shoot!"

Presently Anana's white face came around the hillock of shaggy, horned carcasses. She smiled at him and shouted back, "It's all right! I got all of them!"

He could see the outflung hand of the Beller who had been approaching her. Kickaha walked toward her, but he felt apprehensive.

Now that she had a beamer and a craft—part of a craft, anyway—would she need him?

Before he had taken four more steps, he knew that she still needed him. He increased his pace and smiled. She did not know this world as he did, and the forces against her were extremely powerful. She wasn't going to turn on such a valuable ally.

Anana said, "How in Shambarimen's name did you manage to live through all that? I would have sworn that you had been cut off by the herd and that the Half-Horses would get you."

"The Half-Horses were even more confident," he said, and he grinned. He told her what had happened. She was silent for a moment, then she asked, "Are you sure you're not a Lord?"

"No, I'm human and a mere Hoosier, though not so mere at that, come to think of it."

"You're shaking," she said.

"I'm naturally high-strung," he said, still grinning. "You look like you're related to an aspen leaf, yourself."

She glanced at the beamer, quivering in her hand, and smiled grimly. "We've both been through a lot."

"There's nothing to apologize for, for chrissakes," he said. "Okay, let's see what we have here."

The Tishquetmoac men were small figures in the distance. They had begun running when Anana had started beaming, and they evidently did not plan on returning. Kickaha was glad. He had no plans for them and did not want to be appealed to for help.

Anana said, "I played dead, and I threw a spear at him and killed him. The Bellers in the craft were so surprised that they froze. I picked up the beamer and killed them."

It was a nice, clean, simple story. Kickaha did not believe it. She had not been helped by a disturbance, as he had, and he could not see how she could have gotten up and thrown a spear before the beamer went into action. The Beller was pierced in the hollow of the throat with the spear, but there was little blood from the wound, and there was no wound that could have been made by a beamer. Kickaha was certain that a close investigation would find a small hole bored through the corpse somewhere. Probably through the armor too, because the Beller wore chain-mail shirt and skirt and a conical helmet.

It wouldn't do to poke around the body and let her know his suspicions, though. He followed her to the craft, the two sections of which still hung two feet from the ground. A dead Beller sprawled in each part, and in the front section, huddled in a charred mass, was a Tishquetmoac priest, the Bellers' interpreter. Kickaha pulled the bodies out and examined the aircraft. There were four rows of two seats each with a narrow aisle running down between them. The front row was where the pilot and copilot or navigator sat. There were many instruments and indicators of various sorts on a panel. These were marked with hieroglyphs, which Anana told him were from the Lords' classic writing and used rarely.

"This craft is from my palace," she said. "I had four. I suppose the Bellers dismantled all four and brought them through."

She told him that the two parts did not fall because the keel-plate had been charged with gravitons in stasis when the craft halted. The operating equipment was in the front section, which could still be flown as if it were a whole craft. The rear part would continue to hover above the ground for some time. Then, as the graviton field decayed, it would slowly sink.

"It'd be a shame to waste the rear projector or let it fall into the hands of somebody else," Kickaha said. "And we've only got two good hand-beamers; the others were ruined when you rayed the ship. Let's take it with us."

"And where are we going?" she said.

"To Podarge, the Harpy-queen of the green eagles," he said. "She's the only useful ally I can think of at this moment. If I can stop her from trying to kill us long enough to talk to us, she may agree to help."

He climbed into the rear section and took some tools out of the storage compartment. He began to disconnect the big projector from the pivot, but suddenly stopped. He grinned and said to Anana, "I can't wait to see the expressions on your face and Podarge's! You will be looking at yourselves!"

She did not answer. She was using the beamer and the knife to cut off parts of a buffalo calf. Later, they would fly the meat to a spring and cook it. Both were so hungry, they felt as if their bellies were ravening animals eating up their own bodies. They had to feed them swiftly or lose their flesh to their flesh.

Though they were so tired they had trouble moving their arms and legs, Kickaha insisted that they fly on after eating. He wanted to get to the nearest mountain range. There they could hide the craft in a cave or ledge and sleep. It was too dangerous to remain on the prairie. If the Bellers had other craft around, they might detect them and investigate. Or try to communicate with them.

Anana agreed that he was right, and she fell asleep. Kickaha had learned from her how to operate the craft, so he took it toward the mountains as swiftly as it would go. The wind did not strike him directly, since the cowling protected him, but it did curve in through the open rear part, and it howled and beat at him—at least it kept him awake.

XII

THEY GOT TO THE MOUNTAINS JUST AS THE SUN WENT AROUND THE monolith, and he flew around for fifteen minutes before finding exactly what he wanted. This was a shallow cave with an opening about twenty feet high; it was located two thousand feet up on the face of a sheer cliff. Kickaha backed the craft into the cave, turned off the controls, lay down on the floor of the aisle, and passed out.

Even in his exhaustion and in the safety of the cave, he did not sleep deeply; he swam just below the surface of unconsciousness. He dreamed much and awoke with a start at least a dozen times. Nevertheless, he slept better than he had thought, because the sun was quartering the sky before he fully awoke.

He breakfasted on buffalo steak and some round biscuits he had found in a compartment under one of the seats. Since this was the only food in the craft, he deduced that the fliers had been operating out of a camp not too far away from the scene of the stampede. Or else the craft had been out for a long time and rations were short. Or there might be another explanation.

If there was one thing certain in both worlds, it was uncertainty.

By the time Anana awoke, she found that her companion had eaten, exercised vigorously to remove the stiffness from his muscles, and had dabbed water on his face and hands. He had bathed in the spring the evening before and so was presentable enough. He did not worry about shaving, since he had applied a chemical which retarded beard growth for months, just before he left the Hrowakas' village. It was a gift from Wolff. It could be neutralized at any time by another chemical if he wished to have a beard, but this chemical was not available; it was in a cabin in the Hrowakas' village.

Anana had the ability to wake up looking as if she were getting ready to go to a party. She did complain, however, about a bad taste in her mouth. She also voiced dislike for the lack of privacy in excretion.

Kickaha shrugged and said that a ten thousand year old woman ought to be above such human inhibitions. She did not respond angrily, but merely said, "Do we take off now? Or could we rest today?"

He was surprised that she seemed to give him authority. It was not what he would have expected from a Lord. But apparently she had a certain resiliency and flexibility, a realistic attitude. She recognized that this was his world and that he knew it far better than she did. Also, it must be evident that he had a tremendous capacity for survival. Her true feelings about him were not apparent. She was probably going along with him for her own sake and would drop him if he became a liability rather than an asset—which was an attitude he approved, in some respects. At least, they were operating together smoothly enough. Not too smoothly, since she had made it obvious that she would never think of letting him make love to her.

"I'm all for resting," he said. "But I think we'll be better off if we rest among the Hrowakas. We can hide this boat in a cave near their village. And while we're living there, we can talk to my people. I'm planning on using them against the Bellers, if they're willing. And they will be. They love a fight."

Shortly afterward, Anana noticed a light flashing on the instrument panel. She said, "Another craft is trying to call this one or perhaps the headquarters in Jadawin's palace. They must be alarmed because it hasn't reported in."

"I'd bluff by talking to them, but I'm not fluent enough in Lord-speech to fool them," Kickaha said. "And you could try, but I don't think they'd accept a woman's voice either. Let it flash. But one thing does bother me: do the Bellers have any means for tracking down this craft?"

"Only if we transmit a message for several minutes," she said. "Or if the craft is in a line-of-sight position. These are my machines and I had them equipped with some protection devices. But not many."

"Yes, but they have the devices of four palaces to draw on," he said. "Wolff's, yours, Nimstowl's, and Judubra's. They may have removed devices from these to equip their crafts."

She pointed out that, if they had, they had not equipped this one. She yawned and got ready to take a catnap. Kickaha shouted that she had slept over twelve hours already, and she should get up off her beautiful rump. If they were to survive, they had better get in gear, stir their stumps, and so on with a number of earthier and more personal clichés.

She admitted he was right. This surprised him but did not put him off guard. She got into the pilot's seat, put on the stasis harness, and said that she was ready.

The machine slid parallel to the face of the mountain and then headed for the edge of the level, keeping a few feet above the surface of the jagged terrain. It took two hours to get out of the range, by which time they were on the lip of the monolith on which rested the Amerind level. The stone cliff dropped vertically—more or less—for over a hundred thousand feet. At its base was Okeanos, which was not an ocean but a sea shaped like a ring, girdling the monolith and never more than three hundred miles wide.

On the other side of Okeanos, entirely visible from this height, was the strip of land which ran around the bottom of this planet. The strip was actually fifty miles across, but from the edge of the monolith, it looked thread-thin. On its comparatively smooth, well-treed surface lived human beings and half-human creatures and fabulous beasts. Many of them were the products of Jadawin's biolab; all owed their longevity and unfading youth to him. There were mermen and mermaids, goat-hoofed and goat-horned satyrs, hairy-legged and horned fauns, small centaurs, and other creatures which Jadawin had made to resemble the beings of Greek mythology. The strip was a type of Paradeisos and Garden of Eden with, in addition, a number of extra-terrestrial, extra-universal touches.

On the other side of the Garden strip was the edge of the bottom of the world. Kickaha had been down there several times on what he called "vacations" and once when he had been pursued by the horrible *gworl*, who wanted to kill him for the Horn of Shambarimen. He had looked over the edge and been thrilled and scared. The green abyss below—nothing beneath the planet—nothing but green sky and a sense that he would fall forever if he lost his hold.

Kickaha told her of this and said, "We could hide down there for a long time. It's a great place—no wars, no bloodshed beyond an occasional bloody nose or two. It's strictly for sensual pleasure, no intellectualism, and it gets wearisome after a few weeks, unless you want to be an alcoholic or drug addict. But the Bellers'll be down there eventually. And by that time, they may be much stronger."

"You can be sure of that," she said. "They have started making new Bellers. I suppose that one of the palaces has facilities for doing this. Mine hasn't, but . . ."

"Wolff's has," he replied. "Even so, it'll take ten years for a Beller to mature and be educated enough to take its place in Beller society, right? Meantime, the Bellers are restricted to the original fifty. Forty-four, I mean."

"Forty-four or four, they won't stop until we three Lords, and you, are captured or killed. I doubt they'll invade any more universes until then. They've got all of us cornered in this world, and they'll keep hunting until they've got us."

"Or we've got them," Kickaha said.

She smiled and said, "That's what I like about you. I wish that you were a Lord. Then . . ."

He did not ask her to elaborate. He directed her to fly the machine down the monolith. As they descended, they saw that its seemingly smooth surface was broken, gnarled, and flattened in many places. There were ledges and projections which furnished roads for many familiar and many strange creatures. There were fissures which sometimes widened to become comparatively large valleys. There were streams in the valleys and cataracts hurled out of holes in the steep side and there was a half mile wide river which roared out of a large cave at the end of a valley-fissure and then fell over the edge and onto the sea seventy-five thousand feet below.

Kickaha explained that the surface area on all the levels of this planet, that is, the horizontal area on the tops of the monoliths, equaled the surface area of the watery bodies of Earth. This made the land area more than that of Earth. In addition, the habitable areas on the verticalities of the monoliths were considerable. These alone probably equaled the land area of Earth's Africa. Moreover, there were immense subterranean territories, great caverns in vast networks that ran under the earth everywhere. And in these were various peoples and beasts and plants adapted to underground life.

"And when you consider all this, plus the fact that there are no arid deserts or ice- and snow-covered areas, you can see that the inhabitable land of this planet is about four times that of Earth."

Anana said that she had been on Earth briefly only and that she didn't remember its exact size. The planet in her own universe, however, was, if she remembered correctly, about the size of Earth.

Kickaha said, "Take my word for it, this is a hell of a big place. I've traveled a lot in the twenty-three years I've been here, but I've seen only a small part. I have a lot ahead of me to see. If I live, of course."

The machine had descended swiftly and now hovered about ten feet above the rolling waves of Okeanos. The surf shattered with a white bellow against the reefs or directly against the butt of the monolith.

Kickaha wanted to make sure that the water was deep enough. He had Anana fly the craft two miles further out. Here he dumped the four caskets and bell-shaped contents into the sea. The water was pure and the angle of sunlight just right. He could see the caskets a long way before the darkness swallowed them. They fell through schools of fish that glowed all hues of all colors and by a Brobdingnagian octopus, striped purple and white, that reached out a tentacle to touch a casket as it went by.

Dumping the bells here was not really necessary, since they were empty. But Anana would not feel easy until they were sunk out of reach of any sentients.

"Six down. Forty-four to go," Kickaha said. "Now to the village of the Hrowakas, the Bear People. My people."

The craft followed the curve of the monolith base for about seven hundred miles. Then Kickaha took over the controls. He flew the craft up and in ten minutes had climbed a little over twelve miles of precipitousness to the edge of the Amerind level. Another hour of cautious threading through the valleys and passes of the mountain ranges and half an hour of reconnoitering brought them to the little hill on top of which was the village of the Hrowakas.

Kickaha felt as if a warlance had driven into his skull. The tall sharp-pointed logs that formed the wall around the village were gone. Here and there, a blackened stump poked through the ashes.

The great V-roofed council hall, the lodge for bachelor warriors, the bear pens, the horse barns, the granary storage, the smokehouses, and the log-cabin family dwellings—all were gone. Burned into gray mounds.

It had rained the night before, but smoke rose weakly from a few piles.

On the hillside were a dozen widely scattered charred corpses of women and children and the burned carcasses of a few bears and dogs. These had been fleeing when rayed down.

He had no doubt that the Black Bellers had done this. But how had they connected him with the Hrowakas?

His thoughts, wounded, moved slowly. Finally, he remembered that the Tishquetmoac knew that he came from the Hrowakas. However, they did not know even the approximate location of the village. The Hrowaka men always traveled at least two hundred miles from the village before stopping along the Great Trade Path. Here they waited for the Tishquetmoac caravan. And though the Bear People were talkers, they would not reveal the place of their village.

Of course, there were old enemies of the Bear People, and perhaps the Bellers had been informed by these. And there were also films of the village and of Kickaha, taken by Wolff and stored in his palace. The Bellers could have run these off and so found the Hrowakas, since the location was shown on a map in the film.

Why had they burned down the village and all in it? What could serve the Bellers by this act?

With a heavy halting voice, he asked Anana the same question. She replied in a sympathetic tone, and if he had not been so stunned, he would have been agreeably surprised at her reaction.

"The Bellers did not do this out of vindictiveness," she said. "They are cold and alien to our way of thinking. You must remember that while they are products of human beings"—Kickaha was not so stunned that he did not notice her identification of Lords with human beings at this time—"and were raised and educated by human beings, they are, in essence, mechanical life. They have self-consciousness, to be sure, which makes them *not* mere machines. But they were born of metal and in metal. They are as cruel as any human. But the cruelty is cold and mechanical. Cruelty is used only when they can get something desired through it. They can know passion, that is, sexual desire, when they are in the brain of a man or woman, just as they get hungry because their host-body is hungry.

"But they don't take illogical vengeance as a human would. That is, they wouldn't destroy a tribe just because it happened to be loved by you. No, they must have had a good reason—to them, anyway—for doing this."

"Perhaps they wanted to make sure I didn't take refuge here," he said. "They would have been smarter to have waited until I did and then move in."

They could be hiding someplace up on the mountains where they could observe everything. However, Kickaha insisted on scouting the area before he approached the village. If Bellers were spying on them, they were well concealed indeed. In fact, since the heat-and-mass detector on the craft indicated nothing except some small animals and birds, the Bellers would have to be behind something large. In which case, they couldn't see their quarry either.

It was more probable that the Beller machine, after destroying the village, had searched this area. Failing to find him, it had gone elsewhere.

"I'll take over the controls," Anana said softly. "You tell me how to get to Podarge."

He was still too sluggish to react to her unusual solicitude. Later, he would think about it.

Now he told her to go to the edge of the level again and to descend about fifty thousand feet. Then she was to take the craft westward at 150 MPH until he told her to stop.

The trip was silent except for the howling of the wind at the open rear end. Not until the machine stopped below an enormous overhang of shiny black rock did he speak.

"I could have buried the bodies," he said, "but it would have taken too long. The Bellers might have checked back."

"You're still thinking about them," she said with a trace of incredulity. "I mean, you're worrying because you couldn't keep the carrion eaters off them? Don't! They're dead; you can do nothing for them."

"You don't understand," he said. "When I called them my people, I meant it. I loved them, and they loved me. They were a strange people when I first met them, strange to me. I was a young, mid-twentieth century, Midwestern American citizen, from another universe, in fact. And they were descendants of Amerinds who had been brought to this universe some twenty thousand years ago. Even the ways of an Indian of America are alien and near-incomprehensible to a white American. But I'm very adaptable and flexible. I learned their ways and came to think something like them. I was at ease with them and they with me. And I was Kickaha, the Trickster, the man of many turns. Their Kickaha, the scourge of the enemy of the Bear People.

"This village was my home, and they were my friends, the best I've ever had, and I also had two beautiful and loving wives. No children, though Awiwisha thought she might be pregnant. It's true that I'd established other identities on two other levels, especially that of the outlaw Baron Horst von Horstmann. But that was fading away. I'd been gone so long from Dracheland.

"The Hrowakas were my people, dammit! I loved them, and they loved me!"

And then he began to sob loudly. The cries tore the flesh as they mounted upward with spurs toward his throat. And even after he had quit crying, he hurt from deep within him. He did not want to move for fear he would hurt even more. But Anana finally cleared her throat and moved uneasily.

Then he said, "All right. I'm better. Set her down on that ledge there. The entrance to Podarge's cave is about ten miles westward. It'll be dangerous to get near it any time, but especially at night. The only time

I was there was two or three years ago when Wolff and I talked Podarge into letting us out of her cage."

He grinned and said, "The price was that I should make love to her. Other captives had been required to do this, too, but a lot of them couldn't because they were too frightened, or too repulsed or both. When this happened, she'd shred them as if they were paper with her great sharp talons.

"And so, Anana," he continued, "in a way I've already made love to you. At least to a woman—a thing with a woman's face—with your face."

"You must be feeling better," she said, "if you can talk like that."

"I have to joke a little, to talk about things far removed from death," he said. "Can't you understand that?"

She nodded but did not say anything. He was silent, too, for a long while. They ate cold meat and biscuits—it would be wise not to make a fire. Lights might attract the Bellers or the green eagles. Or other things that would be crawling around the cliffs.

XIII

THE NIGHT PASSED WITHOUT INCIDENT, ALTHOUGH THEY WERE awakened from time to time by roars, screams, whoops, bellows, trumpetings, and whistlings, all at a distance.

After breakfast, they set out slowly in the craft along the cliffside. Kickaha saw an eagle out above the sea. He piloted the craft toward her, hoping she would not try to escape or attack. Her curiosity won over whatever other emotions she had. She circled the machine, which remained motionless. Suddenly, she swept past them, crying, "Kickaha-a-a!" and plunged down. He expected her to wing full speed toward Podarge's cave. Instead, behaving unexpectedly, as might be expected from a female—so he said to Anana—she climbed back up. Kickaha indicated that he was going to land on a ledge, where he would like to talk to her.

Perhaps she thought that this would give her a chance to attack him. She settled down beside the machine with a small blast of closing wings. She towered over him, her yellow hooked beak and glaring black red-rimmed eyes above his head. The cowling was open, but he held the beamer, and on seeing it, she stepped back. She squawked, "Podarge?" but said nothing more about Anana's face.

One eagle looked like another to Kickaha. She, however, remembered when he had been in the cage with Wolff and when the eagles had stormed the palace on top of the highest monolith, the pinnacle of the planet.

"I am Thyweste," she said in the great parrot's voice of the green eagle. "What are you doing here, Trickster? Don't you know that Podarge sentenced you to death? And torture before death, if possible?"

"If that's so, why don't you try to kill me," he said.

"Because Podarge has learned from Dewiwanira that you released her and Antiope from the Tishquetmoac cage. And she knows that something is gravely amiss in Talanac, but she hasn't been able to find out what yet. She has temporarily suspended the sentence on you—though not on Jadawin-Wolff—until she discovers the truth. The orders are that you shall be escorted to her if you show up begging for an audience. Although I will be fair, Kickaha, and warn you that you may never leave the cave, once you've entered it."

"I'm not *begging* for an audience," he said. "And if I go in, I go inside this craft and fully armed. Will you tell Podarge that? But also tell her that if she wants revenge on the Tishquetmoac for having killed and imprisoned many of her pets, then I will be able to help her. Also, tell her there is a great evil abroad. The evil does not threaten her—yet. But it will. It will close its cold fingers upon her and her eagles and their nestlings. I will tell her of this when—or if—I get to see her."

Thyweste promised to repeat what he had told her, and she flapped off. Several hours passed. Kickaha got increasingly nervous. He told Anana that Podarge was so insane that she was liable to act against her own interests. He wouldn't be surprised to see a horde of the giant eagles plunging down out of the camouflaging green sky.

But it was a single eagle who appeared. Thyweste said that he should come in the flying machine and bring the human female with him. He could bring all the weapons he wished; much good they would do him if he tried to lie or trick Podarge. Kickaha translated for Anana, since they spoke the degenerate descendant of Mycenaean Greek, the speech used by Odysseus and Agamemnon and Helen of Troy.

Anana was startled and then scornful. "*Human* female! Doesn't this stinking bird know a Lord when she sees one?"

"Evidently not," he replied. "After all, you look exactly like a human. In fact, you can breed with humans, so I would say that you are human, even if you do have a different origin. Or do you? Wolff has some interesting theories about that."

She muttered some invective or pejorative in Lord-speech. Kickaha sent the craft up and followed Thyweste to the entrance of the cave, where Podarge had kept house and court for five hundred years or so. She had chosen the site well. The cliff above the entrance slanted gently outward for several thousand feet and was almost as smooth as a mirror. There was a broad ledge in front of the cave, and the cave could be approached on the ledge from only one side. But this path was always guarded by forty giant eagles. Below the ledge, the cliff slanted inward. No creature could climb up to or down from the cave. An army of determined men could have dropped ropes from above to let themselves down to the cave, but they would have been open to attack.

The entrance was a round hole about ten feet in diameter. It opened to a long curving corridor of rock polished from five centuries of rubbing by feathered bodies.

The craft had to be driven through the tunnel with much grating and squealing. After fifty yards of such progress, it came out into an immense cavern. This was lit by torches and by huge plants resembling feathers, which glowed whitely. There were thousands of them hanging down from the ceiling and sticking out from the walls, their roots driven into the rock.

From somewhere, air brushed Kickaha's cheek softly.

The great chamber was much as he remembered it except that there was more order. Apparently, Podarge had done some housecleaning. The garbage on the floor had been removed, and the hundreds of large chests and caskets containing jewels, *objets d'art,* and gold and silver coins and other treasures had been stacked alongside the walls or carried elsewhere.

Two columns of eagles formed an aisle for the craft, the aisle crossed fifty yards of smooth granite floor to end at a platform of stone. This was ten feet high and attained by a flight of steps made from blocks of quartz. The old rock-carved chair was gone. In its place was a great chair of gold set with diamonds, formed in the shape of a phoenix with outstretched wings that was placed in the middle of the platform. The chair had been that of the Rhadamanthus of Atlantis, ruler of the next-to-highest level of this planet. Podarge had taken the chair in a raid on the capital city some four hundred years ago. Now there was no Rhadamanthus, almost no Atlanteans left alive, and the great city was shattered. And the plans of Wolff for recolonizing the land were interrupted by the appearance of the Black Bellers and by his disappearance.

Podarge sat upon the edge of the throne. Her body was that of a Harpy's as conceived by Wolff-as-Jadawin 3,200 years ago. The legs were long and avian, thicker than an ostrich's, so they could bear the weight of her body. The lower part of the body was also avian, green-feathered and long-tailed. The upper part was that of a woman with magnificent white breasts, long white neck, and the achingly beautiful face. Her hair was long and black; her eyes were mad. She had no arms —she had wings, very long and broad wings with green and crimson feathers.

Podarge called to Kickaha in a rich husky voice, "Stop your aerial car there! It may approach no closer!"

Kickaha asked for permission to get out of the machine and come to the foot of the steps. She said that would be granted. He told Anana to follow him and then walked with just a hint of a swagger to the steps. Podarge's eyes were wide on seeing Anana's face. She said, "Two-legged female, are you a creation of Jadawin's? He has given you a face that is modeled on mine!"

Anana knew that the situation was just the reverse, and her pride must have been pierced deeply. But she was not stupid in her arrogance. She replied, "I believe so. I do not know my origin. I have just been, that's all. For some fifty years, I think."

"Poor infant! Then you were the plaything of that monster Jadawin! How did you get away from him! Did he tire of you and let you loose on this evil world, to live or die as events determined?"

"I do not know," Anana said. "It may be. Kickaha thinks that Jadawin was merciful in that he removed part of my memory, so that I do not remember him or my life in his palace, if indeed I had one."

Kickaha approved of her story. She was as adept at lying as he. And then he thought, *Oh! Oh! She tripped up!* Fifty years ago, Jadawin wasn't even in the palace or in this universe. He was living in America as a young amnesiac who had been adopted by a man named Wolff. The Lord in the palace was Arwoor then.

But, he reassured himself, this made no difference. If Anana pretended to have no memory of her origin or of the palace, then she wouldn't know who had been Lord.

Podarge apparently wasn't thinking about this. She said to Kickaha, "Dewiwanira has told me of how you freed her and Antiope from the cage in Talanac."

"Did she also tell you that she tried to kill me in payment for having given her her freedom?" he said.

She raised her wings a little and glared. "She had her orders! Gratitude had nothing to do with it! You were the right-hand man of Jadawin, who now calls himself Wolff!"

She folded her wings and seemed to relax, but Kickaha was not deceived. "By the way, where is Jadawin? What is happening in Talanac? Who are these Drachelanders?" she asked.

Kickaha told her. He left out the two Lords, Nimstowl and Judubra, and made it appear that Anana had been gated through a long time ago to the Amerind level and had been a slave in Talanac. Podarge was insanely hostile to the Lords. If she found out that Anana was one, and especially if she suspected that Anana might be Wolff's sister, she would have ordered her killed. This would have put Kickaha into a predicament which he would have to settle within one or two seconds. He would either choose to live and so be able to fight the Bellers but have to let Anana die, or he could back Anana and so die himself. That the two of them could slaughter many eagles before they were overwhelmed was no consolation.

Or perhaps, he thought, *just perhaps, we might be able to escape. If I were to shoot Podarge quickly enough and so create confusion among the eagles and then get into the craft quickly enough and bring the big projectors to bear, maybe we could fight our way out.*

Kickaha knew in that moment that he had chosen for Anana.

Podarge said, "Then Jadawin may be dead? I would not like that, because I have planned for a long time on capturing him. I want him to live for a long long time while he suffers! While he pays! And pays! And pays!"

Podarge was standing up on her bird legs, her talons outspread, and she was screeching at Kickaha. He spoke from the corner of his mouth to Anana. "Oh, oh! I think she's cracked! Get ready to start shooting!"

But Podarge stopped yelling and began striding back and forth, like a great nightmare bird in a cage. Finally, she stopped and said, "Trickster! Why should I help you in your war against the enemies of Jadawin! Aside from the fact that they may have cheated me of my revenge?"

"Because they are your enemies, too," he said. "It is true that, so far, they have used only human bodies as hosts. But do you think that the Bellers won't be thinking of eagles as hosts? Men are earthbound creatures. What could compare with being housed in the body of a green eagle, of flying far above the planet, into the house of the sun, of hovering godlike above all beasts of earth and the houses and cities of man, of being unreachable, yet seeing and knowing all, taking in a thousand miles with one sweep of the eye?

"Do you think that the Black Bellers won't realize this? And that when they do, they won't capture your eagles, perhaps you, Podarge, and will place the bell shape over your heads, and empty your brains of your thoughts and memory, uncoil you into death, and then possess your brains and bodies for their use?

"The Black Bellers use the bodies of flesh and blood creatures as we humans wear garments. When the garments are worn out, they are discarded. And so will you be discarded, thrown onto the trash heap, though of course it won't matter to you, since *you* will have died long before your body dies."

He stopped speaking for a moment. The eagles, ten foot high green towers, shifted uneasily and made tearing sounds in their throats. Podarge's expression was undecipherable, but Kickaha was sure she was thinking hard.

"There are only forty-four Black Bellers now in existence," he said. "They have great power, yes, but they are few. Now is the time to make sure they do not become a far greater threat. Because they will be making more infant Bellers in the laboratories of the Lords' palaces—you may be sure of that. The time will come when the Black Bellers will number thousands, millions perhaps, because they will want to ensure survival of their kind. And in numbers is survival of kind.

"The time will come when the Bellers will be so numerous and powerful that they will be irresistible. They can then do as they please. And if they want to enjoy the bodies of the green eagles, they will do so without a by-your-leave."

After a long silence, Podarge said, "You have spoken well, Trickster. I know a little about what is happening in Talanac because some of my pets have seized Tishquetmoacs and forced them to talk. They did not reveal much. For instance, they have never heard of the Black Bellers. But they say that the Talanac priests claim that their ruler is possessed by a demon. And the presence of this flying machine and of others which my pets have seen substantiates your story. It is too bad that you did not bring the captured bells here so that we could see them, instead of dumping them into the sea as you did."

"I am not always as clever as I think I am," Kickaha said.

"There is another thing to consider, even if your story is only half true or entirely a lie," Podarge said. "That is, I have long been planning revenge against the Tishquetmoac because they have killed some of my pets and caged others as if they were common beasts. They began to do that when the present ruler, Quotshaml, inherited the throne. That was only three years ago, and since then he has ignored the ancient understanding between his people and mine. In his crazed zeal to add specimens to that zoo of his and to mount stuffed creatures in that museum, he has waged war against us. I sent word that he should stop immediately, and he imprisoned my messengers. He is mad, and he is doomed!"

Podarge talked on. Apparently she tired of the eagles' conversation and longed for strangers with interesting news. Now that Kickaha had brought probably the most exciting news she had ever heard, aside from the call to storm the palace of the Lord three years before, she wanted to talk and talk. And she did so with a disregard for the feelings of her guests which only an absolute monarch could display. She had food and drink brought in and joined them at a great table. They were glad for the nourishment, but after a while Anana became sleepy. Kickaha just became more exhilarated. He suggested to Anana that it would be wise if she did sleep. She guessed what he meant but did not comment. She rose and went to the craft and stretched out on the floor on a rug provided by Podarge.

XIV

WHEN SHE AWOKE, SHE SAW KICKAHA SLEEPING BESIDE HER. HIS SHORT-nosed, long-upper-lipped face looked like a baby's, but his breath stank of wine and he smelled of some exotic perfume. Suddenly, he stopped snoring and opened one eye. Its leaf-green iris shot out fine red lightning veins. He grinned and said, "Good morning! Although I think it's closer to afternoon!"

Then he sat up and patted her shoulder. She jerked herself away from his touch. He smiled more broadly. "Could it be that the arrogant superwoman Lord, Anana the Bright, could be a trifle jealous? Unthinkable!"

"Unthinkable is correct," she said. "How could I possibly care? How? Why?"

He stretched and yawned. "That's up to you to figure out. After all, you are a woman, even if you deny being human, and we've been in close, almost too-intimate, contact, if I do say so myself. I'm a handsome fellow and a daredevil and a mighty warrior—if I do say so myself and I do, though I'm just repeating what thousands have said. You couldn't help being attracted, even if you had some self-contempt for thinking of a *leblabbiy* as attractive in any way."

"Have any women ever tried to kill you?" she snarled.

"At least a dozen. In fact, I've come closer to death from wounds inflicted by women than by all the great warriors put together."

He fingered two scars over his ribs. "Twice, they came very close to doing what my most determined enemies could not do. And both claimed they loved me. Give me your honest, open hate anytime!"

"I neither hate nor love you, of course," she said loftily. "I am a Lord, and . . ."

She was interrupted by an eagle, who said that Podarge wanted to talk to them while they breakfasted. The eagle was upset when Anana said that she wanted to bathe first and were any cosmetics, perfumes, etc., available in all these treasures? Kickaha smiled slightly and said he would go ahead to Podarge and would take the responsibility for her not showing up immediately. The eagle strode still-legged ahead of Anana to a corner of the cave where an ornately filigreed dresser held what she wanted.

Podarge was not displeased at Anana's coming late because she had other things to consider. She greeted Kickaha as if she held him in high regard and then said that she had some interesting news. An eagle had flown in at dawn with a tale of a great fleet of warriors on the river which the Tishquetmoac called Petchotakl. It was the broad and winding stream that ran along the edge of the Trees of Many Shadows.

There were one hundred longboats with about fifty men each. So the fleet would total about five thousand of the Red Beards, who called themselves the Thyuda, that is, People. Kickaha said that he had heard of them from the Tishquetmoac, who complained of increasing raids by the Red Beards on the frontier posts and towns. But what was a fleet this size intending to do? Surely, it must mean a raid on, perhaps a siege of, Talanac itself?

She said that the Thyuda came from a great sea to the west, beyond the Glittering Mountains. Kickaha said that he had not yet crossed the Glittering Mountains, though he had long intended to. But he did know that the sea was about a thousand miles long and three hundred wide. He had always thought that Amerinds, people like those on the Plains, lived on its shore.

No, Podarge said, self-satisfied because of the extent of her knowledge and power. No, her eagles reported that a long, long time ago there were feather-caps (Amerinds) there. But then Jadawin let in from Earth a tribe of tall light-skinned people with long beards. These settled down on the eastern shore and built fort-towns and ships. In time, they conquered and absorbed the dark-skins into the population. The dark-skins were slaves at first but eventually they became equals and they blended with the Thyuda, became Thyuda, in fact. The language became a simplified one, basically Thyuda but pidginized and with many aboriginal loan-words.

The eastern end of the sea had been a federation under the joint kingship of Brakya, which meant Strife, and of Saurga, which meant Sorrow. But there had been a long hard civil war, and Brakya had been forced to flee with a loyal band of warriors and women. They had come over the Glittering Mountains and settled along the upper river. During the years they had increased in numbers and strength and begun their raiding of Tishquetmoac posts and riverboats and sometimes even caravans. They often encountered the Half-Horses and did not always win against them, as they did against all other enemies, but, for the most part, they thrived.

The Tishquetmoac had sent out several punitive expeditions, one of which had destroyed a river-town; the others had been cut to pieces. And now it looked as if the Red Beards were making a big move against the people of Talanac. They were a well-disciplined body of tall, fierce warriors, but they apparently did not realize the size or the defenses of the nation against which they were marching.

"Perhaps," Kickaha said, "but by the time they get to Talanac, they will find the defenses greatly weakened. We will have attacked and perhaps conquered the City of Jade by then."

Podarge lost her good humor. "We will attack the Red Beards first and scatter them like sparrows before a hawk! I will not make their way easy for them!"

"Why not make them our allies?" Kickaha said. "The battle against Bellers, Tishquetmoac, and Drachelanders will not be easy, especially when you consider the aircraft and the beamers they have. We need all the help we can get. I suggest we get them on our side. There will be plenty of killing and loot for all, more than enough."

Podarge stood up from her chair and with a sweep of a wing dashed the tableware onto the floor. Her magnificent breasts rose and fell with fury. She glared at him with eyes from which reason had flown. Kickaha could not help shrinking inwardly, though he faced her boldly enough and spoke up.

"Let the Red Beards kill our enemies and die for us," he said. "You claim to love your eagles; you call them your pets. Why not save many of their lives by strengthening ourselves with the Red Beards?"

Podarge screamed at him, and then she began to rave. He knew he had made a serious mistake by not agreeing with her in every particular, but it was too late to undo the harm. Moreover, he felt his own reason slipping away in a suddenly unleashed hatred of her and her arrogant, inhumanly cruel ways.

He shoved away his anger before it could bring him down into the dust from which no man gets up. He said, "I bow to your superior wisdom, not to mention strength and power, O Podarge! Have it your way, as it should be!"

But he was thoughtful afterward and determined to talk to Podarge again when she seemed more reasonable.

The first thing he did after breakfast was to take the craft outside and up fifty thousand feet to the top of the monolith. Then he flew to the top of a mountain peak in a high range near the edge of the monolith. Here he and Anana sat in the craft while they talked loudly of what had happened recently and also slipped in descriptions of the entrance to Podarge's cave. He had turned on the radio so that their conversation was being broadcast. She had set the various detecting apparatus. After several hours had passed, Anana suddenly pretended to notice that the radio was on. She rebuked Kickaha savagely for being so awkward and stupid, and she snapped it off. An indicator was showing the blips of two aircraft approaching from the edge of the monolith which rose from the center of the Amerind level. Both had come from the palace of the Lord on top of the apical monolith of the planet.

Since the two vessels had undoubtedly located them with their instruments, they would be able to locate the area into which their quarry would disappear. Kickaha took the vessel at top speed back over the edge of the level and on down. He hovered before the cave entrance until the first of the two pursuers shot over the edge. Then he snapped the craft into the cave and through the tunnel without heeding the scraping noises.

After that, they could only wait. The big projectors and hand-beamers were in the claws of the eagles gliding back and forth some distance above the cave. When they saw the two vessels before the cave entrance, they were to drop out of the green of the sky. The Bellers would detect the eagles above them, of course, but they would pay no attention to them. After identifying them, they would concentrate on sending their rays into the cave.

Those in the cave did not have long to wait. An eagle, carrying a beamer in her beak, entered to report. The Bellers, three in each vessel, had been completely surprised. They were fried, and the crafts were floating where they had stopped, undamaged except for some burned seats and slightly melted metal here and there.

Kickaha suggested to Podarge that the two vessels be brought into the cave. There should be at least one craft yet in the Bellers' possession, and they might send that one down to investigate the disappearance of these. Also, there might be more than one, because Nimstowl and Judubra could have had such vessels.

"Twelve Bellers down. Thirty-eight to go," Kickaha said. "And we now have some power and transportation."

He and Anana went out in the half-craft. He transferred into a vessel, brought it into the cave, then came out again to bring in the second. When all three vessels were side by side in the huge cavern, Podarge insisted that the two instruct her and some chosen eagles in the operation of the vessels. Kickaha asked, first, for the return of their hand-beamers and the projectors that went with the half-craft. Podarge hesitated so long that Kickaha thought she was going to turn against him then and there. He and Anana were helpess because they had loaned their weapons out to ensure the success of the plan. He did have his knife, which he was determined to throw into the Harpy's solar plexus if she showed any sign of ordering the eagles to seize them. This would not save him and Anana, but he at least would have taken Podarge along with him.

The Harpy, however, finally gave the desired order to her subjects. The beamers were returned; the projectors were put back into the half-craft. Still, he felt uneasy. Podarge was not going to forgive him for being Wolff's friend, no matter what services he rendered her. As soon as his usefulness ended, so would his life. That could be thirty minutes or thirty days from now.

When he had a chance to speak to Anana alone, he told her what to expect.

"It's what I thought would happen," she said. "Even if you weren't Jadawin's friend, you would be in danger because you have been her lover. She must know that, despite her beautiful face and beautiful breasts, she is a hybrid monster and therefore disgusting to the human males she forces to make love to her. She cannot forgive that; she must eliminate the man who secretly despises her. And I am in danger because, one, I have a woman's body, and she must hate all women because she is condemned to her half-bird body. Two, I have her face, and she's not going to let a woman with my body and her face live long to enjoy it. Three, she is insane! She frightens me!"

"You, a Lord, admit you're scared!" he said.

"Even after ten thousand years, I'm scared of some things. Torture is one of them, and I'm sure that she will torture me horribly—if she gets a chance. Moreover, I worry about you."

He was startled. "About me? A *leblabbiy?*"

"You aren't an ordinary human," she said. "Are you sure you're not at least half-Lord? Perhaps Wolff's son?"

"I'm sure I'm not," he said, grinning. "You wouldn't be feeling the emotions of a human woman, would you? Perhaps you're just a little bit fond of me? Maybe a trifle attracted to me? Possibly, perish the thought, you even desire me? Possibly, O most hideous idea, even love me a little? That is, if a Lord is capable of love?"

"You're as mad as the Harpy!" she said, glaring. "Because I admire your abilities and courage doesn't mean that I would possibly consider you as a mate, my equal!"

"Of course not," he said. "If it weren't for me, you'd have been dead a dozen times or would now be screaming in a torture chamber. I'll tell you what. When you're ready to confess you're wrong, I'll save you embarrassment. Just call me lover, that's all. No need for apologies or tears of contrition. Just call me lover. I can't promise I'll be in love with you, but I will consider, just consider, mind you, the prospect of being your lover. You're damnably attractive, physically, anyway. And I wouldn't want to offend Wolff by turning his sister down, although, come to think of it, he didn't speak very fondly of you."

He had expected fury. Instead, she laughed. But he wasn't sure that the laughter wasn't a cover-up.

They had little time to talk thereafter. Podarge kept them busy teaching the eagles about the crafts and weapons. She also questioned both about the layout of Talanac, where she could expect the most resistance, the weak points of the city, etc. She herself was interrupted by the need to give orders and receive information. Hundreds of messengers had been sent out to bring in other eagles for the campaign. The early-arriving recruits, however, were to assemble at the confluence of the Petchotakl river and the small Kwakoyoml river. Here the eagles were to marshal to await the Red Beard fleet. There were many problems for her to solve. The feeding of the army that would gather required logistical reorganization. At one time, the eagles had been an army as thoroughly disciplined and hierarchical as any human organization. But the onslaught on the palace several years before had killed so many of her officers that she had never bothered to reorganize it. Now, she was faced with this immediate, almost overwhelmingly large, problem.

She appointed a certain number of hunters. Since the river areas of the Great Plains were full of large game, they should afford all the food needed for the army. The result, however, was that two eagles out of ten would be absent hunting most of the time.

The fourth morning, Kickaha dared to argue again. He told her that it was not intelligent to waste the weapons on the Red Beards, that she should save them for the place where they were absolutely required—

that is, at Talanac, where the Bellers had weapons which could only be put out of commission by similar weapons.

Moreover, she had enough eagles at her command now to launch an attack on the Tishquetmoac. Feeding them was a big enough headache without waiting to add more. Also . . .

He got no farther. The Harpy screamed at him to keep quiet, unless he wanted his eyes torn out. She was tired of his arrogance and presumptuousness. He had lived too long, bragged too much of his trickster ways. Moreover, she could not stand Anana, assuredly a most repulsive creature. Let him trick his way out of the cave now, if he could; let the woman go jump off the cliff into the sea. Let them both try.

Kickaha kept quiet, but she was not pacified. She continued to scream at him for at least half an hour. Suddenly, she stopped. She smiled at him. Cold thrummed a chord deep in him; his skin seemed to fold, as if one ridge were trying to cover itself with another.

There was a time to await developments, and there was a time to anticipate them. He reared up from his chair, heaving up his end of the table, heavy though it was, so that it turned over on Podarge. The Harpy shrieked as she was pressed between chair and table. Her head stuck out from above the edge, and her wings flapped.

He would have burned her head off then, but she was no immediate danger personally. The two attendant eagles were, since they carried beamers in their beaks. But they had to drop these to catch them with one foot, and in the interim, Kickaha shot one. His beamer, on half-power, set the green feathers ablaze.

Anana had pulled out her beamer, and her ray intersected with his on the second eagle.

He yelled at her and ran toward the nearest craft. She was close behind him in his dive into it, and, without a word from him, she seized the big projector. He sat down before the control panel and activated the motors. The craft rose a foot and shot toward the entrance to the tunnel. Three eagles tried to stop it with their bodies. The vessel went thump . . . thump . . . thump, jarring Kickaha each time. Then he was thrown forward and banged his chest on the panel—no time to strap himself in—as the vessel jammed into the narrow bore of stone. He increased the power. Metal squealed against granite as the vessel rammed through like a rod cleaning out a cannon.

For a second, the bright round of the cave exit was partially blocked by a great bird; there was a thump and then a bump and the vessel was out in the bright yellow sun and bright green sky with the blue-white surf-edge sea fifty thousand feet below.

Kickaha restrained his desire to run away. He brought the craft up and back and down, hovering over the top of the entrance. And, as he had expected, a craft slid out. This was the one captured by the eagles; it was followed by the half-craft. Anana split both along the longitudinal axis with the projector on at full-power. Each side of the craft broke away and fell, the sliced eagles with them, and the halves and green bodies were visible for a long time before being swallowed up in the blue of the distance.

Kickaha lowered the craft and shot the nose-projector at full-power into the tunnel. Screams from within told him that he might have killed some eagles and at least panicked them for a long time. He thought then of cutting out rocks above the entrance and blocking it off but decided that it would take too much power. By then the eagle patrols outside the monolith face and the newcomers were swarming through the air. He rammed the craft through their midst, knocking many to one side while Anana burned others. Soon they were through the flock and going at full speed over the mountain range which blocked off the edge of the level from the Great Plains.

XV

THEN HE WAS SWOOPING OVER THE PRAIRIE, HEDGEHOPPING BECAUSE, the closer he stayed to the surface, the less chance there was of being detected by a Beller craft. Kickaha flew just above the grass and the swelling hills and the trees and the great gray mammoths and mastodons and the giant shaggy black buffalo and the wild horses and the gawky, skinny, scared-faced Plains camels; the nine hundred pound tawny Felis Atrox, the atrocious lion, the long-legged, dogfaced cheetah-lions, the saber-toothed smilodons and the shaggy, dumb-looking megatherium; a sloth as large as an elephant, the dire wolf, six feet high at the shoulder, and the twenty-one foot high archaic ass-headed baluchitherium; the megaceros, deer with an antler spread of twelve feet, and thousands of species of antelopes including one queer species that had a long forked horn sticking up from its snout; the "terrible hog" which stood six feet at the shoulder, and the dread-making earth-shaking brontotherium, recreated in the biolabs of Wolff and released on the Great Plains, gray, fifteen feet long and eight feet high at the shoulder, with a large flat bone horn at the end of its nose; and the coyote, the fox, an ostrich-like bird, the ducks, geese, swans, herons, storks, pigeons, vultures, buzzards, hawks—many thousands of species of beasts and birds and millions, millions of proliferations of life, all these Kickaha shot over and past, seeing within three hours what he could not have seen in five years of travel on the ground.

He passed near several camps of the Nations of the Plains. The tepees and round lodges of the Wingashutah, the Khaikhowa, the Takotita and once over a cavalcade of Half-Horses, the fierce warriors guarding all sides and the females dragging on poles the tribal property and the young gamboling, frisking like colts.

Kickaha thrilled at these sights. He alone of all Earthmen had been favored with living in this world. He had been very lucky so far and if he were to die at this moment, he could not say that he had wasted his life. On the contrary, he had been granted what very few men had been granted, and ho was grateful. Despite this, he intended to keep on living. There was much yet to visit and explore and wonder at and great talk and lovely loving women. And enemies to fight to the death.

This last thought had no sooner passed than he saw a strange band on the prairie. He slowed down and ascended to about fifty feet. They were mounted Drachelanders with a small troop of Tishquetmoac cavalry. And three Bellers. He could see the silver caskets attached to the saddles of their horses.

They reined in, doubtless thinking that the craft contained other Bellers. Kickaha did not give them much time to remain in error. He dropped down and Anana cut all three in half. The others took off in panic. Kickaha picked up the caskets, and later dropped them into the broad Petchotakl river. He could not figure out how the party had gotten so far from Talanac even if they had ridden night and day. Moreover, they were coming from the opposite direction.

It struck him then that they must have been gated through to this area. He remembered a gate hidden in a cave in a group of low but steep-sided hills and rocky hills about fifty miles inland. He took the craft there and found what he had expected. The Bellers had left a heavy guard to make sure that Kickaha did not use it. He took them by surprise, burned them all down, and rammed the craft into the cave. A Beller was a few feet from the large single-unit gate-ring toward which he was running. Kickaha bored a hole through him before he reached the gate.

"Sixteen down. Thirty-four to go," Kickaha said. "And maybe a lot more down in the next few minutes."

"You're not thinking about going through the gate?" she said.

"It must be connected to the temple-gate in Talanac," he said. "But maybe we should save it for later, when we have some reserve force." He did not explain but instead told her to help him get rid of the bodies. "We're going to be gone awhile. If any more Bellers gate through here, they won't know what's happened—if anything."

Kickaha's plan had a good chance of being successful, but only if he could talk effectively in its next phase. The two flew up the river until they saw a fleet of many boats, two abreast, being rowed down the river. These reminded him of Viking ships with their carved dragon heads, and the sailors also looked from a distance like Norsemen. They were big and broad-shouldered and wore horned or winged helmets and shaggy breeches and carried double-axes and broadswords and heavy spears and round shields. Most of them had long red-dyed beards, but there were a number clean-shaven.

A glut of arrows greeted him as he dropped down. He persisted in getting close to the lead boat on which a man in the long white and red-collared robes of a priest stood. This boat had used up all its arrows, and the craft stayed just out of axe range. Spears flashed by or even struck the craft, but Kickaha maneuvered the vessel to avoid any coming into the open cockpit. He called to the priest in Lord-speech and presently the king, Brakya, agreed through the priest to talk to Kickaha. He met him on the banks of the river.

There was a good reason for the Red Beards' hostility. Only a week ago, a craft had set fire to several of their towns and had killed a number of young men. All of the marauders had a superficial resemblance to Kickaha. He explained what was happening, although it took him two days to complete this. He was slowed by the necessity of speaking through the *alkhsguma,* as the priest was called in Thyuda. Kickaha gained in the estimation of Brakya when Withrus, the priest, explained that Kickaha was the righthand man of *Allwaldands,* The Almighty.

The progress of the entire fleet down the river was held up for another day while the chiefs and Withrus were taken via air-car to the cave of the gate. Here Kickaha restated his plan. Brakya wanted a practical demonstration of gating, but Kickaha said that this would warn the Bellers in Talanac that the gate was open to invaders.

Several more days went by while Kickaha outlined and then detailed how five thousand warriors could be marched through the gate. It would take exact timing to get so many men into the gate at a time, because mistiming would result in men in the rear being cut in half when the gate activated. But he pointed out that the Bellers and Drache-landers had come out in a large body, so the Thyuda could go in.

Meantime, he was very exasperated and impatient and uneasy, but he dared not show it. Podarge must have taken her huge winged armada to attack Talanac. If she meant to destroy the Red Beards first, she would have descended upon the fleet before this.

Brakya and the chiefs were by this time eager to get going. Kickaha's colorful and enthusiastic descriptions of the Talanac treasures had converted them to zealots.

Kickaha had a mock-up of the big gate in the cave built outside it and he and the chiefs put the men through a training which took three days and a good part of the nights. By the time that the men seemed to be skilled in the necessities, everybody was exhausted and hot-tempered.

Brakya decided they needed a day of rest. Rest meant rolling out great barrels of beer and a flame-threaded liquor from the boats into the camp and drinking these while deer and buffalo and wild horses and bear were roasted. There was much singing, yelling, laughing, boasting, and quite a few fights which ended in severe wounds or deaths.

Kickaha made Anana stay in her tent, mostly because Brakya had made little effort to hide his lust for her. And while he had never offered anything but compliments that bordered on the obscene (perfectly acceptable in Thyuda society, the priest said), he might take action if alcohol uninhibited him. That meant that Kickaha would have to fight him, since everybody had taken it for granted that she was his woman. In fact, they had had to share the same tent to keep up the pretense. Kickaha engaged Brakya that night in a drinking duel, since he would lose face if he refused the king's challenge. Brakya intended, of course, to drink him into unconsciousness and then go to Anana's tent. He weighed perhaps forty pounds more than Kickaha and should have been able to outdrink him. However, Brakya fell asleep about dawn—to the great amusement of those few Red Beards who had not passed out before then.

In the afternoon, Kickaha crawled out of his tent with a head which felt as if he had tried to outbutt a bull bison. Brakya woke up later and almost tore some muscles in his sides laughing at himself. He was not angry at Kickaha and when Anana appeared he greeted her in a subdued manner. Kickaha was glad that was settled, but he did not want to launch the attack that day, as originally planned. The army was in no shape to battle women, let alone the enemies that awaited them in Talanac.

Brakya ordered more barrels rolled out, and the drinking began all over again. At this time, a raven, a bird the size of a bald eagle of Earth, one of Wolff's Eyes, lit on a branch above Kickaha. It spoke in a harsh croaking voice. "Hail, Kickaha! Long have I looked for you! Wolff, the Lord, sent me out to tell you that he has to leave the palace for another universe. Someone has stolen his Chryseis from him, and he is going to find the thief and kill him and then bring his woman back."

The raven Eye proceeded to describe what traps had been left active, what gates were open, and how he could get into and out of the palace safely if he wished. Kickaha informed the Eye that all had changed, and he told him of the Bellers' occupancy of the palace. The raven was not too startled by this. He had just been to Talanac, because he had heard that Kickaha was there. He had seen the Bellers, though he did not know, of course, who they were then. He also had seen the green eagles and Podarge on their way to attack Talanac. They cast a mighty shadow that inked the ground with a signature of doom and the beat of their wings was like the drums of the day of last judgment. Kickaha, questioning him, judged that the armada had fallen upon Talanac the preceding day.

He went after Brakya and told him the news. By then the whole camp was yelling-laughing drunk. Brakya gave the orders; the great horns were blown; the war drums were beaten; the warriors arranged themselves in ragged but recognizable ranks. Brakya and the chiefs were to go first with Kickaha and Anana, who carried a big projector from the craft. Next was a band of the great warriors, two of whom handled the second projector. After them, the clean-shaven youths, who could not grow a beard and dye it red until they had killed a man in battle. Then the rest of the army.

Kickaha, Anana, Brakya, and six chiefs quick-stepped into the circle of gray metal. The chief of the band behind them had started counting to check that the activation time was correct. Abruptly, the group was in a room which was not the vast chamber in the temple which Kickaha had expected. It was a smaller room, though still large by most standards. He recognized it instantly as the gate-chamber near the middle of the city, the one which he had not been able to get to when being pursued by the Bellers. He shoved the Thyuda on out of the circle; they had frozen at the seemingly magical passage.

Thereafter, events happened swiftly, though they consumed many hours and much energy and many lives. The old city seemed to be aflame; fires raged everywhere. These came from torches which the eagles had dropped. There was little material in the jade city burning, but there were thousands of eagles sputtering or smoldering. These had been caught by the Bellers' projectors. The bodies of the big birds, of Tishquetmoac warriors, and Drachelanders lay in the streets and on the housetops. Most of the fighting was now taking place near the top of the city, around the temple and palace.

The defenders and the eagles were so occupied with the struggle, they did not notice the Red Beards until there were three thousand gated into Talanac. By then, it was too late to stop the remaining two thousand from coming through. Hundreds of eagles turned from the city-top battle to attack the Thyuda, and from then on, Kickaha remembered only firing the projector and advancing up each bloody, smoky, burning level. The time came when the power packs of the projector had been used up, and from then on the handbeamers were used. Before the summit was gained, these were useless, and it was swords then.

In the temple, he came across a group of charred bodies recognizable as Bellers only because of the silver caskets strapped to their backs. There were six of them, and they had been caught in a cross fire from eagles with handbeamers. This must have been at the very beginning, perhaps the first few moments of the surprise attack. The eagles with the beamers had been killed by projectors, but they had taken a toll catastrophic to the Bellers.

He counted four more dead Bellers before he and Anana and Brakya and other Thyuda burst into the immense room in which the Bellers had installed a large permanent gate. Podarge and her eagles, those left to fight, had cornered a number of Drachelanders, Tishquetmoac and two, no, three, Bellers. There were von Turbat, von Swindebarn, and the emperor of the Tishquetmoac, Quotshaml. They were surrounded by their warriors, who were rapidly dwindling in numbers under the fury of the Harpy and the big birds.

Kickaha, with Anana behind him, and the Red Beards to one side, attacked. He slashed at the eagles from the rear; blood and feathers and flesh flew. He shouted with exultation; the end was near for his enemies.

And then, in the melee that followed, he saw the three Bellers desert their fellows and run for the big circle of metal, the gate, in one corner. Podarge and some eagles raced after them. Kickaha ran after the eagles. The Bellers disappeared; Podarge followed them; the eagles close behind her flashed out of existence.

He was so disappointed he wanted to weep, but he did not intend to go after them. No doubt the Bellers had set a trap for any pursuers, and the Harpy and eagles should be in it. He was not going to get caught, no matter how much he wanted to get hold of the Bellers.

He started to turn away but had to defend himself against two of the great birds. He managed to wound them enough to make them uneager to close with him, but they persisted and slowly backed him toward the big gate in the corner of the room. One advanced and chopped at him with her beak; he slashed out to make the beak draw short. The other eagle would then move up a little and feint at him, and he would have to slash at her to be sure that it was only a feint.

He could not call for help, since the others were similarly occupied. Suddenly, he knew he was going to be forced to take the gate. If he did not, he would be struck by one of those huge sharp-hooked beaks. The two birds were now separating; one was circling to a position behind him, or perhaps they would both attack from his flanks, so, even if he got one, he would go down under the beak of the other.

Despairingly, he glanced about the room, saw that Anana and the Red Beards were still busy, and so he did what he must. He whirled, leaped onto the plate, whirled around to defend himself for the few seconds needed before the gate would activate, and then something—a wing perhaps—struck his head and knocked him half-unconscious.

XVI

HE OPENED HIS EYES UPON A STRANGE AND WEIRD LANDSCAPE.

He was in a broad and shallow valley. The ground on which he sat and the hills roundabout were covered with a yellow moss-like vegetation.

The sky was not the green of the world he had just left. It was a blue so dark that it trembled on the edge of blackness. He would have thought it was late dusk if the sun were not just past its zenith. To his left, a colossal tower shape hung in the sky. It was predominantly green with dark blue and light blue patched here and there and white woolly masses over large areas. It leaned as the Tower of Pisa leans.

The sight of this brought Kickaha out of his daze. He had been here before, and only the blow on his head had delayed recognition. He was on the moon, the round satellite of the stepped planet of this universe.

Forgetting his previous experiences, he jumped to his feet and soared into the air, sprawling, and landed on his face and then his elbows and knees. The impact was softened by the cushiony ocher moss-stuff, but he was still jarred.

Cautiously, he got to his hands and knees and shook his head. It was then that he saw von Turbat, von Swindebarn, and Quotshaml running with Podarge and the four eagles after them. Running defined the intent, however, not the performance. The three men were going in incredibly long leaps which ended frequently in their feet sliding out from under them when they landed on the vegetation, or a loss of balance while going through the high arcs. Their desperation added to their awkwardness, and under other circumstances, their situation would have been comical to them.

It was comical to Kickaha, who was in no immediate danger. He laughed for a few seconds, then sobered up as he realized that his own situation was likely to be as dangerous. Perhaps more so, because the three seemed to be striving for a goal that might take them away from their pursuers.

He could just see the edge of a thin round stone set in the moss. This, he suddenly knew, must be a gate of some kind. The three had known they would be gated from the temple-room in Talanac to this gate on the moon. They must have deliberately set it up for this purpose, so that they could maroon any pursuers on the moon, while they gated back to Talanac or, more likely, to the Lord's palace.

Undoubtedly, that gate toward which they were racing was a one-time unit. It would receive and transmit the first to step into it. After that, it would be shut off until reactivated. And the means for reactivation, of course, were not at hand.

The trap was one that Kickaha appreciated, since he liked to set such himself and quite often had. But the trapper might become the trapped. Podarge and the eagles were a type of pursuer not reckoned on. Although handicapped also by their unfamiliarity with the low gravity and the shock of finding themselves here, they were using their wings to aid themselves in control and in braking on landing. Moreover, they were covering ground much more swiftly than the men because they were gliding.

Von Turbat and von Swindebarn, jumping simultaneously and holding hands, came down exactly upon the rock. And they disappeared.

Quotshaml was five seconds behind them, and when he landed on the rock, he remained in sight. His cry of desperation sounded in the quiet and lifeless air.

Podarge, wings spread out to check her descent, came down upon his back, and he fell under her weight. Podarge screamed long and loudly, like a great bird in agony instead of triumph, as she tore gobbets of flesh from the man's back. Then the eagles landed and strode forward and circled Podarge and the writhing victim, and they bent down and slashed with their beaks whenever they got a chance.

The casket which Quotshaml had been carrying on his back had been torn off and now lay to one side near the rock.

Twenty-three Bellers to go.

Kickaha rose slowly to his feet. As soon as Podarge and her pets had finished their work, they would look around. And they would see him unless he quickly got out of sight. The prospects for this were not excellent. The ruins of the city of Korad lay a mile away. The great white buildings gleamed in the sun like a distant hope. But even if he did get to it in time, he would find it to be not a hope but a prison. The only gate nearby which he could use was not in the city but hidden in a cave in the hills. Podarge and the eagles were between him and the cave.

Kickaha took advantage of their concentration on their fun to relearn how to run. He had been here many times for some lengthy periods. Thus, the adaptation was almost like swimming after years of desert living. Once learned, the ability does not go away. However, the analogy was only that, an analogy. A man thrown into the water immediately begins to swim. Kickaha took several minutes to teach himself the proper coordination again.

During this time, he gained a quarter of a mile. Then he heard screams which contained a different emotion than that of bloodletting and revenge gratified. He looked behind him. Podarge and the four birds had seen him and were speeding after him. They were launching themselves upward and covering long stretches in glides, like flying fish. Apparently, they did not trust themselves to try flying yet.

As if they were reading his mind, they quit their hopgliding and took completely to the air. They rose upward far more swiftly than they would have on the planet, and again they screamed. This time, the cries were of frustration. Their flying had actually lost them ground.

Kickaha knew this only because he risked swift glances behind him as he soared through the air. Then he lost ground as his feet slipped on landing and he shot forward and up again and turned over twice. He tried to land on his feet or feet and hands but slammed into the ground hard. His breath was knocked out and he whooshed for air, writhed, and forced himself to get up before he was completely recovered.

During his next leap, he pulled his sword from the sheath. It looked now as if he might need it before he got to the city. Podarge and one eagle were ahead of him, though still very high. They were banking, and then they were coming in toward him in a long flat glide. The other eagles were above him and were now plunging toward him, their wings almost completely folded.

Undoubtedly, the falling birds and the Harpy had automatically computed the ends of their descents to coincide with his forward leap. Kickaha continued forward. A glance upward showed him the bodies of the eagles swelling as they shot toward him. Their yellow claws were spread out, the legs stiff, like great shock absorbers set for the impact of his body. Podarge and friend were coming in now almost parallel to the ground; they had flapped their wings a few times to straighten out the dive. They were about six feet above the moss and expected to clutch him as he rose in the first leg of the arc of a jump.

Podarge was showing almost all her teeth in triumph and anticipation. Her claws dripped blood, and her mouth and teeth were red with blood. Her chin was wet with red.

"Kickaha-a-a-a!" she screamed. "At la-a-a-ast!"

Kickaha wondered if she did not see the sword in his hand or if she was so crazed that she just did not care.

It did not matter. He came down and then went up again in a leap that should have continued on and so brought him into the range of Podarge's claws. But this time he leaped straight upward as hard as he could. It was a prodigious bound, and it carried him up past a very surprised Podarge and eagle. Their screams of fury wailed off like a train whistle.

Then, there were more screams. Panic and fright. Thuds. Wings clapping thunder as the falling eagles tried to check their hurtling.

Kickaha came down and continued his forward movement. On the second bound, he risked a look over his shoulder. Podarge and eagles were on the ground. Green feathers, dislodged by the collision of the Harpy and four mammoth eagle bodies, flew here and there. Podarge was on her back, her legs sticking up. One eagle was unconscious; two were up and staggering around in a daze. The fourth was trying to get onto her talons, but she kept falling over and fluttering and shrieking.

Despite the accident and the new headstart he gained, he still got into the safety of an entrance only a few feet ahead of Podarge. Then he turned and struck her with his sword, and she danced backward, wings flapping, and screamed at him. Her mouth was bloodied and her eyes were pulled wide by insane anger. She was losing blood from a big gash in her side just below her right breast. During the collision or the melee afterward, she had been wounded by a talon.

Kickaha, seeing that only three eagles were following her, and these still at a distance, ran out from the doorway, his sword raised. Podarge was so startled by this that some reason came back to her. She whirled and leaped up and beat her wings. He was close to her and his sword swished out and cut off several long tail feathers. Then he fell to the ground and had to take refuge in the doorway again. The eagles were trying to get to him now.

He wounded two slightly, and they withdrew. Podarge turned to glide back beside them. Kickaha fled through a large hall and across a tremendous room with many ornately carved desks and chairs. He got across the room, down another hall, across a big courtyard and into another building just in time. An eagle came through the doorway of the building he had just left, and the Harpy and another eagle came around the corner of the building. As he had expected, he would have been rushed from the rear if he had stayed in the original doorway.

He came to a room which he knew had only one entrance and hesitated. Should he take a stand here or try for the underground pits? He might get away from them in the dark labyrinths. On the other hand, the eagles would be able to smell him out wherever he hid. And there were things down in the pits that were as deadly as the eagles and far more loathsome. Their existence had been his idea, and Wolff had created them and set them there.

A scream. He jumped through the door and turned to defend it. His mind was made up for him. He had no choice to get to the pits. Now that he had no chance, he wished he had not paused but had kept on going. As long as he was free to move, he felt that he could outwit his pursuers and somehow win out. But now he was trapped, and he could not see, at this moment, how he could win. Not that that meant he had given up. And Podarge was as trapped as he. She had no idea of how to get off the moon and back to the planet, and he did. There could be a trade, if he were forced to deal with her. Meantime, he would see what developed.

The room was large and was of marble. It had a bed of intricately worked silver and gold swinging from a large gold chain which hung down from the center of the ceiling. The walls were decorated with brightly colored paintings of a light-skinned, well-built, and handsomely featured people with graceful robes and many ornaments of metal and gems. The men were beardless, and both sexes had beautiful long yellow or bronze hair. They were playing at various games. Through the windows of some of the painted buildings a painted blue sea was visible.

The murals had been done by Wolff himself, who had talent, perhaps genius. They were inspired, however, by Kickaha, who had, in fact, inspired everything about the moon except the ball of the moon itself.

Shortly after the palace had been retaken, and Wolff had established himself as the Lord, he had mentioned to Kickaha that it had been a long time since he had been on the moon. Kickaha was intrigued, and he had insisted that they visit it. Wolff said that there was nothing to see except grassy plains and a few hills and small mountains. Nevertheless, they had picnicked there, going via one of the gates. Chryseis, the huge-eyed, tiger-haired dryad wife of Wolff, had prepared a basket full of goodies and liquors, just as if she had been a terrestrial American housewife preparing for a jaunt into the park on the edge of town. However, they did take weapons and several taloses, the half-protein robots which looked like knights in armor. Even there, a Lord could not relax absolutely. He must always be on guard against attack from another Lord.

They had a good time. Kickaha pointed out that there was more to see than Wolff had said. There was the glorious, and scary, spectacle of the planet hanging in the sky; this alone was worth making the trip. And then there was the fun of leaping like a grasshopper.

Toward the end of the day, while he was half-drunk on wine that Earth had never been fortunate enough to know, he got the idea for what he called *Project Barsoom*. He and Wolff had been talking about Earth and some of the books they had loved to read. Kickaha said that when he was young Paul Janus Finnegan and living on a farm outside Terre Haute, Indiana, he had loved the works of Edgar Rice Burroughs. He loved especially Tarzan and David Innes and John Carter and couldn't say that he had favored one over the others. Perhaps he had just a bit more love for John Carter.

It was then he had sat up so suddenly that he had spilled his glass of wine. He had said, "I have it! Barsoom! You said this moon is about the size of Mars, right? And you still have tremendous potentialities for biological 'miracles' in your labs, don't you? What about creating Barsoom?"

He had been so exhilarated he had leaped high up into the air but had been unable to pilot himself accurately and so had come down on the picnic lunch. Fortunately, they had eaten most of it. Kickaha was streaked with food and wine, but he was so full of glee he did not notice it.

Wolff listened patiently and smiled often, but his reply sobered Kickaha.

"I could make a reasonable facsimile of Barsoom," he said. "And I find your desire to be John Carter amusing. But I refuse to play God any more with sentient beings."

Kickaha pleaded with him, though not for very long. Wolff was as strong-minded a man as he had ever known. Kickaha was stubborn, too, but arguing with Wolff when his mind was made up was like trying to erode granite by flicking water off one's finger-ends against the stone.

Wolff did say, however, that he would plant a quick-growing yellow moss-like vegetation on the moon. It would soon kill the green grass and cover the moon from ice-capped north pole to ice-capped south pole.

He would do more, since he did not want to disappoint Kickaha just to be arbitrary. And the project did interest him. He would fashion *thoats, banths,* and other Barsoomian animals in his biolabs. Kickaha must realize, however, that this would take a long time and the results might differ from his specifications.

He would even try to create a Tree of Life, and he would build several ruined cities. He would dig canals.

But he would *not* create green *Tharks* or red, black, yellow, and white *Barsoomians*. As Jadawin, he would not have hesitated. As Wolff, he could not.

Aside from his refusal to play God, the scientific and technical problems and the work involved in creating whole peoples and cultures from scratch was staggering. The project would take over a hundred Earth years just to get started.

Did Kickaha realize, for instance, the complexities of the Martian eggs? These were small when laid, of course, probably no bigger than a football at the largest and possibly smaller, since Burroughs had not described the size when they were first ejected by the female. These were supposed to be placed in incubators in the light of the sun. After five years, the egg hatched. But in the meantime they had grown to be about two and a half feet long. At least, the green-Martian eggs were, although these could be supposed to be larger than those of the normal-sized human-type Martians.

Where did the eggs get the energy to grow? If the energy derived from the yolk, the embryo would never develop. The egg was a self-contained system; it did not get food for a long period of time from the mother as an embryo did through the umbilical cord. The implication was that the eggs picked up energy by absorbing the sun's rays. They could do so, theoretically, but the energy gained by this would be very minute, considering the small receptive area of the egg.

Wolff could not, at this moment, imagine what biological mechanisms could bring about this phenomenal rate of growth. There had to be an input of energy from someplace, and since Burroughs did not say what it was, it would be up to Wolff and the giant protein computers in his palace to find out.

"Fortunately," Wolff said, smiling, "I don't have to solve that problem, since there aren't going to be any sentient Martians, green or otherwise. But I might tackle it just to see if it could be solved."

There were other matters which required compromises in the effort to make the moon like Mars. The air was as thick as that on the planet, and though Wolff could make it thinner, he didn't think Kickaha would like to live in it. Presumably, the atmospheric density of Barsoom was equivalent to that found about ten thousand feet above Earth's surface. Moreover, there was the specification of Mars' two moons, Deimos and

Phobos. If two bodies of comparable size were set in orbits similar to the two moonlets, they would burn up in a short time. The atmosphere of the moon extended out to the gravitational warp which existed between the moon and planet. Wolff did, however, orbit two energy configurations which shone as brightly as Deimos and Phobos and circled the moon with the same speed and in the same directions.

Later, after sober reflection, Kickaha realized that Wolff was right. Even if it would have been possible to set biolab creations down here and educate them in cultures based on the hints in Burroughs' Martian books, it would not have been a good thing to do. You shouldn't try to play God. Wolff had done that as Jadawin and had caused much misery and suffering.

Or could you do this? After all, Kickaha had thought, the Martians would be given life and they would have as much chance as sentients anywhere else in this world or the next to love, to hope, and so on. It was true that they would suffer and know pain and madness and spiritual agony, but wasn't it better to be given a chance at life than to be sealed in unrealization forever? Just because somebody thought they would be better off if they didn't chance suffering? Wouldn't Wolff himself say that it had been better to have lived, no matter what he had endured and might endure, than never to have existed?

Wolff admitted that this was true. But he said that Kickaha was rationalizing. Kickaha wanted to play John Carter just as he had when he was a kid on a Hoosier farm. Well, Wolff wasn't going to all the labor and pains and time of making a living, breathing, thinking green Martian or red *Zodangan* just so Kickaha could run him through with a sword. Or vice versa.

Kickaha had sighed and then grinned and thanked Wolff for what he had done and gated on up to the moon and had a fine time for a week. He had hunted. *banth* and roped a small *thoat* and broken it in and prowled through the ruins of Korad and Thark, as he called the cities which Wolff's taloses had built. Then he became lonely and went back to the planet. Several times he came back for "vacations," once with his Drachelander wife and several Teutoniac knights, and once with a band of Hrowakas. Everybody except him had been uneasy on the moon, close to panic, and the vacations had been failures.

XVII

IT HAD BEEN THREE YEARS SINCE HE HAD GATED THROUGH TO THE MOON. Now he was back in circumstances he could never have fantasized. The Harpy and eagles were outside the room and he was trapped inside. Standoff. He could not get out, but they could not attack without serious, maybe total, loss. However, they had an advantage. They could get food and water. If they wanted to put in the time, they could wait until he was too weak from thirst and hunger to resist or until he could no longer fight off sleep. There was no reason why they should not take the time. Nobody was pressing them.

Of course, somebody soon could be. It seemed likely, or at least somewhat probable, the Bellers would be returning through other gates. And this time they would come in force.

If Podarge thought he'd stay in the room until he passed out, she was mistaken. He'd try a few tricks and, if these didn't work, he'd come out fighting. There was a slight chance that he might defeat them or get by them to the pits. It wasn't likely; the beaks and talons were swift and terrible. But then he wasn't to be sneered at, either.

He decided to make it even tougher for them. He rolled the wheel-like door from the space between the walls until only a narrow opening was left. Through this, he shouted at Podarge.

"You may think you have me now! But even if you do, then what? Are you going to spend the rest of your life on this desolate place? There are no mountains worthy of the name here for your aeries! And the topography is depressingly flat! And your food won't be easy to get! All the animals that live in the open are monstrously big and savage fighters!

"As for you, Podarge, you won't be able to queen it over your hundreds of thousands! If your virgin eagles do lay their eggs so your subjects may increase, they'll have a hard time with the little egg-eating animals that abound here! Not to mention the great white apes, which love eggs! And flesh, including eagle flesh, I'm sure!

"Ah, yes, the great white apes! You haven't met up with them yet, have you?"

He waited a while for them to think about his words. Then he said, "You're stuck here until you die! Unless you make a truce with me! I can show you how to get back to the planet! I know where the gates are hidden!"

More silence. Then a subdued conversation among the eagles and the Harpy. Finally, Podarge said, "Your words were very tempting, Trickster! But they don't fool me! All we have to do is wait until you fall asleep or become too thirst-torn to stand it! Then we will take you alive, and we will torture you until you tell us what we need to know. Then we kill you. What do you think of that?"

"Not much," he muttered. He yelled, "I will kill myself first! Podarge, slut-queen of the big bird-brains, what do you think of that?"

Her scream and the flapping of huge wings told him that she thought as little of his words as he of hers.

"I know where the gates are! But you'll never be able to find them without me! Make up your so-called mind fast, Podarge! I'll give you half an hour! Then I act!"

He rolled the door entirely shut and sat down with his back against the red-brown, highly polished hardwood. They could not move it without giving him plenty of time to be up and ready for them. And he could rest for a while. The long hard battle in Talanac, the shock of being hurled onto the moon, and the subsequent chase had exhausted him. And he lusted for water.

He must have nodded off. Up out of black half-oily waters he surged. His mouth was dry, dripping dust. His eyes felt as if hot hard-boiled eggs had just been inserted in his sockets. Since the door was not moving, he did not know what had awakened him. Perhaps it was his sense of vigilance belatedly acting.

He let his head fall back against the door. Faintly, screams and roars vibrated through, and he knew what had cannoned him from sleep. He jumped up and rolled the door halfway back into the inner-wall space. With the thick barrier removed, the sounds of the battle in the corridor struck full force.

Podarge and the three eagles were facing three huge, tawny, catlike beasts with ten legs. Two were maned males; the third was a sleek-necked female. These were *banths,* the Martian lions described by Burroughs and created by Wolff in his biolab and set down on this moon. They preyed on *thoats* and *zitidar* calves and the great white apes and anything else they could catch. Normally, they were night hunters, but hunger must have sent them prowling the daytime city. Or they may have been roused by all the noise and attracted by the blood.

Whatever their reasons, they had cornered the cornerers. They had killed one eagle, probably in the first surprise attack, Kickaha surmised. A green eagle was a fighter formidable enough to run off a tiger or two without losing a feather. So far, though the *banths* had killed one and inflicted enough wounds on the others to cover them with blood, they were bleeding from cuts and gashed all over their bodies and heads.

Now, roaring, they had separated from their intended prey. They paced back and forth in the corridor and then one would hurl himself at an eagle. Sometimes the charges were bluffs and fell just short of the range of beaks as deadly as battle-axes. Other times, they struck one of the two remaining eagles with a huge scythe-clawed paw, and then there would be a flurry of saberish canines, yellow beaks, yellow or scarlet talons, patches of tawny hide flying or mane hairs torn out by the bunch, green feathers whirling through the air, distended eyeballs green or yellow or red, blood spurting, roars, screams. And then the lion would disengage and run back to his companions.

Podarge stayed behind the twin green towers of her eagles.

Kickaha watched and waited. And presently all three lions attacked simultaneously. A male and an eagle rolled into the door with a crash. Kickaha jumped back, then stepped forward and ran his sword forward into the mass. He did not care which he stabbed, lion or eagle, although he rather hoped it would be an eagle. They were more intelligent and capable of greater concentration and devotion to an end—principally his.

But the two rolled away and only the tip of his sword entered flesh. Both were making so much noise that he could not tell which was hurt by the sword.

For just a moment, he had a clear avenue of escape down the center of the corridor. Both eagles were engaged with the lions, the Podarge was backed against the wall, her talons keeping the enraged female at bay. The lioness was bleeding from both eyes and her nose, which was half torn off. Blinded by blood, she was hesitant about closing in on the Harpy.

Kickaha dashed down the aisle, then leaped over two bodies as they rolled over to close off his route. His foot came down hard on a tawny muscle-ridged back, and he soared into the air. Unfortunately, he had put so much effort into his leap that he banged his head against the marble ceiling, cutting his temple open on a large diamond set in the marble.

Half stunned, he staggered on. At that moment, he was vulnerable. If eagle or lion had fallen on him, it could have killed him as a wolf kills a sick rabbit. But they were too busy trying to kill each other, and soon he was out of the building. Within a few minutes, he was free of the city and making great leaps toward the hills.

He bounded past the torn body of the eagle crippled from the collision. Another body, ripped up, lay near it. This was a *banth,* which must have attacked the eagle with the expectation of an easy kill. But it had been mistaken and had paid for the mistake.

Then he was soaring over the body of Quotshaml—rather, parts of the body, because they were scattered. The head, legs, arms, entrails, lungs, and pieces thereof.

He leaped up the hill, which was so tall that it could almost be dignified with the name of mountain. Two-thirds of the way up, hidden behind a curving outcrop of quartz-shot granite, was the entrance to the cave. There seemed no reason why he could not make it; only a few minutes ago all luck seemed to have leaked out of him, and now it was trickling back.

A scream told him that good fortune might only have seemed to return. He looked over his shoulder. A quarter of a mile away, Podarge and the two eagles were flapping swiftly toward him. No *banths* were in sight. Evidently, they had not been able to keep Podarge and the eagles in a corner. Perhaps the great cats had been glad to let them escape. That way, the *banths* could keep on living for sure and could enjoy eating the one eagle they had killed.

Whatever had happened, he was in danger of being caught in the open again. His pursuers had learned how to fly effectively in the lesser gravity. As a result, they were traveling a third faster than they would have on the planet—or so it seemed to Kickaha. Actually, the fighting and the loss of blood they had endured had to slow them down.

Podarge and one eagle, at a second look, did seem to be crippled. Their wings had slowed down since the first look, and they were lagging behind the other eagle. This one, though covered with blood over the green feathers, did not seem to be as deeply hurt. She overtook Kickaha and came down like a hawk on a gopher.

The gopher, however, was armed with a sword and had determined what action he would take. Calculating in advance when her onslaught would coincide with his bound, he whirled around in mid-air. He came down facing backwards, and the eagle's outstretched talons were within reach of the blade. She screamed and spread her wings to brake her speed, but he slashed out. His sword did not have the force that his sure footing on the ground would have given it, and the stroke spun him further than he wanted to go and threw him off balance for the landing. Nevertheless, the blade chopped through one foot at the juncture of talons and leg and halfway through the other foot. Then Kickaha struck the earth and fell on his side, and the breath exploded from him.

He was up again sobbing and wheezing like a damaged bagpipe. He managed to pick up his sword where he had dropped it. The eagle was flopping on the ground now like a wounded chicken and did not even see him when he brought the sword down on her neck. The head fell off, and one black, scarlet-encircled eye glared at him and then became dull and cold.

He was still sucking in air when he bounded through the cave entrance twenty yards ahead of Podarge and the last eagle. He landed just inside the hole in the hillside and then leaped toward the end of the cave, a granite wall forty feet away.

He had interrupted a domestic scene: a family of great white apes. Papa, ten feet tall, four-armed, white and hairless except for an immense roach of white hair on top of his breadloaf-shaped skull, gorilla-faced, pink-eyed, was squatting against the wall to the right. He was tearing with his protruding canines and sharp teeth at the ripped-off leg of a small *thoat*. Mama was ripping the flesh of the head of the *thoat* and at the same time was suckling twin babies.

(Wolff and Kickaha had goofed in designing the great white apes. They had forgotten that the only mammals on Burroughs' Mars were a small creature and man. By the time they perceived their mistake, they agreed that it was too late. Several thousand of the apes had been placed on the moon, and it did not seem worthwhile to destroy the first projects of the biolabs and create a new nonmammalian species.)

The colossal simians were as surprised as he, but he had the advantage of being in motion. Still, there was the delaying business of rolling a small key boulder out of a socket of stone and then pushing in on a heavy section of the back wall. This resulted in part of the wall swinging out and part swinging in to reveal a chamber. This was a square about twenty feet across. There were seven crescents set into the granite floor near the back wall. To the right were a number of pegs at eye-level, on which were placed seven of the silvery metallic crescents. Each of these was to be matched to the appropriate crescent on the floor by comparing the similarity of hieroglyphs on the crescents.

When two crescents were joined at their ends to form a circle, they became a gate to a preset place on the planet. Two of the gates were traps. The unwary person who used them would find himself transmitted to an inescapable prison in Wolff's palace.

Kickaha scanned the hieroglyphs with a haste that he did not like but could not help. The light was dusky in the rear chamber, and he could barely make out the markings. He knew now that he should have stored a light device here when the cave was set up. It was too late even for regret—he had no time for anything but instant unconsidered reaction.

The cavern was as noisy as the inside of a kettledrum. The two adult apes had gotten to their bowed and comparatively short legs and were roaring at him while the two upper arms beat on their chests and the two intermediary arms slapped their stomachs. Before they could advance on him, they were almost knocked over by Podarge and the eagle, who blasted in like a charge from a double-barreled shotgun.

They had hoped to catch a cornered and relatively helpless Kickaha, although their experience with him should have taught them caution. Instead, they had exchanged three wounded and tiring, perhaps reluctant, *banths* for two monstrously large, refreshed, and enraged great white apes.

Kickaha would have liked to watch the battle and cheer the apes, but he did not want to chance wearing his luck through, since it had already given indications of going threadbare. So he threw the two "trap" crescents on the floor and picked the other five up. Four he put under his arm with the intention of taking them with him. If the Harpy did escape the apes and tried to use a crescent, she would end up in the palace prison.

Kickaha lingered when he knew better, delayed his up-and-going too long. Podarge suddenly broke loose—perhaps thrown was a more exact description of her method of departure from the ape—and she shot like a basketball across the cave. She came into the chamber so swiftly that he had to drop the crescents to bring up his sword for defense. She hit him with her talons first, and he was slammed against the wall with a liver-hurting, kidney-paining jolt. He could not bring the sword down because, one, she was too close and, two, he was too hurt at the moment to use the sword.

Then they were rolling over and over with her talons clenched in his thighs. The pain was agonizing, and she was beating him in the face, the head, the neck, and the shoulders with the forward edges of her wings.

Despite the pain and the shock of the wing-blows, he managed to hit her in the chin with a fist and then to bang the hilt of the sword against the side of her head.

Her eyes crossed and glazed. Blood flowed from her nose. She fell backward, her wings stretched like outflung arms. Her talons, however, remained sunk in his thighs; he had to pry them loose one by one. Blood ran down his legs and pooled out around his feet. Just as he pulled the last talon loose, the male ape charged on all sixes into the chamber. Kickaha picked up his sword with both hands and brought it down on an outstretched paw. The shock ran up his hand and arm and almost made him lose his grip. But the paw, severed at the wrist, fell on the floor. The stump shot blood all over him, momentarily blinding him. He wiped the blood off in time to see the ape flee shrieking on two feet and three of its paws. It ran headlong into the last eagle, which had just finished disemboweling the female ape with its beak and talons. They locked and went over and over.

At that moment Podarge recovered her senses. She soared from the floor with a shriek and a frantic beating of wings. Kickaha picked up a crescent from the floor, saw that the hieroglyph on its center matched the nearest one in the floor, and set the two end against end. Then he whirled and slashed at Podarge, who was dancing around, trying to frenzy herself enough to attack him. She dodged back and he stepped into the ring formed by the two crescents.

"Goodbye, Podarge!" he cried. "Stay here and rot!"

XVIII

HE HAD GOTTEN NO FURTHER THAN HER NAME WHEN THE GATE activated. He was out of the cave with no sense of passage—as always—and was in another place, standing inside another ring of two crescents. The contact of the two crescents in the cave, plus the entrance of his mass into the field radiated by the crescents, had activated the gate after a delay of three seconds. He and the loose crescent had been transferred to the crescent which matched the frequency of the crescent in the cave, at the other end of the undercontinuum.

He had escaped, although he would bleed to death soon if he did not find something to staunch the flow.

Then he saw what mistake he had made by acting so quickly because of pressure from Podarge. He had picked up the wrong crescent after dropping the five when attacked by the Harpy. During the struggle, one of the trap crescents must have been kicked out of its corner and among the others. And he had picked it up and used it to gate out.

He was in the prison cell of the palace of the Lord.

Once, he had bragged to Wolff that he could escape from the so-called escape-proof cell if he were ever in it. He did not think that any prison anywhere could hold a man who was clever and determined. The escape might take a long time, but it could be done.

He groaned now and wished he had not been so big-mouthed. Wolff had arranged the prison very well. It was set under eighty feet of solid stone and had no direct physical connection to the outside world. It was an entirely self-enclosed, self-sustaining system except for one thing: food and water for the prisoner were transmitted from the palace kitchen through a gate too small to admit anything larger than a tray.

There were gates in the prison through which the prisoner could be brought up to a prison cell in the palace. But this could be activated only by someone cognizant in the palace above.

The room was cylindrical and was about forty feet long. Light was seemingly sourceless and there were no shadows. The walls were painted by Wolff with scenes from the ancient ancestral planet of the Lords. Wolff had not expected any prisoners other than Lords and so had done these paintings for their benefit. There was some cruelty in the settings of the murals—all depicted the wide and beautiful outdoors and hence could not help reminding the prisoner of his narrow and enclosed space.

The furniture was magnificent and was in the style known among the Lords as Pre-Exodus Middle Thyamarzan. The doors of the great bureaus and cabinets housed many devices for the amusement and education of the prisoner. Originally, these had not been in the cells. But when Wolff had rewon the palace, he had placed these in the prison—he no longer believed in torturing his captives even with boredom. And he provided them with much because he was sometimes gone for long periods and would not be able to release them.

Until now, this room had held no prisoners. It was ironical and sourly amusing that its first prize should be the jailer's best friend and that the jailer knew nothing of it.

The Bellers in the palace would not know of him either, he hoped. Lights would be flashing in three places to indicate that the buried cell now housed someone: a light would be pulsing in Wolff's bedroom; a second, on an instrument panel in the great control room; a third, in the kitchen.

If the Black Bellers were observing any of these, they must be alarmed or, at the least, edgy and uncertain. They would have no way of knowing what the lights meant. The kitchen taloses would know, but even if they were asked, they could not reply. They heard orders but had mouths for tasting and eating only, not for talking.

Kickaha, thinking about this, looked for first aid devices in the cabinets. He soon came across antiseptics, local anesthetics, drugs, bandages, all he needed. After cleaning his wounds, he prepared films of pseudoflesh and applied them to stop the bleeding. They began their healing efforts immediately.

He got a drink of water then and also opened a bottle of cold beer. He took a long shower, dried off, and searched for and found a pill which would dull his overstimulated nerves so he could get a restful sleep. The pill would have to wait, however, until he had eaten and finished exploring this place.

It was true that he should not, perhaps, be thinking of rest. Time was vital. There was no telling what was happening in Talanac with Anana and the Red Beards. They might be under attack this very moment by a Beller flying machine with powerful beamers. And what was von Turbat doing now? After he had escaped Podarge, he and von Swindebarn must have gated back to the palace. Would they be content to hole up in it? Or would they, as seemed more likely to Kickaha, go back to the moon through another gate? They would suppose him to be marooned there and so out of action. But they also must have some doubts. It was probable that they would take at least one craft and a number of men to hunt him down.

He laughed. They would be up there, frantically trying to locate him, and all the time he would be underfoot, so to speak. There was, of course, the possibility that they would find the cave near Korad. In which case, they would test all the crescents left there, and one Beller at least would soon be in this cell. Perhaps he was making a mistake in sleeping. Maybe he ought to keep on going, get out of this cell as soon as possible.

Kickaha decided that he *had* to sleep. If he didn't, he would collapse or be slowed down so much he would be too vulnerable. Light-headed from a bottle of beer and three glasses of wine, he went to a little door in the wall, over which a topaz was flashing a yellow light. He opened the door and took a silver tray from the hollow in the wall. There were ten silver-colored, jewel-encrusted dishes on the tray, each holding excellent foods. He emptied every dish and then returned the tray and contents to the hollow. Nothing happened until he closed the little door. He raised it again a second later. The hollow was empty. The tray had been gated up to the kitchen, where a talos would wash and polish the dishes and the tray. Six hours from now, the talos would place another tray of food in the kitchen gate and so send it to the stone-buried cell.

Kickaha wanted to be up and ready when the tray came through the next time. Unfortunately, there were no clocks in the prison, so he would have to depend on his biological clock. That, in its present condition, was undependable.

He shrugged and told himself what the hell. He could only try. If he didn't make it this time, he would the next. He had to get sleep because he did not know what would be required of him if he ever got out of prison. Actually, this was the best place for him in the universe—if the Bellers did not find the cave of gates on the moon.

First, he had to explore the rest of the prison to make sure that all was right there and also to use anything he might find helpful. He went to a door in one end of the cell and opened it. He stepped into a small bare anteroom. He opened the door on its opposite wall and went into another cylindrical cell about forty feet long. This was luxuriously decorated and furnished in a different style. However, the furniture kept changing shape, and whenever he moved near to a divan, a chair, or table, it slid away from him. When he increased his pace, the piece of furniture increased its speed just enough to keep out of reach. And the other furniture slid out of its way if they veered toward it.

The room had been designed to amuse, puzzle, and perhaps eventually enrage the prisoner. It was supposed to help him keep his mind off his basic predicament.

Kickaha gave up trying to capture a divan and left the room at the door at the opposite end. It closed behind him as the others had done. He knew that the doors could not be opened from this side, but he kept trying, just in case Wolff had made a mistake. It refused to move, too. The door ahead swung open to a small anteroom. The room beyond it was an art studio. The next room was four times as large as the previous and was mainly a swimming pool. It had a steady supply of cool fresh water, gated through from the palace water supply above and also gated out. Inflow was through a barred hole in the center of the pool's floor. Kickaha studied the setup of the pool and then went on to the next room.

This was the size of the first. It contained gymnastic equipment and was in a gravitic field one-half that of the planet's, the field of which was equivalent to Earth's. Much of the equipment was exotic, even to a man who traveled as much as Kickaha. The only things to hold his interest were some ropes, which were strung from ceiling hooks or bars for climbing exercises.

He fashioned a lasso from one rope and coiled several more over his shoulder to take with him. In all, he passed through twenty-four chambers, each different from the others. Eventually, he was back in the original.

Any other prisoner would have supposed that the rooms were connected to form a circular chain. He knew that there was no physical connection between the rooms. Each was separated from the next by forty feet of granite.

Passage from one to the next was effected by gates set inside the doorways of the anterooms. When the door was swung open, the gate was activated and the prisoner was transmitted instantaneously to another anteroom which looked just like the one he thought he was entering.

Kickaha entered the original cell cautiously. He wanted to make sure that no Beller had been gated here from the cave on the moon while he was exploring. The room was empty, but he could not be sure that a Beller had not come here and gone investigating, as he had. He stacked three chairs on top of each other and, carrying them, walked through into the next room, the one with the shape-shifting elusive furniture. He picked out a divan and lassoed a grotesquely decorated projection on top of its back. The projection changed form, but it could metamorphose only within certain limits, and the lasso held snugly. The divan did move away when he walked toward it, but he lay down and then pulled himself along the lasso while the divan fled here and there. The thick rugs kept him from being skinned, although he did get rug-burns. Finally he clutched the divan and hauled himself up onto it. It stopped then, seemed to quiver, solidified, and became as quiescent and permanent as ordinary furniture. However, it would resume its peculiar properties if he left it.

Kickaha tied one end of the lasso to the projection. He then snared the top of a chair which had been innocently standing nearby. The chair did not move until Kickaha pulled it on the rope. Then it tried to get away. He jumped off the divan and went through a series of maneuvers to herd the divan and chair, still connected by the rope, near the entrance. With the other ropes and various objects used as weights, he rigged a Rube Goldberg device. The idea was that anyone coming through the entrance would step inside the noose laid on the floor. The nearby mass of the intruder would then send both divan and chair away in flight, and this would draw the noose tight around the intruder's ankle. One end of the noose was tied to the rope stretched between the divan and chair. Another rope connected the projection on the divan to a chandelier of gold set with emeralds and turquoise. Kickaha, standing on the topmost of the three chairs he'd carried, had performed a balancing act while withdrawing the kingpin that secured the chandelier to the ceiling fixture. He did not entirely remove the kingpin but left just enough to keep the chandelier from falling. When the divan and chair pulled away from the intruder, the strain on the rope tied to the kingpin would yank it the rest of the way out, he hoped. The chandelier would come crashing down onto the floor. And, if his calculations were correct, it would fall on whoever was being dragged along by the noose around his leg.

Actually, he did not expect it to work. He did not think anybody would be imperceptive enough not to see the noose. Still, there was a chance. This world and the next were full of fools and clumsy idiots.

He went to the next room, the art studio. Here he picked up a large ball of plastic. This was extremely malleable and could be fixed to retain a desired shape by shooting a chemical hypodermically into the stuff. He took the ball and needle syringe into the swimming pool room. He dived to the bottom of the pool and jammed the plastic down over the outlet. He molded the plastic into a disc which covered the hole and then fixed it with the hypo. After this, he rose to the surface and drew himself up onto the pool edge. The water level began to rise immediately. It was as he had hoped: there was no regulation or feedback between inflow and outflow, so water continued to pour in even when the outlet was blocked. Wolff had overlooked this. Of course, there was no reason why he should have been concerned about it. If a prisoner wanted to drown himself, he was free to do so.

Kickaha walked into the next room. Here he piled some furniture and statues against the door, dried himself, and lay down to sleep. He was confident that no one would enter the room without having had much difficulty getting there. And no one could enter without making a lot of noise.

He awoke with a jerk and a feeling that bells attached to his nerves were jingling. His heart was drumming like a grouse's wings on takeoff. Something had crashed into his dreams. No, into the room. He jumped up from behind the divan, the sword in his hand. He came up just in time to see a man strike the floor in a wave of water. Then the door automatically shut. The man was gasping as though he had been holding his breath for a long time.

He was a long-legged, powerfully built fellow with pale skin, large freckles, and dark hair that would be red-blond when it dried. He carried no hand-beamers. His only weapons seemed to be a dagger and a short sword. He was unarmored. He wore a short-sleeved red shirt, a big leather belt, and yellow tights striped along the seams.

Kickaha bounded out from behind the divan and ran up with his sword raised. The man, shocked and seeing that he could not get up in time to defend himself, and that Kickaha was giving him a chance to surrender, took the only course a wise man could. Kickaha spoke to him in Lordspeech. The man looked puzzled and answered in German. Kickaha repeated the order in German, then let him get up so he could sit down in a chair. The man was shivering from the cold water and possibly from the thought of what Kickaha might yet do to him.

The fact that the man spoke German fluently was enough to convince Kickaha that he could not be a Beller. His speech was that of a native of the Einhorner Mountains. Evidently, the Bellers had not wanted to expose themselves to the unknown dangers of the gates and so had sent in expendables.

Pal Do Shuptarp told Kickaha everything he knew. He was a baronet who was in command of the castle garrison of King von Turbat of Eggesheim. He had stayed behind while the invasion of Talanac was taking place. Suddenly, von Turbat and von Swindebarn had reappeared. They came from somewhere inside the castle. They ordered the garrison and a number of other troops to follow them into a "magic" room in the castle. Von Turbat had explained that their archenemy Kickaha was now on the moon and that it was necessary to go by sorcery—white magic, of course—to track him down. Von Turbat did not say anything of what had happened to the soldiers in Talanac.

"They're all dead," Kickaha said. "But how did von Turbat talk to you?"

"Through a priest, as he has done for some time," Do Shuptarp said.

"And you didn't think that was peculiar?"

Do Shuptarp shrugged and said, "So many peculiar things were happening all of a sudden that this was just one more. Besides, von Turbat claimed to have received a divine revelation from the Lord. He said he had been given the gift of being able to speak the holy tongue. And he was forbidden to speak anything else because the Lord wanted everyone to know that von Turbat was favored of the Lord."

"A pretty good rationalization and excuse," Kickaha said.

"A magical flying machine appeared above the castle," Do Shuptarp said. "It landed, and we helped take it apart and carried the pieces into the room where we were to be transported magically to the moon."

It was a terrifying experience to be transported instantaneously to the moon and to see the planet they had been on just a moment before now hanging in the sky, threatening to fall down on the moon and crush them all.

But a man could get used to almost anything.

The cave in the hillside had been discovered by the searchers when they came across the carcass of an eagle minus her feet and head. The cave held two dead adult apes, and another dead eagle. There were five loose crescents on the floor. Kickaha, hearing this, knew that Podarge had escaped via a gate.

Von Turbat had selected ten of his best knights to use the gates, two to a circle. He hoped that some would find and kill Kickaha.

"Two of you?"

"Karl von Rothadler came with me," Do Shuptarp said. "He's dead.

He did not step into the noose, although he stormed into that room so fast he almost got caught in it. A great one for charging in, swinging a sword, and to hell with finding out first what's going on. He ran in and so that divan and chair moved away swiftly. I don't know how you bewitched them, but you must be a powerful magician. They pulled the kingpin loose and the chandelier fell on his head."

"So the trap worked, though not exactly as planned," Kickaha said. "How did you get through the room filled with water?"

"After Karl was killed, I tried to go back the way I'd come. The door wouldn't open. So I went on. When I came to the door to the water-filled room, I had to push with all my strength to open it. Water sprayed out of the opening. I quit pushing. But I couldn't go back; I had to go ahead. I pushed the door open again. The pressure of the water was very strong. I couldn't get the door open all the way, and the water spurting out almost knocked me down. But I managed to get through—I am very strong. The anteroom was almost full of water by the time I did get through, and the door closed as soon as I was inside the big room.

"The water was clear and the light was bright. Otherwise, I might have drowned before I found the other door. I swam to the ceiling, hoping there would be a space there with air, but there wasn't any. So I swam to the other end of the room. The water pressure had opened the door there and let some water into the next anteroom. But the door had closed itself again. In fact, it must have been doing this for some time. The anteroom was more than half full when I got into it.

"By then, the pressure was also opening the door into this room. I waited once while it closed. Then, when it began to open a little again, I shoved with my feet braced on the floor. And I came out like a marooned sailor cast up by a storm on a desert island, as you saw."

Kickaha did not comment for a minute. He was thinking of the predicament in which he had put himself—and this fellow—by causing the pool to overflow. Eventually, every room of the twenty-four would be flooded.

"Okay," he said. "If I can't figure a way to get out fast, we've had it!"

Do Shuptarp asked what he had said. Kickaha explained. Do Shuptarp got even paler. Kickaha then proceeded to outline much of what was behind the recent events. He went into some detail about the Black Bellers.

Do Shuptarp said, "Now I understand much of what was incomprehensible to me—to all of us—at the time. One day, life was proceeding normally. I was getting ready to lead a dragon-hunting expedition. Then von Turbat and von Swindebarn proclaimed a holy war. They said that the Lord, Herr Gutt, was directing us to attack the city on the level below us. And we were to find and kill the three heretics hiding there.

"Most of us had never heard of Talanac or the Tishquetmoac or of Kickaha. We had heard of the robber baron Horst von Horstmann, of course. Then von Turbat told us that the Lord had given us magical means to go from one level to the next. He explained why he used only the speech of the Lord.

"And now you tell me that the souls of my king and of von Swindebarn and a few others have been eaten up. And that their bodies are possessed by demons."

Kickaha saw that the soldier did not fully understand yet, but he did not try to disabuse him. If he wanted to think in superstitious modes, let him. The important thing was that he knew that the two kings were now terrible perils in disguise.

"Can I trust you?" he said to Do Shuptarp. "Will you help me, now that you know the truth? Are you convinced that it is the truth? Of course, all this doesn't matter unless I can figure out a way to get us up into the palace before we drown."

"I will swear eternal fealty to you!"

Kickaha wasn't convinced, but he didn't want to kill him. And Do Shuptarp might be helpful. He told him to pick up his weapons and to lead the way back to the cell in which they had arrived. On getting back there, Kickaha looked for a recording device and found one. This was one of many machines with which a prisoner could entertain himself. Kickaha, however, had another purpose than amusement in mind. He took the glossy black cube, which was three inches across, pressed the red spot on its underside, and spoke a few words in Lord-speech at it. Then he pressed a white spot on its side, and his words were emitted back to him.

Kickaha waited for what seemed like hours until the topaz above the little door in the wall began flashing. He removed the tray, which contained enough food for two. Two lights were now flashing in the kitchen, and the talos, noting this, had made suitable provisions.

"Eat!" Kickaha said to Do Shuptarp. "Your next meal may be a long way off—if you ever get one!"

Do Shuptarp winced. Kickaha tried to eat slowly, but the sudden slight opening of the door and spurt of water caused him to gobble. The door shut but almost immediately opened a few inches again to spew in more water.

He put the dishes on the tray and set it in the wallchamber. He hoped that the talos would not have something more pressing to do. If they delayed gating the tray back, it might be too late for the prisoners.

Also, the cube he had put on the tray had started replaying his instructions. It was set for sixty times by pressing the white spot three times, but the talos might not take in the tray until after the recordings were finished.

The topaz quit flashing. He lifted the door. The tray was gone. "If the talos does what I tell him to, we're okay," he said to the Teutoniac. "At least, we'll be out of here. If the talos doesn't obey me, then it's glub, glub, glub, and an end to our worries."

He told Do Shuptarp to follow him into the anteroom. There they stood for perhaps sixty seconds. Kickaha said, "If nothing happens soon, we might as well kiss our . . ."

XIX

THEY WERE STANDING ON A ROUND PLATE OF GRAY METAL IN A LARGE room. The furniture was exotic, Early Rhadamanthean Period. The walls and floor were of rose-red and jet-veined stone. There were no doors or windows, although one wall seemed to be a window which gave a view of the outside.

"There'll be lights to indicate that we're now in this cell," Kickaha said. "Let's hope the Bellers won't figure out what they mean."

With all these unexplained lights on, the Bellers must be in a panic. Undoubtedly, they were prowling the palace to find out what—if anything—was wrong.

Presently, a section of the seemingly solid wall moved and disappeared into the wall itself. Kickaha led the way out. A talos, six and a half feet tall, armored like a knight, waited for them. It handed him the black-cube recorder.

Kickaha said, "Thank you," and then, "Observe us closely. I am your master. This man is my servant. Both of us are to be served by you unless this man, my servant, does something that might harm me. Then you are to stop him from trying to harm me.

"The other beings in this palace are my enemies, and you are to attack and kill any as soon as you see one or more than one. First, though, you will take this cube, after I have spoken a message into it, and you will let the other taloses hear it. It will tell them to attack and kill my enemies. Do you understand fully?"

The talos saluted, indicating that he comprehended. Kickaha spoke into the cube, set it to repeat the message a thousand times, and gave it to the talos. The armored thing saluted again, turned, and marched off

Kickaha said, "They carry out orders superbly, but the last one to ge their ear is their master. Wolff knew this, but he didn't want to change their setup. He said that this characteristic might actually work out to his advantage someday, and it wasn't likely that any invader would know about it."

Kickaha next told Do Shuptarp how to handle a beamer if he should get his hands on one, then they set out for the armory of the palace. To get to it, they had to cross one entire floor of this wing and then descend six stories. Kickaha took the staircases, since the Bellers would be using the elevators.

Do Shuptarp was awed at the grandeur of the palace. The great size of the rooms and their furnishings, each containing treasure enough to have bought all the kingdoms in Dracheland, reduced him to a gasping, slavering, creeping creature. He wanted to stop so he could look and feel and, perhaps, fill his pockets. Then he became cowed, because the absolute quiet and the richness made him feel as if he were in an extremely sacred place.

"We could wander for days and never meet another soul," he said.

Kickaha said, "We could if I didn't know where I was going." He wondered how effective the fellow would be. He was probably a first-rate warrior under normal circumstances. His handling of himself in the water-filled chamber proved that he was courageous and adaptable. But to be in the palace of the Lord was for him as frightening, as numinous an experience, as it would be for a terrestrial Christian to be transported to the City of God—and to discover that devils had taken over.

Near the foot of the staircase, Kickaha smelled melted metal and plastic and burned protoplasm. Cautiously, he stuck his head around the corner. About a hundred feet down the hall, a talos lay sprawled on its front. An armored arm, burned off at the shoulder by a beamer, lay nearby.

Two Black Bellers, or so Kickaha presumed they were from the caskets attached to their backs by harnesses, lay dead. Their necks were twisted almost completely around. Two Bellers, each holding a hand-beamer, were talking excitedly. One held what was left of the black cube in his hand. Kickaha grinned on seeing it. It had been damaged by the beamer and so must have stopped its relay. Thus, the Bellers would not know why the talos had attacked them or what the message was in the cube.

"Twenty-nine down. Twenty-one to go," Kickaha said. He withdrew his head.

"They'll be on their guard now," he muttered. "The armory would've been unguarded, probably, if this hadn't happened. But now that they know something's stalking upwind, they'll guard it for sure. Well, we'll try another way. It could be dangerous, but then what isn't? Let's go back up the stairs."

He led Do Shuptarp to a room on the sixth story. This was about six hundred feet long and three hundred feet wide and contained stuffed animals, and some stuffed sentients, from many universes. They passed a transparent cube in which was embedded, like a dragonfly in amber, a creature that seemed to be half-insect, half-man. It had antennae and huge but quite human eyes, a narrow waist, skinny legs covered with a pinkish fuzz, four skinny arms, a great humped back, and four butterfly-like wings radiating from the hump.

Despite the urgency of action, Do Shuptarp stopped to look at the strangeling. Kickaha said, "That exhibit is ten thousand years old. That *kwiswas,* coleopter-man, is the product of Anana's biolabs, or so I was told, anyway. The Lord of this world made a raid on his sister's world and secured some specimens for his museum. This *kwiswas,* I understand, was Anana's lover at that time, but you can't believe everything you hear, especially if one Lord is telling it about another. And all that, of course, was some time ago."

The monstrously large eyes had been staring through the thick plastic for ten millennia, five thousand years before civilization had set in on Earth. Though Kickaha had seen it before, he still felt an awe, an uneasiness, and insignificance before it. How strongly and cleverly had this creature fought to preserve its life, just as Kickaha was now fighting for his? Perhaps as vigorously and wildly. And then it had died, as he must, too, and it had been stuffed and set up to observe with unseeing eyes the struggles of others. All passed . . .

He shook his head and blinked his eyes. To philosophize was fine, if you did so under appropriate circumstances. These were not appropriate. Besides, so death came to all, even to those who avoided it as ingeniously and powerfully as he! So what? One extra minute of life was worth scrapping for, provided that the minutes that had gone before had been worthy minutes.

"I wonder what this thing's story was?" Do Shuptarp muttered.

"Our story will come to a similar end if we don't get a move on," Kickaha said.

At the end wall of the room, he twisted a projection that looked as fixed as the rest of the decorations. He turned the projection to the right 160 degrees, then to the left 160, and then spun it completely around twice to the right. A section of wall slid back. Kickaha breathed out tension of uncertainty. He had not been sure that he remembered the proper code. The possibility was strong that a wrong manipulation would have resulted in anything from a cloud of poisonous gas or vapor to a beam which would cut him in half.

He pulled in Do Shuptarp after him. The Teutoniac started to protest. Then he began to scream as both fell down a lightless shaft. Kickaha clapped his hand over Do Shuptarp's mouth and said, "Quiet! We won't be hurt!"

The wind of their descent snatched his words away. Do Shuptarp continued to struggle, but he subsided when they began to slow down in their fall. Presently, they seemed to be motionless. The walls suddenly lit up, and they could see that they were falling slowly. The shaft a few feet above them and a few feet below them was dark. The light accompanied them as they descended. Then they were at the bottom of the shaft. There was no dust, although the darkness above the silence felt as if the place had not seen a living creature for hundreds of years.

Angrily, the Teutoniac said, "I may have heart failure yet."

Kickaha said, "I had to do it that way. If you knew how you were going to fall, you'd never have gone through with it on your own. It would have been too much to ask you."

"You jumped," Do Shuptarp said.

"Sure. And I've practiced it a score of times. I didn't have the guts either until I'd seen Wolff—the Lord—do it several times."

He smiled. "Even so, this time, I wasn't sure that the field was on. The Bellers could have turned it off. Wouldn't that have been a good joke on us?"

Do Shuptarp did not seem to think it was funny. Kickaha turned from him to the business of getting out of the shaft. This demanded beating a code with his knuckles on the shaft wall. A section slid out, and they entered a whitewalled room about thirty feet square and well illuminated. It was bare except for a dozen crescents set in the stone floor and a dozen hanging on wall-pegs. The crescents were unmarked.

Kickaha put out a hand to restrain Do Shuptarp. "Not a step more! This room is dangerous unless you go through an undeviating ritual. And I'm not sure I remember it all!"

The Teutoniac was sweating, although the air was cool and moving slightly. "I was going to ask why we didn't come here in the first place," he said, "instead of walking through the corridors. Now, I see."

"Let's hope you continue to see," Kickaha said ambiguously. He advanced three steps forward straight from the entrance. Then he walked sideways until he was even with the extreme right-end crescent on the wall. He turned around once and walked to the crescent, his right arm extended stiffly at right angles to the floor. As soon as his fingertips touched the crescent, he said, "Okay, soldier. You can walk about as you please now—I think."

But he lost his smile as he studied the crescents. He said, "One of these will gate us to inside the armory. But I can't remember which. The second from the right or the third?"

Do Shuptarp asked what would happen if the wrong crescent were chosen.

"One of these—I don't know which—would gate us into the control room," he said. "I'd choose that if I had a beamer or if I thought the Bellers hadn't rigged extra-mass-intrusion alarms in the control room. And if I knew which it was.

"One will gate us right back to the underground prison from which we just came. A third would gate us to the moon. A fifth, to the Atlantean level. I forget exactly what the others will do, except that one would put you into a universe that is, to say the least, undesirable."

Do Shuptarp shivered and said, "I am a brave man. I've proved that on the battlefield. But I feel like a baby lost in a forest full of wolves."

Kickaha didn't answer, although he approved of Do Shuptarp's frankness. He could not make up his mind about the second or third crescent. He had to pick one because there was no getting back up the shaft—like so many routes in the palace, it was one-way.

Finally, he said, "I'm fairly sure it's the third. Wolff's mind favors threes or multiples thereof. But . . ."

He shrugged and said, "What the hell. We can't stand here forever."

He matched the third right-hand crescent with the third from the left on the floor. "I do remember that the loose crescents go with opposing fixed ones," he said. He carefully explained to Do Shuptarp the procedure for using a gate and what they might expect. Then the two stepped into the circle formed by the two crescents. They waited for about three seconds. There was no sensation of movement or flicker of passage before their eyes, but, abruptly, they were in a room about three hundred feet square. Familiar and exotic weapons and armor were in shelves or the walls or in racks and stands on the floor.

"We made it," Kickaha said. He stepped out of the circle and said "We'll get some hand-beamers and power-packs, some rope, and a spy missile guider and goggles. Oh, yes, some short-range neutron hand grenades, too."

He also picked two well-balanced knives for throwing. Do Shuptarp tried out his beamer on a small target at the armory rear. The meta disc, which was six inches thick, melted away within five seconds. Kickaha strapped a metal box to his back in a harness. This contained several spy-missiles, power broadcasting-receiving apparatus for the missiles, and the video-audio goggles.

Kickaha hoped that the Bellers had not come across these yet. If they had guards who were looking around corners or prowling the corridors with the missiles, it was goodbye.

The door had been locked by Wolff, and, as nearly as Kickaha could determine, no one had unlocked it. It had many safeguards to prevent access by unauthorized persons from the outside, but there was nothing to prevent a person on the inside from leaving without hindrance. Kickaha was relieved. The Bellers had not been able to penetrate this, which meant they had no spy-missiles. Unless, that is, they had brought some in from the other universes. But since the crafts had used none, he did not think they had any.

He put on the goggles over his eyes and ears and, holding the control box in his hands, guided a missile out the open doors. The missile was about three inches long and was shaped like a schoolboy's folded-paper airplane. It was transparent, and the tiny colored parts could be seen in a strong light at certain angles. Its nose contained an "eye," through which Kickaha could get a peculiar and limited view and an "ear" through which he could hear noises, muted or amplified as he wished.

He turned the missile this way and that, saw that no one was in the hall, and shoved the goggles up on top of his head. When he left the armory, he closed the door, knowing that it would automatically lock and arm itself. He used his eyes to guide the missile on the straightaway, and when he wanted to look around corners, he slipped the goggles down.

Kickaha and Do Shuptarp, with the missile, covered about six miles of horizontal and vertical travel, leaving one wing and crossing another to get to the building containing the control room. The trip took longer than a mere hike because of their caution.

Once, they passed by a colossal window close to the edge of the monolith on which the palace sat. Do Shuptarp almost fainted when he saw the sun. It was *below* him. He had to look downward to see it. Seeing the level of Atlantis spread out flatly for a five hundred mile radius, and then a piece of the level below that, and a shard of still a lower one, made him turn white.

Kickaha pulled him away from the window and tried to explain the tower structure of the planet and the rotation of the tiny sun about it. Since the palace was on top of the highest monolith of the planet, it was actually above the sun, which was at the level of the middle monolith.

The Teutoniac said he understood this. But he had never seen the sun except from his native level. And, of course, from the moon. But both times the sun had seemed high.

"If you think that was a frightening experience," Kickaha said, "you should look over the edge of the world sometime from the bottom level, the Garden level."

They entered the central massif of the building, which housed the control room. Here they proceeded even more slowly. They walked down a Brobdingnagian hall lined with mirrors which gave, not the outer physical reflection, but the inner physical reflection. Rather, as Kickaha explained, each mirror detected the waves of a different area of the brain and then synthesized these with music and colors and subsonics and gave them back as visual images. Some were hideous and some beautiful and some outrageously obscene and some almost numinously threatening.

"They don't mean anything," Kickaha said, "unless the viewer wants to interpret what they mean to him. They have no objective meaning."

Do Shuptarp was glad to get on. Then Kickaha took a staircase broad enough for ten platoons of soldiers almost to march up. This wound up and up and seemed never to end, as if it were the staircase to Heaven itself.

XX

FINALLY, THE TEUTONIAC BEGGED FOR A REST; KICKAHA CONSENTED.
He sent the spy-missile up for another look. There were no Bellers on
the floor below that on which the control room was. There were the
burned and melted bodies of ten taloses, all on the first six steps of the
staircase. Apparently, they had been marching up to attack the Bellers
in the control room, and they had been beamed down. The device
which may have done this was crouching at the top of the stairs. It was
a small black box on wheels with a long thin neck of gray metal. At its
end was a tiny bulb. This bulb could detect and beam a moving mass at
a maximum distance of forty feet.

It moved the long neck back and forth to sweep the staircase. It did
not notice the missile as it sped overhead, which meant that the snake-
neck, as Kickaha termed it, was set to detect only larger masses. Kickaha turned the missile and sent it down the hall toward the double
doors of the control room. These were closed. He did see, through the
missile's "eye," that there were many small discs stuck on the walls all
along the corridor—mass-detectors. Their fields were limited, however.
A narrow aisle would be left down the center of the corridor so that the
warned might walk in it without setting off alarms. And there must be
visual devices of some sort out here, too, since the Bellers would not
neglect these. He moved the missile very slowly along the ceiling because he did not want it seen. And then he spotted devices. They were
hidden in the hollowed-out heads of two busts on tops of pedestals. The
hollowing-out had been done by the Bellers.

Kickaha brought the missile back carefully and took off the goggles,
then led Do Shuptarp up the staircase. They had not gone far before

they smelled the burned protoplasm and plastic. When they were on the floor with the carnage, Kickaha stopped the Teutoniac.

"As near as I can figure out," he said, "they're all holed up now in the control room. It's up to us to smoke them out or rush them before they get us. I want you to watch our rear at all times. Keep looking! There are many gates in the control room which transmit you to other places in the palace. If the Bellers have figured them out, they'll be using them. So watch it!"

He was just out of range of the vision and beamer of the snake-neck at the top of the steps. He sat down and frayed out the fibers at one end of his thinnest rope and tied these around the missile. Then he put the goggles back on and directed the missile up the steps. It moved slowly because of the weight of the rope. The snake-neck continued to sweep the field before it, but did not send a beam at the missile or rope. Though this meant that it was set to react to greater masses, it did not mean that it wasn't transmitting a picture to the Bellers in the control room. If they saw the missile and the rope, they might come charging out and shoot down over the railing. Kickaha told Do Shuptarp to watch above, too, and shoot if anything moved.

The missile slid by the snake-neck and then around it, drawing the rope with it. It then came back down the steps. Kickaha removed the goggles, untied the rope, seized the ends of the rope, pulled to make sure he had a snug fit, and yanked. The snake-neck came forward and tumbled halfway down the steps. It lay on its side, its neck-and-eye moving back and forth but turned away from the right side of the staircase. Kickaha approached it from the back and turned it off by twisting a dial at its rear.

He carried the machine back up under one arm while he held a beamer ready in his right hand. Near the top, he got down against the steps and slid the machine onto the floor. Here he turned it so it faced the bust at the end of the hall past the control room doors. He set the dials and then watched it roll out of sight. Presently, there was a loud crash. He dropped the goggles down and sent the missile to take a look. As he had hoped, the snake-neck had gone down the hall until the mass of the pedestal and its bust had set it off. Its beamer had burned through the hollow stone pedestal until it fell over. The bust was lying on its side with the transmitter camera looking at the wall. The snake-neck had turned its beam on the fallen bust.

He went back down the staircase and down the hall until he was out of sight of anyone who might come to the top of the steps or look down the side of the well. He replaced the goggles and took the missile to position above the double doors. The missile, flat against the wall, was standing on its nose and looking straight down.

He waited. Minutes went by. He wanted to take the goggles off so he could make sure that Do Shuptarp was watching everywhere. He restrained the impulse—he had to be ready if the doors opened.

Presently, they did open. A periscopic tube was stuck out and turned in both directions. Then it withdrew and a blond head slowly emerged. The body followed it soon. The Beller ran over to the snake-head and turned it off. Kickaha was disappointed because he had hoped the machine would beam the Beller. However, it scanned and reacted only to objects in front of it.

The bust was completely melted. The Beller looked at it for a while, then picked up the snake-neck and took it into the control room. Kickaha sent the missile in through the upper part of the doorway and up into the high parts of the room, which was large enough to contain an aircraft carrier of 1945 vintage. He shot the missile across the ceiling and down the opposite wall and low to the floor to a place behind a control console. The vision and audio became fuzzy and limited then, which made him think that the doors had been shut. Although the missile could transmit through material objects within a limited range, it lost much of its effectiveness.

Zymathol was telling Arswurd of the strange behavior of the snake-neck. He had replaced it with another, which he hoped would not also malfunction. He had not replaced the camera. The other at the opposite end of the hall could do what was needed. Zymathol regretted that they had been so busy trying to get laser-beam or radio contact with von Turbat on the moon. Otherwise, they might have been watching the monitor screens and seen what had happened.

Kickaha wanted to continue listening, but he had to keep his campaign going. He switched off the missile in the control room and tied the end of the rope to another missile. This he sent up and around the new snake-neck and pulled it down. It tumbled much farther, bringing up short against the pile of talos bodies at the staircase foot. It was pointed up in the air. Kickaha crawled up to it, reached over the bodies, and turned it off. He took it back up the steps and sent it against the pedestal and bust at the other end of the hall. He was down the steps and had his goggles on and another missile on its way before the crash sounded. The crash came to his ears via the missile.

Its eye showed him that the same thing had happened. He turned it to watch the door, but nothing happened for a long time. Finally, he switched to the missile in the control room. Zymathol was arguing that the malfunctioning of the second machine was too coincidental. There was something suspicious happening, something therefore dangerous. He did not want to go outside again to investigate.

Arswurd said that, like it or not, they couldn't stay here and let an invader prowl around. He had to be killed—and the invader was probably Kickaha. Who else could have gotten inside the palace when all the defenses were set up to make it impregnable?

Zymathol said that it couldn't be Kickaha. Would von Turbat and von Swindebarn be up on the moon looking for him if he weren't there?

This puzzled Kickaha. What was von Turbat doing there when he must know that his enemy had escaped via the gate in the cave-chamber? Or was von Turbat so suspicious of his archenemy's wiliness that he thought Kickaha might have gated something through to make it look as if he were no longer on the moon? If so, what could make him think that there was anything on the moon to keep Kickaha there?

He became upset and a trifle frightened then. Could Anana have gated up there after him? Was she being chased by the Bellers? It was a possibility, and it made him anxious.

Zymathol said that only Kickaha could have turned the taloses against them. Arswurd replied that that was all the more reason for getting rid of such a danger. Zymathol asked how.

"Not by cowering in here," Arswurd said.

"Then you go look for him," Zymathol said.

"I will," Arswurd answered.

Kickaha found it interesting that the conversation was so human. The Bellers might be born of metal complexes, but they were not like machines off an assembly line. They had all the differences of personality of humans.

Arswurd started to go to the door, but Zymathol called him back. Zymathol said that their duty demanded they not take unnecessary chances. There were so few of them now that the death of even one greatly lessened their hope of conquest. In fact, instead of aiming for conquest now, they were fighting for survival. Who would have thought that a mere *leblabbiy* could have killed them so ingeniously and relentlessly? Why, Kickaha was not even a Lord—he was only a human being.

Zymathol said they must wait until their two leaders returned. They could not be contacted; something was interfering with attempts to communicate. Kickaha could have told them why their efforts were useless. The structure of the space-time fabric of this universe made a peculiar deformation which would prevent the undistorted transmission of radio or laser. If an aircraft, for instance, were to try to fly between planet and moon, it would break up in a narrow zone partway between the two bodies. The only way to travel from one to the other was by a gate.

The two Bellers talked nervously of many things. Twenty-nine of the original Bellers were dead. There were two here, two in Nimstowl's universe, two in Anana's, two in Judubra's. Zymathol thought that these ought to be recalled to help. Or, better, that the Bellers in this universe should leave and seal off all gates. There were plenty of other universes; why not cut this one off forever? If Kickaha wanted it, he could have it. Meanwhile, in a safe place, they could make millions of new Bellers. In ten years, they would be ready to sweep out the Lords everywhere.

But von Turbat, whom they called Graumgrass, was extraordinarily stubborn. He would refuse to quit. Both agreed on that.

It became evident to Kickaha that Arswurd, despite his insistence on the necessity of leaving the room to find the invader, really did not want to and, in fact, had no intention of doing so. He did need, however, to sound brave to himself.

The two did not seem the unhuman, cold, strictly logical, utterly emotionless beings described to him by Anana. If certain elements were removed from their conversation, they could have been just two soldiers of any nation or universe talking.

For a moment, he wondered if the Bellers could not be reasoned with, if they could be content to take a place in this world as other sentients did.

That feeling passed quickly. The Bellers preferred to take over bodies of human beings; they would not remain enclosed in their metal bells. The delights and advantages of flesh were too tempting. No, they would not be satisfied to remain in the bells; they would keep on stripping human brains and moving into the dispossessed somas.

The war would have to be to the end, that is, until all Bellers or Kickaha died.

At that moment, he felt as if the entire world were a burden on him alone. If they killed him, they could move ahead as they wished, because only a few knew their identities and purposes, and these few would also die. This was his world, as he had bragged, and he was the luckiest man in two worlds, because he alone of Earthmen had been able to get through the wall between the worlds. This, to him, was a world far superior to Earth and he had made it his in a way that even Wolff, the Lord, had not been able to do.

Now, the delights and rewards were gone, replaced by a responsibility so tremendous that he had not thought about it because he could not endure to do so.

For a man with such responsibility, he had acted recklessly.

That was, however, why he had survived so long. If he had proceeded with great caution because he was so important, he probably would have been caught and killed by now. Or he would have escaped but would be totally ineffective, because he would be afraid to take any action. Reckless or not, he would proceed now as he had in the past. If he misjudged, he became part of the past, and the Bellers took over the present and future. So be it.

He switched back to a third missile and placed it against the wall just above the doors. Then he laid the control box and goggles beside him. He told Do Shuptarp what he meant to do next. The Teutoniac thought it was a crazy idea, but he agreed. He didn't have any ideas of his own. They picked up a talos and dragged the body, which possibly weighed five hundred pounds, up the steps. They pulled it down the hall in the aisle between the detector fields and propped it up in front of the doors. Then they retreated hastily but carefully to the floor below.

After taking a quick look, Kickaha replaced the goggles. He lowered the missile above the door, positioned it to one side of the sitting talos, and hurled the missile against the helmet-head of the talos. The impact ruined the missile so that he could not observe its effect. But he quickly sent another up and stationed this above the doors. The talos had fallen as he had wished. Its head and shoulders were within the detector field. The alarms must be ringing wildly inside the control room.

Nothing happened. The doors did not open. He waited until he could endure the suspense no longer. Though it was essential that he keep the missile posted above the doors, he sent it to the floor and then switched back to the missile inside the control room. He could see nothing except the rear of the control console, and he could hear nothing. There were no alarms whooping, so these must have been turned off. The Bellers were not talking or making a sound of any kind, even though he turned the audio amplification up.

He switched back to the missile outside the doors. The doors were closed, so he returned to the device in the room. There was still no noise.

What was going on?

Were they playing a game of Who's-Got-The-Coolest-Nerves? Did they want him to come charging on in?

He returned to the missile in the room and sent it back along the floor to the wall. It went slowly up the wall, the area just ahead of i clear for a foot and then fuzzy beyond that. He intended to put it against the ceiling and then lower it with the hopes that he would see the Bellers before they saw the missile. The missile could be used to kill as a bullet kills, but his range of vision was so limited that he had to be very close. If a Beller yelled, he would betray his position by sound and Kickaha might be able to send the missile at him before the Beller burned the missile down. It was a long chance which he was willing to take now.

He had brought the device down approximately where the control console it had hidden behind should be. The missile came straight down to the floor without seeing or hearing anything. It then rose and circled the area without detecting the Bellers. He expanded the territory of search. The Bellers, of course, could be aware of the missile and could be retreating beyond its range or hiding. This did not make sense unless they wanted to keep the operator of the missile busy while one or more left the room to search for him. They probably did not know exactly how the missile worked, but they must realize that its transmission was limited and that the operator had to be comparatively close.

Kickaha told Do Shuptarp to be especially alert for the appearance of Bellers at the top of the staircase—and to remember to use the neutron grenades if he got a chance. He had no sooner finished saying this than Do Shuptarp yelled. Kickaha was so startled that he threw his hands up. The control box went flying. So did Kickaha. Yanking off the goggles, he rolled over and over at the same time, to spoil the aim of anybody who might be trying to shoot at him. He had no idea of what had made the Teutoniac shout, nor was he going to sit still while he looked around for the source of the alarm.

A beam scorched the rug as it shot on by him. It came from an unexpected place, the far end of the hall. A head and a hand holding a beamer were projecting from a corner. Luckily, Do Shuptarp had fired as soon as he saw the Beller, so the Beller could only get off a wild beam. Then he dodged back. At this distance, a beamer's effectiveness was considerably reduced. At short range it could melt through twelve inches of steel and cook a man through to the gizzard in a second. At this distance it could only give him a third degree burn on his skin or blind him if it struck the eyes.

Do Shuptarp had retreated to the first few bottom steps of the staircase where he was lodged behind the pile of talos bodies. Kickaha ran down the hall away from the opposite end, wary of what might pop out from the near side. One or both of the Bellers in the control room had gated to another part of the palace and had made a flank attack. Or one or both had gated elsewhere to get help from other Bellers.

Kickaha cursed, wheeled, and ran back toward the abandoned goggles and control box. The Beller at the far end popped his head out close to the floor and fired. Do Shuptarp, at a wider angle to the Beller because he was on the staircase, replied with his beam. Kickaha shot, too. The Beller withdrew before the rays, advancing along the rug, could intersect at the corner. The nonflammable rug melted where the beams had made tracks.

The three grenades were too far away to risk time to go for them. Kickaha scooped up the box and goggles, whirled, and dashed back along the corridor. He expected somebody to appear at the near end, so he was ready to pop into the nearest doorway. When he was two doorways from the end, he saw a head coming around a corner. He triggered off a beam, played it along the molding, and then up the corner. The head, however, jerked back before the ray could hit it. Kickaha crouched against the wall and fired past the corner, hoping that some energy would bounce off and perhaps warm up the person or persons hidden around the corner. A yell told him that he had scared or perhaps scorched someone.

He grinned and went back into the doorway before the Bellers would try the same trick on him. This was no grinning business, but he could not help being savagely amused when he put one over on his enemies.

XXI

THE ROOM INTO WHICH HE HAD RETREATED WAS COMPARATIVELY SMALL.
It was like hundreds of others in the palace, its main purpose being to
store art treasures. These were tastefully arranged, however, as if the
room were lived in or at least much visited.

He looked swiftly around for evidence of gates, since there were so
many hidden in the palace that he could not remember more than a
fraction of them. He saw nothing suspicious. This itself meant nothing,
but at this time he had to take things on evidence. Otherwise, he would
not be able to act.

He slipped on the goggles, hating to do so because it left him blind
and deaf to events in the hall. He switched to the missile in the control
room. It was still in the air, circling in obedience to the last order. No
Bellers came within its range. He then transferred to the missile outside
the doors and brought it down the staircase and along the corridor. The
closer it came to him, the stronger its transmission of sight and sound
was. And the better his control.

Do Shuptarp was keeping the Beller at the far end from coming out.
Whoever was at the near end was the immediate danger. He sent the
missile close to the ceiling and around the corner. There were three
Bellers there, each with hand-beamers. The face of one was slightly reddish, as if sunburned. At a distance were two coming down the hall and
pushing a gravsled before them. This bore a huge beamer, the equivalent
of a cannon. Its ray could be sent past the corner to splash off the wall
and keep Kickaha at a distance while the others fired with the hand-
beamers. And then, under the covering fire, the big projector would be
pushed around the corner and its full effect hurled along the length of the
hall. It would burn or melt anything in its path.

Kickaha did not hesitate. He sent the missile at full speed toward the right-hand man pushing the sled. His vision was blurred with the sudden increase of velocity, then the scene went black. The missile had buried itself in the flesh of the Beller or had hit something else so hard it had wrecked itself. He took another missile from the box, which he had unharnessed from his back and laid beside him, and he sent it up out of the room and along the ceiling. Abruptly, a Beller, yelling to disconcert anyone who might be in the hall, sprang out from around the corner. He saw the missile and raised his beamer. Kickaha sent it toward him, pressing the full-speed button on the control box. The scene went black. It was deep in the target's flesh, or ruined against the hard floor or wall, or melted by the beamer.

He did not dare to take the time to send another missile out to look. If the Beller had escaped it, he would be looking into the doorways now for the operator of the missile. And he probably had called the others out to help him.

Kickaha snatched off the goggles and, beamer in one hand and goggles in the other, strode to the door. He had left the door open for better control and vision of the missile. In a way, this was a good thing because the Beller would look in the rooms with closed doors first. But, as he neared the doorway, he confronted a Beller. Kickaha was holding his beamer in front of his chest; he squeezed the trigger as the man's shoulder came in sight. The Beller turned black, smoke rose from skin frying and shredding away in layers, the whites of the eyes became a deep brown and then the aqueous humor in the balls shot out boiling, the hair went up in a stinking flame, the white teeth became black, the lips swelled and then disappeared in layers, the ears became ragged and ran together in rolls of gristle. The clothes, fireproof, melted away.

All this took place in four seconds. Kickaha kicked the door shut and pressed the plate to lock it. Then he was across the room and pushing the plate which turned off the energy field across the window. He threw the missile box out so it could not be used by the Bellers. He tied one end of the rope to a post on a bureau and he crawled out the window. Below was a hundred thousand feet of air. This part of the palace projected over the edge of the monolith; if he cared to, he could sweep almost half its area with a turn of his head. At this moment, he did not want to think about the long, long fall. He kept his eyes on the little ledge about six feet below the end of the rope. He slid down the rope until he was near the end, then he swung out a little and let loose as he swung back in. He dropped with both feet firmly on the ledge and both hands braced against the sides of the window. His knees, bent slightly forward, were perilously close to the invisible force field.

Keeping one hand against the side of the window, he removed his shirt, wrapped a hand in it and then took a knife out. Slowly he moved the knife in the shirt-wrapped hand forward. His head was turned away and his eyes were shut. The force field, activated by the knife, would burn it, and the energy would probably lash out and burn the cloth and the hand beneath. The energy might even hurl the knife away with such violence that it would jerk his arm and him along with it on out the window.

He did have hopes, however, that the field would not be on. This did not seem likely, since Wolff surely would have set all guards and traps before leaving—if he had time. And the Bellers certainly would have done so if Wolff had failed.

A light burned even through his shut eyelids. A flame licked at his face and his bare shoulders and ribs and legs. The knife bucked in his hand, but he kept it within range of the field even when the cloth smoldered and burst into flames and his hand felt as if it had been thrust in an oven.

Then he plunged on through the window and onto the floor. There was a two-second pause before recharge of the field after activation, and he had jumped to coincide with it, he hoped. That he was still alive, though hurt, was proof that he had timed himself correctly. The knife was a twist of red-hot metal on the floor. The shirt was charred off, and his hand was blackened and beginning to blister. At another time, he would have been concerned with this. Now, he had no truck with anything except major crippling injuries. Or with death.

At that moment, the rope fell by the window, its end smoking. The projector had burned through the door and burned off the rope. In a moment, the Bellers would be coming downstairs after him. As for poor Do Shuptarp, he had better look out for himself and fast. The big projector would undoubtedly be used on him first to clear him out of the way. If only he had sense enough to get up the staircase and away, he could cause the Bellers to split their forces.

Kickaha looked out the doorway, saw no one, and fled down the corridor. On coming to the foot of the staircase, he looked upward before crossing in front of it. No Bellers were in sight yet. He ran on down the hall and then down the unusually long staircase and on across the corridor and past the hall of retropsychical mirrors. He had passed several elevators but did not enter them because they might be booby-trapped or at least have monitoring devices. His goal was a room which contained a secret gate he had not wished to use before this. Nor would he use it now unless he was forced to do so. But he wanted to be near it in case he was cornered.

In the room, he disassembled a chair that looked solid and pulled out a crescent from a recess under the seat.

Another crescent came from under the base of a thick pedestal for a statue. Both, though they looked as if each weighed half a ton, were light and easy to move. He stuck the two crescents into the back of his belt and tightened the belt to hold them. They were awkward but were insurance, worth the inconvenience.

There were thousands of such hidden gate-halves all over the palace and other thousands unmarked, in open places. The latter could be used by anybody, but the user would not know what waited for him at the other end of the passage. Even Wolff could not remember where all were hidden or the destinations of all the unconcealed ones. He had them all listed in a code-recorder but the recorder was itself disguised and in the control room.

Kickaha had run fast and gone far but not swiftly enough. A Beller appeared at the far end of the corridor as he stepped out of the room. Another looked around the corner of the corridor at the opposite end. They must have caught sight of him as he ran and had come this way with the hope of catching him. One at least had been intelligent enough to run on past where he was and come down the staircase to intercept him.

Kickaha retreated, deactivated the force field, and looked out the window. There was a ledge about fifty feet below, but he had nothing with which to lower himself. And he did not want to test another field unless he absolutely had to do so. He went back to the door and stuck the beamer out without putting his head out first, and fired in both directions. There were yells, but they were so far away that he was sure he had not hit anyone. The door of the room across from his was closed. He could dash across the hall and into it on the chance that it might offer a better route of escape. But if the door was locked, and it could easily be, then he would be exposed to fire from both sides, and they would have a better chance to catch him during the recrossing.

It was too late for regrets now. If he had not stopped to get the gate, he could have still been ahead of them. Again he was cornered, and though he had a way out, he did not want to use it. Getting back into the palace would be far more difficult a second time. And Do Shuptarp would be left on his own. Kickaha felt as if he were deserting him, but he could not help it.

He put the two crescents together to form a circle. He straightened up just as a grenade struck the inside of the doorway and ricocheted inside the room. It rolled about five feet and stopped, spinning on its axis. It was about thirty feet from him, which meant that he was out of range of the neutrons. But there would be others tossed in, the two he had left behind, and perhaps the Bellers had more. In any event, they would be bringing up the big projector. No use putting off the inevitable until it was too late to do even that.

XXII

HE STEPPED INTO THE GATE. AND HE WAS IN THE TEMPLE-CHAMBER OF Talanac. Anana and the Red Beards and a number of Tishquetmoac were there. They were standing to one side and talking. They saw him and jumped or yelled or just looked startled. He started to step forward and then they were gone. The sky was starless, but a small glowing object raced across the sky from west to east and a slower one plodded along to the west. The leaning Tower of Pisa mass of the planet hung bright in the heavens. At a distance, the marble buildings of Korad gleamed whitely in the planet-light. A hundred yards away, a platoon of Drachelander soldiers were becoming aware that someone had appeared in the gate. And over a hill a dark object was rising. The Beller aircraft.

Then all was gone. He was in a cave about ten feet across and eight feet high. The sun shone brightly against the entrance. A giant, crazily angled tree with huge azure hexagram-shaped leaves stood in the distance. Beyond it were some scarlet bushes and green vines that rose seemingly without support, like a rope rising into the air at the music of a Hindu sorcerer. Beyond those were a thin blue line and a white thread and a thin black line. The sea, surf, and a black sand beach.

He had been here several times before. This was one of the gates he used to get to the lowest level, the Garden level, on his "vacations."

Though numbed, he knew that he had been caught in a resonant circuit. Somewhere, somebody had set up a device which would trap a person who stepped into any of the gates in the circuit. The caught one could not step out because the activation time was too short. That is, he could but he would be cut in half, one part left behind, the other gated on to the next circle.

The cave disappeared, and he was on top of a high narrow peak set among other peaks. Far to one side, visible through a pass, was what looked like the Great Plains. Certainly, that must be an immense herd of buffalo which covered the brown-green prairie like a black sea. A hawk soared by, screaming at him. It had an emerald-green head and spiraling feathers down its legs. As far as he knew, this hawk was confined to the Amerind level.

Then that was gone, and he was in a cave again. This was larger than the Garden cave and darker. There were wires clipped to the crescents of the gate; these ran across the dirt floor and behind a huge boulder about twenty feet away. Somewhere, an alarm was ringing. There was a cabinet with open doors by the far wall. The shelves contained weapons and devices of various kinds. He recognized this cave and also knew that here must be where the resonance originated. But the trapper was not in sight, though he soon would be, if he were within earshot of the alarms.

Then that was gone, and he was in a chamber of stone slabs which were leaning in one direction as if they had been pushed by a giant hand, and part of the roof was fallen in. The sky was a bright green. The monolith of which he could see part was thin and black and soaring, so he knew by this that he was in an Atlantean chamber and that the shaft of stone was that which supported the palace of the Lord, a hundred thousand feet up.

Then that was gone, and he was where he had started his hopscotch willy-nilly journey. He was standing in the crescents in the room in the palace. Two Bellers were goggling at him, and then they were raising their beamers. He shot first, because he expected to have to use his weapon, bringing the ray across the chests of both.

Thirty-four down. Sixteen to go.

That was gone. Anana and the Thyuda were standing by the gate now. He shouted to her, "Resonant circuit! Trapped!" and he was back on the moon. The aircraft was a little closer now, coming down the hillside. Probably the occupants had not seen him yet, but they would on the next go-around or the one after that. And all they had to do then was to keep a ray across the gate, and he would be cut down as soon as he appeared.

The Drachelander soldiers were running toward him now; several were standing still but were winding up the wires of their crossbows. Kickaha, not wishing to attract the attention of the Bellers in the craft, refrained from discouraging the soldiers with his beamer.

He followed the Garden cave. And then he was upon the top of the peak in the Amerind level and very startled because the hawk flew into the area of the gate just as he appeared. The hawk was as startled as he. It screamed and landed on his chest and sank its talons in. Kickaha placed one hand before his face to protect it, felt agony as the hawk's beak sank into the hand which was burned, and he shoved outward. The hawk was torn loose by the push, but it took gobbets of flesh of chest and hand with it. It was propelled out of the circle but was not cut in half. The feathers of one wing-tip were sheared off, and that was all. Its movement coincided with the border of the field as the gate action commenced. And it passed over the border in the cave on the Dracheland level, and into the chamber itself.

It was unplanned split-second timing.

The enormously fat man who had just entered the cave was holding a dead, half-charred rabbit in one hand and a beamer in the other. He had expected a man or woman to appear though he could not, of course, know just when. But he had not expected a shrieking fury of talons and beak in his face.

Kickaha got a chance to see Judubra drop the rabbit and beamer and throw his hands up in front of his face. Then he was in the ruins of the Atlantean chamber. He squatted down and leaped upward as high and as straight as he could so no part of him would be outside the limits of the circle. He was at the height of his leap, with his legs pulled up, when he appeared in the palace room. His leap, designed to take him above a ray which might be shot across the circle to cut him in half, was unnecessary. The two Bellers lay on the floor, blackened, their clothes burned off. The odor of deeply burned flesh choked the room. He did not know what had happened, but the next time around, there should be Bellers in this room. They would not, he hoped, know any more than he did about what was happening. They would be mystified, but they would have to be stupid not to know that the killer had popped back into the gate and then popped out again. They would be waiting.

He was in the gate of the temple in Talanac. Anana was gone. The priest, Withrus, shouted at him, "She jumped in! She's caught, too, and she . . ."

He was on the moon. The craft was closer but had not increased its speed. And then a beam of light shot out from its nose and centered full on him. The Bellers in the craft had suddenly noticed the excitement of the troops running toward the gate and the crossbowmen aiming at it. They had turned on the light to find out the cause of the uproar.

There was a twang as the crossbowmen released their darts. And he was in the cave on the Garden level. Next stop, the little flat area on top of the peak. He looked down at his chest, which was dripping blood, and at his hand, which was also bloody. He hurt but not as much as he would later. He was still numb to lesser pains; the big pain was his situation and the inevitable end. Either the fat man in the cave would get him or the Bellers would. The fat man, after ridding himself of the hawk, could hide behind the boulder and beam him as he appeared. Of course, there was the hope that the fat man wanted to capture him.

He was in the cave. The hawk and the fat man lay dead, blackened, and the odor of fried feathers and flesh jammed his nostrils. There was only one explanation: Anana, riding ahead of him in the circuit, had beamed both of them. The fat man must still have been struggling with the hawk and so Anana had caught him.

If he had doubted that she loved him, he now had proof that she did —she had been willing to sacrifice her life in an effort to save him. She had done so with almost no thought; there had been very little time for her to see what was happening, but she had done it quickly and even more quickly she had hurled herself into the gate. She must have known that only if she went through exactly after activation would she get through unsevered. And she had no way of telling the exact moment to jump; she had seen him appear and disappear and then taken the chance.

She loved him for sure, he thought.

And if she could get in without being hurt, then he could get out.

The Atlantean ruins materialized like a gigantic pop-up, and he leaped outward. He landed on the floor of the room in the palace, but not untouched. His heel hurt as if a rat had gashed it. A sliver of skin at the edge of the heel had been taken off by the deactivating field.

Then something appeared. Anana. She said, "Objects! Throw them in . . ." and was gone.

He did not have to stop to think what she meant because he had hoped before that she would take these means to stop the resonant circuit. Aside from turning off the activating device, the only way to stop the circuit was to put objects with enough mass into an empty gate. Eventually, when all the gates were occupied, the circuit would stop.

The obvious method of separating the crescents of a gate would not work in this case. A resonant circuit set up a magnetic attraction between the crescents of the gates that could not be broken except by some devices in the palace. And these would be locked up in the armory.

Keeping his eye on the door, and with the beamer ready, he dragged the body of a Beller by one hand to the crescent. He was counting the seconds in an effort to figure the approximate time when she would next appear here. And while he was counting, he saw out of the side of his eye, five objects come into being in the gates and go out of being. There was a barrel, the torso of a Drachelander soldier severed at the belly, half a large silver coffer with jewels spilling out of it, a large statue of jade, and the headless, legless, almost wingless body of a green eagle.

He was in a frenzy of anxiety. The Thyuda in Talanac must be obeying her orders, given just before she leaped into the gate. They were throwing objects into the gate as fast as possible. But the circuit might stop now when she was on the moon, and if it did, she would assuredly be caught or killed.

And then as he was about to topple the body of the Beller into the gate, Anana appeared. And she did not vanish again.

Kickaha was so delighted that he almost forgot to watch the doorway. "Luck's holding out!" he cried and then, realizing that he might be heard outside the room, said softly, "The chances for the circuit stopping while you were here were almost nothing! I . . ."

"It wasn't chance," she said. She stepped out of the gate and put her arms around him and kissed him. He would have been delighted at any other time. Now he said, "Later, Anana. The Bellers!"

She stepped away and said, "Nimstowl will be here in a second. Don't shoot."

The little man was there all of a sudden. He held a beamer in one hand and a beamer in his belt. He also wore a knife and carried a rope coiled around one shoulder. Kickaha had turned his beamer away from the door and held it on Nimstowl. The Lord said, "No need for that. I'm your ally."

"Until . . . ?" Kickaha said.

"All I want to do is to get back to my own world," Nimstowl said. "I've had more than enough of this killing and almost being killed. In the name of Shambarimen, isn't one world enough for one man?"

Kickaha did not believe him, but he decided that Nimstowl could be trusted until the last of the Bellers was dead. He said, "I don't know what's going on out there. I had expected an attack, but it would have been launched before now. They had a large beamer out there; they could have shot it in here by now and cooked us out."

He asked Anana what had happened, though he could guess part of it. She replied that Nimstowl had come into the cave to find his partner dead, caught by the one he had trapped. Nimstowl had decided that he was tired of hiding out in this cave. He wanted a chance to get back to his own world and, of course, as every Lord should, to wipe out the Bellers. He had turned the resonating device off when Anana had appeared again. It had taken only a few seconds after that to set the resonator so it would deliver two people, at safe intervals, into the palace where Anana had seen Kickaha.

He said, "What do you mean? I had to jump out! I got out but lost the skin off my heel."

"Of course, you had no way of knowing," she said. "But if you had not jumped, you could have stepped out quite safely a moment later."

"Anyway, you came after me," he said. "That's what counts."

She was looking at him with concern. He was burned and bleeding, still dripping blood on the floor. But she said nothing. There was nothing to do for him until they found some aid. And that could be close enough, if they could get out of this room.

Somebody had to stick his head out of the room. Nimstowl wasn't going to volunteer and Kickaha did not want Anana to do it. So he looked out. Instead of the beam he expected, he saw a deserted corridor. He motioned for them to come after him and led the way to a room about a quarter of a mile down the corridor. Here he sterilized his wounds and burns, put pseudoflesh over them, and drank potions to unshock him and to accelerate blood replenishment. They also ate and drank while they discussed what to do.

There wasn't much to talk about. The only thing to do was to explore until they found out what was going on.

XXIII

NOT UNTIL THEY CAME TO THE GREAT STAIRCASE WHICH LED UP TO THE floor of the control room did they find anything. There was a dead Beller, his legs almost entirely burned off. And behind a charred divan lay another Beller. This one was burned on the side, but the degree of burn indicated that the beam's energy had been partially absorbed before striking him. He was still alive.

Kickaha approached him cautiously and, after making sure he wasn't playing possum, Kickaha knelt down by him. He intended to use rough methods to bring him to consciousness so he could question him. But the Beller opened his eyes when his head was raised.

"Luvah!" Anana cried. "It's Luvah! My brother! One of my brothers! But what's he doing here? How . . . ?"

She was holding an object which she must have picked up from behind the divan or some other piece of furniture. It was about two and a half feet long, was of some silvery material, and was curved and shaped much like the horn of an African buffalo. It did flare out widely at the mouth, however, and the tip was fitted with a mouthpiece of some soft golden material. Seven little buttons sat on top of the horn in a row.

He recognized the Horn of Shambarimen. Hope lifted him to his feet with a surge. He said, "Wolff is back!"

"Wolff?" Anana said. "Oh, Jadawin! Yes, perhaps. But what is Luvah doing here?"

Luvah had a face that, under normal circumstances, would have been appealing. He was a Lord, but he could easily have passed for a certain type of Irishman with his snub nose and broad upper lip and freckles and pale blue eyes.

Kickaha said, "You talk to him. Maybe he'll . . ."

She got to her knees by Luvah and spoke to him. He seemed to recognize her, but his expression could have meant anything. She said, "He may not remember me in his condition. Or he may be frightened. He could think I'm going to kill him. I am a Lord, remember."

Kickaha ran down the hall and into a room where he could get water. He brought a pitcher of it back and Luvah drank eagerly. Luvah then whispered his story to Anana. She rose a few minutes later and said, "He was caught in a trap set by Urizen, our father. Or so he thought at the time, though actually it was Vala, our sister. He and Jadawin—Wolff —became friends. Wolff and his woman Chryseis were trapped with others, another brother and some cousins. He says it's too long a story to tell now. But only Luvah and Wolff and Chryseis survived. They returned by using the Horn; it can match the resonance of any gate, you know, unless that gate is set for intermittent resonance at random.

"They were gated back into a secret compartment of the control room. Wolff then took a look into the control room via a monitor. No one was in it. He tapped in on other videos and saw a number of dead men and taloses. Of course, he didn't know that the men were Black Bellers, at first; then he saw the caskets. He still didn't get the connection—after all, it's been, what, ten thousand years? But he gated into the control room with Chryseis. Just to have additional insurance, he gated Luvah into a room on a lower floor. If somebody attacked them in the control room, Luvah could slip up behind them."

"Wolff's cagey," said Kickaha. He had wondered why Wolff didn't see the live Bellers, but remembered that the palace was so huge that Wolff could have spent days looking into every room. He was probably so eager to get some rest after his undoubtedly harrowing adventures and so glad to be home that he had rushed things somewhat. Besides, the control room and the surrounding area were unoccupied.

"Luvah said he came up the staircase and was going to enter the control room to tell Wolff all was clear. At that very moment, two men appeared in an especially big gate that had been set up by the dead men. By the Bellers, of course. There were pieces of a disassembled craft with them and a big projector."

"Von Turbat and von Swindebarn!" Kickaha said.

"It must have been," Anana said. "They knew something was wrong, what with your appearance and disappearance in the gate on the moon and then mine. They gave up their search, and—"

"Tell me the rest while I'm carrying Luvah," he said. "We'll get him to a room where we can treat his burns."

With Nimstowl covering their rear and Anana their front, he lugged the unconscious Lord to the room where he had treated himself a short while ago. Here he applied antishock medicines, blood replenishers, and pseudoflesh to Luvah.

Anana meanwhile finished Luvah's story. The two chief Bellers, it seemed, had expected trouble and were ready. They fired their big projector and forced Wolff and Chryseis to take refuge among the many titanic consoles and machines. Luvah had dived for cover behind a console near the doorway. The two Bellers had kept up a covering fire while a number of troops came through. And with them was a creature that seemed strange to Luvah but Anana recognized the description as that of Podarge. From the glimpse Luvah got of her, she seemed to be unconscious. She was being carried by several soldiers.

"Podarge! But I thought she had used one of the gates in the cave to get off the moon," Kickaha said. "I wonder. . . . Do you suppose?"

Despite the seriousness of the situation, he couldn't help chuckling. One of the gates would have taken her to a cave in a mountain on the Atlantean level. There would have been six or seven gates there, all marked to indicate the level to which they would transport the user. But all lied, and only Kickaha, Wolff, and Chryseis knew the code. So she had used a crescent which would presumably take her to the Amerind level, where she would be comparatively close to her home.

But she found herself back on the moon, in the very same cave.

Why, then, were there only four crescents, when her return should have made the number five?

Podarge was crafty, too. She must have gated out something to leave only four crescents. And since Do Shuptarp had not mentioned finding great white ape cubs in the cave, she must have gated them out. Why didn't she try some of the other crescents? Perhaps because she was suspicious and thought that Kickaha had used the only good one. Who knows what motives that mad bird-woman had? In any event, she had elected to remain on the moon. And the Bellers may have been hunting her in the ruins of Korad when Kickaha saw them while he was in the resonant circuit.

Luvah had been forced out of the control room by the soldiers, some of whom had beamers. This surprised Kickaha. The Bellers must have been very desperate to give the Drachelanders these weapons.

So Luvah had had to retreat, but he had killed a number of his pursuers while doing so. Then he had been badly burned but even so had managed to burn down those left. Six of the killed were wearing caskets on their backs.

"Wolff! Chryseis!" Kickaha said. "We have to get up there right now! They may need us!"

Despite his frenzy, he managed to check himself and to proceed cautiously as they neared the control room. They passed charred bodies along the way, evidences of Luvah's good fight.

Kickaha led the others at a pace faster than caution demanded, but he felt that Wolff might be needing him at the moment. The path to the control room was marked with charred corpses and damage to the furniture and walls. The stink of crisped flesh became stronger the closer they got to their goal. He dreaded to enter the room. It would be tragic indeed, and heart-twisting, if Wolff and Chryseis survived so much only to be killed as they came home.

He steeled himself, but, when he ran crouching into the room, the vast place was as silent as a worm in a corpse. There were dead everywhere, including four more Black Bellers, but neither Wolff nor Chryseis were there.

Kickaha was relieved that they had escaped—but to where? A search revealed where they had taken a last stand. It was in a corner of the back wall and behind a huge bank of video monitors. The screens were shattered from the beamer rays, and the metal of the cabinet was cut or melted. Bodies lay here and there behind consoles—Drachelander troops caught by Wolff's or Chryseis' beams.

Von Turbat (Graumgrass) and von Swindebarn were dead, too. They lay by the big projector, which had continued to radiate until its power-pack had run down. The wall it was aimed at had a twelve foot hole in its metal and a still-hot lava puddle at its base. Von Turbat had been cut almost in half; Von Swindebarn was fried from the hips up. Their caskets were still strapped to their backs.

"There's only one Beller unaccounted for," Kickaha said. He returned to the corner where Wolff and Chryseis had fought. A large gray metal disc was attached to the metal floor here. It had to be a new gate which Wolff had placed here since Kickaha's last visit to the palace.

He said, "Anana, maybe we can find out where this gate goes to, if Wolff recorded it in his code book. He must have left a message for me, if he had time. But the Bellers may have destroyed it.

"First, we have to locate that one Beller. If he got out of here, gated back to your universe or Nimstowl's or Judubra's, then we have a real problem."

Anana said, "It's so frightening! Why don't the Lords quit fighting among themselves and unite to get rid of the Beller?"

She edged away. Her anxiety and near-panic at the tolling in her brain, generated by her nearness to the Bellers' caskets, was evident.

"I have to get out of here," she said. "Or at least some distance away."

"I'll look over the corpses again," he said. "You go—hold it! Where's Nimstowl?"

"He was here," she said. "I thought that . . . no, I don't know when he disappeared!"

Kickaha was irked because she had not been keeping her eye on the little Lord. But he did not comment, since nothing was to be gained by expressing anger. Besides, the recent events were enough to sidetrack anyone, and the tolling in her mind had distracted her.

She left the room in a hurry. He went through the room, checking every body, looking everywhere.

"Wolff and Chryseis sure gave a good account of themselves," he muttered. "They really banked their shots to get so many behind the consoles. In fact, they gave too good an account. I don't believe it."

And Podarge?

He went to the doorway, where Anana crouched on sentry duty.

"I can't figure it out," he said. "If Wolff killed all his attackers, a very unlikely thing, why did he and Chryseis have to gate on out? And how the hell did Wolff manage to beam the two Bellers when they should have fried him at the first shot with that projector? And where is Podarge? And the missing Beller?"

"Perhaps she gated out, too, during the fight," Anana said. "Or flew out of the control room."

"Yeah, and where is Nimstowl? Come on. Let's start looking."

Anana groaned. He did not blame her. Both were drained of energy, but they could not stop now. He urged her up and soon they were examining the bodies in the corridors outside the control room on the staircase. He verified that he had killed two Bellers with the spy-missiles. While they were looking at a burned man rayed during the fight with Luvah, they heard a moan.

Beamers ready, they approached an overturned bureau from two directions. They found Nimstowl behind the furniture, sitting with his back against the wall. He was holding his right side while blood dripped through his fingers. Near him lay a man with a casket strapped to his back.

This was the missing Beller. He had a knife up to the hilt in his belly. Nimstowl said, "He had a beamer, but the charge must have been depleted. He tried to sneak up and kill me with a knife. Me! With a knife!"

Kickaha examined Nimstowl's wound. Though the blood was flowing freely, the wound wasn't deep. He helped the little Lord to his feet, then he made sure that Nimstowl had no weapons concealed on him. He half-carried him to the room where Luvah lay sleeping, put pseudoflesh on Nimstowl's wound and gave him some blood replenishers.

Nimstowl said, "He might have gotten me at that, he jumped at me so quickly. But this"—he held up a hand with a large ring just like Anana's—"warned me in time."

"All the Bellers are dead," Anana said.

"It's hard to believe!" he replied. "At last! And I killed the last one!"

Kickaha smiled at that but did not comment. He said, "All right, Nimstowl, on your feet. And don't try anything. I'm locking you up for a while."

Again, he frisked Nimstowl. The little Lord was indignant. He yelled, "Why are you doing this to me?"

"I don't believe in taking chances. I want to check you out. Come on. There's a room down the hall where I can lock you up until I'm sure about you."

Nimstowl protested all the way. Kickaha, before shutting the door on him, said, "What were you doing so far from the control room? You were supposed to be with us. You weren't running out on us, were you?"

"So what if I was?" Nimstowl said. "The fight was won, or at least I thought it was. I meant to get back to my universe before the bitch Anana tried to kill me, now that she didn't need me. I couldn't trust you to control her. Anyway, it's a good thing I did leave you. If I hadn't, that Beller might have gotten away or managed to ambush you."

"You may be right," Kickaha said. "But you stay here for a while, anyway." He shut the door and locked it by pressing a button on the wall.

XXIV

AFTER THAT, HE AND ANANA CONTINUED THE LONG SEARCH. THEY could have cut down the room-to-room legwork if they had been able to use the video monitors in the control room, since many rooms and corridors could be seen through these. But Wolff had deactivated these when he left the palace, knowing that Kickaha was able to turn them on if he revisited the palace. The Bellers had not been able to locate the source of control, and they had not had time or enough hands to disassemble the control console and rewire it. Now Kickaha could not use them because the fight had put them out of commission.

They looked through hundreds of rooms and dozens of corridors and scores of staircases and yet had covered only a small part of the one building. And they had many wings to go.

They decided they had to get food and sleep. They checked in on Luvah, who was sleeping comfortably, and they ordered a meal from the kitchen. There were several taloses there, the only taloses not involved in the attack on the Bellers. These gated a meal through to the two. After eating, Kickaha decided to go up to the control room to make sure nothing important had happened. He had some hopes that Wolff might come back, though this did not seem likely. The chances were high that the gate was one-way unless the Horn of Shambarimen were used, and Luvah had had that.

They trudged back up the staircases, Kickaha did not dare use the elevators until he was certain they were not booby-trapped. Just before they went into the control room, he stopped.

"Did you hear something?"

She shook her head. He gestured to her to cover him and he leaped through the doorway and rolled onto the floor and up behind a control console. Listening, he lay there for a while. Presently, he heard a low moan. Silence followed. Then another moan. He snaked across the floor from console to console, following the sounds. He was surprised, though not shocked, when he found the Harpy, Podarge, slumped against a console. Her feathers were blackened and stinking; her legs were charred so deeply that some of the toes had fallen off. Her breasts were brown-red meat. A half-melted beamer lay near her, a talon clutched around its butt.

She had come into the room while he and Anana were gone, and somebody had beamed her. Still on his belly, he investigated and within a minute found the responsible person. This was the soldier, Do Shuptarp, whom he had supposed was slain by the Bellers. But, now that he thought back, he had not been able to identify any corpse as his. This was not unexpected, since many were too burned to be recognizable.

Do Shuptarp, then, had escaped the Bellers and probably fled to the upper stories. He had returned to find out what was happening. Podarge had also returned after her flight from the room during the battle between the Bellers and Wolff. And the two, who really had no cause for conflict, had fatally burned each other.

Kickaha spoke to the Teutoniac, who muttered something. Kickaha bent close to him. The words were almost unintelligible, but he caught some of them. They were not in German. They were in Lord-speech!

Kickaha returned to Podarge. Her eyes were open and dulling, as if layer upon layer of thin veils were slowly being laid over them. Kickaha said, "Podarge! What happened?"

The Harpy moaned and then said something, and Kickaha was startled again. She spoke, not in Mycenaean, but in Lord-speech!

And after that she died.

He called Anana in. While she stood guard, he tried to question Do Shuptarp. The Teutoniac was in deep shock and dying swiftly. But he seemed to recognize Kickaha for just a moment. Perhaps the lust to live surged up just enough for him to make a plea which would have saved him—if Kickaha had had mercy.

"My bell . . . over there . . . put it . . . my head . . . I'll be . . ."

His lips twitched; something gurgled in his throat. Kickaha said, "You took over Do Shuptarp, didn't you, instead of killing him? Who were you?"

"Ten thousand years," the Beller murmured. "And then . . . you."

The eyes became as if dust had sifted into the brain. The jaw dropped like a drawbridge to release the soul—if a Beller had a soul. And why not, if anyone did? The Bellers were deadly enemies, peculiarly horrible because of their method of possession. But in actuality they were no more vicious or deadly than any human enemy, and though possession seemed especially horrible, it was not so to the victim, whose mind was dead before the Beller moved into the body.

Kickaha said, "A third Beller usurped Do Shuptarp's brain. He must have taken off for the upper stories then, figuring that if his buddies didn't get me, he would later. He thought I'd accept him as Do Shuptarp.

"Now, there's Podarge. I would have said a Beller had transferred to her on the moon, but that couldn't be. There were only two Bellers, von Turbat and von Swindebarn, on the moon. And Luvah said he saw them gate into the control room. So the transference must have taken place after Wolff and Chryseis had gotten away. One of those two Bellers took over Podarge, but not until the two had rayed down the Drachelander troops with them to make it look as if everybody had been killed by Wolff and Chryseis.

"Then they switched to Podarge and one soldier they must have spared for this purpose. And the Beller in that soldier was the one who jumped Nimstowl. So now von Turbat and von Swindebarn are dead, despite their trickery! And the Beller in Podarge's body was to pretend that she had given up the attempt to get me, I'll bet. She was to plead friendship, act as if she'd really repented. And when my guard was down, powie! It's real funny, you know. Neither the Podarge-Beller nor the Do Shuptarp-Beller knew the other was a Beller in disguise. So they killed each other!"

He whooped with laughter. But, suddenly, he became thoughtful.

"Wolff and Chryseis are marooned somewhere. Let's go to his library and look up the code book. If he's logged that gate, then we can know how to operate it and where they are."

They walked toward the door. Kickaha hung back a little because the sight of Podarge saddened him. She had Anana's face, and that alone was enough to make him downcast, because she looked like Anana dead. Moreover, the madness of the Harpy, the torment she had endured for 3,200 years, weighed him down. She could have been put into a woman's body again, if she had accepted Wolff's offer. But she was too deep in her madness; she wanted to suffer and also wanted to get a horrible revenge on the man who had placed her in the Harpy's body.

Anana stopped so suddenly that he almost bumped into her.

"That tolling!" she said. "It's started again!"

She screamed and at the same time brought her beamer up. Kickaha had already fired. He directed his ray perilously close to her, at the doorway, even before anyone appeared in it. It was on full-power now, raised from burning effect to cutting effect. It sliced off a piece of Nimstowl's left shoulder.

Then Nimstowl jumped back.

Kickaha ran to the doorway but did not go through.

"He's von Turbat or von Swindebarn!" Kickaha yelled. He was thinking furiously. One of the two chiefs had possessed Podarge; the other had switched to a soldier. Then they had burned their former bodies and left the control room, each to go his own way with the hopes of killing their enemies.

The one in the soldier's body had attacked Nimstowl. Perhaps he had actually wounded Nimstowl. He had, however, managed to switch to the Lord.

No, that could not be, since it required two Bellers to make a switch. One had to handle the bell-shape for the transfer of the other.

Then Podarge—rather, the Beller in her body—must have been with the one in the soldier's body. She must have performed the transference and then left. The Beller in Nimstowl's body had put a knife in the belly of the soldier, who must have been knocked out before the switch.

The change to Nimstowl might have worked, if Kickaha had not operated on his usual basis of suspicion. Somehow, the Nimstowl-Beller had gotten out of the locked room. With what? A small low-power beamer hidden in a body cavity?

The Nimstowl-Beller had come back hoping to catch Kickaha and Anana unaware. If he had been successful, he would have been able to fulfill the Beller's plans of conquest. But he had not been able to resist taking his bell with him and so Anana had detected its presence just in time.

Podarge may have been the one to help effect the transference for the soldier-Beller into Nimstowl. But if she were not the one, then there was an extra Beller to be identified, located, and killed.

First, the business of the Nimstowl-Beller.

Kickaha had waited long enough. If the Beller were running away, then he could have gotten far enough so that Kickaha could leave the control room safely. If the Beller were lying out in the corridor bleeding to death—or bled to death—then Kickaha could go into the corridor. If the Beller were not too badly wounded, he might be waiting for Kickaha to come out.

Whatever the situation, Kickaha could not wait any longer.

He motioned to Anana to stand aside. He backed up a few paces, then ran forward and leaped through the doorway. He turned as he soared, his beamer already on, its ray flashing along the wall and digging a two inch deep trough in the marble, striking out blindly but ready to move down or outward to catch the Beller.

The Beller was crumpled against the base of the wall with blood pooling from around his shoulder. His beamer lay at his feet, his head was thrown back, and his jaw sagged. His skin was bluish.

Kickaha landed, shut the beamer off, and slowly approached the Beller. Convinced that he was harmless, Kickaha bent over him. Nimstowl looked at him with eyes in which the life was not yet withdrawn.

"We're a doomed people," the Beller croaked. "We had everything in our favor, and yet we've been defeated by one man."

"Who are you?" Kickaha said. "Graumgrass or the one calling himself von Swindebarn?"

"Graumgrass. The king of the Bellers. I was in von Turbat's body and then that soldier's."

"Who helped you transfer to Nimstowl—to this body?" Kickaha said.

The Beller looked surprised. "You don't know?" he said faintly. "Then there is still hope for us."

Anana unsnapped the casket from the Beller's harness. She opened it and, grimacing, removed the big black bell-shape. She said, "You may think you will die without telling us who that Beller is and what he is going to do. But you won't."

She said, "Kickaha, hold his head! I'm going to put the bell on it!"

Graumgrass tried to struggle but was too weak to do anything except writhe a little. Finally, he said, "What are you going to do?"

"Your mind contents will automatically be transferred to the bell," she said. "As you well know. This body will die, but we'll find you a healthy body. And we'll put your mind in it. And when we do, we'll torture you until you tell us what we wish to know."

Graumgrass said, "No! No!" and he tried again to get away. Kickaha held him easily while Anana placed the bell on his head. After a while, Graumgrass's eyes glazed, and death shook a castanet in his throat. Kickaha looked at the bottom of the bell as Anana held it up for his inspection. The two tiny needles were withdrawn into the case.

"I think his mind was taken in before the body died," he said. "But, Anana, I won't let you strip a man's brain just to put this thing in his body so we can get some information. No matter how important that information is."

"I know it," she said. "And I wouldn't do it, either. I've regained some of my lost humanity because of you. Furthermore, there aren't any living bodies available to use."

She paused. He said, "Don't look at me. I haven't the guts."

"I don't blame you," she said. "And I wouldn't want you to do it, anyway. I will do it."

"But . . . !" He stopped. It had to be done, and he supposed that if she had not volunteered, he would have done so, though very reluctantly. He felt a little shame that he was allowing her to be the subject, but not enough to make him insist that he do this. He had more than one share of courage; he would be the first to say so. But this act required more than he had at this moment or was likely to have, as long as someone else would act. The utter helplessness it would produce made a coward of him. He could not stand that feeling.

He said, "There are drugs here which can get the truth, or what the subject thinks is the truth, anyway. It won't be hard to get the facts out of you—out of the Beller, I mean, but do you really think this is necessary?"

He knew that it was. He just could not accept the idea of her submitting to the bell either.

"You know what a horror I have of the bell," she said. "But I'll put my mind into one and let one of those things into my body if it'll track down the last Beller, the last one, for once and all."

He wanted to protest that nothing was worth this, but he kept his mouth shut. It had to be done. And though he called himself a coward because he could not do it, and his flesh rippled with dread for her, he would allow her to use the bell.

Anana clung to him and kissed him fiercely before she submitted. She said, "I love you. I don't want to do this! It seems as if I'm putting myself in a grave, just when I could look forward to loving you."

"We could just make a search of the palace instead," he said. "We'd be bound to flush out the Beller."

"If he got away, we'd know who to look for," she said. "No. Go ahead! Do it! Quickly! I feel as if I'm dying now!"

She was lying on a divan. She closed her eyes while he fitted the bell over her head. He held her then while it did its work. Her breathing, which had been quick and shallow with anxiety, slowed and deepened after a while. Her eyes fluttered open. They looked as if the light in them had become transfixed in time, frozen in some weird polarity.

After waiting some extra minutes to make sure the bell was finished, he gently lifted it off her head. He placed it in a casket on the floor, after which he tied her hands and feet together and then strapped her down tightly. He set the bell containing the mind of Graumgrass on her head. When twenty minutes had passed, he was sure that the transference was complete. Her face worked; the eyes had become as wild as a trapped hawk's. The voice was the lovely voice of Anana but the inflections were different.

"I can tell that I am in a woman's body," she—it—said.

Kickaha nodded and then shot the drug into her arm. He waited sixty seconds before beginning to dredge the information he needed. It took less time to get the facts than it had for the drug to take effect.

The Lords had been mistaken about the exact number of missing Bellers. There had been fifty-one, not fifty, and the Bellers, of course, had not enlightened their enemies. The "extra" one was Thabuuz. He had been down in the palace biolabs most of the time, where he was engaged in creating new Bellers. When the alarm was raised about Kickaha, he had come up from the labs. He did not get a chance to do much, but he was able to help Graumgrass knock out Nimstowl and then transfer him.

Graumgrass, as the little Lord, was to make one more attempt to kill the two remaining enemies of the Bellers. In case he did not succeed, Thabuuz was to gate to Earth with his bell and his knowledge. There, on Earth, that limbo among the universes, hidden in the swarms of mankind, he was to make new Bellers for another attempt at conquest.

"What gate did he use?" Kickaha asked.

"The gate that Wolff and Chryseis used," Graumgrass-Anana said. "It leads to Earth."

"And how do you know it does?"

"We found the code book and cracked the code, and so found that the gate was to Earth. Thabuuz had orders to take it if an emergency required that he get out of the palace to a place where he could hide."

Kickaha was shocked, but, on reflection, he was pleased. Now he had two reasons to go to Earth. One, and the most vital, was to find Thabuuz and kill him before he got his project started. Two, he must find Wolff and Chryseis and tell them they could return home. That is, they could if they wished. Undoubtedly, Wolff would want to help him and Anana hunt down the Beller.

He replaced the bell on Anana's head. In fifteen minutes, the withdrawal of Graumgrass' mind into the bell was completed. Then he put the bell containing Anana's mind on her head. In about twenty minutes, she opened her eyes and cried out his name. She wept for a while as she held him. Being in the bell, she said, was as if her brain had been cut out of her head and placed in a dark void. She kept thinking that something might happen to Kickaha and then she would be locked up forever in that bell. She knew she would go mad, and the idea of being insane forever made her even more frenzied.

Kickaha comforted her, and when she seemed to be calmed, he told her what he had learned. Anana said they must go to Earth. But first, they should dispose of Graumgrass.

"That'll be easy," he said. "I'll embed the bell in a plastic cube and put it in the museum. Later, when I have time—that is, when I come back from Earth—I'll gate him to Talanac. He can be discharged into a condemned criminal and then killed. Meantime, let's get ready for Earth."

He checked the code book for information that the Beller had not given him. The gate transmitted to an ancient gate in southern California, the exact area unspecified. Kickaha said, "I've had some twinges of nostalgia for Earth now and then, but I got over them. This is my world, this world of tiers, of green skies and fabled beasts. Earth seems like a big gray nightmare to me when I think about having to live there permanently. But still, I get just a little homesick now and then."

He paused and then said, "We may be there for some time. We'll need money. I wonder if Wolff has some stored somewhere?"

The memory bank of an underground machine told him where to locate a storage room of terrestrial currency. Kickaha returned from the room with a peculiar grin and a bag in his hand. He dumped the contents on the table. "Lots of U.S. dollar bills," he said. "Many hundred dollar bills and a dozen thousand dollar bills. But the latest was issued in 1875!"

He laughed and said, "We'll take it along, anyway. We might be able to sell it to collectors. And we'll take along some jewels, too."

He set the machines to turn out clothes for himself and Anana. They were designed as he remembered the latest American styles circa 1945. "They'll do until we can buy some new."

While they were getting ready, they moved Luvah to a bigger and more comfortable room and assigned the kitchen taloses to look after him. Kickaha left Anana to talk to her brother while he busied himself collecting the necessities for the Earth trip. He got some medicines, drugs, beamers, charges for the beamers, a throwing knife, and a little stiletto for her with poison on the hollow hilt. The Horn of Shambarimen was in a case.

He carried the case into the room where the two were. "I look like a musician," he said. "I ought to get a haircut as soon as I get a chance after we get there. My hair's so long I look like Tarzan—I don't want to attract attention. Oh, yes, you might as well start calling me Paul from now on. Kickaha is out. It's Paul J. Finnegan again."

They made their farewell with Luvah, who said that he would be the palace guardian while they were gone. He would make sure that the taloses put all the bodies in the incinerators, and he would set the defenses of the palace for marauding Lords. He was ecstatic that Anana had been reunited with him, even if only briefly. He was not, it was obvious, the customary Lord.

Despite which, once they were out of his room, Kickaha said, "Did you talk about old times, as I told you?"

"Yes," she said, "and there were many things he just could not remember."

Kickaha stopped and said, "You think . . . ?"

She shook her head and laughed. "No. There were also many things he did remember, things which a Beller could not possibly know. And he reminded me of some things I had forgotten. He is my brother all the way through; he is not a Beller, as you suspected, my suspicious lover."

He grinned and said, "You thought of the idea the same time as myself, remember?"

He kissed her. Just before they stepped onto the gate, which would be activated by a code-sentence, he said, "You speak English?"

"I spent most of my three years on Earth in Paris and London," she answered. "But I've forgotten all my French and English."

"You'll pick it up again. Meanwhile, let me do the talking."

He paused, as if he hated to begin the journey.

"One thing about going to Earth. We have to track down that Beller. But we won't have to worry about running foul of any Lords."

Anana looked surprised.

"Didn't Wolff tell you? Red Orc is the secret Lord of Earth!"

BEHIND THE WALLS
OF TERRA

This adventure of Kickaha is dedicated to Jack Cordes, who lives in the pocket universes of Peoria and Pekin.

THE SKY HAD BEEN GREEN FOR TWENTY-FOUR YEARS. SUDDENLY, IT was blue.

Kickaha blinked. He was home again. Rather, he was once more on the planet of his birth. He had lived on Earth for twenty-eight years. Then he had lived for twenty-four years in that pocket universe he called The World of Tiers. Now, though he did not care to be here, he was back "home."

He was standing in the shadow of an enormous overhang of rock. The stone floor was swept clean by the wind that traveled along the face of the cliff. Outside the semi-cavern were mountains covered with pine and fir trees. The air was cool but would get warmer, since this was morning of a July day in southern California. Or it should be, if his calculations were correct.

Since he was high on the face of a mountain, he could see very far into the southwest. There was a great valley beyond the nearer smaller valleys, a valley which he supposed was one near the Los Angeles area. It surprised and unnerved him, because it was not at all what he had expected. It was covered with a thick gray poisonous-looking cloud, that gave the impression of being composed of many many thousands of fumes, as if the floor of the valley below the cloud were jammed with geysers boiling and bubbling and pouring out the noxious gases of internal Earth.

He had no idea of what had occurred on Earth since that night in 1946 when he had been transmitted accidentally from this universe to that of Jadawin. Perhaps the great basins of the Los Angeles area were filled with poison gas that some enemy nation had dropped. He could not guess what enemy could do this, since both Germany and Japan had been wrecked and utterly defeated when he left this world, and Russia was sorely wounded.

He shrugged. He would find out in time. The memory banks below the great fortress-palace at the top of the only planet in the universe of the green sky had said that this "gate" opened into a place in the mountains near a lake called Arrowhead.

The gate was a circle of indestructible metal buried a few inches below the rock of the floor. Only a dimly stained ring of purple on the stone marked its presence.

Kickaha (born Paul Janus Finnegan) was six feet one inch in height, weighed one hundred and ninety pounds, and was broad-shouldered, lean-waisted, and massively thighed. His hair was red-bronze, his eyebrows were thick, dark, and arching, his eyes were leaf-green, his nose was straight but short, his upper lip was long, and his chin was deeply cleft. He wore hiking clothes and a bag on his back. In one hand he held the handle of a dark leather case which looked as if it contained a musical instrument, perhaps a horn or trumpet.

His hair was shoulder-length. He had considered cutting it before he returned to Earth, so he would not look strange. But the time had been short, and he had decided to wait until he got to a barber shop. His cover story would be that he and Anana had been in the mountains so long he had not had a chance to clip his hair.

The woman beside him was as beautiful as it was possible for a woman to be. She had long dark wavy hair, a flawless white skin, dark-blue eyes, and a superb figure. She wore hiking garb: boots, Levis, a lumberman's checked shirt, and a cap with a long bill. She also carried a pack on her back in which were shoes, a dress, undergarments, a small handbag, and several devices which would have startled or shocked an Earth scientist. Her hair was done in the style of 1946 as Kickaha remembered it. She wore no makeup nor needed it. Thousands of years ago, she had permanently reddened her lips, as every female Lord had done.

He kissed the woman on the lips and said, "You've been in a number of worlds, Anana, but I'll bet in none more weird than Earth."

"I've seen blue skies before," she said. "Wolff and Chryseis have a five-hour start on us. The Beller has a two-hour start. And all have a big world in which to get lost."

He nodded and said, "There was no reason for Wolff and Chryseis to hang around here, since the gate is one-way. They'll take off for the nearest two-way gate, which is in the Los Angeles area, if the gate still exists. If it doesn't, then the closest ones will be in Kentucky or Hawaii. So we know where they should be going."

He paused and wet his lips and then said, "As for the Beller, who knows? He could have gone anywhere or he may still be around here. He's in an absolutely strange world, he doesn't know anything about Earth, and he can't speak any of the languages."

"We don't know what he looks like, but we'll find him. I know the Bellers," she said. "This one won't cache his bell and then run away to hide with the idea he'll come back later for it. A Beller cannot endure the idea of being very far away from his bell. He'll carry it around as long as he can. And that will be our only means of identifying him."

"I know," Kickaha said. He was having trouble breathing, and his eyes were beginning to swim. Suddenly, he was weeping.

Anana was alarmed for a minute, and then she said, "Cry! I did it when I went back to my home world once. I thought I was dry forever, that tears were for mortals. But coming back home after so long exposed my weakness."

Kickaha dried his tears and took his canteen from his belt, uncapped it and drank deeply.

"I love my world, the green-skied world," he said. "I don't like Earth; I don't remember it with much affection. But I guess I had more love for it than I thought. I'll admit that, every once in a while, I had some nostalgia, some faint longing to see it again, see the people I knew. But . . ."

Below them, perhaps a thousand feet down, a two-lane macadam road curbed around the side of the mountain and continued upward until it was lost around the other side. A car appeared on the upgrade, sped below them, and then was lost with the road. Kickaha's eyes widened, and he said, "I never saw a car like that before. It looked like a little bug. A beetle!"

A hawk swung into view and, riding the currents, passed before them not more than a hundred yards.

Kickaha was delighted, "The first red-tail I've seen since I left Indiana!"

He stepped out onto the ledge, forgetting for a second, but a second only, his caution. Then he jumped back in under the protection of the overhang. He motioned to Anana, and she went to one end of the ledge and looked out while he did so at the other.

There was nobody below, as far as he could see, though the many trees could conceal anybody who did not want to be seen. He went out a little further and looked upward then but could not see past the overhang. The way down was not apparent at first, but investigation revealed projections just below the right side of the ledge. These would have to do for a start, and, once they began climbing down, other hand and footholds had to appear.

Kickaha eased himself backward over the ledge, feeling with his foot for a projection. Then he pulled himself back up and lay down on the ledge and again scrutinized the road and the forest a thousand feet below. A number of bluejays had started screaming somewhere below him; the air acted as a funnel to siphon the faint cries to him.

He took a pair of small binoculars from his shirt pocket and adjusted three dials on their surface. Then he removed an earphone and a thin wire with a male jack on one end and plugged the jack into the receptacle on the side of the binoculars. He began to sweep the forest below and eventually centered it on that spot where the jays were raising such a ruckus.

Through the device, the distant forest suddenly became close, and the faint noises were loud. Something dark moved, and, after he readjusted the binoculars, he saw the face of a man. More sweepings of the device and more adjusting enabled him to see parts of three other men. Each was armed with a rifle with scope, and two had binoculars.

Kickaha gave the device to Anana so she could see for herself. He said, "As far as you know, Red Orc is the only Lord on Earth?"

She put the glasses down and said, "Yes."

"He must know about these gates, then, and he's set up some sort of alarm device, so he knows when they're activated. Maybe his men are stationed close, maybe far off. Maybe Wolff and Chryseis and the Beller got away before his men could get here. Maybe not. In any case, they're waiting for us."

They did not comment about the lack of a permanent trap at the gates or a permanent guard. Red Orc, or whatever Lord was responsible for these men, would make a game out of the invasion of his home territory by other Lords. It was deadly but nevertheless a game.

Kickaha went back to viewing the four beneath the trees. Presently he said, "They've got a walkie-talkie."

He heard a whirring sound above him. He rolled over to look up and saw a strange machine that had just flown down over the mountain to his right.

He said, "An autogyro!" and then the machine was hidden by a spur of the mountain. He jumped up and ran into the cavern with Anana behind him.

The chopping sound of a plane's rotors became a roar and then th machine was hovering before the ledge. Kickaha became aware that the machine was not a true autogyro. As far as he knew, a gyro could not stand still in the air, or, as this was doing, swing from side to side or turn around one spot.

The body of the craft was transparent; he could see the pilot and three men inside, armed with rifles. He and Anana were trapped, they had no place to run or hide.

Undoubtedly, Orc's men had been sent to find out what weapons the intruders carried. Under these conditions, the intruders would have to use their weapons, unless they preferred to be captured. They did not so prefer. They spoke the activating code word, aimed the rings at the machine, and spoke the final word.

The needle-thin golden rays spat once, delivering the full charges in the rings' tiny powerpacks.

The fuselage split in two places, and the plane fell. Kickaha ran out and looked down over the ledge in time to see the pieces strike the side of the mountain below. One section went up in a white and red ball which fissioned into a dozen smaller fire globes. All the pieces eventually fell not too far apart near the bottom and burned fiercely.

The four men under the trees were white-faced, and the man with the walkie-talkie spat words into the transmitter. Kickaha tried to tighten the beam so he could pick them up, but the noise from the burning machine interfered.

Kickaha was glad that he had struck the first blow, but his elation was darkened. He knew that the Lord had deliberately sacrificed the men in the gyro in order to find out how dangerous his opponents were. Kickaha would have preferred to have gotten away undetected. Moreover, getting down the mountainside would be impossible until night fell. In the meantime, the Lord would attack again.

He and Anana recharged their rings with the tiny powerpacks. He kept a watch on the men below while she scanned the sides of the mountain. Presently, a red convertible appeared on the left, going down the mountain road. A man and a woman sat in it. The car stopped near the flaming wreckage and the two got out to investigate. They stood around talking and then they got back into the car and sped off.

Kickaha grinned. No doubt they were going to notify the authorities. That meant that the four men would be powerless to attack. On the other hand, the authorities might climb up here and find him and Anana. He could claim that they were just hikers, and the authorities could not hold them for long. But just to be in custody for a while would enable the Lord to seize them the moment they were released. Also, he and Anana would have a hard time identifying themselves, and it was possible that the authorities might hold them until they could be identified.

They would have no record of Anana, of course, but if they tracked down his fingerprints, they would find something difficult to explain. They would discover that he was Paul Janus Finnegan, born in 1918 near Terre Haute, Indiana, that he had served in a tank corps of the Eighth Army during World War II, and that he had mysteriously disappeared in 1946 from his apartment in a building in Bloomington while he was attending the University of Indiana, and that he had not been seen since.

He could always claim amnesia, of course, but how would he explain that he was fifty-two years old chronologically yet only twenty-five years old physiologically? And how would he explain the origin of the peculiar devices in his backpack?

He cursed softly in Tishquetmoac, in Half-Horse Lakotah, in the Middle High German of Dracheland, in the language of the Lords, and in English. And then he switched his thinking into English, because he had half-forgotten that language and had to get accustomed to its use. If those four men stuck there until the authorities showed up . . .

But the four were not staying. After a long conversation, and obvious receipt of orders from the walkie-talkie, they left. They climbed up onto the road, and within a minute a car appeared from the right. It stopped, and the four got in and drove off.

Kickaha considered that this might be a feint to get him and Anana to climb down the mountain. Then another gyro would catch them on the mountainside, or the men would come back. Or both.

But if he waited until the police showed up, he could not come down until nightfall. Orc's men would be waiting down there, and they might have some of the Lord's advanced weapons to use, because they would not fear to use them at night and in this remote area.

"Come on," he said to Anana in English. "We're going down now. If the police see us, we'll tell them we're just hitchhikers. You leave the talking to me; I'll tell them you're Finnish and don't speak English yet. Let's hope there'll be no Finns among them."

"What?" Anana said. She had spent three and a half years on Earth in the 1880's and had learned some English and more French but had forgotten the little she had known.

Kickaha repeated slowly.

"It's your world," she said in English. "You're the boss."

He grinned at that, because very few female Lords ever admitted there was any situation in which the male was their master. He let himself down again over the ledge. He was beginning to sweat. The sun was coming over the mountain now and shining fully on them, but this did not account for his perspiration. He was sweating out the possible reappearance of the Lord's men.

He and Anana had gotten about one-third of the way down when the first police car appeared. It was black and white and had a big star on the side. Two men got out. Their uniforms looked like those of state police, as he remembered those of the Midwest.

A few minutes later, another patrol car and an ambulance appeared. Then two more cars stopped. After a while, there were ten cars.

Kickaha found a path that was sometimes precarious but led at an angle to the right along the slope. He and Anana could keep hidden from the people below part of the time. If they should be seen, they would not have to stop. The police could come after them, but they would be so far behind that their pursuit would be hopeless.

Or so it seemed until another gyro appeared. This one swept back and forth, apparently looking for bodies or survivors. Kickaha and Anana hid behind a large boulder until the craft landed near the road. Then they continued their sidewise descent of the mountain.

When they reached the road, they drank some water and ate some of the concentrated food they had brought from the other world. Kickaha told her that they would walk along the road, going downward. He also reminded her that Red Orc's men would be cruising up and down the road looking for them.

"Then why don't we hide out until nightfall?" she said.

"Because in the daylight I can spot a car that definitely won't be Orc's. I won't mind being picked up by one of them. But if Orc's men show up and try anything, we have our rays and we can be on guard. At night, you won't know who's stopping to pick you up. We could avoid the road altogether and hike alongside it in the woods, but that's slow going. I don't want Wolff or the Beller to get too far ahead."

"How do we know they didn't both go the other way?" she said. "Or that Red Orc didn't pick them up?"

"We don't," he said. "But I'm betting that this is the way to Los Angeles. It's westward, and it's downhill. Wolff would know this, and the instinct of the Beller would be to go down, I would think. I could be wrong. But I can't stand here forever trying to make up my mind what happened. Let's go."

They started off. The air was sweet and clean; birds sang; a squirrel ran onto the branch of a tall and half-dead pine and watched them with its bright eyes. There were a number of dead or dying pines. Evidently, some plant disease had struck them. The only signs of human beings were the skeletal power transmission towers and aluminum cables going up the side of a mountain. Kickaha explained to Anana what they were; he was going to be doing much explaining from now on. He did not mind. It gave her the opportunity to learn English and him the opportunity to relearn it.

A car passed them from behind. On hearing it, Kickaha and Anana withdrew from the side of the road, ready to shoot their ray rings or to leap down the slope of the mountain if they had to. He gestured with his thumb at the car, which held a man, woman, and two children. The car did not even slow down. Then a big truck pulling a trailer passed them. The driver looked as if he might be going to stop but he kept on going.

Anana said, "These vehicles! So primitive! So noisy! And they stink!"

"Yes, but we *do* have atomic power," Kickaha said. "At least, we had atomic bombs. America did anyway. I thought that by now they'd have atomic-powered cars. They've had a whole generation to develop them."

A cream-colored station wagon with a man and woman and two teenagers passed them. Kickaha stared after the boy. He had hair as long as Kickaha's and considerably less disciplined. The girl had long yellow hair that fell smoothly over her shoulders, and her face was thickly made-up. Like a whore's, he thought. Were those really green eyelids?

The parents, who looked about fifty, seemed normal. Except that she had a hairdo that was definitely not around in 1946. And her makeup had been heavy, too, although not nearly as thick as the girl's.

None of the cars that he had seen were identifiable. Some of them had a GM emblem, but that was the only familiar thing. This was to be expected, of course. But he was startled when the next car to pass was the beetle he had seen when he first looked down from the ledge. Or at least it looked enough like it to be the same. VW? What did that stand for?

He had expected many changes, some of which would not be easy to understand. He could think of no reason why such an ugly cramped car as the VW would be accepted, although he did remember the little Willys of his adolescence. He shrugged. It would take too much energy and time to figure out the reasons for everything he saw. If he were to survive, he would have to concentrate on the immediate problem: getting away from Red Orc's men. If they were Red Orc's.

He and Anana walked swiftly in a loose-jointed gait. She was beginning to relax and to take an interest in the beauty of their surroundings. She smiled and squeezed his hand once and said, "I love you."

He kissed her on the cheek and said, "I love you, too."

She was beginning to sound and act like an Earthwoman, instead of the superaristocratic Lord.

He heard a car coming around the bend a quarter of a mile away and glanced back at it. It was a black and white state police car with two golden-helmeted men. He looked straight ahead but out of the side of his mouth said, "If this car stops, act easy. It's the police. Let me handle things. If I hold up two fingers, run and jump down the side of the mountain. No! On second thought . . . listen, we'll go with them. They can take us into town, or near it, and then we'll stun them with the rings. Got it?"

The car, however, shot by without even slowing. Kickaha breathed relief and said, "We don't look as suspicious as I feel."

They walked on down the road. As they came onto a half-mile stretch, they heard a faint roar behind them. The sound became louder, and then Kickaha grinned with pleasure. "Motorcycles," he said. "Lots of them."

The roaring became very loud. They turned, and saw about twenty big black cycles race like a black cloud around the corner of the mountain. Kickaha was amazed. He had never seen men or women dressed like these. Several of them aroused a reflex he had thought dead since peace was declared in 1945. His hand flew to the handle of the knife in his belt sheath, and he looked for a ditch into which to dive.

Three of the cyclists wore German coalscuttle helmets with big black swastikas painted on the gray metal. They also wore Iron Crosses or metal swastikas on chains around their necks.

All wore dark glasses, and these, coupled with the men's beards or handlebar moustaches and sideburns, and the women's heavy makeup, made their faces seem insectile. Their clothing was dark, although a few men wore dirty once-white T-shirts. Most wore calf-length boots. A woman sported a kepi and a dragoon's bright-red, yellow-piped jacket. Their black leather jackets and T-shirts bore skulls and crossbones that looked like phalluses, and the legend: LUCIFER'S LOUTS.

The cavalcade went roaring by, some gunning their motors or waving at the two and several wove back and forth across the road, leaning far over to both sides with their arms folded. Kickaha grinned appreciatively at that; he had owned and loved a motorcycle when he was going to high school in Terre Haute.

Anana, however, wrinkled up her nose. "The stink of fuel is bad enough," she said. "But did you smell *them?* They haven't bathed for weeks. Or months."

"The Lord of this world has been very lax," Kickaha said.

He referred to the sanitary habits of the human inhabitants of the pocket universes which the other Lords ruled. Although the Lords were often very cruel with their human property, they insisted on cleanliness and beauty. They had established laws and religious precepts which saw to it that cleanliness was part of the base of every culture.

But there were exceptions. Some Lords had allowed their human societies to degenerate into dirt-indifference.

Anana had explained that the Lord of Earth was unique. Red Orc ruled in strictest secrecy and anonymity, although he had not always done so. In the early days, in man's dawn, he had often acted as a god. But he had abandoned that role and gone into hiding—as it were. He had let things go as they would. This accounted for the past, present, and doubtless future mess in which Earthlings were mired.

Kickaha had had little time to learn much about Red Orc, because he had not even known of his existence until a few minutes before he and Anana stepped through the gates into this universe.

"They all looked so ugly," Anana said.

"I told you man had gone to seed here," he said. "There has been no selective breeding, either by a Lord or by humans themselves."

Then they heard the muted roar of the cycles again, and in a minute they saw eight coming back up the road. These held only men.

The cycles passed them, slowed, turned, and came up behind them. Kickaha and Anana continued walking. Three cycles zoomed by them, cutting in so close that he could have knocked them over as they went by. He was beginning to wonder if he should not have done so and therefore cut down the odds immediately. It seemed obvious that they were going to be harassed, if not worse.

Some of the men whistled at Anana and called out invitations, or wishes, in various obscene terms. Anana did not understand the words but she understood the tones and the gestures and grins that went with them. She scowled and made a gesture peculiar to the Lords. Despite their unfamiliarity with it, the cyclists understood. One almost fell off his cycle laughing. Others, however, bared their teeth in half-grins, half-snarls.

Kickaha stopped and faced them. They pulled up around the pair in an enfolding crescent and turned off their motors.

"OK," Kickaha said. "What do you want?"

A big-paunched, thick-necked youth with thick coarse black hair spilling out of the V of his shirt and wearing a goatee and an Afrika Korps hat, spoke up. "Well, now, Red, if we was Satan's Slaves, we'd want you. But we ain't fags, so we'll take your *la belle dame con, voila.*"

"Man, that chick is the most!" said a tall skinny boy with acne scars, big Adam's apple, and a gold ring in a pierced ear. His long lank black hair hung down past his shoulders and fell over his eyes.

"The grooviest!" a bushy-bearded gap-toothed scar-faced man said.

Kickaha knew when to keep silent and when to talk, but he sometimes had a hard time doing what he knew was best. He had no time or inclination for brawls now; his business was serious and important. In fact, it was vital. If the Beller got loose and adapted to Earth well enough to make other bells, he and his kind would literally take over Earth. The Beller was no science-fiction monster; he existed, and if he were not killed, goodbye Earth! Or goodbye mankind! The bodies would survive but the brains would be emptied and alien minds would fill them!

It was unfortunate that salvation could not discriminate. If others were saved, then these would be too.

At the moment, it looked as if there could be some doubt about Kickaha being able to save even himself, let alone the world. The eight had left their cycles and were approaching with various weapons. Three had long chains; two, iron pipes; one, a switchblade knife; one, brass knuckles; another, an ice pick.

"I suppose you think you're going to attack her in broad daylight and with the cops so close?" he said.

The youth with the Afrika Korps cap said, "Man, we wouldn't bother you, ordinarily. But when I saw that chick, it was too much! What a doll! I ain't never seen a chick could wipe her. Too much! We gotta have her! You dig?"

Kickaha did not understand what this last meant but it did not matter. They were brutal men who meant to have what they wanted. "You better be prepared to die," Kickaha said.

They looked surprised. The Afrika Korps youth said, "You got a lotta class, Red, I'll give you that. Listen, we could stomp the guts outta you and enjoy it, really dig it, but I admire your style, friend. Let us have the chick, and we return her in an hour or so."

Then Afrika Korps grinned and said, " 'Course, she may not be in the same condition she is now, but what the hell! Nobody's perfect!"

Kickaha spoke to Anana in the language of the Lords.

"If we get a chance, we'll make off on one of these cycles. It'll get us to Los Angeles."

"Hey, what kinda gook talk is that?" Afrika Korps said. He gestured at the men with the chains, who, grinning, stepped in front of the others. They drew their arms back to lash out with the chains and Kickaha and Anana sprayed the beams from their rings, which were set at "stun" power. The three dropped their chains, grabbed their middles, and bent over. The rays caught them on the tops of their heads then, and they fell forward. Their faces were red with suddenly broken blood vessels. When they recovered, they would be dizzy and sick for days, and their stomachs would be sore and red with ruptured veins and arteries.

The others became motionless and went white with shock.

Kickaha snatched the knife out of his sheath and threw it at the shoulder of Afrika Korps. Afrika Korps screamed and dropped the ice pick. Anana knocked him out with her ray; Kickaha sprayed the remaining men.

Fortunately, no cars came by in the next few minutes. The two dragged the groaning half-conscious men to the edge of the road and pushed them over. They rolled about twenty feet and came to rest on a shelf of rock.

The cycles, except for one, were then pushed over the edge at a place where there was nothing to stop them. They leaped and rolled down the steep incline, turned over and over, came apart, and some burst into flames.

Kickaha regretted this, since he did not want the smoke to attract anybody.

Anana had been told what the group had planned for her. She climbed down the slope to the piled-up bodies. She set the ring at the lowest burn power and burned off the pants, and much outer skin, of every male. They would not forget Anana for a long time. And if they cursed her in aftertimes, they should have blessed Kickaha. He kept her from killing them.

Kickaha took the wallet of Afrika Korps. The driver's license gave his name as Alfred Roger Goodrich. His photograph did not look at all like Kickaha, which could not be helped. Among other things it contained forty dollars.

He instructed Anana in how to ride behind him and what to expect when they were on the road. Within a minute, they were out on the highway, heading toward Los Angeles. The roar of the engine did not resurrect the happy memories of his cycling days in Indiana. The road disturbed him and the reek of gasoline and oil displeased him. He had been in a quiet and sweet-aired world too long.

Anana, clinging to his waist, was silent for a long while. He glanced back once to see her black hair flying. Her lids were half-shut behind the sunglasses she had taken from one of the Louts. The shadows made them impenetrable. Later, she shouted something at him but the wind and the engine noise flicked her words away.

Kickaha tested the cycle out and determined that a number of items had been cut out by the owner, mostly to reduce weight. For one thing, the front brakes had been taken off.

Once he knew what the strengths and weaknesses of the vehicle were, he drove along with his eyes inspecting the road ahead but his thoughts inclined to be elsewhere.

He had come on a long and fantastic road from that campus of the University of Indiana to this road in the mountains of southern California. When he was with the Eighth Army in Germany, he had found that crescent of hard silvery metal in the ruins of a local museum. He took it back with him to Bloomington, and there, one night, a man by the name of Vannax had appeared and offered him a fantastic sum for the crescent. He had refused the money. Later that night he had awakened to find Vannax had broken into his apartment. Vannax was in the act of placing another crescent of metal by his to form a circle. Kickaha had attacked Vannax and accidentally stepped within the circle. The next he knew, he was transported to a very strange place.

The two crescents had formed a gate, a device of the Lords which permitted a sort of teleportation from one universe to another. Kickaha had been transmitted into an artificial universe, a pocket universe, created by a Lord named Jadawin. But Jadawin was no longer in his universe; he had been forced out of it by another Lord, dispossessed and cast into Earth. Jadawin had lost his memory. He became Robert Wolff.

The stories of Wolff (Jadawin) and Kickaha (Finnegan) were long and involved. Wolff was helped back into his universe by Kickaha, and, after a series of adventures, Wolff regained his memory. He also regained his Lordship of the peculiar universe he had constructed, and he settled down with his lover, Chryseis, to rule in the palace on top of the Tower-of-Babel-like planet which hung in the middle of a universe whose "walls" contained a volume less than that within the solar system of Earth.

Recently, Wolff and Chryseis had mysteriously disappeared, probably because of the machinations of some Lord of another universe. Kickaha had run into Anana, who, with two other Lords, was fleeing from the Black Bellers. The Bellers had originally been devices created in the biolabs of the Lords and intended for housing of the minds of the Lords during mind transference from one body to another. But the bell-shaped and indestructible machines had developed into entities with their own intelligence. These had succeeded in transferring their minds into the bodies of Lords and then began to wage a secret war on the Lords. They were found out, and a long and savage struggle began, with all the Bellers supposedly captured and imprisoned in a specially made universe. However, fifty-one had been overlooked, and these, after ten thousand years of dormancy, had gotten into human bodies again and were once more loose.

Kickaha had directly or indirectly killed all but one. This one, its mind in the body of a man called Thabuuz, had gated through to Earth. Wolff and Chryseis had returned to their palace just in time to be attacked by the Bellers and had escaped through the gate which Thabuuz later took.

Now Kickaha and Anana were searching for Wolff and Chryseis. And they were also determined to hunt down and kill the last of the Black Bellers. If Thabuuz succeeded in eluding them, he would, in time, build more of the bells and with these begin a secret war against the humans of Earth, and later, invade the private universes of the Lords and discharge their minds and occupy their bodies also. The Lords had never forgotten the Black Bellers, and every one still wore a ring which could detect the metal bells of their ancient enemies and transmit a warning to a tiny circuit-board and alarm in the brain of every Lord.

The peoples of Earth knew nothing of the Bellers. They knew nothing of the Lords. Kickaha was the only Earthling who had ever become aware of the existence of the Lords and their pocket universes.

The peoples of Earth would be wide open to being taken over, one by one, their minds discharged by the antennas of the bells and the minds of the Bellers possessing the brains. The warfare would be so insidious that only through accident would the humans even know that they were being attacked.

The Black Beller Thabuuz had to be found and killed.

In the meantime, the Lord of Earth, the Lord called Red Orc, had learned that five people had gated through into his domain. He would not know that one of them was the Black Beller. He would be trying to capture all five. And Red Orc could not be notified that a Black Beller was loose on Earth because Red Orc could not be found. Neither Anana nor Kickaha knew where he lived. Indeed, until a few hours ago, Kickaha had not known that Earth had a Lord.

In fifteen minutes, they had come down off the slope onto a plateau. The little village at the crossroads was a pleasant place, though highly commercialized. It was clean and bright with many white houses and buildings. However, as they passed through the main street, they passed a big hamburger stand. And there were the rest of Lucifer's Louts lounging by the picnic tables, eating hamburgers and drinking cokes or beer. They looked up on hearing the familiar Harley-Davidson and then, seeing the two, did a double take. One jumped onto his cycle and kicked over the motor. He was a tall frowzy-haired long-moustachioed youth wearing a Confederate officer's cavalry hat, white silk shirt with frills at the neck and wrists, tight black shiny pants with red seams, and fur-topped boots.

The others quickly followed him. Kickaha did not think they would be going to the police; there was something about them which indicated that their relations with the police were not friendly. They would take vengeance in their own dirty hands. However, it was not likely that they would do anything while still in town.

Kickaha accelerated to top speed.

When they had gone around a curve which took them out of sight of the village, Anana half-turned. She waited until the leader was only ten feet behind her. He was bent over the bars and grinning savagely. Evidently he expected to pass them and either force them to stop or to knock them over. Behind him, side by side so that two rode in the other lane, were five cycles with individual riders. The engines burdened down with couples were some twenty yards behind.

Kickaha glanced back and yelled at Anana. She released the ray just long enough to cut the front wheel of the lead cycle in half. Its front dropped, and the rider shot over the bars, his mouth open in a yell no one could hear. He hit the macadam and slid for a long way on his face and body. The five cycles behind him tried to avoid the first, which lay in their path. They split like a school of fish, but Anana cut the wheels of the two in the lead and all three piled up while two skidded on their sides off the road. The other cycles slowed down in time to avoid hitting the fallen engines and drivers.

Kickaha grinned and shouted, "Good show, Anana!"

And then his grin fell off and he cursed. Around the corner of the road, now a half-mile away, a black and white car with red lights on top had appeared. Any hopes that he had that it would stop to investigate the accident quickly faded. The car swung to the shoulder to avoid the fallen vehicles and riders and then twisted back onto the road and took off after Kickaha, its siren whooping, its red lights flashing.

The car was about fifty yards away when Anana swept the ray down the road and across the front tires. She snapped the ray off so quickly that the wheels were probably only disintegrated a little on the rims, but the tires were cut in two. The car dropped a little but kept going on, though it decreased speed so suddenly that the two policemen were thrown violently forward. The siren died; the lights quit flashing; the car shook to a halt. And Kickaha and Anana sped around a curve and saw the policemen no more.

"If this keeps up, we're going to be out of charges!" Kickaha said. "Hell, I wanted to save them for extreme emergencies! I didn't think we'd be having so much trouble so soon! And we've just started!"

They continued for five miles and then he saw another police car coming toward them. It went down a dip and was lost for a minute. He shouted, "Hang on!" and swung off the road, bouncing across a slight depression toward a wide field that grew more rocks than grass. His goal was a clump of trees about a hundred yards away, and he almost made it before the police came into view. Anana, hanging on, yelled that the police car was coming across the field after them. Kickaha slowed the cycle. Anana ran the ray down the field in front of the advancing car. Burning dirt flew up in dust along a furrow and then the tires exploded and the front of the radiator of the car gushed water and steam.

Kickaha took the cycle back toward the road at an angle away from the car. Two policemen jumped out and, steadying their pistols, fired. The chances of hitting the riders or the machine at that distance were poor, but a bullet did penetrate the rear tire. There was a bang; the cycle began fishtailing. Kickaha cut the motor, and they coasted to a stop. The policemen began running toward them.

"Hell, I don't want to kill them!" Kickaha said. "But . . ."

The policemen were big and blubbery-looking and looked as if they might be between forty and fifty years old. Kickaha and Anana were wearing packs of about thirty pounds, but both were physically about twenty-five years old.

"We'll outrun them," he said, and they fled together toward the road. The two men fired their guns and shouted but they were slowing down swiftly and soon they were trotting. A half-mile later, they were standing together watching the two dwindle.

Kickaha, grinning, circled back toward the car. He looked back once and saw that the two policemen realized that he had led them astray. They were running again but not too swiftly. Their legs and arms were pumping at first but soon the motions became less energetic, and then both were walking toward him.

Kickaha opened the door to the car, tore off the microphone of the transceiver, reached under the dashboard and tore loose all the wires connected to the radio. By that time, Anana had caught up with him.

The keys were still in the ignition lock, and the wheels themselves had not been cut into deeply. He told Anana to jump in, and he got behind the driver's wheel and started the motor. The cops speeded up then and began firing again, but the car pulled away from them and bumped and shook across the field, accelerating all the time. One bullet pierced and starred a rear window, and then the car was bump-bumping down the road.

After two miles of the grinding noise and piston-like movement, Kickaha decided to call it quits. He drove the car to the side of the road, got out, threw the ignition keys into the weeds, and started to hike again. They had walked perhaps fifty yards when they turned at the noise of a vehicle. A bus shot by them. It was painted all over with swirls, dots, squares, circles, and explosions of many bright colors. In bright yellow and orange-trimmed letters was a title along the front and the sides of the bus: THE GNOME KING AND HIS BAD EGGS. Above the title were painted glowing red and yellow quarter notes, bars, small guitars and drums.

For a moment, looking at the faces against the windows, he thought that the bus had picked up Lucifer's Louts. There were long hairs, fuzzy hairs, moustaches, beards, and the heavy makeup and long straight lank hair of the girls.

But the faces were different; they did look wild but not brutish or savage.

The bus slowed down with a squealing of brakes. It stopped, a door swung open, and a youth with a beard and enormous spectacles leaned out and waved at them. They ran to the bus and boarded with the accompaniment of much laughter and the strumming of guitars.

The bus, driven by a youth who looked like Buffalo Bill, started up. Kickaha looked around into the grinning faces of six boys and three girls. Three older men sat at the rear of the bus and played cards on a small collapsible table. They looked up and nodded and then went back to their game. Part of the bus was enclosed; there were, he later found out, a toilet and washroom and two small dressing rooms. Guitars, drums, xylophone, saxophone, flute, and harp, were stored on seats or on the racks above the seats.

Two girls wore skirts that just barely covered their buttocks and dark gray stockings, bright frilly blouses, many varicolored beads, and heavy makeup: green or silver eyelids, artificial eyelashes, panda-like rings around the eyes, and green (!) and pale mauve (!) lips. The third girl had no makeup at all. Long straight black hair fell to her waist and she wore a tight sleeveless green and red striped sweater with a deep cleavage, tight Levis, and sandals. Several of the boys wore bellbottom trousers, very frilly shirts, and all had long hair.

The Gnome King was a very tall, tubercular looking youth with very curly hair, handlebar moustaches, and enormous spectacles perched on the end of his big nose. He also wore an earring. He introduced himself as Lou Baum (born Goldbaum).

Kickaha gave his name as Paul Finnegan and Anana's as Ann Finnegan. She was his wife, he told Baum, and had only recently come from Finnish Lapland. He gave this pedigree because he did not think that it was likely they would run into anyone who could speak Laplander.

"From the Land of the Reindeer?" Baum said. "She's a dear, all right." He whistled and kissed his fingertips and flicked them at Anana. "Groovy, me boy! Too much! Say, either of you play an instrument?" He looked at the case Kickaha was carrying.

Kickaha said that they did not. He did not care to explain that he had once played the flute but not since 1945 or that he had played an instrument like a pan-pipe when he lived with the Bear Folk on the Amerindian level of the World of Tiers. Nor did he think it wise to explain that Anana played a host of instruments, some of which were similar to Earth instruments and some of which were definitely not.

"I'm using this instrument case as a suitcase," Kickaha said. "We've been on the road for some time since leaving Europe. We just spent a month in the mountains, and now we've decided to visit L.A. We've never been there."

"Then you got no place to stay," Baum said. He talked to Kickaha but stared at Anana. His eyes glistened, and his hands kept moving with gestures that seemed to be reshaping Anana out of the air.

"Can she sing?" he said suddenly.

"Not in English," Kickaha replied.

The girl in Levis stood up and said, "Come on, Lou. You aren't going to get anywhere with that chick. Her boy friend'll kill you if you lay a hand on her. Or else she will. That chick can do it, you know."

Lou seemed to be shaken. He came very close and peered into Kickaha's eyes as if he were looking through a microscope. Kickaha smelled a strange acrid odor on his breath. A moment later, he thought he knew what it was. The citizens of the city of Talanac on the Amerind level, carved out of a mountain of jade, smoked a narcotic tobacco which left the same odor on their breath. Kickaha did not know, of course, since he had had no experience on Earth, but he had always suspected that the tobacco was marijuana, and that the Talanacs, descendants of the ancient Olmecs of Mexico, had brought it with them when they had crossed through the gates provided by Wolff.

"You wouldn't put me on?" Lou said to the girl, Moo-Moo Nanssen, after he had backed away from Kickaha's leaf-green eyes.

"There's something very strange about them," Moo-Moo said. "Very attractive, very virile, and very frightening. Alien. Real alien."

Kickaha felt the back of his scalp chill. Anana, moving closer to him, whispered in the language of the Lords, "I don't know what she's saying, but I don't like it. That girl has a gift of seeing things; she is *Zundra.*"

Zundra had no exact or near-exact translation into English. It meant a combination of psychologist, clairvoyant, and witch, with a strain of madness.

Lou Baum shook his head, wiped the sweat off his forehead, and then removed and polished his glasses. His weak, pale-blue eyes blinked.

"The chick is psychic," he said. "Weird. But in the groove. She knows what she's talking about."

"I get vibrations," Moo-Moo said. "They never fail me. I can read character like that!" She snapped her fingers loudly. "But there's something about you two, especially her, I don't get. Maybe like you two ain't from this world, you know. Like you're Martians . . . or something."

A short stocky youth with blond hair and an acne-scarred face, introduced only as Wipe-Out, looked up from his seat, where he was tuning a guitar.

"Finnegan's no Martian," he said, grinning. "He's got a flat Midwestern accent like he came from Indiana, Illinois, or Iowa. A hoosier, I'd guess. Right?"

"I'm a hoosier," Kickaha said.

"Close your eyes, you good people," Wipe-Out said loudly. "Listen to him! Speak again, Finnegan! If his voice isn't a dead ringer for Gary Cooper's, I'll eat the inedible!"

Kickaha said something for their benefit, and the others laughed and said, "Gary Cooper! Did you ever?"

That seemed to shatter the crystal tension that Moo-Moo's words had built. Moo-Moo smiled and sat down again, but her dark eyes flicked glances again and again at the two strangers, and Kickaha knew that she was not satisfied. Lou Baum sat down by Moo-Moo. His Adam's apple worked as if it were the plunger on a pump. His face was set in a heavy, almost stupefied expression, but Kickaha could tell that he was still very curious. He was also afraid.

Apparently, Baum believed in his girl friend's reputation as a psychic. He was also probably a little afraid of her.

Kickaha did not care. Her analysis of the strangers may have been nothing but a maneuver to scare Baum from Anana.

The important thing was to get to Los Angeles as swiftly as possible, with as little chance of being detected by Orc's men as possible. This bus was a lucky thing for him, and as soon as they reached a suitable jumping-off place in the metropolitan area, they would jump. And hail and farewell to the Gnome King and His Bad Eggs.

He inspected the rest of the bus. The three older men playing cards looked up at him but said nothing. He felt a little repulsed by their bald heads and gray hair, their thickening and sagging features, red-veined eyes, wrinkles, dewlaps, and big bellies. He had not seen more than four old people in the twenty-four years he had lived in the universe of Jadawin. Humans lived to be a thousand there if they could avoid accident or homicide, and did not age until the last hundred years. Very few survived that long, however. Thus, Kickaha had forgotten about old men and women. He felt repelled, though not as much as Anana. She had grown up in a world which contained no physically aged people, and though she was now ten thousand years old, she had lived in no universes which contained unhandsome humans. The Lords were an aesthetic people and so they had weeded out the unbeautiful among their chattels and given the survivors the chance for a long long youth.

Baum walked down the aisle and said, "Looking for something?"

"I'm just curious," Kickaha said. "Is there any way out other than the door in front?"

"There's an emergency inside the women's dressing room. Why?"

"I just like to know these things," Kickaha said. He did not see why he should explain that he always made sure he knew exactly the number of exits and their accessibility.

He opened the doors to the two dressing rooms and the toilet and then studied the emergency door so that he would be able to open it immediately.

Baum, behind, said, "You sure got guts, friend. Didn't you know curiosity killed the cat?"

"It's kept this cat alive," Kickaha said.

Baum lowered his voice and came close to Kickaha. He said, "You really hung up on that chick?"

The phrase was new to Kickaha but he had no trouble understanding it.

He said, "Yes. Why?"

"Too bad. I've really flipped for her. No offense, you understand," he said when Kickaha narrowed his eyes. "Moo-Moo's a real doll, but a little weird, you know what I mean. She says you two are weirdos, and there is something a little strange about you, but I like that. But I was going to say, if you need some money, say one or two thousand, and you'd just, say, give me a deed to your chick, in a manner of speaking, let me take over, and you walk out, much richer, you know what I mean."

Kickaha grinned and said, "Two thousand? You must want her pretty bad!"

"Two thousand doesn't grow on the money tree, my friend, but for that doll . . . !"

"Your business must be very good, if you can throw that much away," Kickaha said.

"Man, you kidding!" Baum said, seemingly genuinely surprised. "Ain't you really heard of me and my group before? We're famous! We've been everybody, we've made the top ten thirty-eight times, we got a Golden Record, we've given concerts at the Bowl! And we're on our way to the Bowl again. You don't seem to be with it!"

"I've been away for a long time," Kickaha said. "So what if I take your money and Ann doesn't fall for you? I can't force her to become your woman, you know."

Baum seemed offended. He said, "The chicks offer themselves to me by the dozens every night. I'm not jesting. I got the pick! You saying this Ann, Daughter-of-Reindeer, or whatever her name, is going to turn me down? Baum, the Gnome King?"

Baum's features were not only unharmonious, he had several pimples, and his teeth were crooked.

"Do you have the money on you?"

Baum's voice had been questioning, even wheedling before. Now it became triumphant and, at the same time, slightly scornful.

"I can give you a thousand; maybe Solly, my agent, can give you five hundred. And I'll give you a check for the rest."

"White slavery!" Kickaha said. And then, "You can't be over twenty-five, right? And you can throw money around like that?"

He remembered his own youth during the Depression and how hard he had worked to just survive and how tough so many others had had it.

"You are a weirdo," Baum said. "Don't you know anything? Or are you putting me on?"

His voice was loaded with contempt. Kickaha felt like laughing in his face and also felt like hitting him in his mouth. He did neither. He said, "I'll take the fifteen hundred. But right now. And if Ann spits on you, you don't get the money back."

Baum glanced nervously at Moo-Moo, who had moved over to sit with Anana.

He said, "Wait till we get to L.A. We'll stop off to eat, and then you can take off. I'll give you your money then."

"And you can get up your nerve to tell Moo-Moo that Ann is joining you but I'm taking off?" Kickaha said. "Very well. Except for the money. I want it now! Otherwise, I tell Moo-Moo what you just said."

Baum turned a little pale and his undershot jaw sagged. He said, "You slimy . . . ! You got a nerve!"

"And I want a signed statement explaining why I'm getting the money. Any legitimate excuse will do."

"You think I'd double-cross you, turn you in to the fuzz?"

"That possibility did cross my mind," Kickaha said, wondering if the "fuzz" was the police.

"You may have been out of it for a long time, but you haven't forgotten any of the tricks, have you?" Baum said, not so scornfully now.

"There are people like you every place," Kickaha said.

He knew that he and Anana would need money, and they had no time to go to work to earn it, and he did not want to rob to get it if he could avoid doing so. If this nauseating specimen of arrogance thought he could buy Anana, let him pay for the privilege of finding out whether or not he could.

Baum dug into his jacket and came up with eight one-hundred doll. bills. He handed these to Kickaha and then interrupted his manager, fat bald-headed man with a huge cigar. The manager gestured violentl and shot some hard looks at Kickaha but he gave in. Baum came bacl with five one-hundred dollar bills. He wrote a note on a piece of paper saying that the money was in payment for a debt he owed Paul J. Finnegan. After giving it to Kickaha, he insisted that Kickaha write him receipt for the money. Kickaha also took the check for the rest of the money, although he did not think that he would be able to cash it. Baum would stop payment on it, he was sure of that.

Kickaha left Baum and sat down on a seat on which were a number of magazines, paperback books, and a *Los Angeles Times*. He spent some time reading, and when he had finished he sat for a long time looking out the window.

Earth had certainly changed since 1946.

Pulling himself out of his reverie, he picked up a road map of Los Angeles, which he'd noticed among the magazines. As he studied it, he realized Wolff and Chryseis could be anywhere in the great sprawl of Los Angeles. He was certain they were headed in that direction, though, rather than Nevada or Arizona, since the nearest gate was in the L.A. area. They might even be in a bus only a few miles ahead.

Since Wolff and Chryseis had taken the gate to Earth from the palace in Wolff's universe as an emergency exit to avoid being killed by the invaders, they were dressed in the clothes of the Lords. Chryseis may have been wearing no clothes at all. So the two would have been forced to obtain clothes from others. And they would have had to find some big dark glasses immediately, because anyone seeing Chryseis' enormous violet eyes would have known that she was not Earth-born. Or would have thought her a freak, despite her great beauty.

Both of them were resourceful enough to get along, especially since Wolff had spent more time on Earth as an adult than Kickaha had.

As for the Beller, he would be in an absolutely strange and frightening world. He could speak no word of the language and he would want to cling to his bell, which would be embarrassing and inconvenient for him. But he could have gone in any direction.

The only thing Kickaha could do was to head toward the nearest gate in the hope that Wolff and Chryseis would also be doing that. If they met there, they could team up, consider what to do next, and plan on the best way of locating the Beller. If Wolff and Chryseis did not show, then everything would be up to Kickaha.

Moo-Moo sat down by him. She put her hand on his arm and said, "My, you're muscular!"

"I have a few," he said, grinning. "Now that you've softened me up with your comments on my hardness, what's on your mind?"

She leaned against him, rubbing the side of her large breast against his arm, and said, "That Lou! He sees a new chick that's reasonably good-looking, and he flips every time. He's been talking to you, trying to get you to give your girl friend to him, hasn't he? I'll bet he offered you money for her."

"Some," Kickaha said. "What about it?"

She felt the muscles of his thigh and said, "Two can play at that game."

"You offering me money, too?" he said.

She drew away from him, her eyes widening and then she said, "You're putting me on! *I* should pay *you?*"

At another time, Kickaha might have played the game out to the end. But, corny as it sounded, the fate of the human race on Earth really depended on him. If the Beller adjusted to this world, and succeeded in making other bells, and then the minds in these possessed the bodies of human beings, the time would come when . . . Moo-Moo herself would become a mindless thing and then a body and brain inhabited by another entity.

It might not matter, however. If he were to believe half of what he read in the magazines and newspapers, the human race might well have doomed itself. And all life on the planet. Earth might be better off with humans occupied by the minds of Bellers. Bellers were logical beings, and, given a chance, they would clear up the mess that humans seemed to have made of the entire planet.

Kickaha shuddered a little. Such thinking was dangerous.

There could be no rest until the last of the Bellers died.

"What's the matter with you?" Moo-Moo said, her voice losing its softness. "You don't dig me?"

He patted her thigh and said, "You're a beautiful woman, Moo-Moo, but I love Ann. However, tell you what! If the Gnome King succeeds in turning Ann into one of his Bad Eggs, you and I will make music together. And it won't be the cacophony that radio is vomiting."

She jerked with surprise and then said, "What do you mean? That's the Rolling Stones!"

"No moss gathered here," he said.

"You're not with it," she said. "Man, you're square, square, square! You sure you're not over thirty?"

He shrugged. He had not cared for the popular music of his youth either. But it was sometimes pleasant, when compared to this screeching rhythm which turned his teeth in on himself.

The bus had moved out of the desert country into greener land. I sped along the freeway despite the increasing traffic. The sun was shining down so fiercely now, and the air was hot. The air was also noisy with the roar of cars and stinking with fumes. His eyes stung, and th insides of his nostrils felt needled. A grayish haze was lying ahead; then they were in it, and the air seemed to clear somewhat, and the haze was ahead again.

Moo-Moo said something about the smog really being fierce this time of the year and especially along here. Kickaha had read about smog in one of the magazines, although he did not know the origin of the word as yet. If this was what the people of southern California lived in, he wanted no more to do with it. Anana's eyes were red and teary and she was sniffling and complaining of a headache and clogging sinuses.

Moo-Moo left him, and Anana sat down by him.

"You never said anything about this when you were describing your world to me," she said.

"I didn't know anything about it," he said. "It developed after I left Earth."

The bus had been traveling swiftly and too wildly. It had switched lanes back and forth as it squeezed between cars, tailgating and cutting in ahead madly. The driver crouched over his wheel, his eyes seeming to blaze, his mouth hanging open and his tongue flicking out. He paid no attention to the sound of screeching brakes and blaring horns, but leaned on his own horn when he wanted to scare somebody just ahead of him. The horn was very loud and deep and must have sounded like a locomotive horn to many a startled driver. These usually pulled over to another lane, sometimes doing it so swiftly, they almost sideswiped other cars.

After a while, the press of cars was so heavy that the bus was forced to crawl along or even stop now and then. For miles ahead, traffic was creeping along. The heat and the gray haze thickened.

Moo-Moo said to Baum, "Why can't we get air conditioning on this bus? We certainly make enough money!"

"How often do we get on the freeway?" the manager said.

Kickaha told Anana about Baum's proposal.

Anana said, "I don't know whether to laugh or to throw up."

"A little of both might help you," he said. "Well, I promised I wouldn't try to argue you out of it if you decided to take him in preference to me. Which, by the way, he seemed one hundred percent sure would happen."

"You sell me; you worry a while until I make up my mind," she said.

"Sure. I'll do that," he replied. He rose and sauntered down the aisle and looked out the back of the bus. After a while he came back and sat down again with Anana.

In a low voice, he said, "There's a big black Lincoln Continental, I believe, behind us. I recognized one of the men in it. I saw him through the binoculars when I looked down from the cave."

"How could they have found us?" she said. Her voice was steady but her body was rigid.

"Maybe they didn't," he said. "It might be just a coincidence. They may have no idea they're so close to us. And then, again . . ."

It did not seem at all likely. But how had they caught up with them? Had they been posted along the road and seen them go by in the bus? Or did Orc have such a widespread organization that someone on the bus had reported to him?

He dismissed this last thought as sheer paranoia. Only time would show whether or not it was coincidence.

So far, the men in the car had not seemed interested in the bus. They were having a vigorous dispute. Three of them were dark and between forty and fifty-five years old. The fourth was a young man with blond hair cut in a Julius Caesar style. Kickaha studied them until he had branded their features on his mind. Then he returned to the seat near the front.

After a while, the traffic speeded up. The bus sped by grim industrial sections and the back ends of run-down buildings. The grayish green-tinged smog did not thicken, but its corrosive action became worse. Anana said, "Do your people live in this all the time? They must be very tough!"

"You know as much as I do about it," he said.

Baum suddenly rose from his seat beside Moo-Moo and said to the driver, "Jim, when you get near Civic Center, pull off and look for a hamburger stand. I'm hungry."

The others protested. They could eat at the hotel when they got there. It would only take about a half hour more. What was his hurry?

"I'm hungry!" he shouted. He looked wide-eyed at them and stomped his foot hard. "I'm hungry! I don't want to wait any longer! Besides, if we got to fight our way through the usual mob of teeny-boppers, we may be held up for some time! Let's eat *now!*"

The others shrugged. Evidently they had seen him act this way before. He looked as if he were going to scream and stamp through the floor, like in a tantrum, if he did not get his way.

It was not a whim this time, however. Moo-Moo rolled her eyes and then came up to Kickaha and said, "He's letting you know it's time to bow out, Red. You better take your worldly goods and kiss your girl friend goodbye."

"You've been through this before?" Kickaha said, grinning. "What makes you so sure Ann'll be staying?"

"I'm not so sure about her," Moo-Moo said. "I sensed something weird about you two, and the feeling hasn't gone away. In fact, it's even stronger."

She surprised Kickaha by saying, "You two are running away, aren't you? From the fuzz. And from others. More than the fuzz. Somebody close behind you now. I smell danger."

She squeezed his arm, bent lower, and whispered, "If I can help you, I'll be at the Beverly Hilton for a week, then we go to San Francisco. You call me. I'll tell the hotel to let you through. Any time."

Kickaha felt warmed by her interest and her offer of help. At the same time, he could not keep from considering that she might know more than any would-be friend of his should. Was it possible that she was tied in with Red Orc?

He rejected that. His life had been so full of danger, one perilous situation after another, and he had gotten into the prosurvival habit of always considering the worst and planning possible actions to avoid it. In this case, Moo-Moo could be nothing more than a psychic, or, at least, a very sensitive person.

The bus pulled off the freeway and drove to the Music Center. Kickaha would have liked to study the tall buildings here, which reminded him of those of Manhattan, but he was watching the big black Lincoln and its four occupants. It had turned when the bus turned and was now two cars behind. Kickaha was willing to concede that its getting off the freeway here might be another coincidence. But he doubted it very much.

The bus pulled into a corner of a parking lot in the center of which was a large hamburger stand. The bus doors opened, and the driver got out first. Baum took Anana's hand and led her out. Kickaha noted this out of the corner of his eye; he was watching the Lincoln. It had pulled into a parking place five cars down from the stand.

Baum was immediately surrounded by five or six young girls who shrieked his name and a number of unintelligible exclamations. They also tried to touch him. Baum smiled at them and waved his hands for them to back away. After a minute's struggle, he and the older men succeeded in backing them off.

Kickaha, carrying the instrument case, followed Moo-Moo off the bus and across the lot to the picnic table under a shady awning, where Baum and Anana were seated. The waitress brought hamburgers, hot dogs, milk shakes, and cokes. He salivated when he saw his hamburger.

It had been, God, over twenty-four years since he had tasted a hamburger! He bit down and then chewed slowly. There was something in the meat, some unidentified element, that he did not like. This distasteful substance also seemed to be in the lettuce and tomato.

Anana grimaced and said, in the language of the Lords, "What do you put in this food?"

Kickaha shrugged and said, "Insecticide, maybe, although it doesn't seem possible that we could detect one part in a million or whatever it was. Still, there's something."

They fared better with the chocolate milk shake. This was as thick and creamy and delicious as he remembered it. Anana nodded her approval, too.

The men were still in the Lincoln and were looking at him and Anana. At the group, anyway.

Baum looked across to Kickaha and said, "OK, Finnegan. This is it. Take off!"

Kickaha glanced up at him and said, "The bargain was, I take off if she agrees to go with you."

Baum laughed and said, "Just trying to spare your feelings, my Midwestern rustic. But have it your way. Watch me, maybe you'll learn something."

He leaned over Anana, who was talking with Moo-Moo. Moo-Moo glanced once at Baum's face, then got up, and walked off. Kickaha watched Baum and Anana. The conversation was short; the action, abrupt and explosive.

Anana slapped Baum so hard across the face that its noise could be heard above the gabble of his fans and the roar of the traffic. There was a short silence from everybody around Baum and then a number of shrieks of anger from the girl fans. Baum shouted angrily and swung with his right fist at Anana. She dodged and slid off the bench, but then the people around her blocked Kickaha's view.

He scooped off some change on the table, left by customers. Putting this in his pocket, he jumped into the fray. He was, however, almost knocked down by the press of bodies trying to get away. The girl rammed into him, clawed at him, shrieked, gouged, and kicked.

Suddenly, there was an opening. He saw Baum lying on the cement his legs drawn up and his hands clenching his groin. A girl, bent over was sitting by him and holding her stomach. Another girl was leaning over a wooden table, her back to him and retching.

Kickaha grabbed Anana's hand and shouted, "Come on! This is the chance we've been looking for!"

The instrument case in his other hand, he led her running toward the back of the parking lot. Just before they went down a narrow alley between two tall buildings, he looked back. The car containing his shadowers had pulled into the lot, and three of the men were getting out. They saw their quarry, and ran toward them. But they were not stupid enough to pull out weapons before they caught up with them. Kickaha did not intend that they should catch up with them.

And then, as he ran out of the alley and into the next street, he thought, *Why not? I could spend years trying to find Red Orc but if I can get hold of those who work for him . . . ?*

The next street was as busy as the one they had just left. The two stopped running but did walk swiftly. A police car, proceeding in the same direction, suddenly accelerated, its lights coming into red life. It took the corner with squealing tires, pursued by the curses of an old man who looked like a wino.

He looked behind him. The three men were still following but making no effort to overtake them. One man was talking into something concealed in his hand. He was either speaking to the man in the car or to his boss. Kickaha understood by now that radio sets were much smaller than in 1946 and that the man might be using a quite common miniature transceiver. On the other hand, he might be using a device unknown on Earth except to those who worked for Red Orc.

They continued walking. He looked back once more when they had covered two blocks. The big black Lincoln had stopped, and the three men were getting into it. Kickaha halted before a pawn shop and looked through the dirty plate glass window at the backwash of people's hopes. He said, "We'll give them a chance to try to pick us up. I don't know that they'll have guts enough to do it in broad daylight but if they do, here's what we do. . . ."

The Lincoln drew up even with them and stopped.

Kickaha turned around and grinned at the men in the Lincoln. The front and back doors on the right side opened, and three men got out. They walked toward the couple, their hands in their coat pockets. At that moment, a siren wailed down the street. The three jerked their heads to look at the police car which had suddenly appeared. It shot between cars, swerved sharply to cut around the Lincoln, and went on through the traffic light just as it was turning red. It kept on going; evidently it was not headed for the trouble around the corner.

The three men had turned casually and walked back toward the Lincoln. Kickaha took advantage of their concern over the police car. Before they could turn around again, he was behind them. He shoved his knuckles into the back of the oldest man and said, "I'll burn a hole through you if you make any trouble."

Anana had her ring finger against the back of the young man with the tangled blond hair. He stiffened, and his jaw dropped, as if he could not believe that not only had their hunted turned against them, they were doing so before at least fifty witnesses.

Horns started blaring at the Lincoln. The driver gestured at the three to hurry back, then he saw that Kickaha and Anana were pressed up closely against the backs of two of the men. The third man, who had overheard Kickaha, waved at the driver to go on. The Lincoln took off with a screeching and burning of tires and swung around the corner without coming to a stop first.

"That was a smart move!" Kickaha said to the man just in front of him. "One up for you!"

The third man began to walk away, Kickaha said, "I'll kill this guy if you don't come back!"

"Kill him!" the man said and continued walking.

Kickaha spoke in Lord language to Anana. "Let your man go! We'll keep this one and herd him to a private place where we can talk."

"What's to keep the others from following us?"

"Nothing. I don't care at this moment if they do."

He did, but he did not want the others to think so.

The blond sneered at them and swaggered off. There was something in his walk, however, which betrayed him. He was very relieved to have gotten away unhurt.

Kickaha then told the remaining man just what would happen if he tried to run away. The man said nothing. He seemed very calm. A genuine professional, Kickaha thought. It would have been better to have kept the blond youth, who might not be so tough to crack. It was too late to do anything about that, however.

The problem was: where to take the man for questioning? They were in the center of a vast metropolis unfamiliar to either Kickaha or Anana. There should be some third-rate hotels around here, judging by the appearance of the buildings and many of the pedestrians. It might be possible to rent a room and interrogate their captive there. But he could ruin everything if he opened his mouth and screamed. And even he could be gotten into a hotel room, his buddies would have trailed them there and would call in reinforcements. The hotel room would be a trap.

Kickaha gave the order and the three started walking. He was on one side of the man and Anana was on the other. He studied his captive profile, which looked brutish but strong. The man was about fifty, had a dark sallow skin, brown eyes, a big curved nose, a thick mouth, and a massive chin. Kickaha asked his name, and the man growled, "Mazarin."

"Who do you work for?" Kickaha said.

"Somebody you'd better not mess around with," Mazarin said.

"You tell me who your boss is and how I can get to him, and I'll let you go scot-free," Kickaha said. "Otherwise, I burn you until you tell. You know everybody has their limits, and you might be able to take a lot of burning, but you'll give in eventually."

The man shrugged big shoulders and said, "Sure. What about it?"

"Are you really that loyal?" Kickaha said.

The man looked at him contemptuously, "No, but I don't figure you'll get the chance to do anything. And I don't intend to say anything more."

He clamped his lips shut and turned his eyes away.

They had walked two blocks. Kickaha looked behind him. The Lincoln had come around and picked up the two men and now was proceeding slowly on the lane nearest the sidewalk.

Kickaha did not doubt that the three had gotten into contact with their boss and were waiting for reinforcements. It was an impasse.

Then he grinned again.

He spoke rapidly to Anana, and they directed Mazarin to the edge of the road. They waited until the Lincoln drew even and then stepped out. The three were staring from the car as if they could not believe what they were seeing. They also looked apprehensive. The car stopped when Kickaha waved at them. The two on the right side of the car had their guns out and pointed through the window, although their other hands concealed the barrels as best they could.

Kickaha pushed Mazarin ahead of him, and they walked around in front of the car and to the driver's side. Anana stopped on the right side of the car about five feet away.

Kickaha said, "Get into the car!"

Mazarin looked at him with an unreadable expression. He opened the rear door and began to climb in. Kickaha shoved him on in and came in with him. At the same time, Anana stepped up to the car. The driver had turned around and the other two had turned to watch Kickaha. She pressed the ring, which was set to stun power again, against the head of the man in the front right seat. He slumped over, and at the same time Kickaha stunned Mazarin.

The blond youth in the right rear seat pointed his gun at Kickaha and said, "You must be outta your mind! Don't move or I'll plug you!"

The energy from the ring hit the back of his head and spread out over the bone of the skull, probably giving the skin a first-degree burn through all the layers of cells. His head jerked forward as if a fist had hit it; his finger jerked in reflex. The .38 automatic went off once, sounding loudly inside the car. Mazarin jerked, fell back, his arms flying out and his hand hitting Kickaha in the chest. Then he fell over, slowly, against Kickaha.

The driver yelled and gunned the car. Anana leaped back to keep from being run over. Kickaha shouted at the driver, but the man kept the accelerator pressed to the floor. He screamed back an obscenity. He intended to keep going, even through the red light ahead at the intersection, on the theory that Kickaha would be too frightened of the results if he knocked him out.

Kickaha stunned him anyway, and the car immediately slowed down. It did not stop, however, and so rolled into the rear end of a car waiting for the red light to change. Kickaha had squatted down on the floor behind the driver's seat to cushion the impact. He was thrown forward with the back of the seat and the driver's body taking up most of the energy.

Immediately thereafter, he opened the door and crawled out. The man in the car in front of him was still sitting in his seat, looking stunned. Kickaha reached back into the car and took out Mazarin's wallet from his jacket pocket. He then removed the driver's wallet. The registration card for the car was not on the steering wheel column nor was it in the glove compartment. He could not afford to spend any more time at the scene. Kickaha walked away and then began running when he heard a scream behind him.

He met Anana at the intersection, and they took a left turn around the corner. Only one man had pursued Kickaha, but he had halted when Kickaha had glared at him, and he did not continue his dogging.

He hailed a cab, and they climbed in. Remembering the map of Los Angeles he had studied on the bus, he ordered the driver to drop them off on Lorraine, south of Wilshire.

Anana did not ask him what he was doing because he had told her to keep quiet. He did not want the cab driver to remember a woman who spoke a foreign language, although her beauty and their hiking clothes would make them stand out in his memory.

He picked out an apartment building to stop in front of, paid the driver, and tipped him with a dollar bill. Then he and Anana climbed the steps and went into the lobby, which was empty. Waiting until they were sure the cab would be out of sight, they walked back to Wilshire. Here they took a bus.

After several minutes, Kickaha led Anana off the bus and she said, "What now?" although she did not seem to be too interested at the moment in their next move. She was looking at the gas station across the street. Its architecture was new to Kickaha also. He could compare it only to something out of the Flash Gordon serials. Anana, of course, had seen many different styles. A woman didn't live ten thousand years and in several different universes without seeing a great variety of styles in buildings. But this Earth was such a hodgepodge.

Kickaha told her what he planned next. They would go toward Hollywood and look for a motel or hotel in the cheaper districts. He had learned from a magazine and from newspapers that that area contained many transients—hippies, they called them now—and the wilder younger element. Their clothing and lack of baggage would not cause curiosity.

They caught a cab in two minutes, and it carried them to Sunset Boulevard. Then they walked for quite a while. The sun went down; the lights came on over the city. Sunset Boulevard began to fill up with cars bumper to bumper. The sidewalks were beginning to be crowded, mainly with the "hippies" he'd read about. There were also a number of "characters," which was to be expected in Hollywood.

They stopped and asked some of the aimlessly wandering youths about lodging. A young fellow with shoulder-length hair and a thick 1890 moustache and sideburns, but dressed in expensive looking clothes, gave them some sound information. He wanted to talk some more and even invited them to have dinner with him. It was evident that he was fascinated by Anana, not Kickaha.

Kickaha said to him, "We'll see you around," and they left. A half hour later, they were inside their room in a motel on a side street. The room was not plush, but it was more than adequate for Kickaha, who had spent most of the last twenty-four years in primitive conditions. It was not as quiet as he wished, since a party was going on in the next room. A radio or record player was blasting out one of the more screechy examples of Rock, many feet stomped, and many voices shrieked.

While Anana took a shower, he studied the contents of the wallets he'd taken from the two men. Frederic James Mazarin and Jeffrey Velazquez Ramos, according to their drivers' licenses, lived on Wilshire Boulevard. His map showed him that the address was close to the termination of Wilshire downtown. He suspected that the two lived in a hotel. Mazarin was forty-eight and Ramos was forty-six. The rest of the contents of the wallets were credit cards (almost unknown in 1946, if he remembered correctly), a few pictures of the two with women, a photo of a woman who might have been Ramos' mother, money (three hundred and twenty dollars), and a slip of paper in Mazarin's wallet with ten initials in one column and telephone numbers in others.

Kickaha went into the bathroom and opened the shower door. He told Anana that he was going across the street to the public telephone booth.

"Why don't you use the telephone here?"

"It goes through the motel switchboard," he said. "I just don't want to take any chances of being traced or tapped."

He walked several blocks to a drug store where he got change. He stood for a moment, considering using the drug store phones and then decided to go back to the booth near the motel. That way, he could watch the motel front while making his calls.

He stopped for a moment by the paperback rack. It had been so long since he'd read a book. Well, he had read the Tishquetmoac books, but they didn't publish anything but science and history and theology. The people of the tier called Atlantis had published fiction, but he had spent very little time among them, although he had planned to do so someday. There had been some books in the Semitic civilization of Khamshem and the Germanic civilization of Dracheland, but the number of novels was very small and the variety was limited. Wolff's palace had contained a library of twenty million books—or recordings of books—but Kickaha had not spent enough time there to read very many.

He looked over the selection, aware that he shouldn't be taking the time to do so, and finally picked three. One was a Tom Wolfe book (but not the Thomas Wolfe he had known), which looked as if it would give him information about the zeitgeist of modern times. One was a factual book by Asimov (who was, it seemed, the same man as the science-fiction writer he remembered), and a book on the black revolution. He went to the magazine counter and purchased *Look, Life, The Saturday Review, The New Yorker,* the *Los Angeles* magazine, and a number of science-fiction magazines.

With his books, magazines, and an evening *Times,* he walked back to the telephone booth. He called Anana first to make sure that she was all right. Then he took pencil and paper and dialed each of the numbers on the slip of paper he had found in Mazarin's wallet.

Three of them were women who disclaimed any knowledge of Mazarin. Three of the numbers did not reply. Kickaha marked these fo later calls. One might have been a bookie joint, judging from the talking in the background. The man who answered was as noncommittal as the women. The eighth call got a bartender. Kickaha said he was looking for Mazarin.

The bartender said, "Ain't you heard, friend? Mazarin was killed today!"

"Somebody *killed* him?" Kickaha said, as if he were shocked. "Who done it?"

"Nobody knows. The guy was riding with Fred and some of the boys, and all of a sudden the guy pulls Charley's gun out of his pocket, shoots Fred in the chest with it, and takes off, but only after he knocks out Charley, Ramos, and Ziggy."

"Yeah?" Kickaha said. "Them guys was pros, too. They must've got careless or something. Say, ain't that gonna makes their boss mad? He must be jumping up and down!"

"You kiddin', friend? Nothin' makes Cambring jump up and down. Look, I gotta go, a customer. Drop around, buy me a drink, I'll fill you in on the gory details."

Kickaha wrote the name Cambring down and then looked through the phone book. There was no Cambring in the Los Angeles directory or any of the surrounding cities.

The ninth phone number was that of a Culver City garage. The man who answered said he'd never heard of Mazarin. Kickaha doubted that that was true, but there was nothing he could do about it.

The last number was opposite the letters R.C. Kickaha hoped that these stood for R. Cambring. But the woman who answered was Roma Chalmers. She was as guarded as the others in her replies to his questions.

He called Anana again to make doubly sure that she was all right. Then he returned to the room, where he ordered a meal from the Chicken Delight. He ate everything in the box, but the food had that taste of something disagreeable and of something missing. Anana also ate all of hers but complained.

"Tomorrow's Saturday," he said. "If we haven't found any promising leads, we'll go out and get some clothes."

He took a shower and got dried just before a bottle of Wild Turkey and six bottles of Tuborg were delivered. Anana tried both and settled for the Danish beer. Kickaha sipped a little of the bourbon and made a wry face. The liquor store owner had said that the bourbon was the best in the world. It had been too long since he had tasted whiskey; he would have to learn to like it all over again. If he had time, that is, which he doubted. He decided to drink a bottle or two of the Tuborg, which he found tasty, probably because beer-making was well known on the World of Tiers and he had not gotten out of the habit of drinking it.

He sat in a chair and sipped while he slowly read out loud in English from the newspaper to Anana. Primarily, he was looking for any news about Wolff, Jadawin, or the Beller. He sat up straight when he came across an item about Lucifer's Louts. These had been discovered, half-naked, beaten up, and burned, on the road out of Lake Arrowhead. The story they gave police was that a rival gang had jumped them.

A page later, he found a story about the crash of a helicopter near Lake Arrowhead. The helicopter, out of the Santa Monica airport, was owned by a Mister Cambring, who had once been put on trial, but not convicted, for bribery of city officials in connection with a land deal. Kickaha whooped with delight and then explained to Anana what a break this was.

The news story did not give Cambring's address. Kickaha called the office of Top Hat Enterprises, which Cambring owned. The phone rang for a long time, and he finally gave up. He then called the *Los Angeles Times* and, after a series of transfers from one person and department to another, some of them involving waits of three or four minutes, he got his information. Mr. Roy Arndell Cambring lived on Rimpau Boulevard. A check of the city map showed that the house was several blocks north of Wilshire.

"This helps," he said. "I would have located Cambring if I had to hire a private eye to find him. But that would have taken time. Let's get to bed. We have a lot to do tomorrow."

However, it was an hour before they fell asleep. Anana wanted to lie quietly in his arms while she talked of this and that, about her life before she had met Kickaha but mostly of incidents after she had met him. Actually, they had not known each other more than two months and their life together had been hectic. But she claimed to be in love with Kickaha and acted as if she were. He loved her but had had enough experience with the Lords to wonder how deep a capacity for love anybody ten thousand years old could possess. It was true, though, that some of the Lords could live for the moment far more intensely than anybody he had ever met simply because a man who lived in eternity had to eat up every moment as if it were his last. He could not bear to think about the unending years ahead.

In the meantime, he was happy with her, although he would have been happier if he could have some leisure and peace so he could get to know her better. Which was exactly what she was complaining about. She did not complain too much. She knew that every situation ended sooner or later.

He fell asleep thinking about this. Sometime in the night, he awoke with a jerk. For a second, he thought somebody must be in the room, and he slid out the knife that lay sheathless by his side under the sheet covering him. His eyes adjusted to the darkness, which was not too deep because of the light through the blinds from the bright neon lights outside and the street lamps. He could see no one.

Slowly, so the bed would not creak, he got out and moved cautiously around the room, the bathroom, and then the closet. The windows were still locked on the inside, the door was locked, and the bureau he had shoved against it had not moved. Nor was there anyone under the bed.

He decided that he had been sleeping on a tightwire too long. He expected, even if unconsciously, to fall off.

There must be more to it than that, however. Something working deep inside him had awakened him. He had been dreaming just before he awoke. Of what?

He could not get his hook into it and bring it up out of the unconscious, though he cast many times. He paced back and forth, the knife still in his hand, and tried to recreate the moment just before awakening. After a while he gave up. But he could not sleep when he lay back down again. He rose again, dressed, and then woke Anana up gently. At his tender touch on her face, she came up off the bed, knife in hand.

He had wisely stepped back. He said, "It's all right, lover, I just wanted to tell you that I'm leaving to check out Cambring's house. I can't sleep anymore; I feel as if I have something important to do. I've had this feeling before and it's always paid off."

He did not add that it had sometimes paid off with grave, almost fatal, trouble.

"I'll go with you."

"No, that won't be necessary. I appreciate your offer, but you stay here and sleep. I promise I won't do anything except scout around it, at a safe distance. You won't have anything to worry about."

"All right," she said, half-drowsily. She had full confidence in his abilities. "Kiss me good night again and get on with you. I'm glad I'm not a restless soul."

The lobby was empty. There were no pedestrians outside the motel, although a few cars whizzed by. The droning roar of a jet lowering for International Airport seemed to be directly overhead, but its lights placed it quite a few miles southeastward. He trotted on down the street toward the south and hoped that no cops would cruise by. He under-stood from what he'd read that a man walking at night in the more prosperous districts was also suspect.

He could have taken a taxi to a place near his destination, but he preferred to run. He needed the exercise; if he continued life in this city long, he would be getting soft rapidly.

The smog seemed to have disappeared with the sun. At least, his eyes did not burn and run, although he did get short-winded after having trotted only eight blocks. There must be poisonous oxides hanging in-visibly in the air. Or he was deteriorating faster than he had thought possible.

By the map, the Cambring house lay about three and one-half miles from the motel, not as the crow flies but as a ground-bound human must go.

Once on Rimpau he was in a neighborhood of fairly old mansions. The neighborhood looked as if only rich people had lived here, but it was changing. Some of the grounds and houses had deteriorated, and some had been made into apartment dwellings. But a number were still very well kept up.

The Cambring house was a huge three-story wooden house which looked as if it had been built circa 1920 by someone nostalgic for the architecture popular among the wealthy of the Midwest. It was set up on a high terrace with a walk in the middle of the lawn and a horse-shoe-shaped curving driveway. Three cars were parked in the drive-way. There were a dozen great oaks and several sycamores on the front lawn and many high bushes, beautifully trimmed, set in among the trees. A high brick wall enclosed all but the front part of the property.

There were lights behind closed curtains in the first and second sto-ries. There was also a light in the second story of the garage, which he could partially see. He walked on past the front of the home to the corner. The brick wall ran along the sidewalk here. Part way down the block was another driveway which led to the garage. He stopped before the closed iron gates, which were locked on the inside.

It was possible that there were electronic detecting devices set on the grounds among the trees, but he would have to chance them. Also, it would be well to find out now.

He doubted that this house was lived in by Red Orc. Cambring must be one of Orc's underlings, probably far down in the hierarchy. The Lord of Earth would be ensconced in a truly luxurious dwelling and behind walls which would guard him well.

He set his ring for flesh-piercing powers at up to two hundred fee and placed his knife between his teeth. Instead of returning to the front, he went over the wall on the side of the house. It was more difficult to enter here, but there was better cover.

He backed up into the street and then ran forward, bounded across the sidewalk, and leaped upward. His fingers caught the edge of the wall and he easily pulled himself up and over onto the top of the wall. He lay stretched out on it, watching the house and garage for signs of activity. About four minutes passed. A car, traveling fast, swung around the corner two blocks away and sped down the street. It was possible that the occupants of the house might see him in the beams. He swung on over and dropped onto soft grassy ground behind an oak tree. If he had wished, he could have jumped to the nearest branch, which had been sawed off close to the wall, and descended by the tree. He noted it as a means of escape.

It was now about three in the morning, if his sense of time was good. He had no watch but meant to get one, since he was now in a world where the precise measurement of time was important.

The next ten minutes he spent in quietly exploring the area immediately outside the house and the garage. Three times he went up into a tree to try to look through windows but he could see nothing. He poked around the cars but did not try to open their doors because he thought that they might have alarms. It seemed likely that a gangster like Cambring would be more worried about a bomb being placed in his car than he would about an invasion of his house. The big black Lincoln was not there. He assumed it had been impounded by the police as evidence in the murder. He read the license numbers several times to memorize them, even though he had a pencil and a piece of paper. During his years in the universe next door, he had been forced to rely on his memory. He had developed it to a power that he would have thought incredible twenty-five years ago. Illiteracy had its uses. How many educated men on Earth could recall the exact topography of a hundred places or draw a map of a five-thousand-mile route or recite a three-thousand-line epic?

In fifteen minutes he had checked out everything he could on the outside and knew exactly where things were in relation to each other. Now was the time to leave. He wished he had not promised Anana that he would only observe the exterior. The temptation to get inside was almost overwhelming. If he could get hold of Cambring and force some information from him . . . but he had promised. And she had gone back to sleep because she trusted him to keep his word. That in itself indicated how much she loved him, because if there was one thing a Lord lacked, it was trust in others.

He crouched for a while behind a bush in the side yard, knowing that he should leave but also knowing that he was hoping something would happen which would force him to take action. Minutes passed.

Then he heard a phone ringing inside the house. A light went on in a second-story window behind a curtain. He rose and approached the house and applied a small bell-like device to the side of the house. A cord ran from it to a plug, which he stuck in one ear. Suddenly, a man said, "Yes, sir. I got you. But how did you find them, if I may ask?"

There was a short silence, then the man said, "I'm sorry, sir. I didn't mean to be nosy, of course. Yes, sir, it won't happen again. Yes, sir, I got you the first time. I know exactly what to do. I'll call you when we start the operation, sir. Good night, sir."

Kickaha's heart beat faster. Cambring could be talking directly to Red Orc. In any event, something important was happening. Something ominous.

He heard footsteps and buzzers ringing. The voice said—presumably over an intercom—"Get dressed and up here! On the double! We got work to do! Jump!"

He decided what to do. If he heard anything that indicated that they were not going after him, he would wait until they left and then enter the house. Conditions would have changed so much that it would be stupid for him not to take advantage of their absence. Anana would have to understand that.

If he heard anything that indicated that he and Anana were concerned, he would take off for the nearest public phone booth.

He felt in his pocket for change and cursed. He had one nickel left over from the calls made that previous evening.

Seven minutes later, eight men left by the front door. Kickaha watched them from behind a tree. Four men got into a Mercedes-Benz and four into a Mercury. He could not be sure which was Cambring, because nobody spoke when they left the house. One man did hold the door open for a tall man with a high curly head of hair and a bold sweeping nose. He suspected that that was Cambring. Also, he recognized two: the blond youth and Ramos, the driver of the Lincoln. Ramos had a white bandage over his forehead.

The cars drove off, leaving one car in the driveway. There were also people in the house. He had heard one woman sleepily asking Cambring what was wrong, and a man's voice surlily asking why he had to stay behind. He wanted some action. Cambring had curtly told him to shut up. They were under orders never to leave the house unguarded.

The cars had no sooner disappeared than Kickaha was at the front door. It was locked, but a quick shot of energy from the ring cut through the metal. He swung the door inward slowly, and stepped inside into a room lit only by a light from a stairwell at the far end. When his eyes adjusted, he could see a phone on a table at the far wall. He went to it, lit a match, and by its light, dialed Anana. The phone rang no more than three times before she answered.

He said softly, "Anana! I'm in Cambring's house! He and his gang are on the way to pick us up. You grab your clothes and get out of there, fast, hear! Don't even bother to dress! Put everything in a bag and take off! Dress behind the motel! I'll meet you where we arranged. Got it?"

"Wait!" she said. "Can't you tell me what's happened?"

"No!" he said and softly replaced the receiver on the phone. He had heard footsteps in the hall upstairs and then the creaking caused by a big man descending the steps slowly.

Kickaha reset the ring for stunning power. He needed someone to question, and he doubted that the woman would know as much about operations as this man.

The faint creakings stopped. Kickaha crouched by the foot of the steps and waited. Suddenly, the lights in the great room went on, and a man catapulted outward from behind the wall which had hidden him. He came down off the steps in a leap, whirling as he did so. He held a big automatic, probably a .45, in his right hand. He landed facing Kickaha and then fell backward, unconscious, his head driven backward by the impact of the beam. The gun fell from his hand onto the thick rug.

Kickaha heard the woman upstairs saying, "Walt! What's the matter? Walt? Is anything wrong?"

Kickaha picked up the gun, flicked on the safety, and stuck it in his belt. Then he walked up the steps and got to the head of the stairwell just as the woman did. She opened her mouth to scream, but he clamped his hand over it and held the knife before her eyes. She went limp as if she thought she could placate him by not struggling. She was correct, for the moment, anyway.

She was a tall, very well built blonde, about thirty-five, in a filmy negligee. Her breath stank of whiskey. But good whiskey.

"You and Cambring and everybody else in this house mean only one thing to me," he said. "As a means to getting to the big boss. That's all.

I can let you go without a scratch and care nothing about what you do from then on if you don't bother me. Or I can kill you. Here and now. Unless I get the information I want. You understand me?"

She nodded.

He said, "I'll let you go. But one scream, and I'll rip out your belly. Understand?"

She nodded again. He took his hand away from her mouth. She was pale and trembling.

"Show me a picture of Cambring," he said.

She turned and led him to her bedroom, where she indicated a photograph on her bureau dresser. It was of the man he had suspected was Cambring. "Are you his wife?" he said.

She cleared her throat and said, "Yes."

"Anybody else in this house besides Walt?"

She said huskily, "No."

"Do you know where Cambring went tonight?"

"No," she said. She cleared her throat again. "I don't want to know those things."

"He's gone off to pick up me and my woman for your big boss," Kickaha said. "The big boss would undoubtedly kill us, after he'd tortured us to get everything he wanted to know. So I won't have any mercy on anybody connected with him—if they refuse to cooperate."

"I don't know anything!" she gasped. "Roy never tells me anything! I don't even know who the big boss is!"

"Who's Cambring's immediate superior?"

"I don't know. Please believe me! I don't know! He gets orders from somebody, I'll admit that! But I don't know!"

She was probably telling the truth. So the next thing to do was to rouse Walt and find out what he knew. He did not have much time.

He went downstairs with Cara ahead of him. The man was still unconscious. Kickaha told Cara to get a glass of water from the nearest bathroom. He threw it over Walt's face. Walt recovered a moment later, but he looked too sick to be a threat. He seemed to be on the verge of throwing up. A big black mark was spreading over the skin on his forehead and nose, and his eyes looked a solid red.

The questioning did not last long. The man, whose full name was Walter Erich Vogel, claimed he also did not know who Cambring's boss was. Kickaha believed this, since Cambring had not said anything about the destination. Apparently, he meant to tell his men after they got started. Cambring called his boss now and then but he carried the phone number in his head.

"It's the old Commie cell idea," Vogel said. "So you could torture me from now until doomsday and you wouldn't get anything out of me because I don't know anything."

Kickaha went to the phone again and, while he kept an eye on the two, dialed Anana's number again. He wasn't surprised when Cambring answered.

"Cambring," he said, "this is the man you were sent after. Now hear me out because this message is intended for your big boss. You tell him, or whoever relays messages to him, that a Black Beller is loose on Earth.

There was a silence, one of shock, Kickaha hoped, and then Cambring said, "What? What the hell are you talking about? What's a Black Beller?"

"Just tell your boss that a Black Beller got loose from Jadawin's world. The Beller's in this area, or was yesterday, anyway. Remember, a Black Beller. Came here yesterday from Jadawin's world."

There was another silence and then Cambring said, "Listen. The boss knows you got away. But he said that if I got a chance to talk to you, you should come on in. The boss won't hurt you. He just wants to talk to you."

"You might be right," Kickaha said. "But I can't afford to take the chance. No, you tell your boss something. You tell him that I'm not out to get him; I'm not a Lord. I just want to find another Lord and his woman, who came to this world to escape from the Black Bellers. In fact, I'll tell you who that Lord is. It's Jadawin. Maybe your boss will remember him. It's Jadawin, who's changed very much. Jadawin isn't interested in challenging your boss; he could care less. All he wants to do is get back to his own world. You tell him that, though I doubt it'll do any good. I'll call your home tomorrow about noon, so you can relay more of what I have to say to your boss. I'll call your home. Your boss might want to be there so he can talk to me directly."

"What the hell you gibbering about?" Cambring said. He sounded very angry.

"Just tell your boss what I said. He'll understand," Kickaha said, and he hung up. He was grinning. If there was one thing that scared a Lord, it was a Black Beller.

The sports car was, as he had suspected, hers. She said she would have to go upstairs to get the keys. He said that that was all right, but he and Vogel would go with her. They went into her bedroom, where Kickaha gave Vogel a slight kick in the back of the head with a beam from the ring. He took Vogel's wallet and dragged him into the closet, where he left him snoring. He then demanded money from the woman, and she gave him six hundred dollars in twenties and fifties. It pleased him that he had been able to live off the enemy so far.

To keep her occupied, he tore down some curtains, and set them on fire with a sweep from the ring. She screamed and dashed into the bathroom to get water. A moment later, he was driving the Jaguar off the driveway. Behind him, screams came through the open doorway as she fought the flames.

At a corner a few blocks east from the motel, he flashed his lights twice to alert Anana. A dark figure emerged from between two houses. She approached warily until she recognized him. She threw their packs and the instrument case into the back seat, got in and said, "Where did you get this vehicle?"

"Took it from Cambring." He chuckled and said, "I left a message with Cambring for Red Orc. Told him that a Black Beller was loose. That ought to divert him. It might even scare him into offering an armistice."

"Not Red Orc," she said. "Not unless he's changed. Which is possible. I did. My brother Luvah did. And you say Jadawin did."

He told her about his idea for contacting Wolff. "I should have thought of it sooner, but we have been occupied. And, besides, I've forgotten a lot about Earth."

For the moment, they would look for new lodgings. However, he was not so sure that they could feel safe even there. It was remarkable that they had been located. Red Orc must have set into action a very large organization to have found them.

"How could he do that?" she said.

"For all I know, his men called every hotel and motel in the Los Angeles area. That would be such a tremendous job, though, I doubt they could have gone through more than a small percentage of them. Maybe they were making random spot calls. Or maybe they were going through them all, one by one, and were lucky."

"If that is so, then we won't be safe when we check in at the next place."

"I just don't believe that even the Lord of the Earth would have an organization big enough to check out all the motels and hotels in so short a time," he said. "But we'll leave the area, go to the Valley, as they so quaintly call it here."

When they found a motel in Laurel Canyon, he ran into difficulties.

The clerk wanted his driver's license and the license number of his car. Kickaha did not want to give him the license number, but, since the clerk showed no signs of checking up on him, Kickaha gave him a number made up in his head. He then showed him Ramos' driver's license. The clerk copied down the number and looked once at the photograph. Ramos had a square face with a big beaky nose, black eyes, and a shock of black hair. Despite this, the clerk did not seem to notice.

Kickaha, however, was suspicious. The fellow was too smooth. Perhaps he did not really care whether or not Kickaha was the person he claimed to be, but then, again, he might. Kickaha said nothing, took the keys, and led Anana out of the lobby. Instead of going to their room on the second floor, he stood outside the door, where he could not be seen. A minute later, he heard the clerk talking to somebody. He looked in. The clerk was sitting at the switchboard with his back to the door. Kickaha tiptoed in closer.

". . . not his," the clerk was saying. "Yeah, I checked out the license, soon as they left. The car's parked near here. Listen, you . . ."

He stopped because he had turned his head and had seen Kickaha. He turned it away, slowly, and said, "OK. See you."

He took off the earphones and stood up and said, smiling, "May I help you?"

"We decided to eat before we went to bed; we haven't eaten all day," Kickaha said, also smiling. "Where's the nearest good restaurant?"

The clerk spoke slowly, as if he were trying to think of one that would suit them. Kickaha said, "We're not particular. Any place'll do."

A moment later, he and Anana drove off. The clerk stood in the front door and watched them. He had seen them put their packs and the case in the car, so he probably did not believe that they were coming back.

He was thinking that they could sleep in the car tonight, provided the police weren't looking for it. Tomorrow they would have to buy clothes and a suitcase or two. He would have to get rid of this car, but the problem of renting or buying a car without the proper papers was a big one.

He pulled into a service station and told the attendant to fill her up. The youth was talkative and curious; he wanted to know where they'd been, up in the mountains? He liked hiking, too.

Kickaha made up a story. He and his wife had been bumming around but decided to come down and dig L.A. They didn't have much money; they were thinking about selling the car and getting a second-hand VW. They wanted to stay the night some place where they didn't ask questions if the color of your money was right.

The attendant told them of a motel near Tarzana in Van Nuys which fitted all Kickaha's specifications. He grinned and winked at them, sure they were engaged in something illegal (or rebellious) and wished them luck. Maybe he could get them a good bargain on the Jag.

A half hour later, he and Anana fell into a motel bed and were asleep at once.

He got up at ten. Anana was sleeping soundly. After shaving and showering, he woke her long enough to tell her what he planned. He went across the street to a restaurant, ate a big breakfast, bought a paper, and then returned to the room. Anana was still sleeping. He called the *Los Angeles Times* ad department and dictated an item for the personal column. He gave as his address the motel and also gave a fictitious name. He had thought about using Ramos' name in case the *Times* man checked out the address. But he did not want any tie between the ad and Cambring, if he could help it. He promised to send his check immediately, and then, hanging up, forgot about it.

He checked the personals of the morning's *Times*. There were no messages that could be interpreted as being from Wolff.

When Anana woke, he said, "While you're eating breakfast, I'll use a public phone booth to call Cambring," he said. "I'm sure he's gotten the word to Red Orc."

Cambring answered at once as if he had been waiting by the phone. Kickaha said, "This is your friend of last night, Cambring. Did you pass on my information about the Black Beller?"

Cambring's voice sounded as if he were controlling anger.

"Yes, I did."

"What did he say?"

"*He* said that he'd like to meet you. Have a conference of war."

"Where?"

"Wherever you like."

Good, thought Kickaha. *He doesn't think I'm so dumb that I'd walk into his parlor. But he's confident that he can set up a trap no matter where I meet him. If, that is, he himself shows up. I doubt that. He'd be far too cagy for that. But he'll have to send someone to represent him, and that someone might be higher up than Cambring and a step closer to the Lord.*

"I'll tell you where we'll meet in half an hour," Kickaha said. "But before I hang up, did your boss have anything else to say I should hear?"

"No."

Kickaha clicked the phone down. He found Anana in a booth in the restaurant. He sat down and said, "I don't know whether Orc's got hold of Wolff or not. I don't even know for sure whether Cambring repeated my message about Wolff and Chryseis, but Orc knows the gate was activated twice before we came through and that one of the people coming through was a Black Beller. I don't think he's got Wolff and Chryseis, because if he did, he'd use them as a way to trap me. He'd know I'd be galloping in to save them."

"Perhaps," she said. "But he may feel that he doesn't have to let you know he has Wolff and Chryseis. He may feel confident that he can catch us without saying anything about them. Or perhaps he's withholding his knowledge until a more suitable time."

"You Lords sure figure out the angles," he said. "As suspicious a lot as the stars have ever looked down on."

"Look who's talking!" she said in English.

They returned to their room, picked up their bags and the case, and went to the car. They drove off without checking out, since Kickaha did not think it wise to let anybody know what they were doing if it could be helped. In Tarzana, he went into a department store and checked out clothes for himself and Anana. This took an hour, but he did not mind keeping Cambring waiting. Let him and his boss sweat for a while.

While he was waiting for his trousers to be altered, he made the call. Again, Cambring answered immediately.

"Here's what we'll do," Kickaha said. "I'll be at a place fairly close to your house. I'll call you when I get there, and I'll give you twelve minutes to get to our meeting place. If you aren't there by then, I move on. Or if it looks like a trap, I'll take off, and that'll be the last you'll see of me—at a meeting place, that is. Your boss can take care of the Beller himself."

"What the hell is this Beller you're talking about?" Cambring said angrily.

"Ask your boss," Kickaha said, knowing that Cambring would not dare do this. "Look, I'm going to be in a place where I can see on all sides. I want just two men to meet me. You, because I know you, and your boss. You'll advance no closer than sixty yards, and your boss will then come ahead. Got it? So long!"

At noon, after eating half a hamburger and a glass of milk, he called Cambring. He was at a restaurant only a few blocks from the meeting place. Cambring answered again before the phone had finished its third ring. Kickaha told him where he was to meet him and under what conditions.

"Remember," he said, "if I smell anything fishy, I take off like an Easter bunny with birth pangs."

He hung up. He and Anana drove as quickly as traffic would permit. His destination was the Los Angeles County Art Museum. Kickaha parked the car around the corner and put the keys under the floor mat, in case only one of them could get back to it. They proceeded on foot behind the museum and walked through the parking lot.

Anana had dropped behind him so that anyone watching would not know she was with Kickaha. Her long, glossy black hair was coiled up into a Psyche knot, and she wore a white low-cut frilly blouse and very tight green-and-red striped culottes. Dark glasses covered her eyes, and she carried an artists' sketch pad and pencils. She also carried a big leather purse which contained a number of items that would have startled any scientifically knowledgeable Earthling.

While Kickaha hailed down a cab, she walked slowly across the grass. Kickaha gave the cab driver a twenty-dollar bill as evidence of his good intentions and of the tip to come. He told him to wait in the parking lot, motor running, ready to take off when Kickaha gave the word. The cab driver raised his eyebrows and said, "You aren't planning on robbing the museum?"

"I'm planning on nothing illegal," Kickaha said. "Call me eccentric. I just like to leave in a hurry sometimes."

"If there's any shooting, I'm taking off," the driver said. "With or without you. And I'm reporting to the cops. Just so you know, see?"

Kickaha liked to have more than one avenue of escape. If Cambring's men should be cruising around the neighborhood, they might spot their stolen car and set a trap for Kickaha. In fact, he was betting that they would. But if the way to the cab was blocked, and he had to take the route to the car, and that wasn't blocked, he would use the car.

However, he felt that the driver was untrustworthy, not that he blamed him for feeling suspicious.

He added a ten to the twenty and said, "Call the cops now, if you want. I don't care, I'm clean."

Hoping that the cabbie wouldn't take him up, he turned and strode across the cement of the parking lot and then across the grass to the tar pit. Anana was sitting down on a concrete bench and sketching the mammoth which seemed to be sinking into the black liquid. She was an excellent artist, so that anybody who looked over her shoulder would see that she knew her business.

Kickaha wore dark glasses, a purple sleeveless and neckless shirt, a big leather belt with fancy silver buckle, and Levis. Under his long red hair, against the bone behind his ear, was a receiver. The device he wore on his wrist contained an audio transmitter and a beamer six times as powerful as that in his ring.

Kickaha took his station at the other end of the tar pit. He stood near the fence beyond which was the statue of a huge prehistoric bear. There were about fifty people scattered here and there, none of whom looked as if they would be Cambring's men. This, of course, meant nothing.

A minute later, he saw a large gray Rolls Royce swing into the parking lot. Two men got out and crossed the grass in a straight line toward him. One was Ramos. The other was tall and gangly and wore a business suit, dark glasses, and a hat. When he came closer, Kickaha saw a horse-faced man of about fifty. Kickaha doubted then that he would be Red Orc, because no Lord, not even if he were twenty thousand years old, looked as if he were over thirty.

Anana's voice sounded in his ear. "It's not Red Orc."

He looked around again. There were two men on his left, standing near the fountain by the museum and two men on his right, about twenty yards beyond Anana. They could be Cambring's men.

His heart beat faster. The back of his neck felt chilled. He looked through the fence across the pit at Wilshire Boulevard. Parking was forbidden there at any time. But a car was there, its hood up and a man looking under it. A man sat in the front seat and another in the rear.

"He's going to try to grab me," Kickaha said. "I've spotted seven of his men, I think."

"Do you want to abandon your plan?" she said.

"If I do, you know the word," he said. "Watch it! Here they come!"

Ramos and the gangly man stopped before him. The gangly man said, "Paul?" using the name Kickaha had given Cambring.

Kickaha nodded. He saw another big car enter the parking lot. It was too far for him to distinguish features, but the driver, wearing a hat and dark glasses, could be Cambring. There were three others in his car.

"Are you Red Orc?" Kickaha said, knowing that the tall man was probably carrying a device which would transmit the conversation to the Lord, wherever he was.

"Who? Who's Redark?" the tall man said. "My name is Kleist. Now, Mr. Paul, would you mind telling me what you want?"

Kickaha spoke in the language of the Lords, "Red Orc! I am not a Lord but an Earthling who found a gate to the universe of Jadawin, whom you may remember. I came back to Earth, though I did not want to, to hunt down the Beller. I have no desire to stay here; I wish only to kill the Beller and get back to my adopted world. I have no interest in challenging you."

Kleist said, "What the hell you gibbering about? Speak English, man!"

Ramos looked uneasy. He said, "He's flipped."

Kleist suddenly looked dumbfounded. Kickaha guessed that he was getting orders.

"Mr. Paul," Kleist said, "I am empowered to offer you complete amnesty. Just come with us and we will introduce you to the man you want to see."

"Nothing doing," Kickaha said. "I'll work with your boss, but I won't put myself in his power. He may be all right, but I have no reason to trust him. I would like to cooperate with him, however, in tracking down the Beller."

Kleist's expression showed that he did not understand the reference to the Beller.

Kickaha looked around again. The men on his left and right were drifting closer. The two men in the car on Wilshire had gotten out. One was looking under the hood with the other man, but the third was gazing through the fence at Kickaha. When he saw Kickaha looking at him, he slowly turned away.

Kickaha said angrily, "You were told that only two of you should come! You're trying to spring a trap on me! You surely don't think you can kidnap me here in the middle of all these people?"

"Now, now, Mr. Paul!" Kleist said. "You're mistaken! Don't be nervous! There's only two of us, and we're here to talk to you, only that."

Anana said, "A police car has just pulled up behind that car on the street."

Kleist and Ramos looked at each other; it was evident that they had also seen the police car. But they looked as if they had no intention of leaving.

Kickaha said, "If your boss would like me to help, he'll have to think of some way of guaranteeing me passage back."

He decided he might as well spring his surprise now. The Lord knew that there was a woman with Kickaha, and while he had no way of knowing that she was a Lord, he must suspect it. Kickaha had only been on Earth a short time when the Lord's men had seen her with him. And since he knew that the gate had been activated twice before Kickaha came along, he must suspect that the other party—or parties—was also a Lord.

Now was the time to tell Red Orc about them. This would strengthen

Kickaha's bargaining position and it might stop the effort to take him prisoner just now.

"You tell your boss," he said, "that there are four other Lords now on Earth."

Kickaha was not backward about exaggerating if it might confuse or upset the enemy. There might come a time when he could use the two nonexistent Lords as leverage.

"Also," he added, "there are two Earthlings who have come from Jadawin's world. Myself and a woman who is with Jadawin."

That ought to rock him, he thought. Arouse his curiosity even more. He must be wondering how two Earthlings got into Jadawin's world in the first place and how they got back here.

"You tell your boss," Kickaha said, "that none of us, except for the Beller, mean him any harm. We just want to kill the Beller and get the hell out of this stinking universe."

Kickaha thought that Red Orc should be able to understand that. What Lord in his right mind would want to take control of Earth from another Lord? What Lord would want to stay here when he could go to a much nicer, if much smaller, universe?

Kleist was silent for a moment. His head was slightly cocked as if he were listening to an invisible demon on his shoulder. Then he said, "What difference does it make if there are four Lords?"

It was obvious that Kleist was relaying the message and that he did not understand the references.

Kickaha spoke in the language of the Lords. "Red Orc! You have forgotten the device that every Lord carries in his brain. The alarm that rings in every Lord's head when he gets close to the metal bell of a Beller! With four Lords searching for the Beller, the chances for finding him are greater!"

Kleist had dropped any pretense that he was not in direct communication with his chief. He said, "How does he know that *you* are not the Beller?"

"If I were a Beller, why would I get into contact with you, let you know you had a dangerous enemy loose in your world?"

"He says," Kleist reported, his face becoming blanker as he talked, as if he were turning into a mechanical transceiver, "that a Beller would try to locate all Lords as quickly as possible. After all, a Lord is the only one besides a Beller who knows that Bellers exist. Or who can do anything about them. So you would try to find him, just as you are now doing. Even if it meant your life. Bellers are notorious for sacrificing one of their number if they can gain an advantage thereby.

"He also says, how does he know that these so-called Lords are not your fellow Bellers?"

Kickaha spoke in the Lords' tongue. "Red Orc! You are trying my patience. I have appealed to you because I know of your vast resources! You haven't got much choice, Red Orc! If you force me to cut off contact with you, then you won't know that I'm not a Beller and your sleep will be hideous with nightmares about the Bellers at large! In fact, the only way you can be sure that I'm not a Beller is to work with me, but under my terms! I insist on that!"

The only way to impress a Lord was to be even more arrogant than he.

Anana's voice said, "The car's gone. The police must have scared them out. The police car's going now."

Kickaha raised his arm and muttered into the transceiver, "Where are the others?"

"Closing in. They're standing by the fence and pretending to look at the statues. But they're working toward you."

He looked past Kleist and Ramos across the grass. The two cars he had suspected were now empty, except for one man, whom he thought would be Cambring. The others were among the picnickers on the grass. He saw two men who looked grim and determined and tough; they could be Cambring's.

"We'll take off to my left," he said. "Around the fence and across Wilshire. If they follow us, it'll have to be on foot. At first, at least."

He flicked a look toward Anana. She had gotten up from the bench and was strolling toward him.

Kleist said, "Very well. I am authorized to accept your terms."

He smiled disarmingly and stepped closer. Ramos tensed.

"Couldn't we go elsewhere? It's difficult to carry on a conversation here. But it'll be wherever you say."

Kickaha was disgusted. He had just been about to agree that it would be best to tie in with Red Orc. Through him, the Beller and Wolff and Chryseis might be found, and after that the dam could break and the devil take the hindmost. But the Lord was following the bent of his kind; he was trusting his power, his ability to get anything or anybody he wanted.

Kickaha made one last try. "Hold it! Not a step closer! You ask your boss if he remembers Anana, his niece, or Jadawin, his nephew? Remembers how they looked? If he can identify them, then he'll know I'm telling the truth."

Kleist was silent and then nodded his head. He said, "Of course. My boss agrees. Just let him have a chance to see them."

It was no use. Kickaha knew then what Red Orc was thinking. It should have occurred to Kickaha. The brains of Anana and Wolff could be housing the minds of the Bellers.

Kleist, still smiling, reached into his jacket slowly, so that Kickaha would not be thinking he was reaching for a gun. He brought out a pen and pad of paper and said, "I'll write down this number for you to call, and . . ."

Not for a second did Kickaha believe that the pen was only a pen. Evidently Orc had entrusted Kleist with a beamer. Kleist did not know it, but he was doomed. He had heard too much during the conversation, and he knew about a device which should not be existing on Earth as yet.

There was no time to tell Kleist that in the hope that he could be persuaded to desert the Lord.

Kickaha leaped to one side just as Kleist pointed the pen at him. Kickaha was quick, but he was touched by the beam on the shoulder and hurled sideways to the ground. He rolled on, seeing Kleist throw his hands up into the air, the pen flying away, and then Kleist staggered back one step and fell onto his back. Kickaha leaped up and dived toward the pen, even though his left shoulder and arm felt as if a two-by-four had slammed into it. Ramos, however, made no effort to grab the pen. Probably, he did not know what it really was.

Women were shrieking and men were yelling, and there was much running around.

When he got to his feet, he saw why. Kleist and three of his men were unconscious on the ground. Six men were running toward them—these must have been the latecomers—and were shoving people out of their way.

The fourth man who had been sneaking up on him was pulling a gun from an underarm holster.

Ramos, seeing this, shouted, "No! No guns! You know that!"

Kickaha aimed the beamer-pen, which, fortunately, was activated by pressing a slide, not by code words, and the man seemed to fold up and be lifted off the ground. He sailed back, hit on his buttocks, straightened out, and lay still, arms outspread, his face gray. The gun lay on the ground several feet before him.

Kickaha turned and saw Anana running toward him. She had shot a beam at the same time that Kickaha shot his, and the gunman had gotten a double impact.

Kickaha leaped forward, scooped up the gun, and hurled it over the fence into the tar pit. He and Anana ran around the fence and up the slope onto the sidewalk. There was no crosswalk here, and the traffic was heavy. But it was also slow because the traffic light a half block away was red.

The two ran between the cars, forcing them to slam on their brakes. Horns blatted, and several people yelled at them out the windows.

Once they reached the other side, they looked behind them. The traffic had started up again, and the seven men after them were, for the moment, helpless.

"Things didn't work out right," Kickaha said. "I was hoping that I could grab Kleist and get away with him. He might've been the lead to Red Orc."

Anana laughed, though a little nervously. "Nobody can accuse you of being underconfident," she said. "What now?"

"The cops'll be here pretty quick," he said. "Yeah, look, Cambring's men are all going back. I bet they got orders to get Kleist and the others out before the cops get here."

He grabbed Anana's hand and began running east toward the corner. She said, "What're you doing?"

"We'll cross back at the traffic light while they're busy and then run like hell down Curson Street. Cambring's there!"

She did not ask any more. But to get away from the enemy and then to run right back into his mouth seemed suicidal.

The two were now opposite the men about a hundred yards away. Kickaha looked between the trees lining the street and saw the unwounded men supporting Kleist and three others. In the distance, a siren wailed. From the way Cambring's men hurried, they had no doubt that it was coming after them.

Cambring, looking anxious, was standing by the car. He stiffened when he felt the pen touch his back and heard Kickaha's voice.

Cambring did not look around but got into the front seat as directed. Anana and Kickaha got into the rear seat, and ducked down. Kickaha kept the pen jammed against Cambring's back.

Cambring protested once. "You can't get away with this! You're crazy!"

"Just shut up!" Kickaha said.

Thirty seconds later, Kleist, supported by two men reached the car Kickaha swung out the back door and pointed the pen at them, saying "Put Kleist into the front seat."

The two holding Kleist halted. The others, forming a rear guard reached for their guns, but Kickaha shouted, "I'll kill Kleist and Cambring both! And you, too, with this!"

He waved the pen. The others knew by now that the pen was a weapon of some sort even if they did not know its exact nature. They seemed to fear it more than a gun, probably because its nature was in doubt.

They stopped. Kickaha said, "I'm taking these two! The cops'll be here in a minute! You better take off, look out for yourselves!"

The two holding Kleist carried him forward and shoved him into the front seat. Cambring had to push against Kleist to keep him from falling on him like a sack full of garbage. Kickaha quickly got out of the car and went around to get into the driver's seat, while Anana held the pen on the others.

He started the motor, backed up with a screech of tires, jerked it to a stop, turned, and roared out of the parking lot. The car went up and down violently as they jumped the dip between the lot entrance and the street. Kickaha shouted to Anana, and she reached over the seat, felt behind Kleist's ear, and came up with the transceiver. It was a metal disc thin as a postage stamp and the size of a dime.

She stuck it behind her ear and also removed Kleist's wristwatch and put it on her own wrist.

He now had Cambring and Kleist. What could he do with them?

Anana suddenly gasped and pushed at Cambring, who had slumped over against Kickaha. In a swift reaction, he had shoved out with his elbow, thinking for a second that Cambring was attacking him. Then he understood that Cambring had fallen against him. He was unconscious.

Another look convinced him that Cambring was dead or close to death. His skin was the gray-blue of a corpse.

Anana said, "They're both dead!"

Kickaha pulled the car over to the curb and stopped. He pointed frantically at her. She stared a moment, and then saw what he was trying to communicate. She quickly shed the receiver and Kleist's wristwatch as if she had discovered that she was wearing a leper's clothing.

Kickaha reached over and pulled her close to him and whispered in her ear, "I'll pick up the watch and receiver with a handkerchief and stick them in the trunk until we can get rid of them. I think you'd be able to hear Red Orc's voice now, if you still had that receiver behind your ear. He'd be telling you he'd just killed Cambring and he was going to kill you unless we surrendered to him."

He picked up Cambring's wrist and with a pencil pried up the watch compartment. There was a slight discoloration under it on the skin.

With the pencil, he pried loose the disc from behind Cambring's ear and exposed a brown-blue disc-shaped spot.

Kleist groaned. His eyelids fluttered, and he looked up. Kickaha started the car again and pulled away from the curb, and then turned north. As they drove slowly in the heavy traffic, Kleist managed to straighten himself. To do this, he had to push Cambring over against Kickaha. Anana gave a savage order, and Kleist got Cambring off the seat and onto the floor. Since the body took up so much space, Kleist had to sit with his knees almost up to his chin.

He groaned again and said, "You killed him."

Kickaha explained what had happened. Kleist did not believe him. He said, "What kind of a fool do you think I am?"

Kickaha grinned and said, "Very well, so you don't believe in the efficacy of the devices, the workings of which I've just explained to you. I could put them back on you and so prove the truth of what I've told you. You wouldn't know it, because you'd be dead and your boss would've scored one on us."

He drove on until he saw a sign which indicated a parking lot behind a business building. He drove down the alley and turned into it. The lot was a small one, enclosed on three sides by the building. There were no windows from which he could be seen, and, for the moment, there was no one in the lot or the alley. He parked, then got out and motioned to Kleist to get out. Anana held the pen against his side.

Kickaha dragged Cambring's body out and rolled it under a panel truck. Then they got back into the car and drove off, toward the motel.

Kickaha was worried. He may have pushed Red Orc to the point where he would report the Rolls as stolen. Up to now he had kept the police out of it, but Kickaha did not doubt that the Lord would bring them in if he felt it necessary. The Lord must have great influence, both politically and financially, even if he remained an anonymous figure. With Kickaha and Anana picked up by the police, the Lord could then arrange for his men to seize them. All he had to do was to pay the bail and catch them after they'd gone a few blocks from the police station.

And if Kleist knew anything which might give Kickaha a lead to Red Orc, the Lord might act to make sure that Kleist could not do so.

Kleist, at this moment, was not cooperating. He would not even reply to Kickaha's questions. Finally, he said, "Save your breath. You'll get nothing from me."

When they reached the motel, Kleist got out of the car slowly. He looked around as if he would like to run or shout, but Kickaha had warned him that if he tried anything, he would get enough power from the pen to knock his head off. He stepped into the motel room ahead of Kickaha, who did not even wait for Anana to shut the door before stunning his prisoner with a minimum jolt from the pen.

Before he could recover, Kleist had been injected with a serum that Kickaha had brought from Wolff's palace in that other world.

During the next hour, they learned much about the workings and the people of what Kleist referred to as The Group. His immediate boss was a man named Alfredo Roulini. He lived in Beverly Hills, but Kleist had never been in his home. Always, Roulini gave orders over the phone or met Kleist and other underlings at Kleist's or Cambring's home.

Roulini, as described by Kleist, could not be Red Orc.

Kickaha paced back and forth, frowning, running his fingers through his long red hair.

"Red Orc will know, or at least surmise, that we've gotten Roulini's name and address from Kleist. So he'll warn Roulini, and they'll have a trap set for us. He may have been arrogant and overconfident before, but he knows now we're no pushovers. We've given him too hard a time. We won't be able to get near Roulini, and even if we did, I'll bet we'd find out that he has no more idea of the true identity or location of Red Orc than Kleist."

"That's probably true," Anana said. "So the only thing to do is to force Red Orc to come into the open."

"I'm thinking the same thing," he said. "But how do you flush him out?"

Anana exclaimed, "The Beller!"

Kickaha said, "So far, we don't know where the Beller is, and, much as I hate to think about it, may never."

"Don't say that!" she said. "We have to find him!"

Her determination, he knew, did not originate from concern for the inhabitants of Earth. She was terrified only that the Bellers might one day become powerful enough to gate from Earth into other universes, the pocket worlds owned by the Lords. She was concerned only for herself and, of course, for him. Perhaps for Luvah, the wounded brother left behind to guard Wolff's palace. But she would never be able to sleep easily until she was one hundred percent certain that no Bellers were alive in the one thousand and eight known universes.

Nor would Red Orc sleep any more easily.

Kickaha tied Kleist's hands behind him, tied his feet together, and taped his mouth. Anana could not understand why he didn't just kill the man. Kickaha explained, as he had done a number of times, that he would not do so unless he thought it was necessary. Besides, they were in enough trouble without leaving a corpse behind them.

After removing Kleist's wallet, he put him in the closet. "He can stay there until tomorrow when the cleaning woman comes in. But I think we'll move on. Let's go across the street and eat. We have to put something in our bellies."

They walked across the street at the corner, and went down half a block to the restaurant. They got a booth by the window, from which he could see the motel.

While they were eating, he told her what his plans were. "A Lord will come as swiftly for a pseudo-Beller as for the real thing, because he won't know for sure which is which. We make our own Beller and get some publicity, too, and so make sure that Red Orc finds out about it."

"There's still a good chance that he won't come personally," she said.

"How's he going to know whether or not the Beller is for real unless he does show?" he said. "Or has the Beller brought to him."

"But you couldn't get out then!" she said.

"Maybe I couldn't get out, but I'm not there yet. We've got to play this by ear. I don't see anything else to do, do you?"

They rose, and he stopped at the register to pay their bill. Anana whispered to him to look through the big plate glass window at the motel. A police car was turning into the motel grounds.

Kickaha watched the two policemen get out and look at the license plate on the rear of the Rolls. Then one went into the manager's office while the other checked out the Rolls. In a moment, the officer and the manager came out, and all three went into the motel room that Anana and Kickaha had just left.

"They'll find Kleist in the closet," Kickaha murmured. "We'll take a taxi back to L.A. and find lodging somewhere else."

They had the clothes they were wearing, the case with the Horn of Shambarimen, their beamer rings with a number of power charges, the beamer-pen, their ear receivers and wrist chronometer transmitters, and the money they'd taken from Baum, Cambring, and Kleist. The latter had provided another hundred and thirty-five dollars.

They went outside into the heat and the eye-burning, sinus-searing smog. He picked up the morning *Los Angeles Times* from a corner box and then waited for a taxi. Presently, one came along, and they rode out of the Valley. On the way, he read the personals column, which contained his ad. None of the personals read as if it had been planted by Wolff. The two got out of the taxi, walked two blocks, and took another taxi to a place chosen at random by Kickaha.

They walked around for a while. He got a haircut and purchased a hat and also talked the clerk out of a woman's hatbox. At a drugstore, he bought some hair dye and other items, including shaving equipment, toothbrushes and paste, and a nail file. In a pawnshop he bought two suitcases, a knife which had an excellent balance, and a knife-sheath.

Two blocks away, they checked in at a third-rate hotel. The desk clerk seemed interested only in whether they could pay in advance or not. Kickaha, wearing his hat and dark glasses, hoped that the clerk wasn't paying them much attention. Judging from the stink of cheap whiskey on his breath he was not very perceptive at the moment.

Anana, looking around their room, said, "The place we just left was a hovel. But it's a palace compared to this!"

"I've been in worse," he said. "Just so the cockroaches aren't big enough to carry us off."

They spent some time dying their hair. His red-bronze became a dark brown, and her hair, as black and glossy as a Polynesian maiden's, became corn-yellow.

"It's no improvement, but it's a change," he said. "So, now to a metalworker's."

The telephone books had given the addresses of several in this area. They walked to the nearest place advertising metalworking, where Kickaha gave his specifications and produced the money in advance. During his conversation, he had studied the proprietor's character. He concluded that he was open to any deal where the money was high and the risk low.

He decided to cache the Horn. Much as he hated to have it out of his sight, he no longer cared to risk the chance of Red Orc's getting his hands on it. If he had not carried it with him when he left the motel, it would be in the hands of the police by now. And if Orc heard about it, which he was bound to do, Orc would quickly enough have it.

The two went to the Greyhound Bus station, where he put the case and Horn in a locker.

"I gave that guy an extra twenty bucks to do a rush job," he said. "He promised to have it ready by five. In the meantime, I propose we rest in the tavern across the street from our palatial lodgings. We'll watch our hotel for any interesting activities."

The Blue Bottle Fly was a sleazy beer joint, which did, however, have an unoccupied booth by the front window. This was covered by a dark blind, but there was enough space between the slats for Kickaha to see the front of the hotel. He ordered a Coke for Anana and a beer for himself. He drank almost none of the beer but every fifteen minutes ordered another one just to keep the management happy. While he watched, he questioned Anana about Red Orc. There was so little that he knew about their enemy.

"He's my *krathlrandroon*," Anana said. "My mother's brother. He left the home universe over fifteen thousand Earth years ago to make his own. That was five thousand years before I was born. But we had statues and photos of him, and he came back once when I was about fifteen years old, so I knew how he looked. But I don't remember him now. Despite which, if I were to see him again, I might know him immediately. There is the family resemblance, you know. Very strong. If you should ever see a man who is the male counterpart of me, you will be looking at Red Orc. Except for the hair. His is not black, it is a dark bronze. Like yours. Exactly like yours.

"And now that I come to think of it . . . I wonder why it didn't strike me before . . . you look much like him."

"Come on now!" Kickaha said. "That would mean I'd look like you! I deny that!"

"We could be cousins, I think," she said.

Kickaha laughed, though his face was warm and he felt anxious for some reason.

"Next, you'll be telling me I'm the long-lost son of Red Orc!"

"I don't know that he has any son," she said thoughtfully. "But you could be his child, yes."

"I know who my parents are," he said. "Hoosier farm folk. And they knew who their ancestors were, too. My father was of Irish descent—what else, Finnegan, for God's sake?—and my mother was Norwegian and a quarter Catawba Indian."

"I wasn't trying to prove anything," she said. "I was just commenting on certain undeniable resemblances. Now that I think about it, your eyes are that peculiar leaf-green . . . yes, exactly like it . . . I'd forgotten . . . Red Orc's eyes are yours."

Kickaha put his hand on hers and said, "Hold it!"

He was looking through the slats. She turned and said, "A police car!"

"Yeah, double-parked outside the hotel. They're both going in. They could be checking on someone else. So let's not get panicky."

"Since when did I ever panic?" she said coldly.

"My apologies. That's just my manner of speaking."

Fifteen minutes passed. Then a car pulled up behind the police car. It contained three men in civilian clothes, two of whom got out and went into the hotel. The car drove away.

Kickaha said, "Those two looked like plainclothesmen to me."

The two uniformed policemen came out and drove away. The two suspected detectives did not come out of the hotel for thirty minutes. They walked down to the corner and stood for a minute talking, and then one returned. He did not, however, reenter the hotel. Instead, he crossed the street.

Kickaha said, "He's got the same idea we had! Watch the hotel from here!" He stood up and said, "Come on! Out the back way! Saunter along, but fast!"

The back way was actually a side entrance, which led to a blind alley the open end of which was on the street. The two walked northward toward the metalworking shop.

Kickaha said, "Either the police got their information from Red Orc or they're checking us out because of Kleist. It doesn't matter. We're on the run, and Orc's got the advantage. As long as he can keep pushing us, we aren't going to get any closer to him. Maybe."

They had several hours yet before the metalworker would be finished. Kickaha led Anana into another tavern, much higher class, and they sat down again. He said, "You just barely got started telling me the story of your uncle."

"There really isn't much to tell," she said. "Red Orc was a figure of terror among the Lords for a long time. He successfully invaded the universes of at least ten Lords and killed them. Then he was badly hurt when he got into the world of Vala, my sister. Red Orc is very wily and a man of many resources and great power. But my sister Vala combines all the qualities of a cobra and a tiger. She hurt him badly, as I said, but in doing she got hurt herself. In fact, she almost died. Red Orc escaped, however, and came back to this universe, which was the first one he made after leaving the home world."

Kickaha sat up and said, *"What."*

His hand, flailing out, knocked over his glass of beer. He paid it no attention but stared at her.

"What did you say?"

"You want me to repeat the whole thing?"

"No, no! That final . . . the part where you said he came back to *his* universe, the first one he *made!"*

"Yes? What's so upsetting about that?"

Kickaha did not stutter often. But now he could not quite get the words out.

Finally, he said, "L-listen! I accept the idea of the pocket universes of the Lords, because I've lived in one half my life and I know others exist because I've been told about them by a man who doesn't lie and I've seen the Lords of other universes, including you! And I know there are at least one thousand and eight of these relatively small manufactured universes.

"But I had always thought . . . I still think . . . it's impossible . . . my universe is a natural one, just as you say your home universe, Gardzrintrah, was."

"I didn't say *that*," she said softly. She took his hand and squeezed it. "Dear Kickaha, does it really upset you so much?"

"You must be mistaken, Anana," he said. "Do you have any idea of the *vastness* of *this* universe? In fact, it's infinite! No man could *make* this incredibly complex and gigantic world! My God, the nearest star is four and some light-years away and the most distant is billions of light-years away, and there must be others billions of billions of light-years beyond these!

"And then there is the age of this universe! Why, this planet alone is two and one-half billion years old, the last I heard! That's a hell of a lot older than fifteen thousand years, when the Lords moved out of their home world to make their pocket universes! A hell of a lot older!"

Anana smiled and patted his hand as if she were his grandmother and he a very small child.

"There, there! No reason to get upset, lover. I wonder why Wolff didn't tell you. Probably he forgot it when he lost his memory. And when he got his memory back, he did not get all of it back. Or perhaps he took it so for granted that he never considered that you didn't know, just as I took it for granted."

"How can you explain away the infinite size of this world, and the age of Earth? And the evolution of life?" he said triumphantly. "There, how do you explain evolution? The undeniable record of the fossils? Of carbon-14 dating and potassium-argon dating? I read about these new discoveries in a magazine on that bus, and their evidence is scientifically irrefutable!"

He fell silent as the waitress picked up their empty glasses. As soon as she left, he opened his mouth, and then he closed it again. The TV above the bar was showing the news and there on the screen was a drawing of two faces.

He said to Anana, "Look there!"

She turned just in time to see the screen before the drawing faded away.

"They looked like us!" she said.

"Yeah. Police composites," he said. "The hounds have really got th scent now! Take it easy! If we get up now, people might look at us. But if we sit here and mind our own business, as I hope the other customers are going . . ."

If it had been a color set, the resemblance would have been much less close, since they had dyed their hair. But in black and white, their pictures were almost photographic.

However, no one even looked at them and it was possible that no one except the drunks at the bar had seen the TV set. And they were not about to turn around and face them.

"What did that thing say?" Anana whispered, referring to the TV.

"I don't know. There was too much noise for me to hear it. And I can't ask anybody at the bar."

He was having afterthoughts about his plans. Perhaps he should give up his idea of tricking Red Orc out of hiding. Some things were worth chancing, but with the police actively looking for him, and his and Anana's features in every home in California, he did not want to attract any attention at all. Besides, the idea had been one of those wild hares that leaped through the brier patches of his mind. It was fantastic, too imaginative, but for that very reason might have succeeded. Not now, though. The moment he put his plan into action, he would bring down Orc's men and the police, and Red Orc would not come out himself because he would know where Kickaha was.

"Put on the dark glasses now," he said. "Enough time has gone by that nobody'd get suspicious and connect us with the pictures."

"You don't have to explain everything," she said sharply. "I'm not as unintelligent as your Earthwomen."

He was silent for a moment. Within a few minutes, so many events had dropped on his head like so many anvils. He wanted desperately to pursue the question of the origin and nature of this universe, but there was no time. Survival, finding Wolff and Chryseis, and killing the Beller, these were the important issues. Just now, survival was the most demanding.

"We'll pick up some more luggage," he said. "And the bell, too. I may be able to use it later, who knows?"

He paid the bill, and they walked out. Ten minutes later, they had the bell. The metalworker had done a good enough job. The bell wouldn't stand a close-up inspection by any Lord, of course. But at a reasonable distance, or viewed by someone unfamiliar with it, it would pass for the prized possession of a Beller. It was bell-shaped but the bottom was covered, was one and a half times the size of Kickaha's head, was made of aluminum, and had been sprayed with a quick-dry paint. Kickaha paid the maker of it and put the bell in the hatbox he had gotten from the shop.

A half hour later they walked across MacArthur Park.

Besides the soap-box speakers, there were a number of winos, hippie types, and some motorcycle toughs. And many people who seemed to be there just to enjoy the grass or to watch the unconventionals.

As they rounded a big bush, they stopped.

To their right was a concrete bench. On it sat two bristly-faced, sunken-cheeked, blue-veined winos and a young man. The young man was a well-built fellow with long dirty blond hair and a beard of about three days' growth. He wore clothes that were even dirtier and more ragged than the winos'.

A cardboard carton about a foot and a half square was on the bench by his side.

Anana started to say something and then she stopped.

Her skin turned pale, her eyes widened, she clutched her throat, and she screamed.

The alarm embedded in her brain, the alarm she had carried since she had become an adult ten thousand years ago, was the only thing that could be responsible for this terror.

Nearness to the bell of a Beller touched off that device in her brain. Her nerves wailed as if a siren had been tied into them. The ages-long dread of the Beller had seized her.

The blond man leaped up, grabbed the cardboard box, and ran away.

Kickaha ran after him. Anana screamed. The winos shouted, and many people came running.

At another time, he would have laughed. He had originally planned to take his box and the pseudo-bell into some such place as this, a park where winos and derelicts hung out, and create some kind of commotion, which would make the newspapers. That would have brought Red Orc out of his hole, Kickaha had hoped.

Ironically, he had stumbled across the real Beller.

If the Beller had been intelligent enough to cache his bell some place he would have been safe. Kickaha and Anana would have passed him and never known.

Suddenly, he stopped running. Why chase the Beller, even if he could catch up with him? A chase would draw too much attention.

He took out the beamer disguised as a pen and set the little slide on its barrel for a very narrow flesh-piercing beam. He aimed it at the back of the Beller and, at that moment, as if the Beller realized what must happen, he dropped to the ground. His box went tumbling, he rolled away and then disappeared behind a slight ridge. Kickaha's beam passed over him, struck a tree, drilled a hole into it. Smoke poured out of the bark. Kickaha shut the beamer off. If it was kept on for more than a few seconds, it needed another powerpack.

The Beller's head popped up, and his hand came out with a slender dark object in it. He pointed it at Kickaha, who leaped into the air sideways and at the same time threw the hatbox away. There was a flash of something white along the box, and the box and its contents, both split in half, fell to the ground. The hatbox burst into flames just before it struck.

Kickaha threw himself onto the ground and shot once. The grass on the ridge became brown. The next instant, the Beller was shooting again. Kickaha rolled away and then was up and away, zigzagging.

Anana was running toward him, her hand held up with the huge ring pointed forward. Kickaha whirled to aid her and saw that the Beller, who had retrieved the cardboard box, was running away again. Across the grass toward them, from all sides, people were running. Among them were two policemen.

Kickaha thought that his antics and those of the Beller must have seemed very peculiar to the witnesses. Here were these two youths, each with a box, pointing ballpoint pens at each other, dodging, ducking, playing cowboy and Indian. And the woman who had been screaming as if she had suddenly seen Frankenstein's monster was now in the game.

One of the policemen shouted at them.

Kickaha said, "Don't let them catch us! We'll be done for! Get the Beller!"

They began running at top speed. The cops shouted some more. He looked behind him. Neither had his gun out but it would not be long before they did.

They were overtaking the Beller, and the policemen were dropping behind. He was breathing too hard, though.

Whatever his condition, the Beller's was worse. He was slowing down fast. This meant that very shortly he would turn again, and Kickaha had better be nimble. In a few seconds, he would have the Beller within range of the beamer, and he would take both legs off. And that would be the end of possibly the greatest peril to man, other than man himself, of course.

The Beller ran up concrete steps in a spurt of frantic energy and onto the street above. Kickaha slowed down and stopped before ascending the last few steps. He expected the Beller to be waiting for his head to appear. Anana came up behind him then. Between deep gasps, she said, "Where is he?"

"If I knew, I wouldn't be standing here," he said.

He turned and left the steps to run crouching across the steep slope of the hill. When he was about forty feet away from the steps, he got down on his belly and crawled up to the top of the slope. The Beller would be wondering what he was doing. If he were intelligent, he would know that Kickaha wasn't going to charge up and over the steps. He'd be looking on both sides of the steps for his enemy to pop up.

Kickaha looked to his right. Anana had caught on and was also snaking along. She turned her head and grinned at him and waved. He signaled that they should both look over the edge at the same time. If the Beller was paralyzed for just a second by the double appearance, and couldn't make up his mind which one to shoot first, he was as good as dead.

That is, if the cops behind them didn't interfere. Their shouts were getting louder, and then a gun barked and the dirt near Kickaha flew up.

He signaled, and they both stuck their heads up. At that moment, a gun cracked in the street before them.

The Beller was down on his back in the middle of the street. There was a car beside him, a big black Lincoln, and several men were about to pick the Beller up and load him into the car. One of the men was Kleist.

Kickaha swore. He had run the Beller right into the arms of Orc's men, who were probably cruising this area and looking for a man with a big box. Or maybe somebody had—oh, irony of ironies!—seen Kickaha with his box and thought he was the Beller!

He gestured at Anana and they both jumped up and ran off toward the car. More shouts but no shots from the policemen. The men by the limousine looked up just as they hurled the limp form of the Beller into the car. They climbed in, and the car shot away with a screaming of burning rubber into the temporarily opened lane before it.

Kickaha aimed at the back of the car, hoping to pierce a tire or to set the gasoline tank on fire. Nothing happened, and the car was gone yowling around a corner. His beamer was empty.

There was nothing to do except to run once more, and now the policemen would be calling in for help. The only advantage for the runners was the very heavy rush hour traffic. The cops wouldn't be able to get here too fast in automobiles.

A half hour later, they were in a taxi, and, in another twenty minutes they were outside a motel. The manager looked at them curiously and raised his eyebrows when he saw no luggage. Kickaha said that they were advance agents for a small rock group and their baggage was coming along later. They'd flown in on fifteen minutes' notice from San Francisco.

They took the keys to their room and went down the court and into their room. Here they lay down on the twin beds and, after locking the door and pushing the bureau against it, slept for fifteen minutes. On awakening, they took a shower and put their sweaty clothes back on. Following the manager's directions, they walked down to a shopping area and purchased some more clothes and necessary items.

"If we keep buying clothes and losing them the same day," Kickaha said, "we're going to go broke. And I'll have to turn to robbery again."

When they returned to the motel room, he eagerly opened the latest copy of the *Los Angeles Times* to the personals column. He read down and then, suddenly, said, "Yay!" and leaped into the air. Anana sat up from the bed and said, "What's the matter?"

"Nothing's the matter! This is the first good thing that's happened since we got here! I didn't really believe that it'd work! But he's a crafty old fox, that Wolff! He thinks like me! Look, Anana!"

He shoved the paper at her. Blinking, she moved away so she could focus and then slowly read the words:

Hrowakas Kid. You came through. Stats. Wilshire and San Vicente. 9 P.M. C sends love.

Kickaha pulled her up off the bed and danced her around the room. "We did it! We did it! Once we're all together, nothing'll stop us!"

Anana hugged and kissed him and said, "I'm very happy. Maybe you're right, this is the turning point. My brother Jadawin! Once I would have tried to kill him. But no more. I can hardly wait."

"Well, we won't have long to wait," he said. He forced himself to become sober. "I better find out what's going on."

He turned the TV on. The newscaster of one station apparently was not going to mention them, so Kickaha switched channels. A minute later, he was rewarded.

He and Anana were wanted for questioning about the kidnapping of Kleist. The manager of the motel in which Kleist had been tied up had described the two alleged kidnappers. Kleist himself had made no charges at first, but then Cambring's body had been found. The police had made a connection between Cambring and Kickaha and Anana because of the ruckus at the La Brea Tar Pits. There was also an additional charge: the stealing of Cambring's car.

Kickaha did not like the news but he could not help chuckling a little because of the frustration that Red Orc must feel. The Lord would have wanted some less serious charge, such as the car stealing only, so that he could pay the bail of the two and thus nab them when they walked out of the police station. But on charges such as kidnapping, he might not be able to get them released.

These charges were serious enough, though not enough to warrant their pictures and descriptions on TV newscasts. What made this case so interesting was that the fingerprints of the male in the case had checked out as those of Paul Janus Finnegan, an ex-serviceman who had disappeared in 1946 from his apartment in Bloomington, Indiana, where he had been attending the university.

Twenty-four years later, he had showed up in Van Nuys, California, in very mysterious, or questionable, circumstances. And this was the kicker according to the newscaster—Finnegan was described by witnesses as being about twenty-five, yet he was fifty-two years old!

Moreover, since the first showing of his picture over TV, he had been identified as one of the men in a very mysterious chase in MacArthur Park.

The newscaster ended with a comment supposed to be droll. Perhaps this Finnegan had returned from the Fountain of Youth. Or perhaps the witnesses may have been drinking from a slightly different fountain.

"With all this publicity," Kickaha said, "we're in a bad spot. I hope the motel manager didn't watch this show."

It was eight thirty. They were to meet Wolff at nine at Stats Restaurant on Wilshire and San Vicente. If they took a taxi, they could get there with plenty of time to spare. He decided they should walk. He did not trust the taxis. And while he would use them if he had to, he saw no reason to take one just to avoid a walk. Especially since they needed the exercise.

Anana complained that she was hungry and would like to get to the restaurant as soon as possible. He told her that suffering was good for the soul and grinned as he said it. His own belly was contracting with pangs, and his ribs felt more obtrusive than several days ago. But he was not going to be rushed into anything if he could help it.

While they walked, Kickaha questioned her about Red Orc and the "alleged" creation of Earth.

"There was the universe of the Lords in the beginning, and that was the only one we knew about. Then, after ten thousand years of civilization, my ancestors formulated the theory of artificial universes. Once the mathematics of the concept was realized, it was only a matter o time and will until the first pocket universe was made. Then the same 'space' would hold two worlds of space-matter, but one would be impervious to the inhabitants of the other, because each universe was 'at right angles to the other.' You realize that the term 'right angles' does not mean anything. It is just an attempt to explain something that can really only be explained to one who understands the mathematics of the concept. I myself, though I designed a universe of my own and then built it, never understood the mathematics or even how the world-making machines operated.

"The first artificial universe was constructed about two hundred years before I was born. It was made by a group of Lords—they did not call themselves Lords then, by the way—among whom were my father Urizen and his brother Orc. Orc had already lived the equivalent of two thousand Terrestrial years. He had been a physicist and then a biologist and finally a social scientist.

"The initial step was like blowing a balloon in non-space. Can you conceive that? I can't either, but that's the way it was explained to me. You blow a balloon in non-space. That is, you create a small space or a small universe, one to which you can 'gate' your machines. These expand the space next to, or in, the time-space of the original universe. The new world is expanded so that you can gate even larger machines into it. And these expand the universe more, and you gate more machines into the new larger space.

"From the beginning of this making of a new world, you have set up a world which may have quite different physical 'laws' than the original universe. It's a matter of shaping the space-time-matter so that, say, gravity works differently than in the original world.

"However, the first new universe was crude, you might say. It embodied no new principles. It was, in fact, an exact imitation of the original. Well, not exact in the sense that it was not a copy of the world as it was but as it had been in our past."

"The copy was this—my—world?" Kickaha said. "Earth's?"

She nodded and said, "It—this universe—was the first. And it was made approximately fifteen thousand Earth years ago. This solar system deviated only in small particulars from the solar system of the Lords. This Earth deviated only slightly from the native planet of the Lords."

"You mean . . . ?"

He was silent while they walked a half block, then he said, "So that explains what you meant when you said this world was fairly recent. I knew that that could not be so, because potassium-argon and xenon-argon dating prove irrefutably that this world is more than four and a half billion years old, and hominid fossils have been found which are at least one million seven hundred and fifty thousand years old. And then we have carbon-14 dating, which is supposed to be accurate up to fifty thousand years ago, if I remember that article correctly.

"But you're saying that the rocks of your world, which were four and a half billion years old, were reproduced in this universe. And so, though they were really made only fifteen thousand years ago, they would seem to be four and a half billion years old.

"And we find fossils which prove indubitably that dinosaurs lived sixty million years ago, and we find stone tools and the skeletons of men who lived a million years ago. But these were duplicated from your world."

"That is exactly right," she said.

"But the stars!" he said. "The galaxies, the super-novas, the quasars, the millions, billions of them, billions of light-years away! The millions of stars in this galaxy alone, which is one hundred thousand light-years across! The red shift of light from galaxies receding from us at a quarter of the speed of light and billions of light-years away! The radio stars, the—my God, everything!"

He threw his hands up to indicate the infinity and eternity of the universe. And also to indicate the utter nonsense of her words.

"This universe is the first, and the largest, of the artificial ones," she said. "Well, not the largest, the second one was just as large. Its diameter is three times that of the distance from the sun to the planet Pluto. If men ever build a ship to voyage to the nearest star, they will get past the orbit of Pluto and then to a distance twice that of Pluto from the sun. And then . . ."

"Then?"

"And then the ship will enter an area where it will be destroyed. It will run into a—what shall I call it?—a force field is the only term I can think of. And it will disappear in a blaze of energy. And so will any other ship, or ships, coming after it. The stars are not for men. Mainly because there are no stars."

Kickaha wanted to protest violently. He felt outraged. But he forced himself to say calmly, "How do you explain that?"

"The space-matter outside the orbit of Pluto is a simulacrum. A tiny simulacrum. Relatively tiny, that is."

"The effects of the light from the stars, the nebulas, and so forth? The red shift? The speed of light? All that?"

"There's a warping factor which gives all the necessary illusions."

An extra-Plutonian astronomy, all cosmogony, all cosmology, was false.

"But why did the Lords feel it necessary to set up this simulacrum of an infinite ever-expanding universe with its trillions of heavenly bodies? Why didn't they just leave the sky blank except for the moon and the planets? Why this utterly cruel deception? Or need I ask? I had forgotten for the moment that the Lords *are* cruel."

She patted his hand, looked up into his eyes, and said, "The Lords are not the only cruel ones. You forget that I told you that this universe was an exact copy of ours. I meant exact. From the center, that is, the sun, to the outer walls of this universe, your world is a duplicate of ours. That includes the simulacrum of extra-solar-system space."

He stopped and said, "You mean . . . ? The native world of the Lords was an artificial universe, too?"

"Yes. After three ships had been sent out past our outermost planet, to the nearest star, only four-point-three light-years away—we thought— a fourth ship was sent. But this slowed down when it came near the area where the others had disappeared in a burst of light. It was not destroyed, but it could progress no further than the first three. It was repelled by a force field. Or was turned away by the structure of the space-matter continuum at that point.

"After some study, we reluctantly came to the realization that there were no stars or outer space. Not as we had thought of them.

"This revelation was not accepted by many people. In fact, the impact of this discovery was so great that our civilization was in a near-psychotic state for a long while.

"Some historians have maintained that it was the discovery that we were in an artificial, comparatively finite, universe that spurred us— stung us—into searching for means of making our own synthetic universes. Because, if we were ourselves the product of a people who made our universe, and, therefore, made us, then we, too, could make our worlds. And so . . ."

"Then Earth's world is not even secondhand!" Kickaha said. "It's thirdhand! But who could have made your world? Who are the Lords of the Lords?"

"So far, we do not know," she said. "We have found no trace of them or their native worlds or any other artificial worlds they might have made. They exist on a plane of polarity that was beyond us then, and, as far as I know, will always be beyond us."

Kickaha thought that this discovery should have humbled the Lords.

Perhaps, in the beginning, it did. But they had recovered and gone on to their own making of cosmoses and their solipsist way of life.

And in their search for immortality, they had made the Bellers, those Frankenstein's monsters, and then, after a long war, had conquered the Bellers and disposed of the menace forever—they had thought. But now there was a Beller loose and . . . No, he was not loose. He was in the hands of Red Orc, who surely would see to it that the Beller died and his bell was buried deep somewhere, perhaps at the bottom of the Pacific.

"I'll swallow what you told me," he said, "though I'm choking. But what about the people of Earth? Where did they come from?"

"Your ancestors of fifteen thousand years ago were made in the biolabs of the Lords. One set was made for this Earth and another set, exact duplicates, for the second Earth. Red Orc made two universes which were alike, and he put down on the face of each Earth the same peoples. Exactly the same in every detail.

"Orc set down in various places the infants, the Caucasoids, the Negroids and Negritos, the Mongolians, Amerinds, and Australoids. These were infants who were raised by Lords to be Stone Age peoples. Each group was taught a language, which, by the way, were artificial languages. They were also taught how to make stone and wooden tools, how to hunt, what rules of behavior to adopt, and so forth. And then the Lords disappeared. Most of them returned to the home universe, where they would make plans for building their own universes. Some stayed on the two Earths to see but not be seen. Eventually, all of these were killed or run out of the two universes by Red Orc, but that was a thousand years later."

"Wait a minute," Kickaha said. "I never thought about it, just took it for granted, I guess. But I thought all Lords were Caucasians."

"That is just because it so happened that you only met Caucasoid Lords," she said. "How many have you met, by the way?"

He grinned and said, "Six."

"I would guess that there are about a thousand left, and of these about a third are Negroid and a third Mongolian, to use Terrestrial terms. On our world our equivalent of Australoids became extinct and our equivalent of Polynesians and Amerinds became absorbed by the Mongolians and Caucasoids."

"That other Earth universe?" he said. "Have the peoples there developed on lines similar to ours? Or have they deviated considerably?"

"I couldn't tell you," she said. "Only Red Orc knows."

He had many questions, including why there happened to be a num ber of gates on Earth over which Red Orc had no control. It occurred to him that these might be gates left over from the old days when many Lords were on Earth.

There was no time to ask more questions. They were crossing San Vicente at Wilshire now, and Stats was only a few dozen yards away. It was a low brick and stone building with a big plate glass window in front. His heart was beating fast. The prospect of seeing Wolff and Chryseis again made him happier than he had been for a long time. Nevertheless, he did not lose his wariness.

"We'll walk right on by the first time," he said. "Let's case it."

They were opposite the restaurant. There were about a dozen people eating in it, two waitresses, and a woman at the cash register. Two uniformed policemen were in a booth; their black and white car was in the plaza parking lot west of the building. Neither Wolff nor Chryseis was there.

It was still not quite nine o'clock, however, and Wolff might be approaching cautiously.

They halted before the display window of a dress shop. From their vantage point, they could observe anybody entering or leaving the restaurant. Two customers got up and walked out. The policemen showed no signs of leaving. A car drove into the plaza, pulled into a slot, and turned its lights out. A man and a woman, both white-haired, got out and went in to the restaurant. The man was too short and skinny to be Wolff, and the woman was too tall and bulky to be Chryseis.

A half hour passed. More customers arrived and more left. None of them could be his friends. At a quarter to ten, the two policemen left.

Anana said, "Could we go inside now? I'm so hungry, my stomach is eating itself."

"I don't like the smell of this," he said. "Nothing looks wrong, except Wolff not being here yet. We'll wait a while, give him a chance to show. But we're not going inside that place. It's too much like a trap."

"I see a restaurant way down the street," she said. "Why don't I go down there and get some food and bring it back?"

They went over her pronunciation of two cheeseburgers, everything except onions, and two chocolate milk shakes, very thick. To go. He told her what to expect in change and then told her to hurry.

For a minute, he wondered if he should not tell her to forget it. If something unexpected happened, and he had to take off without her, she'd be in trouble. She still did not know the way of this world.

On the other hand, his own belly was growling.

Reluctantly he said, "Okay. But don't be long, and if anything happens so we get separated, we'll meet back at the motel."

He alternated watching the restaurant to his left and looking down the street for her.

About five minutes later she appeared with a large white paper bag. She crossed the street twice to get back on the same block and started walking toward him. She had taken a few steps from the corner when a car which had passed her stopped. Two men jumped out and ran toward her. Kickaha began running toward them. Anana dropped the bag and then she crumpled. There was no sound of a gun or spurt of flame or anything to indicate that a gun had been used. The two men ran to her. One picked her up; the other turned to face Kickaha.

At the same time, another man got out of the car and ran toward Kickaha. Several cars came up behind the stopped car, honked, and then pulled around it. Their lights revealed one man inside the parked car in the driver's seat.

Kickaha leaped sideways and out into the street. A car blew its horn and swerved away to keep from hitting him. The angry voice of its driver floated back, "You crazy son . . . !"

Kickaha had his beamer-pen out by then. A few hasty words set it for piercing effect. His first concern was to keep from being hit by the beamers of the men and his second was to cripple the car.

He dropped on the street and rolled, catching out of the corner of his eye a flash of needle-thin, sun-hot ray. A beam leaped from his own pen and ran along the wheels of the car on the street side. The tires blew with a bang, and the car listed to one side as the bottom parts of the wheels fell off.

The driver jumped out and ran behind the car.

Kickaha was up and running across the street toward a car parked by the curb. He threw himself forward, hit the macadam hard, and rolled. When he had crawled behind the car and peered from behind it, he saw that a second car was stopped some distance behind the first. Anana was being passed into it by the men from the first car.

He jumped up and shouted, but several cars whizzed by, preventing him from using the beam. By the time they had passed, the second car was making a U-turn. More cars, coming down the other lane, passed between him and the automobile containing her. He had no chance now to beam the back wheels of the departing car. And just then, as if the Fates were against him, a police car approached on the lane on his side and stopped. Kickaha knew that he could not be questioned. Raging, he fled.

Behind him, a siren started whooping. A man shouted at him, and fired into the air.

He increased his pace, and ran out onto San Vicente, almost stopping traffic as he dodged between the streaming cars. He crossed the divider, and as he reached the other side of the street; he spared a glance behind and saw one policeman on the divider, blocked by the stream of cars.

The police car had made a U-turn and was coming across. Kickaha ran on, turned the corner, ran between two houses, and came out behind them on San Vicente again. The cop on foot was getting into the car. Kickaha crouched in the shadows until the car, siren still whooping, took off again. It went around the same corner he had turned.

He doubled to Stats and looked inside. There was no sign of Wolff or Chryseis. Another police car was approaching, its lights flashing but its siren quiet.

He went across the parking lot and around a building. It took him an hour, but by dodging between houses, running across streets, hiding now and then, he had eluded the patrol cars. After a stop at a drive-in to pick up some food, he returned to his motel.

There was a police car parked outside it. Once more, he abandoned his luggage and was gone into the night.

There was one thing he had to do immediately. He knew that Red Orc would give Anana a drug which would make her answer any question Orc asked. It just might happen that Orc would become aware that the Horn of Shambarimen had been brought through into this world and that it now was in a locker in the downtown bus station. He would, of course, send men down to the station, and would not hesitate to have the whole station blown up. Orc would not care what he had to do to get that Horn.

Kickaha caught a taxi and went down to the bus station. After emptying the locker, he walked seven blocks from the bus station before he took another taxi, which carried him to the downtown railroad station. Here he placed the Horn in a locker. He did not want to carry the key with him. He purchased a package of gum and chewed all the sticks until he had a big ball of gum. While he was chewing, he strolled around outside the station, inspected a tree on the edge of the parking lot, and decided he had found an excellent hiding place. He stuck the key, embedded in the ball of gum, into a small hollow in the tree just above the line of his vision.

He took another taxi to the Sunset and Fairfax area.

He awoke about eight o'clock on an old mattress on the bare floor of a big moldy room. Beside him slept Rod (short for Rodriga). Rodriga

Elseed, as she called herself, was a tall thin girl with remarkably large breasts, a pretty but overfreckled face, big dark-blue eyes, and lank yellow-brown hair that fell to her waist. She was wearing a red-and-blue checked lumberman's shirt, dirty bellbottoms, and torn moccasins. Her teeth were white and even, but her breath reeked of too little food and too much marijuana.

While walking along Sunset Boulevard in the Saturday night crowds, Kickaha had seen her sitting on the sidewalk talking to another girl and a boy.

The girl, seeing Kickaha, had smiled at him. She said, "Hello, friend. You look as if you've been running for a long time."

"I hope not," he said, smiling back. "The fuzz might see it, too."

It had been easy to make the acquaintanceship of all three, and when Kickaha said he would buy them something to eat, he felt a definite strengthening of their interest.

After eating they had wandered around Sunset, "grooving" on everything. He learned much about their sub-world that night. When he mentioned that he had no roof over his head, they invited him to stay at their pad. It was a big run-down spooky old house, they said, with about fifty people, give or take ten, living in it and chipping in on the rent and utilities, if they had it. If they didn't, they were welcome until they got some bread.

Rodriga Elseed (he was sure that wasn't her real name) had recently come here from Dayton, Ohio. She had left two uptight parents there. She was seventeen and didn't know what she wanted to be. Just herself for the time being, she said.

Kickaha donated some more money for marijuana, and the other girl, Jackie, disappeared for a while. When she returned, they went to the big house, which they called The Shire, and retired to this room. Kickaha smoked with them, since he had the feeling that he would be a far more accepted comrade if he did. The smoke did not seem to do much except to set him coughing.

After a while, Jackie and the boy, Dar, began to make love. Rodriga and Kickaha went for a walk. She said she liked Kickaha, but did not feel like going to bed with him on such short acquaintance.

Kickaha said that he understood. He was not at all disgruntled. He just wanted to get some sleep. An hour later, they returned to the room, which was then empty and fell asleep on the dirty mattress.

But the night's sleep had not lessened his anxiety. He was depressed because Anana was in Red Orc's hands, and he suspected that Wolff and Chryseis were also his prisoners. Somehow, Red Orc had guessed that the ad was from Kickaha and had answered. But he would not have been able to answer so specifically unless he had Wolf and had gotten out of him what he knew about Kickaha.

Knowing the Lords, Kickaha felt it was likely that Red Orc would torture Wolff and Chryseis first, even though he had only to administer a drug which would make them tell whatever Orc asked for. After that, he would torture them again and finally kill them.

He would do the same with Anana. Even now . . .

He shuddered and said, "No!"

Rodriga opened her eyes and said, "What?"

"Go back to sleep," he said, but she sat up and hugged her knees to her breasts. She rocked back and forth and said, "Something is bugging you, *amigo*. Deeply. Look, I don't want to bug you, too, but if there's anything I can do . . ."

"I've got my own thing to do," he said.

He could not involve her in this even if she could help him in any way. She would be killed the first time they contacted Red Orc's men. She wasn't the fast, extremely tough, many-resourced woman that Anana was. Yes, that's right, he said to himself. *Was*. She might not be alive at this very moment.

Tears came to his eyes.

"Thanks, Rod. I've got to be going now. Dig you later, maybe."

She was up off the floor then and said, "There's something a little strange about you, Paul. You're young but you don't use our lingo quite right, you know what I mean? You seem to me to be just a little weird. I don't mean a creep. I mean, as if you don't quite belong to this world, I know how that is; I get the same feeling quite a lot. That is, I don't belong here, either. But it isn't quite the same thing with you, I mean, you are *really* out of this world. You aren't some being off a flying saucer, are you now?"

"Look, Rod, I appreciate your offer. I really do. But you can't go with me or do anything for me. Not just now. But later, if anything comes up that you can help me with, I sure as hell will let you do something for me and be glad to do so."

He bent over and kissed her forehead and said, "*Hasta la vista,* Rodriga. Maybe *adiós*. Let's hope we see each other again, though."

Kickaha walked until he found a small restaurant. As he ate breakfast he considered the situation.

One thing was certain. The problem of the Beller was solved. It did not matter whether Kickaha or Orc killed him. Just so he was killed and the Bellers forever out of the way.

And Red Orc now had all but one of his enemies in his hands, and he would soon have that last one. Unless that enemy got to him first. Red Orc had not been using all his powers to catch Kickaha because his first concern was the Beller. But now, he could concentrate on the last hold-out.

Somehow, Kickaha had to find the Lord before the Lord got to him. Very soon.

When he had finished eating, he bought a *Times*. As he walked along the street, he scanned the columns of the paper. There was nothing about a girl being kidnapped or a car on Wilshire with the bottom halves of the left wheels sliced off. There was a small item about the police sighting Paul J. Finnegan, the mystery man, his getting away, and a résumé of what was known about him in his pre-1946 life.

He forced himself to settle down and to think calmly. Never before had he been so agitated. He was powerless to stop the very probable torture of his lover and his friends, which might be happening right now.

There *was* one way to get into the Lord's house and face him. If he gave himself up, he could then rely upon his inventiveness and his boldness after he was brought before the Lord.

His sense of reality rescued him. He would be taken in only after a thorough examination to make sure he had no hidden weapons or devices. And he would be brought in bound and helpless.

Unless the Lord followed the custom of always leaving some way open for an exceptionally intelligent and skilled man. Always, no matter how effective and powerful the traps the Lords set about their palaces, they left at least one route open, if the invader was perceptive and audacious enough. That was the rule of the deadly game they had played for thousands of years. It was, in fact, this very rule that had made Red Orc leave the gate in the cave unguarded and untrapped.

Because he had nothing else to do, he went into a public phone booth on a gas station lot and dialed Cambring's number. The phone was picked up so swiftly that Kickaha felt, for a second, that Cambring was still alive and was waiting for his call. It was Cambring's wife who answered, however.

Kickaha said, "Paul Finnegan speaking."

There was a pause and then, "You murderer!" she screamed.

He waited until she was through yelling and cursing him and was sobbing and gasping.

"I didn't kill your husband," he said, "although I would have been justified if I had, as you well know. It was the big boss who killed him."

"You're a liar!" she screamed.

"Tell your big boss I want to speak to him. I'll wait on this line. I know you have several phones you can use."

"Why should I do that?" she said. "I'll do nothing for you!"

"I'll put it this way. If he gets his hands on me, he'll see to it that you get your revenge. But if I don't get into contact with him, right now, I'm taking off for the great unknown. And he'll never find me."

She said, "All right," sniffled, and was gone. About sixty seconds later, she was back. "I got a loudspeaker here, a box, what you call it?" she said. "Anyway, you can speak to him through it."

Kickaha doubted that the man he was going to talk to was actually the "big boss" himself. Although, Mrs. Cambring had revealed that she now had information that she had not possessed when he had drugged her. Could this be because the Lord had calculated that Kickaha would call her?

He felt a chill sweep over the back of his scalp. If Red Orc could anticipate him this well, then he would also know Kickaha's next step.

He shrugged. There was only one way to find out if Red Orc was that clever.

The voice was deep and resonant. Its pronunciation of English was that of a native, and its use of vocabulary seemed to be "right." The speaker did not introduce himself. His tone indicated that he did not need to do so, that just hearing him should convince anyone immediately of his identity. And of his power.

Kickaha felt that this was truly Red Orc, and the longer he heard him the more he identified certain characteristics that reminded him of Anana's voice. There was a resemblance there, which was not surprising, since the family of Urizen was very inbred.

"Finnegan! I have your friends Wolff and Chryseis and your lover, my niece, Anana. They are well. Nothing has happened to them, nothing harmful, that is. As yet! I drugged the truth from them; they have told me everything they know about this."

Then it is good, Kickaha thought, *that Anana does not know where the Horn of Shambarimen really is.*

There was a pause. Kickaha said, "I'm listening."

"I should kill them, after some suitable attentions, of course. But they don't really represent any threat to me; they were as easily caught as just-born rabbits."

A Lord always had to do some bragging. Kickaha said nothing, knowing that the Lord would get to the point when he became short-winded. But Red Orc surprised him.

"I could wait until I caught you, and I would not have to wait very long. But just now time is of the essence, and so I am willing to make a trade."

He paused again. Kickaha said, "I'm all ears."

"I will let the prisoners go and will allow them to return to Jadawin's world. And you may go with them. But on several conditions. First, you will hand over the Horn of Shambarimen to me!"

Kickaha had expected this. The Horn was not only unique in all the universes, it was the most prized item of the Lords. It had been made by the fabled ancestor of all the Lords now living, though it had been in the possession of his equally fabled son so long that it was sometimes referred to as the Horn of Ilmarwolkin. It had a unique utility among gates. It could be used alone. All other gates had to exist in pairs. There had to be one in the universe to be left and a sister, a resonant gate, in the universe to be entered. The majority of these were fixed, though the crescent type was mobile. But the Horn had only to be blown upon, with the keys of the Horn played in the proper coded sequence, and a momentary way between the universes would open. That is, it would do so if the Horn were played near a "resonant" point in the "walls" between the two worlds.

A resonant point was the path between two universes, but these universes never varied. Thus, if a Lord used the Horn without knowing where the resonant point would lead him, he would find himself in whichever universe was on the other side, like it or not.

Kickaha knew of four places where he could blow the Horn and be guaranteed to open the way to the World of Tiers. One was at the gate in the cave near Lake Arrowhead. One was in Kentucky, but he would need Wolff to guide him to it. Another would be in his former apartment in Bloomington, Indiana. And the fourth would be in the closet in the basement of a house in Tempe, Arizona. Wolff knew that, too, but he had described to Kickaha how to get to it from Earth's side, and Kickaha had not forgotten.

Red Orc's voice was impatient. "Come, come! Don't play games with *me,* Earthling! Say yes or say no, but be quick about it!"

"Yes! Provisionally, that is! It depends upon your other conditions!"

"I have only one." Red Orc coughed several times and then said, "And that is, that you and the others first help me catch the Beller!"

Kickaha was shocked, but a thousand experiences in being surprised enabled him to conceal it. Smoothly, he said, "Agreed! In fact, that's something I had wished you would agree to do, but at that time I didn' see working with you. Of course, you had no whip hand then."

So the Beller had either been caught by Orc's men and had then escaped or somebody else had captured him. That somebody else could only be another Lord.

Or perhaps it was another Beller.

At that thought, he became cold.

"What do we do now?" he said, unwilling to state the truth, which was, "What do *you* wish now?"

Orc's voice became crisp and restrainedly triumphant.

"You will present yourself at Mrs. Cambring's house as soon as possible, and my men will conduct you here. How long will it take you to get to Cambring's?"

"About half an hour," Kickaha said. If he could get a taxi at once, he could be there in ten minutes, but he wanted a little more time to plan.

"Very well!" the Lord said. "You must surrender all arms, and you will be thoroughly examined by my men. Understood?"

"Oh, sure."

While he was talking, he had been as vigilant as a bird. He looked out the glass of the booth for anything suspicious, but had seen nothing except cars passing. Now a car stopped by the curb. It was a big dark Cadillac with a single occupant. The man sat for a minute, looked at his wristwatch, and then opened the door and got out. He sauntered toward the booth, looking again at his watch. He was a very well-built youth about six-foot-three and dressed modishly and expensively. The long yellow hair glinted in the sun as if it were flecked with gold. His face was handsome but rugged.

He stopped near the booth and pulled a cigarette case from his jacket. Kickaha continued to listen to the instructions from the phone but he kept his eye on the newcomer. The fellow looked at the world through half-lidded arrogant eyes. He was evidently impatient because the booth was occupied. He glanced at his watch again and then lit his cigarette with a pass of the flame over the tip and a flicking away of the match in one smooth movement.

Kickaha spoke the code which prepared the ring on his finger to be activated for a short piercing beam. He would have to cut through the glass if the fellow were after him.

The voice on the phone kept on and on. It seemed as if he were dictating the terms of surrender to a great nation instead of to a single man. Kickaha must approach the front of the Cambring house and advance only halfway up the front walk and then stand until three men came out of the house and three men in a car parked across the street approached him from behind at the same time. And then . . .

The man outside the booth made a disgusted face as he looked at his watch again and swung away. Evidently he had given up on Kickaha.

But he only took two steps and spun, holding a snubnosed handgun.

Kickaha dropped the phone and ducked, at the same time speaking the word which activated the ring.

The gun barked, the glass of the booth shattered, and Kickaha was enveloped in a white mist. It was so unexpected that he gasped once, knew immediately that he should hold his breath, and did so. He also lunged out of the booth, cutting down the door with the ring. The door fell outward from his weight, but he never heard it strike the ground.

When he recovered consciousness, he was in the dark and hard confines of a moving object. The odor of gas and the cramped space made him believe that he was in the trunk of a car. His hands were tied behind him, his legs were tied at the ankles, and his mouth was taped.

He was sweating from the heat, but there was enough air in the trunk. The car went up an incline and stopped. The motor stopped, doors squeaked, the car lifted as bodies left it, and then the lids of the trunk swung open. Four men were looking down at him, one of whom was the big youth who had fired the gas gun.

They pulled him out and carried him from the garage, the door of which was shut. The exit led directly into the hall of a house, which led to a large room, luxuriously furnished and carpeted. Another hall led them to a room with a ceiling a story and a half high, an immense crystal chandelier, black and white parquet floor, heavy mahogany furniture, and paintings that looked like original old masters.

Here he was set down in a big high-backed chair and his legs were untied. Then he was told by one of the men to walk. A man behind urged him on with something hard and sharp against his back. He followed the others from the room through a doorway set under the great staircase. This led down a flight of twelve steps into a sparsely furnished room. At one end was a big massive iron door which he knew led to his prison cell. And so it was, though a rather comfortable prison. His hands were untied and the tape was taken from his mouth.

The beamer-ring had been removed, and the beamer-pen taken from his shirt pocket. While the big man watched, the others stripped him naked, cutting the shirt and his undershirt off. Then they explored his body cavities for weapons but found nothing.

He offered no resistance since it would have been futile. The big man and another held guns on him. After the inspection, a man closed a shackle around one ankle. The shackle was attached to a chain which was fastened at the other end to a ring in the wall. The chain was very thin and lightweight and long enough to permit him to move anywhere in the room.

The big man smiled when he saw Kickaha eyeing it speculatively and said, "It's as gossamer as a cobweb, my friend, but strong as the chain that bound Fenris."

"I um Loki, not Fenris," Kickaha said, grinning savagely. He knew that the man expected him to be ignorant of the reference to the great wolf of the old Norse religion, and he should have feigned ignorance. The less respect your imprisoner has for you, the more chance you have to escape. But he could not resist the answer.

The big man raised his eyebrows and said, "Ah, yes. And you remember what happened to Loki?"

"I am also Logi," Kickaha said, but he decided that that sort of talk had gone far enough. He fell silent, waiting for the other to tell him who he was and what he meant to do.

The man did not look quite so young now. He seemed to be somewhat over thirty. His voice was heavy, smooth, and very authoritative. His eyes were beautiful; they were large and leaf-green and heavily lashed. His face seemed familiar, though Kickaha was sure that he had never seen it before.

The man gestured, and the others left the room. He closed the door behind him and then sat on the edge of the table. This was bolted down to the floor, as were the other pieces of furniture. He dangled one leg while he held his gun on his lap. It looked like a conventional weapon, not a gas gun or a disguised beamer, but Kickaha had no way of determining its exact type at that moment. He sat down on a chair and waited. It was true that this left the man looking down on him, but Kickaha was not one to allow a matter of relative altitude to give another a psychological advantage.

The man looked steadily at him for several minutes. Kickaha looked back and whistled softly.

"I've been following you for some time," the man suddenly said. "I still don't know who you are. Let me introduce myself. I am Red Orc."

Kickaha stiffened, and he blinked.

The man smiled and said, "Who did you think I was?"

"A Lord who'd gotten stuck in this universe and was looking for a way out," Kickaha said. "Are there two Red Orcs, then?"

The man lost some of his smile. "No, there is only one! I am Red Orc! That other is an impostor! An usurper! I was careless for just one moment! But I got away with my life, and because of his bad luck, I will kill him and get back everything!"

"Who is that other?" Kickaha said. "I had thought . . . but then he never named himself . . . he let me think . . ."

"That he was Red Orc? I thought so! But his name is Urthona, and he was once Lord of the Shifting World. Then that demon-bitch Vala, my niece, drove him from his world, and he fled and came here, to this world, my world. I did not know who it was, although I knew that some Lord had come through a gate in Europe. I hunted for him and did not find him and then I forgot about him. That was a thousand years ago; I presumed he had gotten out through some gate I did not know about or else had been killed.

"But he was lying low and all the time searching for me. And finally, only ten years ago, he found me, surveyed my fortress, my defenses, watched my comings and my goings, and then he struck!

"I had grown careless, but I got away, although all my bodyguards died. And he took over. It was so simple for him because he was in the seat of power, and there was no one to deny him. How could there be anyone to say no to him? I had hidden my face too well. Anyone in the seat of power could issue orders, pull the strings, and he would be obeyed, since the Earthlings who are closest to him do not know his real name or his real face.

"And I could not go to the men who had carried out my orders and say, 'Here I am, your own true Lord! Obey me and kill that fool who is now giving you orders!' I would have been shot down at once, because Urthona had described me to his servants, and they thought I was the enemy of their leader.

"So I went into hiding, just as Urthona had done. But when I strike, I will not miss! And I shall again be in the seat of power!"

There was a pause. Orc seemed to be expecting him to comment. Perhaps he expected praise or awe or terror.

Kickaha said, "Now that he has this seat of power, as you call it, is he Lord of both Earths? Or of this one only?"

Orc seemed set aback by this question. He stared and then his face got red.

"What is that to you?" he finally said.

"I just thought that you might be satisfied with being Lord of the other Earth. Why not let this Urthona rule this world? It looks to me from the short time I've been here, that this world is doomed. The humans are polluting the air and the water and, at any time, they may kill off all life on Earth with an atomic war. Apparently, you are not doing anything to prevent this. So why not let Urthona have this dying world while you keep the other?"

He paused and then said, "Or is Earth Number Two in as bad a condition as this one?"

Red Orc's face had lost its redness. He smiled and said, "No, the other is not as bad off. It's much more desirable, even though it got exactly the same start as this one. But your suggestion that I surrender this world shows you don't know much about us, *leblabbiy*."

"I know enough," Kickaha said. "But even Lords change for the better, and I had hoped . . ."

"I will do nothing to interfere here except to protect myself," Orc said. "If this planet chokes to death on its man-made foulness, or if it all goes out in a thousand bursts of radiation, it will do so without any aid or hindrance from me. I am a scientist, and I do not influence the direction of natural development one way or another on the two planets. Anything I do is on a microscale level and will not disturb macroscale matters.

"That, by the way, is one more reason why I must kill anyone who invades my universes. They might decide to interfere with my grand experiments."

"Not me!" Kickaha said. "Not Wolff or Chryseis or Anana! All we want is to go back to our own worlds! After the Beller is killed, of course. He's the only reason we came here. You must believe that!"

"You don't really expect me to believe that?" Orc said.

Kickaha shrugged and said, "It's true, but I don't expect you to believe it. You Lords are too paranoid to see things clearly."

Red Orc stood up from the table. "You will be kept prisoner here until I have captured the others and defeated Urthona. Then I'll decide what to do with you."

By this, Kickaha knew, he meant just what delicate tortures he could inflict upon him. For a moment, he thought about informing Orc of the Horn of Shambarimen's presence on Earth in this area. Perhaps he could use it for a bargaining point. Then he decided against it. Once Orc knew that it was here, he would just get the information from his captive by torture or drugs.

"Have you killed the Beller yet?" he said.

Orc smiled and said, "No."

He seemed very pleased with himself. "If it becomes necessary, I will threaten Urthona with him. I will tell Urthona that if he does not leave, I will let the Beller loose. That, you understand, is the most horrible thing a Lord could do."

"You would do this? After what you said about getting rid of anybody that might interfere with the natural development?"

"If I knew that my own death was imminent, unavoidable, yes, I would! Why not? What do I care what happens to this world, to all the worlds, if I am dead? Serve them right!"

There were more questions to which Kickaha wanted answers, but he was not controlling the interview. Orc abruptly walked out, leaving by the other door. Kickaha strained at the end of the chain to see through it, but the door swung out toward him and so shut off his view.

He was left with only his thoughts, which were pessimistic. He had always boasted that he could get loose from any prison, but it was, after all, a boast. He had, so far, managed to escape from every place in which he had been imprisoned, but he knew that he would someday find himself in a room with no exit. This was probably it. He was being observed by monitors, electronic or human or both, the chain was unbreakable with bare hands, and it also could be the conductor for some disabling and punishing agent if he did not behave.

This did not prevent him from trying to break it and twist it apart, because he could not afford to take anything for granted. The chain was unharmed, and he supposed that any human monitors would be amused by his efforts.

He stopped struggling, and he used the toilet facilities. Then he lay down on the sofa and thought for a while about his predicament. Though he was naked, he was not uncomfortable. The air was just a few degrees below his body temperature and it moved slowly enough so that it did not chill him. He fell asleep after a while, having found no way out, having thought of no plan that could reasonably work.

When he awoke, the room was as before. The sourceless light still made it high noon, and the air had not changed temperature. However, on sitting up, he saw a tray with dishes and cups and table utensils on top of the small thin-legged wooden table at the end of the sofa. He did not think that anyone could have entered with it unless he had been drugged. It seemed more likely that a gate was embedded in the wooden top and that a tray had been gated through while he slept.

He ate hungrily. The utensils were made of wood, and the dishes and the cups were of pewter and bore stylized octopuses, dolphins, and lobsters. After he ate, he walked back and forth within the range of the chain for about an hour. He tried to think of what he could do with the gate, if there was a gate inside that wooden table top. At the end of the hour, as he turned back toward the table, he saw that the tray was gone. His suspicion was correct; the top did contain a gate.

There had been no sound. The Lords of the old days had solved the problems of noise caused by sudden disappearance of an object. The a did not rush into the vacuum created by the disappearance because the gate arrangement included a simultaneous exchange of air between the gate on one end and that at the other.

About an hour later, Orc entered through the door by which he had left. He was accompanied by two men, one of whom carried a hypodermic needle. They wore kilts. One kilt was striped red and black and the other was white with a stylized black octopus with large blue eyes. Other than the kilts, leather sandals, and beads, they wore nothing. Their skins were dark, their faces looked somewhat Mediterranean but also reminded him of Amerindians, and their straight black hair was twisted into two pigtails. One pigtail fell down the back and the other was coiled on the right side of the head.

Orc spoke to them in a language unknown to Kickaha. It did seem vaguely Hebrew or Arabic to him but that was only because of its sounds. He knew too little of either language to be able to identify them.

While the one with the crossbow stood to one side and aimed it at Kickaha, the other approached from the other side. Orc commanded him to submit to the injection, saying that if he resisted, the crossbow would shoot its hypodermic into him. And the pain that followed would be longlasting and intense. Kickaha obeyed, since there was nothing else he could do.

He felt nothing following the injection. But he answered all of Orc's questions without hesitation. His brain did not feel clouded or bludgeoned. He was thinking as clearly as usual. It was just that he could not resist giving Orc all the information he asked for. But that was what kept him from mentioning the Horn of Shambarimen. Orc did not *ask* him about it nor was there any reason for him to do so. He had no knowledge that it had been in the possession of Wolff, or Jadawin, as Orc knew him.

Orc's questions did, however, cause Kickaha to reveal almost everything else of value to him. He knew something of Kickaha's life on Earth before that night in Bloomington when Paul Janus Finnegan had been accidentally catapulted out of this universe into the World of Tiers. He learned more about Finnegan's life since then, when Finnegan had become Kickaha (and also Horst von Horstmann and a dozen other identities). He learned about Wolff-Jadawin and Chryseis and Anana, the invasion of the Black Bellers, and other matters pertinent. He learned much about Kickaha's and Anana's activities since they had ated into the cavern near Lake Arrowhead.

Orc said, "If I did allow you and Anana and Wolff and Chryseis to go back to your world, would you stay there and not try to get back here?"

"Yes," Kickaha said. "Provided that I knew for sure that the Beller was dead."

"Hmm. But your World of Tiers sounds fascinating. Jadawin always was very creative. I think that I would like to add it to my possessions."

This was what Kickaha expected.

Orc smiled again and said, "I wonder what you would have done if you had found out where I used to live and where Urthona now sits in the seat of power."

"I would have gone into it and killed you or Urthona," Kickaha said. "And I would have rescued Anana and Wolff and Chryseis and then searched for the Beller until I found him and killed him. And then we would have returned to my world; that is, to Wolff's, to be exact."

Orc looked thoughtful and paced back and forth for a while. Suddenly, he stopped and looked at Kickaha. He was smiling as if a brilliant idea were shining through him.

"You make yourself sound very tricky and resourceful," he said. "So tricky that I could almost think you were a Lord, not just a *leblabbiy* Earthling."

"Anana has the crazy idea that I could be the son of a Lord," Kickaha said. "In fact, she thinks I could be your son."

Orc said, "What?" and he looked closely at Kickaha and then began laughing. When he had recovered, he wiped his eyes and said, "That felt good! I haven't laughed like that for . . . how long? Never mind. So you really think *you* could be my child?"

"Not me," Kickaha said. "Anana. And she liked to speculate about it because she still needs some justification for falling in love with a *leblabbiy*. If I could be half-Lord, then I'd be more acceptable. But this idea is one hundred percent wishful thinking, of course."

"I have no children because I want to interfere as little as possible with the natural development here, although a child or two could really make little difference," Orc said. "But you could be the child of another Lord, I suppose. However, you've gotten me off the subject. I was saying that you were very tricky, if I am to believe your account of yourself. Perhaps I could use you."

He fell silent again and paced back and forth once more with his head bent and his hands clasped behind him. Then he stopped, looked at Kickaha, and smiled. "Why not? Let's see how good you are. I can lose by it no matter what happens, and I may gain."

Kickaha had guessed, correctly, what he was going to propose. He would tell him the address of Urthona, would take him there, in fac provide him with some weapons, and allow him to attack Urthona as he wished. And if Kickaha failed, he still might so distract Urthona that Orc could take advantage of the distraction.

In any event, it would be amusing to watch a *leblabbiy* trying to invade the seat of power of a Lord.

"And if I do succeed?" Kickaha said.

"It's not very likely, since I have not had any success yet. Though, of course, I haven't really tried yet. But if you should succeed, and I'm not worried that you will, I will permit you and your lover and your friends to return to your world. Provided that the others also swear, while under the influence of the proper drugs, that they have no intention of returning to either Earth."

Kickaha did not believe this, but he saw no profit in telling Orc so. Once he was out of this cell and had some freedom of action—though closely watched by Orc—he would have some chance against the Lords.

Orc spoke the unknown language into a wristband device, and a moment later another entered. His kilt was red with a black stylized bird with a silver fish in its claws. He carried some papers which he gave to Orc, bowed, and withdrew.

Orc sat down by Kickaha.

The papers turned out to be maps of the central Los Angeles area and of Beverly Hills. Orc circled an area in Beverly Hills.

"That is the house where I lived and where Urthona now lives," he said. "The house you were searching for and where Anana and the others are now undoubtedly held. Or, at least, where they were taken after being captured."

Orc's description of the defenses in the house made Kickaha feel very vulnerable. It was true that Urthona would have changed the defense setup in the house. But, though the configuration of the traps might be different, the traps would remain fundamentally the same.

"Why haven't you tried to attack before this?"

"I have," Red Orc replied. "Several times. My men got into the house, but I never saw them again. The last attempt was made about three years ago.

"If you don't succeed," Orc continued, "I will threaten Urthona with the Beller. I doubt, however, that that will do much good, since he will find it inconceivable that a Lord could do such a thing."

His tone also made it evident that he did not think Kickaha would succeed.

He wanted to know Kickaha's plans, but Kickaha could only tell him that he had none except to improvise. He wanted Orc to use his devices to ensure a minute's distortion of Urthona's detection devices.

Orc objected to loaning Kickaha an antigravity belt. What if it fell into the hands of the Earthlings?

"There's not much chance of that," Kickaha said. "Once I'm in Urthona's territory, I'll either succeed or fail. In either case, the belt isn't going to get into any outsider's hands. And if it did, whoever is Lord will have the influence to see that it is taken out of the hands of whoever has it. I'm sure that even if the FBI had it in their possession, the Lord of the Two Earths could find a way to get it from them. Right?"

"Right," Orc said. "But do you plan on running away with it instead of attacking Urthona?"

"No. I won't stop until I'm dead, or too incapacitated to fight, or have won," Kickaha said.

Orc was satisfied, and by this Kickaha knew that the truth drug was still effective. Orc stood up and said, "I'll prepare things for you. It will take some time, so you might as well rest or do whatever you think best. We'll go into action at midnight tonight."

Kickaha asked if the cord could be taken off him. Orc said, "Why not? You can't get out of here, anyway. The cord was just an extra precaution."

One of the kilted men touched the shackle around his leg with a thin cylinder. The shackle opened and fell off. While the two men backed away from Kickaha, Orc strode out of the room. Then the door was shut, and Kickaha was alone.

He spent the rest of the time thinking, exercising, and eating lunch and supper. Then he bathed and shaved, exercised some more, and lay down to sleep. He would need all his alertness, strength, and quickness and there was no use draining these with worry and sleeplessness.

He did not know how long he had slept. The room was still lighted and everything seemed as when he had lain down. The tray with its empty plates and cups was still on the table, and this, he realized, was a wrong note. It should have been gated out.

The sounds that had awakened him had seemed to be slight tappings When coming out of his sleep, he had dreamed, or thought he dreamed that a woodpecker was rapping a tree trunk.

Now there was only silence.

He rose and walked toward the door used by Orc and his servants. was of metal, as he had ascertained after being loosed from the cor

He placed his ear against it and listened. He could hear nothing. Then he jumped back with an oath. The metal had suddenly become hot!

The floor trembled as if an earthquake had started. The metal of the door gave forth a series of sounds, and he knew where the dream of the woodpecker had originated. Something was striking the door on the other side.

He stepped away from it just as the center of the door became cherry red and began to melt. The redness spread, became white, and then the center disappeared, leaving a hole the size of a dinner plate. By then, Kickaha was crouching behind the sofa and looking out around its corner. He saw an arm reach in through the hole and the hand grope around the side. Evidently it was trying to locate a lock. There was none, so the arm withdrew and a moment later the edge of the door became cherry red. He suspected that a beam was being used on it, and he wondered what the metal was. If it had been the hardest steel, it should have gone up in a puff of smoke at the first touch of a beam.

The door fell inward with a clang. A man jumped in, a big cylinder with a bell-like muzzle and a rifle-type stock in his hands. The man was one of the kilted servants. But he carried on his back a black bell-like object in a net attached to the shoulders with straps.

Kickaha saw all this in a glance and withdrew his head. He crouched on the other side, hoping that the intruder had not seen him and would not, as a matter of precaution, sweep the sofa with the beamer to determine if anyone would be behind it. He knew who the man *now* was. Whatever he *may* have been, he was now the Black Beller, Thabuuz. The mind of the Beller was housed in the brain of the servant of the Lord, and the mind of the servant was discharged.

Somehow, the Beller had gotten the bell and managed to transfer his mind from the wounded body of the Drachelander to the servant of the Lord. He had gotten hold of a powerful beamer, and he was on his way out of the stronghold of Red Orc.

The odor of burned flesh filled the room; there must be bodies in the next room.

Kickaha wanted desperately to find out what the Beller was doing, but he did not dare to try to peek around the corner of the sofa again. He could hear the man's breathing, and then, suddenly, it was gone. After waiting sixty seconds and hearing nothing, Kickaha peeked around the corner. The room seemed to be empty. A moment later, he was sure of it. The other door, the door by which Kickaha and Orc and his men had originally entered, was standing wide open, its lock drilled through.

Kickaha looked cautiously around the side of the opposite door. There were parts of human bodies here, arms, trunks, a head, all burned deeply. There seemed to have been four or five men originally. There was no way of telling which was Red Orc or if he was among the group, since all clothes and hair had been burned off.

Somewhere, softly, an alarm was ringing.

He was torn between the desire to keep on the trail of the Beller so that he would not lose him and by the desire to find out if Red Orc was still alive. He also wanted very much to confirm his suspicions that he was not on the Earth he knew. He suspected that the door through which he had entered was a gate between the two worlds and that this house was on Earth Number Two.

He went into the hallway. There were some knives on the floor, but they were too hot to pick up. He went down the hall and through a doorway into a very large room. It was dome-shaped, its walls white with frescoes of sea life, its furniture wooden and lightly built with carved motifs he did not recognize, and its floor a mosaic of stone with more representations of sea creatures.

He crossed the room and looked out the window. There was enough light from the moon to see a wide porch with tall round wooden pillars, painted white, and beyond that a rocky beach that sloped for a hundred yards from the house to the sea. There was no one in view.

He prowled the rest of the house, trying to combine caution with speed. He found a hand-beamer built to look like a conventional revolver. Its butt bore markings that were not the writing of the Lords or of any language that he knew. He tested it out against a chair, which fell apart down the middle. He could find no batteries to recharge it and had no way of knowing how much charge remained in the battery.

He also found closets with clothes, most of them kilts, sandals, beads and jackets with puffed sleeves. But in one closet he found Earth Number One type clothing, and he put on a shirt and trousers too large for him. Since he could not wear the big shoes, he put on a pair of sandals.

Finally, in a large bedroom luxuriously provided with alien furniture he discovered how Red Orc had escaped. A crescent lay in the center of the floor. The Lord had stepped into a circle formed of two crescents of a gate and been transported elsewhere. That he had done so to save himself was evident. The door and the walls were crisscrossed with the perforations and charred. It was not likely that Orc would be caught without a weapon on him, but he must have thought that the big beam was too much to face.

He had gated, but where? he could have gone back to Earth Numb

One, but not necessarily to the same house. Or he could have gated to another place on Earth Number Two. Or, even, to another room in this house.

Kickaha had to get out of this house and after the Beller.

He ran downstairs, through the big room, down the hall, and into the room where he had been kept prisoner. The door through which the Beller had gone was still open. Kickaha hesitated before it, because the Beller might be waiting for someone to follow. Then it occurred to him that the Beller would think that everybody in the house had fled or gone and that nobody would be following him. He had not known about the other prisoner, of course, or he would have looked around to dispose of him first.

He returned to the hallway. One knife lying on the floor had cooled off by then and seemed to be undamaged. He hefted it, determined that it had a good balance, and stuck it in his belt. He leaped through the doorway, his gun ready if somebody should be waiting for him. There was no one. The short and narrow hallway was quiet. The door beyond had been closed, and he pushed it open gently with the tip of his dagger. After the door had swung open, he waited a minute, listening. Before going through, he inspected the room. It had changed. It was larger, and the gray-blue paper walls were gray smooth stone. He had expected that this might happen. Red Orc would change the resonance of the gates so that if a prisoner did escape, he would find himself in a surprising, and probably unpleasant, place.

Under other circumstances, Kickaha would have turned back and looked for the switch that would set the gate to the frequency he desired. But now his first duty was to those in the hands of Urthona. To hell with the Beller! It would really be best to get back to Earth Number One and to get started on the attack against Urthona.

He turned and started to reenter the room where he had been held, and again he stopped. That room had changed, though he would not have known it if the door to the opposite side had not been removed by the Beller's weapon. This door looked exactly the same, but it was upright and in place. Only this kept Kickaha from stepping into it and so finding himself gated to another place where he would be cut off from both the Beller and Urthona's captives.

He set his teeth together and hissed rage and frustration. Now he would do nothing but take second-best and put himself in with the Beller and hope that he could figure a way out.

He turned and went back through the door after the Beller, though less cautiously.

This room seemed to be safe, but the room beyond that would proba-bly tell him where he was. However, it was just like the one he had left except that there were some black metal boxes, each about six feet square, piled along the walls almost to the ceiling. There were no locks or devices on them to indicate how they were opened.

He opened the next door slowly, looked through, and then leaped in. He was in a large room furnished with chairs, divans, tables, and statu-ary. A big fountain was in the middle. The furniture looked as if it had been made by a Lord; though he did not know the name of the particu-lar style, he recognized it. Part of the ceiling and one side of the right wall were curved and transparent. The ground was not visible for some distance and then it abruptly sprang into view. It sloped down for a thousand feet to end in a valley which ran straight and level for several miles and then became the side of a small mountain.

It was daylight outside, but the light was pale, though it was noon. The sun was smaller than Earth's, and the sky was black. The earth it-self was rocky with some stretches of reddish sand, and there were a few widely separated cactus-looking plants on the slope and in the val-ley. They seemed small, but he realized after a while that they must be enormous.

He examined the room carefully and made sure that the door to the next room was closed. Then he looked through the window again. The scene was desolate and eerie. Nothing moved, and probably nothing had moved here for thousands of years. Or so it seemed to him. He could see past the end of the mountain on which the building stood and the end of the other mountain. The horizon was closer than it should have been.

He had no idea where he was. If he had been gated into another uni-verse, he would probably never know. If he had been gated to another planet in his native universe, or its double, then he was probably on Mars. The size of the sun, the reddish sand, the distance of the horizon, the fact that there was enough air to support plant life—if that was plant life—and, even as he watched, the appearance of a swift whitish body coming from the western sky indicated that this was Mars.

For all he knew, this building had been on Mars for fifteen thousand years, since the creation of this universe.

At that moment, something came flapping over the mountain on the opposite side and then glided toward the bottom of the valley. It had an estimated wing span of fifty yards and looked like a cross between a kite, a pterodactyl, and a balloon. Its wingbones gave the impression of being thin as tin foil, though it was really impossible to be sure at that distance. The skin of the wings looked thinner than tissue paper. Its body was a great sac which gave the impression, again unverifiable, of containing gas. Its tail spread out in a curious configuration like six box kites on a rod. Its lower limbs were exceedingly thin but numerous and spread out below it like a complicated landing gear, which it probably was. Its feet were wide and many-toed.

It glided down very gracefully and swiftly. Even with the lift of its great wings and tail and the lighter-than-air aspect of the swollen gas-containing body, it had to glide at a steep angle. The air must be so thin.

The thing threw an enormous shadow over one of the gigantic cactusoids, and then it was settling down, like a skyscraper falling, on the plant. Red dust flew into the air and came down more swiftly than it would have on Earth.

The plant was completely hidden under the monster's bulk. It thrust its rapier-like beak down between two of its legs and, presumably, into the plant. And there it squatted, as motionless as the cactusoids.

Kickaha watched it until it occurred to him that the Beller might also be watching it. If this were so, it would make it easier for Kickaha to surprise him. He went through the next door in the same manner as the last and found himself in a room ten times as large as the one he had just left. It was filled with great metal boxes and consoles with many screens and instruments. It, too, had a window with a view of the valley.

There was no Beller, however.

Kickaha went into the next room. This was small and furnished with everything a man would need except human companionship. In the middle of the floor lay a skeleton.

There was no evidence of the manner of death. The skeleton was that of a large male. The teeth were in perfect condition. It lay on its back with both bony arms outstretched.

Kickaha thought that it must have been some Lord who had either entered this fortress on Mars from a gate in some other universe or had been trapped elsewhere and transported here by Red Orc. This could have happened ten thousand years ago or fifty years ago.

Kickaha picked the skull up and carried it in his left hand. He might need something to throw as a weapon or as a distraction to his enemy. It amused him to think of using a long-dead Lord, a failed predecessor, against a Beller.

The next room was designed like a grotto. There was a pool of water about sixty yards wide and three hundred long in the center and a small waterfall on the left which came down from the top of a granite cone.

There were several of the stone cones and small hills, strange looking plants growing here and there, a tiny stream flowing from a spring on top of another cone, and huge lilypad-like plants in the pool.

As he walked slowly along the wet and slimy edge of the pool, he was startled by a reddish body leaping from a lilypad. It soared out, its legs trailing behind frog-fashion and then splashed into the water. It arose a moment later and turned to face the man. Its face was frog-like but its eyes were periscopes of bone or cartilage. Its pebbly skin was as red as the dust on the surface outside.

There were several shadowy fish-like bodies in the depths. There had to be something for the frog to eat, and for the prey of the frog to eat. The ecology in this tiny room must be delicately but successfully balanced. He doubted that Red Orc came here very often to check up on it.

He was standing by the edge of the pool when he saw the door at the far end begin to open. He had no time to run forward or backward because of the distance he would have to traverse. There was no hiding place to his right and only the pool close by on his left. Without more than a second's pause, he chose the pool and slid over the slimy edge into the water. It was warm enough not to shock him but felt oily. He stuck the beamer in his belt and, still holding the skull in one hand, submerged with a shove of his sandaled feet against the side of the pool. He went down deep, past the thick stems of the lilypads, and swam as far as he could under the water. When he came up, he did so slowly and alongside the stem of a lily. Emerging, he kept his head under the pad of the plant and hoped that the Beller would not notice the bulge. The other rooms had been bright with the equal-intensity, hidden-source lighting of the Lords. But this room was lit only by the light from the window and so had a twilight atmosphere on this side.

Kickaha clung with one hand to the stem of the plant and peered out from under the lifted edge of the pad. What he saw almost made him gasp. He was fortunate to have restrained himself, because his mouth was under water.

The black bell was floating along the edge of the pool at a height of about seven feet above the floor.

It went by slowly and then stopped at the door. A moment later, the Beller entered and walked confidently toward it.

Kickaha began to get some idea of what had happened in Red Orc's house.

The Beller, while in the laboratories of Wolff, must have equipped his bell with an antigravity device. And he must have added some device for controlling it at a distance with his thoughts. He had not been able to use it while on Earth nor had any reason to do so until he was taken prisoner by Orc. Then, when he had recovered enough from the wound, he saw his chance and summoned the bell to him with his thoughts. Or, to be more exact, by controlled patterns of brainwaves which could be detected by the bell. The control must be rough and limited, but it had been effective enough.

Somehow, the bell, operating at the command of the Beller's brain-wave patterns, had released him. And the Beller had seized one of Orc's men, discharged the neural pattern of the man's mind, and transferred his mind from the wounded body of Thabuuz to the brain of the servant.

The bell could detect the mental call of the Beller when it extended the two tiny drill-antennas from two holes in its base. The stuff of which the bell was made was indestructible, impervious even to radiation. So the antennas must have come out automatically at certain intervals to "listen" for the brainwaves of the Beller. And it had "heard" and had responded. And the Beller had gotten out and obtained a weapon and started to kill. He had succeeded; he may even have killed Red Orc, though Kickaha did not think so.

And then he had been shunted through the escape gate into a building on Mars.

Kickaha watched the Beller approach. Unable to hang onto the skull any longer and handle his gun at the same time, he let the skull drop. It sank silently into the depths while he held onto the stem with his left hand and pulled the beamer from his belt with the other. The Beller went on by him and then stopped at the door. After opening this, he waited until the bell had floated on through ahead of him.

Apparently, the bell could detect other living beings, too. Its range must be limited, otherwise it would have detected Kickaha in the water as it went by. It was possible, of course, that the water and the lilypad shielded him from the bell's probe.

Kickaha pulled himself higher out of the water with his left hand and lifted the beamer above the surface. From under the darkness of the pad, he aimed at the Beller. It would be necessary to get him with the first beam. If it missed, the Beller would get through the door and then Kickaha would be up against a weapon much more powerful than his.

If he missed the Beller, the beam would slice through the wall of the building, and the air would boil out into the thin atmosphere of Mars. And both of them would have had it.

The Beller was presenting his profile. Kickaha held his beamer steadily as he pointed it so that the thread-thin ray would burn a hole through the hip of the man. And then, as he fell, he would be cut in two.

His finger started to squeeze on the trigger. Suddenly, something touched his calf and he opened his mouth to scream. So intense was the pain, it almost shocked him into unconsciousness. He doubled over, and water entered his mouth and nostrils, and he choked. His hand came loose from the plant stem and the beamer fell from the other hand.

In the light-filled water, he saw a frog-like creature swim away swiftly, and he knew that it was this that had bitten him. He swam upward because he had to get air, knowing even as he did that the Beller would easily kill him, if the Beller had heard him.

He came up and, with a massive effort of will, kept himself from blowing out water and air and gasping and thrashing around. His head came up under the pad again, and he eased the water out. He saw that the Beller had disappeared.

But in the next second he doubled over again with agony. The frog had returned and bitten him on the leg again. His blood poured out from the wounds and darkened the water. He swam quickly to the edge of the pool and pulled himself out with a single smooth motion. His legs tingled.

On the walk, he pulled off his shirt and tore it into strips to bind around his wounds. The animal must have had teeth as sharp as a shark's; they had sheared through the cloth of his pants and taken out skin and flesh. But the wounds were not deep.

The Lord must have been greatly amused when he planted the savage little carnivore in this pool.

Kickaha was not amused. He did not know why the Beller was in the next room, but he suspected that he would soon be back. He had to get away, but he also needed his beamer. Not that he would be able to get it. Not while that frog-thing was in the pool.

At least he had the knife. He took it from his belt and put it between his teeth while he splashed water on the walk where his blood had dripped. Then he straightened up and limped past the pool and into the next room.

He passed through a short bare-walled hall. The room beyond was as large as the one with the pool. It was warm and humid and filled with plant life that looked neither Terrestrial nor Martian. It was true that he had not seen any Martian vegetation other than the cactusoids in the valley. But these plants were so tall, green, stinking, fleshy, and so active they just did not look as if they could survive on the rare-aired Mars-scape.

One side of the wall was transparent, and this showed a gray fog. That was all. Strain his eyes as much as he could, he could see nothing but the grayness. And it did not seem to be a watery fog but one composed of thousands upon thousands of exceedingly tiny particles. More like dust of some kind, he thought.

He was surely no longer on Mars. When he had passed from the hall into this room, he had stepped through a gate which had shot him instantaneously into a building on some other planet or satellite. The gravity seemed no different than Earth's so he must be on a planet of similar size. That, plus the cloud, made him think that it must be Venus.

With a start, he realized that the gravity in the Martian building should have been much less than Earth's. How much? A sixth? He did not remember, but he knew that when he had leaped, he should have soared far more than he did.

But that building was on Mars. He was sure of that. This meant that the building had been equipped with a device to ensure an Earth-gravity locally. Which meant that this building could be on, say, Jupiter, and yet the titanic drag of the planet would be nullified by the Lord's machines.

He shrugged. It really did not matter much where he was if he could not survive outside of the building. The problem he had to solve was staying alive and finding a way back to Earth. He went on to another short and bare hall and then into a twilit room the size of Grand Central Station. It was dome-shaped and filled with a silvery gray metal liquid except for a narrow walk around the wall and for a small round island in the middle. The metal looked like mercury, and the walk went all the way around the room. Nowhere along the wall was there any sign of any opening.

The island was about fifty yards from the wall. Its surface was only a foot above the still lake of quicksilver. The island seemed to be of stone, and in its exact center was a huge hoop of metal set vertically in the stone. He knew at once that it was a gate and that if he could get to it, he would be transported to a place where he would at least have a fighting chance. That was the rule of the game. If the prisoner was intelligent enough and strong enough and swift enough—and, above all, lucky enough—he just might get free.

He waited by the door because there was no other place to hide. While he waited, he tried to think of anything in the other rooms that could be converted to a boat. Nothing came to his mind except one of the sofas, and he doubted that it would float. Still, he might try it. But how did you propel a heavy object that was slowly sinking, or perhaps swiftly sinking, through mercury?

He would not know until he tried it. The thought did not cheer him up. And then he thought, could a man swim in mercury? In addition, there were poisonous vapors rising from mercury, if he remembered his chemistry correctly.

Now he remembered some phrases from his high school chemistry class. That was back in 1936 in a long ago and truly different world: *Does not wet glass but forms a convex surface when in a glass container . . . is slightly volatile at ordinary temperatures and a health hazard due to its poisonous effect . . . slowly tarnishes in moist air . . .*

The air in this dome was certainly moist, but the metal was not tarnished. And he could smell no fumes and did not feel any poisonous effects. Not as yet.

Suddenly, he stiffened. He heard, faintly, the slapping of leather on stone. The door had been left open by the Beller, so Kickaha had not moved it. He was on the other side, waiting, hoping that the bell would not enter first.

It did. The black object floated through about four feet off the floor. As soon as it had passed by, it stopped. Kickaha leaped against the door and slammed it shut. The bell continued to hover in the same spot.

The door remained shut. It had no lock, and all the Beller had to do to open it was to kick it. But he was cautious, and he must have been very shaken by finding the door closed. He had no idea who was on the other side or what weapons his enemy had. Furthermore, he was now separated from his bell, his most precious possession. If it was true that the bell could not be destroyed, it was also true that it could be taken away and hidden from him.

Kickaha ran in front of the door, hoping that the Beller would not fire his heavy beamer at it at that moment. He seized the bell in his hands and plunged on. The bell resisted but went backward all the same. It did not, however, give an inch on the vertical.

At that moment, the metal of the edge of the door and the wall began to turn red, and Kickaha knew that the Beller was turning the full power of his beamer on the door and that the metal must be very resistant indeed.

But why didn't the Beller just kick the door open and then fire through it?

Perhaps he was afraid that his enemy might be hiding behind the door when it swung open, so he was making sure that there would be nothing to swing. Whatever his motives, he was giving Kickaha a little more time, not enough though to swim across to the island. The Beller would be through the door about the time he was halfway to the island.

Kickaha took hold of the bell with both hands and pushed it up against the wall. It did not go easily on the horizontal, but he did not have to strain to move it. He pulled it toward him and then away, estimating its resistance. Then he gave it a great shove with both hands in the direction along the wall. It moved at about two feet per second but then slowed as it scraped along the curved wall. Another shove, this time at an angle to take it away from the curve but to keep it from going out over the pool, resulted in its moving for a longer distance.

He looked at the door. The red spot was a hole now with a line of redness below it. Evidently the Beller intended to carve out a large hole or perhaps to cut out the door entirely. He could stop at any moment to peek through the hole, and, if he did, he would see his enemy and the bell. On the other hand, he might be afraid to use the hole just yet because his enemy might be waiting to blast him. Kickaha had one advantage. The Beller did not know what weapons he had.

Kickaha hurried after the bell, seized it again, backed up, stopped at the wall, and then drew his feet up. He hung with his knees and toes almost touching the walk. But the bell did not lose a fraction of altitude.

"Here goes everything!" he said and shoved with all the power of his legs against the wall.

He and the bell shot out over the pool, straight toward the vertical hoop on the island. They went perhaps forty feet and then stopped. He looked down at the gray liquid below and slowly extended his feet until they were in the metal. He pushed against it, and it gave way to his feet, but he and the bell moved forward a few feet. And so he pushed steadily and made progress, though it was slow and the sweat poured out over his body and ran into his eyes and stung them and his legs began to ache as if he had run two miles as fast as he could.

Nevertheless, he got to the island, and he stood upon its stone surface with the hoop towering only a few feet from him. He looked at the door. A thin line ran down one side and across the bottom and up the other side. It curved suddenly and was running across the top of the door. Within a minute or two, the door would fall in and then the Beller would come through.

Kickaha looked back through the hoop. The room was visible on the other side, but he knew that if he stepped through it, he would be gated to some other place, perhaps to another universe. Unless the Lord had set it here for a joke.

He pushed the bell ahead of him and then threw himself to one side so he would not be in front of the hoop. He had had enough experience with the Lords to suspect that the place on the other side was trapped. It was always best to throw something into the trap to spring it.

There was a blast that deafened him. His face and the side of his body were seared with heat. He had shut his eyes, but light flooded them. And then he sat up and opened them in time to see the bell shooting across the pool, though still at its original height. It sped above the mercury pool and the walk and stopped only when it slammed into the wall. There it remained, a few inches from the wall because of its rebound.

Immediately thereafter, the door fell outward and down against the walk. He could not hear it; he could hear only the ringing in his ears from the blast. But he saw the Beller dive through, the beamer held close to him, hit the floor, roll, and come up with the beamer held ready. By then, Kickaha had jumped up. As he saw the Beller look around and suddenly observe him, he leaped through the hoop. He had no choice. He did not think it would be triggered again, since that was not the way the Lords arranged their traps. But if the trap on the other side was reset, it would blow him apart, and his worries would be over.

He was through, and he was falling. There were several thousands of feet of air beneath him, a blue sky above, and a thin horizontal bar just before him. He grabbed it, both hands clamping around smooth cold iron, and he was swinging at arm's length below a bar, the ends of which were set in two metal poles that extended about twenty feet out from a cliff.

It was a triumph of imagination and sadism for Red Orc. If the prisoner was careless enough to go through the hoop without sending in a decoy, he would be blown apart before he could fall to death. And if he did not jump, but stepped through the gate, he would miss the bar.

And, having caught the bar, then what?

A man with lesser nerve or muscle might have fallen. Kickaha did not waste any time. He reached out with one hand and gripped the support bar. And as quickly let loose while he cursed and swung briefly with one hand.

The support pole was almost too hot to touch.

He inched along the bar to the other support pole and touched it. That was just as hot.

The metal was not quite too hot to handle. It pained him so much that Kickaha thought about letting go. But he stuck to it, and finally, hurting so much that tears came to his eyes and he groaned, he pulled himself up over the lip of the cliff. For a minute he lay on the rock ledge and moaned. The palms of his hands and the inner sides of his fingers felt as if they had third-degree burns. They looked, however, as if they had only been briefly near a fire, not in it, and the pain quickly went away.

His investigation of his situation was short because there was not much to see. He was on the bare top of a pillar of hard black rock. The top was wider than the bottom, and the sides were smooth as the barrel of a cannon. All around the pillar, as far as he could see, was a desolate rock plain and a river. The river split the circle described by the horizon and then itself split when it came to the column. On the other side, it merged into itself and continued on toward the horizon.

The sky was blue, and the yellow sun was at its zenith.

Set around the pillar near its base, at each of the cardinal points of the compass, was a gigantic hoop. One of these meant his escape to a place where he might survive if he chose the right one. The others probably meant certain death if he went through them.

They were not an immediate concern. He had to get down off the pillar first, and at the moment he did not know how he was going to do that.

He returned to the bar projecting from the cliff. The Beller could be about ready to come through the gate. Even if he was reluctant, he would have to come through. This was the only way out.

Minutes passed and became an hour, if he could trust his sense of time. The sun curved down from the zenith. He walked back and forth to loosen his muscles and speed the blood in his legs and buttocks. Suddenly a foot and a leg came out of the blue air. The Beller, on the other side of the gate, was testing out the unknown.

The foot reached here and there for substance and found only air. It withdrew, and, a few seconds later, the face of the Beller, like a Cheshire Cat in reverse, appeared out of the air.

Kickaha's knife was a streak of silver shooting toward the face. The face jerked back into the nothingness, and the knife was swallowed by the sky at a point about a foot below where the face had been.

The gate was not one-way. The entrance of the knife showed that. The fact that the Beller could stick part of his body through it and then withdraw it did not have anything to do with the one-way nature of some gates. Even a one-way gate permitted a body to go halfway through and then return. Unless, of course, the Lord who had designed it wished to sever the body of the user.

Several seconds passed. Kickaha cursed. He might never find out if he had thrown true or not.

Abruptly, a head shot out of the blue and was followed by a neck and shoulders and a chest and a solar plexus from which the handle of the knife stuck out.

The rest of the body came in view as the Beller toppled through. He fell through and out and his body became smaller and smaller and then was lost in distance. But Kickaha was able to see the white splash it made as it struck the river.

He took a deep breath and sat down, trembling. The Beller was at last dead, and all the Universes were safe forever from his kind.

And here I am, Kickaha thought. *Probably the only living thing in this universe. As alone as a man can be. And if I don't think of something impossible to do before my nonexistent breakfast, I will soon be one of the only two dead things in this universe.*

He breathed deeply again and then did what he had to do.

It hurt just as much going back out on the pole as it had coming in. When he reached the bar, he rested on it with one arm and one leg over it. After the pain had gone away in his hands and legs, he swung up onto the bar and balanced himself standing on it. His thousands of hours of practicing on tightwires and climbing to great heights paid off. He was able to maintain his equilibrium on the bar while he estimated again the point through which the Beller had fallen. It was only an undefined piece of blue, and he had one chance to hit his target.

He leaped outward and up, and his head came through the hoop and the upper part of his body and then he went "Whoof!" as his belly struck on the edge of the hoop. He reached out and gripped the stone with his fingertips and pulled himself on through. For a while, he lay on the stone until his heart resumed its normal beat. He saw that the bell was above him and the beamer was on the floor of the island only a foot from him.

He rose and examined the bell. It was indestructible, and the tips of the antennas were encased in the same indestructible stuff. When the antennas were withdrawn, the tips plugged up the two tiny holes at the base of the bell. But the antennas themselves were made of less durable metal, and they had suffered damage from the blast. Or so he supposed. He could see no damage. In fact, he could not even see the antennas, they were so thin, though he could feel them. But the fact that the Beller had not sent the bell ahead through the gate proved to Kickaha that something had damaged the bell. Perhaps the blast had only momentarily impaired the relatively delicate brainwave and flight-governing apparatus inside the bell. This was, after all, something new, something which the Beller had not had time to field-test.

Whatever had happened, it was fixed at its altitude above the island. And it still put up a weak resistance against a horizontal push.

Kickaha presumed that its anetannas must still be operative to some degree. Otherwise, the bell would not know how to maintain a constant height from the ground.

It gave him his only chance to get to the ground several thousand feet below. He did not know how much of a chance. It might just stay at this level even if the ground beneath it were to suddenly drop away. If that happened, he still might be able to get to the top of the stone pillar.

He put the strap of the beamer over one shoulder, hugged the bell to his chest, and stepped out through the hoop.

His descent was as swift as if he were dangling at the end of a parachute, a speed better than he had hoped for. From time to time, he had to kick against the sides of the pillar because the bell kept drifting back toward it, as if the mass of the pillar had some attraction for it.

Then he was ten feet above the river and released his hold on the bell. He fell a little faster, hit the water, which was warm, and came up in a strong current. He had to fight to get to shore but managed it. After he had regained some of his strength, he walked along the shore until he saw the bell. It was stopped against the side of the pillar, like a baby beast nuzzling its gigantic mother. There was no way for him to get to it nor did he see any reason why he should.

A few yards on, he found the body of the Beller. It had come to rest against a reef of rock which barely protruded above the surface of the small bay. Its back was split open, and the back of the head was soft, as if it had struck concrete instead of water. The knife was still in its solar plexus. Kickaha pulled it out, and cleaned it on the wet hair of the Beller. The fall had not damaged the knife.

He pulled the body from the river. Then he considered the giant gates set hoop-like in the rock like the smaller one in the island in that other world. Two were on this side of the river and two on the other. Each was at the corner of a square two miles long. He walked to the nearest one and threw a stone into it. The stone went through and landed on the rock on the other side. It was one of Red Orc's jokes. Perhaps all four were just hoops and he would be stuck on this barren world until he starved to death.

The next hoop, in the northeast corner also proved to be just that, a hoop.

Kickaha was beginning to get tired and hungry. He now had to swim over the river, through a very strong current, to get to the other two hoops. The walk from one to the other was two miles, and if he had to test all four, he would walk eight miles. Ordinarily, he would not have minded that at all, but he had been through much in the last few hours.

He sat down for a minute and then he jumped up, exclaiming and cursing himself for a fool. He had forgotten that gates might work when entered in one direction but not work in the other. Picking up a stone, he went around to the other side of the big hoop and cast the stone through it. The hoop was still just a hoop.

There was nothing to do then but to walk back to the first hoop and to test that from the other side. It, too, gave evidence that it was no gate.

He swam the river and got to the other side after having been carried downstream for a half-mile, thus adding to his journey. The beamer made the swimming and the walking more difficult, since it weighed about thirty pounds. But he did not want to leave it behind.

The southwest hoop was only a huge round of metal. He went toward the last one while the sun continued westward and downward. It shone in a silent sky over a silent earth. Even the wind had died down, and the only sound was the rushing of the river, which died as he walked away from it, and his own feet on the rocks and his breathing.

When he got to the northwest hoop, he felt like putting off his rock-throwing for a while. If this proved to be another jest of Red Orc, it might also prove to be the last jest that Kickaha would ever know. So he might as well get this over with.

The first stone went through and struck the rock beyond.

The second went through the other side and fell on the ground beyond.

He jumped up and down and yelled his frustration and hit the palm of one hand with the fist of the other. He kicked at a small boulder and then went howling and hopping away with pain. He pulled his hair and slapped the side of his head and then turned his face toward the blind blue sky and the deaf bright yellow sun and howled like a wolf whose tail was caught in a bear trap.

After a while he became silent and still. He might as well have been made of the light-red rock which was so abundant on this earth, except that his eyelids jumped and his chest rose and fell.

When he broke loose from the mold of contemplation, he walke briskly but unemotionally to the river. Here he drank his fill and then he looked for a sheltered place to spend the night. After fifteen minutes, he found a hollow in the side of a small hill of hard rock that would protect him from the wind. He fell asleep after many unavoidable thoughts of the future.

In the morning, he looked at the Beller's body and wondered if he was going to have to eat it.

To give himself something to do, and also because he never entirely gave up hope or quit trying, he waded around in the shallows of the river and ran his hands through the waters. No fish were touched or scared into revealing their presence. It did not seem likely that there would be any, especially when there was an absolute absence of plant life.

He walked to the top of the hill in the base of which he had slept. He sat on the hard round peak for a while, moving only to ease the discomfort of the stone on his buttocks. His situation was desperate and simple. Either Red Orc had prepared a way for his prisoner to escape if he was clever and agile enough or he had not. If he had not, then the prisoner would die here. If he had, then the prisoner—in this case, Kickaha —was just not bright enough. In which case, the prisoner was going to die soon.

He sat for a long while and then he groaned. What was the matter with his brain? Sure, the stone had gone through the gates, but no flesh had passed through them. He should have tried them himself instead of trickily testing them only with the stones. The gates could be set up to trigger only if matter above a certain mass passed through them or sometimes only if protein passed through them. Or even only if human brainwaves came close enough to set them off. But he had been so concerned with traps on the other side that he had forgotten about this possibility.

However, any activated gate might be adjusted to destroy the first large mass that entered, just as the gate from the room with the mercury pool had been booby-trapped.

He groaned at the thought of the strain and sweat involved, but he had not survived thus far by being lazy. He lifted the body of the Beller onto his shoulder, thanking his fortunes that the man was small, and set off toward the nearest gate.

It was a long, hot, and muscle-trembling day. The lack of food weakened him, and every failure at each gate took more out of him. The swim across the river with the dead weight of the corpse and the beamer drained him of even more. But he cast the body six times through the three gates, once through each side.

And now he was resting beside the fourth. The Beller lay near him, its arms spread out, its face upturned to the hot sun, its eyes open, its mouth open, and a faint odor of corruption rising like invisible flies from it. At least, there were no real flies in this world.

Time passed. He did not feel much stronger. He had to get up and throw the body through both sides. Just rolling it through was out of the question because he did not want to stand in the path of any explosion. It was necessary to stand by the edge of the hoop, lift the body up and throw it through and then leap to one side.

For the seventh time, he did so. The body went through the hoop and sprawled on the ground. He had one last chance, and this time, instead of resting, he picked up the corpse and lifted it up before him until it was chest-high and heaved.

When he raised his head up from his position on the rock, he saw that the body was still visible.

So much for that theory. And so much for him. He was done for.

He sat up instead of just lying there with his eyes closed. This move, made for no motive of which he was aware, saved his life.

Even so, he almost lost it. The tigerish beast that was charging silently over the hard rock roared when it saw him sit up and increased the lengths of its bounds and its speed. Kickaha was so surprised that he froze for a second and thus gave the animal an edge. But he did not give enough. The beamer fired just as the animal rose for its final arc, and the ray bored through its head, sliced it, cut through the neck and chest, took off part of a leg, and drilled into the rock beyond. The body struck the ground and slid into him and knocked him off his feet and rolled him over and over. He hurt in his legs and his back and chest and hands and nose when he arose. Much skin had been burned off by his scraping against the rock, and where the body of the beast had slammed into his legs was a dull pain that was to get sharper.

Nevertheless, the animal looked edible. And he thought he knew where it had come from. After he had cut off several steaks and cooked and eaten them, he would return to the northwest gate and investigate again.

The beast was about a quarter larger than a Siberian tiger, had a cat-like build, thick long fur with a tawny undercoat and pale red zigzag stripes on head and body and black stocking-like fur on the lower part of the legs and the paws. Its eyes were lemonade-yellow, and its teeth were more those of a shark than those of a cat.

The steaks tasted rank, but they filled him with strength. He took the Beller by the arm and dragged him the two miles to the gate. The corpse, by this time, was in a badly damaged condition. It stank even stronger when he lifted it up and threw it through the gate.

This time, it disappeared, and it was followed by a spurt of oil from the gate that would have covered him if he had been standing directly before it within a range of ten yards. Immediately after, the oily substance caught fire and burned for fifteen minutes.

Kickaha waited until long after the fire was out and then he jumped through with his beamer ready. He did not know what to expect. There might be another of the tigers waiting for him. It was evident that the first time he had thrown the Beller through it, he had set off a delaying activation which had released the beast through it some time after he had given up on it. It was a very clever and sadistic device and just the sort of thing he could expect from Red Orc. It seemed to him, however, that Red Orc might have given up setting any more machines. He would believe that it was very unlikely that anybody could have gotten this far.

For a second, he was in a small bare room with a large cage, its door open, and a black dome on three short legs. Then, he was in another room. This one was larger and was made of some hard gray metal or plastic and lacked any decoration and had no furniture except a seatless commode, a washbowl and a single faucet, and a small metal table fastened to the floor with chains.

The transition from one room to the other shocked him, although he could explain how it happened. On jumping through the hoop into this room, he had triggered a delayed gate. This, activated, had sent him into this seemingly blind-alley chamber.

The light had no visible source; it filled the room with equal intensity. It was bright enough so that he could see that there were no cracks or flaws in the walls. There was nothing to indicate a window or door. And the walls were made of sturdy stuff. The ray from the beamer, turned to full power, only warmed the wall and the air in the chamber. He turned the weapon off and looked for the source of air, if there was one.

After an extensive inspection, he determined that fresh air moved in slowly from a point just above the table top. This meant that it was being gated in through a device embedded inside the solid table top. And the air moved out through another gate that had to be embedded in the wall in an upper corner of wall and ceiling. The gates would be operating intermittently and were set for admission only of gases.

He turned the full power of the beamer on the table top, but that was as resistant as the walls. However, unless his captor intended him to starve, he would have provided a gate through which to transmit food to his captive. It probably would be the same gate as that in the table top, but when the time came for the meal, the gate would be automatically set for passage of solid material.

Kickaha considered this for a while and wondered why no one had thought of this idea for escape. Perhaps the Lord had thought of it and was hoping that his prisoner also would. It would be just the kind of joke a Lord would enjoy. Still, it was such a wild idea, it might not have occurred to the Lord.

He imagined that alarms must be flashing and sounding somewhere in the building which housed this chamber. That is, if the chamber was in a building and not in some deserted pocket universe. If, however, the Lord should be away, then he might return too late to keep his prisoner imprisoned.

He had no exact idea of how much time passed, but he estimated that it was about four hours later when the tray appeared on the table. It held Earth food, a steak medium well-done, a salad of lettuce, carrots, onions, and a garlic dressing, three pieces of brown European bread with genuine butter, and a dish of chocolate ice cream.

He felt much better when he finished, indeed, almost grateful to his captor. He did not waste any time after swallowing the last spoonful of ice cream, however. He climbed onto the top of the table, the beamer held on his shoulder with the strap, and the tray in his hands. He then bent over and, balancing on one leg, set the tray down and then stepped onto it. He reasoned that the gate might be activated by the tray and dishes and not by a certain mass. He was betting his life that the influence of the gate would extend upward enough to include him in it. If it did not, somebody on the other end was going to be surprised by half a corpse. If it did, somebody was still going to be surprised and even more unpleasantly.

Suddenly, he was on a table inside a closet lit by one overhead light. If he had not been crouching, he would have been deprived of his head by the ceiling as he materialized.

He got down off the table and swung the door open and stepped out into a very large kitchen. A man was standing with his back to him, but he must have heard the door moving because he wheeled around. His mouth was open, his eyes were wide, and he said, "What the . . . ?"

Kickaha's foot caught him on the point of the chin, and he fell backward, unconscious, onto the floor. After listening to make sure that the noise of the man's fall had not disturbed anyone, Kickaha searched the man's clothes.

He came up with a sawed-off Smith & Wesson .38 in a shoulder holster and a wallet with a hundred and ten dollars in bills, two driver's licenses, the omnipresent credit cards, and a business card. The man's name was Robert di Angelo.

Kickaha put the gun in his belt after checking it and then inspected the kitchen. It was so large that it had to be in a mansion of a wealthy man. He quickly found a small control board behind a sliding panel in the wall which was half open. Several lights were blinking on it.

The fact that di Angelo had sent down a meal to him showed that the dwellers of this house knew they had a prisoner. Or, at least, that the Lord knew it. His men might not be cognizant of gates, but they would have been told to report to Red Orc if the lights on this panel and others flashed out and, undoubtedly, sound alarms were activated. The latter would have been turned off by now, of course.

There must be a visual monitor of the prison, so the Lord, Urthona, in this case, must know whom he held. Why hadn't Urthona at once taken steps to question his captive? He must surely be burning to know how Kickaha had gotten in there.

He ran water into a glass and dashed it in the face of the man on the floor. Di Angelo started and rolled his head and his eyes opened. He jerked again when he saw Kickaha over him and felt the point of the knife at his throat.

"Where is your boss?" Kickaha said.

Di Angelo said, "I don't know."

"Ignorance isn't bliss in your case," Kickaha said. He pushed the knife in so that blood trickled out from the side of the neck.

The man's eyes widened, and he said, "Take it easy," and then, "What difference does it make? You haven't got a chance. Here's what happened . . ."

Di Angelo was the cook, but he was also aware of what was going on in the lower echelons. He had been told long ago to inform the boss, whom he called Mr. Callister, if the alarms were activated in the kitchen. Until tonight, they had been dormant. When they did go off, startling him, he had called Mr. Callister, who was with his gang on business di Angelo knew nothing about. It must have something to do with the recent troubles, those that had come with the appearance of Kickaha and the others. Callister had told him what to do, which was only to prepare a meal, set it on the table in the closet, close the closet door, and press a button on the control panel.

Kickaha asked about Wolff, Chryseis, and Anana. Di Angelo said, "Some of the guys took them into the boss' office and left them there and that's the last anybody's seen of them. Honest to God, I'm telling the truth! If anybody knows where they went, it's Callister. Him and him only!"

Kickaha made di Angelo get up and lead him through the house. They went through some halls and large rooms, all luxuriously furnished, and then up a broad winding marble staircase to the second floor. On the way, di Angelo told him that this house was in a walled estate in Beverly Hills. The address was that which Red Orc had said was Urthona's.

"Where are the servants?" he said.

"They've either gone home or to their quarters over the garage," di Angelo said. "I'm not lying, mister, when I say I'm the only one in the house."

The door to Callister's office was of heavy steel and locked. Kickaha turned the beamer on it and sliced out the lock with a brief quick rotation of the barrel. Di Angelo's eyes bulged, and he turned paler. Evidently he knew nothing of the weapons of the Lord.

Kickaha found some tape in a huge mahogany desk and taped di Angelo's hands behind him and his ankles together. While di Angelo sat in a chair, Kickaha made a quick but efficient search of the office. The control panel for what he hoped were the gates popped out of a section of the big desk when a button in a corner of the desk was pressed. The pushbuttons, dials, and lights were identified by markings that would have mystified any Earthling but Kickaha. These were in the writing of the Lords.

However, he did not know the nature of Gates Number One through Ten nor what would happen if he pressed a button marked with the symbol for *M*. That could mean many thousands of things, but he suspected that it stood for *miyrtso,* meaning death.

The first difficulty in using the panel was that he did not know where the gates were even if he activated them. The second was that he probably could not activate them. The Lord was not foolish enough to leave an operable system which was also relatively accessible. He would carry on his person some device which had to be turned on before the control panel would be energized. But at least Kickaha knew where the panel was so that if he ever got hold of the activator, he could use the panel. That is, if he also located the gates.

It was very frustrating because he was so sure that Anana and his two friends, if they were still alive, were behind one of the ten gates.

The telephone rang. Kickaha was startled but quickly recovered. He picked up the phone and carried it over to di Angelo and put the receiver at a distance between both their ears. Di Angelo did not need to be told what was expected of him. He said, "Hello!"

The voice that answered was Ramos'.

"Di Angelo? Just a minute."

The next voice was that of the man Kickaha had talked to when he thought he was speaking to Red Orc. This must be Urthona, and whatever it was that had brought him out in the open had to be something very important. The only thing that would do that would be a chance to get Red Orc.

"Angelo? I'm getting an alarm transmission here. It's coming from my office. Did you know that?"

Kickaha shook his head and di Angelo said, "No, sir."

"Well, someone is in my office. Where are you?"

"In the kitchen, sir," di Angelo said.

"Get up there and find out what's going on," Urthona said. "I'll leave this line open. And I'm sending over men from the warehouse to help you. Don't take any chances. Shoot to kill unless you're dead certain you can get the drop on him. You understand?"

"Yes, sir," di Angelo said.

The phone clicked. Kickaha did not feel triumphant. Urthona must realize that anyone in the office could have picked up the phone to listen in. He knew this cut down any chance of di Angelo's surprising the intruder and meant that the reinforcements would have to be rushed over as swiftly as possible.

Kickaha taped di Angelo's mouth and locked him in the closet. He then destroyed the control panel for the gates with a flash from the beamer. If Urthona meant to transfer his other prisoners—if he had any —or to do anything to them, he would be stopped for a while. He would have to build another panel—unless he had some duplicates in storage.

His next step was to get out of the house quickly and down to the railroad station, where the Horn was in a locker. He wished that he could have gotten the Horn first, because then he might have been able to use it unhindered. Now, Urthona would be certain to guard his house well.

Kickaha had to leave the house and go downtown. He decided to cache the beamer on the estate grounds. He found a depression in the ground behind a large oleander bush near the wall. The estate was excellently gardened; there were no loose leaves or twigs with which to cover the weapon. He placed it in the depression and left it there. He also decided to leave the gun which he had taken from di Angelo. It was too bulky to conceal under his shirt.

He left without incident except having to return to the beamer's hiding place so he could use it to burn through the lock on the iron gate that was the exit to the street. This was set in a high brick wall with spikes on top. The guardhouse by the big iron gate to the driveway was unoccupied, apparently because Urthona had pulled everybody except di Angelo from the house. There were controls in the guardhouse, and he easily identified those that worked both gates. But the power or the mechanisms had been shut off, and he did not want to take the time to return to the house to question di Angelo. He burned through the lock mechanism and pushed the gate open. Behind him, a siren began whooping and he could see lights flashing on the control board in the guardhouse. If the noise continued, the police would be called in. Kickaha smiled at that thought. Then he lost his smile. He did not want the police interfering any more than Urthona did.

After hiding the beamer behind the bush again, he walked southward. After five blocks, he came to Sunset. He was apprehensive that a police car might notice him, because he understood that any pedestrians in this exclusive and extremely wealthy neighborhood were likely to be stopped by the police. Especially at night.

But his luck held out, and he was able to hail a taxi. The driver did not want to go that far out of Beverly Hills, but Kickaha opened the back door and got into the car. "This is an emergency," he said. "I got a business appointment which involves a lot of money."

He leaned forward and handed the driver a twenty-dollar bill from di Angelo's wallet. "This is yours, over and above the fare and the regular tip. Think you can detour a little?"

"Can do," the cabbie said.

He let Kickaha off three blocks from the railroad station, since Kickaha did not want him to know where he was going if the police should question him. He walked to the station, removed the ball of gum and the key from the hollow in the tree, and then went inside the station.

He removed the instrument case from the locker without interference or attention, other than a four-year-old girl who stared at him with large deep-blue eyes and then said, "Hello!" He patted her on the head as he went by, causing her mother to pull her away and lecture her in a loud voice about being friendly to strangers.

Kickaha grinned, though he did not really think the incident amusing. During his long years on the World of Tiers, he had become used to children being treated as greatly valued and much-loved beings. Since Wolff had put into the waters of that great world a chemical which gave the humans a thousand-year youth but also cut down considerably on the birth rate, he had ensured that children were valued. There were very few cases of child killings, abuses, or deprivation of love. And while this sort of rearing did not keep the children from growing into adults who were quite savage in warfare—but never killed or maltreated children—it did result in people with much fewer neuroses and psychoses than the civilized Earthling. Of course, most societies in Wolff's world were rather homogenous, small, and technologically primitive, not subject to the many-leveled crisscross current modes of life of Earth's highly industrial societies.

Kickaha left the station and walked several blocks before coming to a public phone booth in the corner of a large service station area. He dialed Urthona's number. The phone had rung only once when it was picked up and an unfamiliar voice answered. Kickaha said, "Mr. Callister, please."

"Who is this?" the rough voice said.

"Di Angelo can describe me," Kickaha said. "That is, if you've found him in the closet."

There was an exclamation and then, "Just a minute."

A few seconds later, a voice said, "Callister speaking."

"Otherwise known as Urthona, present Lord of Earth," Kickaha said. "I am the man who was your prisoner."

"How did you . . . ?" Urthona said and then stopped, realizing that he was not going to get a description of the escape.

"I'm Kickaha," Kickaha said. There was no harm in identifying himself, since he was sure that Urthona had gotten both his name and description from Anana. "The Earthling who did what you supposed Lords of Creation could not do. I killed directly, or caused to be killed, all fifty-one of the Bellers. They are no longer a menace. I got out of Red Orc's house in that other Earth, got through all his traps, and got into your house. If you had been there, I would have captured or killed you. Make no mistake about that.

"But I didn't call you just to tell you what I have done. I want only to return in peace to Wolff's world with Wolff, Chryseis, and Anana. You and Red Orc can battle it out here and may the best Lord win. Now that the Beller is dead, there is no reason for us to stay here. Nor for you to keep my friends."

There was a long silence and then Urthona said, "How do I know that the Beller is dead?"

Kickaha described what had happened, although he left out several details that he did not think Urthona should know.

"So you now know how you can check out my story," he said. "You can't follow my original route as I did, since you don't know where Red Orc's house is, and I don't either. But I think that all the gates are two-way, and you can backtrack, starting from that room in which I ended."

He could imagine the alternating delight and alarm Urthona was feeling. He now had a route to get into Red Orc's dwelling, but Red Orc could get into his house through that same route, too.

Urthona said, "You're wrong, I know where Red Orc lives. Did live, that is. One of my men saw him on the street only two hours ago. He thought at first it was me and that I was on some business he'd better keep his nose out of. Then he returned here and saw me and knew I couldn't have gotten here so quickly.

"I realized what good fortune had done for me. I got my men and surrounded the house and we broke in. We had to kill four of his men, but he got away. Gated out, I suppose. And when he did, he eliminated all the gates in the house. There was no way of following him."

"I had thought that one of the burned corpses might be Red Orc's," Kickaha said. "But he is still alive. Well . . ."

"I'm tired of playing this game," Urthona said. "I would like to see my brother become one of those charred corpses. I will make a bargain with you again. If you will get Red Orc for me, deliver him to me in a recognizable condition, I will release your friends and guarantee safe passage back to your World of Tiers. That is, if I can satisfy myself that your story about the Beller is true."

"You know how to do that," Kickaha said. "Let me speak to Anana and Wolff, so that I can be sure they're still alive."

"I can't do that just at this moment," Urthona said. "Give me, say, ten minutes. Call back then."

"Okay," Kickaha said. He hung up and left the phone booth in a hurry. Urthona might or might not have some means of quickly locating the source of the call, but he did not intend to give him a chance. He hailed a taxi and had it drop him off near the La Brea Tar Pit. From there, he walked up Wilshire until he came to another booth. Fifteen, not ten, minutes had passed. Di Angelo answered the phone this time. Although he must have recognized Kickaha's voice, he said nothing except for him to wait while he switched the call. Urthona's voice was the next.

"You can speak to my niece, the *leblabbiy*-lover, first," Urthona said.

Anana's lovely voice said, "Kickaha! Are you all right?"

"Doing fine so far!" Kickaha said. "The Beller is dead! I killed him myself. And Red Orc is on the run. Hang on. We'll get back to the good world yet. I love you!"

"I love you, too," she said.

Urthona's voice, savage and sarcastic, cut in. "Yes, I love you too, *leblabbiy!* Now, do you want to hear from Wolff?"

"I'm not about to take your word that he's O.K.," Kickaha said.

Wolff's voice, deep and melodious, came over the phone. "Kickaha, old friend! I knew you'd be along, sooner or later!"

"Hello, Robert, it's great to hear your voice again! You and Chryseis all right?"

"We're unharmed, yes. What kind of deal are you making with Urthona?"

The Lord said, "That's enough! You satisfied, Earthling?"

"I'm satisfied that they're alive as of this moment," Kickaha said. "And they had better be when the moment of payment comes."

"You don't threaten me!" Urthona said. And then, in a calmer tone, "Very well. I shall assist you in any way I can. What do you need?"

"The address of Red Orc's house," Kickaha said.

"Why would you need that?" Urthona said, surprised.

"I have my reasons. What is the address?"

Urthona gave it to him but he spoke slowly as if he were trying to think of Kickaha's reasons for wanting it. Kickaha said, "That's all I need now. So long."

He hung up. A minute later, he was in a taxi on his way to Urthona's house. Two blocks away, he paid the driver and walked the rest of the way. The small iron gate was chained now, and the lights in the little guardhouse near the big gate showed three men inside. The mansion was also ablaze, although he could see nobody through the windows.

There did not seem to be any way of getting in just then. He was capable of leaping up and grabbing the top of the wall and pulling himself over, but he did not doubt that there would be alarms on top of the wall. On second thought, so what? At this time, he did not intend to invade the house. All he wanted was to get the beamer and then get out. By the time Urthona's men arrived, he could be back over the wall.

It was first necessary to cache the Horn somewhere, because it would be too awkward, in fact, impossible, to take it with him in scaling the wall. He could throw it over the wall first but did not want to do that. A minute's inspection showed him that he could stick the case in the branches of a bush growing on the strip of grass between the sidewalk and the street. He returned to the spot by the wall opposite where he had hidden the beamer. He went across the street, stood there a minute waiting until a car went by, and then dashed full speed across the street. He bounded upward and his fingers closed on the rough edge of the wall. It was easy for him to pull himself upward then. The top of the wall was about a foot and a half across and set with a double row of spikes made of iron and about six inches high. Along these was strung a double row of thin wires which glinted in the light from the mansion.

He stepped gingerly over the wires and turned and let himself down over the edge and then dropped to the soft earth. For a few seconds, he looked at the guardhouse and the mansion and listened. He heard nothing and saw no signs of life.

He ran into the bush and picked up the beamer. Getting back over the wall was a little more difficult with the beamer strapped over his shoulder, but he made it without, as far as he knew, attracting any attention from inside the walls.

With the beamer and the Horn, he walked down toward Sunset again. He waited on a corner for about ten minutes before an empty cab came by. When he entered the taxi, he held the case with the beamer against it so that the driver would not see it. Its barrel was too thick to be mistaken for even a shotgun, but the stock made it look too much like a firearm of some sort.

Red Orc's address was in a wealthy district of Pacific Palisades. The house was, like Urthona's, surrounded by a high brick wall. However, the iron gate to the driveway was open. Kickaha slipped through it and toward the house, which was dark. Urthona had not mentioned whether or not he had left guards there, but it seemed reasonable that he would. He would not want to miss a chance to catch Red Orc if he should return for some reason.

The front and rear main entrances were locked. No light shone anywhere. He crouched by each door, his ear against the wood. He could hear nothing. Finally, he bored a hole through the lock of the rear door and pushed it open. His entry was cautious and slow at first and then he heard some noises from the front. These turned out to have been made by three men sitting in the dark in the huge room at the front of the house. One had fallen asleep and was snoring softly, and the other two were talking in low voices.

He sneaked up the winding staircase, which had marble steps and so did not squeak or groan under his feet. Finding a bedroom, he closed the door and then turned on a lamp. He dialed one of the numbers of the house.

When the phone was answered, Kickaha, an excellent mimic, spoke in an approximation of Ramos' voice.

"The boss is calling you guys in," he said. "Get out here on the double! Something's up, but I can't tell you over the phone!"

He waited until the man had hung up before he himself hung up. Then he went to the window. He saw the three walk down the driveway and go through the gate. A moment later, the headlights of a car came on a half block down. The car pulled away, and he was, as far as he knew, alone in the house. He would not be for more than thirty-five minutes, at least, which was the time it would take the thugs to get to Urthona's, find out they had been tricked, and return with reinforcements.

All he needed was a few minutes. He went downstairs and turned on the lights in the kitchen. Finding a flashlight, he turned the kitchen lights off and went into the big front room. The door under the stairs was open. He stepped through it into the little hall. At its end, he opened the door and cast the flashlight beam inside. The room looked just like the one he had entered when he was Red Orc's prisoner, but it was not. This room really was set inside this house. The gate embedded in the wood and plaster of the doorway had been inactivated.

He opened the instrument case and took the Horn out. In the beams of the flashlight, it glistened silvery. It was shaped like the horn of an African buffalo except at the mouth, where it flared broadly. The tip was fitted with a mouthpiece of soft golden material, and on top along the axis were seven small buttons in a row. Inside the flared mouth was a silvery web of some material. Halfway along the length of the Horn was an inscribed hieroglyph, the mark of Shambarimen, maker of the Horn.

He raised the Horn to his lips and blew softly through it while he pressed the little buttons. The flare on the other end was pointed at the walls, and, as he finished one sequence of notes, he moved it to his left until it pointed at a place on the wall about twelve feet from the first. He hoped that the inactive gates were in this room. If they were, they had set up a resonant point which had weakened the walls between the universes. And so the frequencies from the Horn would act as a skeleton key and open the gates. This was the unique ability of the Horn, the unreproduced device of Shambarimen, greatest of the scientist-inventors of the Lords.

Softly the Horn spoke, and the notes that issued from the mouth seemed golden and magical enough to open doors to fairyland. But none appeared on the north or east walls. Kickaha stopped blowing and listened for sounds of people approaching the house. He heard nothing. He put the mouthpiece to his lips again and once more played the sequence of notes which was guaranteed to spread wide any break in the walls between the worlds.

Suddenly, a spot on the wall became luminous. The white spot enlarged, inched outward, and then sprang to the limits of the circle which defined the entrance. The light faded and was replaced by a softer darker light. He looked into it and saw a hemispherical room with no windows or doors. The walls were scarlet, and the only furniture was a bed which floated a few feet above the floor in the center of the room and a transparent booth, also floating, which contained a washbowl, faucet, and toilet.

Then the walls regrew swiftly, the edges of the hole sliding out toward each other, and, in thirty seconds, the wall was as solid as before.

The Horn swung away, and the white spot appeared again and grew and then the light died to be replaced by the greenish light of a green sun over a green-moss-tinted plain and sharp green mountains on a horizon twice as distant as Earth's. To the right were some animals that looked like gazelles with harp-shaped horns. They were nibbling on the moss.

The third opening revealed a hallway with a closed door at its end. There was nothing else for Kickaha to do but to investigate, since the door might lead to Anana or the others. He jumped through the now swiftly decreasing hole and walked down the hall and then cautiously opened the door. Nothing happened. He looked around the edge of the door into a large chamber. Its floor was stone mosaic, a small pool flush with the floor was in the center, and furniture of airy construction was around it. The light was sourceless.

Anana, unaware that anybody had entered, was sitting on a chair and reading from a big book with thick covers that looked like veined marble. She looked sleek and well fed.

Kickaha watched her for a minute, though he had to restrain himself from running in and grabbing her. He had lived too long in worlds where traps were baited.

His inspection did not reveal anything suspicious, but this meant only that dangers could be well hidden. Finally, he called softly, "Anana!"

She jumped, the book fell out of her hands, and then she was out of the chair and rushing toward him. Tears glimmered in her eyes and on her cheeks though she was smiling. Her arms were held out to him, and she was sobbing with relief and joy.

His desire to run toward her was almost overwhelming. He felt tears in his own eyes and a sob welling up. But he could not get rid of his suspiciousness that Red Orc might have set this room to kill a person who entered without first activating some concealed device. He had been lucky to get this far without tripping off some machine.

"Kickaha!" Anana cried and came through the door and fell into his embrace.

He looked over her shoulder to make sure that the door was swinging shut and then bent his head to kiss her.

The pain on his lips and nose was like that from burning gasoline. The pain on the palms of his hand, where he had pressed it against her back, was like that from sulphuric acid.

He screamed and threw himself away and rolled on the floor in his agony. Yet, half-conscious though he was from the searing, he knew that his tortured hand had grabbed the beamer from the floor, where he had dropped it.

Anana came after him but not swiftly. Her face had melted as if it were wax in the sun; her eyes ran; her mouth drooped and furrowed and made runnels and ridges. Her hands were spread out to seize him, but they were dripping with acid and losing form. The fingers had become elongated, so much so that one had stretched down, like taffy, to her knee. And her beautiful legs were bulging everywhere, giving way to something like gas pressing the skin outward. The feet were splaying out and leaving impresses of something that burned the stone of the floor and gave off faint green wisps of smoke.

The horror of this helped him overcome the pain. Without hesitation, he lifted the beamer and pressed the button that turned its power full on her. Rather, on *it*. She fell into two and then into four parts as the beam crisscrossed. The parts writhed on the floor, silently. Blood squirted out from the trunks and from the legs and turned into a brownish substance which scorched the stone. An odor as of rotten eggs and burning dog excrement filled the room.

Kickaha stepped down the power from piercing to burning. He played the beam like a hose squirting flaming kerosene over the parts, and they went up in smoke. The hair of Anana burned with all the characteristic odor of burning human hair, but that was the only part of her —of it—that gave off a stench of human flesh in the fire. The rest was brimstone and dog droppings.

In the end, after the fire burned out, there were only some gristly threads left. Of bones there was no sign.

Kickaha did not wish to enter the room from which it had come, but he pain in his lips and nose and hand was too intense. Besides, he hought that the Lord should have been satisfied with the fatality of the ning he had created to look like Anana. There was cool-looking water a that room, and he had to have it. It was possible to blow the Horn nd go back into Orc's office, but he did not think he could endure the agony long enough to blow the sequence of notes. Moreover, if he encountered anyone in that office, he wanted to be able to defend himself adequately. In his present condition, he could not.

At the pool he stuck his face and one hand under the water. The coolness seemed to help at once, although when he at last removed his face and breathed, the pain was still intense. With the good hand, he splashed water on his face. After a long while, he rose from the pool. He was unsteady and felt as if he were going to vomit. He also felt a little disengaged from everything. The shock had nudged him one over from reality.

When he raised the Horn gently to his lips, he found that they were swelling. His hand was also swelling. They were getting so big and stiff they were making him clumsy. It was only at the cost of more agony that he could blow upon the Horn and press the little valves, and the wall opened before him. He quickly put the Horn in its case, and shoved it through the opening with his foot, then leaped through with the beamer ready. The office was empty.

He found the bathroom. The medicine cabinet above the washbowl was a broad and deep one with many bottles. A number were of plastic, marked with hieroglyphs. He opened one, smelled the contents, tried to grin with his blistered swollen lips and squeezed out a greenish salve onto his hand. This he rubbed over his nose and lips and on the palm of his burned hand. Immediately, the pain began to dissolve in a soft coolness and the swelling subsided as he watched himself in the mirror.

He squeezed a few drops from another bottle onto his tongue, and a minute later the shakiness and the sense of unreality left him. He recapped the two bottles and put them in the rear pockets of his pants.

The business of the gates and the Anana-thing had taken more time than he could spare. He ran out of the bathroom and directed the Horn at the next spot on the wall. This failed to respond, so he tried the next one. This one opened, but neither this nor the one after it contained those for whom he was looking.

The bedroom yielded a gate at the first place he directed the Horn. The wall parted like an opening mouth, a shark's mouth, because the hillside beyond was set with rows of tall white sharp triangles. The vegetation between the shark's teeth was a purplish vine-complex and the sky beyond was mauve.

The second gate opened to another hallway with a door at its end. Again, he had no choice except to investigate. He pushed the door open silently and peered around it. The room looked exactly like the one in which he had found the thing he had thought was Anana. This time, she was not reading a book, although she was in the chair. She was leaning far forward, her elbows on her thighs and her chin cupped by her hands. Her stare was unmoving and gloomy.

He called to her softly, and she jumped, just like the first Anana. Then she leaped up and ran toward him, tears in her eyes and on her cheeks and her mouth open in a beautiful smile and her arms held toward him. He backed away as she came through the door and harshly told her to stop. He held the beamer on her. She obeyed but looked puzzled and hurt. Then she saw the still slightly swelled and burned lips and nose, and her eyes widened.

"Anana," he said, "what was that ten-thousand-year-old nursery rhyme your mother sang to you so often?"

If this was some facsimile or artificial creature of Red Orc's, it might have a recording of some of what Orc had learned from Anana. It might have a memory of a sort, something that would be sketchy but still adequate enough to fool her lover. But there would be things she had not told Red Orc while under the influence of the drug because he would not think to ask her. And the nursery song was one thing. She had told Kickaha of it when they had been hiding from the Bellers on the Great Plains of the World of Tiers.

Anana was more puzzled for a few seconds, and then she seemed to understand that he felt compelled to test her. She smiled and sang the beautiful little song that her mother had taught her in the days before she grew up and found out how ugly and vicious the adult family life of the Lords was.

Even after this, he felt restrained when he kissed her. Then, as it became apparent that she had to be genuine flesh and blood, and she murmured a few more things that Red Orc was highly unlikely to know, he smiled and melted. They both cried some more, but he stopped first.

"We'll weep a little later," he said. "Do you have any idea where Wolff and Chryseis could be?"

She said no, which was what he had expected.

"Then we'll use the Horn until we've opened every gate in the house. But it's a big house, so . . ."

He explained to her that Urthona and his men would be coming after them. "You look around for weapons, while I blow the Horn."

She joined him ten minutes later and showed him what looked like a pen but was a small beamer. He told her that he had found two more gates but both were disappointments. They passed swiftly through all the rooms in the second story while he played steadily upon the Horn. The walls remained blank.

The first floor of the house was as unrewarding. By then, forty minutes had passed since the men had left the house. Within a few more minutes, Urthona should be here.

"Let's try the room under the stairs again," he said. "It's possible that reactivating the gate might cause it to open onto still another world."

A gate could be set up so that it alternated its resonances slightly and acted as a flipflop entrance. At one activation, it would open to one universe and at the next activation, to another. Some gates could operate as avenues to a dozen or more worlds.

The gates activated upstairs could also be such gates, and they should return to test out the multiple activity of every one. It was too discouraging to think about at that moment, though they would have to run through them again. That is, they would if this gate under the stairs did not give them a pleasant surprise.

Outside the door, he lifted the Horn once more and played the music which trembled the fabric between universes. The room beyond the door suddenly was large and blue-walled with bright lights streaming from chandeliers carved out of single Brobdingnagian jewels: hippopotamus-head-sized diamonds, rubies, emeralds, and garnets. The furniture was also carved out of enormous jewels set together with some kind of golden cement.

Kickaha had seen even more luxurious rooms. What held his attention was the opening of the round door at the far end of the room and the entrance through it of a cylindrical object. This was dark red, and it floated a foot above the floor. At its distant end the top of a blond head appeared. A man was pushing the object toward them.

That head looked like Red Orc's. He seemed to be the only one who would be in another world and bringing toward this gate an object that undoubtedly meant death and destruction to the occupants of this house.

Kickaha had his beamer ready, but he did not fire it. If that cylinder was packed with some powerful explosive, it might go up at the touch of the energy in the ray from a beamer.

Quickly, but silently, he began to close the door. Anana looked puzzled, since she had not seen what he had. He whispered, "Take off out the front door and run as far as you can as fast as you can!"

She shook her head and said, "Why should I?"

"Here!"

He thrust the Horn and the case at her. "Beat it! Don't argue! I he . . ."

The door began to swing open. A thin curved instrument came around the side of the door. Kickaha fired at it, cutting it in half. There was a yell from the other side, cut off by the door slamming. Kickaha had shoved it hard with his foot.

"Run!" he yelled, and he took her hand and pulled her after him. Just as he went through the door, he looked back. There was a crash as the door under the stairs and part of the wall around it fell broken outward, and the cylinder thrust halfway through before stopping.

That was enough for Kickaha. He jumped out onto the porch and down the steps, pulling Anana behind him with one hand, the other holding the beamer. When they reached the brick wall by the sidewalk, he turned to run along it for its protection.

The expected explosion did not come immediately.

At that moment, a car screeched around the corner a block away. It straightened up, swaying under the street lights, and shot toward the driveway of the house they had just left. Kickaha saw the silhouettes of six heads inside it; one might have been Urthona's. Then he was running again. They rounded the corner from which the speeding automobile had come, and still nothing happened. Anana cried out, but he continued to drag her on. They ran a complete block and were crossing the street to go around another corner, when a black and white patrol car came by. It was cruising slowly and so the occupants had plenty of time to see the two runners. Anybody walking on the streets after dark in his area was suspect. A running person was certain to be taken to the station for questioning. Two running persons carrying a large musical instrument case and something that looked like a peculiar shotgun were guaranteed capture by the police. If they could be caught, of course.

Kickaha cursed and darted toward the house nearest them. Its lights were on, and the front door was open, though the screen door was probably locked. Behind them, brakes squealed as the patrol car slid to stop. A loud voice told them to stop.

They continued to run. They ran onto the porch and Kickaha pulled on the screen door. He intended to go right through the house and out the back door, figuring that the police were not likely to shoot at them if innocents were in the way.

Kickaha cursed, gave the handle of the screen door a yank that tore the lock out. He plunged through with Anana right behind him. They shot through a vestibule and into a large room with a chandelier and a broad winding staircase to the second story. There were about ten men and women standing or sitting, all dressed semiformally. The women screamed; the men yelled. The two intruders ran through them, unhindered while the shouts of the policemen rose above the noise of the occupants.

The next moment, all human noise was shattered. The blast smashed in the glass of the windows and shook the house as if a tidal wave had struck it. All were hurled to the floor by the impact.

Kickaha had been expecting this, and Anana had expected something enormously powerful by his behavior. They jumped up before anybody else could regain their wits and were going out the back door in a few seconds. Kickaha doubled back, running toward the front along the side of the house. There was much broken glass on the walk, flicked there by the explosion from some nearby house. A few bushes and some lawn furniture also lay twisted on the sidewalk.

The patrol car, its motor running, and lights on, was still by the curb. Anana threw the instrument case into the rear seat and got in and Kickaha laid the beamer on the floor and climbed in. They strapped themselves in, and he turned the car around and took off. In the course of the next four blocks, he found the button switches to set the siren off and the light whirling and flashing.

"We'll get to Urthona's house, near it, anyway," he yelled, "and then we'll abandon this. I think Red Orc'll be there now to find out if Urthona was among those who entered the house when that mine went off!"

Anana shook her head and pointed at her ears. She was still deaf.

It was no wonder. He could just faintly hear the siren which must be screaming in their ears.

A few minutes later, as they shot through a red light, they passed a patrol car, lights flashing, going the other way. Anana ducked down so that she would not be seen, but evidently the car had received notice by radio that this car was stolen. It screamed as it slowed down and turned on the broad intersection and started after Kickaha and Anana. sports car which had sped through the intersections, as if its driver intended to ignore the flashing red lights and sirens, turned away to avoid a collision, did not quite make it, scraped against the rear of the police car, and caromed off over the curbing, and up onto the sidewalk.

Kickaha saw this in the mirror as he accelerated. A few minutes later he went through a stop sign south of a very broad intersection with stop signs on all corners. A big Cadillac stopped in the middle of the intersection so suddenly that its driver went up over the wheel. Before he could sit back and continue, the patrol car came through the stop sign

Kickaha said, "Can you hear me now?"

She said, "Yes. You don't have to shout quite so loudly!"

"We're in Beverly Hills now. We'll take this car as far as we can and then we'll abandon it, on the run," he said. "We'll have to lose them on foot. That is, if we make it."

A second patrol car had joined them. It had come out of a side street, ignoring a stop sign, causing another car to wheel away and ram into the curbing. Its driver had hoped to cut across in front of them and bar their way, but he had not been quite fast enough. Kickaha had the car up to eighty now, which was far too fast on this street with its many intersecting side streets.

Then the business section of Beverly Hills was ahead. The light changed to yellow just as Kickaha zoomed through. He blasted the horn and went around a sports car and skidded a little and then the car hit a dip and bounced into the air. He had, however, put on the brakes to slow to sixty. Even so, the car swayed so that he feared they were going over.

Ahead of them, a patrol car was approaching. It swung broadside when over a half block away and barred most of the street. There was very little clearance at either end of the patrol car, but Kickaha took the rear.

Both uniformed policemen were out of the car, one behind the hood with a shotgun and the other standing between the front of the car and the parked cars. Kickaha told Anana to duck and took the car through the narrow space on the other side. There was a crash, the car struck the side of the bumper of the patrol car and the other struck the side of a parked car. But they were through with a grinding and clashing of metal. The shotgun boomed; the rear window starred.

At the same time, another patrol car swung around the corner on their left. The car angled across the street. Kickaha slammed on the brakes. They screamed, and he was pushed forward against his belt and the wheel. The car fishtailed, rocked, and then it slammed at an obtuse angle into the front of the patrol car.

Both cars were out of commission. Kickaha and Anana were stunned, but they reacted on pure reflex. They were out of the car on either side, Kickaha holding the beamer, and Anana the instrument case. They ran across the street, between two parked cars, and across the sidewalk before they heard the shouts of the policemen behind them. Then they were between two tall buildings on a narrow sidewalk bordered by trees and bushes. They dashed down this until they came out at the next street. Here Kickaha led her northward, saw another opening between buildings, and took that. There was an overhang of prestressed concrete about eight feet up over a doorway. He threw his beamer upon it, threw the instrument case up, turned, held his locked hands out, and she put her foot in it and went up as he heaved. She caught the edge of the overhang; he pushed, and she was up on it. He leaped and swung on up, lying down just in time.

Feet pounded; several men, breathing hard, passed under them. He risked a peep over the edge and saw three policemen at the far end of the passageway, outlined by the streetlights. They were talking, obviously puzzled by the disappearance of their quarry. Then one started back, and Kickaha flattened out. The other two went around the corner of the building.

But as the man passed below him, Kickaha, taken by a sudden idea, rose and leaped upon the man. He knocked him sprawling, hitting the man so hard he knocked the wind out of him. He followed this with a kick on the jaw.

Kickaha put the officer's cap on and emptied the .38 which he took from his holster. Anana swung down after having dropped the beamer and the Horn to him. She said, "Why did you do this?"

"He would have blocked our retreat. Besides, there's a car that isn't damaged, and we're going to take that."

The fourth policeman was sitting in the car and talking over a microphone. He did not see Kickaha until he was about forty paces away. He dropped the microphone and grabbed for the shotgun on the seat. The beamer, set for stunning power, hit him in the shoulder and knocked him against the car. He slumped down, the shotgun falling on the street.

Kickaha pulled the officer away from the car, noting that blood was seeping through his shirt sleeve. The beamer, even when set on "stun" power, could smash bone, tear skin, and rupture blood vessels.

As soon as Anana was in the car, Kickaha turned it northward. Down the street, coming swiftly toward him, on the wrong side because the other lane was blocked, were two police cars.

At the intersection ahead, as Kickaha shot past the red light, he checked his rear view mirror and saw the police cars had turned and were speeding after him.

Ahead the traffic was so heavy, he had no chance of getting onto it or across it. There was nothing to do but to take the alley to the right or the left, and he took the left. This was by the two-story brick wall of grocery store building.

Then he was down the alley. Kickaha applied his brakes so hard, the car swerved, scraping against the brick wall. Anana scrambled out after Kickaha on his side of the car.

The police cars, moving more slowly than Kickaha's had when

took the corner into the alley, turned in. Just as the first straightened out to enter, Kickaha shot at the tires. The front of the lead car dropped as if it had driven off a curb, and there was a squeal of brakes. The car rocked up and down, and then its front doors opened like the wings of a bird just before taking off.

Kickaha ran away with Anana close behind him. He led her at an angle across the parking lot of the grocery store, and through the driveway out onto the street.

The light was red now, and the cars were stopped. Kickaha ran up behind a sports car in which sat a small youth with long black hair, huge round spectacles, a hawkish nose, and a bristly black moustache. He was tapping on the instrument panel with his right hand to the raucous cacophonous radio music, which was like Scylla and Charybdis rubbing against each other. He stiffened when Kickaha's arm shot down, as unexpectedly as a lightning stroke from a clear sky, over his shoulder and onto his lap. Before he could do more than squeak and turn his head, the safety belt was unbuckled. Like a sack of flour, he came out of the seat at the end of Kickaha's arm and was hurled onto the sidewalk. The dispossessed driver lay stunned for a moment and then leaped screaming with fury to his feet. By then, Kickaha and Anana were in his car, on their way.

Anana, looking behind, said, "We got away just in time."

"Any police cars after us?" he said.

"No, not yet."

"Good. We only have a couple of miles to go."

There was no sign of the police from there on until Kickaha parked the car a block and a half from Urthona's.

He said, "I've described the layout of the house, so you won't get confused when we're in it. Once we get in, things may go fast and furious. I think Red Orc will be there. I believe he's gated there just to make sure that Urthona is dead. He may be alive, though, because he's a fox. He should have scented a trap. I know I would've been skittish about going into that house unless I'd sniffed around a lot."

The house was well lit, but there was no sign of occupants. They walked boldly up the front walk and onto the porch. Kickaha tried the door and found it locked. A quick circling of the beamer muzzle with piercing power turned on removed the lock mechanism. They entered a silent house and when they were through exploring it, they had found only a parrot in a cage and it broke the silence only once to give a muffled squawk.

Kickaha removed the Horn from the case and began to test for resonant points as he had at Red Orc's. He went from room to room, working out from Urthona's bedroom and office because the gates were most likely to be there. The Horn sent out its melodious notes in vain, however, until he stuck it into a large closet downstairs just off the bottom of the staircase. The wall issued a tiny white spot, like a tear of light, and then it expanded and suddenly became a hole into another world.

Kickaha got a glimpse of a room that was a duplicate of the closet in the house in which he stood. Anana cried out softly then and pulled at his arm. He turned, hearing the noise that had caused her alarm. There were footsteps on the porch, followed by the chiming of the doorbell. He strode across the room, stopped halfway, turned and tossed the Horn to her, and said, "Keep that gate open!" While the notes of the Horn traveled lightly across the room, he lifted the curtain a little. Three uniformed policemen were on the porch and a plainclothesman was just going around the side. On the street were two patrol cars and an unmarked automobile.

Kickaha returned to her and said, "Urthona must have had a man outside watching for us. He called the cops. They must have the place surrounded!"

They could try to fight their way out, surrender, or go through the gate. To do the first was to kill men whose only fault was to mistake Kickaha for a criminal.

If Kickaha surrendered, he would sentence himself and Anana to death. Once either of the Lords knew they were in prison, they would get to their helpless victims one way or the other and murder them.

He did not want to go through the gate without taking some precautions, but he had no choice. He said, "Let's go," and leaped through the contracting hole with his beamer ready. Anana, holding onto the Horn followed him.

He kicked the door open and jumped back. After a minute of waiting, he stepped through it. The closet was set near the bottom of a staircase, just like its counterpart on Earth. The room was huge with marble walls on which were bright murals and a many-colored marble mosaic floor. It was night outside, the light inside came from many oil-burning lamps and cressets on the walls and the fluted marble pillars around the edges of the room. Beyond, in the shadows cast by the pillars, were entrances to other rooms and to the outside.

There was no sound except for a hissing and sputtering from the flames at the ends of the cressets.

Kickaha walked across the room between the pillars and through an antechamber, the walls of which were decorated with dolphins and o topuses. It was these that made him expect the scene that met him when he stepped out upon the great pillared porch. He was back on Earth Number Two.

At least, it seemed that he was. Certainly, the full moon near the zenith was Earth's moon. And, looking down from the porch, which was near the edge of a small mountain, he would swear that he was looking down on the duplicate of that part of southern California on which Los Angeles of Earth Number One was built. As nearly as he could tell in the darkness, it had the same topography. The unfamiliarity was caused by the differences in the two cities. This one was smaller than Los Angeles; the lights were not so many nor so bright, and were more widely spaced. He would guess that the population of this valley was about one thirty-second of Earth Number One's.

The air looked clear; the stars and the moon were large and bright. There was no hint of the odor of gasoline. He could smell a little horse manure, but that was pleasant, very pleasant. Of course, he was basing his beliefs on very small evidence, but it seemed that the technology of this Earth had not advanced nearly as swiftly as that of his native planet.

Evidently, Urthona had found gates leading to this world.

He heard voices then from the big room into which he had emerged from the closet. He took Anana's arm and pulled her with him into the shadow of a pillar. Immediately thereafter, three people stepped out onto the porch. Two were men, wearing kilts and sandals and cloth jackets with flared-out collars, puffed sleeves, and swallow tails. One was short, dark and Mediterranean, like the servants of Red Orc. The other was tall, ruddy-faced and reddish-haired. The woman was a short blonde with a chunky figure. She wore a kilt, buskins and a jacket also, but the jacket, unbuttoned, revealed bare breasts held up by a stiff shelf projecting from a flaming red corselet. Her hair was piled high in an ornate coiffure, and her face was heavily made up. She shivered, said something in a Semitic-sounding language, and buttoned up the jacket.

If these were servants, they were able to ride in style. A carriage like cabriolet, drawn by two handsome horses, came around the corner and stopped before the porch. The coachman jumped down and assisted them into the carriage. He wore a tall tricorn hat with a bright red feather, a jacket with huge gold buttons and scarlet piping, a heavy blue kilt, and calf-length boots.

The three got into the carriage and drove off. Kickaha watched the oil-burning lamps on the cabriolet until they were out of sight on the road that wound down the mountain.

This world, Kickaha thought, would be fascinating to investigate. Physically, it had been exactly like the other Earth when it had started. And its peoples, created fifteen thousand years ago, had been exactly like those of the other Earth. Twins, they had been placed in the same locations, given the same languages and the same rearing, and then were left to themselves. He supposed that the deviations of the humans here from those on his world had started almost immediately. Fifteen millennia had resulted in very different histories and cultures.

He would like to stay here and wander over the face of this Earth. But now, he had to find Wolff and Chryseis and to do this he would have to find and capture Urthona. The only action available was to use the Horn, and to hope it would reveal the right gate to the Lord.

This was not going to be easy, as he found out a few minutes later. The Horn, though not loud, attracted several servants. Kickaha fired the beamer once at a pillar near them. They saw the hole appear in the stone and, shouting and screaming, fled. Kickaha urged Anana to continue blowing the Horn, but the uproar from the interior convinced him that they could not remain here. This building was too huge for them to leisurely investigate the first story. The most likely places for gates were in the bedroom or office of the master, and these were probably on the second story.

When they were halfway up the steps, a number of men with steel conical helmets, small round shields, and swords and spears appeared. There were, however, three men who carried big heavy clumsy-looking firearms with flared muzzles, wooden stocks, and flintlocks.

Kickaha cut the end of one blunderbuss off with the beamer. The men scattered, but they regrouped before Kickaha and Anana had reached the top of the steps. Kickaha cut through the bottom of a marble pillar and then through the top. The pillar fell over with a crash that shook the house, and the armed men fled.

It was a costly rout, because a little knob on the side of the beamer suddenly flashed a red light. There was not much charge left, and he did not have another powerpack.

They found a bedroom that seemed to be that of the Lord. It was certainly magnificent enough, but everything in this mansion was magnificent. It contained a number of weapons, swords, axes, daggers, throwing knives, maces, rapiers, and—delight!—bows and a quiver of arrows. While Anana probed the walls and floors with the Horn, Kickaha chose a knife with a good balance for her and then strung a bow. He shouldered a quiver and felt much better. The beamer had enough left in it for several seconds of full piercing power or a dozen or so rays of burn power or several score rays of stun power. After that, he would have to depend on his primitive weapons.

He also chose a light ax that seemed suitable for throwing for Anana. She was proficient in the use of all weapons and, while she was not as strong as he, she was as skillful.

She stopped blowing the Horn. There was a bed which hung by golden chains from the ceiling, and beyond it on the wall was a spreading circle of light. The light dissolved to show delicate pillars supporting a frescoed ceiling and, beyond, many trees.

Anana cried out with surprise in which was an anguished delight. She started forward but was held back by Kickaha.

He said, "What's the hurry?"

"It's home!" she said. "Home!"

Her whole being seemed to radiate light.

"Your world?" he said.

"Oh, no! Home! Where I was born! The world where the Lords originated!"

There did not seem to be any traps, but that meant nothing. However, the hubbub outside the room indicated that they had better move on or expect to fight. Since the beamer was so depleted, he could not fight them off for long, not if they were persistent.

He said, "Here we go!" and leaped through. Anana had to bend low and scoot through swiftly, because the circle was closing. When she got up on her feet, she said, "Do you remember that tall building on Wilshire, near the tar pits? The big one with the sign, *California Federal*? It was always ablaze with lights at night?"

He nodded and she said, "This summerhouse is exactly on that spot. I mean, on the place that corresponds to that spot."

There was no sign of anything corresponding to Wilshire Boulevard, nothing resembling a road or even a foot path here. The number of trees here certainly did take away from the southern California lowlands look, but she explained that the Lords had created rivers and brooks here so that this forest could grow. The summerhouse was one of many built so that the family could stop for the night or retire for meditation or the doing of whatever virtue or vice they felt like. The main dwellings were all on the beach.

There had never been many people in this valley, and, when Anana was born, only three families lived here. Later, at least as far as she knew, all the Lords had left this valley. In fact, they had left this world to occupy their own artificial universes and from thence to wage their wars upon each other.

Kickaha allowed her to wander around while she exclaimed softly to herself or called to him to look at something that she suddenly remembered. He wondered that she remembered anything at all, since her last visit here had been three thousand and two hundred years ago. When he thought of this, he asked her where the gate was through which she had entered at that time.

"It's on top of a boulder about a half mile from here," she said. "There are a number of gates, all disguised, of course. And nobody knows how many others here. I didn't know about the one under the stone floor of the summerhouse, of course. Urthona must have put it there long ago, maybe ten thousand years ago."

"This summerhouse is that old?"

"That old. It contains self-renewing and self-cleaning equipment, of course. And equipment to keep the forest and the land in its primeval state is under the surface. Erosion and buildup of land are compensated for."

"Are there any weapons hidden here for your use?" he said.

"There are a number just within the gate," she said. "But the charges will have trickled off to nothing by now, and, besides, I don't have an activator. . . ."

She stopped and said, "I forgot about the Horn. It can activate the gate, of course, but there's really nothing in it to help us."

"Where does the gate lead to?"

"It leads to a room which contains another gate, and this one opens directly to the interior of the palace of my own world. But it is trapped. I had to leave my deactivator behind when the Bellers invaded my world and I escaped through another gate into Jadawin's world."

"Show me where the boulder is, anyway. If we have to, we could take refuge inside its gate and come back out later."

First, they must eat and, if possible, take a nap. Anana took him into the house, although she first studied it for a long time for traps. The kitchen contained an exquisitely sculptured marble cabinet. This, in turn, housed a fabricator, the larger part of which was buried under the house. Anana opened it cautiously and set the controls, closed it, and a few minutes later opened it again. There were two trays with dishes and cups of delicious food and drink. The energy-matter converters below the earth had been waiting for thousands of years to serve this meal and would wait another hundred thousand years to serve the next one events so proceeded.

After eating, they stretched out on a bed which hung on chains from the ceiling. Kickaha questioned her about the layout of the land. Sh was about to go to sleep when he said, "I've had the feeling that we got here not entirely by accident. I think either Urthona or Red Orc set it up so that we'd get here if we were fast and clever enough. And he also set it up so that the other Lord, his enemy, would be here, if the other Lord is alive. I feel that this is the showdown, and that Urthona or Orc arranged to have it here for poetic or aesthetic reasons. It would be like a Lord to bring his enemies back to the home planet to kill them—if he could. This is just a feeling, but I'm going to act as if it were definite knowledge."

"You'd act that way, anyway," she said. "But I think you may be right."

She fell asleep. He left the bed and went to the front room to watch. The sun started down from the zenith. Beautiful birds, most of whose ancestors must have been made in the biolabs of the Lords, gathered around the fountain and pool before the house. Once, a large brown bear ambled through the trees and near the house. Another time, he heard a sound that tingled his nerves and filled him with joy. It was the shrill trumpet of a mammoth. Its cry reminded him of the Amerind tier of Wolff's world, where mammoths and mastodons by the millions roamed the plains and the forests of an area larger than all of North and South America. He felt homesick and wondered when—if—he would ever see that world again. The Hrowakas, the Bear People, the beautiful and the great Amerinds who had adopted him, were dead now, murdered by the Bellers. But there were other tribes who would be eager to adopt him, even those who called him their greatest enemy and had been trying for years to lift his scalp or his head.

He returned to the bedroom and awoke Anana, telling her to rouse him in about an hour. She did so, and though he would have liked to sleep for the rest of the day and half the night, he forced himself to get up.

They ate some more food and packed more in a small basket. They set off through the woods, which were thick with trees but only moderately grown with underbrush. They came onto a trail which had been trampled by mammoths, as the tracks and droppings showed. They followed this, sensitive for the trumpetings or squealings of the big beasts. There were no flies or mosquitoes, but there was a variety of large beetles and other insects on which the birds fed.

Once, they heard a savage yowl. They stopped, then continued after it was not repeated. Both recognized the cry of the sabertooth.

"If this was the estate of your family, why did they keep the big dangerous beasts around?" he said.

"You should know that. The Lords like danger; it is the only spice of eternity. Immortality is nothing unless it can be taken away from you at any moment."

That was true. Only those who had immortality could appreciate that. But he wished, sometimes, that there were not so much spice. Lately, he did not seem to be getting enough rest, and his nerves were raw from the chafing of continuous peril.

"Do you think that anybody else would know about the gate in the boulder?"

"Nothing is sure," she replied. "But I do not think so. Why? Do you think that Urthona will know that we'll be going to the boulder?"

"It seems highly probable. Otherwise, he would have set up a trap for us at the summerhouse. I think that he may expect and want us to go to the boulder because he is also leading another toward the same place. It's to be a trysting place for us and our two enemies."

"You don't know that. It's just your highly suspicious mind believing that things are as you would arrange them if you were a Lord."

"Look who's calling who paranoid," he said, smiling. "Maybe you're right. But I've been through so much that I can hear the tumblers of other people's minds clicking."

He decided that Anana should handle the beamer and he would have his bow and arrows ready.

Near the edge of the clearing, Kickaha noted a slight swelling in the earth. It was about a quarter inch high and two inches wide, and it ran for several feet, then disappeared. He moved in a zigzagging path for several yards and finally found another swelling which described a small part of a very large circle before it disappeared, too.

He went back to Anana, who had been watching him with a puzzled expression.

"Do you know of any underground work done around here?" he said.

"No," she said. "Why?"

"Maybe an earthquake did it," he said and did not comment any more on the swelling.

The boulder was about the size of a one-bedroom bungalow and was set near the edge of a clearing. It was of red and black granite and had been transported here from the north along with thousands of other boulders to add variety to the landscape. It was about a hundred yards northeast of a tar pit. This pit, Kickaha realized, was the same size and in the same location as the tar pit in Hancock Park on Earth Number One.

They got down on their bellies and snaked slowly toward the boul der. When they were within thirty yards of it, Kickaha crawled around until he was able to see all sides of the huge rock. Coming back, he said, "I didn't think he'd be dumb enough to hide *behind* it. But *in* it would be a good move. Or maybe he's out in the woods and waiting for us to open the gate because he's trapped it."

"If you're right and he's waiting for a third party to show . . ."

She stopped and clutched his arm and said, "I saw someone! There!"

She pointed across the clearing at the thick woods where the Los Angeles County Art Museum would have been if this had been Earth Number One. He looked but could see nothing.

"It was a man, I'm sure of that," she said. "A tall man. I think he was Red Orc!"

"See any weapon? A beamer?"

"No, I just got a glimpse, and then he was gone behind a tree."

Kickaha began to get even more uneasy.

He watched the birds and noticed that a raven was cawing madly near where Anana thought she had seen Red Orc. Suddenly, the bird fell off its branch and was seen and heard no more. Kickaha grinned. The Lord had realized it might be giving him away and had shot it.

A hundred yards to their left near the edge of the tar pit, several bluejays screamed and swooped down again and again at something in the tall grass. Kickaha watched them, but in a minute a red fox trotted out of the grass and headed into the woods southward. The jays followed him.

With their departure, a relative quiet arrived. It was hot in the tall saw-bladed grass. Occasionally, a large insect buzzed nearby. Once, a shadow flashed by them, and Kickaha, looking upward, saw a dragon fly, shimmering golden-green, transparent copper-veined wings at least two feet from tip to tip, zooming by.

Now and then, a trumpeting floated to them and a wolf-like howl came from far beyond. And, once, a big bird high above screamed harshly.

Neither saw a sign of the man Anana had thought was Red Orc. Yet, he must be out there somewhere. He might even have spotted them and be crawling toward their hiding place. This caused Kickaha to move away from their position near the boulder. They did this very slowly so they would shake the tall grasses as unviolently as possible. When they had gotten under the trees at the edge of the clearing, he said, "We shouldn't stay together. I'm going to go back into the woods about fifty feet or so. I can get a better view."

He kissed her cheek and crawled off. After looking around, he decided to take a post behind a bush on a slight rise in the ground. There was a tree behind it which would hide him from anybody approaching in that direction. It also had the disadvantage that it could hide the approaching person from him, but he took the chance. And the small height gave him a better view while the bush hid him from those below.

He could not see Anana even though he knew her exact position. Several times, the grasses moved just a little bit contrary to the direction of the breeze. If Orc or Urthona were watching, they would note this and perhaps . . .

He froze. The grass was bending, very slightly and slowly and at irregular intervals, about twenty yards to the right of Anana. There was no movement for what seemed like ten minutes, and then the grass bent again. It pointed toward Anana and moved back up gently, as if somebody were slowly releasing it. A few minutes later, it moved again.

Kickaha was absorbed in watching the progress of the person in the grass, but he did not allow it to distract him from observation elsewhere. During one of his many glances behind him, he saw a flash of white skin through the branches of a bush about sixty feet to his left. At first, he considered moving away from his position to another. But if he did so, he would very probably be seen by the newcomer. It was possible that he had been seen already. The best action just now was no action.

The sun slid on down the sky, and the shadows lengthened. The person creeping toward Anana moved rarely and very slowly but within an hour he was about twelve feet from her. Whether or not she knew it, Kickaha could not tell.

He removed the Horn from its case. And he placed the nock of an arrow in the string of the bow and waited. Again, the grass bent down toward Anana, and the person moved a foot closer.

Behind him, nothing showed except the flash of a bright blue-and-red bird swooping between two trees.

Presently, on the other side of the clearing, keeping close to the trees on its edge, a huge black wolf trotted. It stood at least four and a half feet high at the shoulder, and it could remove the leg of a man at the ankle bone with one bite. It was a dire wolf, extinct on Earth some ten thousand years, but plentiful on Jadawin's world and recreated in the Lords' biolabs for restocking of this area. The giant he-wolf trotted along as stealthily and vibrantly as a tiger, its red tongue hanging out like a flag after a heavy rain. It trotted warily but confidently along for twenty yards and then froze. For a few seconds, it turned its head to scan a quarter of the compass, and then it moved ahead, but crouch ingly. Kickaha watched it, while keeping tabs on the persons unknown before and behind him—or tried to do so. Thus, he almost missed the quick action of the wolf.

It suddenly charged toward a spot inside the woods and just as suddenly abandoned its charge and fled yowling across the clearing toward Anana. The fur on its back and hind legs was aflame.

Kickaha grasped immediately that a fifth person was in the game and that he had tried to scare the wolf away with a brief power-reduced shot from a beamer. But in his haste he had set the power too high and had burned the wolf instead of just stunning him.

Or perhaps the burning was done deliberately. The newcomer might have set the beast on fire and be guiding him this way with stabs of beamer power to see what he could flush up.

Whatever his intent, he had upset the plans of the person sneaking up on Anana. He had also upset Anana, who, hearing the frantic yowls approaching her with great speed, could not resist raising her head just high enough to see what was happening.

Kickaha wanted to take another quick look behind him, but he did not have time. He rose, bent the bow and released the shaft just as something dark reared up a little way above the grass about forty feet from Anana. It was dressed in black and had a black helmet with a dark faceplate, just like the helmets with visors that the Los Angeles motorcyclists wore. The man held the stock of a short-barreled beamer to his shoulder.

At the same time, the wolf ran howling by, the flames leaping off onto the dry grass and the grass catching fire. The arrow streaked across the space between the trees and the edge of the clearing, the sun sparkling off the metal head. It struck the man just under the left arm, which was raised to hold the barrel of the beamer. The arrow bounced off, but the man, although protected by some sort of flexible armor, was knocked over by the impact of the arrow.

The beamer fell out of his hands. Since it had just been turned on, it cut a fiery tunnel through the grass. It also cut off the front legs of the wolf, which fell down howling but became silent as the beam sliced through its body. The fire, originating from the two sources, quickly spread. Smoke poured out, but Kickaha could see that Anana had not been hit and that she was crawling swiftly through the grass toward the fallen man and the beamer.

Kickaha whirled then, drawing another arrow from the quiver and starting to set it to the bowstring. He saw the tall figure of the man lean from around behind the trunk of a tree. A hand beamer was sticking out, pointing toward Kickaha. Kickaha jumped behind his tree and crouched, knowing that he could not get off an arrow swiftly or accurately enough.

There was a burning odor, a thump. He looked up. The beam had cut through the trunk, and the upper part of the tree had dropped straight down for two inches, its smoothly chopped butt against the top of the stump.

Kickaha stepped to the left side of the tree and shot with all the accuracy of thousands of hours of practice under deliberately difficult conditions and scores of hours in combat. The arrow was so close to the tree, it was deflected by the slightest contact. It zoomed off, just missing the arm of the man holding the beamer. The beamer withdrew as the man jumped back. And then the tree above Kickaha fell over, pulled to one side by the unevenness of the branches' weight. It came down on Kickaha, who jumped back and so escaped the main weight of the trunk. But a branch struck him, and everything became as black and unknowing as the inside of a tree.

When he saw light again, he also saw that not much time had passed. The sun had not moved far. His head hurt as if a root had grown into it and was entangled with the most sensitive nerves. A branch pressed down his chest, and his legs felt as if another branch was weighing them down. He could move his arms a little to one side and turn his head, but otherwise he was as unable to move as if he were buried under a landslide.

Smoke drifted by and made him cough. Flames crackled, and he could feel some heat on the bottom of his feet. The realization that he might burn to death sent him into a frenzy of motion. The result was that his head hurt even more and he had not been able to get out from under the branches at all.

He thought of the others. What had happened to Anana? Why wasn't she here trying to get him free? And the man who had severed the tree? Was he sneaking up now, not sure that he had hit the archer? And then there was the man in black he'd knocked down with the arrow and the person across the clearing who had set fire to the wolf and precipitated the action. Where were they?

If Anana did not do something quickly, she might as well forget about him. The smoke was getting thicker, and his feet and the lower part of his legs were getting very uncomfortable. It would be a question of whether he choked to death from smoke or burned first. Could this be the end? The end came to everybody, even those Lords who had sur vived fifteen thousand years. But if he had to die, let him do it in his beloved adopted world, the World of Tiers.

Then he stopped thinking such thoughts. He was not dead and he was not going to quit struggling. Somehow, he would get this tree off his chest and legs and would crawl away to where the fire could not reach him and where he would be hidden from his enemies. But where was Anana?

A voice made him start. It came a foot away from his left ear. He turned his head and saw the grinning face of Red Orc.

"So the fox was caught in my deadfall," Red Orc said in English.

"Of course, you planned it that way," Kickaha said.

The Lords were cruel, and this one would want him to die slowly. Moreover, Orc would want him to fully savor the taste of defeat. A Lord never killed a foe swiftly if he could avoid it.

He must keep Red Orc talking as long as he could. If Anana were trying to get close, she would be helped if Red Orc were distracted.

The Lord wanted to talk, to taunt his victim, but he had not relaxed his vigilance. While he lay near Kickaha, he held his beamer ready, and he looked this way and that as nervously as if he were a bird.

"So you've won?" Kickaha said, although he did not believe that Red Orc had won and would not think so until he was dead.

"Over you, yes," Red Orc said. "Over the others, not yet. But I will."

"Then Urthona is still out there," Kickaha said. "Tell me, who set up this trap? You or Urthona?"

Red Orc lost his smile. He said, "I'm not sure. The trap may be so subtle that I was led into thinking that I set it. And then, again, perhaps I did. What does it matter? We were all led here, for one reason or another, to this final battleground. It has been a good battle, because we are not fighting through our underlings, the *leblabbiy*. We are fighting directly, as we should. You are the only Earthling in this battle, and I'm convinced that you may be half-Lord. You certainly do have some family resemblances to us. I could be your father. Or Urthona. Or Uriel. Or even that dark one, Jadawin. After all, he had the genes for red hair."

Red Orc paused and smiled, then said, "And it's possible that Anana could be your mother, too. In which case, you might be all-Lord. That would explain your amazing abilities and your successes."

A thick arm of smoke came down over Kickaha's face and set him coughing again. Red Orc looked alarmed and he backed away a little, turning his back to Kickaha, who was recovering from another coughing fit. Something had happened to his legs. Suddenly, they no longer felt the heat. It was as if dirt had been piled on them.

Kickaha said, "I don't know what you're getting at, Orc, but Anana could not possibly be my mother. Anyway, I know who my parents are. They were Indiana farmers who come from old American stock, including the oldest, and also from Scotch, Norwegian, German, and Irish immigrants. I was born in the very small rural village of North Terre Haute, and there is no mystery. . . ."

He stopped, because there had been a mystery. His parents had moved from Kentucky to Indiana before he was born, and, suddenly, he remembered the mysterious Uncle Robert who had visited their farm from time to time when he was very young. And then there was the trouble with his birth certificate when he had volunteered for the Army cavalry. And when he had returned to Indiana after the war, he had been left ten thousand dollars from an unknown benefactor. It was to put him through college and there had been a vague promise of more to come.

"There is no mystery?" Red Orc said. "I know far more about you than you would dream possible. When I found out that your natal name was Paul Janus Finnegan, I remembered something, and I checked it out. And so . . ."

Kickaha began coughing again. Orc quit talking. A second later, a shape appeared through the smoke above him, coming from the other side of the tree where he had thought nothing could be living. It dived through the cloud and sprawled on top of Red Orc, knocking him on his back and tearing the beamer from his hands.

Orc yelled with the surprise and shock and tried to roll after the beamer, but the attacker, in a muffled voice, said, "Hold it! Or I cut you in half!"

Kickaha bent his head as far to one side and as far back as he could. The voice he knew, of course, but he still could not believe it. Then he realized that Anana had piled dirt on his legs or covered them up with something.

But what had kept her from coughing and giving herself away?

She turned toward him then, though still keeping the beamer turned on Red Orc. A cloth was tied around her nose and mouth. It was wet with some liquid which he suspected was urine. Anana had always been adaptable, making do with whatever was handy.

She gestured at Orc to move away from his beamer. He scooted away backward on his hands and buttocks, eyeing her malevolently.

Anana stepped forward, tossed her beamer away with one hand as she picked up Orc's with the other. Then, aiming the weapon at him with one hand, she slipped the cloth from her face to around her neck. She smiled slightly and said, "Thanks for your beamer, Uncle. Mine was discharged."

Orc looked shocked.

Anana crouched down and said, "All right, Uncle. Get that tree off him. And quick!"

Orc said, "I can't lift that! Even if I broke my back doing it, I couldn't lift it!"

"Try," she said.

His face set stubbornly. "Why should I bother? You'll kill me, anyway. Do it now."

"I'll burn your legs and scorch your eyes out," she said, "and leave you here legless and blind if you don't get him from under that tree."

"Come on, Anana," Kickaha said. "I know you want to make him suffer, but not at my expense. Cut the branches off me with the beamer so he won't have so much weight to lift. Don't play around! There are two others out there, you know."

Anana moved away from the smoke and said, "Stand to one side, Uncle!" She made three passes with the ray from the beamer. The huge branch on his chest was cut in two places; he could not see what she had done to the branch on his legs. Orc had no difficulty removing the trunk and dragging him out of the smoke. He lifted him in his arms and carried him into the woods, where the grass was sparser and shorter.

He let Kickaha down very gently and then put his hands behind his neck at her orders.

"The stranger is out on the boulder," she said. "He got up and staggered away just after I got his beamer. He ran there to get away from me and the fire. I didn't kill him; maybe I should have. But I was curious about him and thought I could question him later."

That curiosity had made more than one Lord lose the upper hand, Kickaha thought. But he did not comment, since the deed was done and, besides, he understood the curiosity. He had enough of it to sympathize.

"Do you know where Urthona is?" he said, wheezing and feeling a pain in his chest as if a cancer had grown there within the last few seconds. His legs were numb but life was returning in them. And with the life, pain.

"I'm not going to be much good, Anana," he said. "I'm hurting pretty badly inside. I'll do what I can to help, but the rest is up to you."

Anana said, "I don't know where Urthona is. Except he's out there.

I'm sure he was the one who set the wolf on fire. And set this up for us. Even the great Red Orc, Lord of the Two Earths, was lured into this."

"I knew it was a trap," Orc said. "I came into it, anyway. I thought that surely I . . . I . . ."

"Yes, Uncle, if I were you I wouldn't brag," she said. "The only question, the big question, anyway, is how we get away from him."

"The Horn," Kickaha said. He sat up with great effort, despite the clenching of a dragon's claw inside his chest. Smoke drifted under the trees and made him cough again. The pain intensified.

Anana said, "Oh!" She looked distressed. "I forgot about it."

"We'll have to get it. It must be under the tree back there," he said. "And we'll open the gate in the boulder. If worse comes to worse, we'll go through it."

"But the second room past it is trapped!" she said. "I told you I'll need a deactivator to get through it."

"We can come out later," he said. "Urthona can't follow us, and he won't hang around, because he'll think we definitely escaped into another universe."

He stopped talking because the effort pained him so much.

Red Orc, at Anana's orders, helped him up. He did it so roughly that a low cry was forced from Kickaha. Anana, glaring, said, "Uncle, you be gentle, or I'll kill you right now!"

"If you do," Orc said, "you'll have to carry him yourself. And what kind of position will that put you into?"

Anana looked as if she were going to shoot him anyway. Before Kickaha could say anything, he saw the muzzle end of the beamer fall onto the ground. Anana was left with half a weapon in her hand.

A voice called out from the trees behind them. "You will do as I tell you now! Walk to that boulder and wait there for further orders!"

Why should he want us to do that? Kickaha thought. *Does he know about the trap inside the gate, know that we'll be stuck there if he doesn't go away as I'd planned? Is he hoping we'll decide to run the trap and so get ourselves killed? He will wait outside the boulder while we agonize inside, and he'll get his sadistic amusement thinking about our dilemma.*

Clearly, Urthona thought he had them in his power, and clearly he did. But he was not going to expose himself or get closer.

That's the way to manage it, Kickaha thought. Be cagy, be foxy, never take anything for granted. That was how he had survived through so much. Survive? It looked as if his days were about ended.

"Walk to the boulder!" Urthona shouted. "At once! Or I burn you a little!"

Anana went to Kickaha's other side and helped Orc move him. Every step flicked pain through Kickaha, but he shut his mouth and turned his groans into silence. The smoke still spread over the air and made him cough again and caused even deeper pain.

Then they passed the tree where the Horn was sticking out from a partially burned branch.

"Has Urthona come out from the trees yet?" he asked.

Anana looked around slowly, then said, "No more than a step or two."

"I'm going to stumble. Let me fall."

"It'll hurt you," she said.

"So what? Let me go! Now!"

"Gladly!" Orc said and released him. Anana was not so fast, and she tried to support his full weight for a second. They went down together, she taking most of the impact. Nevertheless, the fall seemed to end on sharpened stakes in his chest, and he almost fainted.

There was a shout from Urthona. Red Orc froze and slowly raised his hands above his head. Kickaha tried to get up and crawl to the Horn, but Anana was there before him.

"Blow on it now!" he said.

"Why?" Red Orc and Anana said in unison.

"Just do what I say! I'll tell you later! If there is a later!"

She lifted the mouthpiece to her lips and loudly blew the sequence of seven notes that made the skeleton key to turn the lock of any gate of the Lords within range of its vibrations.

There was a shout from Urthona, who had begun running toward them when they had fallen. But as the first note blared out, and he saw what Anana held in her mouth, he screamed.

Kickaha expected him to shoot. Instead, Urthona whirled and, still yelling, ran away toward the woods.

Red Orc said, "What is happening?"

The last of the golden notes faded away.

Urthona stopped running and threw his beamer down on the ground and jumped up and down.

The immediate area around them remained the same. There was the clearing with its burned grasses, the boulder on top of which the darkly clothed stranger sat, the fallen tree, and the trees on the edge of the clearing.

But the sky had become an angry red without a sun.

The land beyond the edge of the clearing had become high hills covered with a rusty grass and queer-looking bushes with green and red striped swastika-shaped leaves. There were trees on the hills beyond the nearest ones; these were tall and round and had zebra stripes of black, white, and red. They swayed as if they were at the bottom of a sea responding to a current.

Urthona's jumping up and down had resulted in his attaining heights of at least six feet. Now he picked up his beamer and ran in great bounds toward them. He seemed in perfect control of himself.

Not so with Red Orc, who started to whirl toward them, his mouth open to ask what had happened. The motion carried him on around and toppled him over. But he did not fall heavily.

"Stay down," Kickaha said to Anana. "I don't know where we are, but the gravity's less than Earth's."

Urthona stopped before them. His face was almost as red as the sky. His green eyes were wild.

"The Horn of Shambarimen!" he screamed. "I wondered what you had in that case! If I had known! If I had known!"

"Then you would have stayed outside the rim of the giant gate you set around the clearing," Kickaha said. "Tell me, Urthona, why did you step inside it? Why did you drive us toward the boulder, when we were already inside the gate?"

"How did you know?" Urthona screamed. "How could you know?"

"I didn't really *know*," Kickaha said. "I saw the slight ridge of earth at several places on the edge of the clearing before we came on in. It didn't mean much, although I was suspicious. I'm suspicious of everything that I can't explain at once.

"Then you hung back, and that in itself wasn't too suspicious, because you wouldn't want to get too close until you were certain we had no hidden weapons. But you wanted to do more than just get us inside this giant gate and then spring it on us. You wanted to drive us into our own gate, in the boulder, where we'd be trapped. You wanted us to hide inside there and think we'd fooled you and then come out after a while, only to find ourselves in this world.

"But you didn't know that Anana had no activator and you didn't know that we had the Horn. There was no reason why you would think of it even if you saw the instrument case, because it must be thousands of years since you last saw it. And you didn't know Jadawin had it, or you would have connected that with the instrument case, since I am Jadawin's friend.

"So I got Anana to blow the Horn even if she didn't know why she was doing it. I didn't want to go into your world, but if I could take you with me, I'd do it."

Anana got up slowly and carefully and said, "The Shifting World! Urthona's world!"

In the east, or what was the east in the world they'd just left, a massive red body appeared over the hills. It rose swiftly and revealed itself as a body about four times the size of the Earth's moon. It was not round but oblong with several blobby tentacles extending out from it. Kickaha thought that it was changing shape slightly.

He felt the earth under him tilting. His head was getting lower than his feet. And the edge of the high hills in the distance was sagging.

Kickaha sat up. The pains seemed to be slightly attenuated. Perhaps it was because the pull of gravity was so much reduced. He said, "This is a one-way gate, of course, Urthona?"

"Of course," Urthona said. "Otherwise I would have taken the Horn and reopened the gate."

"And where is the nearest gate out of this world?"

"There's no harm in telling you," Urthona said. "Especially since you won't know any more than you do now when I tell you. The only gate out is in my palace, which is somewhere on the surface of this mass. Or perhaps on that," he added, pointing at the reddish metamorphosing body in the sky. "This planet splits up and changes shape and recombines and splits off again. The only analogy I can think of is a lavalite. This is a lavalite world."

Red Orc went into action then. His leap was prodigious and he almost went over Urthona's head. But he rammed into him and both went cartwheeling. The beamer, knocked out of Urthona's hands by the impact, flew off to one side. Anana dived after it, got it, and landed so awkwardly and heavily that Kickaha feared for her. She rose somewhat shakily but grinning. Urthona walked back to them; Red Orc crawled.

"Now, Uncles," she said, "I could shoot you and perhaps I should. But I need someone to carry Kickaha, so you two will do it. You should be thankful that the lesser gravity will make the task easier. And I need you, Urthona, because you know something of this world. You should, since you designed it and made it. You two will make a stretcher for Kickaha, and then we'll start out."

"Start out where?" growled Urthona. "There's no place to go to. Nothing is fixed here. Can't you understand that?"

"If we have to search every inch of this world, we'll do it," she said. "Now get to work!"

"Just one moment," Kickaha said. "What did you do with Wolff and Chryseis?"

"I gated them through to this world. They are somewhere on its surface. Or on that mass. Or perhaps another mass we haven't seen yet. I thought that it would be the worst thing I could do to them. And, of course, they do have some chance of finding my palace. Although. . . ."

"Although even if they do, they'll run into some traps?" Kickaha said.

"There are other things on this world . . ."

"Big predators? Hostile human beings?"

Urthona nodded and said, "Yes. We'll need the beamer. I hope its charge lasts. And . . ."

Kickaha said, "Don't leave us in suspense."

"I hope that we don't take too long finding my palace. If you're not a native, you're driven crazy by this world!"

THE LAVALITE WORLD

For Roger Zelazny, The Golden Spinner

My thanks to J. T. Edson, author of the Dusty Fog sagas, for his kind permission to integrate the Texas Fogs with the British Foggs.

—Philip José Farmer

I

KICKAHA WAS A QUICKSILVER PROTEUS.

Few could match his speed in adapting to change. But on Earth and on other planets of the pocket universes, the hills, mountains, valleys, plains, the rivers, lakes, and seas, seldom altered. Their permanence of form and location were taken for granted.

There were small local changes. Floods, earthquakes, avalanches, tidal waves reshaped the earth. But the effects were, in the time scale of an individual, in the lifetime of a nation, minute.

A mountain might walk, but the hundreds of thousands of generations living at its foot would not know it. Only God or a geologist would see its movements as the dash of a mouse for a hole.

Not here.

Even cocksure, unfazed Kickaha, who could react to change as quickly as a mirror reflects an image, was nervous. But he wasn't going to let anyone else know it. To the others he seemed insanely cool. That was because they were going mad.

II

THEY HAD GONE TO SLEEP DURING THE "NIGHT." KICKAHA HAD TAKEN the first watch. Urthona, Orc, Anana, and McKay had made themselves as comfortable as they could on the rusty-red tough grass and soon had fallen asleep. Their camp was at the bottom of a shallow valley ringed by low hills. Grass was the only vegetation in the valley. The tops of the hills, however, were lined with the silhouettes of trees. These were about ten feet tall. Though there was little breeze, they swayed back and forth.

When he had started the watch, he had seen only a few on the hilltops. As time passed, more and more had appeared. They had ranged themselves beside the early comers until they were a solid line. There was no telling how many were on the other side of the hills. What he was sure of was that the trees were waiting until "dawn." Then, if the humans did not come to them, they would come down the hills after them.

The sky was a uniform dark red except for a few black slowly floating shapes. Clouds. The enormous reddish mass, visually six times the size of Earth's moon, had disappeared from the sky. It would be back, though he didn't know when.

He sat down and rubbed his legs. They still hurt from the accident that had taken place twelve "days" ago. The pain in his chest had almost ceased, however. He was recovering, but he was not as agile and strong as he needed to be.

That the gravity was less than Earth's helped him, though.

He lay down for a minute. No enemy, human or beast, was going to attack. They would have to get through those killer trees first. Only the elephants and the giant variety of moosoids were big enough to do that. He wished that some of these would show up. They fed upon trees

However, at this distance Kickaha couldn't determine just what type of killer plants they were. Some were so fearsomely armed that even the big beasts avoided them.

How in hell had the trees detected the little party? They had a keen olfactory sense, but he doubted that the wind was strong enough to carry the odor of the party up over the hills. The visual ability of the plants was limited. They could see shapes through the multifaceted insectine eyes ringing the upper parts of their trunks. But at this distance and in this light, they might as well be blind.

One or more of their scouts must have come up a hill and caught a molecule or two of human odor. That was, after all, nothing to be surprised about. He and the others stank. The little water they had been able to find was used for drinking only. If they didn't locate more water tomorrow, they'd have to start drinking their own urine. It could be recycled twice before it became poisonous.

Also, if they didn't kill something soon, they would be too weak from hunger to walk.

He rubbed the barrel of the hand-beamer with the fingers of his left hand. Its battery had only a few full-power discharges available. Then it would be exhausted. So far, he and Anana had refrained from using any of the power. It was the only thing that allowed them to keep the upper hand over the other three. It was also their only strong defense against the big predators. But when "dawn" came, he was going to go hunting. They had to eat, and they could drink blood to quench their thirst.

First, though, they had to get through the trees. Doing that might use up the battery. It also might not be enough. There could be a thousand trees on the other side of the hills.

The clouds were thickening. Perhaps, at long last, rain would come. If it rained as hard as Urthona said it did, it might fill this cup-shaped valley. They'd have to drown or charge into the trees. Some choice.

He lay on his back for a few minutes. Now he could hear faint creaks and groans and an occasional mutter. The earth was moving under him. Heat flowed along his back and his legs. It felt almost as warm as a human body. Under the densely packed blades and the thick tangle of roots, energy was being dissipated. The earth was shifting slowly. In what direction, toward what shapes, he did not know.

He could wait. One of his virtues was an almost-animal patience. Be leopard, a wolf. Lie still and evaluate the situation. When action was called for, he would explode. Unfortunately, his injured leg and his weakness handicapped him. Where he had once been dynamite, he was now only black gunpowder.

He sat up and looked around. The dark reddish light smoldered around him. The trees formed a waving wall on the hilltops. The others of the party lay on their sides or their backs. McKay was snoring. Anana was muttering something in her native language, a speech older than Earth itself. Urthona's eyes were open, and he was looking directly at Kickaha. Was he hoping to catch him unawares and get hold of the beamer?

No. He was sleeping, his mouth and eyes open. Kickaha, having risen and come close to him, could hear the gentle burbling from his dry lips. The eyes looked glazed.

Kickaha licked his own sandpaper lips and swallowed. He brought the wristwatch, which he'd borrowed from Anana, close to his eyes. He pressed the minute stud on its side, and four glowing figures appeared briefly on the face. They were the numerical signs of the Lords. In Earth numerals, 15:12. They did not mean anything here. There was no sun; the sky provided light and some heat. In any event, this planet had no steady rotation on any one plane, and there were no stars. The great reddish mass that had moved slowly across the sky, becoming larger every day, was no genuine moon. It was a temporary satellite, and it was falling.

There were no shadows except under one peculiar condition. There was no north, south, east, and west. Anana's watch had compass capabilities, but they were useless. This great body on which he stood had no nickel-steel core, no electromagnetic field, no north or south pole. Properly speaking, it wasn't a planet.

And the ground was rising now. He could not detect that by its motion, since that was so slow. But the hills had definitely become lower.

The watch had one useful function. It did mark the forward movement of time. It would tell him when his hour and a half of sentinel duty was over.

When it was time to rouse Anana, he walked to her. But she sat up before he was within twelve feet. She knew that it was her turn. She had told herself to wake at the proper time, and a well-developed sense, a sort of biological clock within her, had set off its alarm.

Anana was beautiful, but she was beginning to look gaunt. Her cheekbones protruded, her cheeks were beginning to sink in, her large dark-blue eyes were ringed with the shadows of fatigue. Her lips were cracked, and that once soft white skin was dirty and rough-looking. Though she had sweated much in the twelve days they'd been here, there were still traces of smoke on her neck.

"You don't look so good yourself," she said, smiling.

Normally, her voice was a rich contralto, but now it was gravelly.

She stood up. She was slim but broad-shouldered and full-breasted. She was only two inches shorter than his six feet one inch, was as strong as any man her weight, and inside fifty yards she could outrun him. Why not? She had had ten thousand years to develop her physical potentialities.

She took a comb from the back pocket of her torn bellbottom trousers and straightened out her long hair, as black as a Crow Indian's.

"There. Is that better?" she said, smiling. Her teeth were very white and perfect. Only thirty years ago, she'd had tooth buds implanted, the hundredth set in a series.

"Not bad for a starving dehydrated old woman," he said. "In fact, if I was up to it . . ."

He quit grinning, and he waved his hand to indicate the hilltops. "We've got visitors."

It was difficult in this light to see if she'd turned pale. Her voice was steady. "If they're bearing fruit, we'll eat."

He thought it better not to say that they might be eaten instead.

He handed her the beamer. It looked like a six-shooter revolver. But the cartridges were batteries, of which only one now had a charge. The barrel contained a mechanism which could be adjusted to shoot a ray that could cut through a tree or inflict a slight burn or a stunning blow.

Kickaha went back to where his bow and a quiver of arrows lay. He was an excellent archer, but so far only two of his arrows had struck game. The animals were wary, and it had been impossible, except twice, to get close enough to any to shoot. Both kills had been small gazelles, not enough to fill the bellies of five adults in twelve days. Anana had gotten a hare with a throw of her light axe, but a long-legged baboon had dashed out from behind a hill, scooped it up, and run off with it.

Kickaha picked up the bow and quiver, and they walked three hundred feet away from the sleepers. Here he lay down and went to sleep. His knife was thrust upright into the ground, ready to be snatched in case of attack. Anana had her beamer, a light throwing axe, and a knife for defense.

They were not worried at this time about the trees. They just wanted to keep distance between them and the others. When Anana's watch was over, she would wake up McKay. Then she'd return to lie down by Kickaha. She and her mate were not overly concerned about one of the others trying to sneak up on them while they slept. Anana had told them that her wristwatch had a device which would sound an alarm if anybody with a mass large enough to be dangerous came close. She was lying, though the device was something that a Lord could have. They probably wondered if she was deceiving them. However, they did not care to test her. She had said that if anyone tried to attack them, she would kill him immediately. They knew that she would do so.

III

HE AWOKE, SWEATING FROM THE HEAT, THE BRIGHT LIGHT OF "DAY" plucking at his eyes. The sky had become a fiery light red. The clouds were gone, taking their precious moisture elsewhere. But he was no longer in a valley. The hills had come down, flattened out into a plain. And the party was now on a small hill.

He was surprised. The rate of change had been greater than he'd expected. Urthona, however, had said that the reshaping occasionally accelerated. Nothing was constant or predictable here. So, he shouldn't have been surprised.

The trees still ringed them. There were several thousand, and now some scouts were advancing toward the just-born hill. They were about ten feet tall. The trunks were barrel-shaped and covered with a smooth greenish bark. Large round dark eyes circled the trunk near its top. On one side was an opening, the mouth. Inside it was soft flexible tissue and two hard ridges holding shark-like teeth. According to Urthona, the plants were half-protein, and the digestive system was much like an animal's. The anus was the terminus of the digestive system, but it was also located in the mouth.

Urthona should know. He had designed them.

"They don't have any diseases, so there's no reason why the feces shouldn't pass through the mouth," Urthona had said.

"They must have bad breath," Kickaha had said. "But then nobody's going to kiss them, are they?"

He, Anana, and McKay had laughed. Urthona and Red Orc had looked disgusted. Their sense of humor had atrophied. Or perhaps they'd never had much.

Above the head of the tree was a growth of many slender stems rising two feet straight up. Broad green leaves, heart-shaped, covered the stems. From the trunk radiated six short branches, each three feet long, a pair on each side, in three ranks. These had short twigs supporting large round leaves. Between each ring of branches was a tentacle, about twelve feet long and as supple as an octopus's. A pair of tentacles also grew from the base.

The latter helped balance the trunk as it moved on two short kneeless legs ending in huge round barky toeless feet. When the tree temporarily changed from an ambulatory to sedentary state, the lower tentacles bored into the soil, grew roots, and sucked sustenance from the ground. The roots could be easily broken off and the tentacles withdrawn when the tree decided to move on.

Kickaha had asked Urthona why he had had such a clumsy unnatural monster made in his biolabs.

"It pleased me to do so."

Urthona probably was wishing he hadn't done so. He had wakened the others, and all were staring at the weird—and frightening—creatures.

Kickaha walked up to him. "How do they communicate?"

"Through pheromones. Various substances they emit. There are about thirty of these, and a tree smelling them receives various signals. They don't think; their brains are about the size of a dinosaur's. They react on the instinctive—or robotic—level. They have a well-developed herd instinct, though."

"Any of these pheromones stimulate fear?"

"Yes. But you have to make one of them afraid, and there's nothing in this situation to scare them."

"I was thinking," Kickaha said, "that it's too bad you don't carry around a vial of fear-pheromones."

"I used to," Urthona said.

The nearest scout had halted thirty feet away. Kickaha looked a Anana, who was sixty feet from the group. Her beamer was ready fo trouble from the three men or the tree.

Kickaha walked to the scout and stopped ten feet from it. It wave its greenish tentacles. Others were coming to join it, though not on run. He estimated that with those legs they could go perhaps a mile a hour. But then he didn't know their full potentiality. Urthona didn remember how fast they could go.

Even as he walked down toward the tree, he could feel the ear swelling beneath him, could see the rate of its shaping increase. The a became warmer, and spaces had appeared between the blades of gra The earth was black and greasy-looking. If the shaping stopped, a there was no change for three days, the grass would grow enough to fill in the bare spots.

The thousand or so plants were still moving but more slowly. They leaned forward on their rigid legs, their tentacles extended to support them.

Kickaha looked closely at the nearest one and saw about a dozen apple-red spheres dangling from the branches. He called to Urthona. "Is their fruit good to eat?"

"For birds, yes," Urthona said. "I don't remember. But I can't think why I should have made them poisonous for humans."

"Knowing you, I'd say you could have done it for laughs," Kickaha said.

He motioned to Angus McKay to come to him. The black came to him warily, though his caution was engendered by the tree, not Kickaha.

McKay was an inch shorter than Kickaha but about thirty pounds heavier. Not much of the additional weight was fat, though. He was dressed in black levis, socks, and boots. He'd long ago shed his shirt and the leather jacket of the motorcyclist, but he still carried his helmet. Kickaha had insisted that it be retained to catch rainwater in, if for nothing else.

McKay was a professional criminal, a product of Detroit who'd come out to Los Angeles to be one of Urthona's hired killers. Of course, he had not known then that Urthona was a Lord. He had never been sure what Urthona, whom he knew as Mr. Callister, did. But he'd been paid well, and if Mr. Callister wasn't in a business which competed with other mobs, that was all to the good. And Mr. Callister certainly seemed to know how to handle the police.

That day which seemed so long ago, he'd had a free afternoon. He'd started drinking in a tavern in Watts. After picking up a good-looking if loud-mouthed woman, he'd driven her to his apartment in Hollywood. They'd gone to bed almost at once, after which he fell asleep. The telephone woke him up. It was Callister, excited, obviously in some kind of trouble. Emergency, though he didn't say what it was. McKay was to come to him at once. He was to bring his .45 automatic with him.

That helped to sober him up. Mr. Callister must really be in trouble if he would say openly, over a phone that could be tapped, that he was to be armed. Then the first of the troubles started. The woman was gone, and with her his wallet—five hundred dollars and his credit cards—and his car keys.

When he looked out the window into the parking space behind the building, he saw that the car was gone, too. If it hadn't been that he was needed so quickly, he would have laughed. Ripped off by a hooker! A dumb one at that, since he would be tracking her down. He'd get his wallet back and its contents, if they were still around. And his car, too. He wouldn't kill the woman, but he would rough her up a bit to teach her a lesson. He was a professional, and professionals didn't kill except for money or in self-defense.

So he'd put on his bike clothes and wheeled out on it, speeding along in the night, ready to outrun the pigs if they saw him. Callister was waiting for him. The other bodyguards weren't around. He didn't ask Callister where they were, since the boss didn't like questions. But Callister volunteered, anyway. The others were in a car which had been wrecked while chasing a man and a woman. They were not dead, but they were too injured to be of any use.

Callister then had described the couple he was after, but he didn't say why he wanted them.

Callister had stood for a moment, biting his lip. He was a big handsome honky, his curly hair yellow, his eyes a strange bright green, his face something like the movie actor's, Paul Newman. Abruptly, he went to a cabinet, pulled a little box about the size of a sugar cube from his pocket, held it over the lock, and the door swung open.

Callister removed a strange-looking device from the cabinet. McKay had never seen anything like it before, but he knew it was a weapon. It had a gunstock to which was affixed a short thick barrel, like a sawed-off shotgun.

"I've changed my mind," Callister said. "Use this, leave your .45 here. We may be where we won't want anybody to hear gunfire. Here, I'll show you how to use it."

McKay, watching him demonstrate, began to feel a little numb. It was the first step into a series of events which made him feel as if he'd been magically transformed into an actor in a science-fiction movie. If he'd had any sense, he would have taken off then. But there wasn't one man on Earth that could have foreseen that five minutes later he wouldn't even *be* on Earth.

He was still goggle-eyed when, demonstrating the "beamer," Callister had cut a chair in half. He was handed a metal vest. At least, it looked and felt like steel. But it was flexible.

Callister put one on, too, and then he said something in a foreign language. A large circular area on the wall began glowing, then the glow disappeared, and he was staring into another world.

"Step through the gate," Callister said. He was holding a han weapon disguised as a revolver. It wasn't pointed at McKay, but McKay felt that it would be if he refused.

Callister followed him in. McKay guessed that Callister was using him as a shield, but he didn't protest. If he did, he might be sliced in half.

They went through another "gate" and were in still another world or dimension or whatever. And then things really began to happen. While Callister was sneaking up on their quarry, McKay circled around through the trees. All of a sudden, hell broke loose. There was this big red-haired guy with, believe it or not, a bow and arrows.

He was behind a tree, and McKay sliced the branches of the tree off on one side. That was to scare the archer, since Callister had said that he wanted the guy—his name was Kickaha, crazy!—alive. But Kickaha had shot an arrow and McKay certainly knew where it had been aimed. Only a part of his body was not hidden by the tree behind which he was concealed. But the arrow had struck McKay on the only part showing, his shoulder.

If he hadn't been wearing that vest, he'd have been skewered. Even as it was, the shock of the arrow knocked him down. His beamer flew away from his opening hands, and, its power still on, it rolled away.

Then, the biggest wolf—a wolf!—McKay had ever seen had gotten caught in the ray, and it had died, cut into four different parts. McKay was lucky. If the beamer had fallen pointing the other way, it would have severed him. Though he was stunned, his shoulder and arm completely numb, he managed to get up and to run, crouching over, to another tree. He was cursing because Callister had made him leave his automatic behind. He sure as hell wasn't going into the clearing after the beamer. Not when Kickaha could shoot an arrow like that.

Besides, he felt that he was in over his head about fifty fathoms.

There was a hell of a lot of action after that, but McKay didn't see much of it. He climbed up on a house-sized boulder, using the projections and holes in it, hauling himself up with one hand. Later he wondered why he'd gone up where he could be trapped. But he had been in a complete panic, and it had seemed a logical thing to do. Maybe no one would think of looking for him up there. He could lie down flat and hide until things settled down. If the boss won, he'd come down. He could claim then that he'd gone up there to get a bird's-eye view of the terrain so he could call out to Callister the location of his enemies.

Meanwhile, his beamer burned itself out, half-melting a large boulder fifty feet from it while doing so.

He saw Callister running toward the couple and another man, and he thought Callister had control of the situation. Then the red-haired Kickaha, who was lying on the ground, had said something to the woman. And she'd lifted a funny-looking trumpet to her lips and started blowing some notes. Callister had suddenly stopped, yelled something, and then he'd run like a striped-ass ape away from them.

And suddenly they were in *another* world. If things had been bad before, they were now about as bad as they could be. Well, maybe not quite as bad. At least, he was alive. But there had been times when he'd wished he wasn't.

So here he was, twelve "days" later. Much had been explained to him, mostly by Kickaha. But he still couldn't believe that Callister, whose real name was Urthona, and Red Orc and Anana were thousands of years old. Nor that they had come from another world, what Kickaha called a pocket universe. That is, an artificial continuum, what the science-fiction movies called the fourth dimension, something like that.

The Lords, as they called themselves, claimed to have made Earth. Not only that, the sun, the other planets, the stars—which weren't really stars, they just looked like they were—the whole damn universe.

In fact, they claimed to have created the ancestors of all Earth people in laboratories.

Not only that—it made his brain bob up and down, like a cork on an ocean wave—there were many artificial pocket universes. They'd been constructed to have different physical laws than those on Earth's universe.

Apparently, some ten thousand or so years ago, the Lords had split. Each had gone off to his or her own little world to rule it. And they'd become enemies, out to get each other's ass.

Which explained why Urthona and Orc, Anana's own uncles, had tried to kill her and each other.

Then there was Kickaha. He'd been born Paul Janus Finnegan in 1918 in some small town in Indiana. After World War II he'd gone to the University of Indiana as a freshman, but before a year was up he was involved with the Lords. He'd first lived on a peculiar world he called the World of Tiers. There he'd gotten the name of Kickaha from a tribe of Indians that lived on one level of the planet, which seemed to be constructed like the tower of Babel or the leaning tower of Pisa. Or whatever.

Indians? Yes, because the Lord of that world, Jadawin, had populated various levels with people he'd abducted from Earth.

It was very confusing. Jadawin hadn't always lived on the home planet of the Lords or in his own private cosmos. For a while he'd been a citizen of Earth, and he hadn't even known it because of amnesia. Then . . . to hell with it. It made McKay's head ache to think about it. But some day, when there was time enough, if he lived long enough, he'd get it all straightened out. If he wasn't completely nuts before then.

IV

KICKAHA SAID, "I'M A HOOSIER APPLEKNOCKER, ANGUS. SO I'M GOING TO get us some fresh fruit. But I need your help. We can't get close because of those tentacles. However, the tree has one weak point in its defense. Like a lot of people, it can't keep its mouth shut.

"So, I'm going to shoot an arrow into its mouth. It may not kill it, but it's going to hurt it. Hopefully, the impact will knock it over. This bow packs a hell of a wallop. As soon as the thing's hit, you run up and throw this axe at a branch. Try to hit a cluster of apples if you can. Then I'll decoy it away from the apples on the ground."

He handed Anana's light throwing axe to McKay.

"What about those?" McKay said, pointing at three trees which were only twenty feet below their intended victim. They were coming slowly but steadily.

"Maybe we can get their apples, too. We need that fruit, Angus. We need the nourishment, and we need the water in them."

"You don't have to explain that," McKay said.

"I'm like the tree. I can't keep my mouth shut," Kickaha said, smiling.

He fitted an arrow to the string, aimed, and released it. It shot true plunging deep into the O-shaped orifice. The plant had just raised the two tentacles to take another step upward and then to fall slightly forward to catch itself on the rubbery extensions. Kickaha had loosed the shaft just as it was off balance. It fell backward, and it lay on its hinder part. The tentacles threshed, but it could not get up by itself. The branches extending from its side prevented its rolling over even if it had been capable, otherwise, of doing so.

Kickaha gave a whoop and put a hand on McKay's shoulder.

"Never mind throwing the axe. The apples are knocked off. Hot damn!"

The three trees below it had stopped for a moment. They moved on up. There had not been a sound from their mouths, but to the two men the many rolling eyes seemed to indicate some sort of communication. According to Urthona, however, the creatures were incapable of thought. But they did cooperate on an instinctual level, as ants did. Now they were evidently coming to assist their fallen mate.

Kickaha ran ahead of McKay, who had hesitated. He looked behind him. The two male Lords were standing about sixty feet above them. Anana, beamer in hand, was watching, her head moving back and forth to keep all within eye-range.

Urthona had, of course, told McKay to kill Anana and Kickaha if he ever got a chance. But if he hit the redhead from behind with the axe, he'd be shot down by Anana. Besides, he was beginning to think that he had a better chance of survival if he joined up with Anana and Kickaha. Anyway, Kickaha was the only one who didn't treat him as if he was a nigger. Not that the Lords had any feeling for blacks as such. They regarded *everybody* but Lords as some sort of nigger. And they weren't friendly with their own kind.

McKay ran forward and stopped just out of reach of a threshing tentacle. He picked up eight apples, stuffing four in the pockets of his levis and holding two in each hand.

When he straightened up, he gasped. That crazy Kickaha had leaped onto the fallen tree and was now pulling the arrow from the hole. As he raised the shaft, its head dripping with a pale sticky fluid, he was enwrapped by a tentacle around his waist. Instead of fighting it, he rammed his right foot deep into the hole. And he twisted sideways.

The next moment he was flying backward toward McKay, flung by a convulsive motion of the tentacle, no doubt caused by intense pain.

McKay, instead of ducking, grabbed Kickaha and they both went down. The catcher suffered more punishment than the caught, but for a minute or more they both lay on the ground, Kickaha on top of McKay. Then the redhead rolled off and got to his feet.

He looked down at McKay. "You okay?"

McKay sat up and said, "I don't think I broke anything."

"Thanks. If you hadn't softened my fall, I might have broken my back. Maybe. I'm pretty agile. Man, there's real power in those tentacles."

Anana was with them by then. She cried, "Are you hurt, Kickaha?"

"No. Black Angus here, he seems okay, too."

McKay said, "Black Angus? Why, you son of a bitch!"

Kickaha laughed. "It's an inevitable pun. Especially if you've been raised on a farm. No offense, McKay."

Kickaha turned. The three advance scouts were no closer. The swelling hill had steepened its slopes, making it even more difficult for them to maintain their balance. The horde behind them was also stalled.

"We don't have to retreat up the hill," Kickaha said. "It's withdrawing for us."

However, the slope was becoming so steep that, if its rate of change continued, it would precipitate everybody to the bottom. The forty-five degree angle to the horizontal could become ninety degrees within fifteen minutes.

"We're in a storm of matter-change," Kickaha said. "If it blows over quickly, we're all right, if not . . ."

The tree's tentacles were moving feebly. Apparently, Kickaha's foot had injured it considerably. Pale fluid oozed out of its mouth.

Kickaha picked up the axe that McKay had dropped. He went to the tree and began chopping at its branches. Two strokes per limb sufficed to sever them. He cut at the tentacles, which were tougher. Four chops each amputated these.

He dropped the axe and lifted one end of the trunk and swung it around so that it could be rolled down the slope.

Anana said, "You're wasting your energy."

Kickaha said, "Waiting to see what's going to happen burns up more energy. At this moment, anyway. There's a time for patience and a time for energy."

He placed himself at the middle of the trunk and pushed it. It began rolling slowly, picked up speed, and presently, flying off a slight hump, flew into a group of trees. These fell backward, some rolling, breaking their branches, others flying up and out as if shot out of a cannon.

The effect was incremental and geometrical. When it was done, at least five hundred of the things lay in a tangled heap in the ravine at the foot of the slope. Not one could get up by itself. It looked like the results of a combination of avalanche and flood.

"It's a log jam!" Kickaha said.

No log jam, however, on Earth featured the wavings of innumerable octopus-tentacles. Nor had any forest ever hastened to the aid of its stricken members.

"Birnam Wood on the march," Kickaha said.

Neither Anana nor McKay understood the reference, but they were too tired and anxious to ask him to explain it.

By now the humans were having a hard time keeping from falling down the slope. They clung to the grass while the three advance guards slid down on their "backs" toward the mess in the hollow at the base.

"I'm getting down," Kickaha said. He turned and began sliding down on the seat of his pants. The others followed him. When the friction became too great on their buttocks, they dug in their heels to brake. Half way down they had to halt and turn over so their bottoms could cool off. Their trouser seats were worn away in several spots.

"Did you see that water?" Kickaha said. He pointed to his right.

Anana said, "I thought I did. But I assumed it was a mirage of some sort."

"No. Just before we started down, I saw a big body of water that way. It must be about fifteen miles away, at least. But you know how deceiving distances are here."

Directly below them, about two hundred feet away, was the living log jam. The humans resumed their rolling but at an angle across the ever-steepening slope. McKay's helmet, Kickaha's bow and quiver, and Anana's beamer and axe, impeded their movements but they managed. They fell the last ten feet, landing on their feet or on all fours.

The trees paid them no attention. Apparently, the instinct to save their fellows was dominating the need to kill and eat. However, the plants were so closely spaced that there was no room for the five people to get through the ranks.

They looked up the hill. This side was vertical now and beginning to bulge at the top. Hot air radiated from the hill.

"The roots of the grass will keep that overhang from falling right away," Kickaha said. "But for how long? When it does come down, we'll be wiped out."

The plants moved toward the tangle, side by side, the tips of their branches touching. Those nearest the humans moved a little to their right to avoid bumping into them. But the outreaching tentacles made the humans nervous.

After five minutes, the apex of the hill was beginning to look like a mushroom top. It wouldn't be long before a huge chunk tore loose and fell upon them.

Anana said, "Like it or not, Kickaha, we have to use the beamer."

"You're thinking the same thing I am? Maybe we won't have to cut through every one between us and open ground. Maybe those things burn."

Urthona said, "Are you crazy? We could get caught in the fire!"

"You got a better suggestion?"

"Yes. I think we should adjust the beamer to cutting and try to slice our way out."

"I don't think there's enough charge left to do that," Anana said. "We'd find ourselves in the middle of this mess. The plants might attack us then. We'd be helpless."

"Burn a couple," Kickaha said. "But not too near us."

Anana rotated the dial in the inset at the bottom of the grip. She aimed the weapon at the back of a tree five yards to her right. For a few seconds there was no result. Then the bark began smoking. Ten seconds later, it burst into flames. The plant did not seem immediately aware of what was happening. It continued waddling toward the tangle. But those just behind stopped. They must have smelled the smoke, and now their survival instinct—or program—was taking over.

Anana set three others on fire. Abruptly, the nearest ranks behind the flaming plants toppled. Those behind them kept on moving, rammed into them, and knocked a number down.

The ranks behind these were stopped, their tentacles waving. Then, as if they were a military unit obeying a soundless trumpet call to retreat, they turned. And they began going as fast as they could in the opposite direction.

The blazing plants had stopped walking, but their frantically thrashing tentacles showed that they were aware of what was happening. The flames covered their trunks, curled and browned the leaves, shot off from the leaf-covered stems projecting from the tops of the trunks. Their dozen eyes burned, melted, ran like sap down the trunk, hissed away in the smoke.

One fell and lay like a Yule log in a fireplace. A second later, the other two crashed. Their legs moved up and down, the broad round heels striking the ground.

The stink of burning wood and flesh sickened the humans.

But those ahead of the fiery plants had not known what was happening. The wind was carrying both the smoke and the pheromones of panic away from them. They continued to the jam until the press of bodies stopped them. Those in the front ranks were trying to pull up the fallen, but the lack of room prevented them.

"Burn them all!" Red Orc shouted, and he was seconded by his brother, Urthona.

"What good would that do?" Kickaha said, looking disgustedly at them. "Besides, they do feel pain, even if they don't make a sound. Isn't that right, Urthona?"

"No more than a grasshopper would," the Lord said.

"Have you ever been a grasshopper?" Anana said.

Kickaha started trotting, and the others followed him. The passage opened was about twenty feet broad, widening as the retreaters moved slowly away. Suddenly, McKay shouted, "It's falling!"

They didn't need to ask what *it* was. They sprinted as fast as they could. Kickaha, in the lead, was quickly left behind. His legs still hurt, and the pain in his chest increased. Anana took his hand and pulled him along.

A crash sounded behind them. Just in front of them a gigantic ball of greasy earth mixed with rusty grass-blades had slammed into the ground. It was a piece broken off and thrown upward by the impact. It struck so closely that they could not stop. Both plunged into it and for a moment felt the oily earth and the scratch of the blades. But the mass was soft enough to absorb the energy of their impact, to give way somewhat. It was not like running into a brick wall.

They got up and went around the fragment, which was about the size of a one-car garage. Kickaha spared a glance behind him. The main mass had struck only a few yards behind them. Sticking out of its front were a few branches, tentacles, and kicking feet.

They were safe now. He stopped, and Anana also halted.

The others were forty feet ahead of them, staring at the great pile of dirt that ringed the base of the hill. Even as they watched, more of the mushrooming top broke off and buried the previous fallen mass.

Perhaps a hundred of the trees had survived. They were still waddling away in their slow flight.

Kickaha said, "We'll snare us some of the trees in their rear ranks. Knock off some more apples. We're going to need them to sustain us until we can get to that body of water."

Though they were all shaken, they went after the trees at once. Anana threw her axe and McKay his helmet. Presently they had more fruit than they could carry. Each ate a dozen, filling their bellies with food and moisture.

Then they headed toward the water. They hoped they were going in the right direction. It was so easy to lose their bearings in a world of no sun and constantly changing landscape. A mountain used as a mark could become a valley within one day.

Anana, walking by Kickaha's side, spoke softly.

"Drop back."

He slowed down, with no reluctance at all, until the others were forty feet ahead. "What is it?"

She held up the beamer so that he could see the bottom of the grip.

The dial in the inset was flashing a red light. She turned the dial, and the light ceased.

"There's just enough charge left for one cutting beam lasting three seconds at a range of sixty feet. Of course, if I just use mild burning or stun power, the charge will last longer."

"I don't think they'd try anything against us if they did know about it. They need us to survive even more than we need them. But when—if —we ever find Urthona's home, then we'd better watch our backs. What bothers me is that we may need the beamer for other things."

He paused and stared past Anana's head.

"Like them."

She turned her head.

Silhouetted on top of a ridge about two miles away was a long line of moving objects. Even at this distance and in this light, she could see that they were a mixture of large animals and human beings.

"Natives," he said.

U

THE THREE MEN HAD STOPPED AND WERE LOOKING SUSPICIOUSLY AT
them. When the two came up to them, Red Orc greeted them.

"What the hell are you two plotting?"

Kickaha laughed. "It's sure nice traveling with you paranoiacs. We
were discussing that," and he pointed toward the ridge.

McKay groaned and said, "What next?"

Anana said, "Are all the natives hostile to strangers?"

"I don't know," Urthona said. "I do know that they all have very
strong tribal feelings. I used to cruise around in my flier and observe
them, and I never saw two tribes meet without conflict of some kind. But
they have no territorial aggressions. How could they?"

Anana smiled at Urthona. "Well, Uncle, I wonder how they'd feel if
you were introduced to them as the Lord of this world. The one who
made this terrible place and abducted their ancestors from Earth."

Urthona paled, but he said, "They're used to this world. They don't
know any better."

"Is their lifespan a thousand years, as on Jadawin's world?"

"No. It's about a hundred years, but they don't suffer from disease."

"They must see us," Kickaha said. "Anyway, we'll just keep on
going in the same direction."

They resumed their march, occasionally looking at the ridge. After
two hours, the caravan disappeared over the other side. The ridge had
not changed shape during that time. It was one of the areas in which
topological mutation went at a slower rate.

"Night" came again. The bright red of the sky became streaked with
darker bands, all horizontal, some broader than others. As the minutes

passed, the bands enlarged and became even darker. When they had all merged, the sky was a uniform dull red, angry-looking, menacing.

They were on a flat plain extending as far as they could see. The mountains had disappeared, though whether because they had collapsed or because they were hidden in the darkness, they could not determine. They were not alone. Nearby, but out of reach, were thousands of animals: many types of antelopes, gazelles, a herd of the tuskless elephants in the distance, a small group of the giant moosoids.

Urthona said that there must also be big cats and wild dogs in the neighborhood. But the cats would be leaving, since they had no chance of catching prey on this treeless plain. There were smaller felines, a sort of cheetah, which could run down anything but the ostrich-like birds. None of these was in sight.

Kickaha had tried to walk very slowly up to the antelopes. He'd hoped they would not be alarmed enough to move out of arrow range. They didn't cooperate.

Then, abruptly, a wild chittering swept down from some direction, and there was a stampede. Thousands of hooves evoked thunder from the plain. There was no dust; the greasy earth just did not dry enough for that, except when an area was undergoing a very swift change and the heat drove the moisture out of the surface.

Kickaha stood still while thousands of running or bounding beasts raced by him or even over him. Then, as the ranks thinned, he shot an arrow and skewered a gazelle. Anana, who'd been standing two hundred yards away, ran toward him, her beamer in hand. A moment later he saw why she was alarmed. The chittering noise got louder, and out of the darkness came a pack of long-legged baboons. These were truly quadrupedal, their front and back limbs of the same length, their "hands" in nowise differentiated from their "feet."

They were big brutes, the largest weighing perhaps a hundred pounds. They sped by him, their mouths open, the wicked-looking canines dripping saliva. Then they were gone, a hundred or so, the babies clinging to the long hair on their mothers' backs.

Kickaha sighed with relief as he watched the last merge into the darkness. According to Urthona, they would have no hesitation in attacking humans under certain conditions. Fortunately, when they were chasing the antelopes, they were single-minded. But if they had no success, they might return to try their luck with the group.

Kickaha used his knife to cut up the gazelle. Orc said, "I'm getting sick of eating raw meat! I'm very hungry, but just thinking about that bloody mess makes my stomach boil with acid!"

Kickaha, grinning, offered him a dripping cut.

"You could become a vegetarian. Nuts to the nuts, fruits to the fruits, and a big raspberry to you."

McKay, grimacing, said, "I don't like it either. I keep feeling like the stuff's alive. It tries to crawl back up my throat."

"Try one of these kidneys," Kickaha said. "They're really delicious. Tender, too. Or you might prefer a testicle."

"You really are disgusting," Anana said. "You should see yourself, the blood dripping down your chin."

But she took the proffered testicle and cut off a piece. She chewed on it without expression.

Kickaha smiled. "Not bad, eh? Starvation makes it taste good."

They were silent for a while. Kickaha finished eating first. Belching, he rose with his knife in his hand. Anana gave him her axe, and he began the work of cutting off the horns of the antelope. These were slim straight weapons two feet high. After he had cut them off from the skull, he stuck them in his belt.

"When we find some branches, we'll make spear shafts and fix these at their tips."

Something gobbled in the darkness, causing all to get to their feet and look around. Presently the gobbling became louder. A giant figure loomed out of the dark red light. It was what Kickaha called a "moa," and it did look like the extinct New Zealand bird. It was twelve feet high and had rudimentary wings, long thick legs with two clawed toes, and a great head with a beak like a scimitar.

Kickaha threw the antelope's head and two of its legs as far as he could. The lesser gravity enabled him to hurl them much further than he could have on Earth. The huge bird had been loping along toward them. When the severed pieces flew through the air, it veered away from them. However, it stopped about forty feet away, looked at them with one eye, then trotted up to the offerings. After making sure that the humans were not moving toward it, it scooped up the legs in its beak, and it ran off.

Kickaha picked up a foreleg and suggested that the others bring along a part, too. "We might need a midnight snack. I wouldn't recommend eating the meat after that. In this heat meat is going to spoil fast."

"Man, I wish we had some water," McKay said. "I'm still thirsty, but I'd like to wash off this blood."

"You can do that when we get to the lake," Kickaha said. "Fortunately, the flies are bedding down for the night. But if morning comes before we get to the water, we're going to be covered with clouds of insects."

They pushed on. They thought they'd covered about ten miles from the hill. Another two hours should bring them to the lake, if they'd estimated its distance correctly. But three hours later, by Anana's watch, they still saw no sign of water.

"It must be further than we thought," Kickaha said. "Or we've not been going in a straight line."

The plain had begun sinking in along their direction of travel. After the first hour, they were in a shallow depression four feet deep, almost a mile wide, and extending ahead and behind as far as they could see. By the end of the second hour, the edges of the depression were just above their heads. When they stopped to rest, they were at the bottom of a trough twelve feet high but now only half a mile wide.

Its walls were steep though not so much they were unclimbable. Not yet, anyway.

What Kickaha found ominous was that all the animal life, and most of the vegetable life, had gotten out of the depression.

"I think we'd better get our tails up onto the plain," he said. "I have a funny feeling about staying here."

Urthona said, "That means walking just that much farther. I'm so tired I can hardly take another step."

"Stay here then," the redhead said. He stood up. "Come on, Anana."

At that moment he felt wetness cover his feet. The others, exclaiming, scrambled up and stared around. Water, looking black in the light, was flowing over the bottom. In the short time after they'd become aware of it, it had risen to their ankles.

"Oh, oh!" Kickaha said. "There's an opening to the lake now! Run like hell, everybody!"

The nearest bank was an eighth of a mile, six hundred and sixty feet away. Kickaha left the antelope leg behind him. The quiver and bow slung over his shoulder, the strap of the instrument case over the other, he ran for the bank. The others passed him, but Anana, once more, grabbed his hand to help him. By the time they had gotten halfway to safety, the stream was up to their knees. This slowed them down, but they slogged through. And then Kickaha, glancing to his left, saw a wall of water racing toward them, its blackish front twice as high as he.

Urthona was the first to reach the top of the bank. He got down on his knees and grabbed one of McKay's hands and pulled him on up

Red Orc grabbed at the black's ankle but missed. He slid back down the slope, then scrambled back up. McKay started to reach down to help, but Urthona spoke to him, and he withdrew his hand.

Nevertheless, Orc climbed over the edge by himself. The water was now up to the waists of Kickaha and Anana. They got to the bank, where she let go of his hand. He slipped and fell back but was up at once. By now he could feel the ground trembling under his feet, sonic forerunners of the vast oncoming mass of water.

He grabbed Anana's legs, boosted her on up, and then began climbing after her. She grabbed his left wrist and pulled. His other hand clutched the grass on the lip of the bank, and he came on up. The other three were standing near her, watching them keenly. He cursed them because they'd not tried to help.

Orc shrugged. Urthona grinned. Suddenly, Urthona ran at Orc and pushed him. Orc screamed and fell sideways. McKay deftly pulled the beamer from Anana's belt. At the same time, he pushed with the flat of his hand against her back. Shrieking, she, too, went into the stream.

Urthona whirled and said, "The Horn of Shambarimen! Give it to me!"

Kickaha was stunned at the sudden sequence of events. He had expected treachery, but not so soon.

"To hell with you!" he said. He had no time to look for Anana, though he could hear her nearby. She was yelling and, though he couldn't see her, must be climbing up the bank. There wasn't a sound from Red Orc.

He lifted the shoulder strap of the instrument case holding the Horn and slipped it down his arm. Urthona grinned again, but he stopped when Kickaha held the case over the water.

"Get Anana up here! Quickly! Or I drop this!"

"Shoot him, McKay!" Urthona yelled.

"Hell, man, you didn't tell me how to operate this thing!" McKay said.

"You utter imbecile!"

Urthona leaped to grab the weapon from the black man. Kickaha swung the instrument case with his left hand behind him and dropped it. Hopefully, Anana would catch it. He dived toward McKay, who, though he didn't know how to fire the beamer, was quick enough to use it as a club. Its barrel struck Kickaha on the top of his head, and his face smacked into the ground.

Half-stunned, he lay for a few seconds, trying to get his legs and arms to moving. Even in his condition, he felt the earth shaking under him. A roaring surged around him, though he did not know if that was the flood or the result of the blow.

It didn't matter. Something hit his jaw as he began to get up. The next he knew, he was in the water.

The coldness brought him somewhat out of his daze. But he was lifted up, then down, totally immersed, fighting for breath, trying to swim. Something smashed into him—the bottom of the channel, he realized dimly—and then he was raised again. Tumbling over and over, not knowing which way was up or down, and incapable of doing anything about it if he had known, he was carried along. Once more he was brought hard against the bottom. This time he was rolled along. When he thought that he could no longer hold his breath—his head roared, his lungs ached for air, his mouth desperately wanted to open—he was shot upward.

For a moment his head cleared the surface, and he sucked in air. Then he was plunged downward and something struck his head.

VI

KICKAHA AWOKE ON HIS BACK. THE SKY WAS BEGINNING TO TAKE ON horizontal bands of alternating dark-red and fiery-red. It was "dawn."

He was lying in water which rose halfway up his body. He rolled over and got to all-fours. His head hurt abominably, and his ribs felt as if he'd gone twelve rounds in a boxing match. He stood up, weaving somewhat, and looked around. He was on shore, of course. The roaring wave had carried him up and over the end of the channel and then retreated, leaving him here with other bodies. These were a dozen or so animals that had not gotten out of the channel in time.

Nearby was a boulder, a round-shaped granite rock the size of a house. It reminded him of the one in the clearing in Anana's world. In this world there were no rock strata such as on Earth. But here were any number of small stones and occasionally boulders, courtesy of the Lord of the lavalite planet, Urthona.

He remembered Anana's speculation that some of these could conceal "gates." With the proper verbal or tactile code, these might be opened to give entrance into Urthona's castle somewhere on this world. Or to other pocket universes. Urthona, of course, would neither verify nor deny this speculation.

If he had the Horn of Shambarimen, he could sound the sequence of seven notes to determine if the rock did contain a gate. He didn't have it. It was either lost in the flood or Anana had gotten up the bank with it. If the latter had happened, Urthona now had the Horn.

A mile beyond the boulder was a mountain. It was conical, the side nearest him lower than the other, revealing a hollow. It would not be a volcano, since these did not exist here. At the moment, it did not seem to be changing shape.

There were tall hills in the distance, all lining the channel. Most of the plain was gone, which meant that the mutations had taken place at an accelerating speed.

His bow and quiver were gone, torn from him while he was being scraped against the channel bottom. He still had his belt and hunting knife, however.

His shirt was missing. The undershirt was only a rag. His trousers had holes and rips, and his shoes had departed.

Woozily, he went to the edge of the water and searched for other bodies. He found none. That was good, since it gave him hope, however slight, that Anana had survived. It wasn't likely, but if he could survive, she might.

Though he felt better, he was in no mood to whistle while he worked. He cut a leg off an antelope and skinned it. Hordes of large black green-headed flies settled on the carcass and him and began working. The bite of one fly was endurable, but a hundred at once made him feel as if he were being sandpapered all over. However, as long as he kept moving he wasn't covered by them. Every time he moved an arm or turned his head or shifted his position, he was relieved of their attack. But they zoomed back at once and began crawling, buzzing, and biting.

Finally, he was able to walk off with the antelope leg over one shoulder. Half of the flies stayed behind to nibble on the carcass. The others decided after a while that the leg he carried was more edible and also not as active. Still, he had to bat at his face to keep them from crawling over his eyes or up his nose.

Kickaha vented some of his irritation by cursing the Lord of this world. When he'd made this world and decreed its ecosystems, did he have to include flies?

It was a question that had occurred more than once to the people of Earth.

Despite feeling that he'd had enough water to last him a lifetime, he soon got thirsty. He knelt down on the channelbank and scooped up the liquid. It was fresh. According to Urthona, even the oceans here were drinkable. He ate some meat, wishing that he could get hold of fruit or vegetables to balance his diet.

The next day, some mobile plants came along. These were about six feet high. Their trunks bore spiral red-and-white-and-blue stripes, and some orange fruit dangled from their branches. Unlike the plants he'd encountered the day before, these had legs with knees. They lacked tentacles, but they might have another method of defense.

Fortunately, he was cautious about approaching them. Each plant had a large hole on each side, situated halfway down the length. He neared one that was separated from the others, and as he did so, it turned to present one of the holes. The thing had no eyes, but it must have had keen hearing. Or, for all he knew, it had a sonic transceiver, perhaps on the order of a bat's.

Whatever its biological mechanisms, it turned as he circled it. He took a few more steps toward it, then stopped. Something dark appeared in the hole, something pulsed, then a black-red mass of flesh extruded. In the center was a hole, from which, in a few seconds, protruded a short pipe of cartilage or bony material.

It looked too much like a gun to him. He threw himself down on the ground, though it hurt his ribs and head when he did so. There was a popping sound, and something shot over his head. He rolled to one side, got up, and ran after the missile. It was a dart made of bone, feathered at one end, and sharp enough to pierce flesh at the other. Something green and sticky coated the point.

The plants were carnivorous, unless the compressed-air propelled dart was used only for self-defense. This didn't seem likely.

Staying out of range, Kickaha moved around the plants. The one who'd shot at him was taking in air with loud gulping sounds. The others turned as he circled.

They had neither eyes nor tentacles. But they could "see" him, and they must have some way of getting the meat of their prey into their bodies for digestion. He'd wait and find out.

It didn't take long. The plants moved up to the now-rotting carcasses of the antelopes and gazelles. The first to get there straddled the bodies and then sat down on them. He watched for a while before he understood just how they ate. A pair of flexible lips protruded from the bottom of the trunks and tore at the meat. Evidently, the lips were lined with tiny but sharp teeth.

Urthona had not mentioned this type of flesh-eating tree. Maybe he hadn't done so because he was hoping that Kickaha and Anana would venture within range of the poison-tipped darts.

Kickaha decided to move on. He had recovered enough to walk at a fairly fast pace. But first he needed some more weapons.

It wasn't difficult to collect them. He would walk to just within range of a plant, run toward it a few steps, and then duck down. The maneuvers caused him some pain, but they were worth it. After collecting a dozen darts, he cut off a piece of his trousers with his knife, and wrapped the missiles in it. He stuck the package in his rear pocket, and, waving a jaunty thanks to the plants, started along the channel.

By now the area was beginning to fill up with animals. They'd scented the water, come running, and were drinking their fill. He went around a herd of thirty elephants which were sucking up the water into their trunks, then squirting it into their mouths. Some of the babies were swimming around and playing with each other. The leader, a big mother, eyed him warily but made no short threatening charges.

These tuskless pachyderms were as tall as African elephants but longer-legged and less massively bodied.

A half an hour later, he came across a herd attacking a "grove" of the missile-shooting plants. These spat the tiny darts into the thick hides of the elephants, which ignored them. Apparently the poison did not affect them. The adults rammed into the plants, knocked them over, and then began stripping the short branches with their trunks. After that the plants were lifted by the trunks and stuck crosswise into the great mouths. The munching began, the giant molars crushing the barky bodies until they were severed. The elephant then picked up one of the sections and masticated this. Everything, the vegetable and the protein parts, went down the great throats.

The young weaned beasts seized the fallen parts and ate these.

Some of the plants waddled away unpursued by the elephants. These became victims to a family of the giant moosoids, which also seemed impervious to the darts' poison. Their attackers, which looked like blue-haired, antlerless Canadian moose, tore the fallen plants apart with their teeth.

Kickaha, who was able to get closer to them than to the pachyderms, noted that the moosoids were careful about one thing. When they came to an organ which he supposed contained the darts, they pushed it aside. Everything else, including the fleshy-looking legs, went into their gullets.

Kickaha waited until he could grab one of the sacs. He cut it open and found a dozen darts inside it, each inside a tubule. He put these into the cloth, and went on his way.

Several times families of lion-sized rusty-colored sabertooth cats crossed his path. He discreetly waited until they had gone by. They saw him but were not, for the moment at least, interested in him. They also ignored the hoofed beasts. Evidently, their most immediate concern was water.

A pack of wild dogs trotted near him, their red tongues hanging out, their emerald eyes glowing. They were about two and a half feet tall, built like cheetahs, spotted like leopards.

Once he encountered a family of kangaroo-like beasts as tall as he

Their heads, however, looked like those of giant rabbits and their teeth were rodentine. The females bore fleshy hair-covered pouches on their abdomens; the heads of the young "rabaroos" stuck out of the pouches.

He was interested in the animal life, of course. But he also scanned the waterway. Once he thought he saw a human body floating in the middle of the channel, and his heart seemed to turn over. A closer look showed that it was some kind of hairless water animal. It suddenly disappeared, its bilobed tail resembling a pair of human legs held close together. A moment later, it emerged, a wriggling fish between long-whiskered jaws. The prey had four short thick legs, the head of a fish, and the vertical tail-fins of a fish. It uttered a gargling sound.

Urthona had said that all fish were amphibians, except for some that inhabited the stable sea-lands.

All life here, except for the grass, was mobile. It had to be to survive.

An hour later, one of the causes for the locomotive character of life on this world rose above the horizon. The reddish temporary moon moved slowly but when fully in view filled half of the sky. It was not directly overhead, being far enough away for Kickaha to see it edge-on. Its shape was that of two convex lenses placed back to back. A very extended oval. It rotated on its longitudinal axis so slowly that it had not traversed more than two degrees in a horizontal circle within two hours.

Finally, Kickaha quit watching it.

Urthona had said that it was one of the very small splitoffs. These occurred after every twelve major splitoffs. Though it looked huge, it was actually very small, not more than a hundred kilometers long. It seemed so big because it was so close to the surface.

Kickaha's knowledge of physics and celestial objects was limited to what he'd learned in high school, plus some reading of his own. He knew, however, that no object of that mass could go slowly in an orbit so near the planet without falling at once. Not in Earth's universe.

But his ideas of what was possible had been greatly extended when he had been gated into Jadawin's world many years ago. And now that he was in Urthona's world he was getting an even broader education. Different arrangements of space-matter, even of matter-energy conversion, were not only possible, they'd been realized by the Lords.

Some day, Terrestrials, if they survived long enough, would discover this. Then their scientists would make pocket universes in bubbles in space-matter outside of yet paradoxically within Earth's universe. But that would come after the shock of discovering that their extra-solar system astronomy was completely wrong.

How long would it be before the secondary returned to the primary?

Urthona hadn't known; he'd forgotten. But he had said that the fact that they'd seen it every other day meant that they must be near the planet's north pole. Or perhaps the south pole. In any event, the splitoff was making a spiral orbit which would carry it southward or northward, as the case might be.

That vast thing cruising through the skies made Kickaha uneasy. It would soon fall to the main mass. Perhaps its orbit would end in one more passage around the planet. When it came down, it would do swiftly. Urthona had said that he did remember that, once it came within twelve thousand feet of the surface, it descended at about a foot every two seconds. A counterrepulsive force slowed its fall so that its impact would not turn it and the area beneath and around it into a fiery mass. Indeed, the final moment before collision could be termed an "easing" rather than a crash.

But there would be a release of energy. Hot air would roar out from the fallen body, air hot enough to fry any living thing fifty miles away. And there would be major earthquakes.

There would be animals and birds and fish and plants on the moon, life forms trapped on it when the splitoff occurred. Those on the underside would be ground into bits and the bits burned. Those on the upper surface would have a fifty-fifty chance of surviving, if they weren't near the edges.

Urthona had said, however, that the splitoff masses never fell in the neighborhood of the oceans. These were in a relatively stable area; the changes in the land surrounding them were slower.

Kickaha hoped that he was near one of the five oceans.

Of all the manifestations of life, the aerial was the most noticeable. He had passed at least a million birds and winged mammals, and the sky was often blackened by flocks that must have numbered hundreds of thousands. These included many birds that had surely been brought in from Earth. There were some, also, that looked just like those he'd known in Jadawin's world. And many were so strange, often grotesque, that he supposed their ancestors had been made in Urthona's biolabs.

Wherever they came from, they were a noisy bunch—as on Earth. Their cawings, croakings, screams, pipings, warblings, whistlings, chatterings filled the air. Some were fish-eaters, either diving into the water from a height or surface swimmers who plunged after fish or frog-like creatures. Others settled down on the elephants and moosoids and pecked at parasites. Others picked food from the teeth of enormous crocodiloids. Many settled down on the branches of various plants and ate the fruit or seeds. The trees did not object to this. But sometimes the weight of the birds was so heavy that a plant would fall over, and the birds, squawking and screaming, would soar up from the fallen like smoke from a burning log.

The tentacled plants would hasten to lift their helpless fellows upright again. The untentacled were left to their fate. More often than not this was being devoured by the pachyderms and moosoids.

Three hours passed, and the menacing mass above him became tiny. It was the only thing on this world that threw a shadow, and even that was pale compared to the shades of Earth. Physically pale, that is. The emotional shadow it cast, the anxiety and near-panic, was seldom matched by anything in Kickaha's native world. A smoking volcano, a violent earthquake, a roaring hurricane were the only comparable events.

However, he had carefully observed the reactions of the birds and animals while it was overhead. They didn't seem to be disturbed by it. This meant to him they somehow "knew" that it posed no threat. Not, at least, this time.

Had Urthona given them the instinctive mechanism to enable them to predict the area in which the splitoff would fall? If he had, then that meant that there was a pattern to the splitting off and the merging of the bodies. However, what about those creatures not made in his biolabs: those which had been brought in from other universes? They hadn't been here long enough for evolution to develop any such instinctive knowledge.

Maybe the importees observed the natives and took their cue from these.

He would ask Urthona about that when he found him. If he found him. Shortly before he killed him.

Kickaha cut off some slices of the antelope leg, and, brushing away the flies, ate the meat. It was getting strong, so he threw the rest of the limb away after his belly was satisfied. A number of scarlet crows settled down on it at once. These had gotten no more than a few pieces when two large purple green-winged eagles with yellow legs drove them off.

Watching them made him wonder where birds laid their eggs. In this world, no nest would be safe. A cranny in a mountain side could be closed up or on a plain in a few days.

He had plenty of time to observe, to get the answers to his questions about the zoology of this world. If he lived long enough.

"Day" passed while he walked steadily along the edge of the channel. Near "dusk" it had begun widening. He drove off some birds from some fruit fallen from a plant and ate the half-devoured "papayas." In the middle of the "night" some smaller varieties of the rabaroos hopped by him, two long-legged baboons after them. He threw his knife into the neck of a rabaroo male as it went by. The creature fell over, causing the baboons to return for this easier prey. Kickaha pulled the knife out and threatened the primates. They barked and showed their wicked-looking canines. One tried to get behind him while the other made short charges at him.

Kickaha didn't want to tangle with them if he could help it. He cut off the legs of the rabaroo and walked away, leaving the rest to the baboons. They were satisfied with the arrangement.

Finding a safe place to sleep was almost impossible. Not only was the night alive with prowling predators, the spreading water was a menace. Twice he awoke inches deep in it and had to retreat several hundred feet to keep from drowning. Finally, he walked to the base of the nearest mountain, which had been only a hill when he had first sighted it. There were several large boulders on its slope. He lay down just above one. When the slope got too steep, the boulder would roll. The movement would awaken him—he hoped. Also, most of the action seemed to be taking place in the valley. The big cats, dogs, and baboons were out, trying to sneak up on or run down the hoofed and hopping beasts.

Kickaha awoke frequently as roars, barks, growls, and screams came up from the valley. None of them seemed to be near, though. Nor was he sure that he hadn't dreamed some of the noises.

Shortly before "dawn" he sat up, gasping, his heart thudding. There was a rumbling noise. Earthquake? No, the ground was not trembling. Then he saw that the boulder had rolled away. It wasn't the only one. About half a dozen were hurtling down the slope, which was ever steeper now, shooting off swellings, thumping as they hit the surface again, gathering speed, headed toward the valley floor.

That floor, however, was now all water. The only beasts there were a few big cats, up to their bellies in water, staying only to eat as much of their kills as possible before they were forced to take off. There were millions of birds, though, among them an estimated two hundred thousand long-legged flamingoes, green instead of pink like their Terrestrial counterparts. They were eating voraciously in the boiling water. Boiling not with heat but with life. Fish by the millions.

It was time to get up even if he had not had enough rest. The slope was tilting so that he would soon be sent rolling down it.

He scrambled down and went into the water up to his knees and the got down and drank from it. It was still fresh, though muddied by all the activity. One of the flamingoes came scooting through the water, following a trail of something fleeing under the surface. It stopped when Kickaha rose, and it screamed angrily. He ignored it and plunged his knife down. Its point went into the thing the flamingo had been chasing. He brought up a skewered thing which looked like a mud puppy. It did not taste like mud puppy, however. It had a flavor of trout.

Apparently, the water level was not going to rise higher. Not for a while, anyway. After filling his belly and washing his body, he slogged through knee-deep water along the base of the mountain. In an hour he'd gotten by that and was walking on a plain. About "noon" the plain was tilting to one side, about ten degrees to the horizontal, and the water was running down it. Three hours later, it was beginning to tilt the other way. He ate the rest of the mud puppy and threw the bones, with much meat attached, on the ground. Scarlet crows settled down on it to dispute about the tidbits.

The splitoff had not appeared again. He hoped that when it did fall, it would be far far away from him. It would form an enormous pile, a suddenly born mountain range of super-Himalayan proportions, on the surface. Then, according to Urthona, within several months it would have merged with the larger mass, itself changing shape during the process.

Some months later, another splitoff would occur somewhere else. But this would be a major one. Its volume would be about one-sixteenth of that of the planet.

God help those caught on it at liftoff. God help those on it when it returned to the mother planet.

One-sixteenth of this world's mass! A wedge-shaped mass the thin edge of which would rip out of the planet's center. Roughly, over 57,700,000,000 cubic kilometers.

He shuddered. Imagine the cataclysms, the earthquakes, the staggeringly colossal hole. Imagine the healing process as the walls of the hole slid down to fill it and the rest of the planet moved to compensate. It was unimaginable.

It was a wonder that any life at all remained. Yet there was plenty. Just before "dusk" he came through a pass between two monolithic mountains that had not changed shape for a day. The channel lay in its center, the surface of the water a few inches below the tops of the banks. There was room on both sides of the channel for ten men abreast. He walked along the channel looking now and then at the towering wall of the mountain on the right.

Its base curved slowly, the channel also curving with it. He didn't want to settle down for the night, since there was little room to avoid any of the big predators. Or, for that matter, to keep from being trampled if a herd of the hoofed beasts was stampeded.

He pushed on, slowing now and then to get as near the mountain as possible when big cats or wild dogs came along. Fortunately, they paid him no attention. It could be that they had run into human beings before and so dreaded them. Which said much for the dangerousness of Homo sapiens here. Probably, though, they found him to be a strange thing and so were wary.

In any event, they might not be able to resist the temptation to attack him if they found him sleeping on the ground. He pushed on. By dawn he was staggering with weariness. His legs hurt. His belly told him it needed more food.

Finally, the mountain ceased. The channel ran almost straight for as far as he could see. He had a great plain to cross before reaching a row of conical mountains in the far distance. There were many plants here, few of them now moving, and herds of animals and the ubiquitous birds. At the moment all seemed peaceful. If there were predators, they were quiet.

The channel ran straight for as far as he could see. He wondered how long it was from its beginning to its end. He'd assumed that the flood had carried him for perhaps ten miles. But now it was apparent that he could have been borne for fifty miles. Or more.

The earth had suddenly split on a straight line as if the edge of an axe of a colossus bigger than a mountain had smashed into the ground. Water had poured from the sea into the trench, and he'd been carried on its front to the end of the channel and deposited there. He was very lucky not to have been ground into bits on the bottom or drowned.

No, he hadn't experienced great luck. He'd experienced a miracle.

He left the mountain pass and started across the plain. But he stopped after a hundred yards. He turned toward the hoofbeats that had suddenly alerted him.

Around the corner of the mountain to his right, concealed until then by a bulge of the mountain-wall, came a score of moosoids. Men were mounted on them, men who carried long spears.

Aware that he now saw them, they whooped and urged their beasts into a gallop.

For him to run was useless. They also serve who only stand and wait. However, this wasn't a tennis match.

VII

THE MOOSOIDS WERE OF THE SMALLER VARIETY, A TRIFLE LARGER THAN a thoroughbred horse. Like their wild cousins, they were of different colors, roan, black, blue, chestnut, and piebald. They were fitted with reins, and their riders were on leather saddles with stirrups.

The men were naked from the waist up, wearing leather tousers which kept their legs from chafing. Some of them had feathers affixed to their long hair, but they were not Amerindians. Their skins were too light, and they were heavily bearded. As they got close enough, he saw that their faces bore tribal scars.

Some of the spears were poles the ends of which had been sharpened and fire-hardened. Others were tipped with flint or chert or antelope horns or lion teeth. There were no bows, but some carried stone axes and heavy war boomerangs in the belts at their waists. There were also round leather-covered shields, but these hung from leather strings tied to the saddle. Evidently they thought they didn't need them against Kickaha. They were right.

The first to arrive halted their beasts. The others spread out and round him.

Their chief, a gray-haired stocky man, urged his animal closer to Kickaha. The moosoid obeyed, but his wide rolling eyes showed he didn't like the idea.

By then the main body of the tribe was beginning to come from round the bend of the mountain. They consisted of armed outriders and a caravan of women, children, dogs, and moosoids drawing travois in which were piled heaps of skins, gourds, wood poles, and other materials.

The chief spoke to Kickaha in an unknown language. Of course. Not expecting them to understand him, Kickaha used test phrases in twenty different languages, Lord, English, French, German, Tishquetmoac, Hrowakas, the degraded High German of Dracheland, several Half-Horse Lakota dialects, a Mycenaean dialect, and some phrases of Latin, Greek, Italian, and Spanish he knew.

The chief didn't understand any of them. That was to be expected, though Kickaha had hoped that if their ancestors came from Earth they might speak a tongue that he at least could identify.

One good thing had happened. They hadn't killed him at once.

But they could intend to torture him first. Knowing what the tribes on the Amerind level of Jadawin's world did to their captives, he wasn't very optimistic.

The chief waved his feathered spear and said something to two men. These got down off their beasts and approached him warily. Kickaha smiled and held out his hands, palms up.

The two didn't smile back. Their spears ready for thrusting, they moved toward him slowly.

If Kickaha had been in his usual excellent physical condition, he would have tried to make a run for the nearest moosoid with an empty saddle. Even then, he would have had only one chance in twenty of fighting his way through the ring. The odds had been heavier against him in past situations, but then he had felt capable of anything. Not now. He was too stiff and too tired.

Both men were shorter than he, one being about five feet six inches tall and the other about an inch higher. The bigger man held his spear in one hand while the other reached out. Kickaha thought that he wanted him to hand his knife to him.

Shrugging, Kickaha slowly obeyed. There was a second when he thought of throwing the knife into the man's throat. He could grab the spear, snatch the knife out, run for . . . No, forget it.

The man took the knife and backed away. It was evident from his expression, and those of the others, that he had never seen metal before.

The chief said something. The man ran to him and gave him the knife. The gray-headed graybeard turned it over, gingerly felt its edge with his palm, and then tried it on a leather string holding his warshield.

All exclaimed when the string fell apart so easily.

The chief asked Kickaha something. Probably, he wanted to know where his captive had gotten it.

Kickaha wasn't backward about lying if it would save his life. He pointed at the mountains toward which he had been traveling.

The chief looked as if he were straining his mind. Then he spoke again, and the two dismounted men tied Kickaha's hands in front of him with a leather cord. The chief spoke again, and the scouts moved on ahead. The chief and the two aides got down off their beasts and waited. In about fifteen minutes, the front of the caravan caught up with them.

The chief seemed to be explaining the situation to his people, making frequent gestures with his spear toward the direction indicated by his captive. There was a babel of excited talk then. Finally, the chief told them to shut up. During this Kickaha had been counting the tribe. Including the scouts, there were about ninety. Thirty men, forty women, and twenty children.

The latter ranged from several babes in arms to preadolescents. The women, like the men, were black- or brown-haired. The general eye color was a light brown. Some had hazel; a few, blue eyes. Some of the women weren't bad-looking. They wore only short kilts of tanned leather. The children were naked and, like their elders, dirty. All stank as if they'd been bathless for a month or so.

Some of the beasts of burden, however, carried big water skins of water. A woman milked a cow during the brief stop.

The travois, in addition to the piles of skins and weapons, carried a form of pemmican. There were no tents, which meant that when it rained the tribe just endured it.

While several men pointed spears at him, he was stripped by others. The chief was given the ragged levis and worn boots. From his expression and the tones of his voice, he had never seen anything like them before. When he tried to put on the levis, he found that his wide buttocks and bulging paunch would not accommodate them. He solved this problem by slitting them with the knife around the waist. The boots were too large for his feet, but he wore them anyway.

Finding the package of poison darts in the rear pocket of the levis, he passed them out to men whose spears lacked flint or chert tips. These tied the darts on the ends with rawhide cords and then had a good time play-jabbing at each other, laughing as they leaped away.

The only possessions left to Kickaha were his holey and dirty jockey shorts.

A big female moosoid was pulled out from the herd, fitted with reins and a saddle, and Kickaha was urged to mount it. He did so, holding the reins in his hands. The chief then said something, and a man tied the ends of a long thong under the beast's belly to Kickaha's ankles. The caravan started up then, an old woman—the only old person he saw

—blowing a strange tune on a flute made from a long bone. Probably it was the legbone of a moa.

The ride lasted about an hour. Then the tribe camped—if you call such a simple quick procedure camping—by the channel. While Kickaha sat on the animal, ignored by everybody except a single guard, the people took their turn bathing.

Kickaha wondered if they meant to keep him on the moosoid until they moved on. After half an hour, during which time he was savagely bitten by a horde of blue flies, his guard decided to untie the leg thongs. Kickaha got down stiffly and waited. The guard leaned on his spear waiting until he was relieved to take a bath.

Kickaha gestured that he would like a drink of water. The guard, a slim youth, nodded. Kickaha went to the edge of the channel and got down on his knees to scoop up water with his hands. The next moment, he was in the water, propelled by a kick on his buttocks.

He came up to find everybody laughing at this splendid joke.

Kickaha swam forward until his feet touched the bottom. He turned around and cast one longing glance at the other side. It lay about three hundred feet away. He could get over to the opposite shore even with his hands tied before him. His pursuers could swim or ride across on swimming beasts. But he could beat them. If only there had been a wood nearby or a mountain, he would have tried for escape. However, there was a plain about two miles broad there. His captors would ride him down before he got to it.

Reluctantly, he hauled himself onto the bank. He stood up, looking expressionlessly at the youth. That one laughed and said something to the others, and they broke into uproarious laughter. Whatever it was he said, it wasn't complimentary to the prisoner.

Kickaha decided he might as well start his language lessons now. He pointed at the spear and asked its name. At first the youth didn't understand him. When he caught on, he said, *"Gabol."*

Gabol, as it turned out, was not a generic term. It meant a spear with a fire-hardened tip. A spear with a stone tip was a *baros;* with a antelope-horn tip, a *yava;* with a lion-tooth tip, a *grados.*

He learned later that there was no word for humankind. The trib called itself by a word which meant, simply, The People. Other huma beings were The Enemy. Children, whatever their sex, were summe under one word which meant "unformed." Adult males were disti guished by three terms: one for a warrior who had slain an enem tribesman, one for a youth who had not yet been blooded, and a thi for a sterile man. It made no difference if the sterile man had killed b enemy. He was still a *tairu.* If, however, he managed to steal a child from another tribe, then he was a full *wiru,* a blooded warrior.

Women were in three classes. If she had borne a child, she was in the top class. If she was sterile but had killed two enemy, male or female, she was in the second rank. If sterile and unblooded, she was a *shonka,* a name which originally was that of some kind of low animal.

Two days and nights passed while the tribe traveled leisurely along the channel. This was, except for the great conical mountains far ahead of them, the only permanent feature of the landscape. Sometimes it broadened and shallowed, sometimes narrowed and deepened. But it continued to run straight as an Indian chief's back for as far as the eye could see in either direction.

Hunting parties went out while the rest of the tribe either camped or moved at the rate of a mile an hour. Sometimes the younger women went with the men. Unlike the primitives who lived on the World of Tiers, the women of this tribe were not engaged from dawn to dusk in making artifacts, growing food, preparing meals, and raising children. They tended herd and shared the child-raising, and sometimes they fashioned wooden poles into spears or carved boomerangs. Otherwise, they had little to do. The stronger of the young women went hunting and, sometimes, on the raiding parties.

The hunters returned with antelope, gazelle, ostrich, and moa meat. Once, a party killed a young elephant which had been separated from its herd. Then the tribe traveled two miles across the plain to the carcass. There they stripped it to the bone, gorging on the raw meat until their bellies looked like balloons.

The cutting of the meat was done with flint or chert knives. Kickaha would find out that these rare stones came from nodules which occasionally appeared when the earth opened up to deliver them. Except for the boulders, these were the only solid mineral known.

The diet included fruit and nuts from various trees. These were usually knocked off by the boomerangs as the hunters rode out of range of tentacle or dart.

Kickaha, though an enthusiastic and quick-learning linguist, took more than a week to master the rudiments of the tribe's speech. Though the tribe had a technology that an Ice Age caveman would have ranked as low, they spoke a complex language. The vocabulary was not great, but the shades of meaning, mostly indicated by subtle internal vowel changes, baffled his ear at first. It also had a feature he'd never encountered before. The final consonant of a word could alter the initial consonant of the succeeding word in a phrase. There was a rule to learn about this, but, as in all living languages, the rule had many exceptions. Besides, the possible combinations were many.

Kickaha thought he remembered reading something about a similar consonant change in the Celtic languages. How similar, he didn't know.

Sometimes he wondered if the Thana, as the tribe called itself, could be descended from ancient Celts. If they were, however, no modern Celt would have understood them. In the course of many thousand years, the speech must have changed considerably. A male moosoid, used for riding, for instance, was called a *hikwu*. Could that possibly be related to the ancient Latin *equus?* If he remembered his reading, done so many years ago, *equus* was related to a similar word in Celtic and also to the Greek *hippos*.

He didn't know. It didn't really matter, except as an item of curiosity. Anyway, why would the original tribe brought in here have named a moose after a horse? That could be because the *hikwu* functioned more like a horse than any animal the tribe had encountered.

During the day Kickaha either rode, his hands bound, on a *merk,* a female riding-moosoid, or he lazed around camp. When he was in the saddle, he kept an eye out for signs of Anana. So far, he didn't know the language well enough to ask anybody if they had seen pale strangers like himself or a black man.

The tenth day, they came through a mountain pass which seemed to be a permanent feature. And there, beyond a long slope, beyond a broad plain, was the ocean.

The mountains on this side and the flat land were covered with permanently rooted trees. Kickaha almost cried when he saw them. They were over a hundred feet tall, of a score of genuses, plants like pines, oaks, cottonwoods, many fruit and nut-bearing.

The first question occurring to him was: if this land was unchanging, why didn't the Thana put down their roots here? Why did they roam the evermutating country outside the ocean-ringing peaks?

On the way down, clouds formed, and before they were halfway down the slope, thunder bellowed. The Thana halted, and the chief, Wergenget, conferred with the council. Then he gave the order to turn about and pass beyond the mountains.

Kickaha spoke to Lukyo, a young woman whose personality, not to mention her figure, had attracted him.

"Why are we going back?"

Lukyo looked pale and her eyes rolled like a frightened horse. "We're too early. The Lord's wrath hasn't cooled off yet."

At that moment the first of the lightning struck. A tree two hundr feet away split down the middle, one side falling, one remaining upright. The chief shouted orders to hurry up, but his urging wasn't needed. The retreat almost became a stampede. The moosoids bolted, riders frantically trying to pull them up, the travois bumping up and down, dislodging their burdens. Kickaha and Lukyo were left standing alone. Not quite. A six-year-old child was crying under a tree. Apparently, she had wandered off for a minute, and her parents, who were mounted, were being carried off against their will.

Kickaha managed to pick up the little girl despite the handicap of his bound wrists. He walked as fast as he could with the burden while Lukyo ran ahead of him. More thunder, more strokes of lightning. A bolt crashed behind him, dazzling him. The child threw her arms around his neck and buried her face against his shoulder.

Kickaha swore. This was the worst lightning storm he had ever been in. Yet, despite the danger of the bolts, he would have fled into it. It was his first good chance to escape. But he couldn't abandon the child.

The rain came then, striking with great force. He increased his pace, his head low while water poured over him as if he were taking a shower. The frequent bolts showed that Lukyo, propelled by fear, was drawing ahead of him. Even unburdened and in good physical condition, he might have had trouble keeping up with her. She ran like an Olympic champion.

Then she slipped and fell and slid face down on the wet grass for a few feet uphill. She was up again. But not for long. A crash deafened him; whiteness blinded him. Darkness for a few seconds. A score or more of blasts, all fortunately not as near as the last bolt. He saw Lukyo down again. She was not moving.

When he got near her, he could smell the burned flesh. He put the child down, though she fought against leaving him. Lukyo's body was burned black.

He picked up the little girl and began running as fast as he could. Then, out of the flickering checkerboard of day-turned-night he saw a ghostly figure. He stopped. What the hell? All of a sudden he was in a nightmare. No wonder the whole tribe had fled in panic, forgetting even the child.

But the figure came closer, and now he saw that it was two beings. Vergenget on his *hikwu*. The chief had managed to get control of the beast, and he had come back for them. It must not have been easy for him to conquer his fear. It certainly was difficult for him to keep the moosoid from running away. The poor animal must have thought his master was mad to venture into that bellowing death-filled valley after having escaped from it.

Now Kickaha understood why Wergenget was the chief.

The graybeard stopped his beast, which trembled violently, its upper lip drawn back, its eyes rotating. Kickaha shouted at him and pointed at the corpse. Wergenget nodded that he understood. He lifted up the girl and placed her on the saddle before him. Kickaha fully expected him to take off then. Why should he risk his life and the child's for a stranger?

But Wergenget controlled the *hikwu* until Kickaha could get up behind the chief. Then he turned it and let it go, and the beast was not at all reluctant. Though burdened with the three, it made speed. Presently, they were in the pass. Here there was no rain; the thunder and the lightning boomed and exploded but at a safe distance away.

VIII

Wergenget handed the child to its weeping wailing mother. The father kissed his daughter, too, but his expression was hangdog. He was ashamed because he had allowed his fear to overcome him.

"We stay here until the Lord is through rampaging," the chief said.

Kickaha slid off the animal. Wergenget followed him. For a moment Kickaha thought about snatching the knife from the chief's belt. With it he could flee into a storm where no man dared venture. And he could lose himself in the forest. If he escaped being struck by lightning, he would be so far away the tribe would never find him.

But there was more to his decision not to run for it just now.

The truth was that he didn't want to be alone.

Much of his life, he'd been a loner. Yet he was neither asocial nor antisocial. He'd had no trouble mixing with his playmates, the neighboring farmers' children, when he was a child nor with his peers at the country schoolhouse and community high school.

Because of his intense curiosity, athletic abilities, and linguistic ability, he'd been both popular and a leader. But he was a voracious reader, and, quite often, when he had a choice between recreation with others or reading, he decided on the latter. His time was limited because a farmer's son was kept very busy. Also, he studied hard to get good grades in school. Even at a young age he'd decided he didn't want to be a farmer. He had dreams of traveling to exotic places, of becoming a zoologist or curator of a natural history museum and going to those fabulous places, deepest Africa or South America or Malaya. But that required a Ph.D. and to get that he'd have to have high grades through high school and college. Besides, he liked to learn.

So he read everything he could get his hands on.

His schoolmates had kidded him about "always having his nose stuck in a book." Not nastily and not too jeeringly, since they respected his quick temper and quicker fists. But they did not comprehend his lust for learning.

An outsider, observing him from the ages of seventeen through twenty-two, would not have known that he was often with his peers but not of them. They would have seen a star athlete and superior student who palled around with the roughest, raced around the country roads on a motorcycle, tumbled many girls in the hay, literally, got disgustingly drunk, and once was jailed for running a police roadblock. His parents had been mortified, his mother weeping, his father raging. That he had escaped from jail just to show how easy it was and then voluntarily returned to it had upset them even more.

His male peers thought this was admirable and amusing, his female peers found it fascinating though scarey, and his teachers thought it alarming. The judge, who found him reading Gibbon's *Decline and Fall of the Roman Empire* in his cell, decided that he was just a high-spirited youth with much potentiality who'd fallen among evil companions. The charges were dropped, but Paul was put on unofficial probation by the judge. The young man gave his word that he would behave as a decent respectable citizen should—during the probation period, anyway—and he had kept his word.

Paul seldom left the farm during the probation period. He didn't want to be tempted into evil by those companions whose evil had mostly come from their willingness to follow him into it. Besides, his parents had been hurt enough. He worked, studied, and sometimes hunted in the woods. He didn't mind being alone for long periods. He threw himself into solitariness with the same zest he threw himself into companionship.

And then Mr. and Mrs. Finnegan, perhaps in an effort to straighten him out even more, perhaps in an unconscious desire to hurt him as he'd hurt them, revealed something that shocked him.

He was an adopted child.

Paul was stunned. Like most children, he had gone through a phase when he believed that he was adopted. But he had not kept to the fantasy, which children conceive during periods when they think their parents don't love them. But it was true, and he didn't want to believe it.

According to his step-parents, his real mother was an Englishwoman with the quaint name of Philea Jane Fogg-Fog. Under other circumstances, he would have thought this hilarious. Not now.

Philea Jane's parents were of the English landed gentry, though h great-grandfather had married a Parsi woman. The Parsis, he knew, were Persians who had fled to India and settled there when the Moslems invaded their homeland. So . . . he was actually one-eighth Indian. But it wasn't American Indian among whom his step-mother counted ancestors. It was Asiatic Indian, though only in naturalization. The Parsis usually did not marry their Hindu neighbors.

His mother's mother, Roxana Fogg, was the one who'd picked up the hyphenated name of Fogg-Fog. She'd married a distant relative, an American named Fog. A branch of the Foggs had emigrated to the colony of Virginia in the 1600's. In the early 1800's some of their descendants had moved to the then-Mexican territory of Texas. By then the extra "g" had been dropped from the family name. Paul's maternal grandfather, Hardin Blaze Fog, was born on a ranch in the sovereign state, the Republic of Texas.

Roxana Fogg had married an Englishman at the age of twenty. He died when she was thirty-eight, leaving two children. Two years later she went with her son to Texas to look over some of the extensive ranch property he would inherit when he came of age. She also met some of the relatives there, including the famous Confederate war hero and Western gunfighter, Dustine "Dusty" Edward Marsden Fog. She was introduced to Hardin Blaze Fog, several years younger than herself. They fell in love, and he accompanied her back to England. She got the family's approval, despite his barbarian origins, since she announced she was going to marry him anyway and he was a wealthy shipping magnate. Blaze settled down in London to run the British office. When Roxana was forty-three years old, she surprised everybody, including herself, by conceiving. The baby was named Philea Jane.

Philea Jane Fogg-Fog was born in 1880. In 1900 she married an English physician, Doctor Reginald Syn. He died in 1910 under mysterious circumstances, leaving no children. Philea did not remarry until 1916. She had met in London a handsome well-to-do man from Indiana, Park Joseph Finnegan. The Foggs didn't like him because, one, he was of Irish descent, two, he was not an Episcopalian, and three, he had been seen with various ladies of the evening in gambling halls before he'd asked Philea to marry him. She married him anyway and went to Terre Haute, which her relatives thought was still subject to raids by the redskins.

Park Joseph Finnegan made Philea happy for the first six months, despite her difficulty in adjusting to a small Hoosier town. At least, she lived in a big house, and she suffered for no lack of material things.

Then life became hell. Finnegan resumed his spending of his fortune on women, booze, and poker games. Within a short time he'd lost his fortune, and when he found out his thirty-eight year old wife was pregnant, he deserted her. He announced he was going West to make another fortune, but she never heard from him again.

Too proud and too ashamed to return to England, Philea had gone to work as a housekeeper for a relative of her husband's. It was a terrible comedown for her, but she labored without complaint and kept a British stiff upper lip.

Paul was six months old when the gasoline-burning apparatus used to heat an iron exploded in his mother's face. The house burned down, and the infant would have perished with his mother if a young man had not dashed in through the flames and rescued him.

The relative whose house had burned died of a heart attack shortly after. Paul was scheduled to go to an orphanage. But Ralph Finnegan, a cousin of Park's, a Kentucky farmer, and his wife decided to adopt Paul. His fostermother gave him her maiden family name, Janus, as his middle name.

The revelation had shaken Paul terribly. It was after this that he began to suffer from a sense of loneliness. Or perhaps a sense of having been abandoned. Once he'd learned all the details he wanted to know about his true parents, he never spoke of them again. When he mentioned his parents to others, he spoke only of the man and woman who'd reared him.

Two years after Kickaha learned about his true parents, Mr. Finnegan fell ill with cancer and died in six months. That was grief enough, but three months after the burial, his mother had also fallen victim to the same disease. She took a longer time dying, and now Paul had no time to do anything except farm, attend school, and help take care of her. Finally, after much pain, she had died, the day before he was to graduate from high school.

Mingled with his grief was guilt. In some mysterious fashion, he thought, the shame they'd felt when he'd been arrested had caused the cancer. Considered rationally, the idea did not seem plausible. But guilt often had irrational origins. In fact, there were even times when he wondered if he hadn't somehow been responsible for his real father's having deserted his real mother and for her death.

His plans to go to college and major in zoology or in anthropology—he couldn't make up his mind—had been deferred. The farm had been mortgaged to pay for the heavy medical expenses of his parents, and Paul had to work the farm and take a part-time job in Terre Haute as a car mechanic. Nevertheless, despite the long hours of work, the lack o money, he had some time to express his innate exuberance. He would drop in occasionally at Fisher's Tavern, where some of the old gang still hung out. They'd go roaring off into the night on their motorcycles, their girls riding behind them, and finally end up in Indian Meadow, where there'd be a continuation of the beer blast and some fighting and love-making.

One of the girls wanted him to marry her, but he shied away from that. He wasn't in love with her, and he couldn't see himself spending the rest of his life with a woman with no intellectual interests whatever. Then she got pregnant, though fortunately not by him, and she departed to Chicago for a new life. Shortly thereafter, the gang began to drift apart.

He became alone and lonely again. But he liked to ride a horse wildly through the meadows or his chopper over the country roads. It was a good way to blow off steam.

Meantime, he had visits from an uncle who was a knife-thrower, juggler, and circus acrobat. Paul learned much from him and became proficient at knife-throwing. When he felt gloomy he would go out into the backyard and practice throwing knives at a target. He knew he was working off his depression, guilt, and resentment at the lot cast for him by the fates with this harmless form of mayhem.

Five years went by swiftly. Suddenly, he was twenty-three. The farm still wasn't paid off. He couldn't see himself as a farmer the rest of his life, so he sold the farm at a very small profit. But now it was evident that his hopes of entering college and becoming an anthropologist—he'd decided by then his choice of career—would once more have to be set aside. The United States would be getting into the war in a year or two.

Loving horses so much, he enlisted in the cavalry. To his surprise and chagrin, he soon found himself driving a tank instead. Then there was a three-months' period in officers candidate training school. Though he wasn't a college graduate, he'd taken an examination which qualified him to enter it. Pearl Harbor tilted the nation into the conflict, and eventually he was with the Eighth Army and in combat.

One day, during a brief respite in the advance of Patton's forces, Paul had looked through the ruins of a small museum in a German town he'd helped clean out. He found a curious object, a crescent of some silvery metal. It was so hard that a hammer couldn't dent it or an acetylene torch melt it. He added it to his souvenirs.

Discharged from the Army, he returned to Terre Haute, where he didn't plan to stay long. A few days later, he was called into the office of his lawyer. To his surprise, Mr. Tubb handed him a check for ten thousand dollars.

"It's from your father," the lawyer said.

"My father? He didn't have a pot to pee in. You know that," Paul had said.

"Not the man who adopted you," Mr. Tubb had said. "It's from your real father."

"Where is he?" Paul had said. "I'll kill him."

"You wouldn't want to go where he is," fat old Tubb said. "He's six feet under. Buried in a church cemetery in Oregon. He got religion years ago and became a fire-eating brimstone-drinking hallelujah-shouting revivalist. But the old bastard must've had some conscience left. He willed all his estate to you."

For a minute, Paul thought about tearing up the check. Then he told himself that old Park Finnegan owed him. Much more than this, true. But it was enough to enable him to get his Ph.D.

"I'll take it," he said. "Will the bank cash it if there's spit on it?"

"According to the law, the bank must accept it even if you crapped on it. Have a snort of bourbon, son."

Paul had entered the University of Indiana and rented a small but comfortable apartment off-campus. Paul told a friend of his, a newspaper reporter, about the mysterious crescent he'd found in Germany. The story was in the Bloomington paper and picked up by a syndicate which printed the story nationally. The university physicists, however, didn't seem interested in it.

Three days after the story appeared, a man calling himself Mr. Vannax appeared at Paul's apartment. He spoke English fluently but with a slight foreign accent. He asked to see the crescent; Paul obliged. Vannax became very excited, and he offered ten thousand dollars for the crescent. Paul became suspicious. He pumped the sum up to one hundred thousand dollars. Though Vannax was angry, he said he'd come back in twenty-four hours. Paul knew he had something, but he didn' know what.

"Make it three hundred thousand dollars, and it's yours," Paul said "Since that's such a big sum, I'll give you an additional twenty-fou hours to round up the money.

"But first, you have to tell me what this is all about."

Vannax became so troublesome that Paul forced him to leave. Abou two in the morning, he caught Vannax in his apartment. His crescer was lying on the floor, and so was another.

Vannax had placed the two so that their ends met, forming a circle. He was about to step into the circle.

Paul forced him away by firing a pistol over his head. Vannax backed away, babbling, offering Paul half a million dollars for his crescent.

Following him across the room, Paul stepped into the circle. As he did so, Vannax cried out in panic for him to stay away from the crescents. Too late. The apartment and Vannax disappeared, and Paul found himself in another world.

He was standing in a circle formed by crescents just like those he'd left. But he was in a tremendous palace, as splendid as anything out of the Arabian Nights. This was, literally, on top of the new world to which Paul had been transported. It was the castle of the Lord who'd made the universe of the World of Tiers.

Paul figured out that the crescents formed some sort of "gate," a temporary opening through what he called the "fourth dimension" for lack of a better term. Vannax, he was to discover, was a Lord who'd been stranded in Earth's universe. He'd had one crescent but needed another to make a gate so he could get into a pocket universe.

Paul soon found himself not alone. Creatures called gworls came through a gate. They'd been sent by a Lord of another world to steal the Horn of Shambarimen. This was a device made ten millennia ago, when the pocket universes were just beginning to be created. Using it as a sort of sonic skeleton key, a person could unlock any gate. Paul didn't know this, of course, but while hiding he saw a gworl open a gate to one of the tiers on this planet with the Horn. Paul pushed the gworl into a pool and dived through the gate with the Horn in his hand.

In the years that passed, as he traveled from level to level, the gworl trailing him, he became well acquainted with many sectors of this planet. On the Dracheland level he took the disguise of Baron Horst von Horstmann. But it was on the Amerind level that he was Kickaha, the name he preferred to be known by. Paul Janus Finnegan was someone in his distant past. Memories of Earth grew dim. He made no effort to go back to his home universe. This was a world he loved, though its dangers were many.

Then an Earthman, Robert Wolff, retired in Phoenix, Arizona, was inspecting the basement of a house for sale when the wall opened. He looked into another world and saw Kickaha surrounded by some gworl who'd finally caught up with him. Kickaha couldn't escape through the gate, but he did throw the Horn through so that the gworl couldn't have it. Wolff might have thought he was crazy or hallucinating, but the Horn was physical evidence that he wasn't.

Wolff was unhappy; he didn't like his Earthly situation. So he blew the Horn, pressing on the buttons to make notes, and he went through the gate. He found himself on the lowest level of the planet, which looked at first like Eden. As time passed, he became rejuvenated, eventually attaining the body he had had when he was twenty-five.

He also fell in love with a woman called Chryseis. Pursued by the gworl, they fled to the next level, meeting Kickaha on the way. Finally, after many adventures, Wolff reached the palace on top of the world, and he discovered that he was Jadawin, the Lord who'd made this little universe.

Later, he and Chryseis were precipitated into a series of adventures in which he met a number of the Lords. He also had to pass through a series of pocket worlds, all of which were traps designed to catch and kill other Lords.

Meanwhile, Kickaha was engaged in a battle with the Bellers, creatures of artificial origin which could transfer their minds to the bodies of human beings. He also met and fell in love with Anana, a female Lord.

While chasing the last survivor of the Bellers, Kickaha and Anana were gated through to Earth. Kickaha liked Earth even less than he remembered liking it. It was getting overcrowded and polluted. Most of the changes in the twenty years since he'd left it were, in his opinion, for the worse.

Red Orc, the secret Lord of the Two Earths, found out that he and Anana were in his domain. Urthona, another Lord, stranded on Earth for some time, also became Kickaha's deadly enemy. Kickaha found out that Wolff, or Jadawin, and Chryseis were prisoners of Red Orc. But they'd escaped through a gate to the lavalite world. Now Jadawin and Chryseis were roaming somewhere on its everchanging surface, if they were still alive. And he, Kickaha, had lost the Horn of Shambarimen and Anana. He'd never get out of this unpleasant nerve-stretching world unless he somehow found a gate. Finding it wasn't going to do him any good unless he had some open-sesame to activate the gate, though. And he couldn't leave then unless he found Anana, alive or dead.

For that matter, he couldn't leave until he found Wolff and Chryseis. Kickaha was a very bad enemy but a very good friend.

He had also always been extremely independent, self-assured, and adaptable. He'd lived for over twenty years without any roots, though he had been a warrior in the tribe of Hrowakas and thought of them as his people. But they were all gone now, slaughtered by the Bellers. He was in love with the beautiful Anana, who, though a Lord, had become more human because of his influence.

For some time now he'd been wanting to quit this wandering always-changing-identities life. He wanted to establish himself and Anana some place, among a people who'd respect and maybe even love him. There he and Anna would settle down, perhaps adopt some children. Make a home and a family.

Then he'd lost her, and the only means he had to get out of this terrible place was also lost.

It was no wonder that Kickaha, the man sufficient unto himself, the ever-adaptable, the one who could find comfort even in hell, was now lonely.

This was why he suddenly decided to adopt the miserable wretches of the Thana as his people. If they'd have him.

There was also the desire not to be killed. But it was the wish to be part of a community that most strongly drove him.

IX

IN HIS STILL LIMITED THANA, HE SPOKE TO WERGENGET OF THIS. THE chief didn't look surprised. He smiled, and Kickaha saw in this a pleasure.

"You could have escaped us; you still could," Wergenget said. "I saw the intent in your face briefly, though it closed almost immediately, like a fist.

"I'll tell you, Kickaha, why you have lived so long among us. Usually, we kill an enemy at once. Or, if he or she seems to be a brave person, we honor him or her with torture. But sometimes, if the person is not of a tribe familiar to us, that is, not an old enemy, we adopt him or her. Death strikes often, and we don't have enough children to replace the dead. Our tribe has been getting smaller for some time now. Therefore, I will decree that you be adopted. You have shown courage, and all of us are grateful that you saved one of our precious children."

Kickaha began to feel a little less lonely.

Several hours later, the storm ceased. The tribe ventured again into the valley and retrieved the body of Lukyo. She was carried into camp with much wailing by the women. The rest of the day was spent in mourning while her body, washed clean, her hair combed, lay on top of a pile of skins. At "dusk" she was carried on a litter borne on the shoulders of four men to a place a mile from the camp. Here her corpse was placed on the ground, and the shaman, Oshullain, danced around her, chanting, waving a three-tined stick in ritualistic gestures. Then, singing a sad song, the whole tribe, except for some mounted guards, walked back to the camp.

Kickaha looked back once. Vultures were gliding toward her, and a band of long-legged baboons was racing to beat them to the feast

About a quarter of a mile away a pride of the maneless lions was trotting toward the body. Doubtless, they'd try to drive the baboons away, and there would be a hell of a ruckus. When the simians were in great numbers, they would harass the big cats until they forced them to abandon the meat.

On getting back to camp, the shaman recited a short poem he'd composed. It was in honor of Lukyo, and it was designed to keep her memory fresh among the tribe. It would be on everybody's lips for a while, then they'd cease singing it. And, after a while, she would be forgotten except in the memories of her child and parents. The child would forget, too, with the passage of time, and the parents would have other more pressing things to think about.

Only those who'd done some mighty deed still had songs sung about them. The others were forgotten.

The tribe stayed outside the sea-country for another day. Wergenget explained that the storm season was almost always over by now. But it had been extended by the Lord, for some reason, and the tribe had made a fatal miscalculation.

"Or, perhaps," the chief said, "we have somehow offended the Lord, and he kept the lightning from going back to the heavens for a day."

Kickaha didn't comment on this. He was usually discreet about getting into arguments about religion. There was also no sense in offending the chief when it might make him change his mind about adopting him.

Wergenget called in the whole tribe and made a speech. Kickaha understood about half of the words, but the tones and the gestures were easily interpreted. Though the Lord had taken away Lukyo with one hand, he had given them Kickaha with the other. The tribe had offended the Lord. Or perhaps it was only Lukyo who had done this. In any event, the Lord still did not hate them altogether. By slaying Lukyo, the Lord had vented his wrath. To show the tribe that it was still in his favor, he'd sent Kickaha, a warrior, to the tribe. So it was up to the tribe to take him in.

The only one who objected to this was the youth, Toini, who had kicked Kickaha when he was bending over the channel. He suggested that perhaps the Lord wanted the tribe to sacrifice Kickaha to him. This, plus Lukyo's death, would satisfy the Lord.

Kickaha didn't know why Toini had it in for him. The only explanation was reactive chemistry. Some people just took an instant and unreasonable dislike to certain people in the first minute of acquaintanceship.

Toini's speech didn't exactly cause an uproar, but it did result in considerable loud argument. The chief was silent during the squabble, but apparently Toini had given him some doubts.

Kickaha, seeing that Toini might swing public opinion to his way of thinking, asked the chief if he could speak. Wergenget shouted for silence.

Kickaha, knowing that height gave a speaker a psychological advantage, mounted a *hikwu*.

"I wasn't going to say anything about a certain matter until after I was adopted by the tribe," he said. "But now I see that I must speak about it."

He paused and looked around as if he were about to reveal something which perhaps he shouldn't.

"But since there are some doubters of the Lord here, I believe that I should tell you about this now, instead of later."

They were hanging on his words now. His grave manner and the serious tones made them think that he knew something they should know about.

"Shortly before you came upon me," Kickaha said, "I met a man. He approached me, not walking, but gliding over the earth. He was in the air above the ground at twice my height."

Many gasped, and the eyes of all but Toini widened. His became narrow.

"The man was very tall, the tallest I've ever seen in my life. His skin was very white, and his hair was very red. And there was a glow about him as if he were wrapped in lightning. I waited for him, of course, since he was not the sort of person you would run away from or attack.

"When he was close to me he stopped, and then he sank to the ground. I am a brave man, people of the Thana, but he frightened me. Also, he awed me. So I sank to my knees and waited for him to speak or to act. I knew that he was no ordinary man, since what man can float through the air?

"He walked up to me, and he said, 'Do not be afraid, Kickaha. I will not harm you. You are favored in my eyes, Kickaha. Rise, Kickaha.'

"I did as he ordered, but I was still scared. Who could this be, this stranger who soared like a bird and who knew my name, though I had never seen him before?"

Some in the crowd moaned, and others murmured prayers. They knew who this stranger was. Or at least they thought they did.

"Then the stranger said, 'I am the Lord of this world, Kickaha.'

"And I said, 'I thought so, Lord.'

"And he said, 'Kickaha, the tribe of the Thana will soon be taking you prisoner. If they are kind to you, then they will gain favor in my eyes, since I have in mind something great for you to do. You will be my servant, Kickaha, a tool to effect a deed which I wish to be done.'

" 'But if they try to kill or torture you, Kickaha, then I will know they are unworthy. And I will blast them all from the face of this earth. As a matter of fact, I will kill one of them as testimony that I am keeping an eye on them to demonstrate my power. If they are not convinced by this, then I will slay one more, the man who will try to keep you from being adopted by the tribe.' "

Toini had been grinning crookedly up to this moment. It was evident that he was going to denounce the captive as a prevaricator the moment he ceased speaking. But now he turned pale and began to shiver and his teeth started chattering. The others moved away from him.

The shaman was the only one who was looking doubtful. Perhaps, like Toini, he thought that Kickaha was lying to save his neck. If so, he was waiting for more developments before he gave his opinion.

"So I said, 'I am grateful, Lord, that you are honoring me by using me as your servant and tool. May I ask what task you have in mind for me?'

"And he said, 'I will reveal that to you in the proper time, Kickaha. In the meantime, let us see how the Thana treat you. If they act as I wish, then they will go on to great glory and will prosper and thrive as no other tribe has ever done. But if they mistreat you, then I will destroy them, men, women, children, and beasts. Not even their bones will be left for the scavengers to gnaw.'

"And then he turned and rose into the air and moved swiftly around the side of the mountatin. A few minutes later, you showed up. You know what happened after that."

The effect of his lie was such that Kickaha almost began to believe in it. The tribe surged around him, fighting to touch him as if to draw to them the power he must have absorbed just by being close to the Lord. And they begged him to consider them as his friends. When the shaman, Oshullain, pushed through the mob and seized Kickaha's foot and held on as if he were absorbing the power, Kickaha knew he'd won.

Then the chief said loudly, "Kickaha! Did the Lord say anything about you leading us?"

Wergenget was concerned about his own position.

"No, the Lord did not. I believe that he just wanted me to take a place in the tribe as a warrior. If he had wanted me to be chief, he would have said so."

Wergenget looked relieved. He said, "And what about this wretch, Toini, who said that perhaps you should be sacrificed?"

"I think he knows he was very wrong," Kickaha said. "Isn't that right, Toini?"

Toini, on his knees, sobbing, said, "Forgive me, Kickaha! I didn't know what I was doing."

"I forgive you," Kickaha said. "And now, chief, what should we do?"

Wergenget said that since it was now obvious that the Lord was no longer angry, it was safe to go into the sea-country. Kickaha hoped that the thunderstorm season was indeed over. If another storm occurred, then the tribe would know he'd been lying. Which meant it'd probably tear him apart.

For the moment, he was safe. But if anything went wrong, if it became evident that the tribe wasn't favored by the Lord, then he'd have to think up another lie fast. And if he wasn't believed, curtains for Kickaha.

Also, what if they should run into Urthona, the real Lord of this universe?

Well, he'd deal with that situation when it happened.

Anyway, if he saw any sign of Anana, any evidence that she was in the sea-land, he'd desert the Thana. It seemed to him that if she'd survived, she would have gone to this area. She'd know that if he'd lived, he would go there too.

Also, Urthona and McKay would go to where the land was relatively stable and where there'd be plenty of water. And where they were, the Horn would be.

He wondered if Orc had been caught in the flashflood which had carried him away. Or had he only been swept a little distance, enough to take him out of reach of Urthona and McKay.

Such thoughts occupied him until the caravan reached the sea. There they drank the water and let the moosoids satisfy their thirst. Some of the women and children gathered nuts and berries from the trees and bushes. The men waded around in the waves and jabbed their spears at the elusive fish. A few were successful.

Kickaha got a small portion of the raw fish, which he examined for worms before eating.

Then the Thana formed a caravan again and began the march over the white fine sand of the beach. They had come in on the right side of the channel, so they turned right. To cross the channel where it emerges from the sea, they would have had to swim a quarter mile of deep water. They passed many trees and animals felled by the lightning. The carcasses were covered with scaly amphibians, teeth flashing or dripping blood, tails flailing to sweep their competitors away, grunting and croaking, snapping. The birds were busy, too, and at many places the uproar was almost deafening.

When the tribe came across a lightning-blasted female elephant and calf, it drove away the multitude of sea, land, and air life and carved up the bodies for itself. Kickaha took some large cuts but put off eating them. When "night" came he piled branches and twigs to make a fire and he fashioned a bow-drill to start a fire. The others gathered around to watch. He worked away until the friction of the drill generated smoke, then added twigs and presently had a small fire going.

Kickaha borrowed a flint knife and cut off some smaller portions. After cooking a piece of leg and letting it cool off, he began eating as if he'd never stop. The chief and shaman accepted his invitation to dine. Though they were suspicious of cooked meat, their fears were overcome by the savory odors.

"Did the Lord teach you how to make that great heat?" Oshullain said.

"No. Where I come from all people know how to make this . . . fire. We call it fire. In fact, your ancestors knew how to make fire. But you have forgotten how to do it.

"I think that your ancestors, when first brought here, must have wandered for many generations before finding a sea-land. By then the scarcity of wood had made your people forget all about fire. Still, I can't understand why you didn't re-invent fire-making when you did find the sea-land, which has plenty of trees."

He didn't say that the most primitive of humans had had fire. Wergenget might have thought he was insulting him. Which he was.

He thought about Urthona. What a sadist he was. Why, if he had to make a world and then place humans on it, had he set up such a barebones world? The potentiality of Homo sapiens could not be realized if it had almost nothing to work with. Also, the necessity to keep on the move, the never-ending changing of the earth, the limiting of human activity to constant travel while at the same time seeking for food and water, had reduced them almost to the level of beasts.

Despite which, they were human. They had a culture, one which was probably more complex than he thought. The riches of which he would learn when he became proficient in the language and knew both the customs of the tribe and its individual members.

He said, "Fires are also good for keeping the big beasts away at night. I'll show you how to keep the fires fed."

The chief was silent for a while. Besides his food, he was digesting a new concept. It seemed to be causing him some mental unease. After a while he said, "Since you are the favored of the Lord, and this tribe is to be yours, you wouldn't bring in any evil to us? Would you?"

Kickaha assured him that he wouldn't—unless the Lord told him to do so.

The chief rose from his squatting position and bellowed orders. In a short while, there were a dozen large fires around the perimeter of the camp. Sleep, however, didn't come easily to it. Some big cats and dogs, their eyes shining in the reflected light, prowled around the edges of the camp. And the Thana weren't sure that the fires wouldn't attack them after they went to sleep. However, Kickaha set an example by closing his eyes, and his simulated snores soon told everybody that he, at least, wasn't worried. After a while the children slept, and then their elders decided that it was safe.

In the morning Kickaha showed the women how to cook the meat. Half of the tribe took to the new way of preparing food with enthusiasm . . . The other decided to stick to eating the meat raw. But Kickaha was certain that before long the entire tribe, except for some dietary diehards, would have adapted.

He wasn't too sure, though, that he should have introduced cooking. When the storm season started again, the tribe would have to go outside the great valley again. Out there, because of the scarcity of firewood, it would have to eat its meat raw again. They might become discontented, then resentful and frustrated because they could do nothing to ease their discontent.

Prometheuses weren't always beneficial.

That was their problem. He didn't plan on being around when they left the valley.

In the "morning" the caravan went on the march again. Wergenget got them to moving faster than the day before. He was nervous because other tribes would be moving in, and he didn't want his to run into one on the beach. Near the end of the day, they reached their goal. This was a high hill about a half a mile inland from the shore. Though it changed shape somewhat, like the rest of the land in the valley, it did so very slowly. And it always remained a hill, though its form might alter.

On its top was a jumble of logs. This had been the walls of a stockade the last time the tribe had seen it. The mutations of the hill had lifted the circular wall a number of times and had broken the vine which held it. The tribe set to work digging new holes with sticks and flint-tipped shovels, then reset the logs. Vines were cut and dragged in and bound to hold the logs together. By the end of the third day, the wooden fortress was restored. Within the walls were a number of leantos in which the families could take shelter from the rains and sleep. During the rest of the season the tribe would stay in here at night. During the day, various parties would sally out to fish and hunt and gather nuts and berries. Lookouts would watch for dangerous beasts or the even more dangerous humans.

But, before they started to rest and get fat, it was necessary to initiate Kickaha into the tribe.

This was a great honor, but it was also rough on the initiate. After a long dance and recitation of numerous chants and songs, during which drums beat and bone flutes shrilled, the chief used a flint knife to cut the identification symbols of the tribe on Kickaha's chest. He was supposed to endure this without flinching or outcry.

Then he had to run a gauntlet of men, who struck at him with long sticks. Aferward, he had to wrestle the strongest man in the tribe, Mekdillong. He'd recovered entirely from his injuries by then, and he knew a hundred tricks Mekdillong was ignorant of. But he didn't want to humiliate him, so he allowed it to appear that Mekdillong was giving him a hard time. Finally, tired of the charade, he threw Mekdillong through the air with a cross-buttock. Poor Mek, the wind knocked out of him, writhed on the ground, sucking for air.

The worst part was having to prove his potency. Impotent men were driven from the tribe to wander until they died. In Kickaha's case, since he was not of the tribe born, he would have been killed. That is, he would have been if it wasn't so evident that the Lord had sent him. But, as the chief said, if the Lord had sent him, then he wouldn't fail.

Kickaha didn't try to argue with this logic. But he thought that the custom was wrong. No man could be blamed for being nervous if he knew he'd be exiled or slain if he failed. The very nervousness would cause impotency.

At least, the Thana did not demand, as did some tribes, that he prove himself publicly. He was allowed to go into a leanto surrounded by thick branches set upright into the ground. He chose the best-looking woman in the tribe for the test, and she came out several hours later looking tired but happy and announced that he'd more than passed the test.

Kickaha had some pangs of conscience about the incident, though he had enjoyed it very much. He didn't think that Anana would get angry about this trifling infidelity, especially since the circumstances were such that he couldn't avoid it.

However, it would be best not to mention this to her.

That is, if he ever found her.

That was the end of the trials. The chief and the shaman each chanted an initiation song, and then the whole tribe feasted until their bellies swelled and they could scarcely move.

Before going to sleep Wergenget told Kickaha that he'd have to pick a wife from the eligible females. There were five nubiles, all of whom had stated that they would be happy to have him as a mate. Theoretically, a woman could reject any suitor, but in practice it didn't work that way. Social pressure insisted that a woman marry as soon as she was of childbearing age. If any woman was lucky enough to have more than one suitor, then she had a choice. Otherwise, she had to take whoever asked her.

The same pressure was on a man. Even if he didn't care for any of the women available, he had to pick one. It was absolutely necessary that the tribe maintain its population.

Two of the five candidates for matrimony were pretty and well-figured. One of these was bold and brassy and looked as if she were brimming over with the juices of passion. So, if he had to take unto himself a wife, he'd choose her. It was possible she'd turn him down, but, according to the chief, all five were panting for him.

Given his pick, he'd have wived the woman he'd proved his manhood on. But she was only borrowed for the occasion, as was the custom, and her husband would try to kill Kickaha if he followed up with a repeat performance.

As it was, the woman, Shima, could make trouble. She'd told Kickaha she'd like to get together with him again. There wasn't going to be much opportunity for that, since she couldn't disappear into the woods by herself without half the tribe knowing it.

Ah, well, he'd deal with the various situations as they came along.

Kickaha looked around. Except for the sentinel on top of a platform on top of a high pole in the middle of the fort, and another stationed near the apex of the giant tree, the tribe was snoring. He could open the gate and get away and be long gone before the guards could rouse the others. In their present stuffed condition, they could never catch him.

At the same time he wanted to get out and look for Anana, he felt counterdesire to stay with these people, miserable and wretched as they were. His moment of weakness, of longing for a home of some sort, still had him in its grip. Some moment! It could go on for years.

Logically, it was just as likely that if he stayed here, she'd be coming along. If he set out on a search, he could go in the wrong direction and have to travel the circuit of this body of water. It could be as big as Lake Michigan or the Mediterranean for all he knew. And Anana could be going in the same direction as he but always behind him. If she were alive . . .

One of these days, he'd have to leave. Meanwhile, he'd do some scouting around. He might run across some clues in this neighborhood.

He yawned and headed for the leanto assigned him by the chief. Just as he got to it, he heard giggles. Turning, he saw Shila and Gween, his two top choices for wife. Their normally flat bellies were bulging, but they hadn't eaten so much they couldn't see straight. And they'd been pretending to be asleep.

Shila, smiling, said, "Gween and I know you're going to marry one of us."

He smiled and said, "How'd you know?"

"We're the most desirable. So, we thought maybe . . ." she giggled again . . . "we'd give you a chance to see whom you like most. There'll never be another chance to find out."

"You must be joking," he said. "I've had a long hard day. The rites, the hours with Shima, the feast . . ."

"Oh, we think you have it in you. You must be a great *wiru*. Anyway, it can't hurt to try, can it?"

"I don't see how it could," Kickaha said, and he took the hand of each. "My place is rather exposed. Where shall we go?"

He didn't know how long he'd been sleeping when he was wakened by a loud hubbub. He rose on one elbow and looked around. Both girls were still sleeping. He crawled out and removed the brush in front of the leanto and stood up. Everybody was running around shouting or sitting up and rubbing their eyes and asking what was going on. The man on top of the platform was yelling something and pointing out toward the sea. The sentinel in the tree was shouting.

Wergenget, his eyes still heavy with sleep, stumbled up to Kickaha. "What's Opwel saying?"

Kickaha said the sentinel's voice was being drowned out. Wergenget began yelling for everybody to shut up, and in a minute he'd subdued them. Opwel, able to make himself understood, relayed the message of the man in the tree.

"A man and a woman ran by on the beach. And then, a minute later, warriors of the tribe of Thans came along after them. They seemed to be chasing the man and the woman."

Kickaha hollered. "Did the woman have long hair as black as the wing of a crow?"

"Yes!"

"And was the hair of the man yellow or red?"

"Onil says the man was black-skinned and his hair was the curliest he'd ever seen. Onil said the man was black all over."

Kickaha groaned, and said, "Anana! And McKay!"

He ran for the gate, shouting, "Anana!"

Wergenget yelled an order, and two men seized Kickaha. The chief huffed and puffed up to him, and, panting, said, "Are you crazy! You can't go out there alone! The Thans will kill you!"

"Let me loose!" Kickaha said. "That's my woman out there! I'm going to help her!"

"Don't be stupid," Wergenget said. "You wouldn't have a chance."

"Are you just going to sit here and let her be run down?" Kickaha yelled.

Wergenget turned and shouted at Opwel. He yelled at Olin, who replied. Opwel relayed the message.

"Onil says he counted twenty."

The chief rubbed his hands and smiled. "Good. We outnumber them." He began giving orders then. The men grabbed their weapons, saddled the moosoids, and mounted. Kickaha got on his own, and the moment the gate was open he urged it out through the opening. After him came Wergenget and the rest of the warriors.

X

AFTER BEING KNOCKED BACK INTO THE CHANNEL, ANANA HAD BEGUN
scrambling back up. The water by then was to her breasts, but she
clawed back up the side, grabbing the grass, pulling it out, grabbing
more handfuls.

Above her were yells, and then something struck her head. It didn't
hurt her much, didn't even cause her to lose her grip. She looked down
to see what had hit her. The case containing the Horn of Shambarimen.

She looked toward the black wall of water rushing toward her. It
would hit within ten seconds. Perhaps less. But she couldn't let the
Horn be lost. Without it their chances of ever getting out of this
wretched world would be slight indeed.

She let herself slide back into the water and then swam after it. It
floated ahead of her, carried by the current of the stream rising ahead of
the flash flood. A few strokes got her to it. Her hand closed around
the handle, and she stroked with one hand to the bank. The level had
risen above her head now, but she did not have to stand up. She seized
a tuftful of grass, shifted the handle from hand to teeth, and then began
climbing again.

By then the ground was shaking with the weight of the immense body
of water racing toward her. There was no time to look at it, however.
Again she pulled herself up the wet slippery bank, holding her head
high so the case wouldn't interfere with her arms.

But she did catch out of the corner of her eye a falling body. By then
the roar of the advancing water was too loud for her to hear the splash
the body made. Who had fallen? Kickaha? That was the only one she
cared about.

The next moment the rumble and the roar were upon her. She was just about to shove the case over the edge of the bank and draw herself up after it when the mass struck. Despite her furious last-second attempt to reach safety, the surface waters caught her legs. And she was carried, crying out desperately, into the flood.

But she managed to hold onto the Horn. And though she was hurled swiftly along, she was not in the forefront of the water. She went under several times but succeeded in getting back to the surface. Perhaps the buoyancy of the case enabled her to keep to the surface.

In any event, something, maybe a current hurled upward by an obstruction on the bottom, sent her sprawling onto the edge of the bank. For a minute she thought she'd slip back, but she writhed ahead and presently her legs were out of reach of the current.

She released the case and rolled over and got shakily to her feet.

About a half a mile behind her were three figures. Urthona. Orc. McKay.

Kickaha was missing. So, it would have been he that had fallen over into the stream. It also would have been he who'd dropped the Horn into it. She guessed that he must have threatened to throw it in if the others didn't allow her to get out of the channel again.

Then they'd rushed him, and he'd released it and gone into the stream after it. Either on his own volition, which didn't seem likely, or he had been pushed into it.

She could see no sign of him.

He was under the surface somewhere, either drowned or fighting.

She found it difficult to believe that he was dead. He'd come through so much, fought so hard, been so wily. He was of the stuff o' survival.

Still, all men and women must die sometime.

No, she wouldn't allow herself to give up hope for him. But even i he were still struggling, he would by now have been swept out of sight

The only thing to do was to follow the channel to its end and hop that she'd run across him somewhere along it.

Red Orc was by now running away. He was going at full speed in th opposite direction. McKay had run after him but had stopped. Ev dently, he either couldn't catch him or Urthona had called him bacl Whatever had happened, the two were now trotting toward her. Sh had the Horn, and they wanted it.

She started trotting, too. After a while she was panting, but she ke on and her second wind came. If she stayed by the channel, she couldn lose them. They'd keep going, though they had no chance with h head start of catching her. Not until utter fatigue forced her to sleep. If they somehow could keep on going, they'd find her.

She believed that she had as much endurance as they. They'd have to lie down and rest, too, perhaps before she did. But if they pushed themselves, rose earlier from sleep, then they might come across her while she slept.

As long as she followed the channel, she couldn't lose them, ever. But across the plains, in the mountains, she might. Then she could cut back to the channel.

There was a chance, also, that she could get lost, especially when the landmarks kept changing. She'd have to risk that.

She turned and started across the plain. Now they would angle across, reducing the lead she had. Too bad. Though she felt the urge to break into a run, she resisted it. As long as she could keep ahead, out of range of the beamer, she'd be all right.

It was difficult to estimate distances in this air, which was so clear because of the almost-total lack of dust and of this light. She thought the nearest of the mountains was about five miles away. Even with the speed with which landscape changed around here, it would still be a respectably sized mountain by the time she got there.

Between her and her goal were groves of the ambulatory trees. None were so large that she couldn't go around them. There were also herds of grazing antelopes and gazelles. A herd of elephants was about a half a mile away, trotting toward the nearest grove. To her right, in the other direction, some of the giant moosoids were nearing another group of plants. She caught a glimpse of two lions a quarter of a mile away. They were using a grove as cover while sneaking up on some antelopes.

Far in the distance was the tiny figure of a moa. It didn't seem to be chasing anything, but her line of flight would lead her near to it. She changed it, heading for the other end of the base of the mountain.

She looked to her left. The two men were running now. Evidently they hoped to put on a burst of speed and make her run until she dropped.

She stepped up her pace but she did not sprint. She could maintain this pace for quite a while. Seldom in her many thousands of years of life had she gotten out of shape. She had developed a wind and an endurance that would have surprised an Olympic marathoner. Whatever her physical potential was, she had realized it to the full. Now she'd find out what its limits were.

One mile. Two miles. She was sweating, but while she wasn't exactly breathing easy, she knew she had a lot of reserve wind. Her legs weren't leaden yet. She felt that she could reach the mountain and still have plenty of strength left. Her uncle was a strong man, but he was heavier, and he'd probably indulged himself on Earth. Any fat he'd had had been melted by their ordeal here, where food hadn't been plentiful. But she doubted that he'd kept himself in tiptop condition on Earth.

The black man was powerfully built, but he wasn't the long-distance runner type. In fact, sparing a look back, she could see that he'd dropped behind Urthona. Not that her uncle had gained any on her.

The case and its contents, however, did weigh about four pounds. Needing every advantage she could get, she decided to get rid of some of it. She slowed down while she undid the clasps, removed the Horn, and dropped the case. Now, carrying the instrument in one hand, she increased her speed. In ten minutes, Urthona had lost fifty yards. McKay was even further behind his boss now.

Another mile. Now she was wishing she could abandon the throwing axe and the knife. But that was out. She'd need both weapons when it came to a showdown. Not to mention that even if she got away from them, she had to consider the predators. A knife and an axe weren't much against a lion, but they could wound, perhaps discourage it.

Another half a mile. She looked back. Urthona was half a mile away. McKay was behind Urthona by a quarter of a mile. Both had slowed considerably. They were trotting steadily, but they didn't have a chance of catching her. However, as long as they kept her in sight, they wouldn't stop.

The lions had disappeared around the other side of the trees. These were moving slowly along, headed for the channel. The wind was blowing toward them, carrying molecules of water to their sensors. When they got to the channel they would draw up along it in a row and extend their tentacles into the water to suck it up.

The antelopes and gazelles stopped eating as she approached, watched her for a moment, their heads up, black eyes bright, then bounded away as one. But they only moved to what they considered a safe distance and resumed grazing.

Anana was in the center of antelopes, with tall straight horns which abruptly curved at the tips, when they stampeded. She stopped and then crouched as big black-and-brown-checkered bodies leaped over her and thundered by. She was sure that she hadn't caused the panic. The antelopes had regarded her as not dangerous but something it was better not to let get too close.

Then she heard a roar, and she saw a flash of brownish-yellow after a half-grown antelope.

One lion had shot out of the trees after the young beast. The other was racing along parallel with its mate. It was somewhat smaller and faster. As the male cut off to one side, the female bent its path slightly inward. The prey had turned to its left to get away from the big male, then saw the other cat angling toward it. It turned away from the new peril and so lost some ground.

The male roared and frightened the antelope into changing its direction of flight again. The female cut in toward it; the poor beast turned toward the male. Anana expected that the chase would not last long. Either the cats would get their kill in the next few seconds or their endurance would peter out and the antelope would race away. If the quarry had enough sense just to run in a straight line, it would elude its pursuers. But it didn't. It kept zigzagging, losing ground each time, and then the female was on it. There was a flurry of kicking legs, and the creature was dead, its neck broken.

The male, roaring, trotted up, his sides heaving, saliva dripping from his fangs, his eyes a bright green. The female growled at him but backed off until he had disemboweled the carcass.

Then she settled down on the other side of the body, and they began tearing off chunks of meat. The herd had stopped running by then. Indifferent to the fate of the young beast, knowing that there was no more danger for the present, they resumed their feeding.

Anana was only forty feet away from the lions, but she kept on going. The cats wouldn't be interested in her unless she got too close, and she had no intention of doing that.

The trees were a species she'd not seen before. About twelve feet high, they had bark which was covered with spiral white and red streaks like a barber pole. The branches were short and thick and sprouting broad heart-shaped green leaves. Each plant had only four "eyes," round, unblinking, multifaceted, green as emeralds. They also had tentacles. But they must not be dangerous. The lions had walked through them unharmed.

Or was there some sort of special arrangement between the cats and the trees? Had Urthona implanted in them an instinct-mechanism which made them ignore the big cats but not people? It would be like her uncle to do this. He'd be amused at seeing the nomads decide that it was safe to venture among the trees because they'd seen other animals do so. And then, stepping inside the moving forest, suddenly find themselves attacked.

For a moment she thought about taking a chance. If she plunged into that mobile forest, she could play hide-and-seek with her hunters. But that would be too risky, and she would really gain nothing by it.

She looked behind her. The two men had gained a little on her. She stepped up the pace of her trotting. When she'd passed the last of the trees she turned to her left and went past their backs. Maybe Urthona and McKay would try to go through the trees.

No, they wouldn't. It was doubtful that her uncle would remember just what their nature was. He might think that she had taken refuge in them. So, the two would have to separate to make sure. McKay would go along one side and Urthona on the other. They'd look down the rows to make sure she wasn't there, and then would meet at the rear.

By then, keeping the trees between her and the others, moving in a straight line toward the mountain from the plants, she'd be out of their sight for a while. And they would lose more ground.

She turned and headed toward her goal.

But she slowed. A half a mile away, coming toward her, was a pack of baboons. There were twenty, the males acting as outriders, the females in the middle, some with babies clinging to their backs. Was she their prey? Or had they been attracted by the roaring of the lion and were racing to the kill?

She shifted the Horn to her left hand and pulled the axe from her belt. Her path and theirs would intersect if she kept on going. She stopped and waited. They continued on in the same direction, silently their broad, short-digited paws striking the ground in unison as if they were trained soldiers on the march. Their long legs moved them swiftly though they could not match the hoofed plains beasts for speed. They would pick out their prey, a young calf or an injured adult. They would spread out and form a circle. The leader would rush at the quarry, and the frenzied bounding and barking of the others would stampede the herd. The pack would dart in and out of the running leaping antelopes under their very hooves, often forced to jump sideways to avoid being trampled. But their general direction was toward their intended kill, and the circle would draw tighter. Suddenly, the running calf or limping adult would find itself surrounded. Several of the heavy powerful male simians would leap upon it and bring it to the ground. The others excepting the mothers carrying infants, would close in.

When within twenty feet of her, the leader barked, and the pack slowed down. Had their chief decided that she would be less trouble than running off two hungry lions?

No. They were still moving, heading toward the corner of the square formed by the marching plants.

She waited until the last of the pack was gone by, then resumed trotting.

There was a sudden commotion behind her. She slowed again and turned to one side so she could see what was going on. She didn't like what she saw. Urthona and McKay had burst out of the woods. They'd not circled the plants, as she'd expected, but had instead gone in a straight line through them. So, Urthona had remembered that these were no danger to human beings. Hoping to catch her by surprise, they'd probably run at top speed.

They'd succeeded. However, they were themselves surprised. They'd come out of the trees and run headlong into the baboons. The chief simian was hurling himself toward Urthona, and three big males were loping toward McKay.

Her uncle had no choice but to use his beamer. Its ray sliced the leader from top to bottom. The two halves, smoking, skidded to a halt several feet from him. If he'd been just a little slower reacting, he'd have found the baboon's teeth in his throat.

Too bad, thought Anana.

XI

NOW HER UNCLE WAS BEING FORCED TO DISCHARGE EVEN MORE OF TH[E] precious energy. McKay would be downed within a few seconds. Th[e] black was crouched, ready to fight, but he was also screaming at U[r]thona to shoot. Her uncle hesitated a second or two—he hated to use th[e] beamer because he was saving its charges for his niece—but he did n[o] want to be left alone to continue the chase. Three males tumbled ove[r] and over until they came to rest—or their halves did—just at McKay['s] feet. Under his dark pigment, McKay was gray.

The other baboons halted and began jumping up and down a[nd] screaming. They were only angry and frustrated. They wouldn't atta[ck] any more.

She turned and began running again. A few minutes later, she look[ed] back. Her pursuers were moving toward her slowly. They didn't da[re] run with their backs to the simians. These were following them at a [re]spectable distance, waiting for a chance to rush them. Urthona w[as] shouting and waving the beamer at them, hoping to scare them [off]. Every few seconds, he would stop and turn to face them. The baboo[ns] would withdraw, snarling, barking, but they wouldn't stop trailing the[m].

Anana grinned. She would get a big lead on the two men.

When she reached the foot of the mountain, which rose abru[ptly] from the plain, she stopped to rest. By then the baboons had given [up]. Another one of the pack lay dead, and this loss had made up th[e] minds for them. Now some were gathered around the latest casu[alty] and tearing him apart. The others were racing to see who could ge[t to] the remaining carcasses first. A half a mile away, a giant scimi[tar]-beaked "moa" was speeding toward the commotion. It would atte[mpt] to scare the simians from a body. Above were vultures hoping to get a share of the meat.

The slope here was a little more than a forty-five degree angle to the horizontal. Here and there were swellings, like great gas bubbles pushing out the surface of the peak. She'd have to go around these. She began climbing, leaning forward slightly. There were no trees or bushes for her to hide among. She'd have to keep going until she got to the top. From there she might be able to spot some kind of cover. It was doubtful that she would. But if she went down the other side swiftly enough, she might be able to get around the base of another mountain. And then her chasers wouldn't know where she was.

The peak was perhaps a thousand and a half feet above the plain. By the time she got there, she was breathing very heavily. Her legs felt as if they were thickly coated with cement. She was shaking with fatigue; her lungs seemed to burn. The two men would be in the same, if not worse, condition.

When she'd started ascending, the top of the peak had been as sharply pointed as the tip of an ice cream cone. Now it had slumped and become a plateau about sixty feet in diameter. The ground felt hot, indicating an increase in rate of shape-mutation.

Urthona and McKay were almost a quarter of the way up the slope. They were sitting down, facing away from her. Just above them the surface was swelling so rapidly that they would soon be hidden from her sight. If the protuberance spread out, they'd have to go around it. Which meant they'd be slowed down even more.

Her view of the plain was considerably broader now. She looked along the channel, hoping to see a tiny figure that would be Kickaha. There was none.

Even from her height, she could not see the end of the channel. About twenty miles beyond the point at which she'd left it, young mountains had grown to cut off her view. There was no telling how far the channel extended.

Where was Red Orc? In all the excitement, she had forgotten about him.

Wherever he was, he wasn't visible to her.

She scanned the area beyond her perch. There were mountains beyond mountains. But between them were, as of now, passes, and here and there were ridges connecting them. On one of the ridges was a band of green contrasting with the rusty grass. It moved slowly but not so much that she didn't know the green was an army of migrating trees. It looked as if it were five miles away.

Scattered along the slopes and in the valleys were dark splotches. These would be composed of antelopes and other large herbivores. Though basically plains creatures, they adapted readily to the mountains. They could climb like goats when the occasion demanded.

Having attained the top, should she wait a while and see what her pursuers would do? Climbing after her was very exhausting. They might think she'd try to double back on them, come down one side of the mountain, around the corner where they couldn't see her. That wasn't a bad idea.

If the two should split up, each going around the mountain to meet in the middle, then she'd just go straight back down as soon as they got out of sight.

However, if they didn't take action soon, she'd have to do so. The plateau was growing outward and downward. Sinking rather. If she stayed here, she might find herself on the plain again.

No. That process would take at least a day. Perhaps two. And her uncle and his thug would be doing something in the meantime.

She began to get hungry and thirsty. When she'd started for the mountain, she'd hoped to find water on its other side. From what she could see, she was going to stay thirsty unless she went back to the channel. Or unless those wisps of clouds became thick black rainclouds.

She waited and watched. The edge of the plateau on which she sat slowly extended outwards. Finally, she knew she had to get off of it. In an hour or so it would begin crumbling along its rim. The apex of the cone was becoming a pancake. She'd have a hard time getting off i without being precipitated down the slope with a piece of it.

There was an advantage. The two men below would have to dodg falling masses. There might be so many they'd be forced to retreat t the plain. If she were lucky, they might even be struck by a hurtlin; bounding clump.

She went to the other side—the diameter of the circle was now a hun dred feet. After dropping the Horn and the axe, she let herself dow cautiously. Her feet dangled for a moment, and she let loose. That wa the only way to get down, even though she had to fall thirty feet. Sh struck the slope, which was still at a forty-five-degree angle, and sli down for a long way. The grass burned her hands as she grabbe handholds; the friction against the seat of her pants and the legs didr make the cloth smoke. But she was sure that if she hadn't succeeded stopping when she did, the fabric would have been hot enough to bur into flames. At least, she felt that it would.

After retrieving the Horn and axe, she walked down the slope, lea

ing back now. Occasionally her shoes would slip on the grass, and she'd sit down hard and slide for a few feet before she was able to brake to a stop. Once a mass of the dark greasy earth, grass blades sticking from it, thumped by her. If it had hit her, it would have crushed her.

Near the bottom she had to hurry up her descent. More great masses were rolling down the slope. One missed her only because it struck a swelling and leaped into the air over her head.

Reaching the base, she ran across the valley until she was sure she was beyond the place where the masses would roll. By then "night" had come. She was so thirsty she thought she'd die if she didn't get water in the next half hour. She was also very tired.

There was nothing else to do but to turn back. She had to have water. Fortunately, in this light, she couldn't be seen by anybody a thousand feet from her. Maybe five hundred. So she could sneak back to the channel without being detected. It was true that the two men might have figured out she'd try it and be waiting on the other side of the mountain. But she'd force herself to take an indirect route to the channel.

She headed along the valley, skirting the foot of the mountain beyond that which she'd climbed. There were housesized masses here also, these having fallen off the second mountain, too. Passing one, she scared something out which had been hiding under an overhang. She shrieked. Then, in swift reaction, she snatched out her axe and threw it at the long low scuttler.

The axehead struck it, rolling it over and over. It got to its short bowed legs, and, hissing, ran off. The blow had hurt it, though; it didn't move as quickly as before. She ran to her axe, picked it up, set herself, and hurled it again. This time the weapon broke the thing's back.

She snatched out her knife, ran to the creature—a lizardlike reptile two feet long—and she cut its throat. While it bled to death she held it up by its tail and drank the precious fluid pouring from it. It ran over her chin and throat and breasts, but she got most of it.

She skinned it and cut off portions and ate the still quivering meat. She felt much stronger afterward. Though still thirsty, she felt she could endure it, And she was in better shape than the two men—unless they had also managed to kill something.

As she headed toward the plain, she was enshrouded in deeper darkness. Rainclouds had come swiftly with a cooling wind. Before she had gone ten paces onto the flatland, she was deluged. The only illumination was lightning, which struck again and again around her. For a moment she thought about retreating. But she was always one to take a chance if the situation demanded it. She walked steadily onward, blind between the bolts, deaf because of the thunder. Now and then she looked behind her. She could see only animals running madly, attempting to get away from the deadly strokes but with no place to hide.

By the time she'd reached the channel, she was knee-deep in water. This increased the danger of being electrocuted, since a bolt did not now have to hit her directly. There was no turning back.

The side of the channel nearer her had lowered a few inches. The stream, flooding with the torrential downpour, was gushing water onto the plain. Four-legged fish and some creatures with tentacles—not large —were sliding down the slope. She speared two of the smaller amphibians with her knife and skinned and ate one. After cutting the other's head off and gutting it, she carried it by its tail. It could provide breakfast or lunch or both.

By then the storm was over, and within twenty minutes the clouds had rushed off. Ankle-deep in water, she stood on the ridge and pondered. Should she walk toward the other end of the channel and look for Kickaha? Or should she go toward the sea?

For all she knew, the channel extended a hundred miles or more. While she was searching for her man, the channel might close up. Or it might broaden out into a lake. Kickaha could be dead, injured, or alive and healthy. If hurt, he might need help. If he was dead, she might find his bones and thus satisfy herself about his fate.

On the other hand, if she went to the mountain pass to the sea, she could wait there, and if he was able he'd be along after a while.

Also, her uncle and the black man would surely go to the sea. In which case, she might be able to ambush them and get the beamer.

While standing in water and indecision, she had her mind made up for her. Out of the duskiness two figures emerged. They were too distant to be identified, but they were human. They had to be her pursuers.

Also, they were on the wrong side if she wanted to look for Kickaha. Her only path of flight, unless she ran for the mountains again, was toward the sea.

She set out trotting, the water splashing up to her knees. Occasionally, she looked back. The vague figures were drawing no closer but they weren't losing ground either.

Time, unmeasured except by an increasing weariness, passed. She came to the channel, which had by now risen to its former height. She dived in, swam to the other side, and climbed up the bank. Standing there, she could hear Urthona and McKay swimming towards her.

would seem that she'd never been able to get far enough ahead of them to lose herself in the darkness.

She turned and went on towards the mountains. Now she was wolf-trotting, trotting for a hundred paces, then walking a hundred. The counting of paces helped the time to go by and took her mind from her fatigue. The men behind her must be doing the same thing, unable to summon a burst of speed to catch up with her.

The plain, now drained of water, moved squishily under her. She took a passage between the two mountains and emerged into another plain. After a mile of this, she found another waterway barring her path. Perhaps, at this time, many fissures opened from the sea to the area beyond the ringing mountains to form many channels. Anyone high enough above ground might see the territory as a sort of millipus, the sea and its circling mountains as the body, the waterways as tentacles.

This channel was only about three hundred yards across, but she was too tired to swim. Floating on her back, she propelled herself backwards with an occasional hand-stroke or up-and-down movement of legs.

When she reached the opposite side, she found that the water next to the bank came only to her waist. While standing there and regaining her wind, she stared into the darkness. She could neither see nor hear her pursuers. Had she finally lost them? If she had, she'd wait a while, then return to the first channel.

An estimated five minutes later, she heard two men gasping. She slid down until the water was just below her nose. Now she could distinguish them, two darker darknesses in the night. Their voices came clearly across the water to her.

Her uncle, between wheezes, said, "Do you think we got away from them?"

"Them?" she thought.

"Not so loud," McKay said, and she could no longer hear them.

They stood on the bank for a few minutes, apparently conferring. Then a man, not one of them, shouted. Thudding noises came from somewhere, and suddenly giant figures loomed behind the two. Her uncle and McKay didn't move for a moment. In the meantime, the first of the "day" bands paled in the sky. McKay, speaking loudly, said, "Let's swim for it!"

"No!" Urthona said. "I'm tired of running. I'll use the beamer!"

The sky became quickly brighter. The two men and the figures behind them were silhouetted more clearly, but she thought that she still couldn't be seen. She crouched, half of her head sticking out of the water, one hand hanging on to the grass of the bank, the other holding the Horn. She could see that newcomers were not giants but men riding moosoids. They held long spears.

Urthona's voice, his words indistinguishable, came to her. He was shouting some sort of defiance. The riders split, some disappearing below the edge of the bank. Evidently these were going around to cut off the flight of the two. The others halted along the channel in Indian file.

Urthona aimed the beamer, and the two beasts nearest him fell to the ground, their legs cut off. One of the riders fell into the channel. The other rolled out of sight.

There were yells. The beasts and their riders behind the stricken two disappeared down the ridge. Suddenly, two came into sight on the other side. Their spears were leveled at Urthona, and they were screaming in a tongue unknown to Anana.

One of the riders, somewhat in the lead of the other, fell off, his head bouncing into the channel, his body on the edge, blood jetting from the neck. The other's beast fell, precipitating his rider over his head. McKay slammed the edge of a hand against his neck and picked up the man's spear.

Urthona gave a yell of despair, threw the beamer down, and retrieved the spear of the beheaded warrior.

The beamer's battery was exhausted. It was two against eight now the outcome, in no doubt.

Four riders came up onto the bank. McKay and Urthona thrust their spears into the beasts and then were knocked backward into the channel by the wounded beasts. The savages dismounted and went into the water after their victims. The remaining four rode up and shouted encouragement.

Anana had to admire the fight her uncle and his aide put up. But they were eventually slugged into unconsciousness and hauled up onto the bank. When they recovered, their hands were tied behind them and they were urged ahead of the riders with heavy blows on their backs and shoulders from spear butts.

A moment later, the first of a long caravan emerged from the darkness. Presently, the whole cavalcade was in sight. Some of the men dismounted to tie the dead beasts and dead men to moosoids. These were dragged behind the beasts while their owners walked. Evidently the carcasses were to be food. And for all she knew, so were the corpses. Urthona had said that some of the nomadic tribes were cannibals.

As her uncle and McKay were being driven past the point just opposite her, she felt something slimy grab her ankle. She repressed a cry. But, when sharp teeth ripped her ankle, she had to take action. She lowered her head below the surface, bent over, withdrew her knife, and drove it several times into a soft body. The tentacle withdrew, and the teeth quit biting. But the thing was back in a moment, attacking her other leg.

Though she didn't want to, she had to drop the Horn and the amphibian to free her other hand. She felt along the tentacle, found where it joined the body, and sawed away with the knife. Suddenly, the thing was gone, but both her legs felt as if they had been torn open. Also, she had to breathe. She came up out of the water as slowly as possible, stopping when her nose was just above the surface. A body broke the water a few feet from her, dark blood welling out.

She went under again, groped around, found the Horn, and came back up. The savages had noticed the wounded creature by then. And they saw her head emerge, of course. They began yelling and pointing. Presently, several cast their spears at her. These fell short of their mark. But they weren't going to let her escape. Four men slid down the bank and began swimming toward her.

She threw the Horn upon the bank and began clawing her way up it. Her pursuers couldn't chase her on their beasts on this side. The big creatures could never get up the bank. She could get a head start on the men. But when she rolled over on the top of the bank, she saw that her wounds were deeper than she had thought. Blood was welling out over her feet. It was impossible to run any distance with those wounds.

Still . . . she put her axe in one hand and her knife in the other. The first man to come up fell back with a split skull. The second slid back with two fingers chopped off. The others decided that it was best to retreat. They went back into the water and split into two groups, each swimming a hundred yards in opposite directions. They would come up at the same time, and she could only attack one. That one would dive back into the water while the other came at her on the ground.

By then ten others were swimming across. Some of them were several hundred yards downstream; others, the same distance upstream. She had no chance to get beyond these. Flight to the mountains a mile away on this side of the channel was her only chance. But she'd be caught because of her steady loss of blood.

She shrugged, slipped off her ragged shirt, tore it into strips, and bound them around the wounds. She hoped the tentacled things hadn't injected poison into her.

The Horn and the axe couldn't be hidden. The knife went into a pocket on the inside of the right leg of her levis. She'd sewed the pocket there shortly after she'd entered the gateway into Earth. That was a little more than a month ago, but it seemed like a year.

Then she sat, her arms folded, waiting.

XII

HER CAPTORS WERE A SHORT, SLIM, DARK PEOPLE WHO LOOKED AS IF they were of Mediterranean stock. Their language, however, did not seem to her to be related to any she knew. Perhaps their ancestors had spoken one of the many tongues that had died out after the Indo-Europeans and Semites had invaded the Middle Sea area.

They numbered ninety: thirty-two men, thirty-eight women, and twenty children. The moosoids were one hundred and twenty.

Their chief clothing was a rawhide kilt, though some of the men's were of feathers. All the warriors wore thin bones stuck through their septums, and many bore dried human hands suspended from a cord around their necks. Dried human heads adorned the saddles.

Anana was brought back to the other side of the channel and flung half-drowned upon the ground. The women attacked her at once. A few struck or kicked her, but most were trying to get her jeans and boots. Within a minute, she was left lying on the ground, bleeding, bruised, stunned, and naked.

The man whose two fingers she'd severed staggered up, holding his hand, pain twisting his face. He harangued the chief for a long while. The chief evidently told him to forget it, and the man went off.

Urthona and McKay were sitting slumped on the ground, looking even more thrubbed than she.

The chief had appropriated her axe and the Horn. The woman who'd beaten off the others in order to keep the jeans had managed to get them on. So far, she hadn't paid any attention to the knife inside the leg. Anana hoped that she would not investigate the heavy lump, but there didn't seem much chance of that, human curiosity being what it was.

There was a long conference with many speeches from both men and women. Finally, the chief spoke a few words. The dead men were carried off in travois to a point a mile away. The entire tribe, except for the few guards for the prisoners, followed the dead. After a half an hour of much wailing and weeping, punctuated by the shaman's leapings-about, chanting, and rattling of a gourd containing pebbles or seeds, the tribe returned to the channel.

If these people were cannibals, they didn't eat their own dead.

A woman, probably a wife of one of the deceased, rushed at Anana. Her fingers were out and hooked, ready to tear into the captive's face. Anana lay on her back and kicked the woman in the stomach. The whole tribe laughed, apparently enjoying the screams and writhings of the woman. When the widow had recovered, she scrambled up to resume her attack. The chief said something to a warrior, and he dragged the woman away.

By then, "dawn" had come. Some men ate pieces of one of the moosoids killed by Urthona, drank, and then rode off across the plain. The rest cut off portions for themselves and chewed at the meat with strong teeth. The flesh was supplemented by nuts and berries carried in raw leather bags. None of the captives was offered any food. Anana didn't mind, since she'd eaten but a few hours ago, and the beating hadn't improved her appetite. Also, she was somewhat cheered. If these people did intend to eat her, it seemed likely that they would want to fatten her up. That would take time, and time was her ally.

Another thought palled that consideration. Perhaps they were saving her for lunch, in which case they wouldn't want to waste food on her.

The chief, his mouth and beard bloody, approached. His long hair was in a Psyche knot through which two long red feathers were stuck. A circle of human fingers on a leather plate hung from a neck-cord over his beard. One eye socket was empty except for a few flies. He stopped, belched, then yelled at the tribe to gather around.

Anana, watching him remove his kilt, became sick. A minute later, while the tribe yelled encouragement, and made remarks that were obviously obscene, though she didn't understand a word, he did what she had thought he was going to do. Knowing how useless it was to struggle, she lay back quietly. But she visualized six different ways of killing him and hoped she'd have a chance to carry out one of them.

After the chief, grinning, got up and donned his kilt, the shaman came up to her. He apparently had in mind emulating the chief. The latter, however, pushed him away. She was going to be the chief's prop erty. Anana was glad for at least one favor. The shaman was even dirtier and more repulsive than the chief.

She managed to get up and walked over to Urthona. He looked disgusted. She said, "Well, Uncle, you can be glad you're not a woman."

"I always have been," he said. "You could run now before they could catch you and you could drown yourself in the channel. That is the only way to cleanse yourself."

He spat, "Imagine that! A *leblabbiy* defiling a Lord! It's a wonder to me you didn't die of shame."

He paused, then smiled crookedly. "But then you've been mating with a *leblabbiy* voluntarily, haven't you? You have no more pride than an ape."

Anana kicked him in the jaw with her bare foot. Two minutes passed before he recovered consciousness.

Anana felt a little better. Though she would have preferred to kick the chief (though not in his jaw), she had discharged some of her rage.

"If it weren't for you and Orc," she said, "I wouldn't be in this mess."

She turned and walked away, ignoring his curses.

Shortly thereafter, the tribe resumed its march. The meat was thrown on top of piles on travois, and a more or less orderly caravan was formed. The chief rode at the head of the procession. Since attack from their left was impossible, all the outriders were put on the right.

About three hours before dusk, the men who'd been sent across the plains returned at a gallop. Anana didn't know what they reported, but she guessed that they'd gone up one of the mountains to look for enemies. Obviously, they hadn't seen any.

Why had the tribe been on the move during the night? Anana supposed that it was because many tribes would be going to the sea-country. This people wanted to be first, but they knew that others would have the same idea. So they were on a forced march, day and night, to get through the pass before they ran into enemies.

At "noon," when the sky-illumination was brightest, the caravan stopped. Everybody, including the prisoners, ate. Then they lay down with skins over their faces to shut out the light, and they slept. About six stayed awake to be lookouts. These had slept for several hours on travois, though when they woke up they looked as if they hadn't gotten a wink of sleep.

By then the captives' hands were tied in front so they could feed themselves. When nap-time came, thongs were tied around their ankles to hobble them.

Anana had also been given a kilt to wear.

She lay down near her uncle and McKay. The latter said, "These savages must've never seen a black man before. They stare at me, and they rub my hair. Maybe they think it'll bring them luck. If I get a chance, I'll show them what kind of luck they're going to get!"

Urthona spoke out of lips puffed up by a blow from a spearshaft. "They might never have seen blacks before, but there are black tribes here. I brought in specimens of all the Earth races."

McKay said, slowly, "I wonder what they'd do to you if they knew you were responsible for their being here?"

Urthona turned pale. Anana laughed, and said, "I might tell them— when I learn how to speak their tongue."

"You wouldn't do that, would you?" Urthona said. He looked at her, then said, "Yes, you would. Well, just remember, I'm the only one who can get us into my palace."

"If we ever find it," Anana said. "And if these savages don't eat us first."

She closed her eyes and went to sleep. It seemed like a minute later that she was roused by a kick in the ribs. It was the gray-haired woman in her panties, the chief's woman, who'd taken a special dislike to Anana. Or was it so special? All the women seemed to loathe her. Perhaps, though, that was the way they treated all female captives.

Obviously, the women weren't going to teach her the language. She picked on an adolescent, a short muscular lad who was keeping an eye on her. Since he seemed to be fascinated by her, she would get him to initiate her into the tribal speech. It didn't take long to learn his name, which was Nurgo.

Nurgo was eager to teach her. He rode on a moosoid while she walked, but he told her the names of things and people she pointed out. By the end of the "day," when they stopped for another two-hour snooze, she knew fifty words, and she could construct simple questions and had memorized their answers.

Neither Urthona nor McKay were interested in linguistics. They walked side by side, talking in low tones, obviously discussing methods of escape.

When they resumed their march in the deepening twilight, the chief asked her to demonstrate the use of the Horn. She blew the sequence of notes which would open any "gate"—if there had been one around. After some initial failures, he mastered the trumpet and for a half-hour amused himself by blowing it. Then the shaman said something to him. Anana didn't know what it was. She guessed the shaman was pointing out that the sounds might attract the attention of enemies. Sheepishly, he stuck the Horn into a saddlebag.

Amazingly, the woman with her jeans had so far not been curious about the heavy lump in the leg of the cloth. Since she had never seen this type of apparel before, she must think that all jeans were weighted in this fashion.

Near the end of the "night" the caravan stopped again. Guards were posted, and everybody went to sleep. The moosoids, however, stayed awake and chomped on tree branches. These were carried on the travois or on their backs. The supply was almost gone, which meant that men would have to forage for more. That is, find a grove or forest of walking plants, kill some, and strip off the branches.

At "noon" the following day the two mountains forming the pass to the sea seemed to be very close. But she knew that distance was deceiving here. It might take two more days before the pass was reached. Apparently the tribe knew how far away it was. The beasts wouldn't make it to the sea before they became weak with hunger.

Twenty of the men and some four adolescents rode out onto the plain. As fortune had it, the necessary food was advancing toward them. It was a square of trees which she estimated numbered about a thousand. The riders waited until it was a quarter of a mile from the channel. Then, holding lariats made of fiber, they rode out. Nearing the trees, they formed an Indian file. Like redskins circling a wagon train, they rode whooping around and around it.

The plants were about ten feet high and coniferous, shaped like Christmas trees with extraordinarily broad trunks which bulged out at the botton. About two-thirds of the way up, eyes ringed the boles, and four very long and thin greenish tentacles extended from their centers. When the tribesmen got close, the whole unit stopped, and those on the perimeter turned on four barky legs to face outward.

Anana had noticed that a herd of wild moosoids had ignored them. There must be a reason for this. And as the men rode by, about twenty feet from the outguards, she saw why. Streams of heavy projectiles shot from holes in the trunks. Though a long way from the scene, she could hear the hissing of released air.

From much experience with these plants, the humans knew what the exact range of the darts was. They stayed just outside it, the riders upwind closer than those on the downwind side.

She deduced that they knew what the ammunition count for a tree was. They were shouting short words—undoubtedly numbers—as they rode by. Then the chief, who'd been sitting to one side and listening, yelled an order. This was passed on around the circle so that those out of hearing of his voice could be informed. The riders nearest him turned their beasts and headed toward the perimeter. Meanwhile, as if the plants were a well-trained army, those who'd discharged their missiles stepped backward into spaces afforded by the moving aside of the second rank.

It was evident that those behind them would take their places. But the riders stormed in, swung, and cast their lariats. Some of them missed. The majority caught and tightened around a branch or a tentacle. The mounts wheeled, the ropes stretched, the nooses closed, and the unlucky plants were jerked off their feet. The riders urged their beasts on until the trees had been dragged out of range of the missiles. The other ends of the lariats were fastened to pegs stuck into the rear of the saddles. All but one held. This snapped, and the plant was left only ten feet from the square. No matter. It couldn't get up again.

The mounts halted, the riders jumped down and approached the fallen plants. Taking care to keep out of the way of the waving tentacles, they loosened the lariats and returned to their saddles.

Once more, the procedure was repeated. After that the riders ignored the upright trees. They took their flint or chert tools and chopped off the tentacles. Their animals, now safe from the darts—which she presumed were poisoned—attacked the helpless plants. They grabbed the tentacles between their teeth and jerked them loose. After this, while the moosoids were stripping a branch, their owners chopped away branches with flint or chert tools.

The entire tribe, men, women, children, swarmed around the victims and piled the severed branches upon travois or tied bundles of them to the backs of the beasts.

Later, when she'd learned some vocabulary, Anana asked the youth, Nurgo, if the missiles were poisoned. He nodded and grinned and said, *"Yu, messt gwonaw dendert assessampt."*

She wasn't sure whether the last word meant *deadly* or *poison*. But there was no doubt that it would be better not to be struck by the darts. After the plants had been stripped, the men carefully picked up the missiles. They were about four inches long, slim-bodied, with a feathery construction of vegetable origin at one end and a needlepoint at the other. The point was smeared with a blue-greenish substance.

These were put into a rawhide bag or fixed at the ends of spearshafts.

After the work was done, the caravan resumed marching. Anana looking back, saw half of the surviving plants ranged alongside the channel. From the bottom of each a thick greenish tube was extended into the water, which was being sucked up into these. The other half stood guard.

"You must have had a lot of fun designing those," Anana said to Urthona.

"It was more amusing designing them than watching them in action," her uncle said. "In fact, designing this world entertained me more than living on it. I got bored in less than four years and left it. But I have been back now and then during the past ten thousand years to renew my acquaintance with it."

"When was the last time?"

"Oh, about five hundred years ago, I think."

"Then you must have made another world for your headquarters. One more diversified, more beautiful, I'd imagine."

Urthona smiled. "Of course. Then I also am Lord of three more, worlds which I took over after I'd killed their owners. You remember your cousin Bromion, that bitch Ethinthus, and Antamon? They're dead now, and I, I rule their worlds!"

"Do you indeed now?" Anana said. "I wouldn't say you were sitting on any thrones now. Unless you call captivity, the immediate danger of death and torture, thrones."

Urthona snarled, and said, "I'll do you as I did them, my *leblabbiy*-loving niece! And I'll come back here and wipe out these miserable scum! In fact, I may just wipe out this whole world! Cancel it!"

XIII

ANANA SHOOK HER HEAD. "UNCLE, I WAS ONCE LIKE YOU. THAT IS, utterly unworthy of life. But there was something in me that gave me misgivings. Let us call it a residue of compassion, of empathy. Deep under the coldness and cruelty and arrogance was a spark. And that spark fanned into a great fire, fanned by a *leblabbiy* called Kickaha. He's not a Lord, but he is a *man*. That's more than you ever were or will be. And these brutish miserable creatures who've captured you, and don't know they hold the Lord of their crazy world captive . . . they're more human than you could conceive. That is, they're retarded Lords . . ."

Urthona stared and said, "What in The Spinner's name are you talking about?"

Anana felt like hitting him. But she said, "You wouldn't ever understand. Maybe I shouldn't say *ever*. After all, I came to understand. But that was because I was forced to be among the *leblabbiy* for a long time."

"And this *leblabbiy*, Kickaha, this descendant of an artificial product, corrupted your mind. It's too bad the Council is no longer in effect. You'd be condemned and killed within ten minutes."

Anana ran her gaze up and down him several times, her expression contemptuous. "Don't forget, Uncle, that you, too, may be the descendant of an artificial product. Of creatures created in a laboratory. Don't forget what Shambarimen speculated with much evidence to back his statement. That we, too, the Lords, the *Lords,* may have been made in the laboratories of beings who are as high above us as we are above the *leblabbiy*. Or I should say as high above them as we are *supposed* to be.

"After all, we made the *leblabbiy* in our image. Which means that they are neither above nor below us. They are us. But they don't know that, and they have to live in worlds which we created. Made, rather. We are not creators, any more than writers of fiction or painters are creators. They make worlds, but they are never able to make more than what they know. They can write or paint worlds based on elements of the known, put together in a different order in a way to make them seem to be creators.

"We, the so-called Lords, did no more than poets, writers, and painters and sculptors. We were not, and are not, gods. Though we've come to think of ourselves as such."

"Spare me your lectures," Urthona said. "I don't care for your attempts to justify your degeneracy."

Anana shrugged and said, "You're hopeless. But in a way you're right. The thing to talk about is how we can escape."

"Yeah," McKay said. "Just how we going to do that?"

"However we do it," she said, "we can't go without the axe and the Horn. We'd be helpless in this savage world without them. The chief has the axe and the Horn, so we have to get them away from him."

She didn't think she should say anything about the knife in the jeans. They'd noticed it was gone, but she had told them she'd lost it during her flight from them.

A man untied their hobbles, and they resumed the march with the others. Anana went back to her language lessons with Nurgo.

When the tribe got to the pass, it stopped again. She didn't need to ask why. The country beyond the two mountains was black with clouds in which lived a hell of lightning bolts. It would be committing suicide to venture into it. But when a whole day and night passed, and the storm still raged, she did question the youth.

"The Lord sends down thunder and lightning into this country. He topples trees and slays beasts and any human who is foolish enough to dare him.

"That is why we only go into the sea-country when his wrath has cooled off. Otherwise, we would live there all the time. The land changes shape very slowly and insignificantly. The water is full of fish, and the trees, which do not walk, are full of birds that are good to eat. The trees also bear nuts, and there are bushes, which also do not walk, that are heavy with berries. And the game is plentiful and easier caught than on the open plains.

"If we could live there all the time, we would get fat and our children would thrive and our tribe would become more numerous and powerful. But the Lord, in his great wisdom, has decreed that we can only live there for a little while. Then the clouds gather, and his lightning strikes, and the land is no place for anyone who knows what's good for him."

Anana did not, of course, understand everything he said. But she could supply the meaning from what phrases she had mastered.

She went to Urthona and asked him why he had made such an arrangement in the sea-country.

"Primarily, for my entertainment. I liked to send my palace into that land and watch the fury of the lightning, see the devastation. I was safe and snug in my palace, but I got a joy out of seeing the lightning blaze and crack around me. Then I truly felt like a god.

"Secondarily, if it weren't for their fear of being killed, the humans would crowd in. It'd be fun to watch them fight each other for the territory. In fact, it was fun during the stormless seasons. But if there were nothing to keep them from settling down there, they'd never go back into the shifting areas.

"There are, if I remember correctly, twelve of those areas. The seas and the surrounding land each cover about five million square miles. So in an area of 200,000,000 square miles there are 60,000,000 square miles of relatively stable topography. These are never separated from the main mass, and the splitoffs never occur near the seas.

"The lightning season was designed to drive beast and human out of the sea-country except at certain times. Otherwise, they'd get overcrowded."

He stopped to point at the plain. Anana turned and saw that it was now covered with herds of animals, elephants, moosoids, antelopes, and many small creatures. The mountains were dark with birds that had settled on them. And the skies were black with millions of flying creatures.

"They migrate from near and far," Urthona said. "They come to enjoy the sea and the wooded lands while they can. Then, when the storms start, they leave."

Anana wandered away. As long as she didn't get very far from the camp, she was free to roam around. She approached the chief, who was sitting on the ground and striking the ground with the axe. She squatted down before him.

"When will the storms cease?" she said.

His eyes widened. "You have learned our language very quickly. Good. Now I can ask you some questions."

"I asked one first," she said.

He frowned. "The Lord should have ceased being angry and gone back to his palace before now. Usually, the lightning would have stopped two light-periods ago. For some reason, the Lord is very angry and he is still raging. I hope he gets tired of it and goes home soon. The beasts and the birds are piling up. It's a dangerous situation. If a stampede should start, we could be trampled to death. We would have to jump into the water to save ourselves, and that would be bad because our *grewigg* would be lost along with our supplies."

Grewigg was the plural of *gregg,* the word for a moosoid.

Anana said, "I wondered why you weren't hunting when so many animals were close by."

The chief, Trenn, shuddered. "We're not stupid. Now, what tribe is yours? And is it near here?"

Anana wondered if he would accept the truth. After all, his tribe, the Wendow, might have a tradition of having come from another world.

"We are not natives of this . . . place." She waved a hand to indicate the universe, and the flies, alarmed, rose and whirled around buzzing. They quickly settled back, however, lighting on her body, her face, and her arms. She brushed them away from her face. The chief endured the insects crawling all over him and into his empty eye-socket. Possibly, he wasn't even aware of them.

"We came through a . . ." She paused. She didn't know the word for *gate.* Maybe there wasn't any. "We came through a pass between two . . . I don't know how to say it. We came from beyond the sky. From another place where the sky is . . . the color of that bird there."

She pointed to a small blue bird which had landed by the channel.

The chief's eye got even larger. "Ah, you came from the place where our ancestors lived. The place from which the Lord drove our forefathers countless light-periods ago because they had sinned. Tell me, why did the Lord drive you here, too? What did you do to anger him?"

While she was trying to think how to answer this, the chief bellowed for the shaman, Shakann, to join them. The little gray-bearded man, holding the gourd at the end of a stick to which feathers were tied, came running. Trenn spoke too rapidly for Anana to understand any but a few words. Shakann squatted down by the chief.

Anana considered telling them that they'd entered this world accidentally. But she didn't know their word for accident. In fact, she doubted there was such. From what she'd learned from Nurgo, these people believed that nothing happened accidentally. Events were caused by the Lord or by witchcraft.

She got an inspiration. At least, she hoped it was. Lying might get her into even worse trouble. Ignorant of the tribe's theology, she might offend some article of belief, break some tabu, say something contrary to dogma.

"The Lord was angry with us. He sent us here so that we might lead some deserving tribe, yours, for instance, out of this place. Back to the place where your ancestors lived before they were cast out."

There was a long silence. The chief looked as if he were entertaining joyful thoughts. The shaman was frowning.

Finally, the chief said, "And just how are we to do this? If the Lord wants us to return to *sembart* . . ."

"What is *sembart?*"

The chief tried to define it. Anana got the idea that *sembart* could be translated as paradise or the garden of Eden. In any event, a place much preferable to this world.

Well, Earth was no paradise, but, given her choice, she wouldn't hesitate a second in making it.

"If the Lord wants us to return to *sembart,* then why didn't he come here and take us to there?"

"Because," Anana said, "he wanted me to test you. If you were worthy, then I would lead you from this world."

Trenn spoke so rapidly to Shakann that she could comprehend only half of his speech. The gist, however, was that the tribe had made a bad mistake in not treating the captives as honored guests. Everybody had better jump to straighten out matters.

Shakann, however, cautioned him not to act so swiftly. First, he would ask some questions.

"If you are indeed the Lord's representative, why didn't you come to us in his *shelbett?*"

A *shelbett,* it turned out, was a thing that flew. In the old days, according to legend, the Lord had traveled through the air in this.

Anana, thinking fast, said, "I only obey the Lord. I dare not ask him why he does or doesn't do this or that. No doubt, he had his reasons for not giving us a *shelbett.* One might be that if you had seen us in one, you would have known we were from him. And so you would have treated us well. But the Lord wants to know who is good and who isn't."

"But it is not bad to take captives and then kill them or adopt them into the tribe. So how could we know that we were doing a bad thing? All tribes would have treated you the same."

Anana said, "It's not how you treated us at first. How you treated us when you found out that we came from the Lord will determine whether you are found good or bad in his eyes."

Shakann said, "But any tribe that believed your story would honor you and take care of you as if you were a baby. How would you know whether a tribe was doing this because it is good or because it is pretending to be good from fear of you?"

Anana sighed. The shaman was an ignorant savage. But he was intelligent.

"The Lord has given me some powers. One of them is the ability to look into the . . ."

She paused. What was the word for heart?

"To look inside people and see if they are good or bad. To tell when people are lying."

"Very well," Shakann said. "If you can indeed tell when a person lies, tell me this. I intend to take this sharp hard thing the chief took from you and split your head open. I will do it very shortly. Am I lying or am I telling the truth?"

The chief protested, but Shakann said, "Wait! This is a matter for me, your priest, to decide. You rule the tribe in some things, but the business of the Lord is my concern."

Anana tried to appear cool, but she could feel the sweat pouring from her.

Judging from the chief's expression, she doubted that he would let the shaman have the axe. Also, the shaman must be unsure of himself. He might be a hypocrite, a charlatan, though she did not think so. Preliterate medicine men, witches, sorcerers, whatever their title was, really believed in their religion. Hypocrisy came with civilization. His only doubt was whether or not she did indeed represent the Lord of this wretched cosmos. If she were lying and he allowed her to get away with it, then the Lord might punish him.

He was in as desperate a situation as she. At least, he thought he was.

The issue was: was he lying or did he really intend to test her by trying to kill her? He knew that if she were what she said she was, he might be blasted with a bolt from the sky.

She said, "You don't know yourself whether you're lying or telling the truth. You haven't made up your mind yet what you'll do."

The shaman smiled. She relaxed somewhat.

"That is right. But that doesn't mean that you can see what I'm thinking. A very shrewd person could guess that I felt that way. I'll ask you some more questions.

"For instance, one of the things that makes me think you might be from the Lord is that thing which cut the men and the *grewigg* in half.

With it he could have killed the whole tribe. Why, then, did he throw it away after killing only a few?"

"Because the Lord told him to do so. He was to use the deadly gift of the Lord only to show you that he did not come from this world. But the Lord did not want him to slay an entire tribe. How then could we lead you out of this place to *sembart?*"

"That is well spoken. You may indeed be what you say. Or you might just be a very clever woman. Tell me, how will you lead us to *sembart?*"

Anana said, "I didn't say I will. I said I might. What happens depends upon you and the rest of your tribe. First, you have to cut our bonds and then treat us as vicars of the Lord. However, I will say this. I will guide you to the dwelling place of the Lord. When we get to it, we'll enter it and then go through a pass to *sembart.*"

The shaman raised thick woolly eyebrows. "You know where the Lord's dwelling is?"

She nodded. "It's far away. During the journey, you will be tested."

The chief said, "We saw the dwelling of the Lord once countless light-periods ago. We were frightened when we saw it moving along a plain. It was huge and had many . . . um . . . things like great sticks . . . rising from it. It shone with many lights from many stones. We watched it for a while, then fled, afraid the Lord would be offended and deal harshly with us."

Shakann said, "What is the purpose of the thing that makes music?"

"That will get us into the dwelling of the Lord. By the way, we call his dwelling a palace."

"*Bahdahss?*"

"That's good enough. But the . . . Horn . . . belongs to me. You have no right to it. The Lord won't like your taking it."

"Here!" the chief said, thrusting it at her.

"You wronged me when you raped me. I do not know whether the Lord will forgive you for that or not."

The chief spread his hands out in astonishment. "But, I did no wrong! It is the custom for the chief to mount all female captives. All chiefs do it."

Anana had counted on avenging herself some day. She hadn't known if she'd be satisfied with castrating him or also blinding him. However, if it was the custom . . . he really hadn't thought he was doing anything evil. And if she'd been more objective about it, she would have known that, too.

After all, aside from making her nauseated, he hadn't hurt her. She'd suffered no psychic damage, and there wasn't any venereal disease. Nor could he make her pregnant.

"Very well," she said. "I won't hold that against you."

The chief's expression said, "Why should you?" but he made no comment.

The shaman said, "What about the two men? Are they your husbands? I ask that because some tribes, when they have a shortage of women, allow the women to have more than one husband."

"No! They are under my command."

She might as well get the upper hand on the two while she had the chance. Urthona would rave, but he wouldn't try to usurp her leadership. He wouldn't want to discredit her, since her story had saved his life.

She held out her hands, and the chief used a flint knife to sever the thongs. She rose and ordered the chief's mother to be brought to her. Thikka approached haughtily, then turned pale under the dirt when her son explained the situation to her.

"I won't hurt you," Anana said. "I just want my jeans and boots back."

Thikka didn't know what *jeans* or *boots* meant, so Anana used sign language. When they were off, Anana ordered her to take the jeans to the channel and wash them. Then she said, "No. I'll do it. You probably wouldn't know how."

She was afraid the woman might find the knife.

The chief called the entire tribe in and explained who their captives, ex-captives, really were. There were a lot of oh's and ah's, or the Wendow equivalents, and then the women who'd beaten her fell on their knees and begged forgiveness. Anana magnanimously blessed them.

Urthona's and McKay's bonds were cut. Anana told them how she had gained their freedom. However, as it turned out, they were not as free as they wished. Though the chief gave each a moosoid, he delegated men to be their bodyguards. Anana suspected that the shaman was responsible for this.

"We can try to escape any time there's an opportunity," she told her uncle. "But we'll be safer if we're with them while we're looking for our palace. Once we find it, if we find it, we can outwit them. However, I hope the search doesn't take too long. They might wonder why the emissaries of the Lord are having such a hard time locating it."

She smiled. "Oh, yes. You're my subordinates, so please act as if you are. I don't think that shaman is fully convinced about my story."

Urthona looked outraged. McKay said, "It looks like a good deal to me, Miss Anana. No more beatings, we can ride instead of walking, eat plenty, and three women already said they'd like to have babies by me. One thing about them, they ain't got no color prejudice. That's about all I can say for them, though."

XIV

ANOTHER DAY AND NIGHT PASSED. THE THUNDER AND LIGHTNING showed no signs of diminishing. Anana, watching the inferno from the pass, could not imagine how anything, plants or animals, escaped the fury. The chief told her that only about one sixteenth of the trees were laid low and new trees grew very quickly. Many small beasts, hiding now, in burrows and caves, would emerge when the storms were over.

By then the plains were thick with life and the mountains were zebra-striped with lines of just-arriving migrators. The predators, the baboons, wild dogs, moas, and big cats, were killing as they pleased. But the plain was getting so crowded that there was no room to stampede away from the hunters. Sometimes, the frightened antelopes and elephants ran toward the killers and trampled them.

The valley was a babel of animal and bird cries, screams, trumpet-ings, buglings, croakings, bellowings, mooings, roarings.

At this place the waterway banks were about ten feet above the sur-face. The ground sloped upwards from this point towards the sea-land pass where the banks reached their maximum height above the surface of the water, almost a hundred feet. The chief gave orders to abandon the moosoids and swim across the channel if a stampede headed their way. The children and women jumped into the water and swam to the opposite bank and struggled up its slope. The men stayed behind to control the nervous *grewigg*. These were bellowing, rolling their eyes, drawing their lips back to show their big teeth, and dancing around. The riders were busy trying to quiet them, but it was evident that if the storm didn't stop very soon, the plains animals would bolt and with them the moosoids. As it was, the riders were not far behind the beasts in nervousness. Though they knew that the lightning wouldn't reach out between the mountains and strike them, the "fact" that the Lord was working overtime in his rage made them uneasy.

Anana had crossed the channel with the women and children. She hadn't liked leaving her *gregg* behind. But it was better to be here if a stampede did occur. The only animals on this side were those able to get up the steep banks: baboons, goats, small antelopes, foxes. There were a million birds on this side, however, and more were flying in. The squawking and screaming made it difficult to hear anyone more than five feet away even if you shouted.

Urthona and McKay were on their beasts, since it was expected that all men would handle them. Urthona looked worried. Not because of the imminent danger but because she had the Horn. He fully expected her to run away then. There was no one who could stop her on this side of the channel. It would be impossible for anyone on the other side to run parallel along the channel with the hope of eventually cutting her off. He, or they, could never get through the herds jammed all the way from the channel to the base of the mountains.

Something was going to break at any minute. Anything could start an avalanche on a hundred thousand hooves. She decided that she'd better do something about the tribe. It wasn't that she was concerned about the men. They could be trampled into bloody rags for all she cared. Nor, only two years ago, would she have been concerned about the women and children. But now she would feel—in some irrational obscure way—that she was responsible for them. And she surely did not want to be burdened with them.

She swam back across the channel, the Horn stuck in her belt, and climbed onto the bank. Talking loudly in the chief's ear, she told him what had to be done. She did not request it, she demanded it as if she were indeed the representative of the Lord. If Trenn resented her taking over, he was discreet enough not to show it. He bellowed orders, and the men got down from the *grewigg*. While some restrained the beasts, the others slid down the bank and swam to the other side. Anana went with them and told the women what they should do.

She helped them by digging away at the edge of the bank with her knife. The chief apparently was too dignified to do manual labor ever in an emergency. He loaned his axe to his wife, telling her to set to with it.

The others used their flint and chert tools or the ends of their sticks. It wasn't easy, since the grass was tough and their roots were intertwined deep under the surface. But the blades and the greasy earth finally did give way. Within half an hour a trench, forty-five degrees to the horizontal, had been cut into the bank.

Then the men and Anana swam back, and the moosoids were forced over the bank and into the water. The men swam with them, urging them to make for the trench. The *grewigg* were intelligent enough to understand what the trench was for. They entered it, one by one, and clambered, sometimes slipping, up the trench. The women at the top grabbed the reins and helped pull each beast on up, while the men shoved from behind.

Fortunately, there was very little current in the channel. The *grewigg* were not carried away past the trench.

Before all, including the moosoids, had quit panting, the stampede started. There was no way to know how it started. Of a sudden the thunder of countless hooves reached them, mixed with the same noises they had heard, but louder now. It wasn't a monolithic movement in one direction. About half of the beasts headed toward the pass. The other part raced toward the mountains outside those that ringed the sealand. These had resumed their cone shape of two days ago.

First through the pass was a herd of at least a hundred elephants. Trumpeting, shoulder to shoulder, those behind jamming their trunks against the rears of those ahead, they sped by. Several on the edge of the channel were forced into the water, and these began swimming toward the pass.

Behind the pachyderms came a mass of antelopes with brownish-red bodies, black legs, red necks and heads, and long black horns. The largest were about the size of a racing horse. Their numbers greatly exceeded those of the elephants; they must have been at least a thousand. The front ranks got through and then a beast slipped, those behind fell over or on him, and within a minute at least a hundred were piled up. Many were knocked over into the channel.

Anana expected the rear ranks to turn and charge off along the base of the right-hand mountain. But they kept coming, falling, and others piled up on them. The pass on that side of the channel was blocked, but the frantic beasts leaped upon the fallen and attempted to get over their struggling, kicking, horn-tossing, bleating fellows. Then they too tripped and went down and those behind them climbed over them and fell. And they too were covered.

The water was thick with crazed antelopes which swam until bodies fell on them and then others on them and others on them.

Anana yelled at the chief. He couldn't hear her because of the terrifying bedlam, so loud it smothered the bellow of thunder and explosion of lightning beyond the pass. She ran to him and put her mouth to his ear. "The channel's going to be filled in a minute with bodies! Then the beasts'll leap over the bodies and be here! And we'll be caught!"

Trenn nodded and turned and began bellowing and waving his arms. His people couldn't hear him, but they understood his gestures. All the moosoids were mounted, and the travois were hastily attached to the harness and the skins and goods piled on them. This wasn't easy to do, since the *grewigg* were almost uncontrollable. They reared up, and they kicked out at the people trying to hold them, and some bit any hands or faces that came close.

By then the spill into the channel was taking place as far as they could see. There were thousands of animals, not only antelopes now, but elephants, baboons, dogs, and big cats, pressed despite their struggles into the water. Anana caught a glimpse of a big bull elephant tumbling headfirst off the bank, a lion on its back, its claws digging into the skin.

Now added to the roaring and screaming was the flapping of millions of wings as the birds rose into the air. Among these were the biggest winged birds she'd seen so far, condor-like creatures with an estimated wingspan of twelve feet.

Many of the birds were heading for the mountains. But at least half were scavengers, and these settled down on the top of the piles in the water or in the pass. They began tearing away at the bodies, dead or alive, or attempting to defend their rights or displace others.

Anana had never seen such a scene and hoped she never would again. It was possible that she wouldn't. The sudden lifting of the birds had snapped the moosoids' nerves. They started off, some running toward the birds, some toward the mountains, some toward the pass. Men and women hung onto the reins until they were lifted up, then lowered, their bare feet scraping on the ground until they had to let go. Those mounted pulled back on the reins with all their might but to no avail. Skins and goods bounced off the travois, which then bounced up and down behind the frenzied beasts.

Anana watched Urthona, yelling, his face red, hauling back on the reins, being carried off toward the pass. McKay had let loose of his moosoid as soon as it bolted. He stood there, watching her. Evidently he was waiting to see what she would do. She decided to run for the mountains. She looked back once and saw the black man following her. Either he had orders from her uncle not to let her out of his sight or he trusted her to do the best thing to avoid danger and was following her example.

Possibly, he was going to try to get the Horn from her. He couldn't do that without killing her. He was bigger and stronger than she, but she had her knife. He knew how skilled she was with a knife, not to mention her mastership of the martial arts.

Besides, if he attempted murder in sight of the tribe, he'd be discrediting her story that they were sent by the Lord. He surely wouldn't be that stupid.

The nearest mountain on this side of the channel was only a mile away. It was one of the rare shapes, a monolith, four-sided, about two thousand feet high. The ground around it had sunk to three hundred feet, forming a ditch about six hundred and fifty feet broad. She stopped at the edge and turned. McKay joined her five minutes later. It took him several minutes to catch his normal breathing.

"It sure is a mess, ain't it?"

She agreed with him but didn't say so. She seldom commented on the obvious.

"Why're you sticking with me?"

"Because you got the Horn, and that's the only way to get us out of this miserable place. Also, if anybody's going to survive, you are. I stick with you, I live too."

"Does that mean you're no longer loyal to Urthona?"

He smiled. "He ain't paid me recently. And what's more, he ain't never going to pay me. He's promised a lot to me, but I know that once he's safe, he's going to get rid of me."

She was silent for a while. McKay was a hired killer. He couldn't be trusted, but he could be used.

"I'll do my best to get you back to Earth," she said. "I can't promise it. You might have to settle for some other world. Perhaps Kickaha's."

"Any world's better than this one."

"You wouldn't say that if you'd seen some of them. I give you my word that I'll try my best. However, for the time being, you'll pretend to be in my uncle's employ."

"And tell you what he plans, including any monkey business."

"Of course."

He was probably sincere. It was possible though, that Urthona had put him up to this.

By then some of the tribe had also gotten to the base of the mountain. The others were mostly riders who hadn't so far managed to control their beasts. A few were injured or dead.

The stampede was over. Those animals still on their hooves or paws had scattered. There was more room for them on the plain now. The birds covered the piles of carcasses like flies on a dog turd.

She began walking down to the channel. The tribe followed her, some talking about the unexpected bonus of meat. They would have enough to stuff themselves silly for two days before the bodies got too rank. Or perhaps three days. She didn't know just how fastidious they were. From what she'd seen, not very.

Halfway to the channel, McKay stopped, and said, "Here comes the chief."

She looked toward the pass. Coming down the slope from it was Trenn. Though his *gregg* had bolted and taken him into the valley itself, it was now under control. She was surprised to see that the heavy black clouds over the sea-country were fading away. And the lightning had stopped.

A minute later, several other *grewigg* and riders came over the top of the rise. By the time she got to the channel, they were close enough for her to recognize them. One was her uncle. Until then, the moosoids had been trotting. Now Urthona urged his into a gallop. He pulled the sweating panting saliva-flecked beast up when he got close, and he dismounted swiftly. The animal groaned, crumpled, turned over on its side and died.

Urthona had a strange expression. His green eyes were wide, and he looked pale.

"Anana! Anana!" he cried. "I saw it! I saw it!"

"Saw what?" she said.

He was trembling.

"My palace! It was on the sea! Heading out away from the shore!"

XV

OBVIOUSLY, IF HE'D BEEN ABLE TO CATCH UP TO IT, HE WOULDN'T BE here.

"How fast does it travel?" she said.

"When the drive is on automatic, one kilometer an hour."

"I don't suppose that after all this time you'd have the slightest idea what path it will take?"

He spread out his hands and shrugged his shoulders.

The situation seemed hopeless. There was no time to build a sailing boat, even if tools were available, and to try to catch up with it. But it was possible that the palace would circle around the sea and come back to this area.

"Eventually," Urthona said, "the palace will leave this country. It'll go through one of the passes. Not this one, though. It isn't wide enough."

Anana did not accept this statement as necessarily true. For all she knew, the palace contained devices which could affect the shape-changing. But if Urthona had any reason to think that the palace could come through this pass, he surely would not have told her about seeing it.

There was nothing to be done about the palace at this time. She put it out of her mind for the time being, but her uncle was a worrier. He couldn't stop talking about it, and he probably would dream about it. Just to devil him, she said, "Maybe Orc got to it when it was close to shore. He might be in the palace now. Or, more probably, he's gated through to some other world."

Urthona's fair skin became even whiter. "No! He couldn't! It would be impossible! In the first place, he wouldn't dare venture into the sea during the storm. In the second place, he couldn't get to it. He'd have to swim . . . I think. And in the third place, he doesn't know the entrance-code."

Anana laughed.

Urthona scowled. "You just said that to upset me."

"I did, yes. But now that I think about it, Orc could have done it if he was desperate enough to risk the lightning."

McKay, who had been listening nearby, said, "Why would he take the risk unless he knew the palace was there? And how could he know it was there unless he'd already gone into the sea-land? Which he wouldn't do unless he knew . . ."

Anana said swiftly, "But he could have seen it from the pass, and that might have been enough for him."

She didn't really believe this, but she wasn't too sure. When she walked away from her uncle, she wondered if Orc just might have done it. Her effort to bug Urthona had backfired. Now *she* was worried.

A few minutes later, the storm ceased. The thunder quit rolling; the clouds cleared as if sucked into a giant vacuum cleaner. The shaman and the chief talked together for a while, then approached Anana.

Trenn said, "Agent of the Lord, we have a question. Is the Lord no longer angry? Is it safe for us to go into the sea-land?"

She didn't dare to show any hesitation. Her role called for her to be intimate with the Lord's plans.

If she guessed wrong, she'd lose her credibility.

"The wrath of the Lord is finished," she said. "It'll be safe now."

If the clouds appeared again and lightning struck, she would have to run away as quickly as possible.

The departure did not take place immediately, however. The animals that had bolted had to be caught, the scattered goods collected, and the ceremonies for the dead gone through. About two hours later the tribe headed for the pass. Anana was delighted to be in a country where there were trees that did not walk, and where thick woods and an open sea offered two ready avenues of flight.

The Wendow went down the long slope leading to sand beaches. The chief turned left, and the others followed. According to Nurgo, the destination lay about half a day's travel away. Their stronghold was about fifteen minutes' walk inland from the beach.

"What about the other tribes that come through the pass?" she said.

"Oh, they'll be coming through during the next few light-periods. They'll go even further up the beach, toward their camps. We were lucky that there weren't other tribes waiting at the pass, since the storm lasted longer than usual."

"Do you attack them as they pass by your stronghold?"

"Not unless we outnumber them greatly."

Further questioning cleared up some of her ignorance about their pattern of war. Usually, the tribes avoided any full-scale battles if it was possible. Belligerence was confined to raids by individuals or parties of three to five people. These were conducted during the dark period and were mainly by young unblooded males and sometimes by a young woman accompanied by a male. The youth had to kill a man and bring back his head as proof of his or her manhood or womanhood. The greatest credit, however, was not for a head but for a child. To steal a child and bring it back for adoption into the tribe was the highest feat possible.

Nurgo himself was an adopted child. He'd been snatched not long after he'd started walking. He didn't remember a thing about it, though he did sometimes have nightmares in which he was torn away from a woman without a face.

The caravan came to a place which looked just like the rest of the terrain to Anana. But the tribe recognized it with a cry of joy. Trenn led them into the wooded hills, and after a while they came to a hill higher than the others. Logs lay on its top and down its slope, the ruins of what had been a stockade.

The next few days were spent in fishing, gathering nuts and berries, eating, sleeping, and rebuilding the fort. Anana put some weight back on and began to feel rested. But once she had all her energy back, she became restless.

Urthona was equally fidgety. She observed him talking softly to McKay frequently. She had no doubts about the subject of their conversation, and McKay, reporting to her, gave her the details.

"Your uncle wants to take off at the first chance. But no way is he going to leave without the Horn."

"Is he planning on taking it from me now or when he finds his palace?" she said.

"He says that we, us two, him and me, that is, would have a better chance of surviving if you was to go with us. But he says you're so tricky you might get the upper hand on us when we sight the palace. So he can't make up his mind yet. But he's going to have to do it soon. Every minute passes, the palace is getting further away."

There was a silence. McKay looked as if he was chewing something but didn't know if he should swallow it or spit it out. After a minute, his expression changed.

"I got something to tell you."

He paused, then said, "Urthona told you and Kickaha that this Wolff, or Jadawin, and his woman—Chryseis?—had been gated to this world. Well, that's a lie. They somehow escaped. They're still on Earth!"

Anana did not reply at once. McKay didn't have to tell her this news. Why had he done so? Was it because he wanted to reassure her that he had indeed switched loyalties? Or had Urthona ordered McKay to tell her that so she would think he was betraying Urthona?

In either case, was the story true?

She sighed. All Lords, including herself, were so paranoiac that they would never be able to distinguish between reality and fantasy. Their distrust of motivation made it impossible.

She shrugged. For the moment she'd act as if she believed his story. She looked around the big tree they'd been sitting behind, and she said, "Oh, oh! Here comes my uncle, looking for us. If he sees you with me, he'll get suspicious. You'd better take off."

McKay crawled off into the bushes. When Urthona found her, she said, "Hello, Uncle. Aren't you supposed to be helping the fish spearers?"

"I told them I didn't care to go fishing today. And, of course, since I'm one of the Lord's agents, I wasn't challenged. I could tell they didn't like it, though.

"I was looking for you and McKay. Where is he?"

She lifted her shoulders.

"Well, it doesn't matter."

He squatted down by her.

"I think we've wasted enough time. We should get away the momen we have a chance."

"We?" she said, raising her eyebrows. "Why should I want to go with you?"

He looked exasperated. "You surely don't want to spend the rest o your life here?"

"I don't intend to. But I mean to make sure first that Kickaha is either alive or dead."

"That *leblabbiy* really means that much to you?"

"Yes. Don't look so disgusted. If you should ever feel that much for another human being, which I doubt, then you'll know why I'm makin sure about him. Meanwhile . . ."

He looked incredulous. "You can't stay here."

"Not forever. But if he's alive, he'll be along soon. I'll give him a ce tain time to come. After that, I'll look for his bones."

Urthona bit his lower lip.

He said, "Then you won't come with us now?"

She didn't reply. He knew the answer.

There was a silence for a few minutes. Then he stood up.

"At least, you won't tell the chief what we're planning to do?"

"I'd get no special pleasure out of that," she said. "The only thing is
. . . how do I explain your French leave? How do I account for a representative of the Lord, sent on a special mission to check out the Wendow tribe, my subordinate, sneaking off?"

Her uncle chewed his lips some more. He'd been doing that for ten
thousand years; she remembered when she was a child seeing him gnaw
on it.

Finally, he smiled. "You could tell them McKay and I are off on a
secret mission, the purpose of which you can't divulge now because it's
for the Lord. Actually, it would be fine if you'd say that. We wouldn't
have to sneak off. We could just walk out, and they wouldn't dare prevent us."

"I could do that," she said. "But why should I? If by some chance
you did find the palace right away, you'd just bring it back here and destroy me. Or use one of your fliers. In any event, I'm sure you have all
sorts of weapons in your palace."

He knew it was useless to protest that he wouldn't do that. He said,
"What's the difference? I'm going, one way or the other. You can't tell
the chief I am because then you'd have to explain why I am. You can't
do a thing about it."

"You can do what you want to," she said. "But you can't take this
with you."

She held up the Horn.

His eyes narrowed, and his lips tightened. By that she knew that he
had no intention of leaving without the Horn. There were two reasons
why, one of which was certain. The other might exist.

No Lord would pass up the chance to get his hands on the skeleton
key to the gates of all the universes.

The Horn might also be the ticket to passage from a place on this
planet to his palace. Just possibly, there were gates locked into the
boulders. Not all boulders, of course. Just some. She'd tried the Horn
on the four big rocks she'd encountered so far, and none had contained
any. But there could be gates in others.

If there were, then he wasn't going to risk her finding one and getting
into the palace before he did.

Undoubtedly, or at least probably, he would tell McKay just when he planned to catch her sleeping, kill her, and take the Horn. Would McKay warn her? She couldn't take the chance that he wouldn't.

"All right," she said. "I'll go with you. I have just as much chance finding Kickaha elsewhere. And I am tired of sitting here."

He wasn't as pleased as he should have been. He smelled a trap. Of course, even if she'd been sincere, he would have suspected she was up to something. Just as she wondered if he was telling her the truth or only part of it.

Urthona's handsome face now assumed a smile. In this millennia-long and deadly game the Lords played, artifices that wouldn't work and which both sides knew wouldn't work, were still used. The combats had been partly ritualized.

"We'll do it tonight then," Anana said.

Urthona agreed. He went off to look for McKay and found him within two minutes, since McKay was watching them and saw her signal. They talked for fifteen minutes, after which the two men went down to the beach to help in the fishing. She went out to pick berries and nuts. When she returned on her first trip with two leather bags full, she stood around for a while instead of going out again. She managed to get her hands on three leather-skin waterbags and put these in her leanto. There was little she could do now until late in the night.

The tribe feasted and danced that evening. The shaman chanted for continued prosperity. The bard sang songs of heroes of the olden days. Eventually, the belly-swollen people crawled into their leantos and fell asleep. The only ones probably awake were the sentinels, one in a tree top near the shore, one on a platform in the middle of the stockade, and two men stationed along the path to the stockade.

Urthona, Anana, and McKay had eaten sparingly. They worked inside their leantos, stuffing smoked fish and antelope and fruits and berries and nuts into provision bags. The waterbags would be filled when they got to the lakeshore.

When she could hear only snores and the distant cries of birds and the coughing of a lion, she crawled out of the frail structure. She couldn't see the guard on top of the platform. She hoped he had fallen asleep, too. Certainly, he had stuffed himself enough to make him nod off, whatever his good intentions.

Urthona and McKay crawled out of their respective leantos. Anana signaled to them. She stood up and walked through the dark reddish light of "midnight" until she was far enough away from the sentinel platform to see its occupant. He was lying down, flat on his back. Whether he was asleep or not she couldn't determine, but she suspected he was. He was supposed to stay on his feet and scan the surrounding woods until relieved.

The two men went to the corral which held the moosoids. They got their three beasts out without making too much noise and began to saddle them. Anana carried over the waterbags and a full provision bag. These were tied onto a little leather platform behind the saddle.

Anana whispered, "I have to get my axe."

Urthona grimaced, but he nodded. He and his niece had had a short argument about that earlier. Urthona thought that it was best to forget about the axe, but she had insisted that it was vital to have it. While the two men led the animals to the gate, she walked to the chief's leanto, which was larger than the others. She pushed aside the boughs which surrounded it and crawled into the interior. It was as dark as the inside of a coal mine. The loud snores of Trenn and his wife and son, a half-grown boy, tried to make up for the absence of light with a plenitude of sound. On her hands and knees she groped around, touching first the woman. Then her hand felt his leg. She withdrew it from the flesh and felt along the grass by it. Her fingers came into contact with cold iron.

A moment later she was out of the structure, the throwing axe in one hand. For just a second she'd been tempted to kill Trenn in revenge for his violation of her. But she had resisted. He might make some noise if she did, and, anyway she had already forgiven if not forgotten. Yet . . . something murderous had seized her briefly, made her long to wipe out the injury by wiping the injurer out. Then reason had driven the irrational away.

The gate was a single piece composed of upright poles to which horizontal and transverse bars had been tied with leather cords. Instead of hinges, it was connected to the wall by more leather cords. Several thick strips of leather served as a lock. These were untied, and the heavy gate was lifted up and then turned inward by all three of them.

So far, no one had raised an outcry. The sentinel might wake at any moment. On the other hand, he might sleep all night. He was supposed to be relieved after a two-hour watch. There was no such thing as an "hour" in the tribe's vocabulary, but these people had a rough sense of passage of time. When the sentinel thought that he'd stood watch long enough, he would descend from the platform and wake up the man delegated to succeed him.

The beasts were passed through, the gate lifted and carried back, and the cords retied. The three mounted and rode off slowly in the half-light, heading down the hill. The moosoids grunted now and then, unhappy at being mounted at this ungodly hour. When the three were about a hundred yards from where they knew the first sentinel was placed, they halted. Anana got off and slipped through the brush until she saw the pale figure sitting with its back against the bole of a tree. Snores buzz-sawed from it.

It was an easy matter to walk up to the man and bring down the flat of her axe on top of his head. He fell over, his snores continuing. She ran back and told the two it was safe to continue. Urthona wanted to slit the man's throat, but Anana said it wasn't necessary. The guard would be unconscious for a long while.

The second sentinel was walking back and forth to keep himself awake. He strode down the hill for fifty paces or so, wheeled, and climbed back up the twenty-degree slope. He was muttering a song, something about the heroic deeds of Sheerkun.

In this comparative stillness, it would be difficult to make a detour around him without his hearing them. He had to be gotten out of the way.

Anana waited until he had turned at the end of his round, ran out behind him, and knocked him out with the flat of her axe. She went back and told the others the way was clear for a while.

When they could see the paleness of the white sand shore and the darkness of the sea beyond, they stopped. The last of the sentinels was in a giant tree near the beach. Anana said, "There's no use trying to get to him. But he can yell as loudly as he wishes. There's nobody to relay his message to the village."

They rode out boldly onto the sand. The expected outcry did not come. Either the sentinel was dozing or he did not recognize them and believed some of his tribesmen were there for a legitimate reason. Or perhaps he did recognize them but dared not question the agents of the Lord.

When they were out of his sight, the three stopped. After filling the waterbags, they resumed their flight, if a leisurely pace could be called a flight. They plodded on steadily, silent, each occupied with his or her own thoughts.

There didn't seem to be any danger from Trenn's tribe. By the time one of the stunned men woke up and gave the alarm, the escapee would have too much of a head start to be caught. The only immediate peril, Anana thought, was from Urthona and McKay. Her uncle could try to kill her now to get the Horn in his own hands. But until they found the palace, she was a strong asset. To survive, Urthona needed her.

"Dawn" came with the first paling of the bands in the sky. As the light increased, they continued. They stopped only to excrete or to drink from the sea and to allow their beasts to quench their thirst. At dusk they went into the woods. Finding a hollow surrounded by trees, they slept in it most of the night through. They were wakened several times by the howling of dogs and roars of big cats. However, no predators came near. At "dawn" they resumed their journey. At "noon," they came to the place which would lead them up to the pass.

Here Anana reined in her moosoid. She made sure that she wasn't close to them before she spoke. Her left hand was close to the hilt of her sheathed knife—she was ambidextrous—and if she had to, she could drop the reins and snatch out her axe. The men carried flint-tipped spears and had available some heavy war-boomerangs.

"I'm going up to the pass and look over the valley from there," she said. "For Kickaha, of course."

Urthona opened his mouth as if to protest. Then he smiled, and said, "I doubt it. See." He pointed up the slope.

She didn't look at once. He might be trying to get her to turn her head and thus give him a chance to attack.

McKay's expression, however, indicated that her uncle was pointing at something worth looking at. Or had he arranged beforehand that McKay would pretend to do such if an occasion arose for it?

She turned the beast quickly and moved several yards away. Then she looked away.

From the top of the slope down to the beach was a wide avenue, carpeted by the rust-colored grass. It wasn't a manmade path; nature, or, rather, Urthona, had designed it. It gave her an unobstructed view of the tiny figures just emerging from the pass. Men on moosoids. Behind them, women and children and more beasts.

Another tribe was entering the sea-land.

XVI

"LET'S SPLIT!" MCKAY SAID.

Anana said, "You can if you want to. I'm going to see if Kickaha is with them. Maybe he was captured by them."

Urthona bit his lip. He looked at the black man, then at his niece. Apparently, he decided that now was no time to try to kill her. He said, "Very well. What do you intend to do? Ride up to them and ask if you can check them out?"

Anana said, "Don't be sarcastic, Uncle. We'll hide in the woods and watch them."

She urged her *gregg* into the trees. The others followed her, but she made sure that they did not get too close to her back. When she got to a hill which gave a good view through the trees, she halted. Urthona directed his beast toward her, but she said, "Keep your distance Uncle!"

He smiled, and stopped his moosoid below her. All three sat on their *grewigg* for a while, then, tiring of waiting, got off.

"It'll be an hour before they get here," Urthona said. "And what if those savages turn right? We'll be between the Wendow and this tribe. Caught."

"If Kickaha isn't among them," she said, "I intend to go up the pass after they go by and look for him. I don't care what you want to do. You can go on."

McKay grinned. Urthona grunted. All three understood that as long as she had the Horn they would stay together.

The *grewigg* seized bushes and low treelimbs with their teeth, tore them off, and ground the leaves to pulp. Their empty bellies rumbled as the food passed toward their big bellies. The flies gathered above beasts and humans and settled over them. The big green insects were not as numerous here as on the plains, but there were enough to irritate the three. Since they had not as yet attained the indifference of the natives, their hands and heads and shoulders were in continuous motion, batting, jerking, shrugging.

Then they were free of the devils for a while. A dozen little birds, blue with white breasts, equipped with wide flat almost duckish beaks, swooped down. They swirled around the people and the beasts, catching the insects, gulping them down, narrowly averting aerial collisons in their circles. They came very close to the three, several times brushing them with the woods. In two minutes those flies not eaten had winged off for less dangerous parts.

"I'm glad I invented those birds," Urthona said. "But if I'd known I was going to be in this situation, I'd never have made the flies."

"Lord of the flies," Anana said. "Beelzebub is thy name."

Urthona said, "What?" Then he smiled. "Ah, yes, now I remember."

Anana would have liked to climb a tree so she could get a better view. But she didn't want her uncle to take her *gregg* and leave her stranded. Even if he didn't do that, she'd be at a disadvantage when she got down out of the tree.

After an almost unendurable wait for her, since it was possible, though not very probable, that Kickaha could be coming along, the vanguard came into sight. Soon dark men wearing feathered head-dresses rode by. They carried the same weapons and wore the same type of clothes as the Wendow. Around their necks, suspended by cords, were the bones of human fingers. A big man held aloft a pole on which was a lion skull. Since he was the only one to have such a standard, and he rode in the lead, he must be the chief.

The faces were different from the Wendow's, however, and the skins were even darker. Their features were broad, their noses somewhat bigger and even more aquiline, and the eyes had a slight Mongolian cast. They looked like, and probably were, Amerindians. The chief could have been Sitting Bull if he'd been wearing somewhat different garments and astride a horse.

The foreguard passed out of sight. The outriders and the women and children, most of whom were walking, went by. The women wore their shiny raven's-wing hair piled on top of their heads, and their sole garments were leather skirts of ankle-length. Many wore necklaces of clam shells. A few carried papooses on back packs.

Anana suddenly gave a soft cry. A man on a *gregg* had come into sight. He was tall and much paler than the others and had bright red hair.

Urthona said, "It's not Kickaha! It's Red Orc!"

Anana felt almost sick with disappointment.

Her uncle turned and smiled at her. Anana decided at that moment that she was going to kill him at the first opportunity. Anyone who got that much enjoyment out of the sufferings of others didn't deserve to live.

Her reaction was wholly emotional, of course, she told herself a minute later. She needed him to survive as much as he needed her. But the instant he was of no more use to her . . .

Urthona said, "Well, well. My brother, your uncle, is in a fine pickle, my dear. He looks absolutely downcast. What do you suppose his captors have in mind for him? Torture? It would be almost worthwhile to hang around and watch it."

"He ain't tied up," McKay said. "Maybe he's been adopted, like us."

Urthona shrugged. "Perhaps. In either case, he'll be suffering. He can spend the rest of his life here with those miserable wretches for all I care. The pain won't be so intense, but it'll be much longer lasting."

McKay said, "What're we going to do now we know Kickaha's not with them?"

"We haven't seen all of them," Anana said. "Maybe . . ."

"It isn't likely that the tribe would have caught both of them," Urthona said impatiently. "I think we should go now. By cutting at an angle across the woods, we can be on the beach far ahead of them."

"I'm waiting," she said.

Urthona snorted and then spat. "Your sick lust for that *leblabbiy* makes me sick."

She didn't bother to reply. But presently, as the rearguard passed by, she sighed.

"Now are you ready to go?" Urthona said, grinning.

She nodded, but she said, "It's possible that Orc has seen Kickaha."

"What? You surely aren't thinking of . . . ? Are you crazy?"

"I'm going to trail them and when the chance comes I'll help Orc escape."

"Just because he might know something about your *leblabbiy* lover?"

"Yes."

Urthona's red face was twisted with rage. She knew that it was not just from frustration. Distorting it were also incomprehension, disgust and fear. He could not understand how she could be so much in love, in love at all, with a mere creature, the descendant of beings made in laboratories. That his niece, a Lord, could be enraptured by the creature Kickaha filled him with loathing for her. The fear was not caused by her action in refusing to go with them or the danger she represented if attacked. It was—she believed it was, anyway—a fear that possibly he might someday be so perverted that he, too, would fall in love with a *leblabbiy*. He feared himself.

Or perhaps she was being too analytical—ad absurdum—in her analysis.

Whatever had seized him, it had pushed him past rationality. Snarling, face as red as skin could get without bleeding, eyes tigerish, growling, he sprang at her. Both hands, white with compression, gripped the flint-headed spear.

When he charged, he was ten paces from her. Before he had gone five, he fell back, the spear dropping from his hands, his head and back thudding into the grass. The edge of her axe was sunk into his breastbone.

Almost before the blur of the whirling axe had solidified on Urthona's chest, she had her knife out.

McKay had been caught flat-footed. Whether he would have acted to help her uncle or her would never be determined.

He looked shocked. Not at what had happened to her uncle, of course, but at the speed with which it had occurred.

Whatever his original loyalty was, it was now clear that he had to aid and to depend upon her. He could not find the palace without her or, arriving there, know how to get into it. Or, if he could somehow gain entrance to it, know what to do after he was in it.

From his expression, though, he wasn't thinking of this just now. He was wondering if she meant to kill him, too.

"We're in this together, now," she said. "All the way."

He relaxed, but it was a minute before the blue-gray beneath his pigment faded away.

She stepped forward and wrenched the axe from Urthona's chest. It hadn't gone in deeply, and blood ran out from the wound. His mouth was open; his eyes fixed; his skin was grayish. However, he still breathed.

"The end of a long and unpleasant relationship," she said, wiping the axe on the grass. "Yet . . ."

McKay muttered, "What?"

"When I was a little girl, I loved him. He wasn't then what he became later. For that matter, neither was I. Excessive longevity . . .

solipsism . . . boredom . . . lust for such power as you Earthlings have never known . . ."

Her voice trailed off as if it were receding into an unimaginably distant past.

McKay made no movement to get closer to her. He said, "What're you going to do?" and he pointed at the still form.

Anana looked down. The flies were swarming over Urthona, chiefly on the wound. It wouldn't be long before the predators, attracted by the odor of blood, would be coming in. He'd be torn apart, perhaps while still living.

She couldn't help thinking of those evenings on their native planet, when he had tossed her in the air and kissed her or when he had brought gifts or when he had made his first world and come to visit before going to it. The Lord of several universes had come to this . . . lying on his back, his blood eaten by insects, the flesh soon to be ripped by fangs and claws.

"Ain't you going to put him out of his misery?" McKay said.

"He isn't dead yet, which means that he still has hope," she said. "No, I'm not going to cut his throat. I'll leave his weapons and his *gregg* here. He might make it, though I doubt it. Perhaps I'll regret not making sure of him, but I can't . . ."

"I didn't like him," McKay said, "but he's going to suffer. It don't seem right."

"How many men have you killed in cold blood for money?" she said. "How many have you tortured, again just for money?"

McKay shook his head. "That don't matter. There was a reason then. There ain't no sense to this."

"It's usually emotional sense, not intellectual, that guides us humans," she said. "Come on."

She brushed by McKay, giving him a chance to attack her if he wanted to. She didn't think he would, and he stepped back as if, for some reason, he dreaded her touch.

They mounted and headed at an angle for the beach. Anana didn't look back.

When they broke out of the woods, the only creatures on the beach were birds, dead fish—the only true fish in this world were in the sealands—amphibians, and some foxes. The *grewigg* were breathing hard. The long journey without enough sleep and food had tired them.

Anana let the beasts water in the sea. She said, "We'll go back into the forest. We're near enough to the path to see which way they take. Either direction, we'll follow them at a safe distance."

Presently the tribe came out onto the beach on the night side of the channel. With shouts of joy they ran into the waves, plunged beneath their surface, splashed around playfully. After a while they began to spear fish, and when enough of these had been collected, they held a big feast.

When night came they retreated into the woods on the side of the path near where the two watchers were. Anana and McKay retreated some distance. When it became apparent that the savages were going to bed down, they went even further back into the woods. Anana decided that the tribe would stay put until "dawn" at least. It wasn't likely that it would make this spot a more or less permanent camp. Its members would be afraid of other tribes coming into the area.

Even though she didn't think McKay would harm her, she still went off into the bush to find a sleeping place where he couldn't see her. If he wanted to, he would find her. But he would have to climb a tree to get her. Her bed was some boughs she'd chopped and laid across two branches.

The "night," as all nights here, was not unbroken sleep. Cries of birds and beasts startled her, and twice her dreams woke her.

The first was of her uncle, naked, bleeding from the longitudinal gash in his chest, standing above her on the tree-nest and about to lay his hands on her. She came out of it moaning with terror.

The second was of Kickaha. She'd been wandering around the bleak and shifting landscape of this world when she came across his death-pale body lying in a shallow pool. She started crying, but when she touched him, Kickaha sat up suddenly, grinning, and he cried, "April fool!" He rose and she ran to him and they put their arms around each other and then they were riding swiftly on a horse that bounced rather than ran, like a giant kangaroo. Anana woke up with her hips emulating the up-and-down movement and her whole being joyous.

She wept a little afterward because the dream wasn't true.

McKay was still sleeping where he had lain down. The hobbled moos-soids were tearing off branches about fifty meters away. She bent down and touched his shoulder, and he came up out of sleep like a trout leaping for a dragonfly.

"Don't ever do that again!" he said, scowling.

"Very well. We've got to eat breakfast and then check up on that tribe. Did you hear anything that might indicate they are up and about?"

"Nothing," he said sullenly.

But when they got to the edge of the woods, they saw no sign of the newcomers except for excrement and animal and fish bones. When they rode out onto the white sands, they caught sight, to their right, of the last of the caravan, tiny figures.

After waiting until the Amerinds were out of sight, they followed. Some time later, they came to another channel running out of the sea. This had to be the waterway they had first encountered, the opening of which had swept Kickaha away. It ran straight outwards from the great body of water between the increasingly higher banks of the slope leading up to the pass between the two mountains.

They urged their beasts into the channel and rode them as they swam across. On reaching the other side they had to slide down off, get onto the beach, and pull on the reins to help the moosoids onto the sand. The Amerinds were still not in view.

She looked up the slope. "I'm going up to the pass and take a look. Maybe he's out on the plain."

"If he was trailing them," McKay said, "he would've been here by now. And gone by now, maybe."

"I know, but I'm going up there anyway."

She urged the moosoid up the slope. Twice, she looked back. The first time, McKay was sitting on his motionless *gregg*. The next time, he was coming along slowly.

On reaching the top of the pass, she halted her beast. The plain had changed considerably. Though the channel was still surrounded by flatland for a distance of about a hundred feet on each side, the ground beyond had sunk. The channel now ran through a ridge on both sides of which were very deep and broad hollows. These were about a mile wide. Mountains of all sizes and shapes had risen along its borders, thrusting up from the edges as if carved there. Even as she watched, one of the tops of the mushroom-shaped heights began breaking off at its edges. The huge pieces slid or rotated down the steep slope, some reaching the bottom where they fell into the depressions.

There were few animals along the channel, but these began trotting or running away when the first of the great chunks broke off of the mushroom peak.

On the other side of the mountains was a downward slope cut by the channel banks. On the side on which she sat was a pile of bones, great and small, that extended down into the plain and far out.

Nowhere was any human being in sight.

Softly, she said, "Kickaha?"

It was hard to believe that he could be dead.

She turned and waved to McKay to halt. He did so, and she started her beast towards him. And then she felt the earth shaking around her. Her *gregg* stopped despite her commands to keep going, and it remained locked in position, though quivering. She got down off of it and tried to pull it by the reins, but it dug in, leaning its body back. She mounted again and waited.

The slope was changing swiftly, sinking at the rate of about a foot a minute. The channel was closing up, the sides moving toward each other, and apparently the bottom was moving up, since the water was slopping over its lips.

Heat arose from the ground.

McKay was in the same predicament. His moosoid stubbornly refused to obey despite his rider's beatings with the shaft of his spear.

She turned on the saddle to look behind her. The ridge was becoming a mountain range, a tiny range now but it was evident that if this process didn't stop, it would change into a long and giant barrow. The animals along it were running down its slopes, their destination the ever-increasing depressions along its sides.

However, the two mountains that formed the pass remained solid, immovable.

Anana sighed. There was nothing she could do except sit and wait this out unless she wanted to dismount. The *gregg,* from long experience, must know the right thing to do.

It was like being on a slow-moving elevator, one in which the temperature rose as the elevator fell. Actually, she felt as if the mountains on her side were rising instead of the ground descending.

The entire change lasted about an hour. At the end the channel had disappeared, the ridge had stopped swelling and had sunk, the hollows had been filled, and the plain had been restored to the bases of the mountains just outside the sea-land. The animals which had been desperately scrambling around to adjust to the terrain-change were now grazing upon the grass. The predators were now stalking the meat on the hoof. Business as usual.

Anana tickticked with her tongue to the *gregg,* and it trotted toward the sea. McKay waited for her to come to him. He didn't ask her if she'd seen Kickaha. He knew that if she had she would have said so. He merely shook his head and said, "Crazy country, ain't it?"

"It lost us more than an hour, all things considered," she said. "I don't see any reason to push the *grewigg* though. They're not fully recovered yet. We'll just take it easy. We should find those Indians sometime after dark. They'll be camped for the night."

"Yeah, some place in the woods," he said. "We might just ride on by them and in the morning they'll be on our tails."

About three hours after the bright bands of the sky had darkened, Anana's *gregg* stopped, softly rumbling in its throat. She urged it forward with soft words until she saw, through the half-light, a vague figure. She and McKay retreated for a hundred yards and held a short conference. McKay didn't object when she decided that she would take out the guards while he stayed behind.

"I hope the guard don't make any noise when you dispose of him," he said. "What'll I do if he raises a ruckus?"

"Wait and see if anyone else hears him. If they do, then ride like hell to me, bringing my *gregg,* and we'll take off the way we came. Unless, that is, most of the Indians are in the woods. Maybe there's only a guard or two on the beach itself. But I don't plan on making a mistake."

"You're the boss," McKay said. "Good luck."

She went into the woods, moving swiftly when there was no obstruction, slowly when she had to make her way among thick bushes. At last, she was opposite the guard, close enough to see that he was a short stocky man. In the dim light she couldn't make out his features, but she could hear him muttering to himself. He carried a stone-tipped spear in one hand and a war boomerang was stuck in a belt around his waist. He paced back and forth, generally taking about twenty steps each way.

Anana looked down the beach for other guards. She couldn't see any, but she was certain there would be others stationed along the edge of the woods. For all she knew, there might be one just out of eyesight.

She waited until he had gone past her in the direction of McKay. She rose from behind the bush and walked up behind him. The soft sand made little sound. The flat of her axe came down against the back of his head. He fell forward with a grunt. After waiting for a minute to make sure no one had heard the sound of the axe against the bone, she turned the man over. She had to bend close to him to distinguish his facial features. And she swore quietly.

He was Obran, a warrior of the Wendow.

He wasn't going to regain consciousness for quite a while. She hurried back to McKay, who was sitting on his mount, holding the reins of her beast.

He said, "Man, you scared me! I didn't think you'd be coming back so quick. I thought it was one of them Indians at first."

"Bad news. Those're Trenn's people. They must have come after us after all."

"How in hell did they get by us without us seeing them? Or them Indians?"

"I don't know. Maybe they went by the Indians last night without being detected and then decided to trail them in hopes of getting a trophy or two. No, if they did that they wouldn't bo sleeping here. They'd be stalking the Indian camp now.

"I don't know. It could be that they held a big powwow after we escaped and it took all day for them to get the nerve up to go after us. Somehow, they passed us while we were up in the pass without them seeing us or us seeing them. The point is, they're here, and we have to get by them. You bring the grewigg up to the guard and make sure he doesn't wake up. I'll go ahead and take care of the other guards."

That job lasted fifteen or so minutes. She returned and mounted her beast, and they rode slowly on the white sand, reddish in the light, past another fallen man. When they thought they were out of hearing of the Wendow sleeping in the woods, they galloped for a while. After ten minutes of this, they eased their animals into a trot.

Once more they had to detect the guard before he saw them; Anana slipped off the gregg and knocked out three Amerinds stationed at wide intervals near the edge of the woods.

When she came back, McKay shook his head and muttered, "Lady, you're really something."

When they had first been thrown together, he had been rather contemptuous of her. This was a reflection of his attitude toward women in general. Anana had thought it strange, since he came from a race which had endured prejudice and repression for a long time and still did in 1970. His own experience should have made him wary of prejudice toward other groups, especially women, which included black females. But he thought of all women, regardless of color, as inferior beings, useful only for exploitation.

Anana had shaken this attitude considerably, though he had rationalized that, after all, she was not an Earth female.

She didn't reply. The grewigg were ridden to where the last unconscious sentinel lay, and they were tied to two large bushes where they could feed. She and McKay went into the woods on their bellies and presently came on the first of the sleepers, a woman with a child. Luckily, these people had no dogs to warn them. Anana suspected that the Amerinds probably did own dogs but, judging from their leanness, the tribe had been forced to eat them during the journey to the sea-land.

They snaked through a dozen snorers, moving slowly, stopping to look at each man closely. Once, a woman sat up suddenly, and the two, only a few feet behind her, froze. After some smackings of lips, the woman lay back down and resumed sleeping. A few minutes later, they found Red Orc. He was lying on his side within a circle of five dead-to-the-world men. His hands were tied behind him, and a cord bound his ankles together.

Anana clamped her hand over her uncle's mouth at the same time that McKay pressed his heavy body on him. Red Orc struggled, and almost succeeded in rolling over, until Anana whispered in his native language, "Quiet!"

He became still, though he trembled, and Anana said, "We're here to get you away."

She removed her hand. The black stood up. She cut the rawhide cords, and Orc rose, looked around, walked over to a sleeper and took the spear lying by his side. The three walked out of camp, though slowly, until they came to an unsaddled *gregg*. Cautiously, they got a saddle and reins and put the reins on. Orc carried the saddle while Anana led the beast away. When they got to the two *grewigg* tied to the bushes, Anana told Orc some of what had happened.

The light was a little brighter here on the beach. When she stood close to him she could see that her uncle's face and body were deeply bruised.

"They beat me after they caught me," he said. "The women did, too. That went on for the first day, but after that they only kicked me now and then when I didn't move quickly enough to suit them. I'd like to go back and cut the throats of a few."

"You can do that if you like," she said. "After you've answered a question. Did you see Kickaha or hear anything about him?"

"No, I didn't see him and if those savages said anything about him I wouldn't have known it. I wasn't with them long enough to understand more than a dozen words."

"That's because you didn't try," she said. She was disappointed, though she really hadn't expected anything.

Red Orc walked over to the still unconscious sentinel, got down on his knees, put his hands around the man's neck, and did not remove them until he had strangled the life out of him.

Breathing hard, he rose. "There. That'll show them!"

Anana did not express her disgust. She waited until Orc had saddled up his animal and mounted. Then she moved her animal out ahead, and after ten minutes of a slow walk, she urged her *gregg* into a gallop. After five minutes of this she slowed it to a trot, the others following suit.

Orc rode up beside her.

"Was that why you rescued your beloved uncle? Just so you could ask me about your *leblabbiy* lover?"

"That's the only reason, of course," she said.

"Well, I suppose I owe you for that, not to mention not killing me when you got what you wanted from me. Also, my thanks, though you weren't doing it for my benefit, for taking care of Urthona. But you should have made sure he was dead. He's a tough one."

Anana took her axe from her belt and laid it flat across the side of his face. He dropped from the *gregg* and landed heavily on the sand. McKay said, "What the . . . ?"

"I can't trust him," she said. "I just wanted to get him out of earshot of the Indians."

Orc groaned and struggled to get up. He could only sit up, leaning at an angle on one arm. The other went up to the side of his face.

"Bring his *gregg* along with you," she told McKay, and she commanded hers to start galloping. After about five minutes of this, she made it trot again. The black came up presently, holding the reins of Orc's beast.

"How come you didn't snuff him out, too?"

"There was a time when I would have. I suppose that Kickaha has made me more humane, that is, what a human should be."

"I'd hate to see you when you felt mean," he said, and thereafter for a long time they were silent.

Anana had given up searching for Kickaha. It was useless to run around, as he would have said, "like a chicken with its head cut off." She'd go around the sea, hoping that the palace might be in sight. If she could get in, then she'd take the flying machine, what the Wendow had called the *shelbett*, and look for Kickaha from the air. Her chances of coming across the mobile palace seemed, however, to be little.

No matter. What else was there to do here but to search for it?

For a while they guided their *grewigg* through the shallow water. Then they headed across the beach into the woods, where she cut off a branch and smoothed out their traces with its leaves. For the rest of the night, they holed up on top of a hill deep in the forest.

In the morning the *grewigg* got nasty. They were tired and hungry. After she and McKay had come close to being bitten and kicked, Anana decided to let them have their way. A good part of the day, the animals ate, and their two owners took turns observing from the top of a tall tree. Anana had expected the Indians to come galloping along in hot pursuit. But the daytime period had half-passed before she saw them in the distance. It was a war party, about twenty warriors.

She called McKay and told him to have the *grewigg* ready for travel, whether the animals liked the idea or not.

Now she realized that she should have taken the animals through the water at once after leaving the camp. That way, the Indians wouldn't have known which direction to take in pursuit, and they might have given up. The precaution was too late, like so many things in life.

The warriors went on by. Not for far, though. About two hundred yards past the point where the refugees had entered the woods, the party stopped. There was what looked like a hot argument between two men, one being the man holding the lion skull on the end of the pole. Whoever wanted the party to go back won. They turned their *grewigg* around and headed back at a trot toward the camp.

No, not their camp. Now she could see the first of a caravan. It was coming at the pace of the slowest walker, and the hunters met them. The whole tribe halted while a powwow was held. Then the march resumed.

She told McKay what was happening. He swore, and said, "That means we got to stay here and give them plenty of time to go by."

"We're in no hurry," she said. "But we don't have to wait for them. We'll cut down through the woods and come out way ahead of them."

That was the theory. In practice, her plan turned out otherwise. They emerged from the woods just in time to see, and be seen by, two riders. They must have been sent on ahead as scouts or perhaps they were just young fellows racing for fun. Whatever the reason for their presence, they turned back, their big beasts galloping.

Anana couldn't see the rest of the tribe. She supposed that they were not too far away, hidden by a bend of the shore. Anyway, she and McKay should have a twenty minutes' head start, at the least.

There was nothing else to do but to force the tired animals into a gallop. They rode at full speed for a while, went into a trot for a while, then broke into a gallop again. This lasted, with a few rest periods, until nightfall. Into the woods they went, and they took turns sleeping and standing watch. In the morning, the animals were again reluctant to continue. Nevertheless, after some savage tussles and beatings, the two got the *grewigg* going. It was evident, however, that they weren't up to more than one day's steady travel, if that.

By noon the first of the hunters came into view. They drew steadily though slowly nearer as the day passed.

"The poor beasts have about one more good gallop left in them," Anana said. "And that won't be far."

"Maybe we ought to take to the woods on foot," McKay said.

She had already considered that. But if these Indians were as good trackers as their Terrestrial counterparts were supposed to be, they'd catch up with their quarry eventually.

"Are you a strong swimmer?" she said.

McKay's eyes opened. He jerked a thumb toward the water. "You mean . . . out there?"

"Yes, I doubt very much that the Indians can."

"Yeah, but you don't *know*. I can swim, and I can float, but not all day. Besides, there may be sharks, or worse things, out there."

"We'll ride until the beasts drop and then we'll take to the sea. At least, I will. Once we're out of their sight, we can get back to shore some distance down, maybe a few miles."

"Not me," McKay said. "Noways. I'm heading for the woods."

"Just as you like."

She reached into a bag and withdrew the Horn. She'd have to strap that over her shoulder beforehand, but it didn't weigh much and shouldn't be much of a drag.

After an hour the pursuers were so close that it was necessary to force the *grewigg* to full speed. This wasn't equal to the pace of the less tired animals behind them. It quickly became evident that in a few minutes the Indians would be alongside them.

"No use going on any more!" she shouted. "Get off before they fall down and you break your neck!"

She pulled on the reins. When the sobbing foam-flecked animals began trotting, she rolled off the saddle. The soft sand eased the impact; she was up on her feet immediately. McKay followed a few seconds later. He rose, and shouted, "Now what?"

The warparty was about a hundred yards away and closing the gap swiftly. They whooped as they saw their victims were on foot. Some cut into the woods, evidently assuming that the two would run for it. Anana splashed into the shallow water and, when it was up to her waist, shucked her ragged jeans and boots. McKay was close behind her.

"I thought you were going for the trees?"

"Naw. I'd be too lonely!"

They began swimming with long slow strokes. Anana, looking back, saw that their pursuers were still on the shore. They were yelling with frustration and fury, and some were throwing their spears and hurling boomerangs after them. These fell short.

"You was right about one thing," McKay said as they dogpaddled. "They can't swim. Or maybe they're afraid to. Them sharks . . ."

She started swimming again, heading out toward the horizon. But, another look behind her made her stop.

It was too distant to be sure. But if the redheaded man on the *gregg* charging the Indians by himself wasn't Kickaha, then she was insane. It couldn't be Red Orc; he wouldn't do anything so crazy.

Then she saw other riders emerging from the woods, a big party. Were they chasing Kickaha so they could aid him when they caught up with him or did they want his blood?

Perhaps Kickaha was not charging the Indians singlehandedly, as she'd first thought. He was just running away from those behind him and now it was a case of the crocodile in the water and the tiger on the bank.

Whatever the situation, she was going to help him if she could. She began swimming toward the shore.

XUII

WHEN KICKAHA RODE OUT OF THE WOODS, HE HAD EXPECTED THE PEOPLE chasing Anana to be far ahead of him. He was surprised when he saw them only a hundred yards away. Most of them were dismounted and standing on the shore or in the water, yelling and gesticulating at something out in the sea.

Neither Anana nor McKay was in sight.

The discreet thing to do was to turn the *hikwu* as quickly as possible and take off in the opposite direction. However, the only reason for the strangers—whom he instantly identified as Amerinds—halting and making such a fuss here was that their quarry had taken to the sea. He couldn't see them, but they couldn't be too far out. And his tribe, the Thana, couldn't be very far behind him.

So, repressing a warcry, he rode up and launched a boomerang at the gray-headed, red-eyed man sitting on his *hikwu*. Before the heavy wooden weapon struck the man on the side of the head and knocked him off his seat, Kickaha had transferred the spear from his left hand to his right. By then the few mounted warriors were aware of his presence. They wheeled their beasts, but one, another gray-haired man, didn't complete the turn in time to avoid Kickaha. His spear drove into the man's throat; the man fell backward; Kickaha jerked it out of the flesh, reversed it, and, using the shaft as a club, slammed it alongside the head of a warrior running to his *merk*.

Having run past all the men, he halted his beast, turned it, and charged again. This time he didn't go through the main body but skirted them, charging between them and the woods. A man threw a boomerang; Kickaha ducked; it whirred by, one tip just missing his shoulder. He crouched down, holding the shaft of the spear between his arm and body, Kickaha drove its tip into the back of a man who'd just gotten onto his animal but was having trouble controlling it. The man pitched forward and over the shoulder of his *hikwu*. Kickaha yanked the spear out as the man disappeared from his beast.

By then the first of the Thana had showed up, and the mêlée started. It should have been short work. The Amerinds were outnumbered and demoralized, caught, if not with their pants down, on foot, which was the same thing to them. But just as the last five were fighting furiously, though hopelessly, more whoops and yells were added to the din.

Kickaha looked up and swore. Here came a big body of more Amerinds, enough to outnumber the Thana. Within about eighty seconds, they'd be charging into his group.

He rose on his stirrups and looked out across the waves. At first, he couldn't see anything except a few amphibians. Then he saw a head and arms splashing the water. A few seconds later, he located a second swimmer.

He looked down the beach. A number of riderless *hikwu* had bolted when he'd burst among them, and three were standing at the edge of the forest, tearing off branches. Their first loyalty was to themselves, that is, their bellies.

Speaking of loyalties, what was his? Did he owe the Thana anything? No, not really. It was true that they'd initiated him, made him a sort of blood brother. But his only choice then was to submit or die, which wasn't a real choice. So, he didn't owe his tribe anything.

Still standing up in the stirrups, he waved his spear at the two heads in the waves. A white arm came up and gestured at him. Anana's, no doubt of that. He used the spear to indicate that she should angle to a spot further down the beach. Immediately, she and McKay obeyed.

Good. They would come out of the water some distance from the fight and would be able to grab two of the browsing moosoids. But it would take them some time to do so, and before then the Amerinds might have won. So, it was up to him to attempt to give Anana the needed time.

Yelling, he urged his *hikwu* into a gallop. His spear drove deep into the neck of a redskin who had just knocked a Thana off his saddle with a big club. Once more, Kickaha jerked the spear loose. He swore. The flint point had come off of the wood. Never mind. He rammed its blunt end into the back of the head of another Indian, stunning him enough so that his antagonist could shove his spear into the man's belly.

Then something struck Kickaha on the head, and he fell half-con scious onto the sand. For a moment he lay there while hoofs churned the sand, stomped, missing him narrowly several times, and a body thumped onto the ground beside him. It was a Thana, Toini, the youth who'd given him a hard time. Though blood streamed from his head and his shoulder, Toini wasn't out of the battle. He staggered up, only to be knocked down as a *hikwu* backed into him.

Kickaha got up. For the first time he became aware that he was bleeding. Whatever had struck him on top of the head had opened the scalp. There was no time to take care of that now. He leaped for a mounted Indian who was beating at a Thana with a heavy boomerang, grabbed the man's arm, and yanked him off his saddle. Yelling, the warrior came down on Kickaha, and both fell to the sand.

Kickaha fastened his teeth on the redskin's nose and bit savagely. One groping hand felt around, closed on testicles, and squeezed.

Screaming, the man rolled off. Kickaha released his teeth, spun around on his back, raised his neck to see his enemy, and kicked his head hard with the heels of his feet. The man went limp and silent.

A hoof drove down hard, scraping the side of his upper arm. He rolled over to keep from being trampled. Blood and moosoid manure fell on him, and sand was kicked into his eyes. He got to his hands and knees. Half-blind, he crawled through the fray, was knocked over once by something or other, probably the side of a flailing *hikwu*-leg, got up, and crawled some more, stopped once when a spear drove into the sand just in front of his face, and then, finally, was in the water.

Here he opened his eyes all the way and ducked his head under the surface. It came up in time for him to see two mounted battlers coming toward him, a Thana and an Amerind striking at each other with boomerangs. The male beast of one was pushing the female of the other out into the water. If he stayed where he was he was going to be pounded by the hooves. He dived away, his face and chest scraping against the bottom sand. When he came up, he was about twenty feet away. By then he recognized the Thana who was being driven from the shore. He was the chief, holding in one hand Kickaha's metal knife and in the other a boomerang. But he was outclassed by the younger man. His arms moved slowly as if they were very tired and the redskin was grinning in anticipation of his triumph.

Kickaha stood up to his waist and waded toward them. He got to the chief's side just as a blow from the young man's boomerang made the elder's arm nerveless. The boomerang dropped; the chief thrust with his left but his knife missed; the enemy's wooden weapon came down on his head twice.

Wergenget dropped the knife into the water. Kickaha dived after it, skimmed the bottom, and his groping hands felt the blade. Then something, Wergenget, of course, fell on him. The shock knocked the air out of Kickaha's lungs; he gasped; water filled his throat; he came up out of the sea coughing and choking. He was down again, propelled by the redskin, who had jumped off his *hikwu*. Kickaha was at a definite disadvantage, trying to get his breath, and at the same time feeling for the knife he'd dropped.

His antagonist wasn't as big as he was, but he was certainly strong and quick. His left hand closed over Kickaha's throat, and his right hand came up with the boomerang. Kickaha, looking up through watery eyes, could see death. His right leg came up between the man's legs and his knee drove into the warrior's crotch. Since the leg had to come out of the water, its force wasn't as strong as Kickaha had hoped. Nevertheless, it was enough to cause the redskin some pain. For a moment, his hand loosed the throat, and he straightened up, his face contorted.

Kickaha was still on his back in the water, and his choking hadn't stopped. But his left hand touched something hard, the fingers opened out and closed on the blade. They moved up and gripped the hilt. The Indian reached down to grab the throat of what he thought was still a much-disadvantaged enemy. But he stood to one side so Kickaha couldn't use the crotch kick again.

Kickaha drove the end of the knife into the youth's belly just above the pubic region. It slit open the flesh to the navel; the youth dropped the boomerang, the hand reaching for the throat fell away; he looked surprised, clutched his belly, and fell face forward into the water.

Kickaha spent some time seemingly coughing his lungs out. Then he scanned the scene. The two beasts ridden by the chief and the Indian had bolted. Anana and McKay were still about four hundred feet from the shore and swimming strongly. The battle on the beach had tipped in favor of the Amerinds. But here came more of the Thana, including the women and Onil and Opwel, who had come down from their sentry perches. He doubted that the redskins could stand up under the new forces.

After removing Wergenget's belt and sheath, he wrapped it around his waist. He picked up a boomerang and waded until the water was up to his knees. He followed the line of the beach, got past the action, went ashore, and ran along the sand. When he got near some riderless moosoids, he slowed down, approached them cautiously, seized the reins, and tied them to the bushes. Another unmounted *hikwu* trotted along but slowed enough when Kickaha called to him to allow his rein to be grabbed. Kickaha tied him up and waded out into the sea to help the swimmers. They came along several minutes later. They were panting and tired. He had to support both to get them in to shore without collapsing. They threw themselves down on the sand and puffed like a blacksmith's bellows.

He said, "You've got to get up and on the *hikwu*."

"*Hikwu?*" Anana managed to say.

"The meese. Your steeds await to carry you off from peril."

He jerked a thumb at the beasts.

Anana succeeded in smiling. "Kickaha? Won't you ever quit kidding?"

He pulled her up, and she threw her arms around him and wept a little. "Oh, Kickaha, I thought I'd never see you again!"

"I've never been so happy," he said, "but I can become even happier if we get out of here now."

They ran to the animals, untied them, mounted, and galloped off. The clash and cry of battle faded away, and when they rounded another big bend they lost both sight and sound of it. They settled into a fast trot. Kickaha told her what had happened to him, though he discreetly omitted certain incidents. She then told her tale, slightly censored. Both expected to supply the missing details later, but now did not seem like a good time.

Kickaha said, "At any time, when you were up in a tree, did you see anything that could have been the palace?"

She shook her head.

"Well, I think we ought to climb one of those mountains surrounding the sea and take a look. Some are about five thousand feet high. If we could get to the top of one of those, we could see, hmm, it's been so long I can't remember. Wait a minute, I think from that height the horizon is, ah, around ninety-six statute miles.

"Well, it doesn't matter. We can see a hell of a long ways, and the palace is really big, according to Urthona. On the other hand, the horizon of this planet may not be as far away as Earth's. Anyway, it's worth try."

Anana agreed. McKay didn't comment since the two were going to do what they wanted to do. He followed them into the woods.

It took three days to get to the top of the conical peak. The climb was difficult enough, but they had to take time out to hunt and to allow themselves and the beasts to rest. After hobbling the animals, Anna and Kickaha set out on foot, leaving McKay to make sure the *hikwu* didn't stray too far. The last hundred feet of the ascent was the hardest. The mountain ended in a harp spire that swayed back and forth due to the slightly changing shape of the main mass. The very tip, though it looked needle-sharp from below, actually was a dirt platform about the size of a large dining room table. They stood on it and swept the sea with their gaze and wished they had a pair of binoculars.

After a while, Kickaha said, "Nothing."

"I'm afraid so," Anana said. She turned around to look over the vista outside the sea-land, and she clutched his arm.

"Look!"

Kickaha's eyes sighted along the line indicated by her arm.

"I don't know," he said. "It looks like a big dark rock, or a hill, to me."

"No, it's moving! Wait a minute."

The object could easily have been hidden by one of two mountains if it had been on the left or right for a half a mile. It was moving just beyond a very broad pass and going up a long gentle slope. Kickaha estimated that it was about twenty miles away and of an enormous size.

"That *has* to be the palace!" he said. "It must have come through a pass from the sea-land!"

The only thing damping his joy was that it was so far away. By the time they got down off the mountain, traveled to the next pass and got through it, the palace would be even further away. Not only that, they could not depend upon the two mountains to guide them. By the time they got there, the mountains could be gone or they could have split into four or merged into one. It was so easy to lose your bearings here especially when there was no east or north or south or west.

Still, the range that circled the sea-lands would be behind them and it changed shape very little.

"Let's go!" he said, and he began to let himself backward over the lip of the little plateau.

XVIII

IT WAS ELEVEN DAYS LATER. THE TRIO HOPED THAT WITHIN A FEW DAYS they would be in sight of the palace. The twin peaks between which it had gone had become one breast-shaped giant. Deep hollows had formed around it, and these were full of water from a heavy rain of the day before. It was necessary to go about ten miles around the enormous moat.

Before they rounded it, the mountain grew into a cone, the hollows pushed up, spilling the water out. They decided to climb the mountain then to get another sight of Urthona's ex-abode. Though the climb would delay them even more, they thought it worth it. The mobile structure could have headed on a straight line, turned in either direction, or even be making a great curve to come behind them. According to Anana's uncle, when it was on automatic, its travel path was random.

On top of the mountain, they looked in all directions. Plains and ranges spread out, slowly shifting shape. There was plenty of game and here and there dark masses which were groves and forests of traveling plants. Far off to the right were tiny figures, a line of tribespeople on their way to the sea-land.

All three strained their eyes and finally Kickaha saw a dot moving slowly straight ahead. Was it an army of trees or the palace?

"I don't think you could see it if it was composed of plants," Anana said. "They don't get very high, you know. At this distance that object would have to be something with considerable height."

"Let's hope so," Kickaha said.

McKay groaned. He was tired of pushing themselves and the animals to the limit.

There was nothing to do but go on. Though they traveled faster than their quarry, they had to stop to hunt, eat, drink, and sleep. It continued on at its mild pace, a kilometer an hour, like an enormous mindless untiring turtle in tepid heat looking for a mate. And it left no tracks, since it floated a half-meter above the surface.

For the next three days it rained heavily. They slogged on through, enduring the cold showers, but many broad depressions formed and filled with water, forcing them to go around them. Much mileage was lost.

The sixth day after they'd sighted the palace again, they lost Anana's beast. While they were sleeping, a lion attacked it, and though they drove the lion off, they had to put the badly mauled *hikwu* out of its misery. This provided for their meat supply for several days before it got too rotten to eat, but Anana had to take turns riding behind the two men. And this slowed them down.

The sixteenth day, they climbed another mountain for another sighting. This time they could identify it, but it wasn't much closer than the last time seen.

"We could chase it clear around this world," McKay said disgruntledly.

"If we have to, we have to," Kickaha said cheerfully. "You've been bitching a lot lately, Mac. You're beginning to get on my nerves. I know it's a very hard life, and you haven't had a woman for many months but you'd better grin and bear it. Crack a few jokes, do a cakewalk now and then."

McKay looked sullen. "This ain't no minstrel show."

"True, but Anana and I are doing our best to make light of it. I suggest you change your attitude. You could be worse off. You could be dead. We have a chance, a good one, to get out of here. You might even get back to Earth, though I suppose it'd be best for the people there i you didn't. You've stolen, tortured, killed, and raped. But maybe, if yo were in a different environment, you might change. That's why I don think it'd be a good idea for you to return to Earth."

"How in hell did we get off from my bitching to that subject McKay said.

Kickaha grinned. "One thing leads to another. The point I'm gettir at is that you're a burden. Anana and I could go faster if we didn't hav to carry you on our moosoid."

"Yours?" McKay blazed, sullenness becoming open anger. "She riding on my *gregg!*"

"Actually, it belongs to an Indian. Did, I should say. Now it belon to whoever has the strength to take it. Do I make myself clear?"

"You'd desert me?"

"Rationally, we should. But Anana and I won't as long as you help us. So," he suddenly shouted, "quit your moaning and groaning!"

McKay grinned. "Okay. I guess you're right. I ain't no crybaby, normally, but this . . ." He waved a hand to indicate the whole world. "Too much. But I promise to stop beefing. I guess I ain't been no joy for you two."

Kickaha said, "Okay. Let's go. Now, did I ever tell you about the time I had to hide out in a fully stocked wine cellar in a French town when the Krauts retook it?"

Two months later, the traveling building still had not been caught. They were much closer now. When they occasionally glimpsed it, it was about ten miles away. Even at that distance, it looked enormous, towering an estimated 2600 feet, a little short of half a mile. Its width and length were each about 1200 feet, and its bottom was flat.

Kickaha could see its outline but could not, of course, make out its details. According to Urthona, it would, at close range, look like an ambulatory Arabian Nights city with hundreds of towers, minarets, domes, and arches. From time to time its surface changed color, and once it was swathed in rainbows.

Now, it was halfway on the other side of an enormous plain that had opened out while they were coming down a mountain. The range that had ringed it was flattening out, and the animals that had been on the mountainsides were now great herds on the plains.

"Ten miles away," Kickaha said. "And it must have about thirty miles more to go before it reaches the end of the plain. I say we should try to catch it now. Push until our *hikwu* drop and then chase it on foot. Keep going no matter what."

The others agreed, but they weren't enthusiastic. They'd lost weight, and their faces were hollow-cheeked, their eyes ringed with the dark of near-exhaustion. Nevertheless, they had to make the effort. Once the palace reached the mountains, it would glide easily up over them, maintaining the same speed as it had on the plain. But its pursuers would have to slow down.

As soon as they reached the flatland, they urged the poor devils under them into a gallop. They responded as best they could, but they were far from being in top condition. Nevertheless, the ground was being eaten up. The herds parted before them, the antelopes and gazelles stampeding. During the panic the predators took advantage of the confusion and panic. The dogs, baboons, moas, and lions caught fleeing beasts and dragged them to the ground. Roars, barks, screams drifted by the riders as they raced toward their elusive goal.

Now Kickaha saw before them some very strange creatures. They were mobile plants—perhaps—resembling nothing he'd ever come across before. In essence, they looked like enormous logs with legs. The trunks were horizontal, pale-gray, with short stubby branches bearing six or seven diamond-shaped black-green leaves. From each end rose structures that looked like candelabra. But as he passed one he saw that eyes, enormous eyes, much like human eyes, were at the ends of the candelabra. These turned as the two moosoids galloped by.

More of these weird-looking things lay ahead of them. Each had a closed end and an open end.

Kickaha directed his *hikwu* away from them, and McKay followed suit. Kickaha shouted to Anana, who was seated behind him, "I don't like the looks of those things!"

"Neither do I!"

One of the logoids, about fifty yards to one side, suddenly began tilting up its open end, which was pointed at them. The other end rested on the ground while the forelegs began telescoping upward.

Kickaha got the uneasy impression that the thing resembled a cannon the muzzle of which was being elevated for firing.

A moment later, the dark hole in its raised end shot out black smoke. From the smoke something black and blurred described an arc and fell about twenty feet to their right.

It struck the rusty grass, and it exploded.

The moosoid screamed and increased its gallop as if it had summoned energy from somewhere within it.

Kickaha was half-deafened for a moment. But he wasn't so stunned he didn't recognize the odor of the smoke. Black gunpowder!

Anana said, "Kickaha, you're bleeding!"

He didn't feel anything, and now was no time to stop to find out where he'd been hit. He yelled more encouragement to his *hikwu*. But that yell was drowned the next moment when at least a dozen explosions circled him. The smoke blinded him for a moment, then he was out of it. Now he couldn't hear at all. Anana's hands were still around his waist, though, so he knew she was still with him.

He looked back over his shoulder. Here came McKay on his beast flying out of black clouds. And behind him came a projectile, a shell-shaped black object, drifting along lazily, or so it seemed. It fell behind McKay, struck, went up with a roar, a cloud of smoke in the center of which fire flashed. The black man's *hikwu* went over, hooves of hooves. McKay flew off the saddle, struck the ground, and rolled. The big body of his *hikwu* flipflopped by, narrowly missing him.

But McKay was up and running.

Kickaha pulled his *hikwu* up, stopping it.

Through the drifting smoke he could see that a dozen of the plants had erected their front open ends and pointed them toward the humans. Out of the cannonlike muzzles of two shot more smoke, noise, and projectiles. These blew up behind McKay at a distance of forty feet. He threw himself on the ground—too late, of course to escape their effects—but he was up and running as soon as they had gone off.

Behind him were two small craters in the ground.

Miraculously, McKay's moosoid had not broken its neck or any legs. It scrambled up, its lips drawn back to reveal all its big long teeth, its eyes seemingly twice as large. It sped by McKay whose mouth opened as he shouted curses that Kickaha couldn't hear.

Anana had already grasped what had to be done. She had slipped off the saddle and was making motions to Kickaha, knowing he couldn't hear her. He kicked the sides of the beast and yelled at it, though he supposed it was as deaf as he. It responded and went after McKay's fleeing beast. The chase was a long one, however, and ended when McKay's mount stopped running. Foam spread from its mouth and dappled its front, and its sides swelled and shrank like a bellows. It crumpled, rolled over on its side, and died.

Its rear parts were covered with blood.

Kickaha rode back to where Anana and McKay stood. They were wounded, too, mainly in the back. Blood welled from a score of little objects half-buried in the skin. Now he became aware that blood was coming from just behind and above his right elbow.

He grabbed the thing stuck in his skin and pulled it out. Rubbing the blood from its surface, he looked at it. It was a six-pointed crystalline star.

"Craziest shrapnel I ever saw," he said. No one heard him.

The plants, which he had at once named cannonlabra, had observed that their shelling had failed to get the passersby. They were now heading away, traveling slowly on their hundred or so pairs of thin bigfooted legs. Fifteen minutes later he was to see several lay their explosive eggs near enough to an elephant calf to kill it. Some of the things then climbed over the carcass and began tearing at it with claws which appeared from within the feet. The foremost limbs dropped pieces of meat into an aperture on the side.

Apparently McKay's dead animal was too far away to be observed.

Anana and McKay spent the next ten minutes painfully pulling the "shrapnel" from their skins. Pieces of grass were applied to the wounds to stop the bleeding.

"I'd sure like to stuff Urthona down the muzzle of one of those," Kickaha said. "It'd be a pleasure to see him riding its shell. He must have had a lot of sadistic pleasure out of designing those things."

He didn't know how the creature could convert its food into black gunpowder. It took charcoal, sodium or potassium nitrate, and sulfur to make the explosive. That was one mystery. Another was how the things "grew" shell-casings. A third was how they ignited the charge that propelled the shells.

There was no time to investigate. A half-hour had been lost in the chase, and McKay had no steed.

"Now, you two, don't argue with me," he said. He got off the *hikwu.* "Anana, you ride like hell after the palace. You can go faster if I'm not on it, and you're the lightest one so you'll be the least burden for the *hikwu.* I was thinking for a minute that maybe McKay and I could run alongside you, hanging onto the saddle. But we'd start bleeding again, so that's out.

"You take off now. If you catch up with the palace, you might be able to get inside and stop it. It's a slim chance, but it's all we got.

"We'll be moseying along."

Anana said, "That makes sense. Wish me luck."

She said, "*Heekhyu!*", the Wendow word for "Giddap!", and the moosoid trotted off. Presently, under Anana's lashings, it was galloping.

McKay and Kickaha started walking. The flies settled on their wounds. Behind them explosions sounded as the cannonlabra laid down an artillery barrage in the midst of an antelope herd.

An hour passed. They were trotting now, but their leaden legs and heavy breathing had convinced them they couldn't keep up the pace. Still, the palace was bigger. They were gaining on it. The tiny figures of Anana and her beast had merged into the rusty grass of what seemed never-ending plain.

They stopped to drink bad-tasting water from the bag McKay had taken off of his dead *hikwu.* McKay said, "Man, if she don't catch the palace, we'll be stranded here for the rest of our lives."

"Maybe it'll reverse its course," Kickaha said. He didn't sound very optimistic.

Just as he was lifting the bag to pour water into his open mouth, he felt the earth shaking. Refusing to be interrupted, he quenched his thirst. But as he put the bag down he realized that this was no ordinary tremor caused by shape-shifting. It was a genuine earthquake. The ground was lifting up and down, and he felt as if he were standing on a plate in an enormous bowl of jelly being shaken by a giant. The effect was scary and nauseating.

McKay had thrown himself down on the earth. Kickaha decided he might as well do so, too. There was no use wasting energy trying to stand up. He faced toward the palace, however, so he could see what was happening in that direction. This was really rotten luck. While this big tremblor was going on, Anana would not be able to ride after the palace.

The shaking up-and-down movement continued. The animals had fled for the mountains, the worst place for them if the quake continued. The birds were taking off, millions salt-and-peppering the sky, then coalescing to form one great cloud. They were all heading toward the direction of the palace.

Presently, he saw a dot coming toward him. In a few minutes it became a microscopic Anana and *hikwu*. Then the two separated, both rolling on the ground. Only Anana got up. She ran toward him or tried to do so, rather. The waves of grass-covered earth were like swells in the sea. They rose beneath her and propelled her forward down their slope, casting her on her face. She got up and ran some more, and, once, she disappeared behind a big roller, just like a small boat in a heavy sea.

"I'm going to get sick," McKay said. He did. Up to then Kickaha had been able to manage his own nausea, but the sound of the black man's heavings and retchings sparked off his own vomit.

Now, above the sounds he was making, he heard a noise that was as loud as if the world were cracking apart. He was more frightened than he'd ever been in his life. Nevertheless, he got to his hands and knees and stared out toward where Anana had been. He couldn't see her, but he could see just beyond where she'd been.

The earth was curling up like a scroll about to be rolled. Its edges were somewhat beyond where he'd last seen Anana. But she could have fallen into the gigantic fissure.

He got to his feet and cried, "Anana! Anana!" He tried to run toward her, but he was pitched up so violently that he rose a foot into the air. When he came down he slid on his face down the slope of a roller.

He struggled up again. For a moment he was even more confused and bewildered, his sense of unreality increasing. The mountains in the far distance seemed to be sliding downward as if the planet had opened to swallow them.

Then he realized that they were not falling down.

The ground on which he stood was rising.

He was on a mass being torn away to make a temporary satellite for the main body of the planet.

The palace was out of sight now, but he had seen that it was still on the main body. The fissure had missed by a mile or so marooning it with its pursuers.

XIX

THE SPLITOFF NOW WAS ONE HUNDRED MILES ABOVE THE PRIMARY AND in a stable, if temporary, orbit. It would take about four hundred days before the lesser mass started to fall into the greater. And that descent would be a slow one.

The air seemed no less thick than that on the surface of the planet. The atmosphere had the same pressure at an altitude of 528,000 feet as it had at ground zero. Urthona had never explained the physical principles of this phenomenon. This was probably because he didn't know them. Though he had made the specifications for the pocket universe, he had left it up to a team of scientists to make his world work. The scientists were dead millennia ago, and the knowledge long lost. But their manufactures survived and apparently would until all the universes ran down.

The earthquakes had not ceased once the splitoff had torn itself away. It had started readjusting, shaping from a wedgeform into a globe. This cataclysmic process had taken twelve days, during which its marooned life had had to move around much and swiftly to keep from being buried. Much of it had not succeeded. The heat of energy released during the transformation had been terrible, but it had been alleviated by one rainstorm after another. For almost a fortnight, Kickaha and his companions had been living in a Turkish bath. All they wanted to do was to lie down and pant. But they had been forced to keep moving, sometimes vigorously.

On the other hand, because of the much weaker gravity, only one-sixteenth that of the primary, their expenditure of energy took them much more swiftly and further than it would have on the planet. And there were so many carcasses and dead plants around that they didn't have to hunt for food. Another item of nourishment was the flying seed. When the separation had started, every plant on the moon had released hundreds of seeds which were borne by the wind on tissue-thin alates or masses of threads. These rose, some drifting down towards the parent world, others falling back onto the satellite. They were small, but a score or so made a mouthful and provided a protein-high vegetable. Even the filmy wings and threads could be eaten.

"Nature's, or Urthona's, way of making sure the various species of plants survive the catastrophe," Kickaha said.

But when the mutations of terrain stopped and the carcasses became too stinking to eat, they had to begin hunting. Though the humans could run and jump faster, once they learned the new method of locomotion, the animals were proportionately just as speedy. But Kickaha fashioned a new type of bola, two or three antelope skulls connected by a rawhide cord. He would whirl this around and around and then send it skimming along the ground to entangle the legs of the quarry. McKay and Anana made their own bolas, and all three were quite adept at casting them. They even caught some of the wild moosoids with these.

Those seeds that fell back on the splitoff put down roots, and new plants grew quickly. The grass and the soil around them became bleached as the nutritional elements were sucked up. The plantling would grow a set of legs and pull up the main root or break it off and move on to rich soil. The legs would fall off but a new set, longer and stronger, would grow. After three moves, the plants stayed rooted until they had attained their full growth. Their maturation period was exceedingly swift by Terrestrial standards.

Of course, many were eaten by the elephants, moosoids, and other animals which made plants their main diet. But enough survived to provide countless groves of ambulatory trees and bushes.

The three had their usual troubles with baboons, dogs, and the feline predators. Added to those was a huge bird they'd never seen before. Its wing-spread was fifty feet, though the body was comparatively small. Its head was scarlet; the eyes, cold yellow; the green beak, long, hooked and sharp. The wings and body were bluish, and the short thick heavily taloned legs were ochre. It swooped down from the sky just after dusk struck, and carried its prey off. Since the gravity was comparatively weak here, it could lift a human into the air. Twice, one of them almost got Anana. Only by throwing herself on the ground when Kickaha had cried a warning had she escaped being borne away.

"I can't figure out what it does when there is no satellite," Kickaha

said. "It could never lift a large body from the surface of the primary.
So what does it live on between-times?"

"Maybe it just soars around, living off its fat, until the planet spits up
another part of it," Anana said.

They were silent for a while then, imagining these huge aerial creatures gliding through the air fifty miles up, half-asleep most of the time,
waiting for the mother planet to propel its meat on a moon-sized dish
up to it.

"Yes, but it has to land somewhere on the satellite to eat and to
mate," he said. "I wonder where?"

"Why do you want to know?"

"I got an idea, but it's so crazy I don't want to talk about it yet. It
came to me in a dream last night."

Anana suddenly gripped his arm and pointed upward. He and
McKay looked up. There, perhaps a half a mile above them, the palace
was floating by.

They stood silently watching it until it had disappeared behind some
high mountains.

Kickaha sighed and said, "I guess that when it's on automatic it circles the satellite. Urthona must have set it to do that so that he could
observe the moon. Damn! So near yet so far!"

The Lord must have gotten pleasure out of watching the shifts in the
terrain and the adjustments of people and animals to it. But surely he
hadn't lived alone in it. What had he done for companionship and sex?
Abducted women from time to time, used them, then abandoned them
on the surface? Or kicked them out and watched them fall one hundred
miles, perhaps accompanying them during the descent to see their horror, hear their screams?

It didn't matter now. Urthona's victims and Urthona were all dead
now. What was important was how they were going to survive the
rejoining of primary and secondary.

Anana said that her uncle had told her that about a month prior to
this event, the satellite again mutated form. It changed from a globe to
a rough rectangle of earth, went around the primary five times, and then
lowered until it became part of the mother world again.

Only those animals that happened to be on the upper part had a
chance to live through the impact. Those on the undersurface would be
ground into bits and their pieces burned. And those living in the area of
the primary onto which the satellite fell would also be killed.

Urthona had, however, given some a chance to get out and from
under. He'd given them an instinctive mechanism which made them flee

at their fastest speed from any area over which the satellite came close. It had a set orbital path prior to landing, and as it swung lower every day, the animals "knew" that they had to leave the area. Unfortunately, only those on the outer limits of the impact had time to escape.

The plants were too slow to get out in time, but their instincts made them release their floating seeds.

All of this interested Kickaha. His chief concern, however, was to determine which side of the moon the three would be on when the change from a globe to a rectangle was made. That is, whether they would be on the upper side, that opposite the planet, or on the underside.

"There isn't any way of finding out," Anana said. "We'll just have to trust to luck."

"I've depended on that in the past," he said. "But I don't want to now. You only use luck when there's nothing else left."

He did much thinking about their situation in the days and nights that slid by. The moon rotated slowly, taking about thirty days to complete a single spin. The colossal body of the planet hanging in the sky revealed the healing of the great wound made by the withdrawal of the splitoff. The only thing for which they had gratitude for being on the secondary was that they weren't in the area of greatest shape-change, that near the opening of the hole, which extended to the center of the planet. They saw, when the clouds were missing, the sides fall in, avalanches of an unimaginable but visible magnitude. And the mass shrank before their eyes as adjustments were made all over the planet. Even the sea-lands must be undergoing shakings of terrifying strength, enough to make the minds and souls of the inhabitants reel with the terrain.

"Urthona must have enjoyed the spectacle when he was riding around in his palace," Kickaha said. "Sometimes I wish you hadn't killed him, Anana. He'd be down there now, finding out what a horror he'd subjected his creations to."

One morning Kickaha told his companions about a dream he'd had. It had begun with him enthusiastically telling them about his plan to get them off the moon. They'd thought it was wonderful, and all three had started at once on the project. First, they'd walked to a mountain the top of which was a sleeping place for the giant birds, which they called rocs. They'd climbed to the top and found that it contained a depression in which the rocs rested during the day.

The three had slid down the slope of the hollow, and each had sneaked up on a sleeping roc. Then each had killed his or her bird by driving the knives and a pointed stick through the bird's eye into it brain. Then they'd hidden under a wing of the dead bird until the others had awakened and flown off. After which they'd cut off the wings and tail feathers and carried them back to their camp.

"Why did we do this?" Anana said.

"So we could use the wings and tails to make gliders. We attached them to fuselages of wood, and . . ."

"Excuse me," Anana said, smiling. "You've never mentioned having any glider experience."

"That's because I haven't. But I've read about gliders, and I did take a few hours' private instruction in a Piper Cub, just enough to solo. But I had to quit because I ran out of money."

"I haven't been up in a glider for about thirty years," Anana said. "But I've built many, and I've three thousand hours flight time in them."

"Great! Then you can teach Mac and me how to glide. Anyway, in this dream we attached the wings to the fuselage and, to keep the wings from flexing, we tied wood bars to the wing bones, and we used rawhide strips instead of wires . . ."

Anana interrupted again. "How did you control this makeshift glider?"

"By shifting our weight. That's how John Montgomery and Percy Pilcher and Otto and Gustave Lilienthal did it. They hung under or between the wings, suspended in straps or on a seat, and they did all right. Uh . . . until John and Otto and Percy were killed, that is."

McKay said, "I'm glad this was just a dream."

"Yeah? Dreams are springboards into reality."

McKay groaned, and he said, "I just knew you was in earnest."

Anana, looking as if she was about to break into laughter, said, "Well, we could make gliders out of wood and antelope hide, I suppose. They wouldn't work once we got into the primary's gravity field, though, even if they would work here. So there's no use being serious about this.

"Anyway, even if we could glide down a mountain slope here and catch an updraft, we couldn't go very high. The moon's surface has no variety of terrain to make thermals, no plowed fields, no paved roads, and so on."

"What's the use even talking about this?" McKay said.

"It helps pass the time," she said. "So, Kickaha, how did you plan to get the gliders high enough to get out of the moon's gravity?"

Kickaha said, "Look, if we shoot up, from our viewpoint, we're actually shooting downward from the viewpoint of people on the surface of the primary. All we have to do is get into the field of the primary's gravity, and we'll fall."

McKay, looking alarmed, said, "What do you mean—*shoot?*"

He had good reason to be disturbed. The redhead had gotten him into a number of dangerous situations because of his willingness to take chances.

"Here's how it was in the dream. We located a battery of cannonlabra, killed four of them, and carried them to our camp. We cut off their branches and eyestalks to streamline their bodies. Then . . ."

"Wait a minute," Anana said. "I think I see where you're going. You mean that you converted those cannon-creatures into rockets? And tied the gliders to them and then launched the rockets and after the rockets were high up cut the gliders loose?"

Kickaha nodded. Anana laughed loudly and long.

McKay said, "It's only a dream, ain't it?"

Kickaha, his face red, said, "Listen, I worked it all out. It could be done. What I did . . ."

"It would work in a dream," she said. "But in reality, there'd be no way to control the burning of the gunpowder. To get high enough, you'd have to stuff the barrel with powder to the muzzle. But when the fuel exploded, and it would, all of it at once, the sudden acceleration would tear the glider from the rocket, completely wreck the structure and wings of the glider, and also kill you."

"Look, Anana," Kickaha said, his face even redder, "isn't there some way we could figure out to get controlled explosions?"

"Not with the materials we have available. No, forget it. It was a nice dream, but . . . oh, hah, hah, hah!"

"I'm glad your woman's got some sense," McKay said. "How'd you ever manage to live so long?"

"I guess because I haven't followed through with all my wild ideas I'm only half-crazy, not completely nuts. But we've got to get off o here. If we end up on the under side when it changes shape, we're don for. It's the big kissoff for us."

There was a very long silence. Finally, Anana said, "You're right We have to do something. We must look for materials to make glider that could operate in the primary's field. But getting free of the moon' gravity is something else. I don't see how . . ."

"A hot-air balloon!" Kickaha cried. "It could take us and the glider up and away and out!"

Kickaha thought that, if the proper materials could be found to make a balloon and gliders, the liftoff should take place after the moon changed its shape. It would be spread out then, the attenutation of the body making the local gravity even weaker. The balloon would thus have greater lifting power.

Anana said that he had a good point there. But the dangers from the cataclysmic mutation were too high. They might not survive these. Or, if they did, their balloon might not. And they wouldn't have time after the shape-change to get more materials.

Kickaha finally agreed with her.

Another prolonged discussion was about the gliders. Anana, after some thought, said that they should make parawings instead. She explained that a parawing was a type of parachute, a semi-glider the flight of which could be controlled somewhat.

"The main trouble is still the materials," she said. "A balloon of partially cured antelope hide might lift us enough, considering the far weaker gravity. But how would the panels be held together? We don't have any adhesive, and stitching them together might not, probably will not, work. The hot air would escape through the overlaps. Still . . ."

McKay, who was standing nearby, shouted. They turned to look in the direction at which he was pointing.

Coming from around a pagoda-shaped mountain, moving slowly towards them, was a gigantic object. Urthona's palace. It floated along across the plain at a majestic pace at an estimated altitude of two hundred feet.

They waited for it, and after two hours it reached them. They had retreated to one side far enough for them to get a complete view of it from top to bottom. It seemed to be cut out of a single block of smooth stone or material which looked like stone. This changed color about every fifteen minutes, glowing brightly, running the spectrum, finishing with a rainbow sheen of blue, white, green, and rose-red. Then the cycle started over again.

There were towers, minarets, and bartizans on the walls, thousands of them, and these had windows and doors, square, round, diamond-shaped, hexagonal, octagonal. There were also windows on the flat bottom. Kickaha counted two hundred balconies, then gave up.

Anana said, "I know we can't reach it. But I'm going to try the Horn anyway."

The seven notes floated up. As they expected, no shimmering prelude to the opening of a gate appeared on its walls.

Kickaha said, "We should've choked the codeword out of Urthona. Or cooked him over a fire."

"That wouldn't help us in this situation," she said.

"Hey!" McKay shouted. "Hey! Look!"

Staring from a window on the bottom floor was a face. A man's.

XX

THE WINDOW WAS ROUND AND TALLER THAN THE MAN. EVEN AT THAT distance and though he was moving, they could see that he was not Urthona or Red Orc. It was impossible to tell without reference points how tall the young man was. His hair was brown and pulled tightly back as if it were tied in a pony tail. His features were handsome. He wore a suit of a cut which Kickaha had never seen before, but which Anana would tell him was of a style in fashion among the Lords a long time ago. The jacket glittered as if its threads were pulsing neon tubes. The shirt was ruffled and open at the neck.

Presently the man had passed them, but he reappeared a minute later at another window. Then they saw him racing by the windows. Finally, out of breath, he stopped and put his face to the corner window. After a while, he was out of sight.

"Did you recognize him?" Kickaha said.

"No, but that doesn't mean anything," Anana said. "There were many Lords, and even if I'd known him for a little while, I might have forgotten him after all those years."

"Not mean enough, heh?" Kickaha said. "Well then, if he isn't one of them, what's he doing in Urthona's palace? How'd he get there? And if he's interested in us, which he was from his actions, why didn't he change the controls to manual and stop the palace?"

She shrugged. "How would I know?"

"I didn't really expect you to. Maybe he doesn't know how to operate the controls. He may be trapped. I mean—he gated into the place and doesn't know how to get out."

"Or he's found the control room but is afraid to enter because he knows it'll be trapped."

McKay said, "Maybe he'll figure out a way to get in without getting caught."

"By then he won't be able to find us even if he wants to," she said.

"The palace'll be coming around again," Kickaha said. "Maybe by then . . ."

Anana shook her head. "I doubt the palace stays on the same orbit. It probably spirals around."

On the primary, the palace was only a few feet above the ground. Here, for some reason, it floated about a hundred feet from the surface. Anana speculated that Urthona might've set the automatic controls for this altitude because the palace would accompany the moon when it fell.

"He could go down with it and yet be distant enough so the palace wouldn't be disturbed by the impact."

"If that's so, then the impact must not be too terrible. If it were, the ground could easily buckle to a hundred feet or more. But what about a mountain falling over on it?"

"I don't know. But Urthona had a good reason for doing it. Unfortunately for us, it removes any chance for us to get to the palace while it's on the moon."

They did not see the palace. Evidently, it did follow a spiral path.

The days and sometimes the nights that succeeded the appearance of the building were busy. In addition to hunting, which took much time, they had to knock over and kill trees and skin the antelopes they slew. Branches were cut from the trees and shaped with axe and knife. The skins were scraped and dehaired, though not to Anana's satisfaction. She fashioned needles from wood and sewed the skins together. Then she cut away parts of these to make them the exact shape needed. After this, she sewed the triangular form onto the wooden structure.

The result was a three-cornered kite-shape. The rawhide strips used as substitutes for wires were tied onto the glider.

Anana had hoped to use a triangular trapeze bar for control. But their efforts to make one of three wooden pieces tied at the corner failed. It just wasn't structurally sound enough. It was likely to fall apart when subjected to stress of operation.

Instead, she settled for the parallel bar arrangement. The pilot would place his armpits over the bars and grasp the uprights. Control would be effected, she hoped, through shifting of the pilot's weight.

When the bars and uprights were installed, Anana frowned.

"I don't know if it'll stand up under the stress. Well, only one way to find out."

She got into position underneath the glider. Then, instead of running, as she would have had to do on the planet, she crouched down and leaped into the wind. She rose thirty-five feet, inclined the nose upwards a little to catch the wind, and glided for a short distance. She stalled the machine just before landing and settled down.

The others had bounded after her. She said, grinning, "The first antelope-hide glider in history has just make its first successful flight."

She continued making the short glides, stopping when she had gone two miles. They walked back then, and Kickaha, after receiving instructions again—for the twentieth time—tried his skill. McKay succeeded him without mishap, and they called it a day.

"Tomorrow we'll practice on the plain again," she said. "The day after, we'll go up a mountain a little ways and try our luck there. I want you two to get some practice in handling a glider in a fairly long glide. I don't expect you to become proficient. You just need to get the feel of handling it."

On the fifth day of practice, they tried some turns. Anana had warned them to pick up plenty of speed when they did, since the lower wing in a bank lost velocity. If it slowed down too much, the glider could stall. They followed her prescription faithfully and landed safely.

"It'd be nice if we could jump off a cliff and soar," she said. "That'd really give you practice. But there are no thermals. Still, you'd be able to glide higher. Maybe we should."

The men said that they'd like to give it a go. But they had to wait until a nearby mountain would form just the right shape needed. That is, a mountain with a slope on one side up which they could walk and more or less right-angles verticality on the other side. By the time that happened, she had built her parawing. This was not to be folded for opening when the jump was made. The hide was too stiff for that. It was braced with lightweight wood to form a rigid structure.

They climbed the mountain to the top. Anana, without any hesitation, grabbed the wing, holding it above her head but with its nose pointed down to keep the wind from catching in it. She leaped off the four thousand foot high projection, released her hold, dropped, was caught in the harness, and was off. The two men retreated from the outthrust of earth just in time. With only a slight sound, the ledge gave way and fell.

They watched her descend, more swiftly than in the glider, pull the nose cords to dive faster, release them to allow the nose to lift, and then work the ropes so that she could bank somewhat.

When they saw her land, they turned and went back down the mountain.

The next day McKay jumped and the following day Kickaha went off the mountain. Both landed without accident.

Anana was pleased with their successful jumps. But she said, "The wing is too heavy to use over the primary. We have to find a lighter wood and something that'll be much lighter than the antelope hides for a wing-covering."

By then the covering was stinking badly. It was thrown away for the insects and the dogs to eat.

She did, however, make another wing, installing this time steering slots and antistall nose flaps. They took it up another mountain, the cliffside of which was only a thousand feet high. Anana jumped again and seemed to be doing well when a roc dived out of the sky and fastened its claw in the wing. It lifted then, flapping its wings, which had a breadth of fifty feet, heading for the mountain on which it roosted.

Anana threw her throwing axe upwards. Its point caught on the lower side of the bird's neck, then dropped. But the bird must have decided it had hold of a tough customer. It released the parawing, and she glided swiftly down. For a few minutes the bird followed her. If it had attacked her while she was on the ground, it could have had her in a defenseless situation. But it swooped over her, uttering a harsh cry, and then rose in search of less alien and dangerous prey.

Anana spent an hour looking for the axe, failed to find it, and ran home because a moa had appeared in the distance. The next day the three went back to search for it. After half a day McKay found it behind a boulder that had popped out of the earth while they were looking.

The next stage in the project was to make a small test balloon. First, though, they had to build a windbreak. The wind, created by the passage of the moon through the atmosphere at an estimated ten miles an hour, never stopped blowing. Which meant that they would never be able to finish the inflation of the balloon before it blew away.

The work took four weeks. They dug up the ground with the knives, the axe, and pointed sticks. When they had a semicircle of earth sixteen feet high, they added a roof supported by the trunks of dead plants of a giant species.

Then came the antelope hunting. At the end of two days' exhausting hunting and transportation of skins from widely scattered places, they had a large pile. But the hides were in varying stages of decomposition.

There was no time to rest. They scraped off the fat and partially dehaired the skins. Then they cut them, and Anana and Kickaha sewed the panels together. McKay had cut strips and made a network of them.

Dawn found them red-eyed and weary. But they started the fire on the earthen floor of the little basket. Using a gallows of wood, they hoisted the limp envelope up so that the heat from the fire would go directly into the open neck of the bag. Gradually it inflated. When it seemed on the brink of rising, they grabbed the cords hanging from the network around the bag and pulled it out from under the roof. The wind caught it, sent it scooting across the plain, the basket tilting to one side. Some of the fire was shifted off the earth, and the basket began to burn. But the balloon, the envelope steadily expanding, rose.

Pale-blue smoke curled up from the seams.

Anana shook her head. "I knew it wasn't tight enough."

Nevertheless, the aerostat continued to rise. The basket hanging from the rawhide ropes burned and presently one end swung loose, spilling what remained of the fire. The balloon rose a few more feet, then began to sink, and shortly was falling. By then it was at least five miles away horizontally and perhaps a mile high. It passed beyond the shoulder of a mountain, no doubt to startle the animals there and to provide food for the dogs and the baboons and perhaps the lions.

"I wish I'd had a camera," Kickaha said. "The only rawhide balloon in the history of mankind."

"Even if we find a material suitable for the envelope covering," Anana said, "it'll be from an animal. And it'll rot too quickly."

"The natives know how to partially cure rawhide," he said. "And they might know where we could get the wood and the covering we need. So, we'll find us some natives and interrogate them."

Four weeks later, they were about to give up looking for human beings. They decided to try for three days more. The second day, from the side of a shrinking mountain, they saw a small tribe moving across a swelling plain. Behind them, perhaps a mile away, was a tiny figure sitting in the middle of the immensity.

Several hours later, they came upon the figure. It was covered by a rawhide blanket. Kickaha walked up to it and removed the blanket. A very old woman had been sitting under it, her withered legs crossed, her arms upon her flabby breasts, one hand holding a flint scraper. Her eyes had been closed, but they opened when she felt the blanket move. They became huge. Her toothless mouth opened in horror. Then, to Kickaha's surprise, she smiled, and she closed her eyes again, and she began a high-pitched whining chant.

Anana walked around her, looking at the curved back, the prominent ribs, the bloated stomach, the scanty white locks, and especially at one foot. This had all the appearance of having been chewed on by a lion long ago. Three toes were missing, it was scarred heavily, and it was bent at an unnatural angle.

"She's too old to do any more work or to travel," Anana said.

"So they just left her to starve or be eaten by the animals," Kickaha said. "But they left her this scraper. What do you suppose that's for? So she could cut her wrists?"

Anana said, "Probably. That's why she smiled when she got over her fright. She figures we'll put her out of her misery at once."

She fingered the rawhide. "But she's wrong. She can tell us how to cure skins and maybe tell us a lot more, too. If she isn't senile."

Leaving McKay to guard the old woman, the others went off to hunt. They returned late that day, each bearing part of a gazelle carcass. They also carried a bag full of berries picked from a tree they'd cut out of a grove, though Kickaha's skin had a long red mark from a lashing tentacle. They offered water and berries to the crone, and after some hesitation she accepted. Kickaha pounded a piece of flank to make it more tender for her, and she gummed away on it. Later, he dug a hole in the ground, put water in it, heated some stones, dropped them in the water, and added tiny pieces of meat. The soup wasn't hot, and it wasn't good, but it was warm and thick, and she was able to drink that.

While one stood guard that night, the others slept. In the morning, they made some more soup, adding berries for an experiment, and the old woman drank it all from the proffered gourd. Then the language lessons began. She was an eager teacher once she understood that they weren't just fattening her up so they could eat her.

The next day Kickaha set out after the people who'd abandoned her. Two days later he returned with flint spear heads, axes, and scrapers, and several war-boomerangs.

"It was easy. I sneaked in at night while they were snoring away after a feast of rotten elephant meat. I picked what I wanted and took off. Even the guards were sleeping."

Learning the old woman's language proceeded swiftly. In three weeks Shoobam was telling them jokes. And she was a storehouse of information. A treasure trove, in fact.

Primed with data, the three set to work. While one of the three guarded Shoobam, the others went out to get the materials needed. They killed the plants which she had told them were likely to contain gallotannin, or its equivalent, in certain pathological growths. Another type of tree which they caught and killed had an exceptionally light-weight wood yet was stress-resistant.

Kickaha made a crutch for Shoobam so she could become mobile, and Anana spent some time every day massaging the old woman's semiparalyzed legs. She was not only able to get around better, she began to put on some weight. Still, though she enjoyed talking to the three and felt more important than she had for a long time, she wasn't happy. She missed the tribal life and especially her grandchildren. But she had the stoic toughness of all the natives, who could make a luxury out of what was to the three the barest necessity.

Several months passed. Kickaha and company worked hard from dawn to long past dusk. Finally, they had three parawings much superior in lightness of weight, strength, and durability to the original made by Anana. These were stiffened with wooden ribs and were not to be folded.

Told by Shoobam about a certain type of tree the bark of which contained a powerful poison, Kickaha and Anana searched for a grove. After finding one, they pulled a dozen plants over with lariats and killed them. During the process, however, they narrowly escaped being caught and burned with the poison exuded by the tentacles. The old woman instructed them in the techniques of extracting the poison.

Kickaha was very happy when he discovered that the branches of the poison-plant were similar to those of yew. He made bows with strings from goat intestines. The arrows were fitted with the flint heads he'd stolen from Shoobam's tribe, and these were dipped in the poison.

Now they were in the business of elephant hunting.

Though the pachyderms were immune to the venom on the darts propelled by certain plants, they succumbed to that derived from the "yew" trees. At the end of another month, they had more than the supply of elephant stomach lining needed. The membranes weighed, per square yard, two-thirds less than the gazelle hides. Anana stripped the hides from the parawings and replaced them with the membranes.

"I think the wings'll be light enough now to work in the planet's field," she said. "In fact, I'm sure. I wasn't too certain about the hides."

Another plant yielded, after much hard work and some initial failures, a blue-like substance. This could seal the edges of the strips which would compose the balloon envelope. They sealed some strips of membrane together and tested them over a fire. Even after twenty hours, the glue did not deteriorate. But with thirty hours' of steady temperature, it began to decompose.

"That's fine," Anana said. "We won't be in the balloon more than an hour, I hope. Anyway, we can't carry enough wood to burn for more than an hour's flight."

"It looks like we might make it after all," Kickaha said. "But what about her?"

He gestured at Shoobam.

"She's saved our necks or at least given us a fighting chance. But what're we going to do with her when we lift off? We can't just leave her. But we can't take her with us, either."

Anana said, "Don't worry about that. I've talked with her about it. She knows we'll be leaving some day. But she's grateful that she's lived this long, not to mention that we've given her more food than she's had for a long time."

"Yes? What happens when we go?"

"I've promised to slit her wrists."

Kickaha winced. "You're a better man than I am, Gunga Din. I don't think I could do it."

"You have a better idea?"

"No. If it has to be, so be it. I suppose I would do it, but I'm glad I don't have to."

XXI

ANANA DECIDED THAT IT WOULD BE BETTER TO MAKE THREE SMALLER balloons instead of one large one.

"Here's how it is. To get equal strength the material of a large balloon has to be much stronger and heavier per square inch than that of a smaller balloon. By making three smaller ones, instead of one large one, we gain in strength of material and lose in weight. So, each of us will ascend in his aerostat."

She added, "Also, since the smaller ones won't present as much area to the wind, they'll be easier to handle."

Kickaha had lost too many arguments with her to object.

McKay resented being "bossed" by a woman, but he had to admit that she was the authority.

They worked frantically to make the final preparations. Even Shoobam helped, and the knowledge of what would happen on the day of liftoff did not shadow her cheeriness. At least, if she felt sorrow or dread, she did not show it.

Finally, the time came. The three bags lay on the ground, stretched out behind the wall of the windbreak. A net of thin but tough cured membrane strips enclosed each bag. These, the suspension ropes, were attached directly to the basket. Anana would have liked to have tied them to a suspension hoop below which the basket would be hung by foot ropes. This arrangement afforded better stability.

However, it was almost impossible to carve three rings from wood. Besides, if the ring was made strong enough to stand up under the weight of the basket, its passenger, and the fuel, it would have to be rather heavy.

The ends of the suspension ropes were tied to the corners and along the sides of a rectangular car or basket made of pieces of bark glued together. In the center of the car was a thick layer of earth, on top of which were piled sticks. Wood shavings were packed at the bottom of the pile so the fire could be started easily. A layer of tinder would be ignited by sparks from a flint and a knife or the axe.

The wall of earth serving as a windbreak had been tumbled over four times because of the shape-changing of terrain. The fifth one was almost twice as high and four times as long as the one built for the test balloon. It was roofed over by branches laid on cross-logs supported by uprights.

Three gallows, primitive cranes, stood near the open end of the enclosure. A cable made of twisted cords ran from the upper sides of the horizontal arm to the top of the balloon. One end was tied around the top of the balloon.

The three people pulled the envelopes up, one by one, until all three hung limply below the gallows arms. The ends of the hoist ropes were secured to nearby uprights. McKay, who had wanted to be first to lift off, probably because it made him nervous to wait, lit the fire. Smoke began to ascend into a circular skin hanging down from the neck of the balloon.

When the bag had started to swell from the expanding hot air, Anana lit the fire in her car. Kickaha waited a few minutes and then started a flame in his basket.

The bands of the "dawn" sky began to glow. Snorts and barks and one roar came from the animals on the plains, awakening to another day of feeding and being fed upon. The wind was at an estimated minimum eight miles an hour velocity and without gusts.

McKay's envelope began to inflate. As soon as it was evident that it would stand up by itself, McKay leaped up past the balloon, reached out with his axe, and severed the cable attached to the top. He fell back, landing at the same time the cable did. After rising, he waited another minute, then pulled the balloon from beneath the gallows by the basket.

When Anana's balloon had lifted enough to support itself, she cut the cable, and Kickaha soon did the same to his.

Shoobam, who had been sitting to one side, pulled herself up on the crutch and hobbled over to Anana. She spoke in a low tone, Anana embraced her, then slashed at the wrists held out to her. Kickaha wanted to look away, but he thought that if someone else did the dirty work he could at least observe it.

The old woman sat down by Anana's basket and began wailing a death chant. She didn't seem to notice when he waved farewell.

Tears were running down Anana's cheeks, but she was busy feeding the fire.

McKay shouted, "So long! See you later! I hope!"

He pulled the balloon out until it was past the overhang. Then he climbed quickly aboard the car, threw on some more sticks, and waited. The balloon leaned a little as the edge of the wind coming over the roof struck its top. It began rising, was caught by the full force of the moving air, and rose at an angle.

Anana's craft ascended a few minutes later. Kickaha's followed at the same interval of time.

He looked up the bulge of the envelope. The parawing was still attached to the net and was undamaged. It had been tied to the upper side when the bag had been laid out on the ground. An observer at a distance might have thought it looked like a giant moth plastered against a giant light bulb.

He was thrilled with his flight in an aerostat. There had been no sensation of moving; he could just as well have been on a flying carpet. Except that there was no wind against his face. The balloon moved at the same speed as the air.

Above and beyond him the other two balloons floated. Anana waved once, and he waved back. Then he tended the fire.

Once he looked back at the windbreak. Shoobam was a dim tiny figure who whisked out of sight as the roof intervened.

The area of vision expanded; the horizon rushed outwards. Vistas of mountains and plains and here and there large bodies of water where rain had collected in temporary depressions spread out for him.

Above them hung the vast body of the primary. The great wound made by the splitoff had healed. The mother planet was waiting to receive the baby, waiting for another cataclysm.

Flocks of birds and small winged mammals passed him. They were headed for the planet, which meant that the moon's shape-change wasn't far off. The three had left just in time.

Briefly, his craft went through a layer of winged and threaded seeds, soaring, whirling.

The flames ate up the wood, and the supply began to look rather short to Kickaha. The only consolation was that as the fuel burned, it relieved the balloon of more weight. Hence, the aerostat was lighter and ascended even more swiftly.

At an estimated fifteen miles altitude, Kickaha guessed that he had enough to go another five miles.

McKay's balloon was drifting away from the others. Anana's was about a half a mile from Kickaha's, but it seemed to have stopped moving away from it.

At twenty miles—estimated, of course—Kickaha threw the last stick of wood onto the fire. When it had burned, he scraped the hot ashes over the side, leewards, and then pushed the earth after them. After which he closed the funnel of rawhide which had acted as a deflector. This would help keep the hot air from cooling off so fast.

His work done for the moment, he leaned against the side of the basket. The balloon would quickly begin to fall. If it did, he would have to use the parawing to glide back to the moon. The only chance of survival then would be his good luck in being on the upper side after the shape-change.

Suddenly, he was surrounded by warm air. Grinning, he waved at Anana, though he didn't expect her to see him. The rapid change in the air temperature must mean that the balloon had reached what Urthona called the gravity interface. Here the energy of the counterrepulsive force dissipated or "leaked" somewhat. And the rising current of air would keep the aerostats aloft for a while. He hoped that they would be buoyed long enough.

As the heat became stronger, he untied the funnel, and he cut it away with his knife. The situation was uncertain. Actually, the balloon was falling, but the hot air was pushing it upwards faster than it descended. A certain amount was entering the neck opening as the hotter air within the bag slowly cooled. But the bag was beginning to collapse. It would probably not completely deflate. Nevertheless, it would fall.

Since the balloon was not moving at the speed of the wind now, Kickaha felt it. When the descent became rapid enough, he would hear the wind whistling through the suspension ropes. He didn't want to hear that.

The floor of the car began to tilt slowly. He glanced at Anana's balloon. Yes, her car was swinging slowly upwards, and the gasbag was also beginning to revolve.

They had reached the zone of turnover. He'd have to act swiftly, no hesitations, no fumbles.

Some birds, looking confused but determined, flapped by.

He scrambled up the ropes and onto the net, and as he did so the air became even hotter. It seemed to him that it had risen from an estimated 100° Fahrenheit to 130° within sixty seconds. Sweat ran into his eyes as he reached the parawing and began cutting the cords that bound it to the net. The envelope was hot but not enough to singe his hands and feet. He brushed the sweat away and severed the cords binding the ha

ness and began working his way into it. It wasn't easy to do this, since
he had to keep one foot and hand at all times on the net ropes. Several
times his foot slipped, but he managed to get it back between the rope
and skin of the envelope.

He looked around. While he'd been working, the turnover had been
completed. The great curve of the planet was directly below him; the
smaller curve of the moon, above.

McKay's balloon was lost in the red sky. Anana wasn't in sight,
which meant that she too was on the side of the balloon and trying to
get into the harness.

Suddenly, the air was cooler. And he was even more aware of the
wind. The balloon, its bag shrinking with heart-stopping speed, was
headed for the ground.

The harness tied, the straps between his legs, he cut the cord which
held the nose of the wing to the net. There was one more to sever. This
held the back end, that pointing downward, to the net. Anana had cautioned him many times to be sure to cut the connection at the top before he cut that at the bottom. Otherwise, the uprushing air would catch
the wing on its undersurface. And the wing would rise, though still attached at its nose to the balloon. He'd be swung out at the end of the
shrouds and be left dangling. The wing would flatten its upper surface
against the bag, pushed by the increasingly powerful wind.

He might find it impossible to get back to the ropes and climb up to
the wing and make the final cut.

"Of course," Anana had said, "you do have a long time. It'll be
eighty miles to the ground, and you might work wonders during that
lengthy trip. But I wouldn't bet on it."

Kickaha climbed down the ropes to the rear end of the wing, grabbed
the knot which connected the end to the net, and cut with the knife in
his other hand. Immediately, with a quickness which took his breath
away, he was yanked upwards. The envelope shot by him, and he was
swinging at the end of the shrouds. The straps cut into his thighs.

He pulled on the control cords to depress the nose of the wing. And
he was descending in a fast glide. Or, to put it another way, he was falling relatively slowly.

Where was Anana? For a minute or so, she seemed to be lost in the
reddish sky. Then he located a minute object, but he couldn't be sure
whether it was she or a lone bird. It was below him to his left. He
banked, and he glided towards her or it. An immeasurable time passed.
Then the dot became larger and after a while it shaped itself into the
top of a parawing.

Using the control shrouds to slip air out of the wing, he fell faster and presently was at the same level as Anana. When she saw him she banked. After some jockeying around, they were within twenty feet of each other.

He yelled, "You O.K.?"

She shouted, "Yes!"

"Did you see McKay?"

She shook her head.

Two hours later, he spotted a large bird-shaped object at an estimated two thousand feet below him. Either it was McKay or a roc. But a long squinting at it convinced him that it must be a bird. In any event, it was descending rapidly, and if it continued its angle, it would reach the ground far away from them.

If it was McKay, he would just have to take care of himself. Neither he, Kickaha, nor Anana owed him anything.

A few seconds later he forgot about McKay. The first of a mass migration from the moon passed him. These were large goose-type birds which must have numbered in the millions. After a while they became mixed with other birds, large and small. The air around him was dark with bodies, and the beat of wings, honks, caws, trills, and whistles was clamorous.

Their wings shot through a craggle of cranes which split, one body flapping to the right, one to the left. Kickaha supposed that they'd been frightened by the machines, but a moment later he wasn't sure. Perhaps it was the appearance of an armada of rocs which had scared them.

These airplane-sized avians now accompanied them as if they were a flying escort. The nearest to Anana veered over and glared at her with one cold yellow eye. When it got too close, she screamed at it and gestured with her knife. Whether or not she had frightened it, it pulled away. Kickaha sighed with relief. If one of those giants attacked, its victim would be helpless.

However, the huge birds must have had other things on their minds. They maintained the same altitude while the parawings continued descending. After a while the birds were only specks far above and ahead.

Anana had told him that this would not be the longest trip he'd ever taken, but it would be the most painful. And it would seem to be the longest. She'd detailed what would happen to them and what they must do. He'd listened, and he'd not liked what he heard. But his imagination had fallen short of the reality by a mile.

When used as a glider, the parawing had a sinking speed of an estimated four feet a second. Which meant that, if they glided, it would take them twenty hours to reach the ground. By then, or before that, gangrene would have set into their legs.

But if the wing was used as a parachute, it would sink at twenty feet per second. The descent would be cut to a mere six hours, roughly estimated.

Thus, after locating each other, the two had pulled out some panels, and from then on they were traveling a la parachute. Kickaha worked his legs and arms to increase the circulation, and sometimes he would spill a little air out of the side of the wing to fall even faster. This procedure could only be done at short intervals, however. To go down too fast might jerk the shrouds loose when the wing slowed down again.

By the time they were at an estimated ten thousand feet from the earth, he felt as if his arms and legs had gone off flying back to the moon. He hung like a dummy except when he turned his head to see Anana. She would have been above him because, being lighter, she would not have fallen so fast. That is, she would not have if she had not arranged for her rip-panels to be somewhat larger than his. She, too, hung like a piece of dead meat.

One of the things that had worried him was that they might encounter a strong updraft which would delay their landing even more. But they had continued to fall at an even pace.

Below them were mountains and some small plains. But by the time they'd reached four thousand feet, they were approaching a large body of water. It was one of the many great hollows temporarily filled with rainwater. At the moment the bottom of the depression was tilting. The water was draining out of one end through a pass between two mountains. The animals on land near the lower end were running to avoid being overtaken by the rising water. What seemed like a million amphibians were scrambling ashore or waddling as fast as they could go towards higher ground.

Kickaha wondered why the amphibians were in such a hurry to leave the lake. Then he saw several hundred or so immense animals, crocodilian in shape, thrashing through the water. They were scooping up the fleeing prey.

He yelled at Anana and pointed at the monsters. She shouted back that they should slip out some air from the wings. They didn't want to land anywhere near those beasts.

With a great effort, he pulled on the shrouds. He fell ten seconds later into the water near the shore with Anana two seconds behind him. He had cut the shrouds just in time to slip out of the harness. The water closed over him, he sank, then his feet touched bottom, and he tried to push upwards with them.

They failed to obey him.

His head broke surface as he propelled himself with his fatigue-soaked arms. Anana was already swimming towards the shore, which was about thirty feet away. Her legs were not moving.

They dragged themselves onto the grass like merpeople, their legs trailing. After that was a long period of intense pain as the circulation slowly returned. When they were able, they rose and tottered towards the high ground. Long four-legged and finned creatures, their bodies covered with slime, passed them. Some snapped at them but did not try to bite. The heavier gravity, after their many months of lightness on the moon, pressed upon them. But they had to keep going. The hippopot-amus-sized crocodiles were on land now.

They didn't think they could make it over the shoulder of a moun-tain. But they did, and then they lay down. After they'd quit panting, they closed their eyes and slept. It was too much of an effort to be con-cerned about crocodiles, lions, dogs, or anything that might be inter-ested in eating them. For all they cared, the moon could fall on them.

XXII

KICKAHA AND ANANA RAN AT A PACE THAT THEY COULD MAINTAIN FOR miles and yet not be worn out. They were as naked as the day they came into the world except for the belts holding their knives and the Horn and the device strapped to her wrist. They were sweating and breathing heavily, but they knew that this time they could catch the palace—if nothing interfered.

Another person was also in pursuit of the colossus. He was riding a moosoid. Though he was a half a mile away, his tallness and red-bronze hair identified him. He had to be Red Orc.

Kickaha used some of his valuable breath. "I don't know how he got here, and I don't know what he expects to do when he catches up with the palace. He doesn't know the codewords."

"No," Anana gasped. "But maybe that man we saw will open a door for him."

So far, Orc had not looked back. This was fortunate, because, ten minutes later, a window. French door rather, swung open for him. He grabbed its sill and was helped within by two arms. The moosoid immediately stopped galloping and headed for a grove of moving plants. The door shut.

Kickaha hoped that the unknown tenant would be as helpful to them. But if Orc saw them, he'd be sure to interfere with any efforts to help.

Slowly they neared the towering building. Their bare feet pounded on the grass. Their breaths hissed in and out. Sweat stung their eyes. Their legs were gradually losing their response to their wills. They felt as if they were full of poisons which were killing the muscles. Which, in fact, they were.

To make the situation worse, the palace was heading for a mountain a mile or two away. If it began skimming up its slope, it would proceed at an undiminished speed. But the two chasing it would have to climb. Finally, the bottom right-hand corner was within reach. They slowed down sobbing. They could keep up a kilometer an hour, a walking pace, as long as they were on a flatland. But when the structure started up the mountain, they would have to draw on reserves they didn't have.

There was a tall window at the very corner, its glass or plastic curving to include both sides. However, it was set flush to the building itself. No handholds to draw themselves up.

They forced themselves to break from a walk to a trot. The windows they passed showed a lighted corridor. The walls were of various glowing colors. Many paintings hung on them, and at intervals statues painted flesh colors stood by the doors leading to other rooms within. Then they came to several windows which were part of a large room. Furniture was arranged within it, and a huge fireplace in which a fire burned was at the extreme end.

A robot, about four feet high, dome-shaped, wheeled, was removing dust from a large table. A multi-elbowed metal arm extended a fat disc which moved over the surface of the table. Another arm moved what seemed to be a vacuum cleaner attachment over the rug behind it.

Kickaha increased his pace. Anana kept up with him. He wanted to get to the front before the palace began the ascent. The front would be only a foot from the slope, but, since the building would maintain a horizontal attitude, the rest would be too far from the ground for them to reach it.

Just as the forepart reached the bottom of the mountain, the two attained their objective. But now they had to climb.

None of the windows they had passed had revealed any living being within.

They ran around the corner, which was just like the rear one. And here they saw their first hope for getting a hold. Halfway along the fron' was a large balcony. No doubt Urthona had installed it so that he coul(c) step out into the fresh air and enjoy the view. But it would not be means of access. Not unless the stranger within the palace ha(c) carelessly left it unlocked. That wasn't likely, but at least they coul(stop running.

Almost, they didn't make it. The upward movement of the building combined with their running in front of it, resulted in an angled trave up the slope. But they kept up with it, though once Kickaha stumbled He grabbed the edge of the bottom, clung, was dragged, then release(c) his hold, rolled furiously, got ahead, and was seized by the wrist b(

Anana and yanked forward and upward. She fell backward, but somehow they got up and resumed their race without allowing the palace to
pass over them.

Then they had grabbed the edge of the balcony and swung themselves up and over it. For a long time they lay on the cool metallic floor
and gasped as if each breath of air was the last in the world. When they
were breathing normally, they sat up and looked around. Two French
doors gave entrance to an enormous room, though not for them. Kickaha pushed in on the knobless doors without success. There didn't seem
to be any handles on the inside. Doubtless, they opened to a pushbutton
or a codeword.

Hoping that there were no sensors to give alarm, Kickaha banged
hard with the butt of his knife on the transparent material. The stuff did
not crack or shatter. He hadn't expected it to.

"Well, at least we're riding," he said. He looked up at the balcony
above theirs. It was at least twenty feet higher, thus, out of reach.

"We're stuck. How ironic. We finally make it, and all we can do is
starve to death just outside the door."

They were exhausted and suffering from intense thirst. But they could
not just leave the long-desired place. Yet, what else could they do?

He looked up again, this time at dark clouds forming.

"It should be raining soon. We can drink, anyway. What do you say
ve rest here tonight? Morning may bring an idea."

Anana agreed that that was the best thing to do. Two hours later, the
downpour began, continuing uninterruptedly for several hours. Their
thirst was quenched, but they felt like near-drowned puppies by the
time it was over. They were cold, shivering, wet. By nightfall they'd
dried off, however and they slept wrapped in each other's arms.

By noon the next day their bellies were growling like starving lions in
cage outside which was a pile of steaks. Kickaha said, "We'll have to
go hunting, Anana, before we get too weak. We can always run this
down again, though I hate to think of it. If we could make a rope with a
grapnel, we might be able to get up to that balcony above us. Perhaps
the door there isn't locked. Why should it be?"

"It will be locked because Urthona wouldn't take any chances," she
said. "Anyway, by the time we could make a rope, the palace would be
far ahead of us. We might even lose track of it."

"You're right," he said. He turned to the door and beat on it with his
fists. Inside was a huge room with a large fountain in its center. A marble triton blew water from the horn at its lips.

He stiffened, and said, "Oh, oh! Don't move, Anana! Here comes someone!"

Anana froze. She was standing to one side, out of view of anyone in the room.

"It's Red Orc! He's seen me! It's too late for me to duck! Get over the side of the balcony! There're ornamentations you can hang onto! I don't know what he's going to do to me, but if he comes out here, you might be able to catch him unaware. I'll have to be the sacrificial goat!"

Out of the corner of his eye he watched her slide over the railing and disappear. He stayed where he was, looking steadily at her uncle. Orc was dressed in a splendid outfit of some sparkling material, the calf-length pants very tight, the boots scarlet and with upturned toes, the jacket double-breasted and with flaring sleeves, the shirt ruffled and encrusted with jewels on the broad wing-tipped collar.

He was smiling, and he held a wicked-looking beamer in one hand.

He stopped for a moment just inside the doors. He moved to each side to get a full view of the balcony. His hand moved to the wall, apparently pressing a button. The doors slid straight upward into the wall.

He held the weapon steady, aiming at Kickaha's chest.

"Where's Anana?"

"She's dead," Kickaha said.

Orc smiled and pulled the trigger. Kickaha was knocked back across the balcony, driven hard into the railing. He lay half-sitting, more than half-stunned. Vaguely, he was aware of Orc stepping out onto the balcony and looking over the railing. The red-haired man leaned over and said, "Come on up, Anana. I'm on to your game. But throw your knife away."

A moment later she came slowly over the railing. Orc backed up into the doorway, the beamer directed at her. She looked at Kickaha and said, "Is he dead?"

"No, the beamer's set for low-grade stun. I saw you two last night after the alarm went off. Your *leblabbiy* stud was foolish enough to hammer on the door. The sensors are very sensitive."

Anana said, "So you just watched us. You wanted to know what we'd try?"

Orc smiled again. "Yes, I knew you could do nothing. But I enjoyed watching you trying to figure out something."

He looked at the Horn strapped around her shoulder.

"I've finally got it. I can get out of here now."

He pressed the trigger, and Anana fell back against the railing. Kic aha's senses were by then almost full recovered, though he felt weak. But if Orc got within reach of his hands . . .

The Lord wasn't going to do that. He stepped back, said something, and two robots came through the doorway. At first glance they looked like living human beings. But the dead eyes and the movements, not as graceful as beings of animal origin, showed that metal or plastic lay beneath the seeming skin. One removed Kickaha's knife and threw it over the balcony railing. The other unstrapped the multiuse device from Anana's wrist. Both got hold of the ankles of the two and dragged them inside. To one side stood a large hemisphere of thick criss-crossed wires on a platform with six wheels. The robot picked up Anana and shoved her through a small doorway in the cage. The second did the same to Kickaha. The door was shut, and the two were captives inside what looked like a huge mousetrap.

Orc bent down and reached under the cage. When he straightened up, he said, "I've just turned on the voltage. Don't touch the wires. You won't be killed, but you'll be knocked out."

He told the humanoid robots and the cage to follow him. Carrying the Horn, which he had removed from Anana's shoulder, he strode through the room toward a high-ceilinged wide corridor.

Kickaha crawled to Anana. "Are you okay?"

"I'll be in a minute," she said. "I don't have much strength just now. And I've got a headache."

"Me, too," he said. "Well, at least we're inside."

"Never say die, eh? Sometimes your optimism . . . well, never mind. What do you suppose happened to the man who let Orc in?"

"If he's still alive, he's regretting his kind deed. He can't be a Lord. If he was, he'd not have let himself be taken."

Kickaha called out to Orc, asking him who the stranger was. Orc didn't reply. He stopped at the end of the corridor, which branched off into two others. He said something in a low voice to the wall, a codeword, and a section of wall moved back a little and then slid inside a hollow. Revealed was a room about twenty feet by twenty feet, an elevator.

Orc pressed a button on a panel. The elevator shot swiftly upward. When it stopped, the lighted symbol showed that it was on the fortieth floor. Orc pressed two more buttons and took hold of a small lever. The elevator moved out into a very wide corridor and glided down it. Orc turned the lever, the elevator swiveled around a corner and went down another corridor for about two hundred feet. It stopped, its open front against a door.

Orc removed a little black book from a pocket, opened it, consulted a page, said something that sounded like gibberish, and the door opened. He replaced the book and stood to one side as the cage rolled into a large room. It stopped in the exact center.

Orc spoke some more gibberish. Mechanisms mounted on the walls at a height of ten feet from the floor extended metal arms. At the end of each was a beamer. There were two on each wall, and all pointed at the cage. Above the weapons were small round screens. Undoubtedly, video eyes.

Orc said, "I've heard you boast that there isn't a prison or a trap that can hold you, Kickaha. I don't think you'll ever make that boast again."

"Do you mind telling us what you intend to do with us?" Anana said in a bored voice.

"You're going to starve," he said. "You won't die of thirst since you'll be given enough water to keep you going. At the end of a certain time—which I won't tell you—whether you're still alive or not, the beamers will blow you apart.

"Even if, inconceivably, you could get out of the cage and dodge the beamers, you can't get out of here. There's only one exit, the door you came through. You can't open that unless you know the codeword."

Anana opened her mouth, her expression making it obvious that she was going to appeal. It closed; her expression faded. No matter how desperate the situation, she was not going to humiliate herself if it would be for nothing. But she'd had a moment of weakness.

Kickaha said, "At least you could satisfy our curiosity. Who was the man who let you in? What happened to him?"

Orc grimaced. "He got away from me. I got hold of a beamer and was going to make him my prisoner. But he dived through a trapdoor I hadn't known existed. I suppose by now he's gated to another world. At least, the sensors don't indicate his presence."

Kickaha grinned, and said, "Thank you. But who was he?"

"He claimed to be an Earthman. He spoke English, but it was a quaint sort. It sounded to me like eighteenth-century English. He never told me his name. He began to ramble on and on, told me he'd been trapped here for some time when he gated from Vala's world to get away from her. It had taken him some time to find out how to activate a gate to another universe without being killed. He was just about to do so when he saw me galloping up. He decided to let me in because didn't look like a native of this world.

"I think he was half-crazy."

"He must have been completely insane to trust you, a Lord," Anana said. "Did he say anything about having seen Kickaha, McKay, and myself? He passed over us when we were on the moon."

Orc's eyebrows rose. "You were on the moon? And you survived its fall? No, he said nothing about you. That doesn't mean he wasn't interested or wouldn't have gotten around eventually to telling me about you."

He paused, smiled, and said, "Oh, I almost forgot! If you get hungry enough, one of you can eat the other."

Kickaha and Anana could not hide their shock. Orc broke into laughter then. When he stopped bellowing, he removed a knife from the sheath at his belt. It was about six inches long and looked as if it were made of gold. He shoved it through the wires, where it lay at Anana's feet.

"You'll need a cutting utensil, of course, to carve steaks and chops and so forth. That'll do the job, but don't think for one moment you can use it to short out the wires. It's nonconductive."

Kickaha said, fiercely, "If it wasn't for Anana I'd think all you Lords were totally unreformable, fit only to be killed on sight. But there's one thing I'm sure about. You haven't a spark of decency in you. You're absolutely unhuman."

"If you mean I in no way have the nature of a *leblabbiy* you're right."

Anana picked up the knife and fingered the side, which felt grainy, though its surface was steel-smooth.

"We don't have to starve to death," she said. "We can always kill ourselves first."

Orc shrugged. "That's up to you."

He said something to the humanoid robots, and they followed him through the doorway into the elevator. He turned and waved farewell as the door slid out from the wall recesses.

"Maybe that Englishman is still here," Kickaha said. "He might get us free. Meanwhile, give me the knife."

Anana had anticipated him, however. She was sawing away at a wire where it disappeared into the floor. After working away for ten minutes, she put the blade down.

"Not a scratch. The wire metal is much harder than the knife's."

"Naturally. But we had to try. Well, there's no use putting it off until we're too weak even to slice flesh. Which one of us shall it be?"

Shocked, she turned to look at him. He was grinning.

"Oh, you! Must you joke about even this?"

She saw a section of the cage floor beyond him move upward. He turned at her exclamation. A cube was protruding several inches. The top was rising on one side, though no hinges or bolts were in evidence. Within it was a pool of water.

They drank quickly, since they didn't know how long the cube would remain. Two minutes later, the top closed, and the box sank back flush with the floor.

It reappeared, filled with water, about every three hours. No cup was provided, so they had to get down on their hands and knees and suck it up with their mouths, like animals. Every four hours, the box came up empty. Evidently, they were to excrete in it then. When the box appeared the next time, it was evident that it had not been completely cleaned out.

"Orc must enjoy this little feature," Kickaha said.

There was no way to measure the passage of time since the light did not dim. Anana's sense of time told her, however, that they must have been caged for at least fifty-eight hours. Their bellies caved in, growled, and thundered. Their ribs grew gaunter before their eyes. Their cheeks hollowed; their legs and arms slimmed. And they felt steadily weaker. Anana's full breasts sagged.

"We can't live off our fat because we don't have any," he said. "We were honed down pretty slim from all the ordeals we've gone through."

There were long moments of silence, though both spoke whenever they could think of something worthwhile to say. Silence was too much like the quiet of the dead, which they soon would be.

They had tried to wedge the knife into the crack in the side of the waterbox. They did not know what good this would do, but they might think of something. However, the knife would not penetrate into the crack.

Anana now estimated that they'd been in the cage about seventy hours. Neither had said anything about Orc's suggestion that one of them feast on the other. They had an unspoken agreement that they would not consent to this horror. They also wondered if Orc was watching and listening through video.

Food crammed their dreams if not their bellies. Kickaha was drowsing fitfully, dreaming of eating roast pork, mashed potatoes and gravy and rhubarb pie when a clicking sound awoke him. He lay on his back for a while, wondering why he would dream of such a sound. He was about to fall back into the orgy of eating again when a thought made him sit up as if someone had passed a hot pastrami by his nose.

Had Orc inserted a new element in the torture? It didn't seem possible, but . . .

He got onto his hands and knees and crawled to the little door. He pushed on it, and it swung outward.

The clicking had been the release of its lock.

XXIII

WHILE THEY CLAMBERED DOWN OUT OF THE CAGE, THE BEAMERS ON the wall tracked them. Kickaha started across toward the door. All four weapons spat at once, vivid scarlet rays passing before and behind him. Ordinarily, the rays were invisible, but Orc had colored them so his captors could see how close they were. Beauty, and terror, were in the eye of the beholder.

Anana moaned. "Oh, no! He just let us loose to tantalize us!"

Kickaha unfroze.

"Yeah. But those beamers should be hitting us."

He took another step forward. Again the rays almost touched him.

"To hell with it! They're set now so they'll just miss us! Another one of his refinements!"

He walked steadily to the door while she followed. Two of the beamers swung to her, but their rays shot by millimeters away from her. Nevertheless, it was unnerving to see the scarlet rods shoot just before his eyes. As the two got closer to the door, the rays angled past their cheeks on one side and just behind the head.

They should have drilled through the walls and floor, but these were made of some material invulnerable even to their power.

When he was a few feet from the door, the beamers swung to spray the door just ahead of him. Their contact with the door made a slight hissing, like a poisonous snake about to strike.

The two stood while scarlet flashed and splashed over the door.

"We're not to touch," Kickaha said. "Or is this just a move in the game he's playing to torment us?"

He turned and walked back toward the nearest beamer. It tracked just ahead of him, forcing him to move slowly. But the ray was always just ahead of him.

When he stopped directly before the beamer, it was pointed at his chest. He moved around it until it could no longer follow him. Of course, he was in the line of sight of the other three. But they had stopped firing now.

The weapon was easily unsecured by pulling a thick pin out of a hinge on its rear. He lifted it and tore it loose from the wires connected to its underside. Anana, seeing this, did the same to hers. The other two beamers started shooting again, their rays again just missing them. But these too were soon made harmless.

"So far, we're just doing what Orc wants us to do," he said. "He's programmed this whole setup. Why?"

They went to the door and pushed on it. It swung open, revealing a corridor empty of life or robots. They walked to the branch and went around the corner. At the end of this hall was the open door of the elevator shaft. The cage was within it, as if Orc had sent it there to await them.

They hesitated to enter it. What if Orc had set a trap for them, and the cage stopped halfway between floors or just fell to the bottom of the shaft?

"In that case," Kickaha said, "he would figure that we'd take a stairway. So he'd trap those."

They got into the cage and punched a button for the first floor. Arriving safely, they wandered through some halls and rooms until they came to an enormous luxuriously furnished chamber. The two robots stood by a great table of polished onyx. Anana, in the language of the Lords, ordered a meal. This was brought in five minutes. They ate so much they vomited, but after resting they ate again, though lightly. Two hours later, they had another meal. She directed a robot to show them to an apartment. They bathed in hot water and then went to sleep on a bed that floated three feet above the floor while cool air and soft music flowed over them.

When they woke, the door to the room opened before they could get out of bed. A robot pushed in a table on which were trays filled with hot delicious food and glasses of orange or muskmelon juice. They ate, went to the bathroom, showered, and emerged. The robot was waiting with clothes that fitted them exactly.

Kickaha did not know how the measurements had been taken, but he wasn't curious about it. He had more important things to consider.

"This red carpet treatment worries me. Orc is setting us up just to knock us down again."

The robot knocked on the door. Anana told him to come in. He stopped before Kickaha and handed him a note. Opening it, Kickaha said, "It's in English. I don't know whose handwriting it is, but it has to be Orc."

He read aloud, "Look out a window."

Dreading what they would see, but too curious to put it off, they hastened through several rooms and down a long corridor. The window at its end held a scene that was mostly empty air. But moving slowly across it was a tiny globe. It was the lavalite world.

"That's the kicker!" he said. "Orc's taken the palace into space! And he's marooned us up here, of course, with no way of getting to the ground!"

"And he's also deactivated all the gates, of course," Anana said.

A robot, which had followed them, made a sound exactly like a polite butler wishing to attract his master's attention. They turned, and the robot held out to Kickaha another note. He spoke in English. "Master told me to tell you, sir, that he hopes you enjoy this."

Kickaha read, "The palace is in a decaying orbit."

Kickaha spoke to the robot. "Do you have any other messages for us?"

"No, sir."

"Can you lead us to the central control chamber?"

"Yes, sir."

"Then lead on, MacDuff."

It said, "What does MacDuff mean, sir?"

"Cancel the word. What name are you called by? I mean, what is your designation?"

"One, sir."

"So you're one, too."

"No, sir. Not One-Two. One."

"For Ilmarwolkin's sake," Anana said, "quit your clowning."

They followed One into a large room where there was an open wheeled vehicle large enough for four. The robot got into the driver's seat. They stepped into the back seat, and the car moved away smoothly and silently. After driving through several corridors, the robot steered it into a large elevator. He got out and pressed some buttons, and the cage rose thirty floors. The robot got behind the wheel and drove the vehicle down a corridor almost for a quarter of a mile. The car stopped in front of a door.

"The entrance to the central control chamber, sir."

The robot got out and stood by the door. They followed him. The door had been welded, or sealed to the wall.

"Is this the only entrance?"

"Yes, sir."

It was evident that Orc had made sure that they could not get in. Doubtless, any devices, including beamers, that could remove the door had been jettisoned from the palace. Or was Orc just making it more difficult for them? Perhaps he had deliberately left some tools around, but when they got into the control room, they would find that the controls had been destroyed.

They found a window and looked out into red space. Kickaha said, "It should take some time before this falls onto the planet. Meanwhile, we can eat, drink, make love, sleep. Get our strength back. And look like mad for some way of getting out of this mess. If Orc thinks we're going to suffer while we're falling, he doesn't know us."

"Yes, but the walls and door must be made of the same stuff, *impervium*, as the room that held the cage," she said. "Beamers won't affect it. I don't know how he managed to weld the door to the walls, but he did. So getting in to the controls seems to be out."

First, they had to make a search of the entire building and that would take days even when traveling in the little car. They found the hangar which had once housed five fliers. Orc had not even bothered to close its door. He must have set them to fly out on automatic.

They also located the great power plant. This contained the gravitic machines which now maintained an artificial field within the palace. Otherwise, they would have been floating around in free fall.

"It's a wonder he didn't turn that off," Anana said. "It would have been one more way to torment us."

"Nobody's perfect," Kickaha said.

Their search uncovered no tools which could blast into the control chamber. They hadn't thought it would.

Kickaha conferred with Anana, who knew more about parachutes than he did. Then he gave a number of robots very detailed instruction on how to manufacture two chutes out of silken hangings.

"All we have to do is to jump off and then float down," he said. "But I don't relish the idea of spending the rest of my life on that miserable world. It's better than being dead, but not by much."

There were probably a thousand, maybe two thousand gates in the walls and on the floors and possibly on the ceilings. Without the codewords to activate them, they could neither locate nor use them.

They wondered where the wallpanel was which the Englishman had used to get away from Red Orc. To search for it would take more time than they had. Then Kickaha thought of asking the robots, One and Two, if they had witnessed his escape. To his delight, both had. They led the humans to it. Kickaha pushed in on the panel and saw a metal chute leading downward some distance, then curving.

"Here goes nothing," he said to Anana. He jumped into it sitting up and slid down and around and was shot into a narrow dimly lit hall. He yelled back up the chute to her and told her he was going on. But he was quickly stopped by a dead end.

After tapping and probing around, he went back to the chute and, bracing himself against the sides, climbed back up.

"Either there's another panel I couldn't locate or there's a gate in the end of the hall," he told her.

They sent the robots to the supply room to get a drill and hammers. Though the drills wouldn't work on the material enclosing the control room, they might work on the plastic composing the walls of the hidden hall. After the robots returned, Kickaha and Anana went down the chute with them and bored holes into the walls. After making a circle of many perforations, he knocked the circle through with a sledgehammer.

Light streamed out through it. He cautiously looked within. He gasped.

"Well, I'll be swoggled! Red Orc!"

XXIV

IN THE MIDDLE OF A LARGE BARE ROOM WAS A TRANSPARENT CUBE about twelve feet long. A chair, a narrow bed, and a small red box on the floor by a wall shared the cube with its human occupant, Orc. Kickaha noted that a large pipe ran from the base of the wall of the room to the cube, penetrated the transparent material, and ended in the red box. Presumably, this furnished water and perhaps a semiliquid type of food. A smaller pipe within the large one must provide air.

Red Orc was sitting on the chair before the table, his profile to the watchers through the hole. Evidently, the cube was soundproof, since he had not heard the drilling or pounding. The Horn and a beamer lay on the table before him. From this Kickaha surmised that the cube was invulnerable to the beamer's rays.

Red Orc, once the secret Lord of the Two Earths, looked as dejected as a man could be. No wonder. He had stepped through a gate in the control room, expecting to enter another universe, possessing the Horn, the Lords' greatest treasure, and leaving behind him two of his worst enemies to die. But Urthona had prepared his trap well, and Red Orc had been gated to this prison instead of to freedom.

As far as he knew, no one was aware that he was locked in this room. He was doubtless contemplating how long it would be before the palace fell to Urthona's world and he perished in the smash, caught in his own trap.

Kickaha and Anana cut a larger hole in the wall for entrance. During this procedure, Orc saw them. He rose up from his chair and stared from a pale-gray face. He could expect no mercy. The only change in his situation was that he would die sooner.

His niece and her lover were not so sure that anything had been changed. If he couldn't cut his way out of the cube, they couldn't cut their way in. Especially when they didn't have a beamer. But the pipe which was Orc's life supply was of copper. After the robots got some more tools, Kickaha slicked off the copper at the junction with the *impervium* which projected outside the cube.

This left an opening through which Orc could still get air and also could communicate. Kickaha and Anana did not place themselves directly before the hole, though. Orc might shoot them through it.

Kickaha said, "The rules of the game have been changed, Orc. You need us, and we need you. If you cooperate, I promise to let you go wherever you want to, alive and unharmed. If you don't, you'll die. We might die, too, but what good will that do you?"

"I can't trust you to keep your word," Orc said sullenly.

"If that's the way you want it, so be it. But Anana and I aren't going to be killed. We're having parachutes made. That means we'll be marooned here, but at least we'll be alive."

"Parachutes?" Orc said. It was evident from his expression that he had not thought of their making them.

"Yeah. There's an old American saying that there's more than one way to skin a cat. And I'm a cat-skinner par excellence. I—Anana and I—are going to figure a way out of this mess. But we need information from you. Now, do you want to give it to us and maybe live? Or do you want to sulk like a spoiled child and die?"

Orc gritted his teeth, then said, "Very well. What do you want?"

"A complete description of what happened when you gated from the control chamber to this trap. And anything that might be relevant."

Orc told how he had checked out the immense room and its hundreds of controls. His task had been considerably speeded up by questioning robots One and Two. Then he had found out how to open several gates. He had done so cautiously and before activating them himself he had ordered the robots to do so. Thus, if they were trapped, they would be the victims.

One gate apparently had access to the gates enclosed in various boulders scattered over the planet below. Urthona must have had some means of identifying these. He would have been hoping that, while roaming the planet with the others, he would recognize one. Then, with a simple codeword or two, he would have transported himself to the palace. But Urthona hadn't had any luck.

Orc identified three gates to other worlds. One was to Jadawin's, one to Earth I, and one to dead Urizen's. There were other gates, but Orc hadn't wanted to activate them. He didn't want to push his luck. So far, he hadn't set off any traps. Besides, the gate to Earth I was the one he wanted.

Having made sure that his escape routes were open, Orc had then had the robots, One and Two, seal the control room.

"So you had our torments all fixed up ahead of time?" Anana said.

"Why not?" Orc said. "Wouldn't you have done the same to me?"

"At one time I would have. Actually, you did us a favor by letting us loose so we could savor the terrors of the fall. But you didn't mean to, I'm sure."

"He did himself a favor, too," Kickaha said.

Orc had then activated the gate to Earth I. He had stepped through the hole between the universes, fully expecting to emerge in a cave. He could see through its entrance a valley and a wooded mountain range beyond. He thought that it was possibly the same cave through which Kickaha and Anana had gone in southern California.

But Urthona had set up a simulacrum to lull the unwary. To strengthen its impression, Urthona had also programmed the robots in case a crafty Lord wanted to use the gate. At least, Red Orc supposed he had done so. Orc had ordered the robot called Six to walk through first. Six had done so, had traveled through the cave, stepped outside, looked around, then had returned through the gate.

Satisfied, Orc had ordered the robots, One and Two, to seal up the control room door with *impervium* flux. Then he had stepped through.

"Apparently," Orc said, "that wily *shagg* (a sort of polecat) had counted on the robot being used as a sacrifice. So he had arranged it that the robot would not be affected."

"Urthona always was a sneaky one," Anana said. "But he had depended on his technological defenses too long. Thrown on his own resources, he was not the man he should have been."

She paused, then added, "Just like you, Uncle."

"I haven't done so badly," he said, his face red.

Kickaha and Anana burst out laughing.

"No," she said. "Of course not. Just look where you are."

Orc had been whisked away when he was only a few feet from leaving the cave or what he thought was a cave. The next second he was standing in the cube.

Kickaha drew Anana to a corner of the room to confer quietly. "Somehow, that mysterious Englishman discovered a gateway to another universe in the wall at the end of the corridor," he said. "Maybe he had found Urthona's codebook. Anyway, where one can go through, others can. And the Horn can get us through. But we can't get to the Horn.

"Now, what's to prevent us from getting Orc to blow the notes for us? Then we can make a recording of it and use it to open the gate."

Anana shook her head. "It doesn't work that way. It's been tried before, it's so obvious. But there's something in the machinery in the Horn that adds an element missing in recordings."

"I was afraid of that," he said. "But I had to ask. Look, Anana. Urthona must have planted gates all over this place. We've probably passed dozens without knowing it because they are inside the walls. Logically, many if not most of them will be quick emergency routes from one place in this building to another. So Urthona could outsmart anyone who was close on his heels.

"But there have to be a few which would gate him to another world. Only to be used in cases of direst emergency. One of them is the gate at the end of the corridor next door. I think . . ."

"Not necessarily," Anana said. "For all we know, it leads to the control room or some other place in the palace."

"No. In that case, the sensors would have shown Orc that the Englishman was in the palace."

"No. Urthona might have set up places without sensors where he could hide if an enemy had possession of the control room."

"I'm the A-Number One trickster, but sometimes I think you sneaky Lords put me to shame. Okay. Just a minute. Let me ask Orc a question."

He went to the cube. The Lord, looking very suspicious, said, "What are you two up to now?"

"Nothing that won't help you," Kickaha said, grinning. "We just don't want you to get a chance to get the drop on us. Tell me. Did the sensor displays in the control room indicate that there were hidden auxiliary sensor systems?"

"Why would you want to know?"

"Damn it!" Kickaha said. "You're wasting our time. Remember, I have to spring you if only to get the Horn."

Hesitantly, Orc said, "Yes, there are hidden auxiliary systems. It took me some time to find them. Actually, I wasn't looking for them. I discovered them while I was looking for something else. I checked them out and noted that they were in rooms not covered by the main system. But since nobody was using them, I assumed that no one was in them. It was inconceivable that anyone in a room where they were wouldn't be trying to find out where I was."

"I hope your memory's good. Where are they?"

"My memory is superb," Orc said stiffly. "I am not one of you sub-beings."

Kickaha grimaced. The Lords had the most sensitive and gangrenous egos he'd ever encountered. A good thing for him, though. He'd never have survived his conflicts with them if they hadn't always used part of their minds to feed their own egos. They were never really capable of one hundred percent mental concentration.

Well, he, Kickaha, had a big ego, too. But a healthy one.

The Lord remembered only a few of the locations of the auxiliary sensor systems. He couldn't be blamed for that since there were so many. But he was able to give Kickaha directions to three of them. He also gave him some instructions on how to operate them.

Just to make sure he hadn't been neglecting another source of information, Kickaha asked robots One and Two about the sensors. They were aware of only that in the control room. Urthona had not trusted them with any more data than he thought necessary for his comfort and protection.

Kickaha thought that if he had been master of this palace he would have installed a safety measure in the robots. When asked certain questions, they would have refused to answer them. Or pretended that they didn't know.

Which, now that he thought about it, might be just what was happening. But they'd given him data that Urthona might not want his enemies to have. So possibly, they were not lying.

He took One with him, leaving Anana to keep an eye on her uncle. It wasn't likely that he'd be going any place or doing anything worth noticing. But you never knew.

The hidden system console was in a room behind a wall in a much larger room on the tenth floor. Lacking the codeword to gate through, he and One tore part of the wall down. He turned on the console and, with One's aid, checked out the entire building. It was done swiftly, the glowing diagrams of the rooms flashing by too swiftly on the screen for Kickaha to see anything but a blur. But a computer in One's body sorted them out.

When the operation was complete, One said, "There are one hundred and ten chambers which the sensors do not monitor."

Kickaha groaned and said, "You mean we'd have to get into all of them to make sure no living being is in one of them?"

"That is one method."

"What's the other?"

"This system can monitor the control chamber. It's controlled by that switch there." One pointed. "That also enables the operator to hook into the control-room sensories. These can be used to look into the one hundred and ten chambers. The man named Orc did not know that. The switch is not on the panel in the control room however. It is under the panel and labeled as an energy generator control. Only the master knew about it."

"Then how did you come to know about it?"

"I learned about it while I was scanning the displays here."

"Then why didn't you tell me?"

"You didn't ask me."

Kickaha repressed another groan. The robots were so smart yet so dumb.

"Connect this system with the control room's."

"Yes, master."

One strode ponderously to the control board and turned a switch marked, in Lord lettering, HEAT. Heat for what? Obviously, it was not designated to make any unauthorized operator ignore it. Immediately, lights began pulsing here and there, a switch turned by itself, and one of the large video screens above the panel came to life.

Kickaha looked into the room from a unit apparently high on the wall and pointing downward. It was directed toward the central chair in a row of five or six before the wide panel. In this sat a man with his back to Kickaha.

For a second he thought that it must be the Englishman who had helped Orc. But this man was bigger than the one described by Orc, and his hair was not brown but yellow.

He was looking at a video screen just above him. It showed Kickaha and the robot behind him, looking at the man.

The operator rose with a howl of fury, spun out of his chair, and shook his fist at the unit receiving his image.

He was Urthona.

XXV

THE LORD WAS CLAD ONLY IN A RAGGED SKIN BOUND AROUND HIS WAIST. A longitudinal depression, the scar from the axe wound, ran down the center of his chest. His hair fell over his shoulders to his nipples. His skin was smeared with the oily dirt of his world, and a bump on his forehead indicated a hard contact with some harder object. Moreover, his nose had been broken.

Kickaha was shocked for a few seconds, then he went into action. He ran toward the switch to turn it off. Urthona's voice screamed through the video. "One! Kill him! Kill him!"

"Kill who, master?" One said calmly.

"You blithering metal idiot! That man! Kickaha!"

Kickaha turned the switch and whirled. The robot was ѕdvancing on him, its arms out, fingers half-clenched.

Kickaha drew his knife. Shockingly, Urthona's voice came out of the robot's unmoving lips. "I see you, you leblabay! I'm going to kill you!"

For a second Kickaha didn't know what was happening. Then illumi-ation came. Urthona had switched on a transceiver inside the robot's ody and was speaking through it. Probably, he was also watching his ctim-to-be through One's eyes.

That had one advantage for Kickaha. As long as Urthona was watch-g the conflict from the control room, he wasn't gating here.

Kickaha leaped toward the robot, stopped, jumped back, slashed ith his knife with no purpose but to test the speed of One's reaction. The robot made no attempt to parry with his arm or grab the knife, however. He continued walking toward Kickaha.

Kickaha leaped past One and his blade flickered in and out. Score one. The point had broken the shield painted to look like a human eyeball. But had it destroyed the video sensor behind it?

No time to find out. He came in again, this time on the left side. The robot was still turning when the knife shattered the other eyeball.

By now Kickaha knew that One wasn't quick enough for him. It undoubtedly was far stronger, but here swiftness was the key to victory. He ran around behind One and stopped. The robot continued on its path. It had to be blinded, which meant that Urthona would know this and would at once take some other action.

He looked around quickly. There were stretches of bare wall which could conceal a gate. But wouldn't Urthona place the gate where he could step out hidden from the sight of anyone in the room? Such as, for instance, the space behind the control console. It wasn't against the wall.

He ran to it and stepped behind it. Seconds, a minute, passed. Was Urthona delaying because he wanted to get a weapon first? If so, he would have to go to a hidden cache, since Orc had jettisoned every weapon he could locate.

Or was he staying in the control room, where he was safe? From there he could order all the robots in the palace, and there were several score or more, to converge on this room.

Or had he gated to a room nearby and now was creeping up on his enemy? If so, he would make sure he had a beamer in his hand.

There was a thump as the robot blindly blundered into the wall. At least, Kickaha supposed that was the noise. He didn't want to stick his head out to see.

His only warning was a shimmering, a circle of wavy light taller than a tall man, on the wall to his right. Abruptly, it became a round hole in the wall. Urthona stepped through it, but Kickaha was upon him, hurling him back, desperate to get both of them in the control room before the gate closed.

They fell out onto the floor, Kickaha on top of the Lord, fingers locked on the wrist of the hand that held a beamer. The other laid the edge of the knife against the jugular vein. Urthona's eyes were glazed, the back of his head having thumped against the floor.

Kickaha twisted the wrist; the beamer clattered on the tile floor. He rolled away, grabbed the weapon, and was up on his feet.

Snarling, shaking, Urthona started to get up. He sank down as Kickaha ordered him to stay put.

The robot, Number Six, started towards them. Kickaha quickly ordered Urthona to command Six to take no action. The Lord did so, and the robot retreated to a wall.

Grinning, Kickaha said, "I never thought the day'd come when I'd be glad to see you. But I am. You're the cat's paw that pulled the chestnuts out of the fire for me. Me and Anana."

Urthona looked as if he just couldn't believe that this was happening to him. No wonder. After all he'd endured and the good luck he'd had to find a boulder with a gate in it. For all he knew, his enemies were stranded on his world or more probably dead. He was king of the palace again.

It must have been a shock when he found the door to the control room welded shut. Somebody had gotten in after all. Possibly a Lord of another world who'd managed to gate in, though that wasn't likely. He must have figured that somehow Orc or Anana and Kickaha had gotten in. But they couldn't get into the control room, where the center of power was. The first thing he had probably done, though, was to cancel the decaying orbit of his palace. After setting it in a safe path, he would have started checking the sensory system. The regular one, first. No doubt one of the flashing red lights on the central console indicated that someone was in a trap. He'd checked that and discovered that Orc was in the cube.

But he must also have seen Anana. Had he ordered the robot Two to kill her?

He asked Urthona. The Lord shook his head as if he was trying to throw his troubles out.

"No," he said slowly. "I saw her there, but she wasn't doing anything to endanger me for the moment. I started then to check out the auxiliary sensories just to make sure no one else was aboard. I hadn't gotten to the room in which you were yet. You connected with the control room . . . and . . . damn you! If only I'd gotten here a few minutes earlier."

"It's all in the timing," Kickaha said, smiling. "Now let us get on with it. You're probably thinking I'm going to kill you or perhaps stick you in that wheeled cage and let you starve to death. It's not a bad idea, but I prefer contemplating the theory to putting it into practice.

"I promised Orc I'd let him go if he cooperated. He hasn't done a thing to help, but I can't hold that against him. He hasn't had a chance.

"Now, if you cooperate, too, Urthona, I'll let you live and I won't torture you. I need to get Orc, your beloved brother, out of that trap so I can get my hands on the Horn. But first, let's check that your story is true. God help you if it isn't."

He stood behind the Lord just far enough away so that if he tried to turn and snatch at the beamer he'd be out of reach. The weapon was set on low-stun. Urthona worked the controls, and the concealed TV of the auxiliary system looked into the room with the cube. Orc was still in his prison; Anana and Two were standing by the hole in the wall.

Kickaha called her name. She looked up with a soft cry. He told her not to be frightened, and he outlined what had happened.

"So things are looking good again," he said. "Orc, your brother is going to gate you into the control room. First, though, put the beamer down on the table. Don't try anything. We'll be watching you. Keep hold of the Horn. That's it. Now go to the corner where you appeared in the cube when you were gated through. Okay. Stand still. Don't move or you'll lose a foot or something."

Urthona reached for a button. Kickaha said, "Hold it. I'm not through. Anana, you know where I went. Go up there and stand by the wall behind the control console there. Then step through the gate when it appears. Oh, you'll meet a blind robot, poor old One. I'll order it to stand still so it won't bother you."

Urthona walked stiffly to a console at one end of the enormous room. His hands were tightly clenched; his jaw was clamped; he was quivering.

"You should be jumping with joy," Kickaha said. "You're going to live. You'll get another chance at the three of us some day."

"You don't expect me to believe that?"

"_hy not? Did I ever do anything you anticipated?"

J directed the Lord to show him the unmarked controls which w ld bring Orc back. Urthona stepped back to allow Kickaha to oper a . The redhead, however, said, "You do it."

It was possible that the controls, moved in the manner shown, would end a high voltage through him.

Urthona shrugged. He flipped a toggle switch, pressed a button, and stepped away from the console. To the left, the bare wall shimmered for a few seconds. A hemisphere of swirling colors bulged out from it, an then it collapsed. Red Orc stood with his back almost touching the wal .

Kickaha said, "Put the Horn down and push it with your foot towar me."

The Lord obeyed. Kickaha, keeping an eye on both of them, ber down and picked up the Horn.

"Ha! Mine again!"

Five minutes later, Anana stepped out of the same gate throug which Kickaha and Urthona had fallen.

Her uncles looked as if this was the end of the last act. They fully expected to be slain on the spot. At one time, Kickaha would have been angered because neither had the least notion that he deserved to be executed. There was no use getting upset, however. He had learned long ago not to be disturbed by the self-righteous and the psychopath, if there was any difference between the two.

"Before we part," he said. "I'd like to clear up a few things, if possible. Urthona, do you know anything about an Englishman, supposedly born in the eighteenth century? Red Orc found him living in this place when he entered."

Urthona looked surprised. "Someone else got into here?"

"That tells me how much you know. Well, maybe I'll run across him some other time. Urthona, your niece has explained something about the energy converter that powers this floating fairy castle. She told me that any converter can be set to overload, but an automatic regulator will cut it back to override that. Unless you remove the regulator. I want you to fix the overload to reach its peak in fifteen minutes. You'll cut the regulator out of the line."

Urthona paled. "Why? You . . . you mean to blow me up?"

"No. You'll be long gone from here when it blows. I intend to destroy your palace. You'll never be able to use it again."

Urthona didn't ask what would happen if he refused. Under the keen eye of Anana, he set the controls. A large red light began flashing on a console. A display flashed, in Lord letters, OVERLOAD. A whistle shrilled.

Even Anana looked uneasy. Kickaha smiled, though he was as nervous as anybody.

"Okay. Now open the gates to Earth I and to Jadawin's world."

He had carefully noted the control which could put the overload regulator back into the line if Urthona tried any tricks.

"I know you can't help being treacherous and sneaky, Urthona," Kickaha said. "But repress your natural viciousness. Refrain from pulling a fast one. My beamer's set on cutting. I'll slice you at the first false move."

Urthona did not reply.

On the towering blank wall two circular shimmerings appeared. They cleared away. One showed the inside to a cave, the same one through which Kickaha and Anana had entered southern California. The other revealed the slope of a wooded valley, a broad green river at the foot. And, far away, smoke rising from the chimneys of a tiny village and a stone castle on a rocky bluff above it. The sky was a bright green.

Kickaha looked pleased.

"That looks like Dracheland. The third level, on top of Abharhp-loonta. Either of you ever been there?"

"I've made some forays into Jadawin's world," Urthona said. "I planned someday to . . . to . . ."

"Take over from Jadawin? Forget it. Now, Urthona, activate a gate that'll take you to the surface of your planet."

Urthona gasped and said, "But you said . . . ! Surely . . . ? You're not going to abandon me here?"

"Why not? You made this world. You can live in it the rest of your life. Which will probably be short and undoubtedly will be miserable. As the Terrestrials say, let the punishment fit the crime."

"That isn't right!" Urthona said. "You are letting Orc go back to Earth. It isn't what I'd call a first-rate world, but compared to this, it's a paradise."

"Look who's talking about *right*. You're not going to beg, are you? You, a Lord among the Lords?"

Urthona straightened his shoulders. "No. But if you think you've seen the last of me . . ."

"I know. I've got another think coming. I wouldn't be surprised. I'll bet you have a gate to some other world concealed in a boulder. But you aren't letting on. Think you'll catch me by surprise some day, heh? After you find the boulder—if you do. Good luck. I may be bored and need some stiff competition. Get going."

Urthona walked up to the wall. Anana spoke sharply. "Kickaha! Stop him!"

He yelled at the Lord, "Hold it, or I'll shoot!"

Urthona stopped but did not turn.

"What is it, Anana?"

She glanced at a huge chronometer on a wall.

"Don't you know there's still danger? How do you know what he's up to? What might happen when he gives the codeword? It'll be better to wait until the last minute. Then Orc can go through, and you can shut the gate behind him. After that, we'll go through ours. And then Urthona can gate. But he can do it with no one else around."

"Yeah, you're right," Kickaha said. "I was so eager to get back I rushed things."

He shouted, "Urthona! Turn around and walk back here!"

Kickaha didn't hear Urthona say anything. His voice must have been very soft. But the words were loud enough for whatever sensor was in the wall to detect them.

A loud hissing sounded from the floor and the ceilings and the walls. From thousands of tiny perforations in the inner wall, clouds of greenish gas shot through the room.

Kickaha breathed in just enough of the metallic odor to make him want to choke. He held his breath then, but his eyes watered so that he could not see Urthona making his break. Red Orc was suddenly out of sight, too. Anana, a dim figure in the green mists, stood looking at him. One hand was pinching her nose and the other was over her mouth. She was signalling to him not to breathe.

She would have been too late, however. If he had not acted immediately to shut off his breath, he would, he was sure, be dead by now. Unconscious, anyway.

The gas was not going to harm his skin. He was sure of that. Otherwise, Urthona would have been caught in the deadly trap.

Anana turned and disappeared in the green. She was heading toward the gate to the World of Tiers. He began running too, his eyes burning and streaming water. He caught a glimpse of Red Orc plunging through the gate to Earth I.

And then he saw, dimly, Urthona's back as he sped through the gate to the world which Kickaha loved so much.

Kickaha felt as if he would have to cough. Nevertheless, he fought against the reflex, knowing that if he drew in one full breath, he would be done for.

Then he was through the entrance. He didn't know how high the gate was above the mountain slope, but he had no time for caution. He fell at once, landed on his buttocks, and slid painfully on a jumble of loose rocks. It went at a forty-five degree angle to the horizontal for about two hundred feet, then suddenly dropped off. He rolled over and clawed at the rocks. They cut and tore into his chest and his hands, but he dug in no matter how it hurt.

By then he was coughing. No matter. He was out of the green clouds which now poured out of the hole in the mountain face.

He stopped. Slowly, afraid that if he made a too vigorous movement he'd start the loose stones to sliding, he began crawling upward. A few rocks were dislodged. Then he saw Anana. She had gotten to the side of the gate and was clinging with one hand to a rocky ledge. The other held the Horn. Her eyes were huge, and her face was pale.

She shouted, "Get up here and away! As fast as you can! The converter is going to blow soon!"

He knew that. He yelled at her to get out of the area. He'd be up here in a minute. She looked as if she were thinking of coming down to help him, then she began working her way along the steep slope. He crawled at an angle toward the ledge she had grabbed. Several times he started sliding back, but he managed to stop his descent.

Finally, he got off the apron of stones. He rose to a crouch and, grabbing handfuls of grass, pulled himself up to the ledge. Holding onto this with one hand, he worked his way as swiftly as he dared away from the hole.

Just as he got to a point above a slight projection of the mountain, a stony half-pout, the mountain shook and bellowed. He was hurled outward to land flat on his face on the miniledge.

The loose rocks slid down and over the edge, leaving the stone beneath it as bare as if a giant broom had swept it.

Silence except for the screams of some distant birds and a faint rumble as the stones slid to a halt far below.

Anana said, "It's over, Kickaha."

He turned slowly to see her looking around a spur of rock.

"The gate would have closed the moment its activator was destroyed. We got only a small part of the blast, thank God. Otherwise, the whole mountain would've been blown up."

He got up and looked alongside the slope. Something stuck out from the pile below. An arm?

"Did Urthona get away?"

She shook her head. "No, he went over the edge. He didn't have much of a drop, about twenty feet, before he hit the second slope. But the rocks caught him."

"We'll go down and make sure he's dead," he said. "That trick of his dissolves any promises we made to him."

All that was needed was to pile more rocks on Urthona to keep the birds and the beasts from him.

XXVI

IT WAS A MONTH LATER. THEY WERE STILL ON THE MOUNTAIN, THOUGH on the other side and near its base. The valley was uninhabited by humans, though occasionally hunters ventured into it from the river-village they'd seen on coming from the gate. Kickaha and Anana avoided these.

They'd built a leanto at first. After they'd made bows and arrows from ash, tipped with worked flint, they shot deer, which were plentiful, and tanned the hides. Out of these they made a tepee, well-hidden in a grove of trees. A brook, two hundred yards down the slope, gave them clear cold water. It also provided fine fishing.

They dressed in buckskin hides and slept on bearskin blankets at night. They rested well but exercised often, hiking, berry- and nut-picking, hunting, and making love. They even became a little fat. After being half-starved so long, it was difficult not to stuff themselves. Part of their diet was bread and butter which they'd stolen one night from the village, two large bagfuls.

Kickaha, eavesdropping on the villagers, had validated his assumption that they were in Dracheland. And from a reference overheard, he had learned that the village was in the barony of Ulrich von Neifen.

"His lord, theoretically, anyway, is the duke, or Herzog, Willehalm von Hartmot. I know, generally, where we are. If we go down that river, we'll come to the Pfawe river. We'll travel about three hundred miles, and we'll be in the barony of Siegfried von Listbat. He's a good friend. He should be. I gave him my castle, and he married my divorced wife. It wasn't that Isote and I didn't get along well, you understand. She just wouldn't put up with my absences."

"Which were how long?"

"Oh, they varied from a few months to a few years."

Anana laughed.

"From now on, when you go on trips, I'll be along."

"Sure. You can keep up with me, but Isote couldn't, and she wouldn't have even if she could."

They agreed that they would visit von Listbat for a month or so. Kickaha had wanted to descend to the next level, which he called Amerindia, and find a tribe that would adopt him. Of all the levels, he loved this the most. There were great forest-covered mountains and vast plains, brooks and rivers of purest water, giant buffalo, mammoth, antelope, bear, sabertooths, wild horses, beaver, game birds by the billions. The human population was savage but small, and though the second level covered more territory than North and Central America combined, there were few places where the name of Kickaha, the Trickster, was not known.

But they must get to the palace-fortress on the top of this world, which was shaped like a tower of Babel. There they would gate through, though reluctantly, to Earth again. Reluctantly, because neither cared too much for Earth I. It was overpopulated, polluted, and might at any time perish in atomic-warfare.

"Maybe Wolff and Chryseis will be there by the time we get there. It's possible they're already there. Wouldn't that be great?"

They were on the mountain, above the river-valley, when he said this. Halfway down the slope were the birches from which they would build a canoe. Smoke rose from the chimneys of the tiny village on the bend of the river. The air was pure, and the earth beneath them did not rise and fall. A great black eagle soared nearby, and two hawks slid along the wind, headed for the river and its plentitude of fish. A grizzly bear grunted in a berry patch nearby.

"Anana, this is a beautiful world. Jadawin may be its Lord, but this is really my world, Kickaha's world."